THE
LIGHT
BRINGER

BOOK THREE - GODS & MONSTERS

JANIE MARIE

Paperback ISBN: 9798406803585
Illustration & Cover design by © Thander Lin
Editing by Emily A. Lawrence,
Proofreading by Emily Vaughan

CONTENTS

For all the Jane's

The goddesses who roar
when darkness surrounds them.

"Now give them
death, Sweet Jane . . .
For I am yours
to give."

-Death
The Light Bringer
Book 3 - Gods & Monsters

1

A KING'S QUEEN

Flapping his massive wings, Lucifer cleared the dust and smoke as he emerged from the cave. The ensuing chaos was expected, but finding half his ranks fighting alongside Belial was not.

Asmodeus dropped from the sky, landing beside Lucifer. "My king."

Lucifer didn't respond. He watched Thanatos, who guarded the mouth of the cave.

"You let her go?" Asmodeus asked, glancing at Lucifer's hair. "You took her demon into you?"

"I think that is obvious," Lucifer said, calling forth his sword. "Death has her. She is safe for now. Go, if you wish. I have things to do."

Asmodeus roared as loud as his dragon form could before vanishing into a cloud of red smoke, his legions following shortly after him.

Lucifer nodded to Thanatos. "You know what to do."

"Yes, my king." Thanatos glanced at the battle. "Belial was told about Jane's soul. He is not happy. Half your legions betrayed you once they felt Death's presence."

"I assumed as much," Lucifer said, walking away. "Go. See that everything happens as it should. Do not fail."

"Will she recover?" Thanatos asked.

Lucifer turned and glared at him. "He took her to the vampire. I have no doubt she will thrive between them. Now do as you're told so things fall back into place. You already know what will happen from here."

"Yes, my king," Thanatos said, bowing before vanishing.

Astaroth walked toward him. Those who could not flee in time were incinerated as the huge fallen angel came to stand in front of Lucifer. "My king, what have you done?"

Lucifer flexed his wings, glancing at the battle, snarling when he made eye contact with Lancelot, retreating with the remaining wolves. "I saved my queen."

Astaroth's gaze lifted to Lucifer's hair. "She will be in grave danger, Lucifer. Half souls are rare, and they do not last for long . . . Belial has been given gifts to aid him, and he will receive more. If he gets to her, you will be at his mercy."

"Anything else?" Lucifer asked as the light within him pulsed to a heart-beat that did not match his own.

"Yes." Astaroth looked up at the moon. "Separate her from Death soon. You know what will happen if you do not. Work swiftly."

Lucifer nodded. "Gather those who are with me and be ready."

"Yes, my king." Astaroth bowed before nodding to Beelzebub. Both Fallen glanced at him, signaling for their legions to follow.

Belial came into view. They stared at one another, neither moving to attack.

Lucifer allowed his light to surface, a command for his most loyal men to prepare. "How long have you known about her?"

Belial smirked, stabbing his sword into a fallen angel's back. "I did not know who she was then, but I was told there was a female with unimagin-able darkness and power. Should I or my men locate her, we were instructed to break her. Her identity only made sense when she fucked Lancelot to break your heart."

The High King of Hell kept his expression blank. "Again, how long?"

"I would imagine it was near her fifth birthday. Apparently the beast had a weakness—a pure soul from which she was created. It was said they could not be separated, but for the lovely monster to rule, the pure half needed to be broken. Some of us got there early on." He smiled, his blood-red eyes gleaming with sick joy. "I only wish I had partaken in the fun . . . You know how much Berith enjoys the young ones. So weak and innocent."

Even though he was furious beyond anything he had ever experienced, he smiled. "You think my queen weak? Why do you think Jane needed to be broken for that bitch to be worth your time?" Lucifer laughed, letting his power consume him. He could taste Jane—his queen—as her sweet pres-ence lingered within his light. It wanted her back. "Jane is not weak. She is stronger than you can imagine. I wasn't just freeing her from that darkness. I was unleashing my queen, cleansing her so she could be the great being she was destined to be. At. My. Side."

"You speak like a lovesick fool." Belial pulled his sword free of the dead fallen angel. "If she is still strong, she has not realized it yet, and that is all I need to claim her. It is only a matter of time now. Your kingdom is falling, and your legions will stand behind me as I drag your little queen on a leash until you break with her."

Lucifer released a breath, smoke spilling free from his nostrils as he summoned his powers. "You should know better, Belial . . . Never threaten a king's queen."

2

THEIR MOON

"Brother, are you certain Death is trustworthy?" Guinevere glanced away from Natalie, who was bathing, to where David leaned against the doorway.

Dragging his hand down his face, David sighed and looked over his shoulder to check on Nathan. The little boy was already asleep on Guinevere's bed. "I have no choice, Gwen." He turned back to his sister. "Everything he said makes sense."

She shook her head but smiled at Natalie as the little girl poured a cup of water over her head. "How could he allow such things to happen to her, though? If he was truly present for most of the torment she suffered . . . I simply cannot understand it."

"Because he loves her, sister. He watched because it was his way of being there for her—he suffered as well. Death and Jane are very similar—they make drastic choices to save each other. He was offered the chance to free her or watch her suffer and perhaps lose her to the demon. He took it because he saw no other way. I do not think the archangels lied about Lucifer being the only one able to free her—I trust them."

She gave him a serious look. "It was never a demon, though. You have not expressed your feelings about it being half of Jane's soul. How can you be so calm? It was *her* all along. Not a possession or entity—it was her."

He clenched his jaw, dropping his gaze away from her disapproving stare. "She did not become evil on her own. He said someone split her soul

—he could not say whom—but they corrupted it, gave it power, and placed it back alongside her true soul. Jane is the one who locked it up. Jane did that. It's still not exactly Jane."

"But it is." She drew a sharp breath, adding, "You must accept that and decide if she is still worth sacrificing your heart for."

David slowly raised his gaze to glare at her. "She is worth everything."

His sister smiled sadly. "Do you really believe that? What are you going to do if she does return to you? She still made a bargain with Lucifer, abandoning you and her children."

"She did so to protect us," he said through gritted teeth. "You have never had to look into her eyes and watch her battle that part of her soul. She knows what she's capable of, and she is always ready to sacrifice herself for those she loves. That's what she did."

"But to Lucifer? How could she trust him? You said he was the one torturing her."

He glanced at Natalie. David and Guinevere spoke low enough that she wouldn't hear them, but he knew she had picked up they were talking about her mom. "You don't understand," he told his sister. "Lucifer is a manipulator, and he played the game just right. He tormented her until she was too hurt to fight and then showed her he could control it. She saw him as someone who could save us from what she could do. Everything she has done by leaning on Death or me has been because we helped her be the woman she really is—but Death and I cannot do what Lucifer can."

"That may be, but if she had any sense, she would have told you rather than jumping into the Devil's arms."

David sighed, tired of having the same conversation with multiple people. "She's never seen how much worth she truly has. She does not think as we do. To her, none of us will care if she's gone or what happens to her. She believes she must keep us safe from the darkness inside her—and Lucifer knew that. You never saw how evil that thing was. She didn't think anyone else could save us—and there wasn't."

"It still does not make sense. Why would God pair you with her?"

He glared at her. "Why wouldn't he? I love Jane, sister. With all of my heart."

A sad smile formed on her lips. "But you never had all of hers, brother. She never stopped loving Death—you said so yourself. So how can you possibly say you love her when she does not love you equally?"

"You don't understand." He glanced at Nathan again. "Death was all she had—he truly adores her, and she fell in love with him. She cannot stop because it isn't a simple love they share. I still feel there is so much more to them. They are too unique to describe—but I do not hold her devotion to him against her. The point is, she still chose me."

"Only because he was not there," she said, pissing him off. "You know I am right. Had he never left, she would have chosen him."

David shook his head. "She cared for me already. She had the chance to leave with him, but she turned him down because of me. Still, she had already fallen for Death, and she was married—I have always been third in line. I cannot expect to have her all to myself when she already loved others so fiercely."

"And you are okay with that?" Gwen watched him carefully.

"I have to be," he answered without hesitation. "I love her and want to spend the rest of our lives together. She wants that too. If Death is necessary for Jane, then I will deal with him. I didn't expect my Other to have children either, Gwen, but I love them, and I would never expect her to give them up."

She laughed sadly. "Brother, Death is not her child. He is a man she loves. I have heard about their intimacies from the other wives. She will not stay faithful."

He growled, turning his head away to hide his snarl. "They should not speak of her relationship with Death—they know little of what they mean to one another. She went so long without affection from Jason, and she craved Death's attention after their reunion. I was still a stranger to her. I was jealous at the time, but I see it more clearly now—she needed his attention."

"She should have needed yours. Not his!"

David faced her again. "Do not judge her for loving Death. I dislike him almost all the time, but I accept him. If I'm saying I accept him and what she has with him, so should everyone else. I am not a child—I know our situation is not the norm."

"So, if she wishes to share his bed—just as she offered herself to him— you will sit back and let her go off with him?"

"She offered herself to save Jason's life."

Her eyes were full of pity. "Do you really think that is the only reason? What if she does the same with Lucifer? If it is as Death says, that Lucifer cares enough to save her, how do you know she will not fall for him as well? Will you accept him as a part of her life?"

David glanced at Natalie's little face. She peered over the tub, staring right at him. "I don't know."

6

Guinevere stood, lifting Natalie before wrapping her in a towel. "I suggest you stop basing your decisions on what your heart tells you and start listening to your brain."

"Is that what you did, sister?" He watched her eyes widen and shook his head as he took Natalie from her. "Do not lecture me on matters of the heart. I know what you keep hidden inside yours."

Natalie wrapped her arms around his neck and kissed his cheek. "Love you, David."

"I love you, too, princess." David averted his eyes from his sister's teary gaze as he rubbed Natalie's back and carried her to where Nathan slept. It was a tad difficult, but he managed to lift the little boy without waking him. "If there is news from Arthur for me, see that I get it. Good night, sister."

David finished tucking Nathan into bed while he waited for Natalie to put on her nightgown in his bathroom. He still wasn't comfortable dressing her, but he was sure Jane trusted him with her daughter. He kissed Nathan's hair, wiping the tears from his cheek. "Stay strong with me, little man."

"Which star is Mommy?" Natalie asked softly.

David turned around, finding her standing by the balcony window. "What are you talking about, princess?" He went over to her, kneeling beside her to see what she was looking at.

She pointed to a bright star. "That one is Wendy, Mommy's friend." She pointed to one next to it. "That's Daddy." She scanned the skies, frowning before she sighed. "I can't tell which one she is."

His eyes burned as he hugged her to hide his heartbreak. "Natalie, Mommy isn't a star."

She gasped, pulling back with tears in her eyes. "Why? Did she do something bad?"

He cupped her little cheeks. "No, princess. I did not mean that she didn't deserve to be a star—Mommy would be the prettiest star in the sky. I meant she's not a star because she's alive." He wiped her tears. "She's going to come back to us."

"Are you sure?"

He smiled sadly. "I'm sure. Do you know how Ryder was here? He's Mommy's oldest friend."

Natalie wiped her wet cheeks. "He loves Mommy. Not us."

David kissed her head. "He loves you because you are a part of Mommy, but he cannot express it without her."

"Oh."

He smiled and pointed to the waning crescent moon. "Well, Ryder calls Mommy his moon. Perhaps she is not exactly the moon, but I like to think she's staring at it at the same time I am. That way, she's with me even when she is not."

"It's almost gone," she whispered. "It's all dark."

His throat ached. "Not all the way. And that is only because the moon must go through phases. It always moves around the Earth and the sun. This type of moon means it's actually closer to the sun. It will be dark tomorrow, but that's when it is closest to the sun. It's called a New Moon."

Natalie kept staring at it. "So, she's looking at it right now?"

"Maybe." He rubbed her back, noticing she was trembling and tense, just like Jane when she tried to hold her emotions in. "You can tell her good night."

"Good night, Mommy." Her lip quivered. "I love you. I hope you come home soon."

David smiled at her when she turned to him with glassy eyes. "She loves you, too. Very much."

"Are you still gonna love her? Aunt Gwen didn't think I could hear her, but I did. She told Aunt Elle you should consider marrying a different lady because Mommy didn't stay with you. She said the other lady would make you happy if you gave her a chance. Someone named Art-mis. Do you love Art-mis?"

David picked her up, kissing her hair as he carried her to bed. "Don't listen to Aunt Gwen. She's only worried because I am her younger brother. I know you are not older than Nathan, but you look out for him, don't you?"

"Yes," she whispered.

"That is all she is trying to do."

"But do you love that lady instead of Mommy? Does Mommy not make you happy?"

His chest ached as he smiled. "Mommy makes me very happy, princess. And no, I do not love Artemis. I never will, so I will not give her a chance. My heart belongs to Mommy."

Natalie stared at him for a minute. "Mommy didn't know I could hear her and Daddy in my room. She would tell you to go like she used to tell him when she'd cry. She was sad because he wasn't happy with her. She told him it was okay to leave her."

"I'm not like Daddy, princess. I love her—always. And she makes me very happy."

"You promise?" she asked as he laid her down.

David fixed the comforter around her. "I promise. Get some sleep now."

"Daddy used to promise Mommy he loved her, but he didn't act like it. He always left when she cried in her room. He said she would never get better. Then, at the park, he told her he wasn't in love with her."

David kissed her forehead, realizing Jane's children had suffered with her. They never should've heard these things. "She doesn't need to get better. She just needs to be loved and held together because there are a lot of bad things out there trying to tear her apart. No matter how bad she gets, I'll always love and hold her."

Natalie smiled, rolling on her side. "I guess that's why you were picked for her."

He sat beside her for a moment, staring at her little face. She had fallen asleep before she fully rolled over, and he was curious if she had consciously spoken or was talking in her sleep. He hoped this was God's way of reminding him that he and Jane were no mistake.

David shook his head before leaving his room. He'd promised Nathan he would find the plush dinosaur toy Dagonet had given him so he could sleep with it, but the little boy had fallen asleep on his own. He hated leaving them alone for long, so he quickly pushed open the broken door to the room they'd stayed in with Jason. Gwen had wanted everything destroyed, but he told her to let the kids have some peace without seeing workers tearing apart the room they had thought would be their new home.

After entering the twins' room, he sighed. It was still a mess, and the smell of Jason's blood was still thick. Luckily, he spotted the dinosaur and the doll Dagonet had given the children. He snatched them, relieved they didn't have blood on them, and headed back to his room.

He glanced at Jane's door out of habit, pausing with his hand on the doorknob to his room. It wasn't like she would come walking out, but he could still smell her sweet scent whenever he passed by.

David sighed and looked away, turning the doorknob to his room.

"David."

He froze, staring at his door.

It was just a whisper of his name, but it was who the voice belonged to that had his heart pounding. *Death.*

Turning quickly, his eyes widened at the green glow fading from under her door. He shoved the door to her room open so fast he almost broke it and nearly cried at what he saw.

Death lifted his gaze from Jane's unconscious form to David's. "Hurry. Lucifer had to drain half her blood." He turned, laying her on the bed and uncovering her naked body.

David couldn't move. Her skin was white. Naked. And she smelled like . . .

"Stop staring at her like that! Come here—I need your help." Death glared at him, holding out his hand. "Give me your arm."

David had no idea what Death could do with his arm that would help her, but he sat on Jane's other side and held it out.

Death grabbed his forearm, squeezing tightly but never looking at him.

A cold sensation pulsed several times where Death's hand was before slowly traveling up David's arm to his chest. It spread through his lungs, reminding David of breathing cold air in, but it instantly switched from cold to hot. Too hot. "Death . . . I can't—" He took a huge breath and tried to free his arm, but Death held him tight.

"Don't," was all Death said when he felt his lungs burn and collapse.

David braced himself with his free hand as his lungs burned so painfully he thought he might collapse. He kept trying to breathe as Death leaned over Jane.

"Breathe," Death said, brushing his lips against hers.

More pressure surrounded David's chest. He tried to suck in air, but each time it was stolen, replaced with a fire he could not escape.

David began to panic as he thought Death might be taking him to let Jane live. He would give his life for hers, but he wanted to see her before he died.

When he collapsed, struggling to keep his eyes open, Death loosened his grip, and blue flames erupted from his mouth. They swirled around Jane's lips before Death kissed her, pushing her mouth open enough that they could enter.

The fire inside David's lungs spiked to unbearable heat and then receded down through his arm, dying the instant Death removed his hand. Relief and oxygen filled his body, but all he could do was watch the blue light spread from her lips down to her chest.

"Baby." David almost felt like crying when the light faded and her chest rose.

Death smiled as he leaned away and cupped Jane's face. "Come on,

Jane." He gave David a slight nod, but David was too focused on the rise and fall of her chest to acknowledge him or ask what had just happened.

Finally, she gasped, her eyes flying open, darting all around the room but never to David.

"Easy, Sweet Jane. You're home," Death said, smoothing her hair back.

"Luc?" she cried, tears falling from her eyes. "Luc, my king. My king?" She frantically slapped Death's hands from her face. "Luc?"

"Stop it," Death yelled, grabbing her face and forcing her to look him in the eye. "Baby girl, it's me."

Her eyes darted back and forth between Death's as she continued to cry. "Luc."

Death shook his head. "He's not here."

More tears slipped from her eyes.

"Luc took her out of you, Jane," Death whispered, nuzzling her. "Remember, angel. Remember what happened. You're only disoriented because you stopped breathing for a while."

She sobbed. "My king—he kept me."

Death nodded, kissing her cheek. "I know, angel. He kept a part of you safe so you could come back. He took her out." Death pulled a sheet up to cover her as she wailed. "He didn't want to go as far as he had to."

"Luc!"

David could only stare at her. She was crying, begging Lucifer to come to her. Not for him. Not for Death.

Death lifted his gaze to David and shook his head. "Give her time. She doesn't understand. He had to break her completely to seal her away for me to revive her. His light protected enough of her for me."

He nodded, remembering what Death had told him: Lucifer was the only one who could control and extract Jane's darker soul—imprisoning it within himself. The only problem—the problem that tore Death apart this entire time—was that Lucifer had to destroy Jane. He had to make her fall and not get back up.

"Baby," David said, finally feeling some of his strength return.

Those hazel eyes he loved so much darted to him, and her face scrunched up as she broke down. "David." She tried to move, but she only slumped to the side.

Death lifted her back in place, but she kept crying.

"David, I'm sorry. I tried. I tried to fight her like you said. I'm sorry."

Death kissed her forehead. "Angel, you did great. You weren't supposed to fight anymore. That's why it had to be Luc. That's why I stayed hidden. I'm so sorry."

Jane didn't take her eyes off David. "Kill me."

David shook his head as Death stared at her—frozen.

"Please kill me," she said, her chest wracked with sobs he'd never heard before. "She killed them. I killed them. I killed those babies."

"No, my love," David said, tears escaping his eyes. "That wasn't you."

She shook her head back and forth, her face twisted in agony. "I know you smell him. You smell both of them in me." David closed his eyes as she screamed, "You smell them in me!"

"I'll fix you, Sweet Jane," Death whispered. "It's going to be okay."

David's heart was crushed. He didn't know what to do. He didn't know what to think about her begging for Lucifer and feared to find out why she smelled like two men. Two enemies. She wasn't screaming that she'd been raped. Had she betrayed him? Could he forgive her?

Natalie's voice suddenly filled his mind:

"Daddy used to promise Mommy he loved her, but he didn't act like it. He always left when she cried. He said she would never get better. Then, at the park, he told her he wasn't in love with her."

David's response was as clear as when he'd said it. "She doesn't need to get better, princess. She just needs to be loved and held together because there are a lot of bad things trying to tear her apart. No matter how bad she gets, I'll always love and hold her."

Her voice was loud and clear in his mind. "I guess that's why you were picked for her."

"You don't need to be fixed," David whispered to Jane as he slowly opened his eyes. He smiled as best he could when she stopped screaming. "You just need to be held together. I'll hold you. Don't worry about what I smell. I love you. Always. We'll work through this."

Her tears didn't stop, but she smiled sadly as Death hugged her. The angel stroked her hair, rocking her as he whispered in her ear, "Let him love you, angel. Don't give up. Please don't give up—we only just got you back."

She didn't respond, and she didn't stop staring at David.

"Come here, baby," he said, trying to sit up. David knew he'd need to do this for her because she wouldn't come close to forgiving herself if he judged her. "Death, bring her here. She needs to be fed."

Without hesitation, Death carried her to the side of the bed David was on. He grabbed David's arm and pulled him up before sitting Jane across his lap.

At first, David could only hug her. Her skin felt like ice, and she was covered in tears and sweat, but she leaned against him, breathing in his scent as she held her hand over his heart.

"Home," she whispered almost too quietly to hear, but it meant so much to him.

"Feed, Jane," Death said, moving her hair out of her face. "The energy I gave you will not sustain you for much longer. Feed."

David situated her. She didn't look like his Jane anymore. She looked incomplete. Lost. He would help her find herself again. "Feed, Jane. Everything will be okay."

"I'm sorry," she whispered, lightly kissing his neck before sinking her fangs in.

Death turned away from them, his head hanging low as black feathered wings manifested. They were gone so quickly, David thought he imagined it, but when Death rubbed his shoulder, he knew he'd seen the angel lose control of the illusion he hid behind.

The only one not losing control was Jane. She wasn't reacting to David's blood like she usually did. His touch seemed to stir some recognition within her, but she wasn't moaning or trying to get closer. She fed until she was full, then withdrew her fangs.

She made eye contact with him and touched his lips as hers trembled. "Am I really here with you?" she asked, tracing his lips. "Sometimes he would give me memories of you both to help me sleep."

That seemed out of place for how David viewed Lucifer, but he chose not to think about it just yet. "I'm real. You're home, my love."

"Home," she whispered, her tears never stopping as she lowered her hand. "I don't deserve to be home. I don't deserve to have you hold me."

David shook his head, still struggling to move after Death had weakened him. "Don't think like that. A lot needs to be sorted out, but you are meant to be here. With me." He nodded to Death. "And with this fucker, too."

She smiled faintly. It was the smile he always dreamed of—just a slight curve of her lips, but it meant so much to him.

"You should not even be awake," Death told him as he leaned over to kiss the back of Jane's head. "Your boyfriend is a strong fucker. Promise me you will whisper I'm stronger when he's showing off to you."

David shoved him, chuckling as he finally pulled her close. She smelled of sex, but he knew his baby loved him. He wouldn't throw her away. He caressed her cheek as Death stood and walked to a dresser.

"David, I did bad things," she said, holding his wrist as though she feared he would let go.

He kissed her forehead. "She did those things. I know you feel like it was all your fault, but I know you, Jane. My Jane is good. If you were truly you, you would not have done anything close to what I fear is tormenting your mind and soul. I promise I will help you. We'll both help you. And whatever you confide in us, I swear I will still love you and want you with me. Always, baby."

She didn't say anything. She seemed different, but his heart refused to lose hope. He could tell without the darkness inside her, she was thinking on her own. She didn't have that same look where she always seemed to argue with someone else or listen to a tormentor she could not escape. Now, she tied to accept what he said.

David cupped her cheek, smiling before he kissed her on the lips. It was hard to smell other men on her, but he pressed his lips against hers, keeping it as sweet as he could—simply happy she returned the kiss at all.

"Oh, my sweet little Jane." Death's teasing tone pulled them apart.

David kissed her forehead before they looked at Death.

The angel acted as though he wasn't bothered by watching them kiss and smirked as he held something up. "When did you start wearing thongs?"

David chuckled. "Leave her alone. And give her the cotton ones. Also, don't touch her intimates ever again."

Death only snickered, tucking the thong in his pocket as he held up a cotton pair and walked back to them. He glanced at Jane's face, his smile fading, but he bent and kissed her head again. "Stay with us. We still see our beautiful girl. Our girl did not do what you are seeing. That is her smile —not the one David and I cherish above all sights in the universe."

Death's wording confused David, but it was right then that he saw the beauty of Jane and her angel. He could see it in the sad yet peaceful smiles on their faces. The way they both relaxed at a simple touch from each other. He should have been jealous. He should have been furious that she was comforted by another man, especially while he held her. But he wasn't. He was happy there was someone else who loved Jane. Someone else saw her for who she was and not what had been done to her. Because of Death, she could feel loved when the rest of the world condemned her.

After listening to his sister speak badly of her when she only knew the basics of what Jane had gone through, David could glimpse how Jane must feel. She needed Death, and David vowed to make sure she always had him.

"Thank you," Jane whispered, receiving another kiss on the head from her angel.

Death stood, handing the panties over to David. "I know she likes your shirts. I will check on the twins and give you two a few minutes alone before I bring one back."

David smiled, his heart aching as he saw Death letting her go as much as he could. "Do me a favor, and don't pocket any of my underwear."

Death chuckled, turning away and walking to the door. "I have the better everything between the two of us, but even I will admit the tales of Prince David's ass have me worried I need to add squats to my workout routine." Death turned, grinning at Jane. "Baby girl, do you remember how you teased me about my ass?"

She smiled softly. "I remember."

Death smirked. "As long as she loves my ass, I'm good."

David shook his head. "Thanks, asshole."

"It's never for you, fucker, but you're welcome." Death winked at Jane before shutting the door behind him.

"Are you sure you still want me here, David?" She didn't sound afraid or sad. She was ready to accept his dismissal because she'd already expected it.

He searched those hazel eyes, smiling as he watched the gold and green colors circling each other. "Baby, I want you with me—more than anything. I know it's not going to be easy. We will not be the same as before, but I think we will be better."

"Why?" She touched his lips. "I've hurt you so much."

David kissed her fingers. "I know why you chose to hurt me. I know you felt there was no other way to protect me and everyone else—I cannot be angry about that. I never want you to do it again, but I understand. And I believe we will only grow stronger because we still ended up together again." He studied her face, his heart pounding as he asked, "Do you want to stay here with me? Or has your heart chosen another?" He wanted to punch himself for asking that, especially right now, but it was still something he needed to know. He could tell Jane felt something for Lucifer. For her to scream out for him, even with Death right there, Lucifer had to have done something right in her eyes.

A tear slid down her face. "My heart has been yours for a while now,

David. I just don't think anyone can look past the things I've done—not even you. You have no idea what you'd be keeping." Her lips trembled. "I want to be with you, but I'm afraid to tell you. I know you have to know, though. You'll never look at me the same way, and I'm terrified to see your face when you find out. It's too much to forgive or look past. I'm ruined, my love." She started shaking as she cried, "I'm ruined."

His heart bled, but he smiled as he wiped her tears away. "Minutes before Death brought you back, Natalie pointed to the sky and asked me which star you were." He watched her eyes well up, but she stayed quiet as he went on. "I explained why she could not find your star and promised you'd come home one day. Then I pointed to the moon." He smiled sadly. "I told her Death—Ryder, as she thinks of him—calls you his moon. I don't know if you know what it looks like tonight, but it is a waning crescent. She said it was dark, almost gone, and I told her not all the way. I also explained that this type of moon looks dark, but tomorrow it will be considered a New Moon, the night it is nearest to the sun—when it prepares to shine again—when she comes out of the dark, eventually outshining every star."

David pressed his lips to hers again. "I know you have been in the dark, but you've also come home. You will glow again. It may take a little time, and it will be hard to heal your wounds, but you will shine for all of us and yourself. This is just a chapter of your life ending tonight. Tomorrow, you and I will begin a new chapter. I will be with you for every one, my love. It's only up to you how you want me with you. I promise you I want us. No matter what you end up telling me—and I know it involves sex. I can smell it." He kissed her head when she sobbed. "I know it's going to hurt, but I'm not walking away. I'm holding you—tightly. I won't let go. I am your David even after the end of time."

"Smooth, fucker." Death's annoyed tone made David sigh and look away from Jane.

"Did you check on them?" David asked, holding out his hand for the shirt.

Death tossed it as he walked to sit beside Jane. "They're asleep. So how are we doing this?"

Jane turned to look at Death. "Doing what?"

He pointed to the bed. "It's going to be a tight squeeze, so I say we kick David out."

"And I was just beginning to view you in a more positive light," David said, kissing Jane's head.

"I know who's the best cuddler for her," Death said, winking at her. "But I will leave you two and keep an eye on the twins."

Jane reached out.

Death smiled, lifting her hand to his lips. "It's okay, angel. I know. This is where you belong. Welcome home." Death glanced at him as he stood. "Take care of my girl."

David could only smile.

"Good night, Death," Jane whispered, leaning her head onto David's chest.

Death looked at her—only her. "Good night, my moon."

3

HOME

Rubbing the tears from her cheeks, Jane stood at the foot of the bed and watched David sleep. He looked like he hadn't slept in days, which she figured was the only reason she could get out of bed without waking him.

Another tear fell from her chin to her chest. She didn't deserve him. She knew he'd never forgive her. Once he found out, he would leave. It didn't matter what he said. He would leave because she was ruined.

She covered her mouth to contain her cries and hurried to the bathroom. The scents on her skin made her nauseous, but most of all, they broke her heart. She could still feel Lancelot inside her. She felt sore and disgusted with herself. It might have been the darker side of her who ordered him to fuck her, but she hadn't been able to stop it. She had been too broken by Luc's betrayal to fight back, yet she still felt a part of her soul crying for him to help her. Her demon was gone, but she had been broken, left behind, and she didn't know what to do.

Jane hadn't even realized she was in the shower until she stared at the blood circling down the drain because she had scrubbed her skin raw.

"Baby?" David called out softly.

Choking on her sob, she curled into a ball and hid her face as she sensed him coming closer.

"Jane," he said, pulling the glass door open. His hands were on her in an instant. "Baby, what have you done to yourself?" His hands were shaking as he lightly pulled her legs apart. "Baby." His voice cracked.

She shoved his hands away, curling farther from him, but he pulled her onto his lap. He was completely dressed and getting soaked, but he didn't seem to care.

"Jane, let me help. What did you do?"

"I still feel him in me." She cried, pressing her face into his chest. "I'm sorry."

He kissed her head. "It's okay. It's okay. Let me see if I need to get a doctor."

"No." She tried to crawl off, but he held her to him. "David, don't look at me. Please don't."

His arms wrapped around her as he rocked them from side to side. "Let me help, my love. I need to help you."

"You don't know what I did with them." She cried, sliding a hand between her legs to hide herself. "They're in me."

His body trembled, but he kept rocking her. "Do you want me to help you clean so you don't feel them?"

She lowered her hand and stared at him. His beautiful blue eyes always soothed her, and they did this time as well. "She forced him to fuck me, David." Her lips quivered as agony and fury etched their way across his face. "Luc couldn't stop her. She told me it was to hurt him, too. She was punishing him for caring for me. She made him watch Lancelot fuck me."

David nodded, holding her cheek. "It's going to be okay. I promise I'm not going anywhere."

Jane could barely see him, but now she'd opened her mouth, she couldn't stop. "She made him transform, David. Then she forced me to see. She forced me to see and feel him, and then she still killed his family right in front of him. She killed his baby boy and daughter, just like Melody tried to kill mine." Her heart felt like it had been ripped out of her chest, but she had to tell him about Luc. "I let Lucifer come in my mouth and in me so he could put his scent over yours. I offered myself to him to save those babies, but he still called her. That's why I couldn't fight her."

David covered his face with one hand. "Baby, please stop for a minute. I love you, but give me a minute."

She crawled off his lap, and this time, he let her. She grabbed her bloody washcloth and started scrubbing between her legs again.

"Stop!" He stilled her hands. "Please don't hurt yourself."

"I don't want you to smell them." She tried to pull her hands away, but he held them tightly and gently pulled her back to him.

"Let me do it. I can't watch you hurt yourself. Let me help."

She didn't understand why he wasn't walking away. When she kept staring at him, he tossed the bloody cloth away and grabbed the hand shower head she'd discarded on the floor, positioning her on his lap as he carefully spread her legs. He kissed her shoulder, stared at her bleeding inner thighs, and rinsed the blood away.

"I'm going to rinse between your legs to see how bad it is, okay?" He kissed her head.

She could only nod, not sure what to say. It felt like waking from a dream. The wounds were healing slowly, but she was still bleeding from how hard she had scrubbed.

"I think the bleeding will stop once we stop spraying. Did you do anything inside?" He kissed her cheek. "I love you, Jane. Please stay with me."

Her tears never stopped. "I reached as far as I could with the cloth and my nails."

He nodded, kissing her again. "It's okay. I'm going to spray, and then we need to get you dry and warm."

She blinked, reaching for the body wash. "I need to keep cleaning them out of me."

David grabbed the soap, stopping her. "My love, no one is in you."

"Yes, they came in me. I have to get it out." She gasped. "I need them out."

"Okay. Let me do it so you don't hurt yourself again. I promise I will make them go away." He didn't wait for her to respond, but he was gentle as he slid a soapy hand between her legs. "I love you. Tell me if it hurts too much or if you're panicking."

She covered her face, crying loudly as he washed her. He was being so careful and loving. She didn't deserve it.

"I'm going to rinse inside for you, okay? Is the soap stinging?"

"I don't feel clean."

A rough noise rumbled in his chest before he kissed her head. "You're clean. I promise. I'll help you see." He applied more soap and then slowly pushed two fingers inside her. He held her tight when she tensed up and gently massaged her. "It's me. It's not them. Just tell me if it hurts."

"David, please leave me. I don't deserve this."

He didn't respond. Instead, he pulled his fingers out and replaced them with a spray of water. Jane was afraid to look at him as he lifted he and shut off the water. He carried her to the sink, grabbing a towel and wrapping it around her.

She heard him make a frustrated noise and opened her eyes to find him shirtless, trying to get his wet pants off.

"I don't want to get your bed soaked," he said, finally getting them off. He patted his underwear with a towel and quickly carried her to bed. "Let me check if you're still bleeding."

Jane shook her head as he laid her down, but he kissed her cheek and started to pull the towel away.

"Baby, I need to make sure you're healing. You might need more blood, and I can't feed you again without growing too weak. Be brave, my love. I swear it is me, and I won't hurt you." He pushed her on her back and finished uncovering her. "Are you still with me, Jane?"

"I don't know. I don't feel anymore." She didn't want to see what she'd done to herself or his reaction, so she wasn't expecting his lips to press against her thigh. Nor had she expected to feel her old David's heat seeping into her body until it wrapped around her weeping soul. "What are you doing?"

He lifted his head and smiled. "Baby, you don't smell like them." He didn't look away from her face as he pressed his lips between her legs. It was just a kiss, but somehow he touched her everywhere. "You still smell like me. I don't smell either one of them."

"How?" She watched him kiss her again; then, he licked the blood. She gasped, not sure what was happening when he didn't stop. "David." She never expected it to feel good to have a man touch her, but he made her forget everything in that tiny moment. She moaned, throwing her head back before the truth returned to her, but his words had her hanging on to him.

"You smell like me, my love," he said again, kissing her thighs and licking the abrasions to help them seal. "You smell like me."

"I do?" Tears welled in her eyes as she croaked out her next words, "Baby, are you sure?"

David chuckled and kissed her thighs again. "You still make my heart beat faster when you call me that." He rested his cheek on her leg and inhaled before kissing the skin there again. "Yes, you definitely smell like me. Neither one of them remains. Just me."

Jane wiped her tears away as he kissed his way up her body.

"The cuts are gone already, too. It's just a bit red." His handsome face came into view, and he kissed her softly. "They're not in you, Jane. It's still me. Just like I said before we got together. Do you remember?"

"Yes, but I don't understand," she whispered, searching his eyes for any sign he was lying. "You didn't even go in me."

He chuckled, kissing her nose. "Oh, baby, I've missed your cute way of talking. And I did come a little bit to get my scent on you. And because I could barely keep from climaxing. You felt like a dream."

Her breathing hitched as he gave her that David smile before he went on.

"I don't know how my scent stayed and not theirs, but it makes me very happy."

"Does that mean I'm pregnant?"

His eyes widened, and he looked down at her belly. "I do not think so. You weren't ovulating. Immortals have a bit of a delay before they have their first cycle. I would have known." He glided his fingers over her stomach. "I would know if my baby was growing inside you. It's just my scent entwined with yours." He looked back at her face. "Don't ever hurt yourself like that again. I promise it is only me inside you. When you're ready, I'll make sure you only feel me, even when I'm not with you."

"You still want to be with me?" She couldn't stop her sob, throwing her arms around his neck when he kissed her.

"Always, my love." He brushed his lips over hers. "Do you want me to show you how much I want you? Do you want me to remind you how we feel when we become one? Because we are beautiful. Our first time was rushed and of bad timing, but it was still a beautiful moment between us."

She nodded. "It was."

David gave her a long kiss as he pulled her legs around his waist. He caged her with his body, pressing against her gently but possessively. His heat rolled over her skin before seeping into her pores.

Jane gasped against his mouth when his erection caressed her sex. He was still wearing his wet underwear, which made her even more sensitive.

"Are you okay?" He pushed her hair back and smiled, thrusting his hips forward when she tried to rub herself against him.

"My David," she whispered, smiling through her tears as she touched his lips. "Please make love to me."

Those fiery lips were on hers again as she felt him pushing off his underwear. "My beautiful Jane." He dragged his hand down her thigh, tugging her underneath him more.

She was shaking. She had no idea how he made their bodies fit together, but he knew how to move her and how gentle and rough to be.

David licked her neck slowly. So slowly. And his hands were everywhere. Tender but so strong. So hot and firm. He was so perfect. And he was making her see stars as he grinned against her neck while sliding his shaft along her core.

"Oh, God." Jane closed her eyes even though she wanted to watch his muscles as they flexed around her. She wanted to see his smile, his beautiful eyes as they darkened but still managed to express all he felt for her.

David chuckled, lining up and pushing in just enough to have her coming undone. "Not God, baby." He watched her cling to him as her body tensed and her legs shook. Just as she started to breathe again, he squeezed her ass and pushed his full length into her. "I'm just your David."

Relax," David whispered before placing a kiss behind her ear. "I think they're in the bath anyway. Come on."

He opened the door to his room and pulled her in. He was right; they weren't in there. But Death was.

"Don't ever leave me with them again," he mumbled into the blankets. He was face down on the bed, his muscular legs hanging halfway off the side. "I have no idea how someone so little can have so much energy and be so hungry all at once."

Jane smiled as her angel slowly rolled over and sat up.

He sniffed, shooting David a glare, but smiled when he looked back at her. "I'm glad you two made up. Is it our turn now, Sweet Jane?"

She tilted her head, confused. "Our turn for what?"

David pointed at him. "I won't ask her to behave differently with you, but you will stop putting her in situations where she can't tell you no."

Death laughed. "Calm down. You got her your way, and I will have her mine."

"Death, don't piss him off," Jane scolded as David kissed her head.

"Stay here with him," David told her before glaring at Death. "Keep your lips to yourself."

Death flipped him off, but David kissed her head again before giving her a little nudge toward her angel and entered his bathroom.

"You shouldn't provoke him," Jane whispered, stopping right in front of Death.

He smiled and held his hand out for her to take. Jane didn't hesitate to grab it, and her heart ached when his sad eyes locked with hers. She

23

touched his cheek, smiling but heartbroken for him as he leaned his face against her palm.

Death let out a sigh. "Hi, baby girl."

"Hi, Death."

"You look better," he said, sliding his gaze down her body. "Did you feed again?" Jane nodded, and her chest tightened because of the longing in his eyes. He shook his head, adding, "Don't worry about me."

Her eyes burned, and she quickly hugged him to her chest.

He wrapped his arms around her waist, mumbling against her skin, "You're going to get me in trouble."

"*Shh.*" She struggled not to cry. "Do you hate me?"

"Never," he said, squeezing her tight. "Don't cry. You're about to see your babies."

"Death." She pulled back and held his face in her hands. "I do love you. So much. More than I can describe, but he's—"

"I know, angel." He covered her hand over his cheek and turned to kiss her palm. "David is where you belong. He's a good man."

She whimpered as tears welled up in her eyes. Because Death was a good man too. He was perfect.

He went on, his voice was soft but powerful. "He loves you so much. I won't say more than I do because it doesn't really matter which of us loves you more. You will always have both of us. Anyway, we already came to an agreement before I got you back—we know what the other needs with you and what will be tolerated." He smirked. "I may break his rules, but I think he already knows that. And I love you as well. More than you will ever know. As long as you love me, and we can touch from time to time, I think I will be content."

"I'll never stop loving you."

He smiled the smile that always sat in the back of her mind. "And I will love you longer than always."

Her throat ached as painfully as her heart. "That was incredibly romantic."

He chuckled. "You always forget who I am, babe."

"My Death." Jane stroked his cheek. "I never wanted to hurt you. I was so awful to both of you."

"No. I know you never wanted to hurt me. David knows as well. I hurt you, though. That is why I know he is the man for you. I've failed you again and again, and I have hurt you. David will never do that to you. I believe I have you the way I am meant to. I will always be here to hold you should he

24

slip up." He grinned. "I would love to have a reason to punch his Boy Scout ass." Jane chuckled as he pulled her closer. "It is so good to hold you again."

She stroked his hair and kissed the top of his head. "It feels so good to be held by you."

He laughed and hugged her to him more.

"Jane," David called behind her.

She glanced over her shoulder to see him standing a few feet away. He gave her a tight smile, but she saw the worry in his eyes.

Death chuckled, removing his arms from around her. "I couldn't keep my hands to myself."

David held out his hand for her to take. She smiled at him but looked back down at Death.

He winked before gently pushing her away. "Let him help you with your rugrats. I'm not cut out for the baby thing."

David smiled as he wiped the tears she didn't realize had fallen.

"You were good with me," she said when David kissed her forehead.

"I already told you." Death stood up, smiling the smile he gave only to her. "Only for you."

David turned her head into his muscular chest and wrapped her arms around his waist. "I told them I have a surprise waiting."

She flexed her fingers, fear flooding her system.

David hugged her tighter. "They're going to be so happy, sweetheart. We'll be right here with you. She's not here. I don't see her at all in your eyes or feel her in your touch. She's gone, and she can't hurt them or anyone else."

"Are you sure?" Jane felt pathetic, but she could only imagine the gruesome images of bodies and the brother and sister with blood spilling out of their tiny throats.

"I'm sure, Jane. She's gone." He gave her a sweeter kiss. "You haven't even felt her, have you?"

She opened her eyes, not remembering when she had squeezed them shut, and shook her head at him, her anxiety fading slightly.

"She's gone, angel," Death said. "I promise."

"Okay." She smiled, feeling his presence without needing to see him.

David glanced over her shoulder. There was a slight nod from him to Death before he looked down at her. Then he gave her a soft but long kiss.

Those perfect lips pushed away all her fears, filling her with warmth and strength. There were no images of her attacking her children—no whispers telling her that she was evil, worthless, or that she would destroy them all. There was still sorrow and guilt for what she'd done to everyone she cared about—sadness knowing that she would not hold her kids with Jason by her side again, but when David pulled away, smiling at her, she realized her heart had been with him all along. He'd kept it safe for her so Death could bring her home. He wouldn't replace Jason, but they would be a family together.

Death chuckled behind her, and tingles spread through her chest without him touching her.

"How did you do that?" She gasped, jerking out of David's hold.

Death smirked but stayed quiet.

She rubbed her chest, still feeling that warm sensation tingling there. "Death?"

"What did he do?" David asked, looking between them.

"You do make a beautiful family." Death smiled, clearly knowing something she did not.

"How?" she breathed, touching her chest as the sensation grew stronger.

"You will find out one day," Death said, looking completely at peace. "Your babies are here now."

Jane turned away from him, forgetting about the strange phenomenon, and took in Guinevere standing in the doorway with Nathan and Natalie at her side.

"I could not keep them back any longer," Guinevere said, almost in tears.

"Mommy?" Natalie whispered.

"Hi, babies." Jane's eyes watered upon seeing no hate or sadness. "I'm so sorry I was gone."

David wrapped his arm around her and kissed her temple before holding his hand out for Natalie. Her little girl didn't wait, and neither did Nathan.

"Mommy," Nathan said, running straight to her when she bent down just as David plucked Natalie off the ground and pulled them all into his arms.

Jane cried, unable to do anything else but squeeze them to her and breathe in their baby smell.

"Mommy, home," Nathan mumbled into her shoulder, making David and Death chuckle.

"Yes, Mommy is home," David whispered, tilting Jane's face up and giving her a sweet kiss. "Welcome home, Mommy."

4

QUEEN OF HELL

"Will you be here when we wake up, Mommy?" Natalie asked.

Jane's eyes burned, but she smiled as David sat on the bed, rubbing her back. "I'll be here," she said, brushing Natalie's hair out of her face.

Natalie looked at David. "It's the new moon, right?"

David grinned before kissing Jane's head. "That's right, princess. It's a new journey for the moon, just like it is for Mommy. We will all support her so she can glow again." He tickled Natalie.

Natalie giggled, nodding. "Can Nathan and I help?"

"You two are why Mommy shines the brightest, princess." David reached over, caressing Nathan's cheek. "Are you better, little man?"

"Better," Nathan said, making Jane's heart ache as much as it felt it could burst from joy.

"Good. I want you both to sleep now. Mommy and I have to visit with Ryder, but Aunt Elle is coming to watch over you."

"Are you still mad at Aunt Gwen?" Natalie asked.

Jane glanced at David. He didn't look at her, but judging by his tense posture, he wasn't happy about something that had happened with his sister.

"I'm not mad at her, princess. She just doesn't understand my love for Mommy, but she will." David kissed Jane's head as she looked down, realizing he must have argued with Guinevere over her. "Now, get some sleep. We'll both be here when you wake up."

They nodded, and Jane quickly kissed their heads before letting David lead her out of the room.

Ragnelle already waited in the hall, and she surprised Jane by hugging her tightly. "I'm so happy to have you back home."

Jane glanced at David, unsure of what was happening. "Oh, well, I'm glad I could come back."

Ragnelle smiled sadly. "I know we are not close, but I know how much David and my husband love you. That makes you precious to me as well. I hope we can become friends, but I understand that will take time. Just know that I, and many of the other wives, care a great deal for you. None of us understand the burdens you had to carry or the events in your life that have shaped you into the person who is adored and loved by David and the knights, so we have no right to judge you. Please understand that some may have spoken negatively purely out of concern for David."

"She doesn't know anything, Elle," David said quietly.

"I know, but she will." Elle smiled sadly. "I want her to know she's still very much loved, and the things she may hear are not what all of us think."

Jane gave her another hug. "Thank you. I appreciate it. And I hope we can be friends too."

David gently pulled Jane away, holding the door for Ragnelle. "We shouldn't be too long."

Ragnelle waved him off. "Take your time. I'm sure the angel wishes to spend time with her, but you two should try to have a few hours alone. Just make sure you keep the door shut." She winked and walked into David's room.

"David, is she telling us to have sex before we come back?"

He took her hand, leading her down the hall. "She is."

She gaped at him before glancing at the door. "Why?"

A smirk formed on his sexy face. "She can tell you want me."

Her eyes went wide. "What?"

He laughed, lifting her hand to his lips. "Baby, it's been visible on your face and scent all day."

Heat spread across her skin. "There's nothing on my face or anything different about my scent."

He wrapped his arm around her. "Your eyes are constantly stripping me naked. They all see it."

"Shut up." She smiled because she did indeed see images of his perfect body every time she glanced at him.

David chuckled, making her more aware of the perverted thoughts she'd had throughout the day. She didn't know how many times she'd imagined licking his stomach again and running her hands all over those smooth, hard muscles. She loved watching him tense and hearing his breathing hitch. It never lasted long. David always regained control and reminded her he was powerful—and good. David was good. And he wanted to show her that everything he did was for her.

"You're doing it right now," David said as a sexy smirk teased his lips. "Don't be embarrassed." He stopped long enough to lift and pull her legs around his waist.

"David." She grinned, throwing her arms around his neck as he pulled her into a kiss.

He squeezed her butt, and she sighed, enjoying the feeling of his strong hands on her. "I love that you daydream about me. You have no idea how often I daydream about you."

"You don't daydream about me." She pecked his smiling lips but noticed other vampires walking through the halls. "Shouldn't you put me down? People are watching."

David didn't even look around. He squeezed her butt and kissed her neck. "You're staying right here. I don't care who looks."

"Not even me?" Death asked.

Jane tensed up. "David, put me down."

"No," David said, nipping her lips. "Don't pout your lips unless you want me to bite them."

Death spoke again. "You two are like a pair of horny teenagers. I would ask to join the fun, but we should talk."

Her vampire sighed before pressing a firm kiss to her lips. "Go show him some attention before he starts pouting as well."

Jane's heart melted, and she caressed David's cheek, giving him a long kiss before whispering, "I love you."

He grinned, kissing her once more. "I know you do. Now go see your other love, but remember, he gets punched in the face every time his lips touch yours." He placed her on her feet, smacking her ass as he walked to a bar where Jane knew they kept blood.

"He says that as if I am supposed to be deterred from kissing you." Death grabbed her hand when she got close. "How can I pass up on these lips and a worthy fight with this fucker?"

David chuckled, opening a refrigerator. "You know she will be upset if we fight, though. And, that, you are deterred from."

Death's eyes ignited as he grabbed her chin. "He's a clever fucker." He kissed her forehead. "Come. Let's sit for this conversation." He led her to a chair, and she wasn't surprised when he sat her on his lap and hugged her.

She glanced at David, catching his smile as he nodded to her that it was okay. *I'm the luckiest girl in the world*, she thought, hugging Death back and accepting all the magic of being close to him. "I missed you."

Death slid his fingers down her arm and pulled her hand to his chest before pressing his palm over her heart. "And I missed you." He kissed her forehead again. "You know I never left, right?"

Her heartbeat instantly sped up. "I know. I think I almost saw you a few times, but you never came to me."

He hugged her tight. "I wanted to, angel. Do you understand why?"

Jane shook her head as the painful memories of sensing him watching her suffer and doing nothing crushed her. She had needed him so badly, and he'd just watched.

Death held her tighter, trembling while his heart pounded away with hers.

David ended up being the one to speak. "Baby, Death was told more about the entity after he left you in Texas. She was never an entity—she was half of your soul. He didn't know this when he discovered her. All he knew was he couldn't take her from you without destroying you. So when they told him there was one who could, he listened and accepted the terms."

"Lucifer," she whispered, and Death nodded. She hugged him, caressing his hair while realizing he'd hurt as much as she had during everything.

"Yes, sweetheart," David said. "An offer was made to Lucifer. No one else knew of it, but he agreed to remove that half of your soul. To do it, though, he needed to break the pure half to the point she—you—stopped fighting. Only then would he be able to lock her away for Death to come and release later."

Death finally spoke, "The problem was you never stopped fighting. As long as you kept getting back up, he would never have the chance to trap your pure soul. I would lose you to her even if you never died. You needed to be broken. You had to lose me, David, your family—you had to lose all hope. You had to fall to your darker soul. I could not save you from darkness as I have most of your life. I had to let him unleash his worst on you. If I interfered, there would be consequences.

"The thing is, there is more evil out there than you can imagine. Lucifer agreed, but he wanted something in return. He wanted you to be his queen:

you, Jane, not her. I had witnessed his reluctance to corrupt you when we made our first wager. My instincts told me he would honor this deal after I learned he sought out your old tormentors. He found some, and he destroyed them. Mercilessly.

"All of Hell believed I was being held back because of the wager I made with him before, but it was something else. He desired you, but he was using only wanting the darker half of you to take his place as High King as a ruse. It wasn't her that allowed him to gain power. It was you. I accepted his offer because I believed what I saw when he looked at you that night. You had stirred something good within him, and it was too much of a coincidence that he would be the one with the power to save you. So I agreed because I knew he would make sure you survived. I did not consider he'd double-cross me; I should have, but I had no choice but to trust this plan. If I didn't, I would not have been able to sit back and watch you get destroyed.

"He was supposed to break you, get her out, and leave you for me to revive. I didn't want to make you believe I'd abandoned you, but I had to. I swear, though, I have been by your side through it all. I have been watching and waiting for him to succeed. Even if I had to merely stay with you in our bond, I have been experiencing everything with you. I never left, angel. He wasn't supposed to take you away. He was supposed to take her and let me bring you back to us. But you were so strong."

Jane wiped her tears. "That's why he kept saying that."

"What?" David asked.

She leaned back, cupping Death's cheeks as his agony spread through her. She felt every bit of pain, fear, and helplessness that he went through. "Oh, Death." Her voice shook as he leaned into her hands.

"I'm sorry." His deep voice sent tingles through her body. "I don't mean to let you feel this."

Biting her lip and staring at him through her tears, she nodded. "I know."

His voice was gentle, but his lips never moved. *"Forgive me, Sweet Jane."*

She widened her eyes as she realized what had just happened. He was speaking to her telepathically, and she felt every bit of him as though he was a part of her. "I do." She sobbed, responding to what he'd mentally said as her heart beat as fast as his. She tried comforting him with better memories of them—of the times he had saved her—smiling sadly when his tense muscles relaxed.

The torture burning in his gaze didn't fade, but she felt his relief as he gave her the hug she'd needed from him for so long.

She cried, clutching his shirt as she breathed him in. "This." She curled her fingers into his shirt, gasping from the flood of foreign emotions washing over her. "This. I needed this."

Death cradled her head against his chest. "I know." His hold tightened as he mentally added for her, *"I knew."*

She choked out a sob, clinging to him as that strange warmth spread through her body.

"Jane," David said, waiting.

She squeezed her eyes shut, holding on to Death's shirt tighter. She didn't know if he was jealous or needed her to continue explaining what she'd meant to say before. It was overwhelming, as much as it felt right to experience this with Death.

Death pressed his lips to her hair as his words entered her mind. *"He needs to understand what happened with Lucifer. I need to make sure you understand."*

Pressing her palm against his chest, Jane breathed out. "Lucifer said I wasn't supposed to last. He said it as soon as we'd gotten there. He kept saying it would be easier if I just stopped fighting him. He wanted me to give every bit of myself to him, but I asked him for time. I didn't know he meant it beyond getting what he wanted."

Death let out a frustrated sigh. "He kept relieving your sorrow for reasons I do not understand. Every breath he allowed you to take without her tormenting you helped you grow stronger. I think he had no choice but to take you from us because there was always some part of you fighting, but he had also aided your suffering so much that you could destroy all of us. So he took you."

She couldn't believe Lucifer had intended to save her all along.

"No, angel," Death said, tilting her head back to meet his fiery gaze. "He wanted to keep you for himself. I have spies within Lucifer's ranks, and I learned about many of the lies and games he's been playing. He could not face me or unite his armies without you, so even if he relieved you—he still intended to keep you for himself."

"But he called you?" She couldn't keep up with everything he was saying. Was Lucifer good or bad?

"He fell in love with you, Jane." The fire in Death's eyes simmered. "I think once he realized you would not be broken by him, he desired to keep you under control but at his side. But your darker soul also grew stronger, and she could destroy you at that point. He knew she would do the unthinkable."

32

Her mouth fell open as she thought over her time with Lucifer. "He'd asked me what I wanted most regarding my demon." Her eyes watered. "I told him to be free of her. Always."

Death breathed out a calmer breath. "That's when he chose. He chose you and not himself. He knew nothing in his power could break you, or perhaps he could not bring himself to do it. Either he feared inflicting torment on you or feared you still not breaking. So, he unleashed her to do her worst."

"Baby," David said softly. "You don't have to say what happened. If you wish to talk about it one day, we will listen. Or, as I'm noticing, Death is communicating telepathically with you, so I will understand if you choose to discuss it with him if you are not ready to tell me."

"Perceptive bastard," Death said, chuckling as he kissed Jane's cheek. "I did not intend on letting her know just yet, so keep this knowledge private. Do not even speak of it to Arthur when he returns. I can shield my conversations with her from him, which he already knows, so that should be all he assumes is happening."

Jane smiled, caressing Death's cheek. "How long have you been reading my mind?"

"Not very long. I have always been able to feel you to the point I almost knew what you were thinking, but now I hear you as if you are speaking to me. I wasn't sure I could push my thoughts to you, but it appears our bond is strengthening quickly."

"How far away can we communicate with each other?"

He shrugged. "I'm not sure. I am blocking most of your thoughts, but if we practice, we may be able to communicate with each other anywhere on Earth."

"Are you able to do this because she is free of the darker half?" David asked. "Or has something else allowed you to have this with her?"

"Jealous, vampire prince?" Death smirked.

David didn't hesitate. "Considering I am the man she has improper thoughts about—no."

Jane covered her flushed face.

"Well, since you are going to be a dick, I will leave you to speculate why I can touch her without using my hands."

"Death," Jane said, shaking her head.

He snickered, keeping his mischievous gaze trained on David. "Quiet. This is between the Ds." He winked at her. "Naughty girl. I know what you're thinking without reading your mind."

"Shut up." She smacked his chest before giving David an apologetic look.

He winked at her too. "Don't worry, Jane. I know whose D you like best."

"Fucker," Death said. "Anyway, I cannot say why this is possible between us."

"Asshole," David retorted, chuckling. "Baby, are you okay? You know we are only attempting to cheer you up . . . And you having this with him doesn't bother me. I am slightly jealous, but he is jealous of me as well."

"I don't want to make you guys jealous." She stared at David. "Especially you."

A small smile formed on his lips. "We know, my love. I know you favor me at times, and in other moments, you need this asshole as badly as you need air to breathe. I am learning to accept him more each day. He is doing the same. So don't worry about us, okay? What matters is that we see you recover from all that happened. It's important to Death, and to me, for you to understand he never meant to hurt you. Just like I do, Death makes choices that put you first. For this situation, putting you first meant letting these awful things unfold." He glanced at Death before focusing on her again. "We both believe you learning these truths might help."

It warmed her heart to see them working together. She knew just how alpha male they were, yet they constantly joined forces for her. "I understand. I know both of you always try to do what's best." She bit her lip and looked at Death. "I just don't understand Luc's role. I don't get any of this. Why would it be him?"

Death began running his fingers through her hair. "I don't know why it was him. That is one thing I was not told. What I know—that I can tell you —is Lucifer needed you to ascend to the throne. He stood no chance against me, so this agreement was the only way to get me back off. Now, he is as strong as I am and commanding all of Hell. Well, I do not think all of Hell is with him. There will be a shift in alliances because of the way he let you go."

Jane thought over the last things she remembered with Luc, and her heart cried. "I started to have feelings for him." She watched them momentarily, worried but confident she needed to express these things. "I know it's stupid, and I'm hurting you both by caring for him at all, but there was something between us that I cherished." She sniffled, rubbing under her eyes to not cry. "I get that he made sure I suffered by inflicting my past on me. Not just that, he amplified every memory, making them a million times worse because he knew I could not escape it. But there were little things he did that seemed out of character. I think it was his way of giving me peace from my past. I know it's twisted, but he gave me a chance to think without her burning my mind and soul, and he told me to fight. He told me to be great. He could have fucked me and just pulled her right out or let her rule my body, but he didn't. He hesitated and smiled at me." Jane found herself smiling as she lost sight of David and Death for a moment, just seeing Luc's face when he smiled at her on the battlefield. "It was a real smile," she whispered, remembering how he would squeeze her hand and how his coldness would fade whenever she spoke to him.

A rumble within Death's chest made her blink the image of Lucifer away.

"Sorry." She watched a fire roar inside Death's gaze. "Death, I just think he was giving me the chance to be who I think I can be and fight my own monsters. He told me to stand up to her, even when he knew she was the true wielder, and I saw how proud he was to see me fight. I felt like I was more than his tool. He was my king."

David lowered his head. The muscles in his forearms continuously flexed, worrying her.

Death sighed, rubbing her arm. "She's struggling to describe her feelings, David. Her feelings for him are not what she feels for you or even me. He forced her to consider him king. The entire army bowed to them as king and queen, but she is still yours."

"I know." David looked back up.

"It's just," she said, her voice cracking because David didn't deserve to go through this, but she could not bring herself to betray Lucifer. "I think caring for him is the only way I can forgive my past and heal. He saw that. He saw me healing, and I don't know if he meant for me to or not, but I saw the moment he was happy. He felt something—I saw it. He realized what he was doing, and it made him feel good. It wasn't a trick. But the princes of Hell came. He kept saying he had not expected them yet, and I think it hurt him to let me go. He knew I wouldn't kill Lancelot's family. He knew it would destroy me. I saw his fury and fear briefly, and she laughed at him. She laughed at Lucifer because I was broken."

"That was the point," Death said. "I know what happened. I see it as clearly as you are recalling it. Can you see the way he looked at you when you offered to give yourself to him?"

She covered her mouth and nodded. She saw her king fall in love with her.

Death wiped her tears away. "He was letting you go at that moment. I will still beat the fuck out of him when I see him again, but you see, my love, it had to be him. I could never do what he did to you. It destroyed me to not interfere. And I still did when I showed myself and took you to my realm. That might have been why he needed to take you in the end. It would have been better for you to feel abandoned."

She whined, covering his hand with hers.

"Perhaps you two can discuss this more another time," David murmured. "Unless you need to do this now."

She shook her head. "No. I think later is better. He already knows what happened—that's enough." She kissed Death's palm. "Thank you for being with me as much as you could."

"Always." He pulled her to him, kissing her forehead. "I'm going to eventually need these lips again."

She chuckled sadly and turned to rest her head against his shoulder. "What else is bothering you, Death? I can feel you holding something back. There is something off about you, but I don't know what it could be."

He squeezed her gently. "I must leave for a while."

She gripped his jacket. "You said you'd stay."

Death sighed, pressing his palm over her heart again. "I am always with you. We may not be able to communicate over long distances—perhaps in time, we will, but I will know if you need me. I can return in an instant if you are in danger. I swear nothing will keep me from coming to you again. I did what was necessary to keep you alive—to keep her from destroying you. But she's gone. Luc is the only one who can contain her, and I do not see him wanting to put her back in you. He truly cared for you —I saw it too. Still, I do not trust him. He is stronger now, and he loves you. While it is true he let me take you; he can easily decide he wants you back. So I must find more answers and see to other matters in the upcoming war."

She nodded but felt like a piece of her was being stolen again. "Okay."

"I'm not being stolen from you. I told you I am yours. Only yours." Those tingles began to move over her skin, radiating from his palm, even up to her lips, as if he had pressed his lips there. It was the best feeling ever.

He chuckled and kissed her head. "I'm glad you think so. Shall I elaborate for your prince? I would love to hold this over his head."

"No." She laughed as she glanced at David.

Her vampire winked, reminding her he truly accepted her and Death's relationship.

"Whatever perverted thoughts he is putting in your head are nothing compared to what we share, so it's fine."

"Say that when I steal her from you."

Darkness shuttered David's handsome face. "Try it, Angel of Death. You already know I can leave a fucking mark on you."

Death grinned, clearly ready to test David's patience.

"Boys." Jane gave Death a slight jab with her elbow. "You, stop pushing him. I love when you get along with each other. Don't make me watch you fight."

Her angel continued to stare at David. "What's the matter, vampire prince? You just got her back and are already tired of fighting for her?"

"Death." Jane sat up straighter, ready to throw herself between them. "Stop."

He didn't look at her. "If he cannot take it, he does not deserve you." He smirked at David. "Do you deserve her, Prince David?"

Jane's heart raced as she darted her eyes between them. "David, he's just messing with you."

David held Death's stare. He looked casual enough with his elbows resting on his knees, but he was ready to fight. "No, he's challenging me."

Death grinned, and it was terrifying. "Giving up?"

"Death, stop this." Jane tried to make him look at her, but he didn't budge. "Why are you acting like this? I thought you were getting along."

"We have limits, baby." David still didn't avert his gaze from Death. "If you want to fight me, we fight where she does not see."

"No!" Jane tried to stand, but Death held her.

"Let her go," David growled.

Tears stung Jane's eyes. This was a bad dream. It had to be a bad dream. She kept blinking, trying to wake up, but nothing changed. "Death, what are you doing?"

His chest flexed as he responded telepathically. *"Testing him."*

Her panic halted as she wondered why.

Death's voice was calm when it entered her mind again. *"Because he will not like what he hears about you and Luc. I am strengthening him."*

A growl left David's mouth, and Death smirked.

"David," Jane said, not wanting to watch them fight. "Ignore him. I know you won't give up on me."

His eyes finally shifted to her, and he exhaled, his posture relaxing. "I won't."

A dark chuckle sounded behind her.

"You better not." Death loosened his grip but didn't lift Jane off his lap. "I will take her without hesitation if you do because Lucifer will feel like we did after he took her from us. For him—now the High King of Hell—losing his queen has yet to set in. Every moment you have her, his need to have her will grow, just as ours did."

David snarled. "Are you fucking with me to see if I'll fight that bastard?"

"Yes." Death snickered. "Get over it. She's worth it. Aren't you, High Queen of Hell?"

David looked ready to breathe fire. "Stop calling her his queen."

Death pulled her head to his shoulder. "Jane is the High Queen of Hell. The title has been up for grabs since Lucifer fell from Heaven. She met many princes, including Beelzebub, Astaroth, Asmodeus, Belial, Berith, and Sonneillon. They are demons and fallen angels who have waged war to gain the title of High King. Jane ignited hidden power within Lucifer—his prize—when he claimed her. Then he began acquiring full control of Jane's darker soul and gained the ability to physically harm Earth's Immortals. Word has it, he beat the shit out of Lancelot for the first attack Jane suffered at the hands of his wolves. He is a cruel bastard, but he protects his queen."

"He hated her," Jane said, not looking at David. "I think it was her who was supposed to be his queen. She kept saying that I was not the rightful queen. She was jealous—she wanted him to suffer for the attention he gave me."

"But Jane is not Lucifer's queen," David growled, baring his fangs. "You're mine. I can tolerate Death—barely—but I can't share you with Lucifer. Baby, the things you said he did to you—that you let him—"

Death shook his head. "You have no choice. She is the High Queen. It does not mean they will have a romantic relationship or that she needs to bear him an heir, but she became his queen when she agreed to go with him. Those loyal to Lucifer will recognize her as High Queen, and Lucifer will not choose another. Ever. So it's not entirely a bad thing. One of my spies will follow Jane if he has to choose between her or Lucifer."

She looked at her vampire. "David, a part of me felt like I belonged there. It felt right to stand between my generals and with Luc."

He glared at her. "You don't belong with Hell's army. Or with Lucifer. And his name is Lucifer, not Luc!"

She stayed quiet, knowing it would only upset him if she said more.

"You need to relax," Death told David. "I will handle Lucifer. It is those disloyal to him I am concerned about. They knew I was there when I came for her. Lucifer had control over the darker side of her soul, which kept her hidden from me. It protected the entire army's whereabouts. It was actually not far from Valhalla, but they felt me when he lifted the block."

"Who was he?" Jane asked, trying to distract David from the king and queen matter. "Luc said he would hold *him* back. Who was he talking about, Death?"

"I can't tell you," he murmured. "This is why I must go. The balance will soon shift, and I must do what I can. I'm sorry I cannot tell you more."

"Are you serious?" said David. He had gotten up and was staring out the window.

Death placed a kiss on her head. *"Go to him. He needs you."*

She leaned up and kissed his cheek. "Thank you."

He cupped her cheek, nuzzling her face before helping her off his lap.

It tore her up to walk away from one love to go to the other, but she had to if she wanted to hold on to what they could have together.

"David," she whispered, staring at his back.

He didn't move or acknowledge her, so she wrapped her arms around his waist and kissed his back. Her eyes watered when he stayed tense, but he eventually sighed and placed his hand over hers.

"Don't let her go on missions," Death said. "She is in too much danger."

Finally, David spoke. "She lost her powers, didn't she?"

Jane frowned, not having thought about it.

"Yes," Death answered. "The power belonged to the darker half of Jane's soul—not her pure side. Luc holds that half of her soul and the power she had."

"Can he use it?" David asked, turning and facing her now.

"No," Death said. "Only if he puts it back in Jane. She is the true vessel. It needs her pure half to function. That is why she didn't want to kill Jane. She wanted to break her so she would stop fighting. I fear others might be given the power to control Jane if they are united again. Lucifer broke many agreements to set her free the way he did, and I still have no idea if he intends on using her to destroy his enemies."

"He won't put it back," she whispered, stepping away from David when he finally tried to touch her.

He crossed his arms instead of reaching for her when she moved farther away. "You don't know that."

"He won't." Her heart hurt. She didn't like Death and David pushing each other in a non-playful way, and she already knew if Lucifer ever showed up, he would receive the wrath of both men.

"Calm down." Death took a step toward her.

"No!" She held out her hand, her eyes instantly brimming because she would never be able to stop him. She felt no surge of power. Nothing. She was nothing.

"That's not true." Death gestured to David to back up but focused on her. "Jane, you need time. You need to trust me. Trust in David. We are yours. Although Lucifer may love you, he is not on our side. And this shit you're pulling, feeling worthless without that bitch inside you, is exactly the type of thing he would use to get you to go with him."

"Don't talk badly about him." Her lips trembled, but she lifted her chin when he glared at her.

He stood tall and spoke slowly. "Lucifer is bad, Jane. He saved you, yes, but that Fallen is one of the most evil creatures ever to exist."

"He has good in him." Jane's voice cracked. "You're being mean because you're scared. You're being mean to each other, and you're hurting my heart."

David shook his head. "I love you. We love you. But he's right—Lucifer is bad. I understand you might be confused about your feelings because he did save you, but you must remember he didn't intend to honor the bargain he made with Death. He wanted to keep you. He forced you to—" He growled, clenching his fist. "I can't even say it, Jane."

"I'm sorry." Tears slipped free as she clutched at her heart. "I need to be alone."

"No," David said. "I don't want you to feel like I'm angry with you. I'm not."

"I just need to be alone."

"Jane," Death snapped. "Stop this now."

She glared at him. "You want to kill him, don't you?"

"He's dangerous," was all he said, but it was enough.

Her eyes filled with tears at the instant thought of seeing Luc dead. "You can't. He won't hurt me. I know he won't."

Death's features sharpened for a moment. His eyes burned brighter, and his skin paled before returning to the normal, tanned color. "He might. I know you care for him, but he is a threat to you. I won't let him take you again. If I have to reap your darker soul with his, so be it. I will find a way to keep you alive. No one will take you from us again. Ever!"

"I have to go," she whispered and made to leave, but David grabbed her before she could go anywhere.

He turned her toward him. "Stay with me. I didn't mean to become upset."

"Just let me think by myself." She pushed his hands away. "I need to think about all of this. I didn't even know I had lost my powers. And I know I can't stop Death from his plans with Luc or your feelings toward him, but I don't want to hear either of you talk badly about him. I get it if you need to, but I won't listen to it. So stay and talk to each other about whatever you have to—but I can't listen to you plot his murder." Jane looked back at Death and saw how angry he was with her. "Come to my room when you are ready to leave."

"Fine." Death turned away.

"Baby." David grabbed her again, cupping her cheeks. "Don't be upset. It has been difficult for us to be without you. We are both afraid of losing you."

"I know." She kissed him quickly. "I'm sorry for being this way. Come find me when you're done."

He smoothed her hair back and gave her a quick kiss. "I'll be up in a few minutes."

She didn't look behind her as she headed to her room. She needed to be alone. She needed to figure out how to keep her king alive.

5

THE TRUTH

David's few minutes had come and gone. At least twenty had passed, and Jane was still alone in her old room. It was what she needed, but she was surprised he hadn't come yet.

She watched snow flurries swirl by the window and, when the room's temperature dropped, pressed her hand to the glass and closed her eyes. "I know you're here," she whispered, instantly feeling two arms wrap around her from behind. A tear slipped from her eye when she opened them to see his white sleeves and strong hands resting against her stomach. It filled her with a strange peace, and she felt awful for wanting that feeling.

"My queen." Lucifer hugged her tighter. "Forgive me."

"You know I already have," she sobbed, covering his hands with hers. "Why didn't you tell me? You let me kill—you let him fuck me. Why?"

He breathed her in deeply. "I couldn't tell you, my queen. You know how these things work."

"But those babies." She licked the tears from her lips. "Lancelot. He didn't want to hurt me anymore. I saw it in his eyes. He wanted his children to be safe, and you let her . . . How could you?"

"I did what had to be done," he mumbled. "It gave me no pleasure to watch you breaking inside her. Still, I had to let it happen to have any chance of freeing you from her. You would have forgiven me if I did anything wrong. She knew what to do to break you, so I let her. You have always been your own worst enemy, Jane."

42

It hurt to even breathe. "Why did Death believe you would do things differently?"

"Because he is a fool. He knows very little of the truth—of who you really are."

She held her breath for a few seconds. "And who am I?"

"So many things, little queen."

"Enough of this." She glared at the faint reflection of him in the mirror. For a second, she was confused by the sight of dark gray hair, but then she remembered it had changed after he'd taken half of her soul into him.

The corner of his mouth twitched slightly. "There's my queen."

Jane stared at his reflection in silence, struggling to process the surge of pride that washed over her from hearing him say that. "I like the gray color. It matches your wings."

"So easily distracted." He sighed, but he scanned her reflection too. "You look well."

"Thank you." She tried to see if there were other differences, but he looked the same. "Does she still burn?"

"Constantly, my queen." His gaze softened. "Now I will answer your question." Lucifer caressed her cheek, his eyes never moving from hers as they continued staring at one another's reflections. "A long time ago, after I had fallen, I was told about a weapon that would bring me victory over my enemies. It was to be hidden from me by my father, but I was informed this weapon would eventually make itself known. I simply had to claim it when it revealed itself. Doing this would crown me as the High King of Hell, thus granting me control over all its legions.

"I was drawn to your power when you fought Lancelot's wolves for the first time. I observed you, wondering what lured me to you, and then you unleashed your first wave of energy. I watched your lovely hazel eyes darken and saw my prize—my weapon—smiling at me. It was no surprise that Death would come—after all, you were mortally wounded. He outsmarted me initially, but I knew who you were. It was a glorious revelation to learn he had feelings for you and had hidden you from everyone. I had long awaited the day I could destroy a part of him, and you being my weapon was all I needed to do so.

"I had not expected the vampire to be prophesied to you. I planned to use him, though. Your loyalty to Jason and lust for David would torment you—but you, my little queen, fought your desire for him—and he was incorruptible. So, I waited. You were so beautifully unstable, yet something was captivating about your smile when you stood between your angel and vampire. Your strength to fight darkness intrigued me. You would truly suffer for the sake of others, and you honestly believed you were unworthy of their love. She knew this, too, of course, and she tormented you with it. But you surprised me again when I pushed those memories into you. Do you remember the little boy's burial?"

A tear fell from her eye. "The cold."

His eyes flashed with silver light. "As much as you and Death love one another, he hurts you. I saw this as a way to turn you against him. Instead of doing what I expected, though, you shut off. Somehow you locked yourself and the darker side of you away. It was a setback, but it still allowed me another chance to obtain you. I had intended to numb you so severely that you would be too far gone to fight when I called her forward. Only, you never made it to me that night. I was called to Heaven and forced to abandon my pursuit for the time being."

"I don't understand." She stayed still as he wiped her tears away.

"I waited for you in that cemetery, Jane. When I realized you were under attack, Gabriel came for me. He promised Death would not allow you to perish, and I went with him. This is where I cannot say more."

She bared her fangs, hissing when he merely smirked. "You said you'd tell me."

"And I have told you what I am permitted to." He held her stare.

"I already knew I was a weapon—this is nothing new."

"She was, my queen. Not you."

"I thought she was part of me. Are we not the same?"

"She is half your soul. You were ripped apart well before your birth. When reintroduced, she was too evil to be considered the same soul. She was hidden inside you. It has always been necessary for her to defeat you for me to truly wield her—you. Your constant choice to keep others from feeling the pain you have is what kept her back. Until I found you, that is. My blood gave her strength to rise, but you still tried to cage her, and you did—many times—because of your love for your family and the men in your life."

"That doesn't answer who I am. I want to know. If she is the weapon, and you consider us separate, what role do I have? Why did you let me stay? Why free me of her when you had what you wanted?"

"Because I love you, Jane."

She slowly turned in his arms, but he still held her close. He was so beautiful, and she found the gunmetal gray hair color suited him as much as his pale blond color.

"That is who you are." He stared into her eyes. "You are the woman I would love—I never expected you to be her. Not the vessel containing my weapon."

Jane had to focus on speaking—his aura was pulsing, calling for her to be with him. "You were told you would love me?"

"Yes."

"When?"

His eyes glinted with silver. "Before my fall."

"But you learned of your weapon after?"

"Yes."

"By who?"

"That is the secret, my queen. You will learn the truth when it is time."

She nodded, finally accepting she would only know when they wanted her to. It was easier to be told this by him. It wasn't that she trusted Lucifer more than Death, but she knew Lucifer would answer if he could. With Death, she feared he would hide information that may hurt her. "They fear you will put her back in me."

Fury broke his emotionless mask, and he snarled. "You are my queen, Jane. I will always protect my queen."

"You choose me over your weapon?" She fought hard to suppress her smile, but she saw his eyes capture the moment of happiness his words brought her.

"Yes." He caressed her lip with his thumb. "I did not plan to, but I did, and I will hold her prisoner within me. She despises the light."

She laughed sadly, turning to kiss his palm. "Thank you, Luc."

"I want you to come with me," he said.

"What?" She pushed his hand away, but he grabbed her again, holding her tightly.

"You have no powers. You are still among the strongest made immortals because of David, but you are no match against those coming for you."

Her breaths came faster. "Who's coming?"

"Everyone. My main concern, however, is Belial. I need to keep you safe. If he gets you . . ."

"What is it? What will happen?"

He cupped her cheek. "When your soul was corrupted, a failsafe was left behind—a second wielder. I dismissed this rumor, but he knew once she came forward. He could not wield her if I ruled over you, but he was ready to fight for her after she assumed full control. He wanted nothing to do with you; he saw you as a threat. So he waited for me to unlock all her power."

"Only you freed me of her," she said softly.

"Yes. He did not know I could also imprison her—very few did. Now Belial will do all he can to see her joined with you again."

"But you won't let that happen, right?"

Lucifer let out a breath, removing his hand. "You lost your powers. You lost my light as well. If you were ever captured, I would be at their mercy. They saw my feelings for you, but when I released you to Death, it became clear I would do anything to keep you safe." He searched her eyes. "Anything, my queen."

"If you're saying you'd put her back in me just to keep me alive, you are a bastard." She tried to shove him, but he didn't move an inch. "Don't you even think of it. I would rather you let me suffer and die than ever have her inside me again. I may forgive you for a lot of the things you do, but not for this."

He gritted his teeth. "I would not have to consider it if you just came with me. I can protect you. Together, we are stronger. The legions will see that and fight him rather than join his quest to have her at his side."

"No, Luc! Together, we rule Hell, and you will use me to hurt everyone I love. Together, you risk them forcing you to put her back."

"I will protect you."

She bared her fangs at him. "I am with David."

He snarled. "I know you are with him. I smell his stench on you. I did not expect you to fuck him so quickly."

"Did you expect me to crawl into your bed?" She tried to pull away, but he held her, and she hated that it still felt right to be near him. "You tortured me." She shook her head, trying to make herself hate a part of him, but she couldn't. "You had your reasons, I know. I know you care for me, and I care for you, but I will always choose David. I love him. I want to spend however long I have left in this world with him."

"I already know this." He lifted his angry but sad eyes to stare at her.

"If you truly love me, you won't put her back, and you will support me as I am with David. You will join me here."

He chuckled. "I will not join the knights. Those still loyal will abandon me if I lower myself to one of your bodyguards."

"I'm not asking you to guard me. I'm asking you to fight beside me —beside us."

"And how do you think your boy toys will feel? Do you honestly believe

David and Death will look past what I did with you? We would destroy each other, my queen, and then I would take you because I am stronger than them. And Death will not kill me with half of your soul sitting inside my prison."

"How are you stronger than Death?" Her heart was beating too fast. Death was invincible. He was supposed to be her warrior, her protector, even if she was strong on her own. She couldn't give up that sense of letting Death stand in the way of her demons.

"Because of you, Jane. I cannot say more."

Her eyes watered as she pleaded, "We can work together."

"You know we cannot," he said. "You came here because you feared their plotting against me. You care for me, and that only fuels them to defeat me. They are smiling at you, telling you it is fine because they do not blame you for all that happened—they blame me. I will not get along with them as they do with each other. I doubt they will last in their truce anyway."

"But they don't know about Belial. If you would just tell them, they would understand."

"It will only cause Death to do something drastic." He glanced around the room. "I'm sure they will come for you any moment now. Allow me to take you."

"Why are you even asking me?" She watched a muscle in his jaw twitch.

"I need your permission to bond with you again. We can only form a temporary bond since Death reclaimed his bond after I removed mine."

"You mean you can't teleport with me?"

"Correct."

"Luc." She lifted her hand to his cheek when the cold look returned to his handsome face. "Don't do that. Please."

"I need to keep you safe." He tried to keep that same harsh exterior, and she smiled when he struggled. Finally, Lucifer growled, reaching up to hold her hand in place. "You know I enjoy your smile. Do not use it against me."

She smiled wider, awed by the softness in his eyes now. "You do love me."

"I have told you this already, my queen. I am not your mate—I will not repeat it like a fool simply because I have waited for you to be born."

Jane searched his eyes. "How long have you known about me?"

"I have already said too much. Will you come with me or stay with the imbeciles who do nothing but put you in danger?"

"Don't insult them," she snapped. "And you already know I won't leave David. So now you decide—will you stay and help or leave?"

"Are you dense?" He looked at her like she'd lost her mind. "You will not be able to defend yourself from demons and fallen angels. Before you could—now you are as vulnerable as a child."

She scowled, pulling her hand down, but he held on to it. "Quit being mean."

"I am not your boyfriend." He said it so emotionlessly that she almost forgot he was upset. "Stop acting as if I care about your feelings. I care about my queen being kept safe."

Jane knew he could see the hurt in her eyes, but his blank mask shifted into something cold and cruel, and she raised her chin, ready to show him she wasn't as weak as he made her out to be. "I may have lost everything that made me special, but I can fight. I have David and Death. I have the knights, and I would have you if you stopped being an asshole by trying to keep me for yourself. I'm your queen, not your puppy."

He grabbed her chin, staring into her eyes. "There's my queen." His gaze fell to her lips, and he smirked when she automatically licked them. "Do you desire my kiss? You already know it is yours."

She tried to push his hand off, but he held her tighter, moving his body closer and tilting her face up more. "I don't."

"But you do." He caressed her bottom lip. "Why do you refuse to admit that you love me?"

Her eyes widened. "I don't love you. I love David."

His eyes flashed. "And you love Death."

She knew what he was getting at—she could love all of them. "David accepts my relationship with Death. I've always loved Death."

A sadness danced across his face. "I know you have."

"What do you mean?"

"I meant nothing, my queen." He glanced at the door as it suddenly burst open. In an instant, he pushed her behind him, one hand tightly grasping her forearm.

David and Death entered quickly but stopped in the middle of the room when she managed to get between them. Lucifer didn't let go of her arm, so it looked like he was holding her captive.

"Let her go," David shouted, baring his fangs.

"David, he's not here to hurt me," she said quickly, holding a hand up for him to stay back.

"Jane, get out of the fucking way," David yelled, his eyes almost black. "He's trying to take you with him."

Death pushed David back a bit, appearing calmer than her vampire, but he wasn't happy. He was furious, and Jane hated the terrifying way he stared at Lucifer. She could almost see the thousand ways her angel wanted to kill him.

"Calm down." Death yanked David's shoulder. "You are going to hurt her."

"I won't hurt her," David snarled, shoving Death's hand away.

"I meant her heart, idiot." Death pulled David back when he moved forward.

"He's not here to hurt me." She shook when David's glare settled on her. "He wanted to see that I'm safe."

"Don't you fucking lie for him." David shifted his gaze back to Lucifer. "I heard everything this bastard just said."

"Move away from him, Jane," Death ordered. "We won't fight, but you need to get away."

"He won't hurt me," she cried. "He won't hurt me. Please, David. He loves me—just like you and Death do. He won't hurt me."

"He tortured you. He took you from me, and we all know what he made you do." David growled, clenching his fists. "Don't tell me he's not going to hurt you after everything he did."

"No, he didn't mean to," she said, not knowing what to do. She couldn't sit by and watch them kill Lucifer.

"We won't kill him." Death shook his head. "I promise, angel. We just need you to get away from him."

"You're lying." She shielded Lucifer with her body. "You want to kill him because you're afraid of what he might do."

"Enough, Jane," Lucifer said in that firm tone that somehow always made her feel loved by him. "You are not a weak girl anymore, and you know they are right. I did come here for you, and I did hurt you."

She rubbed her tears but stood taller. "Yes, you hurt me. But it's up to me how you are punished—not them. You are good, Luc. I won't let them hurt you. No one will if I can stop it."

"I'm not good, my queen," he said without any softness. "You know that. If they want to fight, I will fight them. I came to protect you, not to have you beg these two righteous fucks to spare me."

Both Death and David growled loudly.

"Stop it," she shouted at him. "Don't yell at me. I'm trying to keep you safe because I love you!" She stared at David with wide eyes. "Oh, God. David, I'm sorry. I didn't mean to say that."

He looked like he'd been stabbed in the heart.

Jane's lips trembled as Death tightened his hand on David's shoulder.

"You are still her choice." Death pulled David back another step. "It's not the same as it is with you. Understand? He gives her something we cannot, that is all. He gives her the ability to forgive the wrongs committed against her. She doesn't know any other way but to love."

David lifted his gaze to hers. He stayed quiet, taking in her tears as she held her hands over her mouth. She hadn't meant to say that. She hadn't realized she felt that way about Lucifer, but now she'd said it, she realized it was true. She loved him.

Lucifer sighed, letting go of her hand. "Go."

She tore her gaze from David's to slightly meet Lucifer's. "What?"

Her king briefly glanced at David before looking at her. "I freed you and summoned Death so you could return to your knight. Go. If he wishes to fight, I will fight back only because I need to keep you safe. He may be the strongest of your kind, but he is no match for me or the others coming. I won't receive a wound that hinders me from protecting you, so go and let him decide what he must do. I already gave you my word I would not kill him."

Jane searched his emotionless face.

He gently shoved her forward. "Go so we can get on with things. You will not worry for me like this again."

"Jane." Death grabbed her hand and tugged her until she stood between him and David. "We won't fight." He cupped her face, forcing her to look at him rather than Lucifer as his voice filled her mind. *"Snap out of it! David needs you. You should not have said that."*

She slowly lifted her gaze to David. "I'm sorry. I didn't know."

He didn't move to hold her, and his expression emptied like Lucifer's as he spoke. "Choose. You have all three of us in the same fucking room—say who you choose."

Death put his hand on David's shoulder. "Don't make her do that. You've told her you would not make her choose."

Her vampire kept his dark eyes on hers. He was hurt, rightfully so. Even though she refused to watch them kill Lucifer, she was wrong. She was done putting David last. She had to prove here and now—he was it for her.

Not saying anything, she moved in front of him and pulled him down

50

until his lips touched hers. He kissed her back, pulling her close before lifting her into his favorite position to hold her as he ravaged her mouth.

She wanted to cry because she didn't want to hurt Death or Lucifer, but she had chosen David. She was ready to act like it, which meant showing him he came first. "I'm sorry," she whispered, caressing his cheek.

"I know." He breathed in deeply as he nuzzled her, occasionally kissing her lips or cheek.

"Well." Death walked toward Lucifer.

Jane tensed, sensing his rage. "Death, you said you wouldn't fight."

David held her tight, and they watched Death stare Lucifer down. He was taller and more muscular than the King of Hell, but she knew it would be a nasty fight if they chose to.

"Calm down," Death's voice rang through her head, but he didn't move an inch as he kept his gaze fixed on Lucifer.

"Are we going to discuss my reason for coming here?" Lucifer asked.

Death smirked. "You're lucky I knew you couldn't teleport with her."

"And why is that?" Lucifer asked, not looking away from Death's menacing gaze.

Death swung faster than Jane had ever seen a punch given. His fist slammed into Lucifer's jaw, knocking the king to his knees as she screamed.

"Death, stop." She sobbed, trying to get out of David's arms. Lucifer looked up at her as Death loomed over him.

"He's getting off easy." Death walked to the window. His wings manifested, making her gasp and cease her cries as he flapped the massive black wings once before hiding them again.

Lucifer chuckled, standing up and spitting out some blood. "Having trouble with your glamour? I wonder why that would be . . ."

Death didn't turn around, but she could feel his frustration and anger. Even fear laced his emotions. "If you come to her again in an attempt to take her from us, I will rip your wings from your back and watch them burn in Father's light."

"He didn't come here to hurt me," Jane said. "He's worried."

Her angel sighed, shaking his head. "You cannot lie to me. Not that you did often, but it is impossible now. Do not insult me by lying for him."

She bit her lip, staring at Lucifer. He rubbed his jaw, shaking his head at her, and she knew he was saying he was fine, so she smiled sadly before looking down.

"Explain your plans, Lucifer," Death said, still not looking at them. "And tell me why there is another with the ability to control her."

"Belial is a failsafe," Lucifer said calmly.

She had to look up because she expected him to be pissed, but besides redness on his jaw and a drop of blood on his lips, he seemed fine.

"Was her soul aware?" Death asked. "Either of them?"

"I believe the darker one knew once she realized I had developed an attachment to Jane. Not the other."

David kissed her head, wiping her tears before whispering in her ear, "I'm sorry, my love."

Jane shook her head, kissing his palm. "You did nothing wrong."

Death continued staring out the window. "How many are with Belial?"

"I still don't know for sure," Lucifer said. "Perhaps half. Although, she gained followers on her own. I am certain the word is out she was not the same as the other one."

"What do you mean, Luc?" she asked, taking David's hand and intertwining their fingers.

Lucifer stared at her, his gaze falling to her and David's hands before returning to her face. "Your match with Lancelot drew the attention of many. The same can be said of your initial meeting with the other princes. They recognized you as their queen, and it will be difficult for them to break loyalty now it is done. However, when *she* put on her show"—his gaze softened—"not all were pleased with the personality change."

"Which of the princes are loyal?" she asked.

He smirked, his eyes flashing silver when David growled. "You made an impression, my queen. Thanatos remains loyal, and I believe a few others, but I do not wish to get your hopes up until I can confirm them."

"Than is loyal to her?" Death laughed. "He knows nothing of loyalty— don't trust in this, Jane. If he comes near you, call me, and I will destroy him or lock him away."

Lucifer shrugged, still wearing that smirk of his. "You are not a lovely woman with a charming personality, Death. Jane and Than got along quite well, isn't that right, my queen?"

Finally, her angel turned, his green eyes lit ablaze with emerald fire, and his features more prominent, almost too beautiful to stare at. Those eyes darted to her as he let out a low growl.

Death, she thought, imagining herself caressing his gorgeous face. *Let him talk. He's not going to hurt me. Please try. If you try, David will. The more protection I have, the better, right?*

His voice kissed her mind as tingles slid over her lips. *"You trust him?"*

"Yes," she said aloud but added silently, *they care for me. Both. I saw it, and you do too.*

Death slid his gaze to David before looking at Lucifer. "What of Asmodeus?"

Jane turned to Lucifer. "He's on our side, right?"

"He may be on your side, my queen, but I am not sure. He withdrew his army once I returned without you. There was little time to confirm alliances once Belial and Berith freed Lancelot and the wolves. However, Sonneillon and Astaroth stayed until I joined the battle."

"So, they're against you?" she asked.

Lucifer glanced at Death. "No, my queen. When I fight, even demons flee."

"You can stop trying to impress her," David said as he sat on the bed. He slid his hand along her thigh to her ass. "If you had seen what she did to herself because of you, you wouldn't even speak to her."

Jane sighed, kissing David's cheek as he glared at Lucifer.

"I cannot change what has been done." Lucifer held David's stare. "And I have seen what she did to herself, vampire. I will not forgive myself, but it had to be done. Be grateful they did not ask you to destroy her."

"I would never hurt her the way you two have." David shifted his gaze to Death briefly.

Jane stayed quiet as Death and Lucifer eyed one another. She knew there was very little she could do to change David's view on either angel. They would have to decide how they'd get along, and she couldn't show Death or Lucifer preference over David. Protect them from killing each other, yes, but she had to prove to David he was her choice.

"We know." Death crossed his arms as he addressed Lucifer again. "How soon will they come for her?"

"Days." Lucifer tugged his sleeve.

"So, we leave or try to gather followers to fight with us?" Jane asked.

Death shook his head. "You will stay put. Luc and I will hunt Belial together while David convinces the knights to return. We will likely have to move all of you, but we can buy you time by pressuring Belial. He will keep his army close to him, and his is strongest."

"That's stupid," she said, ignoring his glare. "Really, Death? You want to leave me sitting here by myself? I mean, I don't care all that much if I get hurt, but I won't stay here and endanger my babies. If you leave, we come with you."

"I can only take you, Jane." Death shifted his gaze to David. "You must stay close to David for now. I'm sure he will return quickly. I already have someone who will watch over you anyway. He will be here tomorrow morning."

"Who?" she asked at the same time David and Lucifer did.

Her angel smiled at her. "She will be in good hands. Have some faith in me."

"I do, but I don't see the purpose of you leaving. You three are the strongest—why would you leave?"

"You can call me if there is trouble, and I will return," Death said. "It is vital we seek out Belial now. What matters is whether your dark soul is returned. That is why I want Luc with me, and I want Belial destroyed or locked away."

"I still think it's stupid." She shoved David's shoulder. "Aren't you supposed to be on my side?"

He gave her that sexy smile. "Baby, I'm always on your side, but I am the only one fast enough to retrieve Arthur quickly. Even if I asked Death to go to him, Arthur would not listen. They had some disagreements while you were away—I should go in person. And if Death is comfortable leaving you for a short while, I trust him. I know he will not put your life in danger again. You did not see him the way I did, my love. Trust me. I know when to believe him."

Jane looked at Lucifer. "What do you think?"

David growled but said nothing and merely squeezed her tighter.

Lucifer's gaze fell to David's hand. "Your vampire and angel are right. If you wish for the people of Arthur's kingdom and your family to stay alive, you need the knights, and you need to prepare to flee. Then you prepare to fight. I doubt we will catch Belial, but it will buy us time. If Death has a guard for you, I trust him to keep you safe until our return."

"You mean whatever threats make it through while you hunt Belial can be destroyed without you three?"

"Precisely, my queen." Lucifer finally smiled. "You lost the powers she held, but you have gained more if you would only embrace who you truly are."

Death sighed, walking toward her as he told her, "Don't stress yourself out. I promise you will like my replacement. He even brings a surprise for you." He caressed her cheek, then spoke to David. "Stay with her until the morning light, then find Arthur and return. The battles they are engaged in are nothing compared to what will come. Convince him to withdraw and get back to her. Start preparing mass evacuations and perhaps send the weak to safe houses. I swear, if she falls under attack, she will be guarded, and Luc and I can return as well."

"It is Lucifer, little brother." Lucifer fixed his sleeve.

"Whatever, Luc." Death winked at her.

She wanted to smile, but she knew he was only trying to make up with her. "I'm not a baby. If y'all think I can handle things, I'll handle them."

David chuckled, kissing her head. "We know, my love. Still, you are one against countless enemies. It is our nature to worry."

"We should leave," Lucifer said, gaining their attention.

Jane felt awful—he was the odd one out.

Death gave her a look as his voice filled her mind. *"He will not have you the way David and I do. Ever."*

She glared at him and spoke aloud. "Which is why we shouldn't rub it in his face."

Death opened his mouth, but David stopped him, holding up his hand.

"She's right." David kissed her head. "She needs us to work together, and you and I both know what it's like to be the odd one out. If she needs him, she needs him." David shifted his gaze to Lucifer. "I may accept Death and understand she benefits from being close to him, but you are to keep your distance. Unless she needs your immediate aid, you will not touch her again. She made her choice. Understand?"

"He understands." Jane met Lucifer's gaze. "He has said it before: he is my king, not my boyfriend."

Lucifer ran his hand through his hair, and Jane realized she really enjoyed his new look.

Lucifer nodded before asking Death, "Do you wish to waste more time here?"

Death ignored him and David as he bent to kiss her forehead quickly. "Be safe."

"I love you," she whispered, trying to ignore David's rigid posture as she reached for Death's hand.

Death's eyes flicked up to David before looking back at her, his voice entering her mind. *"And I love you, angel. I am sorry for my behavior before. I only worry about losing you again."*

"I know." She squeezed his hand.

He pushed tingles through her, smiling when she sighed. His voice kissed her mind just as sweetly as his touch. *"Take care of David. He needs your love."*

Jane nodded and lifted his hand to her cheek. The sparks kissed her skin, and she smiled when she heard his voice again. *"I will tell Luc that you love him. Do not say it in front of David again; he is still struggling. I may not be happy about your love for Lucy, but I feel what you do and understand it is not the same . . . Do not feel guilty about loving all of us—it will make sense one day. And don't worry about showing me you have chosen David—I know he is where you belong. So does Lucifer."* He rubbed his thumb across her cheek. *"Be happy, baby . . . Just don't get pregnant."*

Jane let out a sad laugh as she reached out to hug him. She felt him nod to David as her knight let her go.

Death hugged her tightly. He slid his fingers through her hair while she silently cried. *"Shh..."* he whispered as those tingles spread throughout her body, calming her.

She always hated how it felt to have him leave. It physically hurt her. "Please hurry back," she murmured, looking over his shoulder to hold Lucifer's stare.

"You will hardly miss me." Death kissed her shoulder. "Are you good now?"

"No." She leaned back as he chuckled. She cupped his cheeks, admiring his beauty as he smiled, tilting his face toward her hand. "Thank you for not giving up on me—for bringing me back home."

His smile fell, and he pulled her close for a kiss. It was impossible not to press her lips back as the tingles came alive, frantically racing over her lips and down to her heart.

"You're welcome." He pecked her once more, chuckling. "He owes me two hits now. Shall I make it three?"

"Since you hit him for me, you get one for free," David said, standing behind her.

Jane glanced at Lucifer and smiled. "Be careful, Luc."

"Of course, my queen." His expression gave away nothing, but he had watched her without blinking once.

Death rolled his eyes and quickly stole another kiss, laughing loudly as David yanked her out of his arms. "Don't be greedy with her."

David kissed her head as he wiped his thumb over her lips. "Next time, Angel of Death. I will pay you back next time."

Death winked at her as he spoke to her through their bond. *"Keep that smile. I'll keep your king safe—as long as he stays true."*

"Thank you, Death." She watched him walk to Lucifer.

They glared at each other until Death darted his gaze back to her.

"Always, Sweet Jane." Death put a hand on Lucifer's shoulder. "Ready?"

Lucifer made eye contact with her. "Be safe, my queen."

"You too," she said, silently adding, *my king.*

Death gave her a stern look.

I'm sorry, she thought to him. *I love you. Please try to get along.*

"Not possible, babe," Death said, squeezing Lucifer's shoulder. Hard.

Then they were gone.

Jane was quiet, but she slowly looked up at David.

He rubbed his thumb over her lips again. "I trust you, Jane, but please try to understand it is not easy to watch you put yourself in danger." He lifted his gaze to hers. "Or listen to you declare your love for another man —for Lucifer."

"I didn't mean to say that." She held his hand to her face. "Or mean to feel that way about him. I swear it's not the same kind of love. I can't describe it, but I swear I never meant to hurt you like this."

"I know." He gave her a tight smile. "Did he kiss you?"

"No." She kissed his palm. "And I'm sorry about kissing Death. I'll stop."

David shook his head, chuckling. "Even if you stop, that fucker will sneak them in, and you will let him. And I see it is simply how the two of you express what you share—maybe something else, but I believe I am supposed to accept it. I don't want you making out with him, but I see it differs from sating lust for one another." He tilted her face up, smiling. "It's hard to accept that you love him so much, but I can't help but want him to show you he loves you. He makes you shine, and I feel like the luckiest man on earth because you choose to direct that light at me."

Her smile hurt. "You really are the bestest."

"So you have said before." He grinned, pressing his lips to hers. The burn was slow and deep. He held her by the hair when he pulled away and spoke again. "Do not allow yourself to be alone with Lucifer again. If he comes to you, contact Death through your bond. I don't trust that Fallen. I know you do, in a way, but I can't. And I cannot forgive the wrongs he has committed against you as you have decided to. I will not tell you to cut him out of your life. Clearly, there is a reason he cares for you and a reason he was given the ability to remove your demon, so I will continue to trust God's plan and see where this goes. If you behave as you do with Death and me with him, though, I will be angry. I don't wish to be mad at you. So please help me where you can. Love him if you must, accept whatever peace his presence gives you—if it's relief from your past—or just the ability to forgive those who've wronged you—take it. I know that benefits you, but be mindful of my feelings. Be mindful of your feelings for him.

"You have such a big heart that I believe is not meant just for me, and I want you to be conscious of your choices. You tend to follow your heart, which is fine, but just be aware of what it causes me or even Death to feel. Decide if that's something you can live with before blindly leaping into another man's arms. You have both of us, and we want to help you. I know together, Death and I can probably find a solution or relieve most of the pain you have. At the very least, explain what you need Lucifer to do since I know he has abilities neither Death nor myself have."

"I will," she said quickly. "I promise. I was just afraid of you two attacking him. I needed to forgive him for what he did and understand, so I didn't call Death."

He smiled, but it wasn't his usual smile. "You looked like a queen when you stood beside him. You looked like *his* queen."

Her heart throbbed. "It feels right."

David sat, pulling her onto his lap. "You are certain I am the man you choose? I don't want to find out later you chose me only to spare my feelings."

"I'm sure." She turned, so she straddled him. "Did I tell you what Lucifer had to force into my mind to make me kiss him?"

He settled his hands on her hips. "I'm going to be cocky and guess it had something to do with me. Perhaps shirtless because you are a silly, hormonal girl."

"I'm your silly, hormonal girl." She lifted her fingers to his lips. "But this is what he pushed into my mind. This smile. He pushed my favorite smiles from you into my mind so I would kiss him and smile for him."

David was quiet for a while, and she worried this was not the right thing to say.

He finally spoke. "He eventually stopped, though."

Jane lowered her hand. "Yes." Her eyes watered as breathing became harder because she didn't know how David could love her anymore. "He refused to continue doing it, and I had to prove I could kiss him and allow him to touch me without looking forced. He threatened to call her if I did not, and I was afraid of letting him do that, so I learned to kiss him, and I even sought out his touch when I was afraid. I'm sorry."

His grip tightened on her hips as his eye color darkened. "You said you gave him oral sex. Why?"

"David, I'm sorry." She tried to climb off his lap.

He shook his head, grabbing her chin as his other hand kept her from moving. "I know I said you didn't have to tell me, but after seeing you with him—looking as if you belonged at his side—I can't stop thinking the worst. You say you choose me, but it's difficult to imagine you not wanting him to touch you. Fuck." He breathed out harshly. "I'm sorry. I just . . . tell me something, Jane. I'm trying to be strong and say it's fine to love him, but it's not, not after seeing you stand that way in front of him. I could practically see the pull between you and him. You wanted to be close to him. I need to know what resulted in his scent on and inside you. Baby, his fucking seed was in you!"

She swallowed hard, and her voice cracked when she answered him. "I know. I'm sorry. I'll tell you because I want you to know you're the man I want this way."

He breathed out a few times, trying to calm down. "Go on."

Jane decided to get it all out. He deserved to know, and his anger would grow stronger if left in the dark. He knew Death knew, and it wasn't right to give him no explanation. So she prepared to witness the end of her relationship with David. "He was angry," she whispered. "He kept saying I wasn't supposed to last and I should give myself to him now, but I asked for time to at least grieve losing you and everyone else. He kept touching me, telling me to prove he wouldn't need her, but he said something like, 'Maybe it's better this way,' and I was plunged into darkness. When I came back, my mouth was around him, and my hands were between my legs." She squeezed her eyes shut because she could not bear to see the fury on his face. "He told me to finish because I would need to cover your scent with his. He said Fallen and demons had stronger senses, so they would smell you, not him, and might even attack. So I finished him like I have always done. He told me to keep it in my mouth and used his fingers to stick it in me."

"Did you enjoy it?"

Her eyes flew open. "No! I gagged when I was aware, and I yelled at him. I mean, I know I'm not innocent, but I chose him because I had no hope of saving you and everyone else. I was crying unless he forced me not to. I can't even figure out how he did that. Even when he made us do more so my scent was on him, I had to imagine you."

He glared at her. "You imagined me to get your scent on him?"

A tear fell before she could stop it. "I asked for time before giving myself to him. I didn't want him to call her and have him do things I had no way of even coming close to stopping, so I did what I thought I had to. He told me to come, so I did. I imagined our time in your room that night before we left, and I was able to pleasure myself enough to have an orgasm for him.

He said he had envied you. I guess he had seen us that night, so he came in me just like you did."

David stopped breathing. He stopped every movement. He was stone.

"Please say something." She sobbed as she held her hands over his heart.

"That was for us." He squeezed his eyes shut, breathing heavily as he asked another question. "I know Lancelot was not done by you, that she made you see, but did you do more with Lucifer? Did you do more that was meant just for him? Did you want it, Jane?"

"Please, David." She touched his cheek. "Look at me."

He did, and he didn't look like David at all. He was the monster inside him. "Answer me!"

"Yes." She wiped a tear even though he still held her chin. "I kissed him. The last day I was there, we talked in the morning. He was upset because I talked about you. He'd already told me not to say your name, but I explained I would always love you. I was trying to figure out his motives because nothing he did made sense, and I saw how he did care for me. He promised she would never hurt you or those I love, and I promised to give myself to him willingly if he gave me more time. I didn't want him to call her again and bring me back mid-sex or find out afterward he'd had sex with her. I wanted to control who I gave my body to."

"So, you willingly kissed him and felt something?" He bared his fangs but breathed out and lowered his gaze to hide them.

She shook as she sobbed. "Yes, but it's not the same. Please . . . I never would have gone with him if I didn't need to. You said you understood."

He let go of her chin and looked away. "I do understand, but it was easier to accept when I didn't think you loved him. When you weren't throwing yourself in front of him like he was yours. Goddammit, you fucking love him!"

Her chest felt like it was caving in when he stayed silent. "Are you breaking up with me?" She didn't know how to fix this. She didn't blame him for being so angry, but a small part of her had hoped he wouldn't react this way after he'd been so supportive earlier.

David didn't say anything. He didn't look at her. He just took his hand off her hip, so she stood and held her breath as she walked to the door.

She glanced down at her chest to see if she bled because the pain was too much. "I understand. I'll go relieve Elle and start packing our stuff to get out of your room."

He still stayed silent, so she left the room as quickly as she could.

Once she was in the hall, though, she collapsed, sobbing loudly. "Oh, God, what have I done?" She tried to stop crying, but she couldn't. She knew he must hear her gasping because David heard everything. She didn't want him to feel bad, but she couldn't stop crying. "Please don't let him hurt. Please, God."

The door opened, and she sat up, wiping her tears as he stared down at her.

"I'm sorry," she whispered, trying to keep her lips from trembling. "I don't mean for you to hear. I just need a minute before I go in there."

He said nothing but bent down, quickly lifting and carrying her back into the room. He didn't look at her as he laid her on the bed and still didn't say a word as he covered her up. He merely kissed her forehead and then walked out the door.

Jane stared at the door for hours, waiting for him to return. For him to do anything but walk away without saying anything, but he never did. It wasn't until the sun peeked through the curtains that she realized how much time had passed.

There was a light knock before the door opened. She held her breath and sobbed. It wasn't David.

"Oh, goodness." Ragnelle rushed to her side. "*Shh*... He just needs some time. It's going to be all right." She grabbed some tissues, dabbing Jane's eyes. "*Shh.*"

"I blew it," Jane said, crying as Elle tried to comfort her. "I didn't mean to love Luc."

Ragnelle nodded. "I know, dear. I know. He will understand. Give him some time. He's been trying so hard to defend you against those who have openly voiced their foolish opinions, and I think that hit him where it hurt —where they warned him you would go. Those who do not know what you endured cannot possibly understand, but I know you love David deeply and didn't want this."

Jane closed her eyes, trying to calm herself. She still had things to tend to. She still had to keep her children safe and prepare to flee with them. "Did he leave?"

"Yes." Ragnelle gave her an apologetic smile. "I tried to convince him to at least say goodbye, but he said he would do something he'd regret. I'm not sure what he meant, but he said he'd be back. He told the children goodbye, though. Gwen is with them right now."

"She's the one who told him I might love Lucifer, isn't she?"

"Yes. He tried not to speak to her about it, but he asked her not to speak to you while he was gone."

Jane nodded, wiping her face as she got up. "Let me wash my face. Is there a way you can have blood brought up?"

She quickly stood and raced to the door, carrying a pitcher of blood. "He asked me to give it to you. He apologized for not bagging it. He just opened his wrist right there."

Jane's lip trembled as she lifted the mug to her lips, still warm. She didn't want to hope things would work out and then have them fail, but she knew David was the man she wanted to spend her life with. It wasn't fair, though. It had never been fair to ask him to take on so much with her.

"He loves you very much." Ragnelle watched her drink his blood. "Don't lose hope. You two have been through so much in such a short amount of time. You have not even had time to be a couple in love. There has always been something pulling you apart. But, if you make it through this, I think nothing will break you."

Jane placed the mug down and proceeded to wash her face. She needed to be rational and not fall apart. She needed to give him time if that's what he needed, or she needed to let him go. "Am I a serious threat to my children? I don't know what to do without him."

"I do not think you are a threat. The way I understood it, you displayed immense control over yourself, but it was always your darker soul, and I suppose Lucifer, increasing your instability. I will stay with you. If you'd like, we can also ask one of the other ladies to help. He, um, explained you no longer had extra abilities, so I am confident we could restrain you if necessary."

She looked in the mirror. "Thank you, Elle."

The pretty blonde stepped beside her, hugging her as they stared at their reflections. "It's going to be all right."

"No," Jane said sadly. "It's going to be painful. But I have to keep going. I can't give up just because my heart is broken."

Ragnelle smiled sadly. "Gawain will talk sense into him. David loves you too much to walk away truly. I think he needs time. Let him have it. Show him you are strong on your own so both of you know it is not the physical need to rely on him—that it is true love. He will remember, just as he has come to accept Death, that there are secrets to your existence that require you to love more than him."

"That's not fair, though."

Ragnelle smiled again. "That is why he is David."

6

SURPRISE

Jane sighed as she picked up several toys from the floor in David's room. It was mid-day, and she was unsure how soon Death's replacement would be here or when David would return. While she prayed things would work out with David, she couldn't get her hopes up. She had to be ready for things to end and still prepare for the war. There was no way she was letting her kids get hurt.

Ragnelle had already gone over what had happened with David. He'd gone and gorged himself on blood and then came to pack, giving Gawain's wife the barest of explanations, but enough for the woman to know he was walking away from her. Now Jane was determined to return his room to how it was before she entered and ruined his life. If he was done with her, she didn't want to cause him more pain by reminding him she'd been there.

"Why do we have to move?" Natalie asked, putting her doll in a box.

Jane gave her daughter a sad smile. "It's time for us to be on our own. Mommy is a lot better now."

"But I thought we were going to live with David." Natalie frowned. "He loves us."

"I know." Jane turned away so Natalie wouldn't see her watery eyes. "It's just time for us to let him get back to his life. I'm sure we'll see him around."

"Natalie, why don't you go help your brother?" Ragnelle asked, entering the room.

"Okay," Natalie muttered, walking over to the little pile of toys Nathan was supposed to be packing.

Jane rubbed her sore eyes. "Thanks."

"You're welcome." Ragnelle took a seat on the bed beside Jane and folded some shirts. "Are you sure you want to do all this now? He may cool off after killing some of the Damned and forget he was upset."

Jane laughed sadly. "I'm sure. I wish it were as simple as him needing to blow off some steam, but it's not. Nothing with me ever is." She let out a choked sob as she came across one of his shirts. She was going through his bags, finding her stuff so he wouldn't have to bring it to her. "Why do I mess everything up? I always hurt him."

Ragnelle took David's shirt from her hands and folded it. "Why don't you take this one? I can tell you have worn it. It might help to let go slowly."

She shook her head, grabbing the shirt to throw in David's dirty pile. "No. I'll only cry every time I smell him."

"What did that fucker do?" came a voice Jane knew all too well.

She gasped, turning around to see Death staring at the mess around her. "What are you doing here?" She jumped up, scanning his dirty clothes. "And what happened to you?"

He smirked as he glanced at himself. "I trekked across the fucking country on foot."

"What?" She looked behind him, expecting to see Lucifer. "You didn't kill him, did you?"

"Luc? No, he's not here." He walked up to her, cupping her cheeks and scanning her face.

She knew he was probing her thoughts and tried to show him what she could.

"That stupid fuck." He pulled her into a hug and kissed the top of her head as she sobbed. "I'll talk to him."

"Don't. Let him figure out what he wants on his own." She hugged his waist, ignoring the dirt and grime.

"I thought he was fine. I wouldn't have left you with him if I thought he would do that. He seemed okay, but I admit, it was hard to see you next to Lucifer like that."

"I know." She grabbed his hand and held it to her cheek. "I know I deserve to feel the pain, but can you please do something to ease some of it? I need to get things done, but I feel like I will throw up and break in half."

Those tingles amplified and raced directly to her bruised heart, surrounding it in his unique warmth.

"You know he's going to calm down." Death rubbed her wet cheek.

"I told him I'd move out before he got back." She looked up. "Where's Luc? Did you already find Belial?"

He kept staring at her, pushing more of his presence into her until she sighed. "Luc and I are still hunting Belial."

She covered his hand, searching his eyes as she tried to understand. "So, you left him to come here? Did you feel me upset or something? I've tried to stay as calm as possible."

"No, I am still with Luc." He smiled at her confusion before glancing at Ragnelle. "Excuse us, and watch the children for a while. We will return in a moment."

"No, don't ask her to do that," Jane said, but he was dragging her to the door.

"It's fine, Jane." Ragnelle giggled, blushing at Death. "He has something to show you. I'll keep them safe and continue packing your things."

Death opened the door, pulling Jane out before she could say anything.

"Death, what's going on? How are you with Luc, hunting, if you're here?"

He stopped walking. "Very few have seen this or even know I can do it, but I can split my soul to carry out important tasks. I can duplicate myself. This me—that you're staring at right now—has been traveling across the United States for some time."

"You can split your soul?" She rubbed her head. "Okay, so what does that mean? Are you hurt? What task?"

"It does inflict an unpleasant sensation, but I am better now. And you will understand what I have been doing very soon."

Jane reached up to touch his chest. "How many times can you split your soul?"

"As many times as I need to. It requires a significant amount of energy and concentration. I don't do it often, but it has been necessary to complete this task while continuing my duties."

"But you mean you could have always been with me?"

His green eyes dulled. "I have come to you often, Jane. Even if it's a tiny part of my soul, enough to simply observe you. I had to let things unravel as they did, though. I have already explained this. If I were to have stayed, Lucifer would never have had the chance to remove her."

"Right." She removed her hand.

"I thought David was going to spend quality time with you, angel." He was calm as he said it, but she saw his hostility. "I would have abandoned one of my efforts to come to you right away. I was trying to stay out of your thoughts, though. I figured you'd be occupied with him."

She shook her head as a pang resonated within her chest. "No, things went bad fast. Anyway, I don't want to talk about it. I need to get back to moving my things so he's not bothered when he gets back."

Death scoffed, taking her hand and leading her down the hall. "We both know he's going to come back to you. Stop thinking so little of your relationship. I would not stand aside if I did not believe in his feelings for you."

"Well, I have a talent for turning good people bad. I guess even without Evil Jane, I'm still a monster capable of bringing down the strongest men."

He cast her an amused look. "That is true, but I am positive if you wait in his bed, either naked or dressed in something that requires little effort to remove, he will get over his tantrum."

"It's not a tantrum." She rubbed her sore eyes. "He's done with me."

"Well, if that is true, I will permanently fuck up his face so he always remembers he fucked things up with you, and then I will take you away. I'll even bring your rugrats with us."

"Don't hurt David. This isn't his fault." She lifted his hand to kiss it. "Thank you, though. I won't leave with you, but I know you mean it."

He focused on her. "I do mean it—more than you want to accept. If I could, I would make you mine, but I know that fucker will come crawling back, and he's better for you than I will ever be."

Shrugging, she tried to hide how hurt she was.

"You can't hide from me." He squeezed her hand as he led her down a different hall. "Stop thinking about him anyway. He's ruining my surprise by making you stress about him."

"I thought you were the surprise."

Death stopped in front of a door she knew opened to the library. "I know I'm always your favorite, but I brought something you lost a long time ago." He pushed the door open as he leaned down to kiss her head. "Surprise, Sweet Jane."

Jane gasped, covering her mouth as tears blurred her vision. "Is he real?"

He tugged her into the room. "He is. Go say hello before I take you all for myself."

She shakily stepped forward, letting go of Death's hand as another was held out to her. "Adam. Oh my God."

"He was telling the truth," her cousin whispered, pulling her into a hug. "The fucking bastard was telling the truth."

Jane cried, hugging him tight. "I didn't think I'd ever see you again."

He tilted her face back, his smile wide even though he was crying. "You're really okay." He glanced at Death. "Thank you, Ryder."

As usual, Death ignored him, but his voice filled her mind. *"He thinks I'm human. Don't tell him who I am unless you want to scare the shit out of him."*

She sent him a silent okay as she reached for Adam's stubbled cheek. "You look so handsome. And buff. Holy cow!"

"Not much to do in prison except work out." He laughed, cupping her cheek. "You look beautiful." His eyes slowly fell over her. "Different."

Jane's smile slipped. "Yeah. Um, maybe we should sit. I'm not sure what Ryder has explained."

Death took her hand. "Sit, Adam. I need to help her while she deals with some things emotionally. If you choose to be upset, it's best I hold her."

Adam studied her, frowning at how close Death held her. "Yeah . . . I thought you said you weren't with her."

"I'm not with anyone," she said, trying to be tough about things with David.

Death chuckled, sitting and gesturing toward the opposite chair for Adam as he pulled her onto his lap. "Stop being dramatic. Although, if David keeps acting like a piece of shit, I'll gladly take his place. I told him you were mine first."

Adam sat, his gaze falling to Death's thumb as it slid up and down her arm.

Death smirked at Adam. "I told you I was close to your cousin."

"Yeah." Adam stretched out his legs. "She's married, though. Or was." He gave Jane a sympathetic smile. "He told me Jason didn't make it. Are you okay?"

Jane stared at her lap as an aching sensation spread through her chest.

Her angel held his hand over her heart as he kissed her head. "Breathe."

She did. It was easier with his presence pulsing through her. "Will you explain things to him? I don't think I can talk about Jason yet."

Death pulled her against his chest. "Damn, I've missed you. It's always better to be the one touching you." He smiled, kissing her hair but looking at Adam. "She hasn't exactly had time to grieve. She has support now, but I don't think this is the time to discuss Jason. So I will first explain your concern over my relationship with her. When we met, I told you I knew her and wanted to reunite both of you. She didn't know I had gone to find you —I wanted it to be a surprise."

"Right," Adam said, smiling as a woman—a human—brought him a glass of water. "Thank you."

Jane glanced at Death when the woman blushed, stuttering as she asked if he'd like refreshments.

Death rolled his eyes. "You should have seen him whenever we came across stragglers. He wanted to bring every one of those giggling women with us. If only they knew who was traveling with them."

She grinned, leaning on his shoulder. "I'm glad you behaved and kept him in line."

"I didn't say I kept him in line." He chuckled before whispering in her ear, "The man has been in prison for years. He needed to—"

"Oh, shush." She smacked his shoulder.

Death laughed, kissing her head. "I behaved."

"What's going on?" Adam asked, taking the small plate given to him by another blushing maid.

"I told her about you coming out of retirement." Death snickered when Jane covered her face.

"Don't tell her that." Adam stuffed a tiny sandwich in his mouth to avoid looking at the two women walking out of the library.

"Just wait until you see her with David." He squeezed her to him. "She thinks they broke up, but that fucker loves her more than his own dick."

Jane shook her head, smiling because she loved how Death and David, no matter how badly they rivaled the other, always took up for each other when it came to her worrying over their love for her.

"So, this David is the one who owns this place?" Adam asked.

"No, his brother-in-law does," Death said. "His name is Arthur. He's a king, actually."

Adam glanced at her. "A King Arthur owns this place?"

Death responded before she could. "Well, he and his wife. Queen Guinevere. They live here with several knights. David is the strongest, though. I wouldn't let my girl go to anyone but second best."

Adam stared at him for a while before he chuckled. "Okay, did you smoke something while I wasn't looking?"

"He's not lying, Adam," Jane said, unsure if she should worry about him having a mental breakdown.

"He'll be fine," Death whispered to her mind.

"Where the fuck is this queen, then?" Adam asked, playing along. "Isn't she supposed to be super-hot?"

"I recommend you not use that language or even think such vulgar things once my husband returns." Guinevere entered the room, two guards flanking her. She briefly glanced at Jane and Death, her gaze lingering on Death's hand placement on Jane's lap and arm.

Death's voice slid into her mind. *"Oh, I see . . . She's the reason David's being a bitch."*

Don't say that, Jane thought in response. *It sucks, but she's right. Maybe you and I are too close for David to handle. Maybe I should sit somewhere else.*

He tightened his grip. *"Stay right where you are. David and I discussed this thoroughly. It is our business—no one else's."*

Adam jumped to his feet. "Oh, I'm sorry. Um, it's a pleasure to meet you —uh, your Majesty?" He rubbed his head. "I'm sorry. I don't know what to call you."

Guinevere smiled kindly. "Guinevere is fine, Adam. I appreciate your consideration. Please sit. You have traveled a great distance. I wanted to welcome you to my home and inform you I am preparing a room for you. Unfortunately, it is quite a distance from your cousin's room."

"You can put him in Jane's room." Death covered Jane's mouth when she tried to say something. "They had a misunderstanding. David will return, and they will stay together." Death held Guinevere's glare. "Do I make myself clear, Queen of Camelot? I will not be happy to find out you had something to do with the doubts in David's mind that led to their recent quarrel."

Guinevere sighed, gently clasping her hands as she responded. "You may be all-powerful, but this is my home, and David is my brother. Your relationship with his Other is inappropriate, as are her feelings for that devil you allowed into my home."

Death pulled Jane to him, his aura pulsing with green light. "Your opinion on our relationship is your own. Your brother has accepted what Jane and I share. She requires and thrives on my affection, and it is not your fucking business why or how I give it to her."

Guinevere gestured to how they were sitting together. "You believe this is natural?"

"For us, it is," Death said, his aura thickening the air. "You forget she is no mere immortal, and while she is free of her darker half, she is still unstable, learning to cope with matters your puny mind will never begin to comprehend, and she's doing all this while grieving her husband and trying to reunite with her mate. Now, do you think you should have stuck your nose into their business?"

Jane shoved Death's hand off, but instead of apologizing to Guinevere, she pulled Death's face to look at her. He was furious, struggling to hold onto his glamour. "*Shh...* It's okay." She stroked his cheek. "She doesn't know us. None of them do, but it's not their fault. She was just trying to protect him."

Death snarled but nuzzled her hand. "They should not speak if they do not know."

"What the fuck is going on?" Adam asked, grimacing as he saw Guinevere cast him a dark look. "I'm sorry. I've seen him mad before, but never like this."

"He doesn't do well when things happen around me." Jane leaned forward, kissing Death's cheek. She could feel something was off with him. It reminded her of her overdoses, disconnected, and something more. "He'll be okay. I'll talk to David when he gets back, and we'll work on things like we're supposed to. And he's right, Guinevere. Although I understand your concern for David, our relationship is our business. You don't know what we've gone through or anything about my relationships with any of them. I've had enough to deal with simply trying to be with David. We need support, not those we love most tearing us apart." She smiled at Death. "And if David can tolerate him, there's really no reason for you to judge us."

Guinevere didn't respond.

Adam did, though. "Can we discuss the fact he said you're immortal?"

"He doesn't act like your friend, Jane," Adam said after Death excused himself.

Several hours had passed since their reunion, and they'd returned to David's room to wait for dinner. Death had insisted she stay there while Adam took up residence in her original room, and she wouldn't argue with him. Something stressed him, and she didn't have it in her to make things more complicated. She had no idea what was involved with splitting a soul, but he'd also reminded her she'd had hers split as well. There were so many questions, but she also didn't have the luxury of discussing that matter while Adam was trying to accept she was a vampire who used to be the strongest of their kind and the fact the legendary King Arthur and the Knights of the Round Table in a palace ruled them.

Jane shrugged, putting away more of her things. "Like he told Guinevere, there's no easy way to explain us. All I can say is he does something for me that no one else can. I know I should be all woman power—I don't need any man to be strong—but I need him. We need each other."

Adam sighed, stretching out on the chaise. "He's in love with you."

"I know," she said, not looking up.

"But you're with some other dude?" He sighed again. "Honey, even I know that's not right. They don't share you, do they?"

She shut the drawer she had been nervously reorganizing. "It's complicated. But I'm not having sex with Ryder if that's what you're asking."

Adam grimaced. "Okay, so what . . . You get to have two boyfriends, but one gets you in bed while the other offers you emotional support? And why can't you explain what he is? I knew something was weird. I mean, he just showed up out of nowhere, killed every fucking zombie in the prison—without any explanation as to how he'd done it—and safely got me from Texas to Canada. Then he emitted some weird ass green light while he looked like he was about to murder the queen."

Jane turned around. "If I told you what he was, you would probably pass out. Just trust me, and don't forget that he did save you. He didn't have to. I didn't even think to ask him if he could get you, but he did. And it's not two boyfriends. David is—or was—my boyfriend. Well, more than that, considering what we are."

"Soul mates." Adam chuckled. "You don't believe in that shit. I mean, say David is some ancient vampire prince—"

"He is," she said.

"Whatever. He's a vampire knight and a prince who was told you were out there, and he was destined to change you . . . It doesn't stop the fact Ryder is madly in love with you, and you're cuddling up next to him like a silly teenager. You're in love with him, too. How is it you can be with the other guy?"

She rolled her eyes, but her heart pounded from guilt. "I haven't seen Ryder in a while. Things have been rough, and I had only reunited with him briefly in Texas before he left again. We have to be together right now. It's just complicated. We're meant to be this way . . . It's more than cuddling."

"Shouldn't you be saying that about your boyfriend? The one you keep getting all teary-eyed over?"

"What do you want me to say?" She crossed her arms. "I love Ryder. I love him more than you can ever understand, but I love David too. They both feel right and make me happy—but when I'm with David, it feels like he's my home. He's the man I want to spend the rest of my life with. And Ryder is the man . . ." She slapped her hands at her sides. "Fuck, I don't know what to say. Just drop it, okay? I don't even know what to do about Ryder and David right now. And this thing with Luc—"

"The guy the queen had the bigger problem with?" Adam asked, peeking over at her.

"Yes. That's an even more complicated issue, but I realized I love him too. And, because I'm stupid, I blurted that out in front of David and Ryder."

"Maybe you don't know what love is," he said, rubbing his eyes. "Maybe you shouldn't be with anyone until you properly mourn Jason."

Her lips trembled.

Death entered the room, glaring at Adam. "Or maybe she loves on a level your puny human mind cannot fathom." He glanced at Jane. "Arm yourself. We must leave."

"What?" Jane quickly walked to the bed where the kids were playing. "What's going on?"

"The village is under attack." Death went to her, cupping her cheeks. "Sweet Jane, Lancelot has made more mutations. He's attacking the town with Ares, Mania, and Berith. Possibly others. They herded the undead as well. Gather your things. We must leave before more of them come. They're here for you."

Jane quickly raced to David's closet, her hands shaking as Ragnelle appeared at her side.

"Is there no way for you to destroy them on your own?" Jane asked, digging through her things.

Death glared at her. "My current separation makes me unstable. I would destroy everything."

She swallowed, not wanting to upset him. "I understand."

"I'll dress the twins, Jane," Ragnelle said, opening another drawer. "Put on your battle attire."

Death growled, turning away from her as he yelled, "Someone get Adam a fucking jacket."

Her hands shook, but she breathed and tried to steady herself. "How are we going to get them out of here? Do we have a plane?"

"It's all right," Adam said, hugging the twins when Jane emerged from the closet.

Ragnelle rushed to them as Guinevere entered the room with clothes for Adam. Several guards shuffled in as screams from outside started echoing around them.

Jane made eye contact with Death. It was hard to see him through her tears. It was hard to see him worried.

He took three steps until he was right in front of her, cupping her face with shaking hands. "I want to take you to my realm again. No one can hurt you there."

She covered his hands. "Why are you afraid? You're not supposed to be afraid."

A strained expression came across his face. "I can't let you get hurt or taken."

"But you're with me."

"I know, but I know you want me to guard your children as well. I will not do both."

"What are you saying?" She pushed his hands off. "You have to keep them safe. Put them above me."

"There is no one above you for me," he snarled. "Let me take you to my realm, and I promise I will return to protect them." He grabbed her before she could go to Nathan and Natalie.

"I won't leave them." She tried to pull away, but he was stronger, and now she had no power to stop him. "I won't leave them. I'd rather die."

"Don't say that." His wings appeared, unfolding and taking up most of the room.

"Holy shit," Adam shouted, almost falling as the guards kneeled. "He's an angel!"

Ragnelle and Guinevere kept dressing the children.

Jane reached up for Death's face. "What's happening to you? I know you're stronger than this."

He ground his teeth together while the screams and growls from outside amplified. He scanned the room, his eyes roaring with emerald fire. Then, when he focused back on her, she wasn't surprised when he bent and pressed his lips to hers. She kissed him back, crying because she'd never seen him like this. She could feel something breaking inside him.

Death ended his kiss but kept her face close. "The balance has been tipped, Jane. Lucifer's throne has been challenged, and many have sided with his opponent . . . They can touch you now. Hell can touch you all."

"What?" she finally whispered.

"The rules are lifted. They can torture and destroy all of you." He smoothed her hair back. "Don't ask me to watch you get taken."

"What about Heaven?"

He shook his head. "They are still forbidden. Every created immortal is still safe from them. Only demons and Fallen can be slaughtered, but they will not interfere yet. Father must be holding them back." He tilted his head to the side. "Lancelot's wolves are attacking the village. He brought the plague to Arthur's steps."

"What about Luc? They fear him."

"He is still with me, but we are engaged with Belial. If we abandon our fight, we might lose him for good. We can't come, and I'm not letting Luc out of my sight. They planned the attack well."

"Okay," she said, wiping her tears. "It's okay. There are still plenty of guards, and you can kill almost everyone by yourself."

"Not while trying to get you out of here on foot." He growled, flapping his wings as more wives rushed into the room.

"Death," she said, forcing him to concentrate on her. "You are not going to fall apart because of me. We'll fight together and save as many as we can. Don't worry about me. Even if they get me, they won't kill me."

He looked like he was about to breathe fire, but he quickly pulled her into another kiss before pushing her back. "Stay with the wives or by my side. Let two of them carry the children. You run—do not look back. Do not go back for anyone. If you so much as think of sacrificing yourself, I will take you without giving you any warning. Understand?"

"I understand." Honestly, she was terrified, and seeing him like this stressed her out. She needed to focus on her kids.

"Focus on yourself. I will worry about them. I swear. As long as you focus on yourself, I'll keep them safe."

"Thank you," she said, going back to hug him.

He sighed, wrapping his arms around her before gently shoving her to the wives. "Get your things ready."

Jane glanced around when she saw her cats run under David's bed. She felt awful for neglecting them. "What about my cats?"

Death's voice pushed into her mind. *I'm sorry, baby girl. We must leave them.*

Her eyes stung, but she nodded, forcing herself to focus on her children.

"My queen." A guard rushed inside toward Guinevere. "They're inside, most armed with silver. We have too many humans to protect—we must flee."

Guinevere nodded, handing Nathan over to one of the wives while Ragnelle did the same with Natalie. They were all dressed similarly to her, wearing the usual black uniform that fit tight against their bodies and carrying swords like hers.

"Clear the exit. We are coming," Guinevere told them.

The guard nodded and left with several others while some stayed outside the door.

Jane rushed to Adam and started attaching holsters and guns to him. "It's silver. Aim for the head, but stay close to us. Don't fall behind."

"I'm fine, Jane." He checked the gun while continuously darted his eyes to where Death stood.

"I told you not to ask what he was." She smiled even though her heart pounded painfully fast.

Death grabbed her by the arm, quickly checking her attire and weapons. "Let me see you kick some ass. My girl always wanted to be a warrior. Are you a warrior?"

Jane grinned, a surge of power pulsing through her. "Yes."

He smirked as he caressed her cheek, pushing more tingles inside her. "Believe in yourself. Let that fearless girl free. But stay safe."

"I will."

"Now give them death, Sweet Jane"—he held out his hand as a flash of emerald light filled the room before revealing his scythe—"for I am yours to give."

Jane nodded and moved to kiss Nathan and Natalie while Death moved for the door.

"Try to keep their eyes covered," she told the women.

Death pointed his scythe at Adam. "Keep her children safe, or I am beating the shit out of you."

Surprisingly, Adam flipped Death off.

Jane cringed and peeked at Death.

He surprised her even more by chuckling before glancing at her as his voice entered her mind. *"I will clear the way for you. Keep up. Love you, angel."*

And I love you, she thought as he took a deep breath and vanished.

7

DEATH'S ANGEL & HEAVEN'S REAPER

There are moments in life when one must decide: fight or flee. For some, they are rare, and fleeing is usually the wisest, most assured choice for survival. For others, turning and engaging in the brutal satisfaction combat can offer or suffering defeat at the hands of a better opponent is the best option.

Jane didn't have the luxury of choosing between bravery or self-preservation. To flee, she had to fight.

Only, at this moment, another urge consumed her: fight alone. There was such a strong pull to stand at the center of a horde, to taunt them into giving her their best shot, but she ignored that hidden desire and prepared to stay close to the wives and her family.

Jane turned to where they were huddled together at one of the castle's exits. Loud shouts and gunfire exploded around them while the wives waited with her. Their guards covered them in the rear, but the front had engaged a large group of vampires on the castle grounds.

When she saw her daughter's tear-stained cheeks, she lifted her mask and stood beside her. The others were all pulling theirs on, and Adam was helping Nathan with his.

"*Shh*, baby." Jane hushed her while Gareth's wife, Lyonesse, fixed Natalie's hair to fit under a small mask. "I want you to close your eyes and think of something happy. Think of our trips to the zoo with Daddy." Jane leaned forward and kissed her head when Natalie closed her eyes. "Do you see us?"

"Yes," Natalie cried as Lyonesse gave Jane a sad look before pulling her mask down to cover her face.

"Good girl," Jane cooed. "Keep watching us. Look at all the animals. I want you to count them—find all the animals for me. When you hear those loud roars, pretend they're the pretty lions and tigers we saw."

Natalie cried. "I want Daddy."

"Baby, Daddy is always with you, and tonight, I will show you his star." A little smile formed on Natalie's lips. "But first, you must keep your eyes closed for Lyonesse and hold on tight. Can you do that?"

Natalie nodded, but heavy little heaves were passing her lips. "Yes, Mama."

"Good girl. I'm so proud of you, and Daddy would be, too."

"And David?" Natalie hiccuped

Jane's heart throbbed. "Yes, baby. David is always so proud of you. Be brave. That's what he tells Mommy. You can be his brave girl, too." Jane kissed her cheek. "Keep your eyes closed. I'm putting your mask on now."

Natalie nodded and squeezed her eyes shut tighter.

"Mommy's going to go help the others now. Love you."

Natalie sniffled. "Love you, Mommy."

Jane's chest tightened, but she turned toward Adam and gave him a quick hug.

"Jane, you're fighting those things?" He looked horrified for her.

She grinned as she handed him his mask. "This is what I've been doing. Don't fall behind." She reached over and kissed Nathan's wet cheek before wiping it. "Mommy loves you, bubby. Keep your eyes closed." She kissed him again, slid his mask on, then looked back at Adam and gave him a wink, exposing her fangs simultaneously. "This is what my men taught me to do." She pulled her sword, as did Guinevere and Elle.

The others all started readying their M12s.

"Aim for the zombies' heads," she told him. "The vampires will be too swift for you, so don't worry about them unless they get close. Shoot the wolves but not the mutated ones. The bullets are wasted on them. They're already dead."

"Who will take care of them?" he asked.

Jane pulled her mask on. "Me."

Death's roar shook the walls.

"And him," she added before walking to the front of the line.

77

Guinevere touched Jane's shoulder. "Please forgive me, Jane. I don't want to run out there with us thinking badly of one another."

She took a deep breath. "I'll always forgive you for loving your brother. Stay safe. Keep my children and cousin safe for me."

Guinevere smiled before pulling on her mask. "With my life." She then pointed to the others. "Jane will lead with the angel. Stay in formation and do not abandon the children. If you become injured, pass them off before you fall. Elle and I are on point. Fight to the death."

"Yes, my queen," the others replied as they got into formation.

Upon hearing those words, Jane half expected to see Thanatos and Asmodeus beside her, but she shook those thoughts away and made her way to the front of the line as gunfire came closer. The castle had been taken, and it was time to leave.

"Go," Guinevere said when the screams and growls echoed around them.

The absolute carnage surprised Jane. It was worse than any battle she'd been in because most were not soldiers and many were against them. There was no time to mourn the mutilated bodies strewn across the once beautiful gardens. Jane was leading their team. She'd been entrusted to give them all a chance to get to safety.

She briefly wondered why no one told her where they were going and feared it was because none of them expected to make it out alive. Or maybe they didn't expect *her* to.

Again, Jane pushed the fear away and ran in the direction she knew Death to be. He would lead her, and it wasn't long before her dark angel came into view. His green eyes connected with hers immediately, and her chest warmed at the sight of her ruthless protector.

He roared, turning away as his scythe split in two. Seeing demons and Fallen drop to their knees around him, writhing in agony while he rotted their skin from their bones, she grinned. His voice filled her mind, *"Run, Jane. Look forward. That direction. I will catch up."* He began unleashing his wrath on the demons surrounding him and enjoyed the destruction he inflicted on them. His roar was the kind of sound that made the hair on the back of your neck stand, the sound that promised you death was near. And that was always the best assurance her entire being could ask for.

But Jane followed his order, slightly awed by the sight of the wives already unleashing a hail of gunfire around them in a wide circle. They looked as organized as the knights. They were warrior goddesses, and she was leading them.

Death pointed toward the town. However, it seemed the worst choice considering it took them right into the swarm.

Her angel's voice penetrated her mind again. *"Focus!"*

She kept running. The path had cleared, thanks to him. *There are too many for me,* she thought, her eyes widening as she saw countless black eyes all concentrated on her as they ran head-on.

"The castle's hidden fortress and safety bunkers are in that direction," he answered, his mental voice ringing through her head. *"Keep going."*

Her heart pounded when the first set of wolves came into view. Dozens of mutated monsters swarmed the homes and ripped through Arthur's army. They weren't alone either. Zombies in the hundreds surrounded and ate the humans who could not escape. The mutated beasts and wolves shocked her most, though. Unlike the slow-moving zombies, these creatures were swift and devastating. There were more than she'd ever seen. They were an unstoppable wave, overwhelming everyone they came close to, either brutally mauling them or simply infecting them, forcing an immediate change in their victims.

Jane glanced behind her. There was more than just her family running. Vampire and human guards were protecting the crying humans carrying their children.

Tightening her hand on her sword, she rushed ahead of everyone else and roared, swinging her sword at the first set of vampires in her way. Guinevere and Elle joined her quickly, hollering as they took out those trying to get around her. They were just as ruthless as David had said they'd be. Their pale gazes were frightening; they left no chance for their victims to stand once they attacked.

"Keep pushing forward, Jane," Guinevere yelled.

Swinging and slicing off the head of the vampire in front of her, Jane kicked his body down and ran again. She constantly felt the urge to throw out her hands to use her abilities but kept her grip tight and snarled, darting too fast for anyone to grab her. She only stopped long enough to cut down her prey, smiling as blood sprayed around her. She was all on her own now. No Evil Jane. No powers.

Just Jane.

Flashing bursts from grenades went off in the trees as their group continued to unleash gunfire, but as it faded, it alerted her she was moving too fast.

Guinevere and Ragnelle caught up to her, though. The queen's fierce battle cry rivaled Jane's. Guinevere cut down a vampire at the center while Jane ran her sword through the second, and Elle claimed another's head.

Jane hissed, yanking her sword free before she delivered a solid kick to the one about to reach her and then sliced the head of a male trying to pass them. But, while their trio mimicked a deadly pride of lionesses, Jane still felt the urge to fight alone.

She looked ahead, adrenaline flooding her veins when the mutated wolves changed direction. Her direction. That was when she saw Lancelot's figure in the distance. Standing tall with his arms crossed, he was looking right at her. As the clouds parted and moonlight bathed the battlefield, his dark eyes glinted with a promise—a promise he wanted her to pay.

"I'm sorry," she whispered.

A flicker of sadness filled his eyes, but it was gone quickly. He whistled, and more of his wolves turned toward her.

Jane didn't blame him for seeking her out, but she wouldn't let him kill her when her family needed her—when others relied on her to protect them.

So, steeling herself from feeling sorry for what she'd done to Lancelot, Jane embraced the calling to destroy. "The mutants will have silver lining their jaws," she told the others as they ran. "Take their heads. There is no other way."

"Protect the children," Guinevere hollered, racing to keep up with her.

Jane was focused, her vision tunneling, but she remained conscious of everything happening around her. The next wave coming at them contained a mixture of vampires, werewolves, and mutated wolves. "I'm their target," she said. "Go around me once they come. Leave me behind."

"No, Jane." Ragnelle panted beside her. "We fight together."

Jane's gaze slid to the side, and she grinned. "Not tonight. Tonight I fight with Death." She leapt through the air, barely missing the jaws snapping at her face as she swung her sword. The wolf's head smacked the frozen ground as she landed. She was in the middle of the pack that had rushed toward them. They growled and snapped their jaws, but she attacked with all the strength David had gifted her. She cut them in half, removing their limbs and smiling at their screams. There was no sorrow as she watched their bodies fall to the ground or as she ran over them. She delivered death.

A feral hiss broke past her lips when a knife dug into the back of her thigh. She turned and grabbed the vampire by the throat as she noticed her family approaching. Jane let out a shout before delivering a devastating punch to the vampire's face, then grabbing his arm, she threw him into the next outfit of vampires and werewolves in their path.

The vampire's body plowed through the frontline, knocking several down and creating a sizable gap for Guinevere and Elle to work through.

She screamed out in pain, hearing a wild howl in the distance. Jane swung her sword around after receiving a massive scratch across her back. It was already healing, but nothing stopped the tears from freezing around her eyes.

"Jane," Guinevere yelled.

"Keep going," Jane hollered, fighting off three armed vampires. Wolves quickly approached her, but she had given them an opening to run through. Jane, however, was surrounded.

"No, stop," Adam shouted. "Don't leave her."

"Take him." Jane swung her sword and smiled when she saw Lucan, one of the guards who'd been with Dagonet, dragging him away.

Their presence faded, and she knew Guinevere had continued without her. Jane was wild, though. That tingle of fear was at the back of her mind, but she let the baneful creature that had always been a part of her soul take over her actions.

"That's my girl." Death's praise caressed her mind. *"Destroy them. I am coming."*

Her body hummed with energy as it flowed into her muscles, increasing her excitement for slaughter. She cut into every monster around her with power that surpassed her imagination. Her movements became more graceful and steady. It was as if every attack was predestined to meet its target. There was no effort to ponder her lethal executions. It was all instinct. Her mind shut off, and she became a death-dealing nightmare.

Throwing out a powerful punch, she completely removed the head of the vampire in front of her, and she was already gripping her sword with both hands before swinging from the ground upward, cutting another from groin to throat. The destroyed body split with a yank of her sword, and she found her next target—a hairy, snarling beast. Jane's lungs shook under the force of her battle cry, but she didn't stop her attack. Within seconds she'd torn the monster in half. One after the next fell under her blade, but they continued to pour around her.

Kicking another down, she smiled and felt Death before she saw him. However, the momentary lapse in her concentration caused her to lower her defenses.

Screaming in agony when a fanged mouth closed around her neck and shoulder from behind, Jane's vision blurred. Their bite tightened, but she kicked those in front of her to keep them from taking her down. The pain was excruciating, but a twisted smile formed on her lips as a black and green cloud soared across the sky.

Death's howl shook the ground, and she fell to her knees as an enormous crash sounded behind her. The creature on her back was ripped away, and Death swung his scythe wildly, forcing his fury onto every monster surrounding them.

The rocks and dirt crumbled under her fingers as she struggled to stay on all fours. Death had moved in front of her and continued his slaughter. His muscles were visible under his tight black cloak. It stretched perfectly over his broad shoulders and glorious body.

Jane coughed up blood clots, gagging because she could feel them in her mouth. She yanked her mask off and spat out the disgusting chunks as the icy wind stung her watery eyes. It dawned on her she'd fucked up. Once again, she'd let herself get hurt, but she smiled anyway. Death was there this time, delivering a beautiful massacre to avenge her.

His crazed, emerald eyes met hers, and she gave him a bloody smile until her arms began to tremble, and she collapsed to her stomach.

Those violent green orbs slanted before he roared toward the heavens.

I'm okay, she thought to calm him as she coughed and rolled onto her side to hold her wound better. *I'm healing.* Hot blood seeped through her fingers, making her aware that she never put gloves on when her numb fingers began to shake. Her wound was healing, but the cursed vampire had gotten a good bite.

Death's spine-chilling roar drew her attention again. Through teary eyes, she saw his wraithlike wings forming around his massive back while he battled the horde around them. A smile formed on her chattering lips as she watched her beautiful Grim Reaper slay monsters for her.

Another howl ripped from Death's mouth, and she noticed his features had become more animal-like. The angles of his face were more prominent while his eyes truly lit with emerald fire.

A blue ball of light burst into view above his head, but Death didn't stop his slaughter when it shot straight into his chest. Instead, his movements quickened and magnified in strength. Somehow, she already knew what she was seeing. Death was feeding on the souls his reapers around the world had claimed. Death's unique nourishment increased his strength, and her body began healing faster.

Jane wheezed out and felt the blood pulsing out of her wound decrease.

Death gripped her arm while the other hand slid under her belly to lift her into his possessive hold. His muscles flexed against her back, and she basked in the tingles that sparked across her body. "Jane." He turned her to face him. He sniffed her neck and surprised her by licking the blood. Relief flashed across his gorgeous face, but the worry didn't leave his eyes.

He's afraid for me.

"I am," he whispered, bringing his face close. "Your wound is healed, but you are drained. Take from me . . . Here." He pressed his lips against hers without warning, and her body jolted as tingles coated in fire slid across her tongue and down her throat.

Death growled, pressing his lips around hers and tugging her against him. The exchange was quick and immediately renewed her with a surge of power pumping through her veins. The screams of torture reached her ears, but she ignored them and smiled when his lips curved up against hers.

"My lips." His voice was everywhere but nowhere at the same time.

She opened her eyes and stared into his vibrant green pair. "Thank you, Death."

He pulled back, caressing her cheek. "Do you feel me?"

Jane grinned, placing her hand over the spot where the tingles always gathered.

Death eyed her hand placement before glancing around. "We fight together now." His gaze settled back on her. "Embrace us. We are meant to do this together."

An immediate *yes* formed in her mind, and she nodded as screams of pain tore her attention from him. All within a twenty-foot radius of them were withering to bone and dust.

Looking back at Death, she chuckled at his deadly grin.

"Their end is more painful this way." His eyes flashed before he ran with her still in his strong arms.

She wrapped her arm around his neck, gasping from the cold wind in her face. "Can you do this to the entire army?"

More of the enemies began falling around them as he ran through the mass in the direction the others had gone. "Not anymore," he said.

"Why?"

He didn't look at her. "Because of you, baby. No more questions." His grip tightened, and he leapt into the air. He wasn't flying, though. With frightening speed, they fell back toward the ground in the middle of a mass of vampires.

They never met the ground or the deadly hands of the Damned. The giant pale horse that manifested out of green flames raced forward. They landed, and Sorrow never stopped.

Death shifted her in front of him. They were already in full gallop, and Sorrow increased his pace. He easily barreled through the mob, leaving a wake of crushed, decaying bodies.

Jane smiled as green flames from Sorrow slid over her hands and legs. They gave her the same tingling sensation as Death's touch. But her brief awe ended when she searched the numerous battles and finally found a huddled mass fighting in a well-formed circle of wives and guards—her children in the center with several other children.

"Death!" She tilted her face up to see him.

He held his hand out, summoning his scythe as his fingers flexed against her stomach before pulling her against him more. "I see them." He swung his scythe, cutting wolves with ease. "This is why you don't take matters into your own hands."

She gritted her teeth, fury flooding her soul.

"*Easy.*" His deep voice vibrated through her. "*You are just not ready yet. Be patient.*"

His response calmed her, and she nodded before putting a hand over his. "Okay."

Death swung his scythe again as his legs tightened around hers when Sorrow sped up, charging toward the overwhelmed group. Her angel sliced at every reachable foe they passed. His heavy breaths against her head and flexing muscles at her back comforted her, and his closeness seemed to cause power to hum through her body. It was as if they were each feeding off the other. As though their bodies were happy to be together.

Death continued his slaughter but let out a purr of agreement.

She didn't overthink what this meant, and her breathing became frantic upon spotting three figures standing in the distance. They were watching her and her horseman. She'd already seen Lancelot but was startled at the sight of Berith and Mania.

"Death," she whispered when hundreds of shadowy figures took flight behind them.

"I know," he said before kissing her head. "Get your children and Adam. Keep them near Sorrow and tell Adam to mount him when I say. Wait for my order, then let the wives lead you to your hideout."

Jane nodded and threaded her fingers through his as she watched demons and Fallen soar through the sky.

Their screeches burned her ears, sending fire through her veins as their dark silhouettes scattered the silvery moonlight across the battlefield.

Death leaned over her slightly, shielding her from the dust kicked up by the thousands of wings from the demonic flock.

"Show no fear," he said before pressing his lips to her hair.

"I won't."

He smiled against her head, and his voice caressed her thoughts. *"You looked amazing out there. I'm proud of you."* She could almost hear the smirk in his voice as he added, *"It's such a turn-on to watch you reap your vengeance on those bastards. I particularly loved seeing the emerald glow in your beautiful eyes."* He nuzzled her and spoke aloud, "I love you."

Jane smiled. "And I love you."

Death said nothing more. He launched himself into the air, leaving her by herself on Sorrow. She watched him land ahead, swinging his scythe, ripping the beasts off his back, and stomping them into the earth. The urge to fight beside him rose, but she tightened her hand on Sorrow's mane as he raced to her family.

"Jane," Adam yelled when Sorrow broke through their circle.

She jumped off and ran to him, checking quickly to see if he was injured. He had blood seeping down his arm and scratches across his torn mask, but he seemed okay.

He confirmed this. "I'm fine. The kids are, too."

Sorrow nudged her back.

"What are we doing?" Adam asked, glancing around the chaos.

"Stay near Sorrow." Jane took Nathan and then Natalie from the arms of Enid and Lyonesse. "When Death says to, get on the horse and follow the wives."

Adam sighed, but he gently pulled the twins from her arms. "Be safe."

"You too." She kissed her babies, refusing to linger because she feared drawing attention to them, and turned away. As she reached back for her sword, she came up empty. "Fuck!" All she had was her M9.

She growled and pulled the gun as she pushed through the circle.

"Thank goodness, Jane," Guinevere greeted her but didn't stop firing her rifle. "I do not know how long we can hold them off."

"We'll hold them long enough." She smiled at Death's slaughter. He had exchanged his scythe for a massive hammer, demolishing all foolish enough to charge their group. "He won't let us fall."

Guinevere gave her a look but said nothing.

Jane fired at a winged creature flying toward them.

"Do not bother shooting," Guinevere said. "Our ammunition does very little damage to them."

Baring her fangs, Jane aimed at a vampire and shot him right between the eyes before shooting two more. "I need a sword."

"I only have mine." Guinevere unleashed a hail of gunfire.

Jane grew jealous for not having one of her rifles. Not that they would take care of the bigger problems. A sword would be ideal, and all she had was a handgun.

Screams erupted from within their unit. Jane spun around, and her mouth fell open. Demons were diving down and ripping guards up from the ground, tossing them to the pack of werewolves.

Death let out a roar, and she turned back to see dozens of wolves pouncing on him. "No!" She tried to run forward, but Guinevere and Elle held her back. His neon eyes met hers, and fire raced through her veins; she needed to be by his side.

He was savage. He didn't stop fighting, but they were crushing him.

Demons flew down, swiping him across his back and arms with their talons. She knew he would be fine, but watching and doing nothing wasn't easy.

A sudden pressure around her head almost caused her knees to buckle. She gripped Elle's shoulder and grabbed her head with her free hand.

"What is it?" Elle shouted.

A sadistic cackle raised the hairs on the back of Jane's neck as she looked across the battlefield. Mania was in the distance, a twisted smile on her doll-like face as images Jane had wished never to see again penetrated her mind, preventing her from seeing what happened around her.

"Jane," Elle yelled as Jane screamed.

"Look what you did, Sweet Jane." Mania laughed in her mind. "You killed those babies."

"No." Jane squeezed her eyes shut, hoping the horror of what she'd done to Lancelot's family would disappear.

Death roared when she sobbed upon watching herself slit Lancelot's children's throats.

"Stop," she screamed as tears spilled free from her eyes.

Mania's laughter grew so loud she could barely hear the shouts coming beside her. Her sins began to play out behind her closed eyes. She saw herself kissing Lucifer, pleasuring him even without her darker soul controlling her.

"*Little whore,*" Mania's voice cut across her heart.

Death howled again, and Jane opened her eyes to see him becoming wilder in his attacks. His hammer morphed back into his scythe, and he was destroying everything.

"Hang on, Jane," Elle said, holding her. "Tell me what to do."

She couldn't answer her. She looked through her teary eyes and realized they were surrounded. Only Death stood between them and Hell.

More screams from their men cut her heart when they were snatched away from the decreasing huddle, and she cried when Death fell to his knees after a huge mass of winged creatures slammed into him. He was weak.

The roar from the wives blasted around her when the enemies advanced on them, but the large crash beside Jane made her eyes fly open despite the horrific images of her bathing in her own children's blood.

"My queen," said a familiar deep voice before hands pulled hers from her ears. Under a black hood, ruby eyes shone back at her. He snarled at the two wives, ready to die for her. "I will not harm my queen."

"Than!" Jane whimpered, happy to see her fallen general beside her.

He returned his glare to her but softened his gaze before slightly bowing. "I told you I would not fail you again."

Jane laughed but clutched her head. A dark look came over his face, and he stood tall before turning toward the demon goddess, then the two others beside her.

"Help Death," she said, trying to push away Mania's torment.

Thanatos watched her for a moment before holding out his hand. His demonic scythe illuminated into view when another ball of fiery smoke came hurtling toward them.

The others screamed but didn't let up on their gunfire when it crashed in front of Jane. Thanatos put a hand out protectively in front of her. She squinted, shocked to see a massive man with long red hair staring down at her. He wore armor that reminded her of a Spartan's, but he didn't wear a helmet.

"Than," the man greeted, surprise in his amber eyes as a massive sword manifested in his hand. "I did not expect to see you here." He smirked before glancing at Jane.

Thanatos growled and extended his wings slightly to hide her.

The man laughed. "I know better than to wish harm onto my brother's . . ." He let his words trail off and smiled. "Shall we aid him? It looks like Heaven is going to sit this one out. But, lucky for us, Father's rules do not apply, do they?"

Thanatos folded his wings in and nodded. "I fight for my queen."

Jane screamed out again. This time, blood dripped from her nose and mouth.

Thanatos growled at the same time Death's howl shook the sky.

She cried, still fighting off the painful images when a flash of green and black announced Death's arrival. He quickly yanked her from Thanatos and pulled her against his chest. "Breathe, Jane. We're not finished." His lips pressed against hers, soothing the burns inside her mind. Those delightful tingles did their wonders and chased the poison away.

She could feel his injuries when they touched, but their bodies comforted and healed one another.

Death leaned away, glancing at the man with red hair. "Brother."

"Brother." The red-haired angel returned his greeting. "I thought you might like a hand now the war has begun. I see your beauty calls more than your terrifying heart to her aid. She even brought your great general to his knees."

Death's lips twitched, and he softly kissed her again.

"I'm fine," she whispered, touching his cheek, worried he still seemed so off.

"I am fine," he promised, his gaze following the blood trail from her nose. He snarled. "She's doing this to you?"

Jane could feel his mind touching hers. "Yes. I can't force her out. But it's better with you."

He caressed her hair before wiping the blood from her nose. "Hold on to what I gave you. Find it."

She knew he was talking about their kiss, and she touched her chest, nodding when it warmed. It spread as he watched her, further pushing away the horror of her past.

"Good girl. Now, where is that bitch?" He looked over his shoulder, a threatening grin stretching over his lips when he locked eyes with Mania.

The demon goddess paled, but she didn't flee.

"Leave Lancelot," Death ordered. "His fight is with David."

Jane was so relieved to have Death by her again that she wrapped her arms around his waist, burying her face against his chest.

He caressed her hair, breathing heavily from his fight, but she could only focus on their bodies reacting to their closeness again. Her fingers flexed on his back the exact moment his did in her hair, but Death didn't acknowledge it, nor did she ponder the relevance of their synchronized movements.

"Leave that bitch for me. She ends today." Death bent down to kiss her head as he pulled her away. "Stay here. I will claim her wicked soul for you."

She touched his chest, smiling at him. "You're okay?"

"I am." He lifted his eyes to her general. "Than." He moved her aside and stepped toe to toe with Thanatos.

Jane moved closer, touching each of their hands.

Both males jumped, darting furious glares down at her.

"Don't fight with each other." She squeezed Death's hand as she silently added, *He came to help me.*

Death's eyes lit up, but he nodded before returning his attention to the true enemy. Thanatos bowed to her and also turned.

"This will be a fun warm-up," the red-haired man said with a menacing smile.

Death snorted at the same time his midnight wings erupted from his back. She smiled at his beauty, and Elle dragged her back into the protective circle.

"Jane, my sweet," Death spoke without looking at her. He flapped his massive wings while the red-haired male revealed a white set of wings, "Meet my brother,"—he folded his wings and nodded his head in the man's direction—"War."

8

WAR

When we are children, our parents often tell us tales of beautiful angels who protect us from evil. They are loving beings of peace and light. They are said to be beautiful and wear crowns in the form of golden halos. Pure, righteous—ethereal beings who keep evil from us and protect our innocent souls.

Jane was told these tales as a little girl, too. Her mother had described them in their white robes with harps, singing songs of praise to God. While Jane listened to her mother and smiled at pictures of chubby, angelic children, her innocent mind formed a darker, more powerful being. Still beautiful and divine, but nothing resembling the gentle creatures painted by her parents.

Jane had been right.

She smiled at the three men standing tall and strong in front of her. The most beautiful—Death—stood at the center. Jane had never been as proud as she was at that moment. He was her angel. Hers. And, even though she'd seen glimpses of him with his wings before, seeing him in all his glory was magical. This time, they were not in a ghostly, skeletal form. Now he stood tall, a gorgeous black-winged warrior, and he was there to fight for her.

Her eyes traveled across his broad shoulders, and though he was cloaked in black, the impressive body of the ultimate killer showed through. Every angry breath he took caused his muscles to stretch and flex under the smooth material. Despite her commitment and love for David, her heart fluttered at the sight of the dangerous angel.

She didn't fully understand their bond, but it was something she never wanted to part with.

Death turned his head in her direction. His face was hidden under his hood, and she smiled as the flash of emerald allowed her to see him. *Perfect.* His smirk made her cheeks heat up because she remembered he was aware of every admiring thought running through her mind.

A single wink from his stunning neon-green eyes filled her chest with the warmth only he could make her feel, then he turned forward again.

Jane shifted her gaze to Death's brother. War looked every bit what she imagined the Red Horseman of the Apocalypse to be. She was awed by his massive size, as he was larger than Death—a hulk. Considering someone larger than Death was hard, but this brute was probably close to seven feet tall. And it didn't look odd on him. He had his own beauty, which was only enhanced by his immense confidence and power.

Destruction. She stared at destruction and couldn't help but think he was there because of her.

His snowy wings flapped, moving his red cloak and exposing his golden armor—a *Spartan.* Jane grinned at the comparison because she always fancied Spartans. And now the most handsome and largest one ever stood beside her angel with an enormous sword that had every vampire shaking in fear.

It was the length of her entire body, but his large hand hanging loosely at his side made it look no different from David holding his sword. He flexed, and Jane made eye contact with Elle as the muscles under his golden skin rippled with strength neither of them had probably ever seen before.

"Oh, my," Elle mouthed.

Jane held back her smile. It was nice to see she wasn't the only one affected by these angels' beauty and strength.

Everything about him seemed horrifying, but she did not fear being so close to him. Perhaps it was the excited smile on his full lips—how his lopsided grin promised a painful death to his victims. Or it could have been the way his long red hair offset the fire in his orange eyes, making them glow brighter, that made her find him charming.

Jane smiled, surprised by the sudden feeling of staring at a younger brother who had grown into a giant of a man.

Death chuckled before turning toward Thanatos. The formal general in his army stared back at him, nodding briefly with a flash of red under his hood.

Then, without warning, Death vanished when Thanatos and War shot up into the sky before they crashed in the center of the massive force ahead of them.

They swung their massive blades, clearing a wide circle for Jane and the others to see. War wielded his sword, completely shattering those in his wake. Blood flew into the air and rained down around him.

Thanatos was just as frightening, but he was more elegant with his scythe. He cut through his victims with swift, graceful sweeps, leaving surprised expressions on those who realized they were taking their last breaths.

Any beauty in his form was forgotten when he and War banished their blades. They began grabbing those within reach, violently hurling them into the crowd.

Jane darted her eyes around, searching for Death. Then, as if he'd roared her name, her eyes shot to Mania, where he materialized in front of the goddess.

He grabbed Mania by her throat before the two males beside her could react. Then, once his powerful choke found its mark, he flapped his massive wings, launching straight into the air with a mixture of emerald and dark smoke billowing out behind him across the sky.

He didn't stay airborne for long. He crashed back to earth with a terrifying roar, landing between War and Thanatos.

Mania's scream was cut off by Death's tight grip when he slammed her onto the ground. Upon hearing the sick crack of her leathery wings crumpling underneath her against the rocky surface, every warrior cried out.

Death growled in her face before yanking her up so she was at eye level with him.

War moved away but continued his massacre of any trying to aid their mistress. Jane knew these were Mania's legions, and they were loyal to their leader. The Red Horseman cared little—he smiled as he destroyed each one trying to save her.

Thanatos no longer battled. He stood silent beside Death as if waiting for an order.

Death grabbed Mania by her curly hair and then turned her to face Jane. He brought his mouth to Mania's ear but spoke loud enough for the entire battlefield to hear. "She is your death, Demon. Enjoy the sight of the beauty that brought your end. I promise you will be haunted for eternity by the sight of her lovely face as she laughs at the torment forced upon you."

"No!" Mania thrashed when Thanatos moved slightly in front of her.

Jane still had a clear view of Mania and Death, and he locked eyes with her. He was empty, but at the same time, he filled Jane's entire being with his devotion to her.

"For you, my love," Death said darkly when Thanatos lifted his hand over Mania's lips and called her wicked soul out.

Jane couldn't breathe, nor could any other witnessing Death's wrath on the one who had tortured her.

No one moved. They could only watch a vile orb of blackness being choked out of Mania's twisted lips before it disappeared with the close of Thanatos' hand.

While her soul was gone, awareness still glowed in the demon's eyes, and they widened in fear when Death growled. His cursed scythe manifested in his free hand when Thanatos' appeared in his.

A strangled scream rang out for a tiny moment before Death forcefully ripped his scythe across her neck, and Thanatos tore his across her belly. Screams from Hell's army shook the ground, but Death's roar was louder. He silenced their cries before releasing what was left of Mania's decapitated head. His eyes stayed on Jane's. She was breathing fast, her chest rising and falling quickly.

Jane finally looked down at Mania's remains. They had ripped her into three parts.

The shock of Mania's death lasted only seconds before roars thundered across the sky. All three angels turned with terrifying roars of their own, facing the enormous legions of monsters without displaying an ounce of fear.

Her three angels charged the army against them, each swinging their preferred weapons to deliver death. They crashed into the demonic bodies, knocking those in front to their backs before slicing anyone close enough to taste their blades.

Death and War made the most prominent circles of destruction around them. Their speed and force were nothing like the huddled crowd behind Jane had ever witnessed. They cut into them like they were nothing but air. The destroyed corpses had not touched the blood-soaked grounds before Death and War dealt death to the next wave of attackers.

It was beautiful to Jane, though. The demons and Fallen were no match to either brother, and the cursed vampire enemies were dwindling or withdrawing into the forest.

Jane bared her fangs as the wolves pulled back and darted her eyes to where Lancelot had been, but he was missing. Rage filled her, and a growl shook her lungs when she saw him and Ares retreating. This fury wasn't her own, though. She didn't want to hurt Lancelot more than she had, but an uncontrollable fire within her wanted to engulf all who would see harm done to her.

"Easy, Jane," Guinevere said.

"I'm fine," Jane whispered, watching the fight continue. Worry filled her heart upon seeing dozens of horned demons flying at Thanatos.

His yell was intimidating as he split his scythe in two and jumped up to cut any who managed to reach him. He quickly landed with a loud bang that sent out blue flames and instantly continued his battle. He started spinning both blades in circles. It almost seemed he was manipulating them by some source besides his hands because their speed was impossible. It took little effort to mow down those who had just overwhelmed him.

A gigantic explosion surprised everyone when the castle burst into flames. The wives screamed, tears running down their faces as they watched their home burn. Jane's throat closed up. The last bits of her home were in there.

Her cats were in there.

The agony over the loss of the castle quickly turned to horror when a giant flaming beast emerged from the ruins with a thunderous bellow.

It only drew a glance from Death while he continued his slaughter.

Jane's heart pounded because the horned demon, easily the size of a house, charged him. She shifted her gaze between Death and the beast and screamed when it was inches from smashing into him. But a sudden blur of gold and red crashed into the fiery monster, sending it flying into the massive army advancing on her three angels.

It stood quickly, pressing its knuckles into the ground, spewing fire at the Red Horseman. War didn't react, but a helmet covered his head, pulling his fiery red hair through a slit down its center, creating a mohawk. She couldn't help but grin at his undeniable similarity to a Spartan Warrior now.

War threw his arms up, taunting the fiery beast while Death and Thanatos kept the others from interrupting the upcoming match. The creature screeched and rushed at War.

The Horseman flew up when he was yards in front of him, avoiding the hellish flames that erupted from the monster's mouth before landing on its back, stabbing his sword in its shoulder. It howled in pain, and War grinned, yanking out his blade before hacking into the monster's back.

Blood flew through the air as the demon reared up on its hind legs.

War leapt down, but he began his assault again. Finally, the creature fell to its belly, and with a mighty swing of his sword, War decapitated the horned head. He hollered over his kill, causing Death and Thanatos to let out their yells of bloodshed.

War didn't celebrate long before launching himself back into the horde. All three continued their carnage, laying waste to dozens in their paths. Jane felt an overwhelming sense of pride as she watched them destroy every soul they chose to take.

But that pride soon turned to panic when black masses formed on the ground. The shadowy blobs quickly morphed into solid, slick black creatures. Her mouth fell open as she watched their monstrous jaws release bloodcurdling howls. These new, four-legged beasts could only be described as dogs, and they were running toward Jane and her group, as well as her three warriors.

"Hellhounds," Thanatos yelled.

The wives and guards quickly unleashed an endless assault of gunfire, but the hellhounds didn't seem fazed. Hysteria began when the first group broke into the side of their circle. They viciously mauled Arthur's guards as more hellhounds started snatching the remaining humans.

People were tossed into the air toward the massive pack, but Arthur's guards quickly cast aside their useless rifles and began using their swords. The wives followed quickly, hissing like wildcats and leaping at the terrifying hounds, cutting them apart with swift, feral attacks.

Jane stared down at her gun and cursed. "Fuck!"

"Stay here, Jane," Guinevere shouted at her and moved out with Elle to keep the monsters away.

Jane focused back at the three angels receiving their attacks from the hounds and the winged forces being commanded by Berith, who stood calmly in the distance.

Loud gunshots sounded from where Death and War fought. Forgetting her frustration with being unable to fight, she stood awed at the guns their swords had transformed into.

Death expertly fired a silver gun at the fast-moving creatures while War used a golden one. Both were devastating and bombarded the swift packs.

Unfortunately, more formed within the darkness, and Jane's fascination with Death's new weapon vanished as the lines broke around her.

Guinevere and Elle appeared to be having the most success dispatching the enemy.

Jane looked around for something to fight with, but horror claimed her heart as one of the hounds broke through and ran straight at Adam and her children. She screamed and raced toward them, not even caring that she had no weapon.

She jumped onto its huge back and dug her nails into its sides to avoid falling off the horse-sized hellhound.

It howled and snapped its razor-sharp jaws at her, rearing up on its hind legs to free itself. But Jane squeezed her thighs around it, hollering as she tried to reach for its throat.

Nathan's cries fueled her madness, and she yelled, finally grabbing its jugular and digging her fingers into its thick flesh.

Blood coated her fingers, but she didn't let go. Death's battle cry echoed in the distance, but her thrumming pulse filled her ears, and she squeezed tighter, never letting her hold weaken.

Death's yells sounded again, almost filling her mind with a command, but she didn't have time to decipher the order. She hollered and started tearing at the now exposed neck. The cold liquid spilled down her arms and sprayed around her face until it fell to its belly. It wasn't dead, though, so Jane continued tearing into him with her bare hands, screaming madly in its revolting face as she did so.

When she realized it was no longer moving, she looked around and locked eyes with Adam. She must have looked wild, but he didn't seem afraid of her. She began to smile but screamed when something smashed into her back.

She tumbled across the ground, gaining cuts and bruises until she finally rolled to a stop and pushed up on all fours. She hissed at her attacker. It was another hellhound. She showed no fear when six others joined their pack mate—all snapping their slimy teeth as they circled her.

Death gave a louder roar when the first hound launched himself at her. She prepared herself for his attack but was surprised when flaming balls of blue and black fell from the sky.

The blue flames revealed a man with shiny black armor similar to Thanatos' and a hooded cloak billowing out behind him. He was tall and lean but still muscular, and his tanned face barely appeared before it was shrouded in darkness again. He looked away and growled, swinging his sword right at the hound that nearly devoured her.

The monster instantly fell to its death, and the man had already delivered more slaughter to the others surrounding them. He was quick and lethal with every strike. Jane marveled at his ferocity before looking around to see more balls of blue fire fall around them. Hooded men and women emerged from the flames, and each entered combat with the demonic forces.

Jane searched the grounds for Death and found him. He was destroying the endless amounts of demons and hellhounds trying to get to her family and the other unarmed humans. His emerald eyes flashed in her direction before he looked away to focus on keeping her children safe.

"They are my reapers," Death said to her mind. *"He has gifts for you. Take them."*

She snapped her eyes away from his brutal slaughter to settle on the man finally finished with her attackers. He faced her, his blue eyes lit up like lightning, revealing a faint smirk, but not long enough to let her see more of his face. "Hello, Death's angel. I am Viduus."

Jane stood there, dumbfounded, before she replied, "Hello. He said you have something for me."

The man nodded and held out his hand. "From my lord."

Jane gasped as she stared at a hellish-looking gun. It was similar to Death's but much smaller.

"This is Death's Angel," he said before holding his other hand out. "And this is Heaven's Reaper." He placed an unearthly dark sword into her shaking hands.

After attaching a holster to her side, he bowed. "I believe he desires you at his side now."

Death's voice caressed her mind, *"Punish them, Sweet Jane."* There was still fear for her safety in his voice, but he was also proud.

"Shall we?" Viduus asked, glancing around the chaos casually before focusing back on her.

Jane squeezed her hand around the hilt of her new sword and watched green flames ignite around it. They sent tingly shocks into her skin, and she grinned. But there wasn't time to waste—hellhounds continued manifesting all over the battlefield. "Let's kick some ass, Viduus."

Without waiting, he turned and headed toward Death. Jane quickly raced behind him, watching him cut a path for her to reach Death.

But soon, Viduus slid to a stop, holding an arm to keep her from passing around him. They were surrounded.

"Hand the girl over, Reaper," said a reddish-colored demon.

Four hellhounds snarled, circling them.

"I must refuse your request, Demon," said Viduus. "Try to take her, and you will perish."

Jane was surprised by the smooth confidence in his voice and looked over, quickly noticing how their ranks were still overwhelmed, including Death, who frantically darted his eyes in her direction.

Stay with my family, she thought for him to hear. She felt his instant desire to refuse, but he growled and became more unrestrained with his attacks.

Jane pushed away his cries for her to be safe and focused on the increasing gathering around her and Viduus. The hounds snarled and snapped their teeth at her. While they wanted to injure her, she felt that orders had been issued to ensure her survival.

"Very well, Reaper," said the demon.

Viduus didn't hesitate. He attacked the supposed leader of the gang, removing his head instantly from his body. He cut down the next one within moments before kicking the gut of a hellhound about to leap at her, then brought down his sword to sever it in half.

Snapping out of her daze, Jane sliced into every monster that lunged at her. She turned to fight back to back with Viduus and swung her new sword—Heaven's Reaper—with expert proficiency.

A scratch to her arm had her crying out, but she yanked her gun from her side, aimed it right between her attacker's eyes, and fired. The shot was thunderous, and her arm shook from the kickback, but she didn't stop. Instead, she lifted her arm and began firing at the others.

More charged them, but she fired her gun, happy it didn't appear to run out of ammunition.

"Jane," Death yelled. "Get your ass over here!"

She felt his panic when a considerable mass started growing ahead of her. "Stay with them," she screamed at him, firing wildly at the formless mass of black clouds.

The reaper behind her turned to look at her quickly, muttering a curse, but couldn't turn to aid her just yet. He still fought the countless horde of devils in front of him.

Someone landed beside her, and she screamed but released a relieved breath when War moved in front of her.

He fired three shots into the growing mass. The shapeless body recoiled but didn't fall. "This will be fun," he said, firing twice before smiling at Jane. "It's time to watch your angel do what he does best." He winked, looking very similar to Death at that moment, and then lifted her into his arms.

He fired several more shots from his massive gun before shoving it in his holster and launching them into the air.

Jane squeezed her arms around his neck and saw he had brought her right to Death. Tingles immediately touched her arm, and another set of muscular arms pulled her close. "Jane," Death said, scanning the sizzling injury to her arm.

"She has venom in her," War told him before he turned away to begin firing at the still encroaching mass.

Jane looked to see that order had been restored, and the wives and remaining guards were again forming a protective barrier around the defenseless humans.

"What about Viduus?" She turned to see the reaper still laying waste to those around him.

"He's fine," Death muttered, holding his hand over her wound.

It felt like her wound had caught fire, and she cried out.

"*Shh*, you're okay." Death whispered in a foreign language as fiery pain spread up her arm.

She screamed, burying her face against his neck as he continued in the strange tongue. "Ow, Death," she whimpered, but he only squeezed her and chanted faster.

War was smiling when she opened her eyes. He seemed to be enjoying the battle itself.

Stinging tears blurred her vision, but she tried to seek out her family, and she luckily found them behind Death and Sorrow, bravely guarding them.

The fire engulfed the area of her shoulder, nearly making its way into her heart. Death spoke even faster. She cried in agony, catching glimpses of the wives working together as they ripped apart the demons attempting to breach their lines. They were savage and showed no fear while slaughtering the threat to their kingdom.

"Ow!" She breathed easier as the fire ebbed and retreated down her arm to where she received her wound.

"Jane?" Death called her.

She lifted her eyes to see him glaring down at her. She panted softly and nodded, offering him a faint smile, but he wasn't happy. "I know," she whispered, reaching under his hood to touch his face. "I will let you come for me next time." His jaw clenched, but he didn't say anything, so she continued. "Thank you for keeping them safe."

He kissed her palm as War grinned at her over his shoulder.

"Brother," War said, "if you don't want that beast, I will gladly dispose of it."

Death pressed another soft kiss to her palm, reaching up to wipe the blood from her forehead. "Than," he said. She quickly felt her general land behind her. "Keep her safe." He made brief eye contact with him. She realized Thanatos must have nodded to him because he was looking at her again. "You can't lose this blade, Jane."

Jane looked to see War handing him her sword.

"It is bonded to you," Death said. "Simply call it with your mind or order it away—no more excuses for losing your weapons. The same goes for your gun. He gave you a holster so you can get used to it."

She smiled at his seriousness and let her mind issue the order. It vanished in a green flame, the glow showing Death's smile.

"Good girl. Stay here now."

Jane didn't argue with him. "Yes, sir."

He chuckled before giving her a sneaky kiss on her lips when he yanked her up to him.

"Death." She shook her head but smiled at him.

His deep chuckle made her body tingle. "I told you you're worth his beating."

She rolled her eyes and received a quick peck before she was handed over to Thanatos.

"Do not leave her alone. She needs time to recover from the venom," he said, caressing her cheek as he kept his eyes on Thanatos.

"She will be safe," Thanatos said before greeting her. "My queen."

Jane looked back at Death.

He summoned his scythe again. Another flash of pale green illuminated his favorite weapon and produced two instead.

A figure dropped down beside Death, but he continued watching her.

"My lord." Viduus greeted him with a bow.

Jane smiled that the reaper had come out unscathed.

"Finish this mess, Viduus. I will take care of that." He never looked away from her, nor did she let her eyes leave his dark face. "Kali?"

A voluptuous woman with beautiful blue hair landed beside him. Her hood was down, revealing her oval-shaped face. She was stunning, but Jane was alarmed by the dark look that flitted across the beauty's eyes when she took in Thanatos holding Jane.

Thanatos let out an irritated rumble and hugged Jane protectively.

The woman's piercing amber eyes narrowed on Jane as a second set of arms manifested from her body, all holding swords.

Jane gasped as Death growled at Kali.

"She's taken, Kali," Death said, his tone chastising. "He views her as his queen."

The female reaper lowered her fierce gaze. "Yes, my lord."

"I would have thought you two were over your ridiculous lovers' spat." Death shook his head and jabbed his finger into Kali's chest. "Round up the hounds while Viduus destroys these demon scum. I want those dogs in ashes when I'm finished."

"Yes, my lord," she said.

Jane glanced at the beautiful woman before turning her face to Thanatos. His scowl softened when he looked at her—until Jane gave him a mischievous smirk, realizing why the woman looked ready to rip her heart out.

Thanatos glared at Jane. "Don't get any ideas, my queen."

She chuckled, returning her focus to Death.

He watched her already. "You're dismissed, Kali. Do what you do best."

"Yes, my lord." Kali nodded and let out a loud whistle before jumping into the air, gracefully extending her snowy wings and disappearing from view.

Death's eyes slid to Thanatos. "Don't make me regret this."

"I said I would not fail her," Thanatos told him.

War chuckled in front of them. "You boys and your women . . . Do you see why I never promise them serious relationships?"

Thanatos snorted, and Jane smiled at how calm the Red Horseman appeared as he continued firing into the crowd.

She struggled to hold onto her happiness when she registered how enormous the rising black mass was in the distance. It was solidifying, but she still couldn't determine what shape it was trying to achieve.

"Don't worry," Death said, getting her attention again. His eyes flashed brightly. "These bastards are my specialty."

"I want the next one," War piped.

"Keep them safe, brother," Death ordered.

War waved him off.

Death tilted his head at her. "See you in a minute, angel." His green eyes angled again, the beast within him coming forward.

"Be careful," she whispered without thinking.

War laughed loudly, and even Thanatos chuckled.

Death winked at her and turned away, flexing his wings. "How many times do I have to tell you who I am?" He paused and twirled one of his scythes.

She smiled. "Always once more, apparently."

He peered over his shoulder, his eyes glowing brightly as his voice entered her mind. *"See you in a few, my green-eyed beauty."*

Jane touched her face, about to ask what he was getting at, but he flapped his wings as he turned forward again and charged.

Demons, Fallen, and vampires swarmed him, but he cut them down and continued toward the creature growing from the black mass. The monster finally stood on all fours, screeching the loudest, most terrifying sound—like a plane and train crash mixed with every roar she could imagine.

The crowd screamed, many covering their ears or falling to their knees. Jane realized Thanatos and War had each placed a hand over her ears. The monster closed its terrifying jaws, and they both removed their hands.

"Bastard," War said, shooting his gun again.

Then Jane saw that many angels and demons who fell to their knees had not gotten up. Their heads had exploded.

"My kids!" Jane turned, realizing the creature's roar had been powerful enough to kill.

"They are fine, my queen," Thanatos said quietly.

"But," she said, searching his eyes as she watched Death get closer.

"A behemoth's cry only affects some this way. Mortals and vampires are safe under God's protection."

Jane darted her eyes toward Death. He was almost there. "But I'm—"

Thanatos shook his head at her.

She opened her mouth to ask him what he was trying to say, but she turned away upon hearing Death's roar.

He had stopped because the beast was spewing a lava-like substance, which Death was staying out of range of.

Her breathing sped up as she took in the monster. It was much larger than the demon War had quickly destroyed, easily ten times its size. And it was scarier all around. Its bony head protruded misshaped spikes that dripped with yellow mucus, which she assumed was venom. Black, oily skin stretched tight over the humongous creature, allowing his many pale, bone-colored horns and spikes to glisten in the moonlight.

"Thanatos, that thing is like a hundred feet tall," she whispered, her heart racing as Death leapt out of the way when it took a step closer in an attempt to spew lava on him.

"One hundred and fifty, my queen." Thanatos chuckled. "This is an alpha male, though, so he is a bit larger."

Jane's mouth fell open.

"Did you think your angel merely sat around reaping human souls all day?" Thanatos pointed ahead. "Watch, my queen. There may come a day you will need to know how to fight these wretched beasts; I believe this one is looking for you."

Jane was filled with dread as she gazed at it swinging its razor-sharp claws at Death. And, as if it had heard Thanatos, soulless, black eyes darted to where she stood. It stepped in her direction, and Death roared, jumping between them. It spewed more lava at him, but he produced a shield and covered his head, sending lava in all directions. Unfortunately, Death failed to see the spiked tail coming at him.

Jane screamed when it hit him and watched as he was knocked amidst the battle, still waging around them.

"Help him," she said, shoving Thanatos.

War laughed in front of her as he produced a ball of fire and threw it at the horde of Fallen racing toward Death. They burst into flames, screaming as the ground erupted into a raging inferno.

Jane panicked. Death was inside the fire. "War, what the fuck?"

The monster started toward them again, but a dark figure surrounded by emerald flames raced out of the blaze War had set.

Just like Sorrow, green flames raged around his body. He was unharmed. But he was pissed.

"Worry not, my queen," Thanatos said. "The Horsemen have ways to protect themselves from each other. He needs only to fuel himself now. His haste to rid this beast for you left him forgetful that he is not whole and has given so much to you already. Look now."

Jane watched her fearless angel block the behemoth's path to her.

"She's mine." Death snarled before tilting his head back, a howl unlike any she had ever heard ripping from his mouth, and then thousands of balls of blue light appeared from all directions, including the mouths of his reapers nearby. They howled with him, then increased their attacks while the spectacular spheres crashed into Death's body.

Death roared louder, and Jane gasped as the outline of a skeleton seeped through his black suit around his hands and forearms, while the wicked glow from his neon eyes revealed a frightening skeletal mask under his hood. It was nothing like a human skull, either. Every angle was exaggerated and menacing, reminding her of the beautiful sharpness she had sometimes caught glimpses of on Death's and Lucifer's faces. He was horrifyingly beautiful.

"The King Reaper, my queen." Thanatos bowed his head. "One of the Angel of Death's many titles. This is the King Reaper's Army. They are feeding him."

"Oh, God," she whispered as Death's scythe ignited in green and gold flames and increased in length and girth until finally revealing a more devilish looking one. This scythe was decorated with ancient-looking symbols, similar to the beautiful markings that painted Lucifer's perfect body. There were also various demonic skulls etched along the enormous blade.

"Not God, little angel," War said. "He is Death. Your Death. Just yours."

Thanatos and War chuckled softly, and she could barely register the loud bangs blasting out of the canon-sized gun in War's hand anymore.

As the last blue orb was absorbed, Death cast her a look over his shoulder. All she could see was part of a skeletal face illuminated by the flames flickering from his body and his scythe.

He was a monster.

He was beautiful.

He winked.

Jane's jaw dropped as he extended his giant wings before he turned forward and ran, leaping into the sky. Green flames trailed behind him, and when he landed on the ten-story devil's back, he roared, swinging his scythe with devastating force into the monster's side.

Instead of blood, lava poured out of the wounds, but Death didn't let up. He kept hacking as he held on to a spike. The beast cried as it reached for him. He was moments away from getting clawed, but he swung his scythe, removing its fingers.

The behemoth let out a thundering bellow.

"Ah, shit," Thanatos said, lifting her.

"Take them," Death hollered, hacking the alpha behemoth.

Jane panicked, her eyes wide as three more behemoths tore through the forest, all spewing lava with hellhounds and other beasts rushing forward.

Thanatos whistled, and Sorrow galloped over. Adam held his hand down for her.

"No," she shouted, turning to see the reapers flying and running toward the new enemies as Death brought down the first behemoth.

Death's gaze connected with hers as Thanatos put her on Sorrow with her kids and Adam.

His voice entered her mind. *"Go, angel. Go with your babies."*

Tears stung her eyes as the flames around Death's body grew, and he turned toward the new behemoths.

"Viduus," Thanatos shouted.

The reaper landed beside Thanatos with two other reapers at his side.

"See that they make it safely to the bunkers. She and her family are not to be captured." Thanatos summoned his scythe as his hood hid all of his face.

"Yes, Lord Thanatos." Viduus motioned for the two reapers to go ahead.

Thanatos glanced at her. "Be safe, my queen."

"Than," Jane said, reaching out to him.

He grabbed her hand and bowed. "We will see you again." With that, he nodded to Sorrow, and the Pale Horse turned, carrying them away from the battle with the rest of their party.

Jane wiped her freezing tears and hugged her children as Adam held her. Her heart throbbed when explosions and screams of death reached her ears.

They ran for hours, a reaper occasionally landing beside them, but none would speak.

Then, finally, the frontline of their party cried out in joy. "We made it."

Jane lifted her head, meeting Viduus' gaze. "Anything?" she asked.

He held out his arms for Natalie. "Not yet, Death's angel. Not yet."

9

NO END

"What do you think will happen when this David guy returns?" Adam ran his fingers through Jane's hair.

She shrugged as best she could from where her head rested on his lap. "I don't know. I always hurt him, and I was trying to put him first for good. I wanted to show him he was the one, but I'm so stupid . . . I can't let go of Death or Luc."

"Especially Death." Adam chuckled. "I never would have guessed the Grim Reaper was real or that he was visiting my baby cousin and loving her."

"I'll never let him go," she whispered. "That's the thing—I think David deserves more than I'll ever be able to give. I guess it's selfish of me to refuse to let Death go, but I won't. And Luc, well, I didn't expect to have feelings for him. I suppose it makes sense, though. Why else would he save me unless he cared for me? Maybe I'm meant to care for him . . . There had been a pull toward him the first time we met. Like I knew there was something good there right away. My instincts, I guess."

Adam nodded. "That makes sense, but if I were David, I'd have a hard time with you loving other guys, too. You have to choose him or let him go."

An unbearable pain radiated through her chest as her lips trembled.

"Or she can choose him, and he can be the man she needs him to be and suck it up," came a voice from the doorway.

Jane sat up quickly, locking eyes with David. "You came back."

He dropped his bag on the floor as he shut the door. "I heard you were injured." His gaze shifted to Adam, but he returned his focus to her. "Has someone checked your wounds?"

"A hellhound bit me, but I'm healing." She wiped a tear that slipped free. "Death removed the venom . . . Are you okay?"

David nodded, rubbing his hand down his face as he glanced at the kids. "The children?"

"They're fine," Jane whispered as she gestured to Adam. "David, this is my cousin Adam. Adam, this is David, my—um—maker."

David's gaze burned into her before sliding to Adam. "Hello, Adam. I am glad to see you made it here safely. Death told me about you coming. It was difficult not to spoil his surprise for her."

Adam glanced at her, confused.

"Don't ask," Jane said, knowing Adam wasn't aware Death could split his soul and he'd also been here with them.

"Well, it's good to see her again," Adam said. "Thanks for saving her back home."

David removed his sword and vest before placing them on a table. "Of course. I do not wish to sound rude, and I know you have just reunited with her, but I must ask that you find a different room to stay in. Jane and I have some things we need to discuss, and it will take a while."

"Are you going to keep being a dick to her?" Adam asked, and Jane widened her eyes, completely shocked.

A faint but deadly smile touched David's lips. "Because you are her cousin, I will show restraint, but I suggest you do not speak to me this way again. Her relationship with me is our business. Not yours. I don't care who you are to her."

Jane patted Adam's hand. "It's okay. I want to talk to him now rather than later. Let me help you find a room, though."

David opened the door and pointed down the hall. "My brothers are at the end of the hall. They are expecting you, but you are welcome to find wherever you are comfortable staying."

Adam kissed her hair, ignoring David. "I thought he was supposed to be your prince charming. He's an even bigger asshole than Ryder. Are you sure about me leaving? You don't have to stay with him."

She gave him a quick hug. "I'll be fine. Find Gawain or Gareth—they're great. And get some rest. I'm sure we'll have a big day tomorrow."

He sighed, kissing her head again, but he stood, grabbing his bag as he walked past David without saying anything.

David shut the door. "He looks well taken care of. Yet another way Death has succeeded in bringing you happiness."

She wasn't expecting that from him. "I didn't think you would see that as a negative thing."

"I don't—I'm happy for you. You know what I have a problem with." He crossed his arms; his expression was unreadable. "Lucifer doesn't deserve your love, and I don't deserve to watch my girlfriend throw herself in front of him after he tortured, manipulated, and raped her. He stole you from me, Jane. But you blurt out you love him and lie for him right to my face."

"I didn't mean to feel that way or blurt it out. That was wrong of me." She could barely look at him; his gaze burned. "And I know you don't deserve to deal with any of this. That's why it's up to you whether our relationship continues." Her face scrunched up as she tried not to cry. "I don't expect you to keep putting up with me—I'm the worst girlfriend and Other ever. I honestly don't blame you if you're done with me. In fact, I'm ready for you to leave me. I can take it, so you don't have to worry about me if that's making you hesitate. I can take you leaving."

"That's part of your problem. You continuously expect the worst from me. You still think the solution is to run away and suffer alone." He shook his head. "Baby, I have told you before—my love for you has no end. All I want is for you to think about me from time to time. You're so ready to fight for them—to not lose them—but when it's me, you're ready to run. You have walked away from me. Twice! To go off with them. Yes, for us to live, but you still left me. Without the fight you're putting up for them. Do I mean less to you?"

"No," she sobbed, covering her face. She was trying to be brave by saying she could handle him leaving, but she wasn't. She never wanted to let him go, but she couldn't stand herself for putting him through so much. "It's because you're better than them. You're the best man I've ever met, and I love you so much it hurts. I want you to be happy, but I see how everyone is right—I'm not good enough for someone like you." She lowered her hands and looked him in the eyes. "Your own sister thinks this way. I tried to be brave when she judged me, but she was right. My relationship with Death is wrong and unfair to you."

Jane rubbed her chest, watching his eyes fall to the movement as she went on. "So, it's not that you mean less—not at all. You mean more, and I'm terrified of losing you. I deserve to, though. I deserve to watch you walk away because I'm selfish for refusing to let go of them. I want you to have the best, but I'm not it. I think I would cease to exist if I tried any harder to be what you deserve because the best for you is me having a life without Death."

Seeing David through her tears became harder, but she kept going. "I can't live without him, David. And I can't stop caring for Luc. So I deserve it. I deserve to lose you, and I will try to be brave when you walk out that door. Just don't come back for me. Ever. Walk away and be happy because I will never deserve you."

He uncrossed his arms and walked to her, squatting as he took one of her hands in his. "Baby, I have never looked at you and thought I deserve better. I have defended you and our relationship, but it hurt to find out you fell in love with Lucifer. He tortured and stole you. He manipulated you so you would jump to him in order to save us. I get why you made the choices you did, and I love that you are so brave and selfless to sacrifice yourself for all of us, but then you throw it in my face that all the shit he did to you was still nothing in your eyes because you learned to love him.

"Death is entirely different. I would not ask you to change anything other than be mindful of how much you allow him to have with you. But this Lucifer thing . . . I cannot turn my head and be at peace with it. I cannot look at you next to him and accept that you still pick me.

"Baby, you looked completely different at his side. You look different at Death's side, too. I don't understand where I come in. I know you love me, but I fear the way you think. Right now, you're ready to throw us away because it's what you think is best for me. It's not. It's the most horrible thing you could do to me. Worst of all, I know you would walk right to Death or Lucifer. That's an unbearable truth, Jane."

"I'm sorry." She wiped her tears away.

He reached up, rubbing his thumb over her cheek when more tears fell. "Why didn't you tell me you loved him?"

"I didn't know I did." She searched his eyes to find home, but it wasn't there. "I guess knowing I was about to watch him get killed forced me to see it."

"We wouldn't have killed him." He kissed her hand. "I know how much you like to protect others you care about, but this has been a knife in my heart, and you're plunging it deeper every time you say you will not stop loving him."

Her face ached as she tried to keep it together. "I don't mean to hurt you. I don't want to hurt you, but I will. And they are why. My love for you doesn't end either, but it is the same for them."

David sighed as he lifted his gaze to the ceiling. "What guts me is this means you were not always forced into your intimacies with Lucifer."

Her hand was shaking. "I swear there were only the two kisses I gave him willingly. They weren't the same as they are for you, either. I felt like a monster for imagining your face so I could give him what he wanted, and I hate that I can't just stop the feelings I developed or change what I did. He kept telling me to prove he didn't have to call her forward. I can't express how terrifying it was for me to be forced into darkness, unable to stop her from destroying anyone and everything she wanted. I didn't want to open my eyes and see the horror she was capable of. So I did what I had to. Then, I guess my feelings changed when Lucifer changed."

"He ached for your kiss and smile," he said quietly.

"How do you know that?"

David gave her a sad smile. "Baby, that was all I wanted from you when you were not mine. To watch Death receive your kiss and smile so easily was torture. It was my heart's greatest desire to have you smile just for me and kiss me without your darker soul using your body."

"That explains why he would tell me to smile like I do for you. He got so mad when he tried to offer me a woman donor, and I told him to bring me a man with dark hair and blue or green eyes. I thought he was going to incinerate me."

"I am sure that pissed him off." He turned his lips toward her palm and kissed it as he chuckled. "I love you."

"I love you." Her voice cracked as tears spilled free.

David pushed her legs apart to reach her and pulled her face to his for a kiss.

Jane eagerly wrapped her arms around his neck and hooked her legs around him. "I'm so sorry," she mumbled against his lips as he gripped her hips and tugged her to the edge of the bed.

"I know." He smiled, cupping her cheek with one hand, wiping her tears away with his thumb. "I'm sorry too. I don't like being harsh with you."

"I deserve it. I deserve worse."

He chuckled before kissing her softly. "We'll work through this, okay?"

She nodded, her heart pounding.

His eyes bored into hers, and she finally found home when he asked, "Are you still certain I am your choice?"

"Yes," she whimpered, touching the corner of his mouth, smiling when he kissed her fingers. "Yes. I will always choose you."

"Good." He sniffed, chuckling as he shook his head. "That bastard knows he's getting hit, right?"

Jane grinned. "Don't hit him too bad. Most of his kisses were from being worried and when I was hurt, but I think he's secretly just itching to spar with you."

"How many times did he kiss you?"

"I wasn't counting. A few times, though." She bit her lip, fearing this would set him off again.

"I'll go a full minute with him, then. Deal?"

"A minute? David, that's a lot." She knew David couldn't kill Death, but he was strong.

"Ten hits. Wherever and whenever I choose."

"Two." She smiled at his glare.

"Fine. Two." He glanced over his shoulder, briefly eyeing her sleeping kids before turning toward her again. He smirked, reaching for the button of her pants. "Death can have your kiss that's his as well as your love for him, and I suppose Lucifer can have your love, but I don't want him getting you like he had you there ever again. I get this." He pulled her against him. "I get your love, your kiss, your smile, and your body. I don't want you giving yourself to him or anyone else to keep me safe. I may not be able to do what they can, but I am no pushover, my love. If anyone wants to kill me, they will have a tough time. So no more sacrificing yourself for me."

He gently pushed her onto her back and unbuttoned her jeans. "Raise your hips if you are mine—if you will only give yourself to me from here on out."

She bit her smiling lips and raised her hips, giggling when he growled, showing his fangs but gently and swiftly ridding her of her pants.

"David, what about the kids?" She sighed at the sight of him pulling his shirt over his head.

"I will hear if they begin to wake." He stood and unbuttoned his pants. "And I'm sure if you want it bad enough, you will find a way to be quiet. Do you wish for us to make up like this? We can wait. But I don't know when we will be alone again."

"No, I want this." She could barely breathe. She had been so sure he'd leave her, but he was there, preparing to make love to her. "I'll be quiet."

"Good." He sat beside her, bending down to remove his boots.

Jane sat up, kneeling behind him. She wanted to touch him, but she was still hesitant.

"You better put those lips on me." He didn't look up and kept untying his other boot. "Now, Jane."

She lightly placed her hands on his muscular back before leaning down and kissing one of his scars. She sighed, pressing her hands and lips harder to his hot skin. "You're sure you want me? I don't think I can take it if you change your mind later. I'd rather lose you now than get my hopes up."

David set his boots aside before turning slightly. He grabbed her hips, smiling as he slid his hands to her ass. "I am always sure about wanting you. You are my only choice—that will never change."

"I love you so much." She caressed his cheek but moaned as he pushed her shirt up and brought his mouth to her breasts.

"Quiet." He nipped her skin and pulled her shirt over her head. "And I love you, too." He quickly popped off her bra and, running a hand up to the back of her neck, yanked her thigh so she'd fall onto her back. "*Shh.*"

Jane covered her breasts as she watched him stand and remove his pants. He was over her, tugging the blanket over them within seconds.

He had been going commando.

She arched her body, exhaling softly as he leaned over her. "Oh God," she whispered. "I don't think I'll ever get tired of feeling us together."

David kissed her nose before putting his weight on his forearm and removing her hands from her breasts. "That's good to know." He chuckled softly, kissing down the column of her neck, pausing when his lips were over her heart. "Jane?"

"Yeah?" She peeked down at him as he lifted his head and pressed his hand over her heart.

He kept his voice low. "When Death touches you here, what do you feel?"

Jane smiled, sliding his hand down a little more. "He touches me here. It's where the tingles go. Like they surround my heart or gather there. I think he feels it, too."

He was quiet for a few seconds before he asked, "Do you feel anything when I touch you?"

Her eyes watered, and she nodded. "I feel your heat . . . But it blankets my heart as well as going inside it. It fills the cracks—it warms the parts that feel cold or bruised so those tingles can attach to my heart. Then I breathe again."

David smiled that beautiful smile of his. "So, I warm your heart—hold it together—and bring your other great love along with me?"

"I don't think we should tell him that." She pulled him down as she angled her pelvis, begging.

Her vampire groaned quietly as he slid the tip of his cock along her slit before guiding himself to her entrance. "Why is that? Are you afraid of him knowing?"

Panting, she shook her head. "I think he already knows. But if you tell him you're bringing him along, he'll take that as an offer to have a three-way."

His eyes darkened, but he smiled and slowly thrust forward.

"Oh, gosh." Jane gasped, digging her fingers into David's shoulders. He always filled her up completely, and it overwhelmed her each time.

He let out a deep sigh and slowly buried himself inside her. "Are you okay?"

She gasped, nodding. "Yes. Keep going. Oh, please, keep going." She moved her hips with his, watching him smirk. Her stomach tightened as she fought moaning out because he always hit the right spot. Her mouth fell open. "Oh, shit. Yes. Fuck." With a shaking hand, she covered her mouth and whimpered.

David growled as he looked down to watch himself moving in and out of her for a few seconds before increasing his speed.

Jane hung onto him and the bed as her entire body tensed up. He always managed to make her climax right away.

"Come, Jane." He went harder and faster. "I want every male—every female—to know you are mine, and I am yours."

"I'm yours." She panted, hanging onto him as he pounded into her.

David gripped the bed frame, squeezing it until the metal stopped squeaking. He sighed, dipping his face down to kiss her cheek. She turned her face up but could only gasp and hang on to him.

He grinned, that sexy grin that made her moan and tingle all over.

"Shh." David glanced over to the kids. Thankfully they were still out. "Fuck, I want to make you scream."

Jane gasped, knowing he was holding back—she wanted him to lose control.

He pulled out, making her whine, but he quickly flipped her onto her stomach as he straddled her legs and grabbed her hip. "Lift your ass a little bit."

Jane peeked over at her kids as she followed his orders.

"They're asleep," he whispered, sliding his cock along her slit. "Bite the mattress if you have to. I'm done holding back."

"I've never done it like this." She was shaking with anticipation as she tightened her fingers into the sheets.

David leaned down, gently kissing her cheek. "It's okay. Turn your head." He gathered her hair and turned her head to reach her lips.

She had no idea how he could be forceful but was still careful that he wasn't causing her pain or discomfort.

He still spoke softly, but he sounded all alpha male at the same time. "Do you know how badly I want to see you pregnant with my child?"

Her eyes widened. "David . . ."

He quieted her with a kiss, gently nudging her with small thrusts. "You are not at risk, but I want it." He let go of her hair to brace himself and slide his other hand down her back. He squeezed her ass cheek, spreading it a little. "Do you think of that? Do you want my child growing in your womb?"

She nodded, pressing her lips together to keep quiet. She had no idea why this was such a turn on. She knew they weren't supposed to have children, but she was imagining everything now.

David thrust forward slowly but pulled back before she could have all of him. "That's what you do to me. You make me fearless of the consequences. You make it possible to allow you to love others. Just having what you grant me is the greatest gift I will ever receive. But I will devour all you give me. This"—he squeezed her ass before sliding his hand along her spine—"is mine. And they will know it."

Jane tore the sheets. Her body was shaking.

He pushed in, growling as he lowered his mouth to her shoulder. He kissed a path to the back of her neck, thrusting hard. "Who gets you this way, Jane? Who gets your body and holds your heart?"

Jane curled her fingers, pulling the sheet. "You. Just you." She loved that he was dominating her. He needed reassurance and to show her exactly who he was. Her David.

"Just me." He entered her again after pulling out. "My Jane."

She closed her eyes, moaning until he tightened his fist in her hair.

"Quiet," he scolded.

She managed only to release soft mewling sounds, smiling when he picked up the pace and started growling. Oh, she'd give anything to see him. She could imagine his sexy ass flexing every time he entered her.

"Ah, fuck." He slowed down and spread her butt cheeks.

She peeked at him, watching him stare down where they became one. He was breathtaking. Every heavy breath he took flexed his delicious muscles, and he had the most possessive expression etched across his handsome face as he scanned her body.

His eyes darted up to hers, and he leaned over her, thrusting slower but deeper.

"I love you," she breathed as his lips brushed her cheek.

He was massive over her, but he kissed her lips and kept his movement. "I love you, Jane." He kissed her again. "I'll never stop."

A happy sob escaped her, but her frantic gasps quickly followed it.

David smirked, moving faster as he whispered, "Stay quiet."

Jane gasped. "You're so deep. I can't."

He kept plunging into her, his chest and stomach flexing against her slick skin, making her shiver.

"You're my home, too," he breathed in her ear, stopping as he ground into her. "This is my home."

She panted, nodding. "Yes." She took a deep breath as he pulled back.

"Do you like having me home?" He thrust in hard again.

It was painful, but a beautiful pain. Just like them. They were beautiful together, but they had to endure pain to hold each other.

"Yes." She found his hand, smiling as he linked their fingers together. "Yes. Please don't leave."

David pressed his lips to her temple, still thrusting. "Never, my love. We are beyond forever. We are always."

"Beyond forever." She smiled, raising her hips the best she could to meet his thrust. "Always."

1 0

THIS PERSON

"And then Ryder kissed Mommy on the lips," Natalie whispered to David.

Jane glanced over at him, her heart racing as he locked gazes with her.

He smirked. "Well, Mommy's kisses are the sweetest. But I will remind Ryder he does not get them all the time, okay?" He zipped her jacket up. "Thank you for watching out for her."

Natalie wrapped her arm around his neck, and David lifted her.

"Mommy said you would be proud of me."

He nodded, walking over to where Jane sat and helped Nathan dress. "I am proud, princess."

"Are you sad about your castle?" she asked. "Mommy was packing our things and said we had to let you get your life back."

Jane met David's stare and had to look away because of the sadness she saw there. She knew Natalie wasn't saying things to be mean, but she could've used a break on the out-mouth-of-babes thing.

Unfortunately, Natalie kept going. "Will we still have to live without you? She said you would visit us."

He pulled Natalie into a hug. "Don't worry about any of that. We will build a new home, and we will be together. Don't worry about anything, okay?"

"Mommy's cats were inside. Ryder wouldn't let us bring them."

David darted his eyes back to Jane. "They might have made it out, baby."

116

Her lip quivered, but she turned to finish dressing Nathan.

He sighed, rubbing Jane's back as he spoke to Natalie. "What matters is you and the others made it here safe. I promise I will not leave again."

"You will," Natalie muttered.

David didn't respond, and Jane stayed quiet, too. She knew there would be more battles, torment, and loss. She and David could not guarantee they'd be with them.

"Sword," Nathan said.

Jane frowned. "I don't have my sword out." She looked around, making sure.

Nathan pointed to her hand. "David."

It dawned on her what Nathan was talking about, and she beamed at him before summoning her sword and gun.

Nathan clapped as she held them up for David to inspect.

His mouth hung open, and he placed Natalie on the bed with Nathan before holding his hand out for her sword. "May I?"

Jane happily handed over her sword, giddy over the amazement shining in his eyes.

"How?" he asked.

"Death."

David took a deep breath. "You lost mine?"

Her happiness vanished. "Um, well, yes. I was overwhelmed a few times and lost it with my rifle. Viduus, one of the reapers I was telling you about, gave these to me. He said Death wanted me to have them. This one"—she pointed to the sword—"is Heaven's Reaper. The gun is called Death's Angel."

David handed her sword back to her and took the gun. "They are etched with the same markings on Death's scythe."

Jane chewed on her lip. "Yes, I don't know what that means. I think it's to do with bonding them to me or the magic they hold."

David aimed the gun at the other side of the room and grinned. "It's small."

Jane smacked his chest. "It's made for me, not you."

He chuckled, handing it back to her. "Does it have unlimited ammunition?"

"Yes." She giggled at his annoyed look.

"Cheaters." He glanced at the twins. "Only Mommy and I touch weapons, right?"

"Right," they said together.

He smiled at them before focusing on her again. "How far is the range?"

"I don't know. They're really powerful. I do prefer holding a rifle, but I think they go further."

He picked Natalie up again. It always stole her breath to see him holding her children.

"So you can summon them? Like he does?" he asked.

"Yes. I don't know how it works or where they go, but I just have to think of them, and they appear." She sent them away, smiling when Nathan clapped again. "War and Thanatos summon weapons too. I think all angels can. It was all that worked on the demons and hellhounds."

David stared at Natalie. "Ryder is trying to win your mommy from me. Perhaps I should get her a gift."

Natalie nodded and whispered in his ear.

Jane thought they looked too cute.

"Oh, wait." He held up a finger and went to his bag. "I did find something. What do you think?" He showed Natalie, and her daughter smiled, covering her mouth as she nodded to David.

"David, you don't have to give me anything," Jane said, but she wanted to know what he had brought for her.

"Close your eyes," he said, in all seriousness now.

"Why?" She searched his face, her heartbeat speeding up as he smiled.

"I want to do this properly," was all he said.

Jane glanced at Natalie and then at Nathan. "Okay." She closed her eyes.

"Hold out your hand." His voice was closer, and she bit her lip as she did as he asked.

He put something cold in it.

"Open."

Jane laughed when she did and held up the Dr Pepper bottle. "I love it. Thank you."

David chuckled, leaning forward to kiss her. She loved that they were holding her kids for this moment. "Enjoy it, my love."

The underground bunker was pleasant, but it was no castle or Valhalla. Plus, it was crowded. They had to squeeze past the bodies shuffling through them constantly. It gave the feeling of being in a refuge shelter—a good quality one, but still, not somewhere Jane wanted to keep the kids for long. Luckily, there was no hiding David's intimidating size and reputation.

Humans and immortals shied away from him, making navigating easier than when she'd walked through the halls earlier without him.

David squeezed her hand while he pulled her through the busy hall. He was carrying Nathan because her little boy had started whining about hunger, which was always hard on her son.

Jane let go of David's hand and pulled Natalie's head to her shoulder as they neared some wounded sitting outside the triage area, waiting for more treatment. It wasn't like Natalie hadn't seen blood or even people dying at this point, but Jane wanted her to feel safe.

"The others are having breakfast," David said. "It sounds like Adam is with them."

The peace she had felt the whole morning vanished as soon as they entered the mess hall. David even stopped and squeezed her hand before pulling her forward.

But Jane wasn't happy. She didn't take her eyes off the scene before her, and she gave David a dirty look when he moved to block her view.

"Baby, don't get upset."

Jane glared at him. "How can you say that? She's not getting anywhere near him."

David pulled her to a stop, his grip tightening as his tone came out far more firm than she expected. "Get a hold of your emotions."

"Move," she growled.

He glared at her. "He's a grown man, and he's only talking to her. You cannot stop him from talking to someone."

"Yes, I can," she snapped. She couldn't believe he was willing to allow what she was seeing. "Are you taking up for her?"

David gave her a stern look. "You know I am not taking up for her, but you can't behave like this. Remember you are holding your child, and they are soaking up everything you say and do. Do not show them this person. I know you think you are protecting Adam, but he doesn't need you to—so stop. You are behaving this way for the wrong reasons."

"Let me go." The wording he used stabbed her heart and fueled her anger. *This person.* She didn't care what he said now and nearly bared her fangs at him.

David growled, tightening his hold when she almost broke free. "Knock it off."

His cold tone made her flinch and halt her efforts to burn a hole through his chest so she could view the two people talking behind him in the distance.

"We are going to go greet your cousin," he said, "and you will be polite and kind to her. If you want to argue with her, do it when your children are not around. Do not behave like this in their presence—or in front of these people. They are mourning several losses and don't need to watch you fight with a woman who is doing nothing wrong."

Jane looked down. It always hurt more when he was the one being firm with her. She was spoiled with his sweet side and felt he'd show her that side more now. But maybe that was her being lovesick. Maybe he finally saw her. Maybe he saw the hate brewing beneath her skin. Maybe he still saw the woman who cheated on him, and now he was looking at Artemis, the woman who likely wouldn't have dared to betray him.

He stepped closer and lowered his voice. "Do you understand me?"

"Yes," she mumbled, hating how she felt with him looking down at her like he was. He was right, but knowing that didn't feel any better. She knew she shouldn't be like this around her kids, but she was seeing red and couldn't make it go away.

David sighed and pulled her to him, but she refused to meet his gaze. "I don't mean to hurt your feelings. You know I only want to be soft with you. But I don't want you to be upset with yourself—like you will be if you go over there and cause a scene."

Ouch.

He let go of her hand and reached up to lift her chin. "I'm sorry."

She nodded, but she wasn't okay. He was reminding her of her life with Jason when things were bad. Jason wanted everything to appear happy no matter what she was feeling. Of course, she knew David's heart was in the right place—he was thinking about the kids and not just wanting her to look pretty for everyone, but it felt like he had just betrayed her. He'd always had her back, but he was saying she was wrong, and she would be the bad guy—that he did not want her to be that way—that her feelings didn't matter.

His lips touched hers, making her realize she had closed her eyes. "I am sorry for talking to you so harshly, but I want my words taken seriously. Just be calm. I'm only trying to ensure you don't get mad at yourself later." He kissed her lips again. "Okay?"

"Yeah." But she still wasn't okay. She would suck it up, though. If she did it with Jason, she could do it with David. She could give him what he wanted, what she knew was the right thing to do, and put her feelings aside. Hide them. Make him happy.

He sighed and took her hand again. "Let's go. I'm starving, and I'm sure the kids are too."

She didn't say anything. She just followed him.

"Hey, guys," Adam greeted them.

"Hello, Adam," David returned his greeting, giving her hand a little squeeze when she kept quiet. "It looks like you got some rest. Were you able to find my brothers?"

David pulled Jane toward a chair and gently pushed her onto it. She kept her eyes down, feeling everyone's stares aimed at her. It made her feel even more ridiculous, so she played with a few curls of Natalie's hair when David kissed her head and sat beside her.

"No," Adam replied slowly, obviously sensing some tension between them. "This beautiful lady found me wandering around and offered me the extra bed in the room she shared with a few others."

His words made Jane's blood boil. *Beautiful lady, my ass.*

"That was kind of you, Artemis," David said. "Thank you."

Jane fought hard not to reach over and slap him. He didn't have to be that fucking nice.

"You know her?" Artemis' disbelieving voice felt like bee stings in her ears.

Unable to contain her vicious feelings for the goddess any longer, Jane jerked her head up and glared at Artemis.

David quickly took Jane's hand and let out a chastising growl.

Fucking traitor! Jane felt like she could cry as much as she was ready to rip Artemis and David to pieces. Thinking about harming David and even Artemis was awful, but every part of the situation hurt her.

"Jane is my cousin," Adam finally muttered. "The one I was telling you about."

Jane stared at the table while David's hand heated around hers. She knew she was in trouble now, but how else was she supposed to react?

"Did I miss something?" Adam asked, looking between the two.

David cleared his throat and handed Nathan off to his sister while he gestured for Ragnelle to take Natalie. "No, everything is fine. She's just a bit tired and hungry."

Jane pressed her lips together and stayed silent as Ragnelle took Natalie. She only took a breath when Ragnelle rubbed her arm before directing all her attention to Natalie.

Luckily, a new set of hands snatched Jane out of her chair.

"I'm so glad you're okay," Gawain whispered in her ear, hugging her.

Tears welled in her eyes, and she squeezed her arms around him. Her new brothers had been away from her for so long, and it was finally crashing down on her. "I'm so glad to see you."

David spoke again, "Arthur, any word on the village?"

She wanted to smack him for brushing off her feelings. It was like he'd turned into a different man.

"Do you want to come sit with us?" Gawain whispered in her ear.

"Yes. I can't stay here right now." She let him guide her away.

"Where are you going?" David asked, but she didn't want them to see her crying, so she kept her head down.

Gawain squeezed her and said, "She's coming to sit with us."

"You need to eat, Jane," David said. "This is not a time to brush off your needs."

"I'll make sure she eats," Gawain snapped. "You can come to find her when you're finished. She doesn't need to deal with this, and you know it."

A cold feeling seeped inside her chest. It wasn't the same as when Lucifer touched her. This was different. It didn't numb her—it was painful.

"There you are," Gareth said, pulling her away from Gawain.

Jane hugged him back and didn't protest when he dragged her away without another word to Gawain. She knew Gawain and David must've had a silent face-off, but she couldn't bring herself to look at them. Her emotions warred within her. Her logical side agreed with everything David said and did, but her heart and soul couldn't handle his attitude toward her or let go of what Artemis had done to her.

"Don't worry about him, darling," Gareth whispered, tucking her under his arm. "He's a big boy. He can deal with the two of you parting for a few minutes. Plus, we missed you. We already told him we'd steal you before he hibernated with you in a bedroom."

"Well, he didn't tell you how we parted." She laughed sadly.

Gareth chuckled. "Oh, he told us, but we told him to suck it up because you two are destined for each other. And you, darling, are destined to have many loves." He grinned. "We just suggested he show you he's alpha, and you'll turn back into a giggly mess of a girl."

"Shut up," she mumbled, finally feeling herself calm with more distance between her and Artemis, but something inside her heart cracked because David hadn't come around on his own.

Gareth laughed and gestured to the knights. "Look who I found about to throw down with a spoiled goddess."

Tristan shook his head at Gareth. "Stop instigating." He then smiled at her before pulling her into a hug. "We are all happy to have you back, Jane."

"It's good to be back." She patted his shoulder before turning to greet Bors and Geraint. She took turns hugging all the knights sitting at that particular table. Bedivere and Kay seemed to be the only ones missing, and she figured they were at the table David was sitting at with Arthur.

"Fucking idiot," Gawain muttered when he stomped back toward them.

Jane had just pulled away from Gaheris when Gawain plopped down. Galahad quickly embraced her before she was finally allowed to sit beside Gawain.

Gawain leaned over, giving her head a hard kiss and handing her the plate Tristan was trying to pass down.

"Thank you," she whispered, smiling at the amused grins on the others' faces as Gawain began angrily shoveling food into his mouth, still grumbling under his breath between bites. She loved they were not upset with her. She'd almost forgotten she'd attacked most of them before leaving.

"Gawain," Gareth drawled. "Care to share what has got you so upset?"

Gawain huffed, and Jane could only smile at his angry face before she realized she was the only woman sitting with them. The wives ate separately, it seemed. She figured it was a habit for them, but she wouldn't sit with the wives when she felt more comfortable with the knights.

"He knows better than to expect her to get along with that little tramp," Gawain snapped, getting snickers from the others. "Just tell me, and I'll beat his ass if he talks to you like that again."

Jane giggled when the others laughed louder. But it did make it worse that everyone had heard him.

"I mean it," Gawain added. "Fuck off, Gareth."

"Thank you, Gawain," Jane whispered, leaning over and pecking his cheek.

"You're welcome, love." He smiled, looking happier to see her not looking so down. "Your dumbass boyfriend just doesn't know anything about women yet." The others laughed again. "Even I wouldn't expect Elle to get along with that little brat. Especially after all of her crap you had to deal with."

"*Shh* . . ." Gareth hushed.

Like children caught doing something naughty, everyone froze.

"Jane," a voice greeted from behind. "Boys."

Jane breathed out in relief that it wasn't David, but she still internally cringed when she found Hades standing over her. "Hello, Hades."

"Don't give her any shit, Hades," Gawain said. "I don't care who you are. I'll still punch the next tool who talks down to her. She's not a robot—she has feelings, too."

An amused smile touched Hades' pale lips. "I realize that and agree. I only came to say welcome back." He held his hand out for Jane while the others laughed at Gawain.

She smiled and stood to hug him. "It's good to see you again, Hades."

Hades whispered in her ear, "David better watch out. It seems *big brother* doesn't like having you disciplined."

Jane scowled at him as Gareth laughed.

"He should know better," Gareth said. "He has seen our women get into catfights loads of times. At least Jane's desire to claw her eyes out is warranted."

Jane bit her lip, trying not to laugh, when Hades glared at Gareth.

"She is still my niece, Gareth," Hades muttered.

"Well, your niece better watch her little attitude," said Gawain. "Our sissy doesn't need to deal with that. We'll hold David so that she can set her straight."

"Shut up, both of you," Tristan said, shaking his head with a smile. "There's no one to hold Hades off from beating your ass."

She felt it was time to stop her knights from digging themselves into holes with any more males in the room. "I'm sorry, Hades."

Hades sighed, placing his hands on her shoulders as he stared into her eyes. "I should have warned your cousin you might be upset. I did not realize who he was, but I should have. She found him wandering around. It's so crowded here—I thought he must have belonged to one of the families who lived in the village. When she offered our spare bunk, I consented . . . She didn't know, Jane."

"It's fine." She sighed. "I'm acting like a child, but I'm just so emotional. So much has changed with me." Everyone nodded to her. "Did he tell you all what Luc did?"

"Yes," Hades replied. "I knew what was meant to happen, but Death did not expect Lucifer to take you. I suppose there is no point pondering why things unfolded as they did. Lucifer ended up keeping his end of the bargain by separating her from you."

"I don't have my powers," she blurted out, worriedly taking in their surprised expressions. "I'm just a regular vampire now."

"You will never be regular," Tristan told her.

Gareth nodded. "You are the greatest immortal ever to be created. You killed the Wolf King, and David said you beat the shit out of Lancelot. Fuck, you even got Lucifer to bow down to you. No other woman can tame all those men and kick as much ass as you do. Powers or no powers, you are great." He grinned at the others. "Now we should definitely hold David down for her—she has gone through far more than he ever has."

Gawain nodded. "Let's do it, bro."

"Thanks, boys," she whispered.

Hades kissed the top of her head. "Welcome back, Jane."

She smiled at him and watched him return to the other table. Her eyes met David's for a moment. His glare was fierce, and it ate her up that it was all aimed at her. There wasn't a hint of regret in his gaze nor a speck of hatred for Artemis.

Jane's chest felt like it had been ripped open when he looked away to answer a question that Artemis must have asked him. He smiled kindly at the goddess and responded to her as if nothing was wrong. Had he forgotten everything that had happened between them? Jane's eyes burned when he chuckled at something Artemis said.

"Don't look at him," Gawain whispered, taking her hand.

She couldn't look away and gasped when Artemis giggled at whatever David replied. Worse, Adam laughed along with them and was all smiles for Artemis, too.

"Fucking idiot," Gareth grumbled under his breath.

She finally turned away when Artemis touched Adam's shoulder.

"It's okay, love." Gawain rubbed her back. The others wore somber expressions and stayed quiet, eating as Gawain added, "He'll realize he needs to stand by you first. He is far too proper sometimes. He means well, even if he is being a complete moron."

Jane wiped the tears that quickly fell. "I know. I just don't see how they laugh at a time like this."

"Exactly." Gawain huffed. "There is no need for them to pretend all is well. Our home is gone. Our people are dead. So what if Jane's not in the mood to be friendly with her."

"Leave her be, Gawain," Gaheris ordered quietly. "We all deal with loss differently."

Jane blew out a shaky breath and focused on her plate. But she could only push the food around. Her appetite was gone entirely.

"So, we heard your angel wasn't the only one who arrived to aid you," Lamorak said.

Jane knew he was trying to get her mind off David. "Yeah. His brother came. He's massive, and he dresses like a Spartan Warrior. Super cool . . . Than came too."

"Than?" Gawain made a face at her. "Since when do you call that demon Than?"

Jane wiped her eyes again and tried to push the laughter behind her out of her mind. "He is an angel, not a demon. And he became Than when he asked for my forgiveness. I am the High Queen of Hell, and he is one of my generals."

Gawain choked on his drink. "High Queen?"

Her chest tightened at the loud laughter from David's table.

The knights shot glares over her head. She figured David must have looked her way.

"I accepted Luc," she said, forcing them to look at her again. "That made me his queen. So I guess I will always hold that title. I'm not really sure, but yeah, Than and I are friends, sort of. Like I said, he's my general. I'm unsure about Asmodeus, but I think he remains loyal. Anyway, despite all the horrible stuff Luc did and the fact he meant to keep me with him and use her, I love him, and he loves me." A little smile came to her lips. She would forever be grateful for what he did and what he suffered still for her. "He saved me."

"What the fuck do you mean you love him?" Gawain asked.

Jane instantly felt defensive. "Exactly what I said. I love him. I won't stop caring about him. He was the only one who could do this for me. He made bad choices but loved me enough to still save me and call Death to bring me home." She glared at the rest of them. "You don't have to like him —I don't expect you to. But he's trying to protect me—just like Death has always done. I need him, and I need you all. Now will you accept that, or do I need to sit by myself?" Her chest heaved. She knew it was a low blow to throw out her feelings for Lucifer, but she knew David could hear her. If she had to watch him put Artemis first, he deserved to watch her defend Luc.

The knights sat there stunned, mouths hanging open, and not one of them uttered a word.

"Fine." She went to stand, but Gawain grabbed her to keep her still.

"Don't leave," he whispered. "It's just a shock. David didn't tell us all of the Lucifer details. We support you, and you know we would all die for you."

The others nodded, but they were confused.

"I won't let any of you die for me," she said. "But thank you for standing by me."

"Of course, love. We are with you always." Gawain gave her another kiss and nodded to her food. "I said we'd make sure you ate. Now eat up."

"I don't think I can," she responded, grimacing at her plate of pancakes and oatmeal.

"Yeah, I know." Gawain squeezed her shoulder. "Just eat what you can. I am sure your appetite will return later."

She sighed before resting her elbows on the table to hold her head. David's table was still having a good time, and her blood boiled every time she heard his voice and Artemis'. She still didn't know how they could laugh at a time like this. Their home had been destroyed, and lives had been lost, yet, they were joking around as though all was well. "Do you think Death and the others are okay?" she mumbled, closing her eyes when David laughed again.

"Are you kidding?" Gareth said with surprise. "That bastard can take on anything. Don't worry about him, Jane. He's Death."

"He always says that." Jane smiled, but she didn't open her eyes. She kept fighting the urge to run to David. She wanted to apologize, but she also wanted to fight. She wanted him to apologize, too. Everything he was doing was deliberately hurting her. Dark thoughts started to form. She wanted to show him—show all of them how much she'd been hurt.

Jane released a deep breath. "Do you guys know the plan for what will happen now?"

"We will not be going back home," Lamorak said. "There are guards watching the perimeter, and we are obviously all staying armed and ready to evacuate if need be."

Jane had already noticed their battle gear and individual packs at their feet.

"Arthur has arranged a small mission, which my team and Tristan's will take with a few other men. Hopefully we will manage to retrieve one of our planes. Thor has been informed of the situation and awaits our arrival in Asgard. We know the cursed armies are nearby, but so are our allies. Most have already begun to arrive. A few men will stay behind to salvage what's left of the castle. Perhaps we can return for them, but this is always something we've had teams prepared for."

"How long will it take to retrieve the plane?"

"We are leaving at daybreak," he said. "At least if Lancelot and Ares are around, we can avoid their attacks since the sun still penetrates the skies here."

Jane let out another breath, clutching her hair in her hands when they began to shake. "Am I wrong for not being able to be nice to her?"

They chuckled at her, and Tristan said, "Not at all. David is not used to being in a relationship, though. He always tries to do what's best, and that is sometimes not seen as the most sensitive approach. He considers all outcomes and sometimes fails to see he should put aside what is right for what is needed. He loves you, so don't doubt that, but I suppose you should try to step away from the situation emotionally when you think about how he's acting. Of course, no one blames you for having the feelings you do— we are still upset with her actions toward you—but David is different. He's thinking about everyone, which includes your children and your cousin. He, like us, knows they will come first for you—so I think this is his backward way of putting you first. Although, he seems more unhinged. None of us expected him to speak down to you or ask you to act as if you had no problem with her, especially with your cousin involved now."

"Mhm," Gareth hummed. "Maybe just give him time. We were horrified to see smoke rising over the trees and to smell so much blood. He was completely panicked as we searched the bodies. He kept muttering about how he shouldn't have left you. He thought you were gone again."

"I didn't know that. Thank you."

"No problem," he replied.

"So," Galahad said. "Aridane told me you ripped apart a hellhound with your bare hands."

Jane chuckled. She didn't talk to him often and was happy he seemed to accept her. "Your wife was far more impressive than me—all of your wives were. It's no wonder Arthur left them behind. He was leaving his best warriors."

Galahad grinned. "While we agree our wives are more skilled than our greatest guards, mine and the others were in awe of what they witnessed from you. They have not spoken of another fighter so admirably since watching David slay a thousand vampires."

A bit of pride swirled within her chest as she realized the wives were impressed with her, but she wasn't sure what to make of her fight yet. She had no powers and still got hurt, but she felt different.

When she realized they were waiting for her to say something, she held out her hands. "Watch this." She summoned her blade and gun.

Gareth let out a whistle. "From Death, I assume?"

Jane handed him her sword. "I met Viduus, one of his reapers. He told me it was from him. There was a Kali as well. She didn't like me. I think she was Than's ex or something—she had four arms."

"Viduus and Kali." Tristan smirked. "His reapers are the 'gods of death' from myths even we were unsure of."

"Really?" She grinned.

Lamorak answered, "Viduus is a god in Roman mythology—the divider —he separates souls from the body after death. So, it's quite fitting he is one of Death's reapers. Kali is the name of the Hindu goddess of death. It's interesting. We have all wondered how he worked. It seems the gods of death are indeed what legends and religions say—but Death is the embodiment of death, which makes him different—more, you could say. They must harvest some souls for him."

Jane felt dumb for not putting that together. "That's really cool," she said, handing her gun to Gawain as they nodded, agreeing. "They said the gun is called Death's Angel, and the sword is Heaven's Reaper. They're bonded to me, and as far as I know, only their guns work against the demons and hounds. Otherwise, you have to be able to use your sword."

"So unfair," Gareth said, handing the sword to Gaheris. "Unlimited ammo, huh?"

Jane beamed at him, getting a laugh from them. "It's better than a video game."

"I need an angel to give me cool toys." Gareth winked at her. "Although I am not as charming as Jane. I do not think I would be so lucky."

"They'd give you a toy gun." Gawain laughed. "You would not know what to do with so much power."

Bors leaned over the table, catching her eye as the brothers started arguing. "Claire said you looked amazing, Jane. We are very proud of you."

"She always fights amazingly," Geraint piped in.

"True, but the women seemed to think there was something different about her," Lamorak said. "What do you suppose they meant, Jane?"

She shrugged. "I don't know, really. I didn't have any powers." She didn't want to tell them about her new connection with Death during her fight or how she seemed to know she would kill with the attacks she delivered.

"Come now, Jane." Gawain gave her a serious look. "You can tell us."

"It was nothing. They've just never seen me fight before. Maybe they thought my style was different."

"Your style is David's," Gareth said quickly. "They know his style."

Jane bit her lip, feeling uncomfortable under their anxious gazes. They weren't judging her, but she feared having them turn on her.

She glanced around, banishing her weapons from their hands as the urge to flee consumed her. The irritating giggles from Artemis reached her ears again, increasing that urge. "Um . . ." She fought the sounds of David's deep voice talking to Arthur and the others. She knew he was busy gathering information on the upcoming missions, but she was suddenly surprised by the thoughts of wanting nothing to do with him. "Um."

"Holy fuck," Gareth shouted.

"My queen is not required to answer what causes her discomfort."

Jane snapped her head around to see Thanatos glaring at the others.

"Than." She quickly stood up and launched into his arms, hearing several chairs scrape back, but she smiled at him. "You're okay."

He stepped out of her hug and bowed. "I am unharmed, my queen."

"Where is Death?" she quickly asked. "Is he fine? War?"

"Both fine. I am sure Death will come to you soon." Thanatos' gaze slid over each knight. "They had some matters to see to; he requested I stay with you in the meantime."

"What kind of matters?" She frowned at him and glared over at David, who stood with an angry look.

Thanatos shifted his stance, taking in those standing, preparing to flee or fight. "Nothing that he would wish those listening to know."

She grabbed his hand. "Can I?"

His gaze softened as it settled on her. "Of course, my queen."

"Good." She tugged him. "Let's go to my room, and you can tell me."

Gawain quickly grabbed her shoulder. "Jane, perhaps that is not a good idea."

She noticed the others all standing now. "He won't hurt me. I want to know where Death is and what he's doing. I'll be back."

"You're not going anywhere," David said, standing behind Thanatos.

Jane spun around, locking eyes with him as Thanatos shifted into a defensive stance in front of her. She moved between them, growling. "Back off, David. I'll be back in a minute. Go sit at your table and keep pretending my feelings don't matter to you."

"Jane, what's wrong?" Adam was also approached.

She tried to lose her viciousness and answered him. "Nothing, as David would say. I just need to speak to my general. I'll be back in a bit."

David growled as he balled his shaking fists. "I apologize for hurting your feelings—you know I only meant to protect you and the children. Please stay here. I don't trust him."

Jane fought the immediate desire to accept his apology but reminded herself she wanted to know what Death was doing. She trusted Thanatos. She didn't care what anyone said about him or her other dark angels. She was dark, too. If no one here could accept them, she had no reason to expect anyone to accept her. "I trust him and want to hear what he needs to tell me. Why don't you go back to being besties with the person who wants me dead?"

David bared his fangs. "You know I am not 'besties' with her. Now be angry with me all you like, but also think things through. You have little reason to trust him, and you know damn well you would be upset with yourself for starting anything in front of your children and cousin."

Jane shifted her gaze around the room, the urge to slaughter everyone rising to dangerous heights. She returned her focus to David, and all she could see was how easily he smiled and laughed with Artemis. Yet when it was her, he stared her down like she was a monster that needed to be stopped. "I trust him to have my back," she said, staring into his blue eyes. "And that's more than I can say for you right now."

David growled, reaching for her, but Thanatos blocked him. "I suggest you give her space. I do not know what has caused her to be upset with you, but I will not let anyone stand in the way of her wishes. And her wish is for you to leave her be."

"Don't talk to me, Fallen," David snapped. "I don't trust you. I've already had your piece of shit master try to steal her from me again."

"I'm telling you," Jane said to David, "I don't care what you say. I am going to go with him—don't follow us. We all know how much it means to you to not cause a scene." Fire burned within her heart. "So I suggest you let me go, or I will make one for you."

David's eyes widened, and Arthur pulled him back.

"Call if you need us, Jane." Arthur gestured for the others to stand down. "She is safe with him."

Thanatos folded her arm in his and walked away without looking back. "Your king would be proud of you. But Death would be more satisfied with that emerald fire glowing in your eyes right now."

Jane reached up to her face. "What do you mean?"

He shrugged. "Nothing, my queen. It is simply the energy he granted you during the battle."

She blew out a breath. "Yeah, right."

Thanatos' lip twitched. "In time, my queen. The answers will be revealed in time."

She sighed. "You know more than you let on, don't you, Than?"

His ruby eyes lit up. "More than I wish to, my queen."

Jane leaned her head against his arm, aware David watched her. "Thank you for being with me. I do trust you, by the way."

He patted her hand. "Always so forgiving, my queen."

Tears stung her eyes, but she smiled up at him. "I do forgive you for letting it happen. I trust you."

His gaze was unreadable as they exited the mess hall. "Thank you, my queen."

11

NOT ABOUT YOU

"Are you sure you are all right?" Thanatos asked, eyeing her while she chewed her lip.

"Yeah." She nodded. "I mean, no."

He shrugged. "It is meant to happen, my queen. Pestilence unleashed the plague. The Horsemen will come—all of them. That means the end for all."

"But War didn't seem bad at all." She paced around the small room. "He helped us."

"He fought a battle, my queen. That is what he does."

She dropped down on the bed. "Well, if he fights on our side, we'll win. I suppose that's what matters."

Thanatos eyed her quietly. "Perhaps."

Jane lifted her eyes to him. "You think we will fail?"

"It matters little what I think," he said, sniffing. "Your vampire's scent is strong. Do you realize he has been attempting to breed with you?"

Jane's eyes widened. "He said I'm not at risk of getting pregnant."

Thanatos' gaze fell to her stomach. "He is correct. Still, it is strange he would behave so recklessly." He tilted his head. "No, I suppose it makes perfect sense. Your relationship with him is unstable, and he is grasping what he can to solidify your bond. A child would do the trick. He likely fears Lucifer or Lancelot could have impregnated you. His instincts demand he ensures that does not happen."

She swallowed. "Oh. I guess I didn't think of that. God, I'm so horrible. I don't even know how he can have sex with me after everything that happened. Now I'm almost damning him to Hell."

Thanatos shrugged. "He makes his own decisions. Try to remember, though, while he is an honorable knight, he is still one of the deadliest monsters on Earth and a male with powerful urges he has suppressed for quite some time. Finally succeeding in bedding his beloved has undoubtedly changed him. He needs to gain control of himself, or you will have more disagreements because of your other relationships. Or worse—he could hurt you, or you could damn each other." He grinned. "At least you have a bit of pull with the King of Hell."

"Than." She shook her head. She couldn't bear the thought of David being damned. "David has great control, unlike me."

"Then I am certain he will figure out what is best. If not, and he threatens you, I will fight him until he is no longer a threat to you."

Jane chuckled. "There will be no need for that. Thank you, though. And, I have to say, I never expected you to be such a willing relationship counselor."

"I'm not. I am simply an ancient being who has seen more than your mind can comprehend. I have witnessed kings and queens destroy one another, and I have torn apart many." He smirked at her gasp. "I am a Fallen, after all."

"It's easy to forget sometimes."

A faint smile teased his lips. "I will take that as a compliment from you. Did your vampire forgive your intimacy with Lucifer? I assume so since you have resumed your couplings. Unless he forced you." His red eyes glowed.

A lump rose in her throat. "He didn't force me. We were working on rebuilding things. I thought he was going to leave me. I'm sure I blew it yet again."

"He should not have disregarded your unease with the other female's presence," he said, focusing on a corner of the room. "I made similar mistakes in my past. The woman you love should always come first. Duty and the comfort of others are always second. Even if what a man is attempting to achieve with his insensitive actions is for her well-being, he must be mindful of what it does to her.

"There is always a better way to approach a difficult situation. And while it should not always require delicate methods from the male, it does not take much effort to show your woman more tenderness to ease her distress. A woman should be shown she matters and is her beloved's priority. Once she feels betrayed or neglected, it can often be too late for him to make amends."

Jane smiled sadly. "She was very pretty, Than."

He shot her an annoyed glare. "Focus on your own relationships, my queen. You have enough male egos to occupy yourself with. Do not add my irreparable romantic past to your list of concerns."

"Fine." She sighed. "I'm just trying to distract myself. I mean, he knows I hate Artemis. She even tried to have me killed. She couldn't have David, so it feels like she's gone after my cousin. I just got him back, and she's stealing him. And now she's taking David anyway."

"Your knight has no interest in the female vampire. She is repulsive to many males, actually. Her infatuation with the prince has reached far beyond the inner circle of the knights."

"Great."

"I did say he has no interest." He smiled. "Your cousin, however, sees a beautiful immortal woman showering him with attention. You will come second to him. Or not at all."

"You really are blunt."

His lip twitched with a smile. "Forgive me. I have little experience reassuring a queen on matters of the heart. Trust me, though, the prince has no intention of straying from you. While he seems to have strong urges to breed—which is not a good thing for either of you—I am confident he only has the desire to do so with you. Another female will become a nuisance to him rather quickly."

"Well, he wasn't acting like she was a nuisance." She rubbed her chest —it felt colder. "It's just that he didn't care about how I felt, you know? I admit, I shouldn't be violent or rude in front of anyone—or at all—but it's her. And he was so mean about it. And then I feel worse for thinking the way I was and still am. He knows I'm a freaking mess already—that's not an excuse, either. But I thought he would get by now that I hurt from stuff like this.

"I try to breathe and understand that he means well, and he's right, but then I'm thinking things I shouldn't. Like, right now, I wish Death were here. He would help me and take my side without worrying what anyone thought."

"Death does not care for others, my queen. Not even your children."

Her throat tightened. "I know. It's not that I want David to not care. I love that he is good, but dammit, just not with her. He didn't have to smile or act like she never tried to have me killed. He could've even made an excuse for us to sit somewhere else. Somewhere where everyone wasn't acting like we were not in a freaking underground bunker after getting attacked and losing everything. It's how I always felt around Jason and my family. Just a bunch of blind cows not caring that the slaughterhouse is beyond the barn."

He chuckled. "I believe they are merely showing strength. In times of sorrow and war, followers look to the royal family for guidance and reassurance. Your vampire is a member of the royal family. He is likely used to this behavior, but he could have explained it to you since you are together and, of course, been kinder since you needed his softness. But I think that was their motive if they behaved as you said. Royals can come off as cruel or great. Your prince has often been described as both."

She scoffed, ignoring the part about David. "Well, Artemis isn't a member of their royal family." Several ways to kill the goddess popped into her head. The favored: feeding her to Lancelot's wolves, just like she would have been to Lycaon's.

"My queen?"

Jane sighed, squeezing her eyes shut. "I'm not good, Than. He's right. I am 'this person' he was trying to keep everyone from seeing. The one who wants—" She growled. "I can't even say. I'm barely keeping them from surfacing completely in my mind, but I know what they are." More thoughts of seeing everyone who'd ever hurt her getting eaten by wolves flickered in her mind.

"Death will return to you soon," Thanatos said. "Try to relax. You are away from them and no longer have to put on a show for the sake of others. Do you know how long you will remain at this location?"

Jane fell back on the bed and covered her eyes. She didn't want him to see more into her. "Whenever they secure a plane. I guess we will leave soon afterward. Why?"

"You should not stay in such simple housing."

She chuckled, uncovering her eyes, relieved the ache in her heart lessened. It was bizarre to feel so comfortable with him. "Than, I stayed in a cave with Luc." She watched his face flicker with rage. "Why are you angry with him?" She had picked up that there was some hostility between the two of them. "You knew what he was doing all along, right?"

"I think that is for your king to disclose to you." His attention darted to the door. "Your vampire waits outside, as does your cousin."

Jane sat up quickly.

"Shall I send them away? I have no problem ordering them away from you."

"No, can you just hide your wings? Adam is still getting used to things." Thanatos quickly folded them behind him until she could no longer see them. She nodded, thankful, and pointed toward the bed her children had slept on. "Sit there. I can't have either of them near me right now. I will sit next to you."

Thanatos sat where she instructed him. "If he threatens you, I'll have no option but to fight him."

Jane came to a stop in the middle of the room. "Than, please just stay calm. If you are, I will be. If anything, it's me you will have to stop. I'm the unstable one."

His eyes glowed. "As you wish."

Her heart pounded painfully fast, but she went to the door, yanking it open to reveal one pissed-off vampire boyfriend and one confused human cousin.

She huffed, turned around without saying anything, and walked to Thanatos. It was too difficult to speak without screaming at David or blurting out her hate for Artemis to Adam.

The door shut softly, and Jane darted her eyes up to Thanatos' red pair before looking at the ground when David's body came into her peripheral vision. He stopped in the center of the small room before walking over to the other bed and sitting. Adam followed behind him and sat as well.

"I take it you are done with your private conversation?" David's tone was even, but there was no mistaking his hatred for Thanatos.

"The matters my queen wished to discuss have been satisfied," Thanatos said. "I advise you to watch your tone with her. She is upset, and I cannot restrain myself from engaging you in a fight should you cause her further discomfort."

"Try me, Fallen," David said.

"David, stop," Jane said, finally lifting her head. "He is only telling you what he has to. How the hell can you act like this to someone who is standing by me but not to someone who is hurting me?"

"She wasn't hurting you." His eyes darkened as deeply as his tone. "She was having breakfast. And if you recall correctly, she has your handprints burned into her flesh. I'd say you're even with her."

Jane's eyes widened before darting to Adam and Thanatos. She didn't know what to say.

"Jane . . ." Adam said slowly. "What's going on?"

137

Two emotions rushed through Jane. The first was hurt. She couldn't believe David would say such a thing. Was he going back to treating her like everything was her fault now he knew her demon was a part of her soul all along? Part of her wanted to cry. She wanted to run away from him —never see him again. She wanted to be away from her children because she was a monster, too dangerous and wicked to be around anyone. She wanted to be utterly alone.

That would never happen, though.

So, the second emotion—rage—won out. Fire sparked under her skin as she focused entirely on David, even though she was answering Adam. "I would tell you, but I don't think David would like that." All she could see was Artemis smiling at these two men and David forever taking Artemis' side because he blamed Jane for hurting her. He didn't care Artemis had never done a good thing for her. All he saw was that she was evil—not Artemis.

"You know I only wanted you to stay calm in front of your children," David said as his eyes shifted to a pale blue. "That is all I was trying to do. I know you don't want anyone to see you like *this*."

"Like what?" She hated he was making her feel like a crazy person. It was the same thing Jason did time after time. And it only pissed her off more that she really was a crazy girl. He was right about her, and she couldn't stand it.

David sighed as his features softened. "You know what I am talking about. This isn't you. You are letting your anger cloud your judgment."

"And you are an idiot," she shouted, unable to stop herself. "Even the boys knew you were being a jerk." David clenched his jaw and looked away from her heated gaze, but she couldn't keep her mouth shut. "But you had to be proper, didn't you? For her."

David snapped his eyes back to her. "It was never for her."

Thanatos shifted at her side, but she touched his shoulder.

It only seemed to anger David more; his voice felt like a blade across her skin. "When will you see I do everything for you? Honestly, Jane, are you going to sit here and tell me that if I let you march up and punch her in the face or scream at her in front of everyone, you would be happy with yourself? I know good and well that if Death had been with you, he'd need only touch you for everything to be fine. Well, I am sorry I don't have his magic touch."

She teared up as complete sorrow and self-hate drowned her.

David spoke again. "You just need to ask yourself: would Nathan and

Natalie look at you with fear, or would they be happy to see their mother attack another woman for no reason?"

"I have every reason to do it," she screamed. "She's trying to take you both from me. You know what she did, and you still sat there smiling at her. You pretended nothing was wrong. You laughed and carried on a conversation as if I wasn't crying." Tears made it impossible to make out his face. "You may be right, but you didn't think about how much it would hurt me. How else did you really expect me to react? You smiled at her and looked at me like—"

She whined, hating how pathetic she sounded. "Anyone but her . . . And now I realize you were only with me last night because of your stupid urges to show you're the one with me. It wasn't that you wanted to be with me. Your brothers told you to dominate me, and you did. You did it because you hate me for needing them, and you wanted to throw in my face how it feels for you." She whimpered, turning her head away from them all. "Well, I get it. I get that I'm . . . You know what? I can't even say what I am except I am *that person* you hate. I'm the woman who embarrasses you, and you would rather not have. I'm the girl you got stuck with. So I'm sorry too. I'm sorry I'm not her."

It was silent for nearly thirty seconds before David spoke, "Baby."

"Don't baby me," she whimpered.

Thanatos' hand on her back startled her, but she tried to relax from his efforts to comfort her.

"You know that is not true," David said. "I did want to be with you last night—don't even think that. My urges are heightened, but I did want to be with you. I always do.

"And no one will ever take me from you, my love. I am sorry I didn't consider you would form that thought. I assumed you would know by now that I am yours—only yours—for all time. I was only trying to protect you from saying or doing something you would regret. I would never pick her over you."

"But you did. You always do."

His jaw clenched. "I was thinking about you and your children. Do they want to see either of us angry? No. I was trying to help you give them what you want them to have. I'm sorry, baby, but you cannot behave like a wild animal around your children because you get jealous." He growled. "I am trying to be kind, but you are making it difficult. It doesn't help that you keep running to angels and demons whenever something doesn't go your way."

Jane wanted to burn him alive. And that horrible desire crushed her more than his words.

The sudden memory of David's decision to lie to her about Melody came forward, and she realized that was another time he had tried to stop her from turning into something evil by standing in the way of what her ugly heart wanted.

I'm still bad. Jane's heart bled. She could see herself standing beside Lucifer, and even then, she wished for Death.

She squeezed her eyes shut to try to stop herself from sobbing.

"Jane?" Adam whispered while she trembled under Thanatos' strong hand.

She was still a terrible person. The darker half of her soul was gone, but she was still a flawed, hate-filled being who could be just as cruel as the evilest creations of Hell.

Adam continued, "I don't know what you both are talking about, but I'm sorry if I did anything to hurt you, and I can see David is too. Please tell me what to do to make this better for you."

His pleading only made her feel worse about herself. She clutched her chest, waving her hand in a gesture for them to leave her. The shame was too great to suffer in front of them. There was no way she could tell them anything now. David was right, and it broke her.

"I believe she wishes for both of you to leave," Thanatos said.

"Jane," David said in a pleading tone.

"Just leave me alone," she whimpered. "I can't be around you. Just go. Go wherever you want—just as long as it's away from me." She was terrified. It was her all along who wanted to hurt him, and even having Adam back—she couldn't help but want to scream at him for letting his brother destroy all her chances of being a normal person. "Both of you leave me in fucking peace."

There was silence for a moment before she finally heard someone stand and march out of the room. She knew it was David, which only caused more tears.

Adam's steps were slower, but he left too.

Sobs immediately ripped out of her lips, and she let Thanatos hold her so she didn't cry alone. He didn't speak, and she didn't want him to.

She was still a hateful person. It had always been her choices that resulted in her final acts of evil and wrongdoings. She'd been the one to kill Melody and cheat on Jason. She'd been the one to leave David for Death and then bargain with Lucifer. She'd practically slept with Lucifer and allowed her darker soul to fuck Lancelot. And the fact she could only wish for Death or Lucifer as she accepted the buried thoughts of hating that Adam and David did not protect her proved how accurate her discovery was. She was a bitter, crazy, jealous woman who was hurting the man she loved because she was evil all on her own. Her demon was never needed.

"Is there anything I can get you, my queen?" Thanatos asked after she continued to cry.

"No," she croaked. "You can go. I'm sorry."

"There is no need to apologize. You apologize too often. If you permit, I wish to stay with you."

"Thank you," she whispered and moved to lie down.

Thanatos stood up and removed the shoes from her feet before covering her. "Rest, my queen. You will feel better when you wake." He gently caressed her hair before she felt him move to sit farther away.

And Jane cried herself into a slumber, beating herself up because, demon or no demon, her wrathful heart was capable of its own evil. The same evil that took Melody's life—the same wicked thoughts of preferring Death to David, the inconsiderate way she regarded her children because she desired vengeance and was jealous of another, and the flickering desire to run away from all her problems—to leave everything and everyone she cared about—still made her the most horrible person.

David could barely fight the urge to bleed every human dry as he stomped toward one of the common rooms. And although he was angry and fuming, it was pain that he felt.

"Are you going to fill me in?" Adam asked once they walked through the entrance and headed to where the knights sat together on the far side of the room.

David didn't slow his stride or lose any of his rage as he answered, "She doesn't want you near Artemis. And she's upset that I prevented her from doing what she wanted instead of understanding how much it would hurt her. I was trying to keep her from making a mistake. But it seems that was the wrong thing to do in her eyes. She can forgive them for torturing her, but I keep her from becoming a monster and—fuck."

"What do you mean? Why wouldn't she want me near Artemis? And who tortured her?"

David grunted and nodded to one of the servants that he wanted blood.

"Telling you anything more will only serve to piss me off." He fought to contain his frightening features.

The servant returned with his blood, and David took it without thanking the trembling man before sitting in one of the single chairs. Every one of his brothers watched him, but he forced himself to drink rather than unleashing his boiling fury on them.

Gawain crossed his arms and leaned back. "Did you see her?"

Unable to keep his violent temper in check, David smashed the empty blood-stained glass against the wall across the room, causing screams from anyone nearby. "What the fuck do you want to say to me?" he roared. "Go on, tell me how much of an asshole you think I am."

"You don't need me to tell you, brother," Gawain replied calmly.

"All she had to do was understand she couldn't cause a scene in front of her children. If that was so hard to understand, she only had to tell me how much it hurt her and why. I don't have the advantage of her fucking angels! But I guess that makes me an asshole, and everything becomes my fault."

There were two separate flashes of green and red light behind him.

"Well, this is not really about you. Now, is it?" Death's deadly voice silenced the room and made David snap his furious gaze around to see him, and who he could only assume was War, standing behind the couch several of the knights were sitting on. Death continued, "But you're too much of a self-centered prick to see that, aren't you?"

"Stay the hell away from her," David growled. "You have no idea how much I am restraining myself from beating the shit out of you."

Death shrugged and walked around the sofa. "Go ahead, Vampire Prince. If that's what it will take for you to see this isn't really about you, then by all means, beat the shit out of me." Death stood merely three feet in front of him—waiting. His emerald eyes had a menacing gleam, but his face was blank of emotion.

"It is about me."

"Not exactly," Death said. "But you are the one who broke her heart five minutes ago. It felt like a rusty knife, by the way. Nice and jagged—made a huge mess of things. And here she thought you were the best of us—the one who would never hurt her."

"Fuck you," David spat.

"I enjoy kissing her sweet lips," Death said. David froze, and Death smirked before continuing, "She loves how much my touch comforts her. You don't come close. My kiss—when I lick and suck on her pink lips—we touch Heaven together." He licked his lips. "*Mm* . . . I still taste her. Berries."

David roared Death, grabbing him by his leather jacket and slamming him against the wall behind them. He punched Death in the face once. Then again, before halting with his fist reared back.

"*Two.*" Jane's sweet voice rang through his thoughts. "*You can hit him twice.*"

Slowly, Death turned his head until they were looking each other in the eye.

David fumed at the situation but held back, taking angry breaths to steady himself.

"Is that all you have in you?" Death asked.

Heat bubbled under David's skin, but he shoved Death and stepped back. "No, but I made her a promise."

Death pushed away from the wall. "One you are going to keep?"

David growled, trying to calm himself. "I promised her I would only hit you twice."

Death chuckled and spat blood from his mouth before lifting his threatening gaze and stepping toward him. "There you go again. Always trying to do what is right. I'll help you since you are too stupid to see it yet." He delivered a punch to the side of his face faster than even David could register.

David hit him back, and they took turns delivering hateful blows to each other.

They slammed each other into walls, floors, and furniture while yells for them to stop filled the room. But they didn't. Every bit of loathing David had for Death's relationship with Jane was delivered in each punch he managed to connect. Death's returned blows only fueled his desire to release all the fury he'd bottled.

"I think that's enough," said War before David was ripped away and shoved into the arms of his brothers.

David thrashed, watching a sadistic smile form on Death's face when War placed a restraining hand on his chest.

"Feel better?" Death asked David, wiping the blood from his lip and shaking his hand out. The hulking man in front of Death removed his hand, seeming satisfied that his brother would not attack again, and moved away.

David stopped struggling to break free. "You wanted me to hit you?"

"It was the only way for you to let your hatred for me out. I know it has been building for a while now. I just wanted to make it a good fight." Death grinned over at War when the huge man laughed. "Maybe now you will see your irritation with me and the others who love her that prevents you from seeing all her suffering. I know it is hard to watch her love another—I was there, remember? You knew she loved me, but it was easier for you then—you didn't have to see it."

David shoved the others off and took a few steps away, shaking his busted hand.

Death glanced around the room. "Everyone out. Now."

David had never seen a room empty so quickly. Only War stayed, yet he looked beyond bored as he plopped down on a bench when Death continued talking.

"You need to accept you are not the only one she needs and that there are things she can't tell even you. You may put her first, but this need to be the only one for her will destroy both of you. And it makes you assume that just because she cannot tell you why she is in pain, it has something to do with you. That is your only fault. That is the only time you put yourself above her, and you take it out on her because deep down, you know you should stop what you are doing. You know your hate toward what she has with me makes you say the things you have to her. You know it hurts her—yet you allow yourself to knock her down so she feels what you do.

"You spout promises that you will allow her to have what she does with me, but you constantly remind her how much it hurts you. She knows it does, but she never does it to inflict pain. She fucking needs me like she needs air to breathe.

"She is not an ordinary woman. I am the only one she will never have to tell her shame and inner hatred to, but I will know them as if they were my thoughts. You cannot handle what's inside her head, little prince. She knows it, too.

"While you've believed her in the past and did not judge those thoughts, she was aware she only told you the tip of her torment and what she has gone through. I am surprised she repeatedly shared so much with you, so you should feel honored, I suppose, but she saw what I did: you could barely take it. On top of all this, she also knows you blamed it all on a demon that wasn't really a demon."

David snapped his eyes over to finally see Death's hate-filled expression.

The angel continued, "That is what she is feeling. You've shown her you loathe what she fears to become—what is so easy for her to embrace. And that is why she can't rely on you to soothe her pained heart or spill her terrible thoughts. You judge her each time she slips a little toward darkness. She's placed you on such a high pedestal, but she doesn't blame you, which feeds into the belief that she is bad."

Death jabbed his finger in the direction of their room. "Her tormentors are gone—no unnatural darkness is left inside her—but that does not stop her from thinking she is just as evil as the bitch who tortured her all these years. There is so much you will never understand—so much hidden inside her. She has to sit there and realize a bitter, wrathful heart still beats inside her chest. She has to know it was there all along and that she was responsible for some of the most terrible things inflicted by her hand or words.

"When you looked at her like you did tonight, she wanted to hurt you. And that destroyed her a thousand times more than the cruel way you treated her. She keeps most of her hate down because she is that fucking strong, but she knows what dark, hidden desires lurk within her. They are so dark and cruel that they would break every one of you if spoken aloud. That is why she needs me. No one besides myself and God will ever know what is inside that mind of hers, and that is how it will always remain.

"You were patient with her when she nearly killed or attacked others because you blamed what you thought was a demon. Where has that patience and understanding gone? She's not a fucking fictional character who miraculously gets over every hardship, doubt, and anxiety because she's immortal and prince charming came into her life. She's always going to go through moments of pure happiness and moments of complete rage and sadness. That will never change, no matter how beautiful and great she is. She has no middle ground.

"Your job is to accept her. You told Jason you accepted all of her, but you always saw her as a pure soul with no shred of darkness, that the evilness was completely separate. When you live the life she has, it never completely fades, David. It's at her fingertips, ready to bury her goodness and destroy all she loves.

"Yet, you focus on how she copes with that side of herself and take it out on her because you're not her savior. Luc saved her. I didn't, and you didn't, and it's eating you up. My poor girl is destroying herself because she hates how much it hurts you. She hates that her getting better meant you had to suffer.

"Let go of that hatred. Understand that others need to hold her for different moments. You have no idea how happy she was when you and I got along. She saw the greatest man because you showed her you wanted her to have my love, and she believed it made you happy. She believed her happiness meant more to you than having her all to yourself."

"I do want her happy," David said.

"You wanted her happy until you saw how much I make her feel and how close we truly are. Is it really so bad that I can touch her and soothe the burns left across her heart, soul, and mind? That she knows she doesn't have to utter her dark thoughts but that I'm there anyway? I told you, you can't handle what's inside her mind. You see it sometimes, and you're starting to give her that look she was so used to seeing from Jason. No one blames you for slipping, but you basically told her what he always did: act pretty and perfect for you and everyone else. Fuck her feelings."

"That's not what I was doing." David bared his fangs. "I was stopping her from doing something she'd regret."

Death shook his head, a cruel smile curling at his lips. "You ignored how she was feeling. She knows damn well it's wrong to behave that way, but you treated her like shit and smiled at another woman when all it took was for you to acknowledge you understood her feelings and possibly take her away from the situation altogether."

The fire grew within David's chest, making it hard to speak. "She knows I disagree with Artemis' choices."

"Really?" Death chuckled. "She's a woman, David. Knowing something goes right out the window when she's hurt. All she sees is how you looked at her compared to how you laughed and smiled at someone who hates her. Artemis is a bitch who has been on your nuts for fucking centuries, a bitch you openly considered instead of waiting for Jane—a bitch who Jane thinks deserves you more than she does."

Death clenched his fist and squeezed his glowing eyes shut for a moment before opening them. "I know you were only trying to protect her, but what she saw is your hate for the being that she is and total acceptance of another woman who hates her guts. She saw things—dark things—and it ruined her to know it was no demon that made her think them. To her, it means it was no demon that made her a bad mother, a cruel monster, and an unworthy woman who doesn't deserve the man she has dreamed of having a life with."

David's muscles flexed painfully. "She dreamed of you. She still does—and she has added Lucifer to the list of men she'd rather run to than me."

Death was quiet. "Never have I heard her think of a life with Luc or me. Even before I could read her mind, I was attuned to her emotions—and her hope for a future didn't rise with me the way it did with you. Her time with

Luc was torture, David. He willed her to perform sexual acts on him because he knew her betraying you was one of the worst things she could imagine doing. He used his power to make her kiss him and perform every vile thing he could think of to make her break. He even forced her to enjoy it. Killing an innocent child practically shattered her, and he couldn't do it on his own. Do you know what that did and still does to her?"

David couldn't respond.

"But he craved for her to truly kiss him. So he granted her the ability to imagine you. He sometimes pushed your face and voice into her head. He mimicked your touch to glimpse what she felt for you. And when he stopped, she fell to her knees in agony."

"She developed feelings for him, though," David said through gritted teeth.

Death shrugged. "As damaged as it is, she still has one of the biggest hearts I have ever witnessed. She searched for good in Luc, and she found it. She saw when he slipped up and cared for her. He gave her a chance to fight her past demons instead of babying her like you and I do."

"But she forgave him without a second thought."

"So?" Death's brows drew together in confusion before his expression emptied. "Would you rather she hate him and torture herself for the rest of her life? Would you prefer to see how much wrath she could unleash? You're telling her not to do that to a woman who tried to have her slaughtered."

When he put it like that, it was hard for David to see a problem with her forgiving anyone and easy to see what a hypocrite he was.

"When Luc summoned me, she was barely conscious, but she looked at him and saw her second-greatest tormentor. But she saw his love for her, too. And it was greater than she could have ever imagined. She saw the pain he was in. She saw it was killing him to let her go and the hate he had for breaking her the way he had. Do you know why his hair is gray now?"

David hadn't thought about it, but he recalled Lucifer had pale blond hair when he'd taken Jane.

"Her soul burns him," Death said. "He trapped that half of Jane's soul in his prison right with his soul, and that bitch has set him on fire. Her flames rival that of God's. Jane always felt that fire. She kept it suppressed for so long, and she realized Luc had taken that torture as his own to free her.

"Imagine her gratitude for someone willingly putting themselves through such agony. The gray hair is the color of ash for a reason. It's from the constant fire burning him inside. Yet, he smiled at her and confessed his love before letting her go. He promised to protect you and her children when even I will not. Because when it comes down to it, even if I protect you or her children during a battle, I will leave you all for her when she is in danger. Without her, I am nothing. But she sees that Lucifer will hold his bargain with her. He would ensure her children are safe and let her go to whatever fate befalls her.

"But you and the others show her nothing but hate for the other man she came to love. You are showing her that when she's not acting like the silly girl we adore, she is pure evil in your eyes. An evil that is not fit to be around anyone—and meaningless enough that her feelings are nothing compared to others. She starts to believe she belongs with Luc. In Hell.

"You helped her believe she could be good. Now she thinks you only excused darkness from her because you blamed that half of her soul. So her fear of not being good enough—of being too evil for you—is coming true. And that means she's a bad person—a bad mother—and a bad Other."

"She's not evil, though," David whispered. "She's not a bad mother or a terrible person. She's the woman I love."

Death's cold expression returned. "I know that. But she will probably never honestly believe it. That is her burden. All I can do is stand by her and soothe the pain when it attacks her. She has never been normal. She will always fear not being enough and be terrified of losing you.

"She knows she will lose everyone eventually—I remind her of that every time she sees me. She knows it's only a matter of time before everyone leaves her, and I'm the one who will take them. How conflicted do you think she feels because of that? She's in a constant state of feeling she must choose between me and everyone else. And it's me she truly cannot live without. I realize that isn't very clear, but it is true. Even free of the dark, she will never be better. She will never escape.

"So when she says she's ready to let you go, she means it. It isn't that you are not enough. You just have to let me hold her hand as she walks through her battles or, if she permits, let you shine a light for her to fight her way to. Luc and I can hold her hand. We can give her strength that you cannot. But you are where she is going. Always. That is a gift, David—one I envy more than you will ever know." Death looked around briefly before returning his heated gaze to him. "Do you understand all of this?"

"I think so," he said, rubbing his chest. The pull Jane emitted was weak. It was weaker every time she was away from him, especially Death.

"Then go in there, suck up your pride, and tell her you're sorry. It wasn't

148

what you said—it was how you said it. Tell her you love her no matter what. She will always need to hear that from you. She will always return to thinking you do not when she watches you disregard her feelings. She can't help it." Death jabbed a finger at him. "You need to show her she can have me and that it doesn't hurt you to share her. She will always be yours, but the way she has me cannot be broken or replaced by you. The way Luc strengthens her against her enemies and gives her peace from her past is not yours or mine to give either—only her pain can give her that. He is her pain. Let him help."

David locked eyes with Death. "Thank you."

"It's never for you." Death grinned as David passed. "Go hold her now, or she will refuse my love, beat herself up for hurting you, and continue torturing herself into believing she is an evil monster who deserves to rot alone."

David sighed and nodded.

"Good. I will be there soon."

He nodded at Death's dismissal, feeling like a bastard for his behavior. He didn't want her to become something evil, but he needed to accept there were dark parts in her even without a demon. He had to remember he was the man chosen for her because God believed he could help her through that. David wasn't supposed to be a man who made her feel worse for everything she internally fought against or one who made her hate herself. He needed to remember that while he would probably always want to be everything to her, he got the best parts of her. She constantly tried to be the best she could be for him and her kids—for everyone but herself. And her angels eased her torment so she could love any of them.

David glanced up at the ceiling as he walked through the halls. Everyone moved out of his way because he'd forgotten himself earlier. He was the one who had become a jealous monster. And he'd done it to the person he loved more than his own life. "I'll make it right," he said, still staring upward. "Forgive me for forgetting my duty to her."

"It is about time you remembered your role." Thanatos stood in the doorway, arms crossed.

David didn't trust him, but he was thankful Jane had someone while he was being an ass. "Will you tell her I wish to see her?"

Thanatos pushed the door open, revealing a bundle covered up on one of the beds. "She cried herself to sleep."

David sighed, rubbing his face. "I've come to apologize."

The fallen was quiet before he finally nodded. "Do it properly this time.

She is fragile after everything that has unfolded. Do not forget that—although it was evil—half of her soul was removed."

He frowned, not having thought about Jane's soul during all this or how that must be affecting her. "Does it hurt her? I thought the darker half hurt more."

An annoyed look flitted over Thanatos' face. "Imagine always being on fire. And then imagine the sensation of that fire being extinguished. What's left behind?" Thanatos moved so David could pass him. "Just because her hair color did not change as Lucifer's did does not mean she was not permanently scarred." Thanatos walked through the door. "She was burned while breathing . . . and then torn in half. If you think hard enough, I'm sure you can discover what it will take for her to rebuild herself." He then jabbed David in the chest. "And for fuck's sake—do not impregnate her to prove a point to the other dicks in her life. They already know you're the one who gets to make love to her."

With those last words, Thanatos shut the door, leaving David alone as he realized how much these angels helped him and Jane.

12

OUR LIGHT

Muffled whispers abruptly cut off as Jane whimpered. She listened, though she didn't care who spoke. She wanted to stay in the dark shadows of her semi-conscious state. That was where she belonged.

A warm tear rolled over the bridge of her nose, but the fiery caress that followed it nearly had her bolting from the room.

But she stayed still when the bed shifted, and David's heat warmed her back. All she wanted was to have him hug her, tell her he still saw the girl he'd fallen in love with, and it was okay—that everything would be okay—even though she knew the end was only drawing closer. She didn't want to fight him anymore. She didn't want to hurt him anymore. She just wanted her David.

Lips pressed against her temple, and she sobbed, her body shaking as she cried. But he was there. He kissed her again before slowly rolling her onto her back. His smile was sad, but it was still the smile that made her heart beat faster—and he was giving it to her.

He cupped her cheek, wiping her tears before kissing her forehead, then hugged her, burying his face against her neck. Jane kept crying, covering her mouth as she stared at the ceiling. Her blubbering sounded ridiculous, and she didn't know what would happen to them. She didn't know if he was saying goodbye or if they needed a break. She didn't know anything anymore.

David didn't lift his head, but he pulled one of her hands to hold close to his face. He moved just enough to kiss her fingers, and she finally put her other hand over his head.

"I'm sorry," he murmured, brushing his lips across her knuckles.

Jane cried harder, hugging him but unable to speak.

He did, though. "I understand now. I should have never treated you like that or said things the way I did. I let my emotions get the best of me and broke my promises to you."

"No," she croaked. "It's my fault. I know you were doing what was right. You were trying to protect me, and you just finally let out everything I was doing to you. It's me. It's not your fault."

He lifted his head and smiled as he cupped her cheek. "No, my love. Even if what I said was true or right, I should have gone about it differently. I should have put your feelings above my own. I should have been my best instead of saying things I knew would hurt you."

She sighed, trying to soak up his heat. "You were trying to protect me from myself. You were trying to protect my babies from me, and that's something I've always asked you to do."

He caressed her cheek with his thumb. "Baby, I knew I would hurt you, and I did it anyway. I have been so consumed with everything that happened with Lucifer and Death—with you leaving and coming back—with your need for Death over me and your instant forgiveness to those who hurt you. I stopped thinking about what you were going through and what you needed. I stopped putting you first because I was angry I was not the only man you needed."

Jane bit her trembling lip.

"Easy." He rubbed his thumb over her lips.

"I'm sorry," she whispered.

He lifted his gaze from her mouth to her eyes. "I know. You don't have to say why—I know, and it's okay. It will be—or, at least, I will try to make sure I do not let it get to me as it did this time."

Her face hurt as she tried to keep from crying more. "You don't deserve to go through this."

"And you don't deserve a fraction of what you have gone through. You deserve what Death gives you—what all of them give you. It has not been my place to do what they can for you. My place is here." He put his hand over her heart. "My place is to ensure you are always shown the love they cannot bring you. My place is to keep your beautiful heart together. Keep it warm when he leaves."

She refused to blink away her tears and kept staring at those blue eyes. That smile. It was there again. She was home.

"I know he brings you to life. I'm jealous, but I will find peace with it again. Because watching you light up is the best sight of my entire existence. That is what he does."

Jane reached up and covered his cheek with her shaking hand. "You really are the bestest."

He chuckled, kissing her palm. "No, my love. But I will try every day from here on out to be my best for you. I will try to be as good as you trust and need me to be. Even when it gets dark, I will never give up on you or us. I will always want you home with me. You can always trust in that. Just look for me, and you will see where to go. I will always call for you and be thankful when your angel helps you find your way back to me.

"Because you are our light, Jane. You may shine brightest with Death, and you may not hurt anymore when you burn for all of us because of Lucifer, but you are the light we need. Each of us surrounds you, but we are nothing without you. We each have our duty to you, but above all, we are meant to light up for you when you weaken—when darkness becomes too great."

"What if I am meant for darkness? Or if I am darkness?"

He shook his head. "You would not glow as you do if you were. You brighten so many lives with just your smile and laugh. Those lucky enough to have earned a place in your heart are awed each time you look their way. So, no, you are not meant to be lost in the dark or even come close to being a dark spot in this universe. Even when you do get lost in darkness, which I know is your pain and past, you are meant to conquer it.

"You may not be able to now, but I have faith in you. Only one who has experienced the darkest of nights can turn night into day."

She smiled sadly. "I'm not that strong, David. I'm nowhere close to being that good either."

"Maybe you have not reached that level, but that is okay. You grow stronger every time I look at you and every time you stand back up after you have been knocked to the ground. It scares me to imagine what you may still have to face to gain that brightest of lights, but I will be with you. When you fade, I will do my best to burn brighter for you. I know you will come roaring out of the dark when you are ready. If a pair of angels or a whole army of them have to share their light with you, I swear, from now on, I will be amazed and proud. My girl, my baby, my kitten—she will roar, giving me the best gift I could ask for: my playful, brave goddess dancing in the dark."

Her lips trembled, and she couldn't speak, so she showed him with her eyes: *I love you.*

That beautiful smile spread over his face. "I love you, too."

She laughed sadly and pulled him down. "Please kiss me."

He didn't make her wait. Those perfect lips pressed against hers, and they both closed their eyes, holding each other tightly as he sent those beautiful flames back to her chilled heart.

Jane gasped, covering her chest as she stared downward.

"What's wrong?"

She breathed slowly, smiling as that lovely heat seeped into the wounds they'd made together. "Nothing."

He watched her briefly before lowering his face to kiss her chest. "Did you stop feeling me?"

"Yes," she said, her voice cracking.

He sighed, kissing her chest again and then her lips. "I won't leave again. I swear I am always in love with you. I always see us beyond forever. I'm always your David—even if I act like an ass for a short time." He grinned. "I will gladly take punishment from your angels if that happens, but I will do my best to be good for you. Just be patient with me, too. I am not the perfect man you expect me to be."

"I don't want them hurting you," she said. "I promise to make a better effort to believe in you and accept you will never hurt me."

His smile fell. "I lost my temper today, Jane. I have not felt so out of control since my youth and first turning. It was only because of you that I paused at all."

"What are you saying?"

He sat up straighter. "We are deadly creatures, my love. We run on instincts quite often, and with the war building, tensions will rise, and numerous challenges will present themselves. There is always a chance I could lose myself again."

Jane touched his lips. "You won't."

"Baby, I wanted to see you pregnant with my child." He swallowed hard. "Not for the right reasons, either. I was upset that you could not conceive at the present time."

Jane's heart pounded. "But we can't have a baby."

He gave her a tender kiss. "I know. That is what I am saying, though. I became so lost I almost damned us."

Her eyes ached, and her nose burned. "You can't get damned. Not you."

"Always thinking about me instead of yourself." He kissed her again. "If I ever become so reckless again, you scream for Death. You scream for Lucifer or Thanatos. Scream for anyone."

She shook her head. "You won't do that."

He caressed her hair. "Jane, just as you fear becoming something monstrous, so do I."

"You're not like me, though. You're not evil."

His expression cracked, and he looked broken for a tiny moment. "Neither of us is evil. Still, we are both capable of evil—just like everyone else. For us, though, the strongest immortals in this world, we could destroy it. So, you see, we are nearly the same. You just have a different war than I do.

"We have to hold on to and believe in each other. I will do everything I can to remind you how great and good you are. And as long as I have you to look forward to, I will stay on my path. I swear it, Jane. You are why I never fell into darkness. I always saw you in my mind—even then. You kept me good even before I saw you in Texas. But never forget I am just as capable of doing unspeakable things as the most vile immortals."

"Please don't talk like this," she said, sliding her fingers over his lips. "You may be the deadliest and capable of unleashing terror, but you are the greatest knight. You are my David—the bestest—and you won't hurt me or anyone you care about."

He smiled and kissed her fingertips. "Then remember that when you start to think the same about yourself. Never will you destroy those you love because you are my Jane—my woman"—he smirked—"my baby, my kitten, my goddess. And you are my light. Our light." He pushed her hand away and gave her a firm kiss, surrounding her in his fire. "Beyond forever. That's a long fucking time I expect to be with you, and I can't wait to be by your side through it all."

"Damn." Death's smooth voice broke her into a fit of giggles. "David, do you have a book published somewhere? Because my horny girly panties just flew across the room."

Smiling, David shook his head, kissing her once more before turning to Death. "You could not give me five more minutes?"

Death chuckled, holding up a paper bag and two stainless steel bottles. "You forgot the goody bag you had made for her. I wanted to make sure she got it while it was still fresh."

David sniffed the air, chuckling again before turning to kiss her again. "He lies, my love."

Jane frowned, peeking over at Death as he stood there in all his magnificent glory.

He winked, and she blushed as tingles teased her heart.

David made her look at him again. "I had nothing to do with your goody bag. Thank your arrogant angel. I will check on the children and give you two some time."

"You don't have to go. You can mentally call Arthur to bring them back, can't you?"

He grinned. "I can, but Death deserves this with you. And I think you both need each other after what happened." He kissed her again. "I promise to return quickly. And don't worry—everything will be okay."

Jane slowly lowered her hands, chewing her lip as he stood, playfully punching Death's shoulder. "Show-off. I did get her a drink all by myself."

Death smirked, walking closer to her. "I know. That's what gave me the idea." He chuckled, heavily sitting on the bed beside Jane and kissing her cheek as he put the bag on her lap. "Hi, angel."

She sighed as he withdrew his lips, feeling like she could finally breathe. "You're okay."

He scoffed. "Sweet Jane, you insult me too often." He gestured to the bag. "Open. It really was him being a soft fool that gave me the idea. I only had to threaten a man handing out rations to get everything."

Jane breathed in the delicious smell as her eyes lit up. "You didn't?"

David chuckled as he opened the door, watching them.

"I did." Death pushed her hair out of her face. "Tell me if it's good. I told that fucker if it tasted like shit, I was coming back for him."

Jane beamed, pulling open the bag, gasping at the sight of crispy, golden fries and a hamburger.

"Did he only put mustard and pickles?" Death peeked at her burger as she teared up.

"Yes." Her voice cracked.

"Good. Here." He plopped the two bottles on her lap. "One is a chocolate shake—or as close as they could make to one. The other is a soda. They didn't have Dr. Pepper, but I told that asswipe it better come close to those twenty-three flavors, or my scythe might find a new pair of balls to dangle from it."

She smiled, laughing with a mixture of happiness, sadness, and hope as she hugged him and peeked over his shoulder, meeting a pair of sapphire eyes. "Thank you, Death."

She kept her eyes on David, smiling as she mouthed, *I love you.*

David winked, mouthing back, *I love you too, baby.*

"I don't know why you're trying to hide what you're saying—I can read your mind." Death chuckled, turning his face toward Jane's. He winked and quickly kissed her on the lips.

Jane's eyes widened, and she locked gazes with David.

He smiled. "It's okay. He's just asking for a rematch. Keep tabs for me."

Death flipped him off. "Leave me alone with my girl. I'll keep your tab, Vampire Prince. Just make sure you bring your A-game."

Jane pulled Death's arm down, but she kept her gaze on David, telling him with her eyes: *I love you.*

"I do too. Enjoy your food. I'll be back." He pointed to Death. "Watch it."

"Yeah, yeah." Death waved him off.

"Wait," Jane shouted. "You're both bruised."

David cringed. "He started it." He quickly shut the door as Death muttered curses in a language she didn't know.

"Death," she said, laughing as he managed to wedge himself behind her.

"Shut up. You already forgave us."

She frowned as he took a fry out and held it up for her. She took it, sighing because it was freaking amazing.

"One more kiss," he said, leaning down.

She was about to tell him no, but she saw a slip in his mask. *Fear.*

"Don't worry about it," he whispered, cupping her cheek and pushing tingles into her almost frantically. "Just allow me one more kiss."

Something roared within her, and she covered his hand, nodding to him. "Always one more, Death."

Relief flickered in his eyes, and he swiftly gave her the kiss that was theirs.

"Close your eyes," he murmured, not pulling his mouth from hers as a light began to glow between them. "Do it now."

She followed his order, sighing as he pushed her mouth open. Her lips warmed before that unique sensation he created flowed down into her belly. Jane knew he wasn't just kissing her to fulfill a bit of lust or rack up points to fight David—he was doing something special.

Her heart jolted as if it had never been beating in the first place, and he held her face, kissing her harder. He was shaking.

"Death? What's happening?"

He sucked her lip, shaking less, but he seemed unwilling to let her go. "I will never lose you. If I do, I will never stop searching for you until I have you back."

Finally, she opened her eyes and smiled through the agony she felt from him and what she was feeling within herself. He and David always did their best to be strong for her, and she would return it with her strength.

"You are strong." Death put his hand over her heart, sighing, and the pain went away.

She brought his hand to her lips. "Thank you, Death."

He lifted her hands to his lips and kissed them. "You're welcome, beautiful girl."

"I know he has a nice ass, baby girl, but can you focus on me for a few minutes?" Death pressed his grinning lips against her cheek.

War chuckled as Jane turned away from watching David across the mess hall. He was getting something special made for Nathan and Natalie, who was currently in the bathroom with Ragnelle. Unfortunately, they weren't stomaching the food being served to everyone, so David said he would take Death's lead and issue threats to get the good stuff.

"Hey." Death nudged her with his nose before raising his hand to cover her eyes.

She laughed that time, pulling his hand down so she could stare at his gorgeous face. "You big baby. I'm just watching him. I'm sitting on your lap, so there's no need to pout."

"Damn right, you're on my lap." He squeezed her, giving her a dramatic kiss on the forehead, and she was sure he was keeping his eyes on David the whole time.

Sure enough, she turned her head in time to see David flipping Death off.

David laughed, switching his obscene hand gesture to a wave as Death made several gestures she'd never seen, but the others must have recognized them because they were laughing.

"Death," she said, chuckling. "Behave."

"You don't even know what I'm saying to him. I could be telling him what a wonderful person I think he is."

"I doubt that's what you told him. And I'm pretty sure that thing you just did with your tongue means someone is giving or receiving oral sex."

"It means David likes to lick lollipops." He smirked.

She laughed, covering his mouth. "Stop."

"Once again," Gareth said, laughing, "I wish I had a phone to record this. I swear, Jane, you make the scariest men do the funniest shit."

Death stopped smiling and glared at Gareth. "Do I look like a fucking comedian to you, Knight?"

Gareth's smile dropped so fast it looked painful. "No, sir."

Jane covered her smile as Death kept up his glare. She knew Gareth saw the Grim Reaper instead of her handsome angel.

Death's lips twitched with a smile. "Lighten up, Shit Ass. I'm just fucking with you."

"Shit Ass?" Jane asked, smacking him. "And don't be mean to Gareth."

Death smirked at Gareth, whose face went red. "Still regretting sneaking into that chili last night?"

Everyone turned their heads in Gareth's direction.

War threw his head back, his bellowing laugh carrying through the mess hall while Gawain fell to his side, laughing as he said, "Death was walking by when I told Gareth through a door I wasn't sharing my supplies with his dirty ass. When he heard Death's voice, he asked him to steal him a roll of your toilet paper."

Jane couldn't stop the peel of laughter that left her mouth. "Oh, Lort."

Again, everyone spun their heads around, mouths hanging open as they stared at her hot face.

"Lort?" Death chuckled.

"Lort, help us all," War said, laughing loudly.

Gawain wheezed. "I can't breathe. Jane's got the Horsemen of the Apocalypse making jokes."

She turned, snorting, only causing their entire group to roar with laughter.

"Oh, thank the Lort for bringing Jane into our lives," Gareth cried, then jumped up, grabbing his stomach as he raced out of the mess hall, shouting, "Oh, Lort!"

Gawain gasped on the floor. "Dear Lort, his asshole has been torn asunder."

"Stop!" Jane smacked Death's chest as it vibrated. He wasn't laughing loud, but he was enjoying her humiliation.

"Dear Lort, Jane," came David's voice, "what have you done now?"

"David made a joke." Gawain still gasped for air. "Oh, Lort, what has the world come to?"

"Stop, my face is hurting." Jane wiped the tears from her eyes as she turned to glare at her vampire, but she shut up when he held something out to her.

"Ah, you fucking cheater." Death kissed her head, lifting her off his lap when she gasped, grabbing the bottle of Dr Pepper from David. "Well played, Pretty Boy."

David grinned, bending to kiss her. "He thinks I'm pretty and says I have a nice ass. You better watch out."

"Y'all need to stop," she said, helping David with the tray of food he had for the kids.

War caught her eye before he shifted his gaze to Death. "I knew you had a thing for Tex when I caught you watching her."

Jane looked between them. "Are y'all talking about me?"

David chuckled, kissing her head. "I believe you just clarified that for everyone, sweetheart."

She blushed. "Y'all are mean. Dammit." She stuck her tongue out at War. "Laugh it up, big guy."

War chuckled again before he settled his gaze on Natalie, who was led over to them by Ragnelle.

Natalie blushed, running to latch onto David's leg as War glared at her.

David chuckled, picking her up. "He's not going to shave your hair off, princess. He was joking."

Jane plucked Nathan up, glancing around for a place to sit with him. Death hooked a finger in her belt loop and pulled her and Nathan onto his lap.

"Death," she said, checking to see what David was doing.

David handed Death a plate. "Help her feed him."

Jane sat in shock as Death held the plate up to Nathan and became even more shocked when Nathan began eating as if eating from the Angel of Death was normal.

Jane peeked at David, smiling when he sat on the ground, putting Natalie on his lap and helping her piece apart her food.

War shook his head at Death. "She has domesticated you, brother."

Death smirked. "You are only jealous you do not have a Sweet Jane."

The Red Horseman winked at her. "Care for another admirer, Tex?"

David whispered in Natalie's ear, and Jane gasped when Natalie threw a nugget at War's forehead.

The room went silent.

Death tightened his hold on Jane, saying, "Watch your daughter. She's been fucking with him ever since she saw him."

"You little monster!" War wiped his forehead.

Natalie stuck her tongue out. "My mommy loves David. She has too many boyfriends. Go away."

"That's not what I told her to say. She said that on her own." David chuckled, kissing Natalie's head. "Thank you, princess. Mommy has many admirers, but it's okay—we know who number one is."

Death scoffed while Natalie huffed, giving War a dark look before she started eating again.

"Vile beast," War muttered, making a flame incinerate the nugget.

"You're a beast," Natalie shot back.

War gave David a dark look, but he ignored Natalie and turned his attention to Death. "So, these boys are heading out for their plane in a few hours. I think I will join them. I am certain there will be some action. I cannot stand sitting still for too long."

"That's not a bad idea." Death placed the plate down when Nathan pointed to a cup on the table beside them. Death handed the cup to Nathan without saying anything, waiting for Nathan to return it to him before he again held the plate up.

Jane smiled, kissing Nathan's head as she glanced over at David. Her vampire watched her already, a faint smile on his lips.

"I assume you are staying with your little woman." War waved his hand toward Jane and grinned when she glared at him. "She's feisty. No wonder you like her."

Death chuckled. "Watch it, she packs a punch, and her little pinch feels like a damn horse bite."

"You're just a baby." Jane smacked his hand when he pinched her side.

"Yes, I'm staying with her from now on," Death finally answered War. "She is too important"—he lifted his eyes to hers—"to me. I want to ensure she reaches Asgard safely. Their allies are unpredictable, but I want them to have numbers should they come under attack. Berith and Lancelot likely know where we are heading and will follow."

"Thank you, Death," she whispered.

"Always, angel." He kissed her head.

She touched his bruised cheek. "Is this from David or the fight?"

Death scowled. "From your boy. Don't worry—I got his ass worse."

"Your obsession with my rear end is disturbing now." David chuckled.

"It is very nice." Jane grinned at Death's annoyed glare. She turned to

War. "So what happened with the battle? I haven't heard what's been going on."

"I got the other two behemoths. He only took two down."

"You were not keeping someone precious to you safe until she was out of sight." Death ran his fingers down her arm, making her sigh from the sparks he left on her skin.

War shrugged. "I told you boys not to settle down. You will find life to be more pleasant, and you will get to enjoy all that battle can offer. Plus, you don't have to deal with their women problems. Simply call the next willing vixen to fill your bed."

Thanatos shimmered into view. "How has that worked out for you, Horseman? Did you not start a war because a male attempted to bed one of your frequent lovers?"

"Hi, Than." Jane grinned over at Thanatos.

"My queen." Thanatos bowed, taking in Death's and David's positions.

War laughed as he addressed Thanatos. "I started a war for fun. Monica had nothing to do with it. She was merely an excuse to destroy."

A sly grin formed on Thanatos' face. "I did not say Monica. If I recall correctly, five of your lovers were present."

Jane giggled, running her fingers through Nathan's hair. "Busted."

Death chuckled, nodding to Nathan. "Finished?"

Nathan focused on Death. "Finish."

Although Death didn't reply or praise him, Jane saw Nathan's satisfaction, as though he was trying to please her angel as he did with David.

"They are more behaved with you guys." She kissed Nathan's head.

Death smirked. "It is because I am scary and demand obedience. You are sweet."

Nathan shifted on her lap and then crawled onto Death's, resting his head on his chest and shutting his eyes.

Jane's mouth fell open, and she darted her eyes to see Death's blank expression. Once again, he only showed emotion when he glanced at her.

He caressed her cheek. "It is who I am, my love."

It hurt he couldn't care for them. "Do you want me to take him?"

"No. War has something to give you." He caressed her cheek again, sending his magic into her.

She sighed but got off his lap as War stood.

Everyone stopped talking as she approached him. She beamed, tilting her head back to see his face.

"Jane," he said, his deep voice practically shaking the room.

"War." She tried to relax her excitement. She wasn't sure she'd get used to having the Red Horseman as an ally.

He chuckled and held out his hand. "If I may, I have a gift for you. It requires forming the Horsemen's bond between us. I can only do this with one being—the one Death has chosen."

She shot her eyes over to Death. "You want me to bond with him?"

He smiled. "Yes. It is not going to change anything you have with me. He will be able to locate you quickly if you call for him."

Jane looked at David. "Are you okay with this?"

"Does it hurt or commit her to anything?" he asked War.

"No, it commits the Horsemen who bond with her to her." War's gaze slid to Death. "She is his choice."

David tapped his fingers on the floor as he focused on Death. "Are you putting her in danger?"

"I am doing what I can to keep her safe. I will never put her in harm's way."

"I want to do it, David," Jane said softly. "I think I'm meant to."

He stared at her for a long while before taking in both children and Death. "You're sure about this?"

"It is her fate," Death said.

He sighed, returning to Jane. "It is your choice, my love. If it feels right, I will not stop you."

"I trust them." Jane darted her eyes at Thanatos, noticing he did not look at them. "Than, do you have anything to say?"

His ruby eyes locked on hers. "It is not my place to interfere with the Horsemen's bond, my queen."

She stared at him for a few seconds and then quickly shifted her gaze to her two children. They didn't say anything, but when Nathan smiled, she turned and took War's hand. "I consent."

War's eyes lit up with red flames, and he pulled her close, raising his other hand to her cheek. "When war finds you, think of me. I am yours to bring, Sweet Jane." He leaned down, his eyes glowing brighter as he kissed her lips. Fire seeped in and immediately sought where Death's tingles always settled. It didn't hurt, but she felt it, like a breathing beast waiting alongside Death's calmer, peaceful presence.

War withdrew his lips. "Havoc Bringer."

Jane gasped as a golden shield appeared in a burst of fiery light.

Everyone jumped to their feet, mouths gaping as Nathan and Natalie clapped.

"You summon it just as you do with Death's gifts," War said, sliding her arm under the leather bands and folding her fingers around a handle on the back of it. "It is the most powerful shield in existence. Even the Archangels and Princes of Hell will cower from you in battle."

"Wouldn't I be fighting alongside Heaven?" She glanced at Thanatos and then Death.

"You will fight whoever attacks you," Death said quietly. "Use it well, Jane."

She smiled, knowing he was still worried and needed her to agree. "I will. Thank you. You too, War. This is incredible."

"I'm glad you like it, Tex."

Grinning, she held it up to show everyone, beaming at David when he smiled.

"Ah, dammit." Gareth marched into the room. "I missed everything. And I told you I needed one of these angels."

"Watch your mouth around them," David said, lifting Natalie and handing her to Gawain before approaching Jane. He touched the markings. "What do these mean?"

War knocked on the shield, and the markings lit up, vibrating the entire shield and room. "The Seal of War. It's the enchantment to bond the chosen wielder with all the power of the Red Horse."

"That's right. You have a horse, too." Jane's heartbeat sprinted from excitement. "Oh, goodness. Can you summon him?"

Death chuckled. "Perhaps it is unwise to showcase the Red Horse in front of survivors, Jane."

"Oh, yes. Sorry." She noticed the anxious looks of humans and vampires who were eating. "Let me send the shield away."

"*Away, Havoc,*" Death's voice entered her mind.

She thought the exact words, sighing as the fire inside her died.

David cupped her cheek, rubbing his thumb over her lips and ignoring War's laugh.

"I didn't know he would do that," she whispered.

He grinned, kissing her firmly. Howls from the knights had her smiling against his mouth, but she wrapped her arms around his neck and kissed him back when he straightened, letting her legs dangle.

"Jane?" Adam's voice broke through the peaceful bubble she and David had created.

David lowered her to her feet and turned. Artemis stood across the room, obviously having returned with Adam.

"If you insist on keeping Artemis around you," David said, "I recommend waiting until Jane is in a state of mind where she can allow her close."

Adam stared at Jane. "Can we talk privately?"

"No," Death answered. "If you wish to know why she has a problem with your new interest, find out elsewhere. I suggest you start by asking that green-eyed brat, and then remember Jane had not been well when she attacked the wannabe goddess on your nuts."

Adam clenched his fist. "Fine, but I really think you three need to think about how it looks to everyone seeing Jane passed between you two."

David pulled Jane's back flush with his body, resting his arms around the top of her chest. "I told you before; our relationship is ours. Do not question us as though you have a say in her decisions. She has enough of a difficult time coping with how to make us work. Your input, and anyone else's, is unwanted. And I will save you the hassle regarding Jane's and Artemis' quarrel since everyone here already knows. Artemis was jealous because she hoped I would choose her as my Other. We were never together, but she, and many others, believed I would choose Artemis." He kissed Jane's head. "Obviously, I did not. And despite Jane saving her life, Artemis tried to ensure Jane would fall in battle to one of the most feared werewolf leaders."

Adam looked at Jane. "Is this true?"

Jane sighed. "I won't tell you what to do. I wanted to, but it's up to you. She did draw attention to me while I was weak."

Adam sighed, shaking his head as he turned, walking past Artemis, throwing his hand up when she tried to grab him.

Tears welled up in Artemis' eyes, and she fled the hall, going in the direction opposite to the one Adam had gone.

David kissed Jane's head again. "Well, he would have found out eventually."

Jane felt terrible as she stared at the empty entrance—like she'd become one of those girls who always tried to break up relationships.

"That's not the same, Sweet Jane," Death's voice caressed her mind. *"She deserves this. If he wishes to have more with her, he would want to know because he cares a great deal for you. You are his family. Not her."*

Arthur walked over. "Tristan's and Lamorak's teams are leaving."

David nodded before turning his focus to War. "Are you still going with them?"

"Yes, it is a bit too lovey-dovey around here for my taste." War smirked

165

at his brother. "It is as though I have entered a Bizarro universe where Death is a daddy and husband."

Death chuckled, noticing Nathan was asleep. "Perhaps in another existence." He waved his hand at War but had his eyes on Jane. "Keep her knights safe."

"Of course," War said with a nod. "Always a pleasure, Than."

Thanatos nodded stiffly. "War."

War bowed to David and then Jane. "Sir David, Jane."

"See you soon." Jane smiled when anyone in War's path scampered away as he followed the knights.

Death stood, gesturing to Ragnelle. "Take him and watch the girl. David and I need to see to Jane for a bit." He pointed at Natalie. "Stay put."

Jane frowned, wishing he could be a tad softer with others. "Where do we have to go?"

David kissed her head. "You need to feed. I'm assuming he wants to cuddle you afterward."

A flash of green fire lit in Death's eyes. "You know me so well, Prince David. Now, let's get this three-way started."

13

GRIEF

Jane grinned as David's lips slid along the back of her neck, and she squirmed on his lap to make him stop. But a bump on the road had him securing his hold on her.

"David," she whispered and shut her eyes as he smiled against her skin and pressed a kiss in the center.

"Yes, baby?" he murmured, gathering her hair in his hand and still not removing his lips.

"Stop." She shivered, tightening her hand on his.

He hugged her, sliding his fingers between hers. "I have missed you, though."

Her smile couldn't be stopped. "I've missed you, too."

He gently pulled her hair to kiss the side of her neck. "Stay quiet," he whispered just before biting down.

She gasped softly, reveling in the heat seeping into her body. An image of her sweet soul flickered in her thoughts, and she smiled, seeing the peaceful smile on her face as what looked like blue fire swirled around her.

"Mm." David stopped sucking her blood and withdrew his fangs.

She opened her eyes as he lapped the blood rolling over her collarbone. The image of her soul smiling inside a blue flame faded, but her smile stayed in place.

"There are children present, David." Death's eyes met Jane's in the visor mirror.

David kissed her neck again before letting go of her hair and hugging her. "Nathan and Natalie are napping. I didn't know I had to take the Angel of Death into consideration."

Death flipped him off.

I'm sorry, Jane thought.

Her angel's eyes darted back to hers. *"I'm just fucking with him, angel. He needs to keep thinking clearly. Make sure he is feeding."*

Jane shifted on David's lap. He was speaking to Gawain, who sat behind them.

What's wrong? I thought he was feeling better.

Death kept his eyes on her as his voice entered her mind again. *"He is, for the moment. Just be mindful of his feeding and mood."*

Okay, she thought, leaning against David more. She sighed when he kissed her head and continued speaking to the other knights. *I love you, Death. Thank you for this.*

He didn't answer, but tingles slid over her lips, and she grinned, noticing he seemed to be smiling too.

Sneaky, she laughed in her mind.

His laugh echoed through hers. *"I have to be. That bastard hits almost as hard as War."*

He is the bestest.

His mental scoff made her giggle.

David brought his mouth near her ear, whispering, "If he's talking dirty to you, he is getting his ass thrown from this van."

"Eat Gawain's ass, David," Death said. "Go back to talking to your boyfriend so I can flirt with my girl, whom you're greedily holding."

David chuckled, kissing her temple. "I worry about your obsession with ass."

"Guess whose sweet ass fits in my hand perfectly and slightly overflows in yours." Death's eyes flashed as he laughed darkly.

Jane covered her face. "Literally everyone in this van can hear your discussion of my tush. If my kids were awake for this, I'd slap both of yours until you feared thinking of mine ever again."

David's hand dropped to what he could grab of her ass. "She loves me."

"Jane," Death said, turning in the front seat to look at her. "Perhaps you should refrain from flirting with me in a van full of women and children. I don't care if you're on his lap. He'll enjoy the show."

"Death." She laughed as David growled. "You're gonna start a fight, and we'll never reach the plane. Then not even David is getting ass."

"Can we stop discussing my cousin's ass being grabbed and fantasized about?" Adam asked, not opening his eyes. He sat next to Gawain.

"No one told you to ride with us." Death chuckled. "And with the amount of ass I, unfortunately, witnessed you hitting on the way here, I'd say this is payback. Especially when you couldn't handle three women, so you left one behind for me to chat with. I'll never forgive you. So suck it up, Speed Racer. I'll motorboat your cousin's ass just to watch you puke."

"Adam was living the dream. Two girls for every boy," Gareth sang the last part before his wife smacked the back of his head. "I'm kidding."

David turned to Adam. "I will hold him so you can get a few hits for his motorboat comment."

Death chuckled. "I'll sit still and close my eyes for you, Adam. And I'll think about Jane's heart-shaped ass the entire time."

David launched his protein bar at Death's head. It flew like a missile, missing Arthur's head as he dodged it without stopping his conversation with his wife.

"Fucker." Death threw the bar back. Harder.

David caught it. "Stop talking about her ass. I mean it."

Everyone quieted at David's dark tone.

Jane kissed his cheek. "He'll stop."

David kissed her on the lips, holding her cheek, warming her up despite the freezing temperatures outside.

"David," Arthur's warning tone broke into their moment.

Her vampire sighed, pulling back but not before pecking her on her nose, cheeks, chin, and forehead.

"One minute out," Tristan said. He was driving one of the twenty vans that had been stored in the bunker.

Jane leaned forward, peeking in on Nathan.

"He is fine." Guinevere caressed his cheek.

She reached over, too, brushing some of his hair back. "His hair is so long now."

Guinevere nodded. "He would not let us cut it."

"Yeah." Jane smiled sadly. "A lot of children with autism struggle with haircuts and stuff. It would take Jason and me holding him still for a hair-stylist with a lot of patience." A tear rolled down her cheek as she thought of Jason. Of all the times he'd smiled when Nathan finally spoke to him and how he'd spoil Nathan by taking him to get a toy after each haircut.

"David," Death said quietly.

David leaned forward, kissing her head. "*Shh . . .*"

"I'm fine," she whispered, wiping her tears. She wasn't. She hadn't mourned Jason properly. She'd lost all of their things and had nothing to keep his memory alive for their children.

The van rolled to a stop, and everyone quietly climbed out. Jane sobbed when tingles crawled up her arm, and David let Death pull her out. Her angel lifted her into his arms, hugging her as he carried her away from everyone's view.

"He's gone." She buried her face into his neck, crying as he rubbed her back.

"He's with you, angel." He kissed her shoulder. "The end is simply a new beginning. He only waits."

She nodded, knowing he meant Jason was waiting for them so they could start their next journey.

Death's hold tightened. "I'm sorry I took him the way I did."

Jane wiped her tears away. "It's my fault. I went crazy."

He chuckled, swaying with her as he finally stopped behind a different van. "Only a bit. It was level ninety on the Jane flipped-her-shit scale."

Jane laughed sadly. "Only ninety?"

He pulled back to see her, rearranging his hold so he could reach up to wipe more of her tears. "He didn't want you to watch. He said it would haunt you, and I agreed."

It hurt to imagine the event of Jason's death, and she didn't think she would have been able to handle it either. "He deserved better than me."

"He didn't think so. Trust me, he loved you fiercely. He simply lost his way. He forgot all he had to do was look up from the haze of his routine and see you shining. Darkness comes in many forms, and for Jason, he concentrated on himself and the helpless feeling of watching the woman he loved suffer. He was not David. He could not bear to watch you that way, so he stopped seeing and allowed more darkness to surround him and separate you from each other. David is a warrior who is unwilling to watch you fade." He rubbed her trembling lips. "So am I."

Jane leaned forward, kissing him softly. "Are you going to be all right?"

He rested his forehead against hers. "Always forgetting who I am."

She grinned. "No. I just like the reminder you are as powerful as you are beautiful."

Death chuckled, glancing around when the plane's engine came to life and more vans arrived. "To answer your question, I will be if you are at peace."

"What is happening to us?" she whispered. "We are changing."

The green fire swirled within his eyes. "Our bond is strengthening."

"Liar. Why won't you tell me?"

He kissed her once more. "It pains me. Do not ask me more, Jane."

Her eyes stung when the wind blew around them, and he unfolded his wings to shield them. "They're beautiful, Death."

"I am the hottest." He laughed, nuzzling her cheek. "Let me take you back now. My brother is requesting to see you."

"You can speak with him telepathically?"

Death hid his wings. "I will with each of my brothers as they arrive. Until they take their place, we know where the other is and avoid coming close."

"So how come you couldn't find Pestilence?"

His facial features sharpened. "Magic."

"Like wizards and witches?"

He gave her an annoyed look. "No. But there are spells powerful beings can conjure. This one hid him from each of us. War had been searching for him for nearly two years when rumor spread he was in danger."

"Did you ever find him?"

"Yes. He is being held somewhere protected."

Jane watched him, asking, "What happened to him?"

"Another time, Jane." He turned his head, looking almost violent. "Close your eyes."

She did quickly. "Are you okay?"

"Yes." He didn't sound okay.

"Brother," War said.

Death huffed. "I see you found what I asked you to."

"You owe me a spar," War said. "Are you going to let her see?"

"Hang on. David? Have them close their eyes and bring them here." Death kissed her head.

Jane tightened her arms around Death. "Are we on board now?"

"Yes," Death said. "Stay quiet."

She smelled David's scent and smiled. "Can I open them?"

Death kissed her forehead. "Thank them, but take these as my apology for not taking your hand when you reached out for me." He kissed her forehead again. "Open."

She did, gasping and covering her mouth at the sight of War holding two very dirty cats by their scruffs. "Oh my gosh!"

"Jules, Belle!" She sobbed, throwing her arms around Death. "Thank you."

He chuckled, hugging her tightly before lowering her to the ground. "Thank my brother and the knights who searched for them."

Jane nodded, but she pecked his cheek before turning to War. She laughed sadly at Lamorak and Tristan. They were holding other objects, and she teared up again, seeing that Lamorak had something special, too.

"May I?" he asked, nodding to Natalie and Nathan, both in David's arms with their eyes closed.

"Yes, thank you."

David instructed the kids to open their eyes. They both gasped, taking the toys from Lamorak: a princess doll and a dinosaur plush—the toys Dagonet had given them.

"Julesy," Nathan said, noticing the cats.

Jane quickly took her cats from War. "Thank you, War."

He helped her fit both cats into her arms, and she cried. They weren't afraid of her.

"You're welcome, Tex." He gestured to Tristan before holding up a wooden crate. "Greet your cats and load them in here. He found something else for you."

After kissing her cats and putting them in the crate filled with blankets, she turned to Tristan.

He smiled as he opened a bag. "Some of them are singed, but I think the best ones are in good condition." He pulled out a photo album, and she fell to her knees, bawling as he opened it to a picture of Jason holding Natalie as she held Nathan. They were at the zoo celebrating the twins' third birthdays.

Tristan kissed her head, handing the album to David as he squatted behind her to let the kids stand. They hugged her, tears running down their faces as they cried, "Daddy."

"Don't cry," she told them, pulling out two pictures. "Look how happy Daddy was with you."

Natalie hiccuped, kissing the picture before hugging it. Nathan stared at the one she gave him.

His eyes watered, and tears rolled down his chubby cheeks. "Daddy gone."

Jane shook her head, hugging him. "No, bubby. He never left you." She leaned back, putting her hand over his heart. "He left his heart with both of you. We will see him again." She teared up, broken, that it would only happen when they each died. "He's just waiting for us."

"Stars?" Nathan asked, looking up at Death.

Death nodded. "In the stars. Smile. He is watching you."

Jane smiled sadly, wiping Nathan's cheeks when he nodded to Death. He hugged the picture of him and Jason waving at the killer whales on one of their trips to an amusement park.

She stood up, rubbing her cheek as she quickly embraced Tristan and Lamorak. "Thank you."

They patted her back before handing her a bag.

"These are just small things we found. But we thought you would like them anyway," Lamorak said.

"Yes, thank you."

David put the bag over his shoulder as he nudged her toward War and thanked his brothers.

Jane walked right up to War, wrapping her arms around his waist. "Thank you."

He chuckled, awkwardly caressing her head. "My brother threatened each of us to search all of Canada. We had little choice."

She smiled, tilting her head up to see his face. "Thank you anyway."

He nodded, picking up the crate. "Give them some attention before they start pouting again. I will put your pets in a safe location."

Jane let him go and turned, smiling at David first, then at Death. Nathan was in his arms now, hugging his dinosaur and falling asleep.

"Thank you for giving them this," she said, walking toward Death.

He cupped her cheek. "It makes you happy."

She knew he meant he only intended this for her, but he indirectly created happiness and peace for her children. *I love you,* she thought, covering his hand with hers.

"And I love you," was his silent reply.

"Let's get to our spot." David picked up Natalie.

Jane stared at the two men, standing side by side, holding her children together. She never wanted to forget it. She hugged her album, returning their smiles with one of her own before following them into the packed plane.

"Does this mean we get to make out later?" Death asked.

David didn't stop walking but smacked Death on the back of the head. "Sure. You can make out with my fist as it smashes your face."

Death grinned at him. "I love it when you talk dirty."

Jane smiled, peeking at the photo on the front of her album. She and Jason were at the park, lying on a merry-go-round. He had held his camera above them as they lay with their faces turned toward each other. Smiling.

A teardrop fell on the picture, and she wiped it away before kissing the photo. "I love you."

David grabbed her hand, and she realized he had put something in it.

"He loved you, too," he said, releasing her hand but still guiding her to sit beside him.

She uncurled her fingers, smiling sadly at the sight of Jason's ring.

"He wanted you to have it." He pulled her next to him, placing a hand on her lap as Death sat on her other side.

"Thank you, David." She held the ring to her chest and received a kiss.

"You're welcome. Just remember it's okay to cry, and there is no rush in grieving someone so dear to you. Don't let anyone ever make you feel bad for being sad. You can cry for a thousand years for all I care—as long as you live each day for the people around you, so the ones waiting in the stars can shine brighter at the sight of your smile." He wiped her tears and even her runny nose.

"Oh, gross." She used her sleeve. "I'm sorry."

He leaned over, kissing her again. "You are never gross. I'll take your runny nose kisses any day."

She laughed, kissing him quickly as she took Natalie's hand. "You okay?"

Natalie hugged David's neck. "Yes."

Jane warmed as David kissed Natalie's head and rocked her, murmuring sweet things to her that Jason had told him.

Tingles spread over her hand, and she turned to Death, lacing their fingers together.

"So, what are the Norse going to think when you show up?" she asked, leaning her head on his shoulder as she watched everyone getting in their final positions for take-off.

Death smirked. "I will let you see how the Norse react to me. Every religion and mythos has its take on who I am. Those who have witnessed the moment their heart stopped have glimpsed me as you see me. The others will see their version of Death until I come for them."

"Sounds kinky." She giggled.

"I saw a secret spot by the blood storage. We can still go make out."

David reached over, smacking Death's head. "Enough."

"Hey!" Natalie lifted her head, glaring at David.

Jane frowned, wondering why she would give David that look.

"Ryder is Mommy's pretty angel. Don't hurt him."

Jane covered her mouth, hiding her laugh at David's shocked expression.

"You tell 'em, baby girl," Death cheered her on. "Tell him who's prettier, too."

Natalie blushed and went back to hiding her face in David's neck.

David glared at him. "You are out for both of my girls."

Jane quickly leaned over to kiss David. "I love you."

He held her chin, kissing her back. "You're glowing again."

She beamed up at him, kissing him again and loving how his eyes searched every part of her as if he would never see enough of her.

Giving her one more kiss, he glanced at Death and said, "Thank you, Death."

"It's never for you, Prince."

David winked at her. "Love you, too, baby. Keep glowing for us."

"Hang on, everybody," a voice came over the speaker. "We have a big storm ahead of us, but The Queen has fought through each one. So hang on to each other. We'll make it."

There was a beep, and the plane's engines roared louder.

David took her other hand, and Jane took a deep breath, squeezing their hands and smiling when they both squeezed hers. "David?" she called him.

"Hm?"

"What is The Queen?"

"It's the name of the plane. This one is different from the one we flew on before."

"Oh." She tightened her hand when the plane started gaining speed.

David held hers tight. "It's okay—I won't let go of you."

"I know," she whispered, closing her eyes as the plane lifted. Her stomach turned, and tingles increased in her belly before teasingly kissing her heart as it pulsed with fire that never burned. "I know," she repeated, sighing. "I'll hang on."

Both of her men raised the hand they were holding to their lips at the same time, and both murmured the same words, "That's my girl."

She opened her eyes, gasping. "David, how are we landing in Asgard this time?"

"Well . . ." David sighed.

"Do not fret, my queen." Thanatos shimmered into view, bowing. "This time, you're jumping in style." He smirked at Death. "Fallen angels have an advantage Light angels do not."

"Right now," Death said, winking at her, "I'll take you for the ride of your life, babe. What do you say?"

Her heart was beating so fast. "You're gonna fly me?"

"If your pretty boy is fine with it," he said.

David shook his head when she spun around to look at him. "Baby, I thought you would want him to hold the children. I can carry you again."

She pouted but nodded. "Yes, I would rather them fly than fall. No offense."

Death chuckled. "Next time, then. I'll let the suspense get you all tingly."

She blushed when some of the wives looked their way. "Do you have to make everything sexual?"

A dangerously sexy smirk spread over his lips. "Yes."

"Mind your business," David snapped.

Jane looked over to see a group of vampires watching them. David's warning was received, and each turned quickly.

"This is going to be fun." Death chuckled.

"Agreed," Thanatos said.

"That's what I'm talking about!" War's voice bellowed from somewhere else on the plane.

The knights started roaring as various people and vampires began clapping. It reminded Jane of a football pep rally.

"Here we come, Valhalla," Gawain shouted. "Hell is going to tremble tonight!"

"Take us to glory, Queen," Gareth hollered, getting more cheers and whistles.

Thanatos' eyes glowed as he bowed to her and said, "My queen." She was about to ask him to ensure this landing did not end like the first time, but he spoke before she could. "I will secure your arrival. See you in Asgard."

Jane smiled, feeling excitement for whatever was coming as the plane's cabin continued to fill with cheers and songs. "Thank you, Than."

He was gone in a burst of red and black smoke.

Death kissed her head. "The world is about to meet Queen Jane. Are you ready to show them who you are?"

She took in everyone's hopeful faces before noticing Nathan's and Natalie's grins. "Yes."

14

HORSEMEN BRINGER

Jane squinted as her hair whipped around her and David. She hadn't had a tie for it—or a mask, and she'd refused to let David give his up. So here she was, clinging to him with her face buried against his neck as they fell to the ground.

"Jane?" David called.

She peeked over his shoulder, noticing the other vampires falling before tilting her head to see the fallen angels hovering above them. Thanatos had brought those loyal to him to carry humans, but they were instructed to stay in the air until Death permitted them to land.

He was staying up, too. He carried her children, whom he'd rendered unconscious with a simple touch as he uttered 'sleep.' She had screamed, startling the entire plane when their little heads dropped to his shoulders. Death had rolled his eyes, telling her he always did this to them. That statement stunned her to silence and awe. He'd been helping her with her children for years.

Jane shook her head to rid herself of these thoughts. There were other matters more important than the realization Death did far more for her than she'd ever known, and those matters involved her general.

David tightened his arms around her. "Stay calm," he said. "Tensions are going to be higher this time. Your angels are only going to cause that tension to increase."

She pushed her hair back to see below them. Thanatos wasn't engaged in battle, but almost a hundred vampires surrounded him. Thor was most visible with his red hair, and she was ready to smack him for causing yet another drama-filled arrival.

"I don't like them treating him this way," she said, feeling her fangs cut her lip.

"You never will." David chuckled. "Thanatos is fine, though. But they are afraid—I do not blame them. They are only holding him until we arrive."

She glared at David. "Thanatos is my general and friend."

"I know. I am referring to their history with demons and fallen angels." He kissed her through his mask. "I have your back no matter what."

Jane kissed his smiling lips through his mask too. "Thank you."

"Hang on." He gripped her tight just before smashing into the rocks.

The knights and other vampires landed, hissing and drawing their swords when some of Thor's men aimed their blades at them.

Thor pushed his way through his soldiers. "You send unwelcome messengers, Arthur."

Jane bared her fangs, walking toward them.

David held her hand, but he didn't say anything when she marched up to Thor with a glare.

"Get your men away from my general." She could barely control her voice. She was enraged and freezing.

Thor frowned, glancing at Arthur before looking back at her. "Jane, you sent this Fallen to my fortress?"

"He's my general," she snapped, not liking how they still looked ready to attack Thanatos.

Thor looked up at the sky, seeing the black wings of more fallen angels. "What has happened to you?"

David shoved Thor backward. "Watch how you speak to her. She sent this angel to ensure we did not arrive in the same mess we did last time." He jabbed his finger toward the sky. "Our cargo is precious. She is not taking risks."

Thor shook his head. "You have turned to darkness, after all."

Arthur moved between them as several hisses from their group erupted. "You should not jump to conclusions. And I request you show less hostility to the angels with us. They are friends of Jane's, therefore, our allies. They aided during the attack on Camelot and wish to continue aiding our fight."

Thor scanned the vampires with them. "Arthur, you did not mention this when you asked for help. He and his fallen brethren cannot stay here. His kind has already attacked us." He pointed his hammer at Thanatos. "He is lucky I did not destroy him when he appeared."

"You would not last two breaths against me, Son of Odin," Thanatos said calmly.

Jane noticed he'd switched into his reaper form. A hood covered his head, but he had not summoned a weapon.

"I have slain your kind, Fallen," Thor spat. "There is no fear in my heart when I look upon you. Demon."

"Perhaps my presence will disagree with you then, Asgardian." Death's smooth voice hushed the snarls and threats hurled at them.

Jane smiled as his presence engulfed her. He stopped at her side and caressed her cheek before walking in front of her.

The fear that flashed in every set of eyes pleased Jane, but she quickly searched for her children.

Death's voice kissed her mind, *"They are with Gawain and Gareth."*

"Grímnir," Thor whispered.

Death chuckled darkly. "Oh, how I miss hearing my old names. It almost hurt when the humans misinterpreted the translations and gave your father my title." He chuckled again. "It has been a fair amount of time since I have bothered revealing myself to your race. A fortunate blessing for you, Damned One." He paused, tilting his head at Thor. "Still longing for redemption, I see. I must say, you are foolish if you assume forgiveness would be granted to one who threatens the only being precious to me."

Thor looked from Death to Jane, confused.

"Not to mention," Death continued, waving a hand toward David, "her mate here can destroy each of you with his bare hands, and the newly crowned High King of Hell, King Lucifer, would rip your black hearts from your bodies simply because you failed to address his queen properly."

"What?" Thor stared at Death in shock.

"Do not question me, Asgardian." Death's voice made all of Thor's followers cower. "Your thick skull prevents you from understanding any explanation I can give you. The only words I want to hear from your mouth are the order for your men to withdraw their weapons and a fitting apology to Jane."

Thor stood silent.

"Hm." Death kept a calm exterior and glanced off to the edge of the crowd. "I wonder if your Nephilim allies agree with your lack of respect toward Jane and her men."

Jane took in the gathering of ethereal-looking men and women. They appeared not to want any association with Thor's army and kept their distance off the side. Some had wings that anyone would assume made them an angel, while others still held the same amount of beauty but no wings. They were not angels, but they were not just vampires either. Their elegant facial features and streamlined bodies made her feel inferior because of her short size and what she still considered a plain face.

A feeling of complete disagreement washed over her as soon as she finished that thought, and she shook the internal dislike of her appearance away before looking back at these angelic-looking people.

She realized she had seen some of them when she focused on them again. They were the elves and fairies that had arrived during their battle with Lancelot's wolves on their last visit. Her wild state back then prevented David from letting others formally meet her, so she had no clue who these individuals were.

A gorgeous man with shoulder-length blond hair stood at the center of them. He turned with very fluid movements and, after taking a few steps toward them, bowed to Death. He kept his head down as he spoke in a low, alluring voice. "An Bás."

Those behind him followed his example, bowing in unison. "An Bás."

Death didn't move to return their greeting, but their leader spoke again.

"We are aware of the circumstances regarding the newly crowned King of Hell and his queen." His vibrant blue eyes darted to Jane's, as did all the others behind him, before looking at Death again.

The way they all moved gracefully and synchronized was a compelling but disturbing sight. Jane had the urge to shiver, but she held her head high and kept her glare fierce.

"Our allegiance remains with the heavens," the leader continued. "You know which of our families remain in darkness, but those of us—here— battle against it. We continue to honor our fallen parentage who seek redemption." He gave Jane a charming smile. "We have no objection to you, Queen of Hell."

"Thank you," she replied with a nod.

"Well, I am glad you have sense, King Finvarra," said Death. He looked at the enchanting redheaded female beside the king and nodded. A jealous feeling filled Jane when the green-eyed woman smiled brightly at Death before bowing her head. Death greeted her, "Queen Oona."

Jane's insides boiled at the way her name rolled off his tongue.

"An Bás," said Queen Oona.

The urge to rip her pretty eyes out consumed Jane while the queen regarded her dismissively. Jane hoped she wouldn't have to deal with women throwing themselves at David or Death. Even if she was with David, she didn't think she'd ever be able to handle the sight of Death flirting or leaving with another woman. In fact, as wrong and unfair as it was to both men, she was certain it would destroy her.

"*Calm yourself,*" Death mentally chastised her. "*She is nothing in my eyes. None of them are—only you.*"

It still bothered her that she could be so possessive of him. Of course, it was wrong, but he would always be hers in her mind.

"*I am,*" he promised.

He addressed Thor again. "I realize they are from superior genetics than yourself. However, you are the new ruler here. I expect the hospitality you and your people show Jane to be satisfying." Death nodded toward her. "She is of the utmost importance, Asgardian. And she is the only reason you receive powerful allies, such as myself and her general. We are hers. We will not be lenient if she, or her family, are treated with hostility. The same can be said for Sir David. So I suggest you take this warning and pass it on to your men.

"Treat her with respect and control your followers. There will be many"—Death seemed to think over his words—"unexpected alliances because of Jane, all of whom she will want to be treated with equal respect. You will not enjoy the reaction you receive from her protectors should this type of behavior be displayed around her again. I can promise you, although I am the most lethal of her many protectors, I am not the most unpleasant."

War shimmered into view at Death's side, causing Thor's and King Finvarra's men to gasp and move back.

A menacing grin stayed on War's lips. "Ah, Norsemen and Nephilim." He looked at Thanatos and chuckled. "I would withdraw your blades, Asgardians. I will not break up the quarrel you began with The Horsemen Bringer's general."

Jane shifted her eyes back to Death.

"*It is what my brothers will call you.*"

Thor's men lowered their swords and moved back.

Thanatos casually walked to them, standing beside War with Death between them. They were an intimidating sight together, even if Thanatos wasn't one of the horsemen.

"As I said, Asgardian." Death held his hand out for Jane. She took it but

181

didn't let go of David's as he pulled them between him and Thanatos. "She has acquired many unpleasant followers."

Each of the fallen from Thanatos' legion dropped down, quickly unloading the humans and supplies they held before falling into defensive positions around their group.

"Should I list them for you?" Death asked.

"No, Grímnir," Thor replied. "My men were only agitated by the presence of a Fallen. We have lost some to an attack we received the night before. King Finvarra advised we hold our attack and trust the Fallen, but I could not let my men put their guard down. The enemy grows daily. We are always on high alert."

Death nodded. "Then let us travel back to your great fortress. It is not safe for their human companions to be exposed like this. They have lost many and will need those left to ensure their survival. Have your men help them with their supplies as well."

Thor bowed and issued a silent order with a single nod, resulting in the withdrawal of his men around them.

Death chuckled and turned toward her. "Than, what have you done to my girl for her to be so fierce on your behalf? I am jealous."

Jane let out a breath. "I don't like seeing my friends under threat."

Thanatos gave her a slight bow. "I am most honored, my queen."

She smiled before searching the crowd. "Where are my kids and Adam?"

David kissed her head. "I'll go find them. Stay with Death."

Her angel pulled her close. "About damn time I get some alone time with my girl."

"Just keep your lips to yourself," David said, walking away.

"Feel like breaking pretty boy's rules?" Death snickered.

"No. Behave." Jane shivered, squeezing closer to Death. "I wish I hadn't lost that good jacket. If I had balls, they'd be frozen."

War laughed loudly, startling some of the people close to them. "Brother, perhaps it is time to give her the cloak? She is already bonded to you, after all."

"You know why I do not want to." Death glared at his brother.

War shrugged. "It will keep her warm and hide her from being seen once she masters it. You know it makes matters easier."

"Like an invisibility cloak?" she asked, almost ready to jump up and down.

"Not in that sense, Sweet Jane." Death caressed her cheek as he revealed his wings with a sigh. He flapped them before plucking a single feather. "May you stay hidden from your enemies"—he held her gaze as he kissed the feather and placed it in her palm—"and Death."

Her eyes widened as she prepared to refuse, but it was too late. The feather seeped into her palm, and black gloves appeared on her hands as her entire body became covered in a black suit. It was skin tight with a corset around her torso. She gasped, reaching up to her face as a mask formed over its lower half. When her hair shifted, she patted her head, realizing a hood covered her now. "Death." She held out her arms. "What does this mean? You can't see me?"

He pushed her mask down. "I see you. When you wish, though, your presence can be hidden from me and any enemy. You have to will it, though."

"Oh." She smiled. "Well, that's fine, I guess. I won't hide from you, but I suppose this is useful."

He was quiet as he took her in.

"She looks good," War said, folding his arms, grinning. "Did you have to add the corset, brother? And skull mask?"

Death smirked. "Yes, I did."

War threw his head back, laughing again as he smacked Thanatos on the back. "Cheer up, Than."

Jane eyed Thanatos. "Do I look bad?"

"No, my queen." He pointed behind her. "Your knight has returned."

She turned, smiling. "Look!"

David shot Death a dirty look. "Your doing?" He took Jane's hand, his eyes darkening as they slowly fell over her body.

Death nudged him. "I don't have to read your mind to know you're thanking me."

David shoved him off. "What does this mean? Another bond?"

"No. It is merely a gift," Death said quickly. His mental voice pushed into her mind. *"Do not disclose its ability to anyone."*

David grunted. "I doubt that is all it is. What does it do?"

"It simply keeps her warm," Death said. "She can summon the suit at will."

"Really?" she asked, wishing it away and then back again. "This is awesome."

David raised her mask, shaking his head. "A skull?"

"She is my girl." Death shrugged. "Just letting the others know."

"Ours. But mostly mine." David smirked before chuckling. He cupped her cheek. "You're warm now?"

She beamed, nodding as Death said, "It's too bad you can't see. It appears she has a smaller version of my wings." His eyes traveled to her side. War and Thanatos were doing the same.

"Wings?" Jane tried to feel beside her. "I don't feel anything."

"You won't." Death's eyes glowed brighter. "Only angels can. If it isn't clear, it shows we are bonded."

David sighed, but he kissed her head. "I'm sure they're beautiful on you."

She kept glancing at her sides and behind her. "I wish I could see."

"The children are with Ragnelle and my sister at the front line." David lowered her mask again. "Let's go meet them. We are about to leave."

Jane took his hand as they walked through the crowd, following Death, War, and Thanatos. It was amusing to see how everyone parted so they could pass and how her angels seemed so casual about their threatening presence.

David pulled her faster, and she smiled as Thanatos immediately moved away so they could stand between the angels, again, with her between Death and David.

"I feel kinda badass," she whispered.

Death chuckled. "Wait until they see you fight wearing this."

"I wish I could see myself."

A flash of green appeared, and Death held out his scythe. She laughed that he was using the blade as a mirror for her while scaring the crap out of everyone in the process.

"Thanks," she said, holding it still. She lifted her mask over her mouth, excited at how great she looked. Her eyes were visible, but the rest of her face was shrouded in darkness and the coolest skeletal mask she'd ever seen; it had a wicked fanged smile. The hood didn't have a cape but more of a wrap around her shoulders. "I look like a video game character."

David's hand slid down to her ass. "Can you summon it without anything underneath? This could actually come in handy."

Thanatos and War chuckled.

Death surprisingly grinned at David. "Only if you want her to feel like I'm touching her. Everywhere."

"Does this mean you feel my hand on your ass right now?" David removed his hand.

"I've been working out," Death said. "Does it show?"

Jane giggled as she finally saw her babies with the wives. "Your bromance is the best thing ever."

They both grunted, then glared at each other, making her laugh again before walking to her family. Adam took in her attire, but he said nothing. He hadn't talked to her much since he learned about Artemis. She figured he was also upset with her for hurting Artemis, but he was staying on her side.

"Mommy, you look pretty," Natalie said, reaching out for her.

"Thanks, baby girl." Jane put her mask up. "Do you like this, too?"

Natalie touched the material, glancing at Death as if she knew it came from him. "It's pretty." She blushed again when she looked at Death before hiding her face.

Jane beamed at her before turning to Nathan. "What do you think, bubby?"

"Pretty." He yawned.

David rubbed Nathan's back, asking his sister if she was fine carrying him.

"I'm cold, Mommy," Natalie whispered, hugging Jane.

"We'll be in a huge fortress in a bit." She rubbed her back, hoping the friction would create some warmth.

"David," Arthur said, hesitating when he saw Jane. "We are about to move out. Thor mentioned strange lights in the forest on their way here. I want you and Jane prepared to fight or do what you discussed before. It will take us some time to get to the fortress with all the humans and our remaining supplies."

Jane hugged Natalie. "I'll carry her."

Death waved Arthur off. "Go, let us handle this."

Hades approached, bowing to Death. "Master, I sent her ahead with Apollo."

"Good," Death said. "Scout ahead. It's happened . . . War."

War vanished without uttering a word.

Jane noticed the others tensing at the sudden departure. "Death?"

He nodded to David, who quickly gestured for Adam to come. "Carry Natalie. Do not let her go."

Adam took Natalie as Jane tried to protest.

"I will prepare my legion." Thanatos vanished.

Death pulled Jane closer as his voice entered her mind. *"I lost Lucifer. That part of my soul just returned."*

"What?" she asked aloud as her heart hammered away.

185

He growled. "I feared he would betray us."

"No, he wouldn't do that." She noticed the Fallen forming ranks around the humans. Thor's men and the knights shouted orders while David spoke to Adam and the wives about protecting the children.

Death turned her face toward him. "Listen to me—Lucifer is not good, Jane. I hoped, for your sake, there was more to his actions regarding you, but it appears to have been another scheme to get you."

"He is good. I saw it!" She tried to shove him off.

"You know that is a damn lie," he snapped. "I have held my tongue because I did not wish to hurt you, and I hoped he would last longer, but he knows Berth and Lancelot attacked you, and he's lost it. He has one goal: to protect his queen. And while he stayed with me, he did so because that was best for you while he eliminated threats. If we could have kept Belial on the run, you would have been safe for a while longer."

Her breathing quickened. "You lost Belial?"

He nodded. "He has grown stronger; his armies are larger than Lucifer's and mine combined."

Her mouth fell open. "But Heaven would give us the advantage. Why can't they come?"

"Heaven would make us even with the army they have amassed. And Heaven cannot join the battle yet."

David walked over to them. "Take her."

Jane panicked when Death's grip tightened. "Take me where?"

"We want you to wait in my realm," Death said.

"No." She began searching for her children. "I know you can't take my family, so that's out of the question. Let go of me."

David pushed her mask down and cupped her cheeks. "Baby, I need to concentrate on keeping our children safe."

Jane gasped as her heart beat faster.

"They're mine, too." He rubbed his thumb over her skin. "Please go. You will be safe. I swear I'll keep them safe, but I cannot fight while fearing someone might take you. It isn't just Belial's army after you. Now Lucifer, and whoever he has loyal to him, can come to grab you before we could ever stop them."

She growled, searching for her children again as she pushed back the sweetness of his claim on them. Her instincts were to stay with her babies. "I'm not leaving my kids."

"It's not safe, Jane!" Death yanked her back to him. "Get it through your head: Lucifer will steal you, and I will never see you again. You won't see David or your children. Do you understand me? You will be gone."

Her eyes watered, not having thought of that. "But I can't leave them. And I have faith in Luc. He has his reasons for doing what he does, but he knows where I want to be. Deep down, he wants me to have what I want."

Death snarled. "Your desires are meaningless if Belial gets you. Lucifer fucking knows you will do anything to keep others safe, and he's going to use that to his advantage. All he cares about is keeping you out of Belial's hands. He will do anything . . . Do not ask me to watch you disappear with him again. I will not lose you!"

Jane hugged him as she whispered, "We are always." She cried, listening to his heart beat faster. "What you feel for me is what I feel for my babies. So don't ask me to sit alone while everyone I love fights and dies."

Death took angry breaths, but he gently held the back of her head, caressing her hair. She knew something was still off with him, and he was scared for a reason she could not ask him to tell her.

"Fight with me, Death. Fight with us, and I will make you proud." She kissed his chest, whispering, "Breathe. We will always find each other." Her eyes and throat hurt as she kept herself from sobbing at the defeat she felt wash through him.

Death held her at arm's length as he searched her eyes. He glanced at David, and she did, too. Her knight looked slightly unhinged, but she saw he had her back in this.

"Let her stay." David glanced at the sky. "She is meant to fight, not sit on the sidelines. We can't keep babying her. She is our Jane—a warrior. We both have to have faith in her. I do."

"Thank you, David," she said, facing Death again.

He breathed harshly before growling. "Do not leave to save anyone. I will take you to my realm without stopping to ask what you want if you consider sacrificing yourself in some way. If I have to, I will take you there and leave you until the war ends. You are everything. Understand?"

"Yes." She touched his chest, rubbing her hand over his heart.

He let out another growl and kissed her forehead before releasing her. "Watch your back and keep moving forward. David and I will get your family if they are in danger. You keep going. Many are looking to you for leadership now. Destroy every fucking bastard in your path. You will know who."

"Wait," she said, grabbing Death's arm. "Can the Fallen carry the humans?"

He shook his head. "It is too risky. Fallen and demons from the other side will attack them, and there are too many. They would steal or kill every human."

She sighed. "Oh."

David led her through the mass of different immortals until they were reunited with their team. She glanced at the front line. Every leader was present with their highest commanders. That meant David for Arthur.

"Brother," David said, patting Arthur on the back. "Jane will lead with us."

Arthur smiled, gesturing for her to get into position. "I assume you will stand between your men?"

Death walked a few paces ahead of the line, scanning the perimeter. "You assume correctly. But David is wrong . . . Jane?"

"Yes?" She realized everyone was watching them.

He pointed to the ground on his right side. "Your place is at my side. Take it."

David tightened his hand around hers but sighed, letting her go.

"David . . ." Death didn't turn around. "Your place is at her side—she is between us. Always. Take your place at her side."

Jane beamed up at David before walking out in front of the line.

David glanced at Death briefly. "Thank you."

"It's never for you," Death said.

Jane rolled her eyes as both of her men kept their gazes forward.

David inhaled deeply, shaking his head. "Their scents are diluted."

Death nodded. "Fallen magic. There are six legions. Fallen, Demons, and Damned. At least there are no wolves this time." He turned to his side. "Come, Sorrow."

Jane smiled brightly as the Pale Horse erupted from emerald flames. There were shocked gasps of fear and amazement.

Death affectionately rubbed Sorrow's muzzle. "Get Adam and the children. You are to carry them. Burn all who attempt to take them." Death moved so Sorrow could reach her. "He needs your blood so your family will not be burned in his flames. Your bloodline will be the only one able to mount him when he transforms. In this form, at least."

Jane took a breath and ordered her suit away to expose her wrist. She summoned her sword, ignoring the whispers as she cut her wrist. Death held her arm still as smoke came out of Sorrow's nostrils, and he lowered his massive head, opening his mouth as green flames formed around her arm and Death's. She hissed as the fire entered her cut. It rushed through her body before settling in her lungs.

"Breathe, it will pass." Death rubbed her arm with his thumb, and Sorrow licked the blood dripping from her wound.

She breathed out, watching smoke leave her nostrils and Death's.

Sorrow whinnied, bowing to her before trotting away.

Death rubbed his thumb over her wrist until it sealed. "He will not leave them. Should they need assistance, I will know."

"Thank you, Death," she whispered, smiling.

"Always, baby girl." He looked to his left as Thanatos appeared.

"Keres are close," he said. "My ranks will target them and the Fallen. We will protect as many humans as possible."

Death nodded. "If needed, retreat with the family so she focuses. She is counting on you."

Thanatos bowed to her. "I will keep them safe, my queen. My legion will follow your command. They are awaiting your signal when you are ready."

Jane smiled, glancing at the sight of the black-winged angels. They reminded her of herself, and she wanted them to see she believed in them. She caught Death's gaze. *Is this right?*

He responded to her mental question aloud. "You are their queen. Lead them."

It felt right, and she was their queen. So, calling her suit back, she summoned her sword and raised it in the air.

The Fallen roared, some rising into the air. Many of them let out flashes of red light, transforming their attire. Most of them now wore armor like Thanatos had under his cloak, but several wore outfits closer to War's Spartan style.

The wives parted as Sorrow marched through the crowd. He lit up in green flames once ahead of the others. Arthur pointed to each side of Sorrow. The wives and knights created an arrow-shaped formation as humans and guards fell got in place behind the Pale Horse.

"You should have fed, David," Death said, summoning his scythe as the group continued to pump themselves up. "Start using your fucking head instead of making out with my girl all the time."

Jane frowned after accepting her family was unharmed in Sorrow's flames and looked up at David. "You're thirsty?"

He shook his head. "I will be fine."

"Can't you take a ration real fast?"

"Apollo and Artemis took a shortcut to the fortress with our heaviest supplies. The blood was with them."

"Why aren't we taking a shortcut?" she asked.

Death grabbed her by the arm to pull her back in place. "It is too difficult for the humans—they'd drag us down or freeze. Focus. You are about to lead this charge with me. David will feed on his kills if he must."

"David?" She didn't want him to do that. He hadn't fed on a person in so long.

"I'll be fine. Now, be brave, my love. I believe in you." He nodded to Death. "Ready?"

Fires began lighting throughout the forest. There were thousands.

"What are they doing?" Jane asked.

Death snarled. "They have archers. They're going to scatter us. This is probably more of an attempt to steal the humans you have and take out commanders as they capture prisoners. Tristan, get your ass up here."

Tristan came to Death's side. "I can't take out this many."

War appeared. "Not yet, you can't." He grinned, holding his palms over Tristan's temples. "Let's see what power we can unlock within you." His orange eyes glowed as he said, "Inferno."

Jane gasped as Tristan and War lit on fire.

"Suck it in, boy," War said, grinning madly.

Tristan fell to his knees as his wife fought to reach him. Arthur held her back as Tristan yelled out in pain, but he began sucking in the flames, roaring as he punched the ground until every flame was within him.

War summoned his helmet and put it on. His flaming red hair pulled through the slit, making a mohawk as he laughed. "It will take some time to get used to it. For now, use their fires to destroy their bows and then extinguish those flames. This is going to be an even fight tonight." He held out a hand for Tristan.

Tristan took his hand, shuddering as he stood. He looked fine—maybe a little scarier with the way smoke rose off his body, but still, Jane wasn't afraid as he walked a few paces ahead and held out his hands.

"Can he not light everyone on fire?" Jane asked, watching Tristan shake under whatever mental strain he was putting on himself with the surge of power pulsing through him.

"Not yet," Death said. "He needs to recover and get used to the sensation of burning. I know you want to fight. Anyway, the army needs to take prisoners to feed on. That's why I will not simply cast Death Field."

"You mean you could kill them all right now?" Jane wanted to smack him.

He smirked. "I can, but I won't. I cannot tell you why."

She sighed, knowing he had some other secret. "But what about them feeding? Those are not humans over there."

David reached over, caressing her cheek. "We can feed on other immortals just like we feed on each other. But we tend to bleed them dry during feedings, or they fight back."

She swallowed when Death's gaze fell on her.

"They either die in battle or live long enough to feed another. You will lose many mortals tonight. Your ranks need this."

She knew he'd put a sound barrier around them. Her heart ached as she glanced at the terrified people behind the knights. Some were soldiers, but they'd also lost entire families to the battle. They were weak and needed hope.

"Then give it to them," Death said, caressing her cheek as he watched the flames roaring in the trees extinguish.

Their enemy's angry snarls and yells shook the sky, and the ground trembled as they began racing across the rocky landscape.

Jane peeked at the humans and her family before walking toward Tristan when he fell to his knees again. He'd done it but hadn't damaged the vast numbers between them and Valhalla.

She patted Tristan's back. "Get back in line and recharge. Geraint, Bors, help him."

They ran forward, putting Tristan's arms over their shoulders as they carried him to his wife, who instantly exposed her neck for him.

Jane smiled at Death and David. "If you think I'm leading y'all in this charge by myself, you're mistaken. Get your asses up here with me." She pointed to Arthur, Thor, the Elf King, and War. "You too. I'm not what I was before."

David and Death flanked her as War came up on Death's left. The other leaders all took their places.

"Baby, you kind of just led us." David leaned down, kissing the top of her head.

She knew they were aware they'd lose many, and for Arthur, it was as essential to keep his humans alive as it was to protect his army.

Jane turned her gaze up to Death. He didn't look at her. He was watching the sky fill with Fallen, Keres, and Demons.

"Help her punch a hole through," he said, stepping forward. "David?"

"I know," David said, confusing Jane.

"Good." He revealed his wings, which caused those in the air to hover in place rather than swoop down. "Sweet Jane, the Fallen await your order. Their queen has been betrayed. Perhaps you should let them deliver punishment for their crime."

Jane nodded, raising her sword. The fallen legion Thanatos had given her took to the air. They hovered, so she grinned, aiming her sword at the enemy and shouting, "Get those fucking traitors!"

"Yes, Queen."

Death chuckled as the Fallen flew with a roar, sending dust over the crowd.

She felt her face heat up. "You put me on the spot. I don't know what I'm supposed to say."

Death pointed at something she couldn't see. "War, stay close to her. Keep an eye out for him."

"I can go," War said.

"No." Death didn't look away from whatever he saw. "He's mine. Do not leave her. None of you fucks let her get taken, or I will come for you myself. And your death will not be peaceful."

"She will be fine," War said, and Death vanished.

Jane looked around, seeing a big explosion of green and red. Her heart pounded as she turned toward the battle approaching and the one taking place in the sky. "War, where'd he go?"

"Belial is here." War made a show of fixing his helmet as he addressed the group. "War and Death are on your side tonight."

The soldiers hollered out in various languages.

War grinned, pointing at the continuous flashes of green and red in the forest. The roars coming from there were Death's, and he was pissed. "If you find yourself staring at some green-eyed bastard wearing black, tell him Sweet Jane sent you, and my fucking brother will carry you to the next life without scaring the fuck out of you."

There were laughs and cheers, but Jane couldn't stop staring at the green light.

David grabbed her hand. "Fight with me this time, Jane."

Although her urge to fight alone rose again, she squeezed his hand before hollering out with the army they'd gathered.

"Ready to go to war with the Red Horseman, Tex?" War winked.

She smiled, releasing David's hand. "Quit standing around, boys!" Then she took off.

David muttered curses and chased after her. He smacked her butt, passing her. "Cheater."

War caught up to her, but the others had not yet. He laughed, watching David already attacking the front line. "He's a beast."

A surge of pride swelled inside her chest for her vampire.

War grabbed her hand. "Havoc Bringer."

Her shield appeared, already in her hold, as he yanked her up. "I'm going to take flight to cover you. Make a hole for your knights, Horsemen Bringer." Then he put his hand on her ass and launched her toward the wall of vampires and demons.

15

RAVAGE

Shimmering red and gold light engulfed Jane as she braced herself for impact. She heard David's roar, felt his presence as she drew closer, and wanted to show her baby what she could do. She wanted all of them to see.

Jane peeked over her shield, seeing who her first victims were: a battalion of vampires. She threw her feet down into the dirt, holding her arm close to her body, and roaring, she hit, throwing her arm outward to send them flying in an arc of bodies, clearing a path she hadn't expected but welcomed nonetheless.

"Yes, Tex," War roared above her, but she didn't look up.

Grinning, she swung her sword as her knights rushed past her. They were a wave of destruction following Sorrow. His flames burst, lighting up the dark sky. She looked up when the humans screamed and saw winged creatures slamming down on the battlefield.

One was about to land on Jane, but a pair of black wings unfolded in front of her, and a grunt sounded.

"Keep moving, my queen." Thanatos tossed the demon across the sky as he fired his gun at the monsters and Fallen around them.

She pointed at the humans. "Get them some protection. If some kid dies from a demon crushing them, I'm gonna be pissed."

Thanatos' red eyes gleamed as he bowed and let out a whistle. "Yes, my queen."

A bloody hand wrapped around her wrist, and she smiled, immediately knowing it was David.

He lifted her as Thanatos shot into the air, his men flanking him as they entered the battle again.

David pulled her legs around his waist and took off running. "I thought you wanted to fight."

She shivered at the raw sound of his voice and touched his cheek. "I got distracted."

"Learn to focus, my love. Now shoot behind me. I'll catch us up to the front."

Jane realized her shield and sword had disappeared at some point, but she summoned her gun and took aim over David's shoulder. She smiled, shooting much quicker than she had ever done before. Her arm almost seemed to move on its own accord, as if it knew who would be her victim next before she did.

Her breathing sped up when David slowed.

"Jane, they're singling us out." His grip on her tightened, and he grunted.

"David?"

"I'm fine!" He kicked a vampire down, running over him as he fired his gun.

"Put me down so I can fight with you!" She gasped, realizing how far behind they were and how many of their enemies had gathered between them and the main group.

"I'm not letting you go. Keep shooting."

She tried to wiggle free, but he was too strong. When she looked over his shoulder, she yelled, summoning the shield to cover David's back as she ducked her head. "You fuckers!" She was furious, but the shield had done its job. Silver bullets bounced off, many flying back toward the enemy.

"Grab Thanatos, Jane!" David yelled, throwing her up in the air.

Thanatos caught her hand, tightly pulling her body against his as he flew away from David.

"No," she screamed, watching David fight the vampires swarming him. "Go back."

"He's fine." Thanatos tightened his hold, flying too fast for her to see clearly.

"Goddammit, Than! Go back." She hit his chest, feeling helpless.

"Fuck," Thanatos roared as something massive hit them.

Jane screamed, clinging to him as they spun out of control, crashing into trees before slamming onto the rocky ground. She jumped up, scanning their surroundings. "Than," she whispered, watching him growl and stand. He had a sizable piece of wood sticking out of his side. He yanked it free, muttering a slew of curses.

"Oh, shit." She rushed to him, but he held his hand up.

"Stay alert." His hand hovered over his wound as a white light left his palm, searing his flesh.

She did as she was told, holding her gun up as she scanned the trees. She could hear the battle, and they were far from it. "Than, where are we?"

"Death wanted you flown past the main battle to attack from the front. Some have already made it to Valhalla's outer gates. They are struggling to hold the line to make room for survivors."

"Where's Death?"

"He is still engaged with Belial and the highest guards," he mumbled as the light faded. He massaged his healing wound. "Apologies, my queen."

"It's fine." She turned her head, pointing to where she could hear David's roar amongst the chaos. "I'm going back for him."

Thanatos grabbed her arm. "Jane, he is not stable."

"What?"

His eyes shifted rapidly between red and black. "It is best you do not get close to him now. Come. We will make our way to the front. The battle has grown in size."

"Then we should rejoin it!" Once again, she turned to head in David's direction.

"He will kill you, my queen. I cannot permit you to go to your mate."

Her hand shook as she balled it. "David won't hurt me. And he is my mate, so I am going back for him. Come or don't."

"We should get to your children."

She paused, staring at the ground as her heart pounded. It wasn't something she ever thought she'd have to do. If David was unwell, which she believed he might be, she needed to protect him. He could be hurt and need her blood. But her children were always her priority.

Thanatos lifted her into his arms. "He is the best for a reason, my queen. He will survive, but he may be lost to you. Your children, however, are relying on you. He would tell you to go to them."

A tear slipped free as she nodded. "I know. Take me to my kids."

Her general leapt into the air, but he stayed close to the tree line and flew away from the sound of David's battle cries.

"Try to use your cloak," Thanatos whispered, flying lower.

"What do I do?"

"Stop existing."

Her eyes went wide.

"Think of ceasing to exist. The enemy is searching for you, and they may pick up our location. I'm wounded, my queen. Death must fight, and War protects your family and the knights."

"Okay." She closed her eyes and did something she hadn't done in a long time. Still, she was familiar with the thought: *what if I never existed?*

"Hold on to it," he said, flying awkwardly.

Jane glanced at his right wing and gasped. It was dripping large amounts of blood, and several feathers had been torn off. "Than, your wing."

"It will heal."

"Jane," David and Death roared at the same time.

She breathed faster. "Than, they're panicking."

"I know." Thanatos' grip loosened.

"You're hurt. Put me down. I can run."

He shook his head. "I'm fine. We're almost there. I'll drop you near Sorrow."

War appeared out of nowhere, causing Thanatos to almost fly into him. "Give her here and go."

Thanatos handed her over without protest and vanished.

The Red Horseman shook his head and quickly flew in the same direction they'd been going.

"Have you seen David?" she asked, wrapping her arms around War's neck.

"He's surrounded. Let's get you some backup, and we'll go back for him. We will make a path from the other side for the others to escape, but we will have some fun showing your enemies who they are facing."

"What about my family? Are they okay?"

"Sorrow will get them to the fortress and return to battle once they are secure."

She grinned. "Thank you."

"Don't thank me yet. My brother isn't going to like this."

"Has he defeated Belial?"

"He will not defeat him," War said calmly.

"Why?"

War gave her a tender but sad smile. "Because of you." He glanced down and said, "Come, Ravage."

Jane's thoughts and emotions had her gasping, but she still focused on the ground as fire engulfed the trees. It moved quickly, racing in the same direction they flew. "What's happening?"

"You must embrace who you are, Jane. Your men need you more than you realize. It has always been you. Fight for them now."

Her eyes went wide as the source of fire became clear.

"The Red Horse wishes to aid you in battle, Horsemen Bringer. Meet Ravage." He smirked. "Now let's go scare the shit out of Hell." He let go of her.

Surprisingly, she didn't scream as she fell. She landed like a pro, smiling widely as Ravage neighed a greeting. He was huge. The color of lava and blood swirled over his body, creating patterns that matched the angelic writing on her shield.

"Hi, boy." She patted his neck, marveling at how the red flames spiraled around her arms. "Let's go get my man."

Two jets of fire erupted from his nose, and he sped up, lighting everything on fire or turning it to ash.

They broke free of the trees, and she grinned, finding War had reached the gate before them. He swung a massive morning star. It sent dozens of vampires and demons into the sky, even incinerating some on contact.

Sorrow came charging through. She sighed in relief as the knights and their wives appeared in his wake. The knights joined War while the wives helped humans and wounded through the gate.

Sorrow's flames died, and Guinevere and Ragnelle raced toward her children.

"Please get them inside," Jane yelled.

Guinevere's eyes widened as Ravage barreled past the crowd. He'd extinguished his flames, but his entire body was smoking.

"I'm going back for David," Jane shouted.

"We'll keep them safe," Ragnelle yelled, pushing Guinevere and Adam past Thor's guards.

"Let's go." Jane patted Ravage's neck again.

War grabbed Tristan by the shoulder and shoved him forward. "Get it, boy."

Tristan nodded and ran ahead as his entire body burst into flames. He roared, jumping into the air—flames shooting from his hands as if each arm was a flamethrower. A Fallen from her army caught him before he fell and flew him in a pattern. They were making a wall to protect the gates, sealing them on the outside.

"Ravage," War yelled. He was at the center, still swinging the morning star as Arthur, Thor, and the fairy king shouted orders to the remaining soldiers.

Arthur rushed forward, delivering an onslaught of attacks; she'd never seen him move so fast. His sword glowed with golden light, and bodies exploded with each strike. He was incredible.

Ravage cut through the ranks and stopped beside War.

"Take her to the knight. Protect them at all costs," War said before looking at her. "Death is with David. You can admire the great king's abilities another day."

"I better get to find out why he just did that."

War grinned. "Secrets, Horsemen Bringer. That is between him and his angel."

"Fine." She pushed aside her curiosity and focused on David. She knew something was wrong with him—she felt it in her gut.

War didn't say anything else, and she sensed he did not wish her to go, but he took to the air, joining the Fallen as they continued the aerial battle.

"Let's go, Jane," Arthur said. "Lead the way."

Ravage took off in a gallop, bursting into flames again when they were well ahead of the knights. The wind whipped past them, sending fiery whirlwinds into the air. The whites of the enemies' eyes widened as she roared and raised her sword. Sorrow joined her and Ravage, his emerald flames glowing eerily against the trees. Thor's men and the elves charged the massive army ahead of them. They would have stood no chance, but she saw their fear from the sight of the horses, and she hollered louder as her Fallen army flew overhead, barely keeping up with Ravage.

A fireball soared past all of them. She knew it was War. The loud boom and shockwave made her tighten her hands on Ravage's reins as her heart threatened to explode because she finally saw them. Death and David fought back to back. They were surrounded.

War was already slaying a whole variety of monsters. Hellhounds ran wild, but there didn't appear to be a single behemoth.

Jane returned her attention to David and Death, gasping when she took in her vampire more carefully. David had removed his mask and fed on every vampire he could grab. Blood dripped down his chin and coated his fangs as he snarled, ripping the man he held in half.

Her breathing sped up, and she realized Death was holding men down under his feet or in his hands. He was waiting for David to finish. He was feeding him.

She glared at them. This was why they didn't want her here. Death was turning David into a monster. She hardly recognized either of them. Their dark eyes were almost black. They were wild.

Jane locked gazes with Death, knowing he didn't recognize her. He was lost to his bloodlust, just as David was. That's when she remembered her suit had cut off his ability to sense her. *He needs to feel me. They both do.*

Well, they weren't going to get her back acting like this.

"Stay clear of David," Arthur shouted behind her. He was telling everyone—but not her. "Jane," he said softer, "be careful."

She nodded, knowing Arthur trusted her to bring David back.

"Ravage, Sorrow," she said, rubbing her hand along the Red Horse's neck. "Make me an opening. Create a circle and burn those fuckers to the ground."

Sorrow took off first, making a massive arc before increasing his flames.

"Thanks for the ride," she said, patting Ravage before putting her mask in place. Then she jumped, summoning her shield in midair. She landed in front of the knights, roaring, not even pausing before she charged with them.

They were a wall of chaos, all taking turns rushing ahead of each other to smash, cut, and destroy.

Jane felt fire roar in her belly when David's murderous gaze fell on her. He bared his fangs and snarled.

Death growled, killing those he'd been holding in his hands. The bodies decayed and fell to the ground as balls of blue fire flew from them into his chest.

"David," she whispered, swinging her sword at the bastards in front of her. She paused only for a moment, catching sight of Ravage and Sorrow passing each other as they made a fiery ring to stop the army from crushing them.

Jane ripped her sword free from a vampire, kicked another down, and then raced toward David. Only Thanatos appeared and tackled her to the ground.

She yelled, punching him.

"My queen." He grabbed her face. "He's going to kill you."

Tears slid into her hair. "Let me go."

War yanked Thanatos off and shoved him away. "They must face each other."

Thanatos summoned his sword and moved between them. "She is my queen. I will keep her safe."

A terrifying grin spread over War's lips, and he looked nothing like the angel she'd joked with.

"Face me or keep her safe by joining the battle. She will face the knight and Death."

Jane looked between them, snarling before rushing around Thanatos. "Hold him, War!"

"Jane," Thanatos yelled, but she cut out the sound of him fighting War.

Racing past the elves, fairies, Norsemen, and knights, Jane focused only on the two men glaring at her. Her men.

Gawain tried to stop her, and so did Gareth, but she squeezed through a gap and found herself alone with the Angel of Death and the deadliest vampire ever to be created.

Death grabbed David but spoke to her in a voice she'd never heard him speak. It echoed but wasn't booming the way an echo would be created. Instead, it was almost as if she could hear multiple versions of him speaking as one. "You are not supposed to be here," he said. "Go."

"No, let him go, Death." She tugged her mask down. "David, baby, look at me."

He snarled, thrashing in Death's hold. "Mine."

"Stop!" Death yanked David backward, but David managed to break free.

Jane's eyes widened as he charged her, and she instinctively held up her shield. She yelled when he grabbed it, tossing her and her shield like they were nothing to him.

A pair of hands caught her before she could hit the ground. She looked up. It was War, and he smirked as Death and David growled at the sight of him holding her.

"Help me," she said, straightening as she watched Thanatos unfold his wings, blocking her.

"You cannot always rely on my brother or me to save you." He let her go.

"Jane." David sounded like himself, only more raw.

She ran to Thanatos' side and saw David on his knees.

"Baby, run." He looked like he was in agony as he struggled to breathe. "War, take her."

Thanatos was the one to grab her, which seemed to be the wrong thing to do as far as Death and David were concerned.

Their gazes darkened. David bared his fangs, standing once again as Death's wings manifested.

War chuckled and charged Death. He tackled him, and they went flying through the crowd into the flames created by Ravage and Sorrow.

Jane's breathing sped up. "Go, Thanatos. He doesn't like you touching me."

Thanatos shook his head and tightened his grip. "I'm taking you back."

"Sorry, Than," she said, punching his wound.

He crumpled to the ground, yelling in pain as he tried to reach for her, but she moved in front of him, taking cautious steps as she watched David fight a group of vampires that jumped him.

She waited for him to finish, slightly worried he'd kill her by mistake if she interfered. Once he ripped his mouth free of a lifeless vampire, he focused on her.

"Jane." His rough voice made her skin prickle painfully. "Go."

She swallowed her cry. "No, I'm not leaving you like this. You just need to calm down. You've fed. You don't need to feed anymore."

He glanced at his bloody hands. "More."

"No, David. You don't need more. Look at me."

His gaze shot up to hers. His eyes turned nearly white before darkening again. They never returned to the beautiful blue that made her feel at home. He was turning into what he had never wanted to be. A monster. "Mine."

"I'm yours," she said, not caring about the sounds of battle. "Always, my love."

He blinked, shaking his head before he spoke in that same raw voice. "Go. I don't want you here."

She fought sobbing. "No, David."

"Go," he roared, aiming his gun at her.

The urge to flee was great, but she shook her head.

He fired at her feet, and she flinched but didn't run.

"Go!" He fired again and again.

Jane cried, but she stayed still. She could see him fighting but knew he'd be lost if she turned and walked away.

So, she summoned her shield and flung it right at him. She screamed when it hit, and a loud crack from his chest reached her ears. He flew about twenty feet before landing on his back. Jane ran to him, jumping on him without thinking too much as she summoned her gun, ready to scare him if she had to.

When she fell on him, his arms instantly came around her.

He hugged her, shaking as he buried his face against her neck. "Baby, forgive me."

She lifted her head and kissed him on the lips. "I do. Oh, God, I didn't know what to do." She touched his chest as he wheezed. "Did I break something?"

He squeezed his eyes shut. "I'll be fine. I'm healing. You should still go. I don't feel in control of myself."

"No." She gave him another kiss. "We stay together beyond forever."

He smiled, but it looked like it caused him pain. "Beyond forever."

Jane pressed her lips to his again, whispering, "I'll knock you on your ass if you shoot at me again."

His eye color shifted constantly. He was struggling. "I'm sorry."

"I said I forgive you." She stood, holding out a hand. "Come on."

David finally glanced around as he got to his feet. He reached for her, bracing himself as he took harsh breaths. "You brought everyone back for me?"

"You bet your sexy ass I did." She knew David wouldn't like her crying over him, so even though she wanted to hug him and get him treated, she kept smiling to hide her worry. "I need my David. Can you fight?"

"Yes. But if I—"

She pulled him down to her as gently as she could and kissed him. "I love you. Now fight with me."

He smiled, wincing when a loud pop sounded in his chest. "I'm okay. Maybe wait another day to hit me with that."

When her lip trembled, he lifted her mask.

"Thank you." He kissed her forehead before pointing at a weak spot. "Come on."

She kept close to him, her shield raised, ready to block him if she had to, but she scowled, realizing they were approaching Thor.

"Sir David," Thor greeted without looking at them.

The fairy queen bumped into Jane's shoulder. It seemed by accident until she saw her gaze slide to where Jane would have Death's wings.

"Watch it," she said when the fairy snarled, summoning her gun and firing into the mass caught between the flames and them.

David pulled her to his other side, separating her from the woman. She was about to smack him, but he squeezed her ass and kissed her head. "Incoming."

She frowned as two loud bangs shook the ground.

"Move out of my fucking way," Death said, shoving Thor and the vampires close to Jane. He pushed her mask down. "Drop the veil. Now."

She nodded quickly, watching how dark his eyes had become. He didn't like not sensing her.

As soon as she focused on thinking the opposite of what she had before —existing for him—existing for them, his eyes lightened, and he relaxed.

"Don't do that to me unless I tell you to." He lifted her mask. "Got it?"

"Yes. I'm sorry."

Death grunted, eyeing David briefly before letting out a whistle. Sorrow circled and came to a stop right in front of Death. She thought he would mount him, but he muttered something and Sorrow's flames went out.

He glanced at David. "Get on with her. You need to preserve your energy with the injury she gave you."

Jane didn't want to make David appear weak. She already felt terrible for hurting him, so she pulled David with her. He lifted her without trouble, but she felt how tense he seemed.

Once he was situated behind her, she sighed, smiling at Death. "Thank you, Death."

He kissed her hand. "Go. Ravage will lead the way."

There were shouts and orders spouted out. Jane saw her Fallen legion hovering above her, and she waved her sword to show she was fine. They roared and took flight toward the fortress, still killing any that tried to attack their group.

"I think you scared the army off," David whispered in her ear.

She scanned the charred land. It was filled with bodies in various states of death, but the army had pretty much disappeared. "I was so focused on you, I didn't notice," she said, threading their fingers together.

He breathed heavily as he hugged her. "Baby, I do not feel right."

Her nose and throat burned. "Just stay with me."

David breathed deeply, scenting her as he spoke, "I haven't killed that way before."

"I know." She squeezed his hand. "It's okay."

Sorrow nickered, and Jane glanced around as they approached the fire wall.

"What happened?" David asked.

"Tristan." She smiled, squeezing his hand. "He made it to keep the gate safe."

David kissed her head as the flames receded from the Fallen flapping their wings.

"Go find the children," David said, getting off Sorrow. "I'll find you later."

"What? No." She turned, watching him walk away. "Where are you going?"

He held his hand up. "Go inside. I'm not safe."

Jane patted Sorrow's neck, and he circled back, blocking David's path.

"Dammit, Jane!" He bared his fangs before closing his eyes.

Sorrow snorted, stomping his hooves.

"Jane," Arthur said, running over. "He may need some time to gather himself."

Her eyes watered, stinging them when the freezing wind blew. "I'm not leaving him alone."

Death shimmered into view between her and David. He tilted his head, observing David as her vampire growled.

"Death, don't fight him," she said, sliding off Sorrow.

Thanatos appeared at her side. He scowled at her but still put a hand out to stop her from getting close.

"Get away from her, Fallen," David shouted.

Jane shoved Thanatos away. "Go. I know you're protecting me, but you're making this worse. Go heal."

"Than," Death said, not looking at them.

Thanatos snarled but vanished.

"Calm yourself," Death said to David, hiding his wings. "She's fine."

Jane pushed past Arthur and the knights as they watched David pace back and forth. He was hurt but still surging with power that none of the others came close to.

His eyes locked onto her once she was at Death's side.

"Take her away," David said, his voice dark and raw.

Death chuckled. "If I take her away, I'm not giving her back."

David snarled and pointed his sword at Death. "Try it, and we will see if Death can die."

Jane shook her head. "David, you were calming down."

"He senses the children, Jane," Arthur said, coming to her side. "He caught their scent when you got close to the gate. He's afraid."

David growled, pacing again. "Take them inside. I'll come later."

Gawain and Gareth tried to pull her away, but she smacked their hands and walked forward.

Death's voice slid into her mind, *"Careful. If he attacks you, I'm killing him."*

She shot him a dirty look. "Try it and see if I forgive you."

"You always forgive me," he said, smiling at David's growl. "Calm him before I knock his ass out."

"I said take her," David roared. "Go, Jane. I mean it. I can't fight this."

"You can." She stepped closer to him. "I'm not leaving you out here."

"I don't want you around me." He bared his fangs. "And don't you fucking throw that shield at me again."

She smiled sadly. "I won't. I'd rather let you bleed me dry than do that to you again."

His face crumpled, and he fell to his knees.

Jane took the chance to run to him, and she wrapped her arms around him. "It's okay."

He shook his head, hugging her. "I can see it."

Death's voice was like ice. "Does this look like a fucking show? Get the fuck out of here!"

Jane watched vampires rush past them.

"Please go," David whispered, kissing her neck. "The things I want to do to you—"

Death lifted Jane off him. "Sounds kinky, Prince David. Mind if I join in?"

David squeezed his eyes shut as Death held her back.

"There you go." Death didn't sound comforting at all. He was threatening her vampire.

"David?" she said, glaring at Death when he was slow to let her go.

"Come on. Let's go to our room," she said, taking his hand.

"Arthur, please keep the children," David said.

Jane shook her head. "No. We stay together."

"Baby, I can't." David's fear broke her heart, and she wondered if she had looked the same as he did.

"We stay together. You won't hurt them, and you won't hurt me." She raised his hand to her lips. "I believe in you."

David glanced at Death. "Please talk to her."

Death stared at her. "She's made up her mind. Just don't fuck up, and I won't have to kill you in the morning." He smacked her on the butt and walked past them. "Go. I have shit to do." His voice entered her mind as he added, *"He'll be fine."*

She smiled, feeling more confident as she wrapped an arm around David's waist. "Come on."

Together, they entered the fortress with the knights, and Jane smiled as the halls filled with cheers.

Thor patted David's back as he walked past. "David, call if you need anything."

David waved him off, but he was shaking the closer they got to the suites where all the knights stayed.

Arthur kissed her on the head. "Well done."

Jane didn't think she'd done anything special but smiled and kept pulling David to the room. She realized all the knights were staying with them, backup in case he did lose it.

"Arthur?" David called.

"They're in there. They saw you feed a few times."

David hesitated, but she kept pulling him.

"Go, everyone. I have this," she said.

Gawain smiled at her. "Arthur and I will stay."

"Fine," she said, knowing that Ragnelle and Guinevere were likely with the kids.

"Baby, please give me time to calm down." David stared at the door as his breathing sped up.

Arthur touched David's shoulder. "Death is in there. He's putting them to sleep."

The door opened, and Death walked out. "I'm going to start charging for my services." He smirked at Jane. "Sweet Jane kisses are the only form of payment I accept."

"Aw, Death," Jane said, smiling. "You put them to sleep for us?"

"You. Only for you." Death glared at David. "I'll collect my fee tomorrow."

David flipped him off, but he had a faint, relieved smile as he peeked in the room to see his sister and Ragnelle situating them on the bed.

"Thank you, Death," Jane said as Death walked past them.

"No problem, babe. Get some rest now."

Guinevere came out, hugging Arthur first and then David. She teared up as she stared into her brother's eyes but smiled. "Good night, brother."

"Good night, sister." David kissed her cheek before nodding to Arthur and Gawain. "Thank you."

"Call if you need anything," Gawain said, patting David's shoulder. "No one thinks less of you."

David nodded and tightened his hand around Jane's as she started to pull him into the room.

Once inside, he let out a sound that held a mixture of pain and relief at the sight of her kids. "Baby, I'm going to shower, okay?"

She locked the door and ordered her suit away. "Okay. I'll just wash my face. I can bathe tomorrow so you don't have to worry."

He kissed her on the forehead. "I'm sorry."

She tilted her head up and kissed him on the lips. "I love you."

"I love you, too." He kissed her again. "Thank you."

"You're welcome." She grinned, gently pushing him into the bathroom as she reached for his shirt.

"Jane, we can't be together right now." He held her hand still.

"I'm checking your wound, horny boy." She lifted his shirt, cringing at the bruising all over him, mainly the center of his chest. "Oh, I'm sorry."

He tugged his shirt off. "You did what I expect you to do if I ever act that way again. Never come for me like that, though. Ever."

She stuck her tongue out and walked to turn the shower on. "I do what I want." She pointed to her head, making a circular motion. "Queen."

He chuckled, taking off his boots and pants. "You're my Jane. That beats Queen of Hell, and I want my baby to stay safe before she puts herself in danger for me."

"I wasn't in danger." She returned to him, touching his cheek as he stood completely nude, leaning against the counter. She swallowed, lifting her eyes to his darkening pair. "Well, I wasn't before. I might be now, though."

He cupped her cheeks and gave her a long kiss. "Brave girl." He gave her another kiss. "I love you so much."

She smiled against his lips. "I'm about to love shower sex if you don't get in there."

He chuckled, pecking her before walking away.

She fanned her cheeks as she stared at his ass.

"I worry about the obsession you and your angel have with my ass." He winked at her over his shoulder before disappearing behind the rock wall.

Jane sighed, leaving. She checked on her kids before quickly washing her hands and face. She undressed and yelped when she noticed Death leaning against the wall, watching her.

He held up a finger and approached her, taking in her body. She looked over her shoulder, afraid David would come charging and attack him.

Death tugged the shirt from her hands and put it over her head. Thankfully, she had already put on fresh panties.

"What are you doing?" she hissed.

He twirled a strand of her hair. "Putting Sweet Jane to sleep so she doesn't make a mistake."

"A mistake?"

He caressed her cheek before pulling her close and lowering his face to hers. "Yes. Now, sleep, Sweet Jane." Then he pressed his lips to hers.

16

HORMONES

Jane smiled as she awoke engulfed in David's heat. His arm tightened around her before his lips pressed against her neck.

"You up?" he murmured, kissing her neck again.

"Unfortunately." She closed her eyes, tilting her head so he'd continue kissing her.

"Why is waking up unfortunate?" His hand slid under her shirt, and he immediately surprised her by grabbing her breast.

"David?" She moaned quietly as he continued kissing along the nape of her neck.

He nibbled and sucked as he massaged and caressed everywhere he could reach. "I'm just saying good morning and hoping this earns me your smile today."

"My smile is yours whenever you like," she whispered, gasping when he grabbed her ass. She'd only gone to sleep in a shirt and panties, and he was acting as if he was contemplating ripping them off. "You won't always be able to bribe me with kisses."

His lips turned up against her neck. "Your ass seeking me out says otherwise."

She covered her face to try to quiet her laugh. "I'm starting to think you like my ass more than me."

"No. I love you more than you will ever know." He pressed a long kiss right in the center of her neck before grabbing her ass and sliding his hand

209

between her legs to tease her core. "Your cute ass and her friend, however, are more like a pair of frisky female felines. I give them attention—they rub all over me—I ignore them, and they rub all over me." He chuckled as her face grew hot.

"Okay, I think that's enough discussing my body as though I'm some weird creation."

"You are not a weird creation." He pulled her tight against him. "You're a masterpiece."

She couldn't stop herself from smiling. "Trying really hard to get into my panties this morning, aren't you?"

"Baby, I'm always hoping you'll throw them in my face."

She giggled, covering her mouth as she lifted her head to check on her kids. Luckily, they were still out because she loved these moments with him.

"I love you," he whispered against her shoulder.

Jane sensed his shift in mood and turned in his arms to face him. "I love you, too. Are you feeling okay? Your chest and everything . . ."

"My injuries are mending well, and I am calmer." He held her cheek as he scanned her face. "I'm proud of you. You fought so well, and your confidence and leadership were both impressive. I wish I had been there to see more. To see my baby leading a charge back to me while she rode the Red Horse of the Apocalypse with the Pale Horse at her side . . . It is no wonder the enemy retreated."

Her chest warmed. "They did look scared. Ravage is just as badass as Sorrow."

He smiled, caressing her cheek. "Jane," he said even softer, "I know you are often disappointed that you must split your heart instead of giving it all to me, but I want you to know how incredibly awed I am by your faith and commitment to me. You didn't have to come back for me. You didn't have to put me first, and you could have walked away after I fired at you—but you didn't. You told everyone to fuck off and made sure I saw your love and trust.

"Baby, I wanted to drain you, possess you, keep everyone from getting near you. The only way for me to have all of you was to destroy you, and you held out your arms and dared me. It was so shocking that I woke up and finally realized what I was doing. It made it clearer that I really don't have to worry about us. Just like last night, having you to myself would mean destroying you. And it will destroy me to watch you fade into nothing. I will still have weak days, and I apologize, but I promise always to hold you when you fall. I pray you will always find me worthy of holding on to in return."

She grinned, throwing her leg over his waist and pulling him until his lips touched hers. "I think you rubbed off on me. And it isn't possible to let go of you."

David held her hip before sliding his hand along her back. She would never get used to his heat, but at the same time, she felt at home under his touch.

"You realize you have always been my reason for staying true, don't you?"

For a moment, Jane saw her soul smile, and she could only kiss David to express her happiness.

He chuckled as he held her still and brushed his lips over hers. "I wish I could make love to you right now."

"Why can't you?" It was a dumb question, but he could take her to the bathroom or something.

"You know the children may wake any moment, which I can work with" —he smirked—"however, I am fairly certain you are close to ovulating. I do not doubt you start today."

She pouted her lips. "I don't like that part of being a real immortal. The movie vampires had it so easy."

He continued brushing his lips over hers, driving her crazy because he never quite kissed her. "It is a drawback. But it makes for exciting fights amongst males and lots of built-up sexual tension between partners. Nearly all couples are ripping clothes off the other by the time the male senses he's in the clear."

Jane giggled. "In the clear?"

He shrugged a shoulder. "Just wait. You will beg me to tell you I am clear to dominate you. And that is all I will desire, even if I cannot have a child with you."

"To dominate me?"

"You will begin to lose my scent, and it will drive me insane because I will be consumed with the need to impregnate you. I suppose it is similar to your fantasies of werewolf mates. So, when it is safe, I will probably be more aggressive."

"Sounds fun." She chuckled, kissing his jaw.

"Very."

"I'm getting tingly."

He laughed before kissing her cheeks, nose, and forehead. "You're about to turn into a cat in heat. This is going to be torture and heaven all at once."

"Can't we have a quickie?" She pressed her lips to his neck. She knew he liked it and grinned when he gripped her waist tighter.

"I don't think we should risk it. I am almost positive you are preparing to ovulate within the hour, and I don't want to risk damning us."

She sighed, nodding as she began rubbing her cheek along his jaw. "I'd love to have a baby with you. A little David would be the most adorable thing ever."

He ran his fingers through her hair as she continued rubbing on him. "That is why I am thankful you had the chance to have the twins. Although, now I am worried about their reaction to me. I know I cannot hide, though."

"They are yours." She kissed his collarbone. "They'll understand. They know we're not human, and they love you. To them, you're a superhero who saved us. I doubt you can do any wrong in their eyes."

"I hope so. I see now why you feared being near them. To have so little control over your mind and body is such a helpless and terrifying thing to experience. Baby, I hope you see now how strong you are. You went through it for so long—I can hardly fathom the mental and emotional strength it took you to keep going."

"Yeah." She kept kissing his neck and tried to get closer to him.

"I was right." He took a deep breath as he rubbed his hands along her back. "You're ovulating, my love."

"Oh." She didn't care what he'd just said. She had to have more of him.

He chuckled as she crawled on top of him, never stopping her kisses. David gathered her hair in one hand, sighing as she ran her hands over his chest. "Jane?"

"Huh?" She licked up his neck.

David shivered as he lifted her to him. "It's a good thing you were asleep when I came out last night."

"Why?" She reached up for his hair and tugged.

"Because I wanted to have my way with you, which would have meant my seed would still be in you."

"Oh, I'd love a baby with you, though."

"I know. You already said so." He chuckled. "But you're saying that mostly because your new hormones demand you breed with the strongest male."

She couldn't help but laugh. "Well, I do have good taste."

"Mhm." He held her away. "I'll arrange for us to have someone watch them later, and I can do my best to satisfy you without risking damnation for the both of us."

"Oh, yes, please." She whimpered when he kept her from moving lower. "I think I'm going to die if you stop touching me."

"Now I see," he murmured, holding her hair back as she leaned over him.

"See what?" She stared into his eyes as she caressed his cheek.

"I see why men fall. We are shown God's greatest creation and told not to touch when she begs to be conquered."

"I don't know how you managed to make me being a sin for you sound so sexy, but I don't even care."

"If you were not at risk of seducing me since I am foolishly considering damning myself because of how you're looking at me right now, I'd speak with my native accent."

Jane gasped. "Oh, goodness. Say something. I always forget you've all hidden your accents."

"Perhaps another time, my love. I can feel you trying to shove my pants down as we speak."

She moved her hand away and pouted at his smile. "Promise you'll do it. Sometimes I hear you sound slightly different, but you already talk so sexy. I'm kinda always a bimbo when you talk."

"I am flattered." He exhaled, glancing down at her breasts and licking his lips. "This is going to be difficult."

"I'll try to be good."

He chuckled. "I was about to tell you to be bad, but I think that makes matters worse for me."

"David, I just thought of something."

"What's that?" He didn't look away from her breasts.

Jane ran her fingers through his hair. "What's your last name? Or did people not have one back then?"

He lifted his eyes to hers. "It would be my father's name. Leodegrance. He was king of Cameliard."

"Oh, you sounded so hot saying that. Say it again."

He smirked and spoke in a smooth voice that slid over her hot skin, touching her in places she'd only asked him to touch. "I am Sir David Leodegrance, Prince of Cameliard, second son of King Leodegrance, High Knight of King Arthur's Court, Jane's David and Other—her Bestest."

She bit her lip to hide her smile. "That was the sexiest and cutest thing I've ever heard in my life. I'm pretty sure I just got pregnant."

He laughed, giving her a quick kiss. "Perhaps in another life, my love. For now, let us be happy with our children and try not to damn ourselves. I promise to talk to you with my native accent when you are less fertile."

She repeatedly kissed his cheek. "Oh, I still want you in me."

"*Shh* . . ." He hugged her when she started moving again. "You are being a bad kitty. Perhaps I should also strive to be Prince David, tamer of needy kittens."

"Just one kitty." She glared at him.

His lips twitched as he caressed her cheek. "Yes, just this beautiful girl."

Just then, the bed dipped, and Jane jumped.

David laughed, holding out his hand as Jules walked right to him. "I forgot they were brought in here while you slept. I think they've been hiding under the bed all night."

Jane held out her hand and almost cried because she had her cats back. "Jules-y Poolsy. Oh, I've missed them. Belle? Bella-Wella? Come here."

David kissed her head as he rubbed her back, and Belle jumped up on the bed with them, greeting her with a head bump before curling up near Nathan.

"No, I should not have yelled at my brothers," David said, tying Natalie's shoes. "It was wrong of me to behave that way, especially in front of you two."

Jane smiled to herself as she buttoned Nathan's shirt. As she had promised David, her babies had been more than understanding of his behavior, and they were reassuring him better than she ever could.

"You won't hurt us." Natalie touched David's cheek.

He grinned, kissing the back of her hand. "Thank you for having faith in me, princess. I will do my best to honor it. But I want you to promise me if I look like that again, you will get away from me and get help. You take Nathan and run. Even if Mommy stays behind—get away."

Natalie frowned, glancing at Nathan. "Take care of Nathan but not Mommy?"

David sighed, rubbing Natalie's little hand. "Princess, you understand I am not like you, right? Mommy, too?"

"I know," Natalie murmured. "But you love us."

"I do," he said quickly. "I love all of you very much, but I am dangerous, just like Mommy was. She still is. We both want you safe, even if you must leave us."

Jane ignored the burning sensation in her eyes and picked Nathan up. Her little boy hugged her, telling her all she needed to know: he understood the situation. She rubbed his back and went to David as he lifted Natalie.

David kissed Natalie's forehead before kissing Nathan's and then Jane on the lips. "I love all of you," he said, rubbing the traitorous tear Jane couldn't hold back. "Everything is going to be harder on all of us. I'm going to fight to end this war, but it won't be easy. There will be more moments when your mother and I struggle with what we are, but we will always love you. I want you to understand we are still dangerous even though we love you. Promise me you will always choose yourselves over me. Please."

Jane put her free arm around his waist, hugging him and kissing his chest. "We promise. And we will always believe in you. Just like you've believed in me."

He smiled down at her, pushing her hair out of her face before kissing her softly. "Glowing for me now."

She beamed up at him. "You make me glow."

David kissed her once more before grinning at the kids. They were already smiling at him, just like they'd done when he'd brought her home to them. "Let's get some breakfast. Mommy and I have some meetings we will have to attend later, and you will go off with Aunt Elle. Okay?"

They sighed but nodded.

"I know," David said, hugging Natalie and rubbing Nathan's back. "We will come to get you as soon as we can. There are a lot of new kids you will be able to play with, though. That will be fun, right?" He took Jane's hand as he led them out.

"Will they like us?" Natalie hugged his neck.

"I am sure they will, but never feel upset if someone is not nice or doesn't want to play, okay? They will be the ones missing out because you two are the best kids I have ever met. And you have so many people who love you both."

Jane smiled, turning to mush because he was saying the sweetest and most encouraging things and keeping their attention on him rather than the hall of vampires they were walking through.

"I hope I can make a friend," Natalie whispered.

Jane's heart ached. She had not taken the kids to any playdates or daycares

215

because she was so afraid something similar to what happened to her would happen to them. While it protected them, they had never had real friends.

David squeezed Jane's hand. "I hope so, too, princess. You always have us, though."

"Okay," Natalie said.

A loud, deep voice spoke around the corner. "Shall we go find you a friend after you eat, little monster?" War stepped out from the hall, smirking at Natalie's red face.

"I'm not a monster," Natalie said, glaring at him.

War tapped his chin. "Are you sure? Some of the best souls I know consider themselves monsters." His eyes slid to Jane before darting to Natalie again. "Many are the most beautiful creatures, too. And I will tell you a secret—monsters have incredibly strong, fierce hearts. But their dark paths trick them into believing they are monsters. One only needs to remember they were an angel all along."

"Really?" Natalie asked. "Like they are good inside?"

He nodded. "If they can find themselves. Some are lucky enough to have help, but I believe they only find themselves when God needs them to." He held out his hands. "Come. Let Mommy and her knight take care of some things. I will take you for breakfast and scare the boys for your daddy." War's eyes darted to David.

David hesitated, handing her over. "They are not to leave your sight. If someone is cruel—"

War bowed. "Of course, Sir David. I shall ensure they are taken care of. Now, give me your little monster and the little prince. My brother waits for you. He is in quite the mood—not a man they should see now, especially while Jane is in her current condition. And I believe you will become less pleasant once you enter the main hall."

"Right," David said, sighing.

"Why does Nathan get to be a prince, and I'm a monster?" Natalie asked as War took Nathan, who went to him without protest.

"Because princesses do not throw food at God's warriors. Nathan is polite and has proper manners like a prince."

Natalie's mouth fell open. "I'm sorry."

War walked away with them. "You do not say you are sorry, little monster. You should ask for forgiveness and prove yourself with your future actions. Saying sorry only benefits you, not those you have wronged." They disappeared around the corner.

Jane had to force her mouth to close. "I think my daughter just became friends with the Red Horseman of the Apocalypse. War is babysitting for us."

David chuckled as he grabbed her hand. "She takes after her mother. I think he fits her personality more than Death does. Death cannot show her affection, which Natalie truly needs from those around her. Nathan is different—he does not appear to need the attention she does. I feel that is why Nathan often reaches for Death. He knows Death loves you, and I think he senses how much of you Death carries in his heart."

"Maybe . . . Do you think Death will be capable of showing affection toward them someday? It's strange to see him not give it to anyone else." Jane smiled at some of the people in the halls and chuckled as most men ran off before she made eye contact with them.

"Baby," David said, "Death does not show emotion toward anyone unless it relates to you. Only when he is speaking or thinking about you does he show emotion. Without you in his thoughts or presence, he is empty. I spent a lot of time with him while you were gone. The children were often there, too. And he paid them no attention unless they spoke of you."

She sighed, leaning her head on his arm. "He really is just for me, isn't he?"

David squeezed her hand. "Yes, my love. It is beautiful and heart-breaking to witness. I am happy you found each other."

Her lips twitched. "My perfect David."

He shook his head. "If you say so."

"So, why will you be unpleasant?" she asked, hugging his arm as she trailed her fingertips along the veins there. "You've been nothing but sweet this morning."

"Because I am about to walk my very fertile Other into a hall full of immortal men." His fangs descended. "Many may require a reminder from me that you are uninterested."

"Can't they smell you on me?" Jane tried to hide her excitement at the thought of watching David being possessive of her.

"Oh, they will be able to pick up my scent. Those wise, controlled, or perhaps committed to another will know not to approach you, look in your direction for too long, and not challenge me. Those who have yet to master restraint must be shown why they should run when my female is ready to conceive."

"Do you have to talk about it like I'm a prize heifer, waiting for the biggest bull to mount me?"

"Baby, I am the biggest bull."

She heard laughter in the distance and blushed like a tomato when she saw Death, Thanatos, and the knights lounging in the banquet hall.

"I thought I was the biggest bull." Death winked at her.

David paused, tightening his hold on her as he addressed Death. "Are you affected by her condition?"

Death took his time as he looked her over. "Do you want me to answer truthfully?" He smirked when David growled. "Do not worry. I can control my desire for her. I must say, I am impressed you have been able to so far this morning. I was prepared to break down your door if you could not."

David grunted, his eyes dark as he scanned the others. Then, finally, he moved her to his other side to put himself between her and Thanatos.

"David, he's my general. He's not interested."

Thanatos eyed her but said nothing as Death chuckled.

She wanted to hide behind David when she noticed various immortals scenting the air.

"I feel awkward," Gareth said, lifting a mug to his lips. "Jane smells mouthwatering."

David and all the others turned to the knight, who was shaking his head as if trying to remove an unpleasant thought.

"What?" David's harsh tone had her squeezing his hand.

Gareth sniffed the air. "I'm just thirsty. It's more a juicy steak than the urge to breed with her. Still, I want to sink—"

Gawain punched Gareth, knocking him out cold. "Whoops."

Jane peered up at David as he stared at Gareth. He almost appeared to be contemplating whether to kill Gareth or let him be.

"*He is,*" Death's voice slid into her mind like a teasing kiss. "*Hi, baby. Sleep well after I put you to bed? I did like those cute panties you were wearing.*"

She felt her cheeks heat as he practically grinned like a cat in her mind. *Stop. I thought that was a fucking dream.*

"*You are mine every damned second.*"

Jane gave him a dark look. *Stop.*

"*Trying to, Sweet Jane.*" He looked away when David glared at him and held his hands up in surrender as he spoke aloud, "Be thankful I am not collecting my kisses while she is like this. I've heard I'm irresistible."

Jane sighed, pushing David to a chair near Gawain. "Do you want me to get you food?"

David pulled her onto his lap when she reached for a chair. "No. Stay with me until this is over. I may slaughter this entire army if you leave my sight." He held her tightly, burying his nose in her hair as he took deep breaths.

"Um," Jane said, covering her face when the others laughed.

"David," Gawain said, shoveling food into his mouth.

"What?" David moved her hair to sniff her neck.

"Brother, I realize this is her first cycle, and those are always fun, but perhaps you could focus on the war rather than claiming her."

Thanatos snorted and tossed David something. "Just use those."

Jane grabbed the box of condoms from David's hand and chucked it back at Thanatos, but Death caught it and glared at her general.

"What the fuck are you doing?" Death spoke calmly, but it was that scary calm that made her nervous.

"Giving them protection. You know the consequence should he successfully mate her. And since she refuses to leave his side, they will struggle."

"What did you give him?" Gawain asked.

Death glared at David. Neither spoke for what felt like an eternity until Gareth sat up with a shout.

"Fuck!" He punched Gawain's shoulder. "As if you're not thinking the same thing, you ass."

Gawain shook his head. "She is our sister. Control yourself, or I will not stop David from ripping your heart out."

"I wouldn't do anything," Gareth muttered as Jane watched them with her mouth hanging open. He made eye contact with her and shrugged. "It's not sexual, darling. You just smell good."

"Enough," David said, holding a hand out toward Death. "Give them back."

"No." Death roughly shoved the box into his pocket. "Focus, or I will take her where you cannot follow."

"Try it," David snarled.

Death smirked. "Afraid she'll find out you're not the biggest bull. Believe me, she already knows."

"Death!" She tried to stand to hit him, but David held her down.

Now David smirked. "She knows how I feel when I'm buried deep inside her, and she's screaming my name."

Jane stared at them in shock. Too many emotions surged within, and she couldn't decide what hurt her most. The fact that they were discussing her in such a way in front of everyone, or that they were both basically pissing on her—challenging the other. "You both need to stop."

David shook his head. "Sorry. He needs to learn his place is not between your legs."

"Are you sure?" Death wore a dangerous grin. "I think she quite enjoyed the feeling of me between her legs when she was bent over, offering me everything."

Jane gasped, covering her mouth.

"Aw, shit," Thanatos said, standing and moving back.

The knights followed his lead, none speaking as the hall went silent.

David trembled with fury, but he kissed her cheek softly as he moved her off his lap and stood up.

"No, David." She grabbed his hand. "He's just feeding off my emotions, I think."

"He is," Thanatos said, folding his arms and shaking his head. "Death, you should consider severing the bond."

"Fuck you, Fallen." Death stood, not looking away from David.

David pushed Jane behind him. "Don't interfere, my love."

"No!" She held his arm as Death smirked down at him. He was just an inch or so taller than David, but he was making a show of it. "You're both being assholes, and it's going to make me mad."

Death didn't look away from David. "Do you know how many nights I've held her when she's like this? Gareth is right; she is mouthwatering— and she was as a human too. So soft and warm. She always got a little warmer to the touch, and, if you haven't noticed yet, her tits are begging to be devoured. Just like her pretty, pink—"

David punched Death before he could finish.

Jane yelped, holding her hands over her mouth as Death slowly turned back toward David. His eyes burned brightly, and his facial features became more defined.

"I am restraining myself for her sake," David said as his entire body shook from rage. "Think about what this is doing to her . . . You are disrespecting her when she trusts you above even me."

Death's gaze fell to where she stood, but he had no emotion on his expression.

It was at that moment several snarls erupted from the hall entrance.

Jane glanced over, as did their entire group, to find three huge men scenting the air.

Gareth chuckled and patted David on the back. "You can take out some of that rage now."

"David," Jane said, clamping her mouth shut quickly when those three males, well, every male immortal, focused on her.

David shifted his stance so that he blocked her from sight. That caused more snarls. Several chairs scraped against the floor, and many men fled the hall. Even when Arthur, Thor, and King Finvarra entered, they hesitated at the sight of David and bowed before walking to the far side of the room.

"Stand down," David said with that raw, animalistic voice again. "She is taken."

She worried he would lose it, but he reached back, grabbed her hand resting on his back, and gave it a gentle caress. In that same instance, she breathed in David's scent. It was stronger. She wanted to live in it, wrap it around her, eat it.

Again, the three men snarled and hissed.

The muscles in David's back flexed as he shot Death a dark look. "Make sure she stays back."

Tingles wrapped around her hand, and she was pulled away.

"Wait!" She tried to go to David, unsure of what was happening, as Death lifted her into his arms. "David?"

"Stay with him." David faced the three vampires.

Death carried her to where he'd been sitting and glared at Thanatos until the general stood, moving farther away but not leaving their sight.

"Death, what's wrong?" she whispered, pressing her lips together when several vampires hissed, turning in her direction.

"What's wrong is you're not pregnant. Yet. And these are fresh immortals." Death sat, pulling her on his lap as he smirked at the vampires closest to them. "Keep staring at her, and I will shove your balls up your asses and your dicks down each other's throats."

They stopped staring, and several of them fled the room.

"Dear heavens," Lyonesse said, sitting beside Death. "I heard I may have to rescue my foolish husband, but it seems fresh immortals have saved his skin."

Jane peered up at Death, but he was glaring at Thanatos and seemingly unconcerned with Gareth's wife.

"They're newly made," Lyonesse said, pulling Jane's attention away from Death.

"Oh," she said before inhaling a deep breath.

Surprisingly, Lyonesse did the same. "Wow."

Jane glared at her. "Wow?"

Lyonesse shrugged. "Forgive me. Like my husband, I often speak before thinking. Your mate released pheromones, claiming you, in a sense. That is why his scent is stronger. Think of it as him marking his territory."

"Like a dog?" Jane asked. "As in, he pretty much pissed on me?"

An amused grin touched Lyonesse's lips. "Basically. He has little choice —it's all instinctual. I think it will be a bit of fun for him, and seeing the boys become more animal than man is always entertaining."

Jane smiled and focused on David. She knew it was wrong for him to lose control, especially after last night, but he was always so proper. It might be good for him to be all instincts for a while.

Death sighed, and Jane remembered this wasn't easy on him.

Forgive my girly hormones? She gave him puppy-dog eyes. *And I'll forgive you for being a prick.*

He glanced down at her, letting her see just how beautiful he was with his long lashes kissing those sinful cheekbones.

"Flattery will only get you thoroughly kissed." His mental voice seemed amused, but his expression went unchanged.

Jane huffed. There was no point in trying to make him happy. He'd get pissed with her in a few minutes when David wanted her back.

"Perhaps you should get off my lap, then," he hissed in her mind.

Her eyes stung, but she did what he said, motioning for Lyonesse to let her sit in her spot.

David must have sensed the tension between her and Death because he turned, taking his attention off the three vampires.

And it was the opening the new immortals needed. They lunged for him as two, who had not been near the three men, lunged at her.

Everything happened so fast. David punched the man in the center, sending him flying into a wall before grabbing one by the throat and pinning the other beneath his foot. He made eye contact with her just as Death held his hand out. The two vampires who had tried to get to her fell to their knees, screaming in agony as their flesh began to rot. Death showed no reaction as Jane covered her mouth and clutched Lyonesse's hand. It was horrific but seemed to satisfy David enough to continue his attack.

He was controlled as he slammed the one he held by the throat to the ground. The loud snaps that proved the guy's spine had been shattered were gruesome. Yet, the man still tried to punch David.

Her vampire growled before tossing the man at the one angrily climbing out of the hole in the wall, then focused on the man he still pinned beneath him.

"Yield," David growled, ignoring the screams from the two men rotting before everyone's eyes.

"Fuck you," the vampire spat, pulling out a knife.

David grabbed the man's wrist and snapped his arm several times before punching and knocking him out.

He stood, casting a glance at Death.

"I suggest you finish the other two before I impress your girl," Death said as black smoke began to swirl around his hands.

David grunted and looked at the two vampires he'd thrown into the wall. They had drawn their swords, and her vampire chuckled. "Those will do you no good."

"You can't take both of us," one of the vampires said.

David grinned. "Do you know who I am?"

Jane glanced between David and Death. Did people really not know who they were?

"You're about to be a dead man if you don't hand her over," the other said.

Death chuckled, but it wasn't the attractive laugh she usually felt across her body. He cut her a look but said nothing as she tried to focus on David.

"I will give you a chance since you are new to this life. I am Prince David, the only immortal to be created by the archangel Michael. I am the strongest of our kind." He flexed, and several women swooned. David pointed at Jane. "She is my Other and mate. You stand no chance against me or with her. Now I say again, stand down."

Jane smiled like an idiot when one of the men dropped his sword and kneeled.

The other, however, kicked his friend away and charged David again.

David didn't move. He stood there, relaxed, and when the man swung for his neck, David caught his arm, squeezing until several cracks made him scream.

"Drop the sword," David said calmly.

The man tried to spit in his face, but David punched him in the stomach, making him choke on his spit and fall to his knees, but still, he kept his sword.

David yanked it from his hand before twisting the arm he held behind the man's back. He pushed him toward the two vampires writhing in pain on the floor at her feet. The man heaved, finally looking at Death with worry.

"Hi, baby," David said, pulling the man's head up so he could see.

She blushed. "Hi."

The knights started howling like wolves, making others in the hall cheer.

"This fellow wishes to take you from me," he said, forcefully yanking the man's head back so hard she worried it might come off.

"I'm not interested," she said quietly.

"There." David turned the man's head to look at him. "Do I need to continue proving to you she is off-limits?"

The man thrashed, snarling. "Fuck you both. She won't complain when I have her bent over your corpse, screaming my name as I fuck her again and again. You can't watch her forever."

David sighed as he gave her an apologetic look. "Watch, my love. This is our world and why I am the way I am around you."

Jane's heartbeat sped as David glanced at Lyonesse.

"The children are away," Lyonesse said, turning her head.

David nodded, grabbing the man's head with both hands and pulling slowly.

The man's screams were horrifying as she watched skin, muscle, and bone tear away until David gave a final tug, removing the man's head.

She covered her mouth as the hall erupted in cheers for David's kill. He tossed the head away before approaching the two vampires, barely conscious on the floor.

Death lowered his hand, and they began to heal. "It's their time. Do it, or I will."

Jane glanced back and forth between her two men in shock.

David bent over them. His fangs were out, but he still seemed in control of himself when he quickly snapped their necks in a way that even immortality couldn't repair.

The crowd roared louder as several men came to carry the bodies away. Five women came forward and started cleaning the mess as if this was nothing out of the ordinary.

"Jane?" David held out his hand for her.

She didn't know what to do.

"He is claiming you the way immortal men do." Death's voice pushed into her mind. *"Take his hand, or he will likely have to repeat this display until word gets around you are claimed."*

She shakily took David's hand, and he pulled her close.

"Mine," he said, leaning down and kissing her.

Jane was stunned that this still turned her on and that she could kiss him back with every bit of passion she felt for him.

David bit his lip and hers, kissing her so their blood mixed for both of them to taste.

The room roared with applause and whistles as David lifted her.

She wrapped her legs around his waist, kissing him frantically as heat surged through her body.

Her vampire chuckled, squeezing her ass as he kissed across her cheek until he whispered in her ear, "I love you."

"I love you," she said, gasping for breath as she leaned back enough to look at him. "Are you okay?"

"Yes." He kissed her tender lips. "Now you're claimed as much as I can without giving you a child."

"Oh." She looked around to see that many of the others had already returned to their meals or conversations. Some were still excited over the event, but she realized it likely happened often.

"That was fun," Gareth said, holding out a hand to his wife.

Lyonesse took it but smacked Gareth on the back of his head. "Fool. You realize that could have been you. Thank goodness Gawain knocked you out before David had to."

Gareth scowled. "I didn't mean anything by it. You knew I was thirsty."

His wife blushed. "Well, you will remain thirsty because you are cut off."

David grunted and carried Jane away from them. She turned her head to see if Death was okay, but he was nowhere to be found.

"He left," David said, sitting at a table far from everyone else.

A woman quickly brought them two plates, including a blood ration.

"Where'd he go?"

David situated her on his lap and shrugged as he began eating. "He needs space, my love. Eat. We have a meeting in a few moments. I'm sure he will be there."

Jane sighed, leaning against David as she picked at her food.

"I did not wish to kill them," David said quietly.

She kissed his cheek. "I know."

He smiled softly, but she saw sadness in his eyes. "I worry about you seeing how I am amongst immortals. I am not the same man you know."

"That's okay." She put some oatmeal in her mouth, grimacing. "This tastes like shit."

David chuckled, kissing her shoulder. "Thank you for accepting me. I know we kill and punish, but I also know you see me as a perfect man. I'm not. I try to be as good as I can, but I also uphold many of our less pleasant traditions."

"That was a tradition?"

He rubbed her leg. "You are fertile. It is the most tempting offer an immortal comes across—more than blood—and very few fear the consequences should they give in to temptation. When an immortal man is committed to a woman, he must strive to not damn either of them by impregnating her. Even though many are already damned, nearly all here hope to be forgiven. So, they try not to breed. Breeding would be grounds for extermination as well. It's simply what is done.

"So, as the male strives to keep from further damning himself and his mate, he also vows to protect her. Those who cannot control themselves will go to any length to take a woman. Many, who are not claimed, are beaten, raped, or killed by uncontrollable males. I, of course, know you can protect yourself, but as you saw, more than one will attack if given the opportunity. I am responsible for protecting you and warning others of what they face should they dare touch my mate.

"Submission is usually enough, but a kill has the greatest impact for a highly desired ovulating immortal. Once threats and challengers are eliminated, the male exchanges blood publicly with his mate with acceptance from the woman. A willing kiss is acceptable. Now, rumor will spread, and hopefully, no further demonstrations will need to occur."

Jane ate the rest of her oatmeal in silence. She wasn't mad, just worried. She worried about David having to do more violent things while he struggled and Death's behavior.

David finished his meal before her and drank down his ration as she put the last bite into her mouth.

"Ready?" he asked, lifting her.

"Yeah."

"What happened between you and Death?" he asked, taking her hand and leading her out of the banquet hall.

"He's just being him."

"Your bond is too strong," David said.

She snapped her head up. "Our bond is fine."

His eyes paled for a fraction of a second. "Jane, you are immortal. This is your first cycle, and you are under constant threat—this isn't something he needs to deal with while he works through whatever is happening to him. You said something is wrong with him."

"Well, it's not like there is anything we can do. We just have to get through these few days, and we'll be fine."

David shook his head. "A few days under these conditions are not going to be easy. I will try to be mindful of my contact with you, but you are my girlfriend, and you need pleasure."

Her cheeks grew hot. "Please don't talk about me like I'm some weird sex freak."

"Not weird." David laughed. "But you are going to get worse. If he is reading your mind, and my head is between your legs, I may end up fighting him in our quarters."

Jane's eyes were wide. "David!"

"What?" He smirked. "You like it, don't you?"

She covered her hot cheeks. "Yes, but . . ."

"Then I will do it—happily—and I'm sure you'll want to do things to me, which I will eagerly agree to, but don't you think it is unfair to have him listening to your thoughts? I have no idea how he managed to hold back from attacking me."

Jane chewed her lip. "I didn't think about that."

"I know." He squeezed her hand. "After he apologizes to you for what he said, I think we should discuss options for blocking some of your bond."

She didn't want to do anything of the sort, but she nodded and hid her face because she knew tears were building. It felt like the worst thing she could do to them.

"Hey," David said, pulling her to the side. They were by a door that several men were entering.

"I'm fine," she said, turning away.

David wrapped his arms around her, hugging her as she cried. "Oh, Jane."

"I'm sorry," she whimpered.

"No. You are more emotional in this state, and I am asking you to do something I cannot comprehend. There is nothing set in stone. I just want the best for both of you. If you hurt, he hurts, and if he hurts, you do. We'll just talk, and I promise to be calm with whatever he says."

She nodded, wiping her tears. She couldn't bear the thought of losing her connection with Death.

"Let's go inside," David said, smoothing her hair back. "I know he must be in there, and you can sit with him if that helps you."

She smiled and stood on her tippy toes to kiss him.

He grinned, cupping her cheeks as he kissed her back. "Smile for him, my love. I see you dimming, and it is breaking my heart."

Jane touched the curve of his lips. "I love you so much, David."

"I know." He kissed her fingers. "And you love that green-eyed bastard just as deeply. So let's go reunite you two."

He's the bestest.

David took her hand and opened the door, and Jane's cooling blood boiled.

She marched forward and pointed across the room. "Get the fuck away from my angel!"

17

MY ANGEL

Every pair of eyes settled on Jane as she practically breathed fire at the sight of the fairy queen touching Death. It wasn't overly inappropriate. Death was sitting in a chair at the far end of the table, and the fairy stood beside him, resting a hand on his shoulder as she caressed the top of his hand with the other. . . No, it was totally inappropriate, as far as Jane was concerned. It was a goddamn declaration of war.

She tried to hide her fangs. She tried to hide that she was almost in tears while on the verge of slaughtering every woman close to Death, and there were quite a few.

Too close.

David took her shaking hand but stayed quiet.

She wanted to beg him to forgive her, but she couldn't. She couldn't even look away from Death or the queen. He held no reaction to seeing her so upset, and the queen glared at Jane as if she had no right to speak to her that way.

Thanatos, who sat beside Death, putting the queen between them, looked at the woman Jane was ready to bleed dry. "Sit somewhere else, fairy."

Death didn't look at the queen. He kept his eyes on Jane, but the fairy queen stared at him as if she expected Death to refuse to let her go.

"Breathe," David whispered, pulling her closer to him.

Everything hurt. Her eyes burned, her throat felt like it was closing, her muscles were ready to explode, and her heart grew weaker. And, worst of all, the light around her soul began to fade.

Make her leave, Jane mentally told Death even though she knew it was wrong of her.

"Death," David said, making everyone dart their attention between them.

You're breaking my heart, she thought sadly when her gaze fell to Death's hand that still rested underneath the queen's. *Not in front of me. Please.*

Finally, Death spoke. "I am here because of Jane, Queen Oona. Not to take you as a lover again. Go."

Again.

Queen Oona gave Jane a dirty look, but she moved away before leaving the room.

Whispers broke out amongst the others, but Jane could only stare at Death. Broken.

Sure, she could probably kill the woman without breaking a sweat, but she knew she should not have these feelings. She had just betrayed David after trying so hard to put him first. It didn't matter that David thought he could handle everything, she wanted to do right by him, and she'd failed after less than a day.

Yet, David was perfect as ever. He kissed her hand and led her toward her angel. Not displaying an ounce of animosity toward Death, he pulled out the chair nearest Death and motioned for her to sit. He sat on her other side, supporting her.

Jane stared at the table, disappointed in herself but too overwhelmed with jealousy and sadness to focus on what her actions might have just caused between her and David. She knew Death had women, but to witness it, just as she feared, was something she was not prepared for. Staring into the eyes of a woman he'd been with who knows how many times, was burning her alive. She couldn't help but wonder if he'd taken this woman while being in her life. Had he fucked her while she cried . . . when she married Jason? Or maybe when she began her relationship with David? None of it should matter, yet it did. And he'd let her see. To hurt her.

Death sighed as he glanced around the table. "Is there a fucking reason you're not conducting the conference you asked me to attend?"

Thor cleared his throat. "I believe you can surmise why we have yet to begin, and she is to your right."

Jane jerked her head up. "Fuck you, Thor."

David grabbed her hand as she clutched the armrest, cracking the wood. Several immortals she didn't know gasped and murmured behind their hands.

Thor's face reddened to almost match his hair. "You dare speak to me this way? In my home? After you sought refuge because it was your blasted fault Camelot was attacked."

"Fuck off," Gawain yelled as the knights shouted at other members around the table.

David pointed at Thor. "You are testing my patience. Speak to her again as though she is one of the insignificant harlots you like to march around this fortress, and I will destroy you. She already proved herself to you before, and you vowed to stand by her."

Thor laughed. "You are blind. Have you no concern that your mate disrespected you by staking a claim on another male? I never thought I would witness such a sight. I did vow to fight beside her, but I can change my mind when I realize I've made a mistake. You are a fool if you cannot see what the rest of us do."

"You don't know of their relationship," came a female's voice from down the table.

Jane turned her head and nearly gaped at the fierce gleam in Artemis' eyes as she stared down the God of Thunder.

"And you do?" Thor laughed loudly. "We all know of your infatuation with David, Virgin Goddess, and I have heard of your pairings with the angel she just claimed. Are you telling me you all share?"

Artemis stood as Apollo reached out to stop her from lunging over the table. "My dealings with Death have been in service of my uncle, you brainless oaf. Do not spout rumors for the sake of upsetting Jane. She has done you no wrong. She avenged your father after I put her in mortal danger. She destroyed a quarter of Lancelot's, Ares', and Hermes' armies with the power she held, and you are preparing to cast her off as a whore who entertains your ranks. How dare you."

"How dare I?" Thor stood. "You foolish girl have as little right to be here as she does. Sit yourself down before you speak more nonsense. No one gives a damn about your tantrums or opinions, especially on sexual matters. You haven't the slightest clue how to please a man."

Apollo's arm lit with flames as he raised it toward Thor. "Say another word—I dare you, Son of Odin."

Thor hesitated, but he still opened his mouth. "If you kill me, you kill your chances at surviving this war. We will all burn in Hell while she"—he pointed to Jane—"laughs at our burning souls from Lucifer's lap."

David's hand shook as he held it up to silence Apollo and pinned Thor with a deadly glare. "You know nothing of Jane's relationship with Death or my feelings regarding it. What ensues between the three of us, or simply them, is not the business of a single soul in this room. Do not discuss it in our presence again. I assure you, I will not feel a shred of remorse as I rip your heart out if you continue disrespecting her. And I will not interfere when Apollo or Hades eliminates you in Artemis' honor. We've been through this shit a dozen times before—Jane is not here to harm any of you."

Thor shook his head as he waved his hand out and spoke to his side of the table. "Do you see now? The rumors are true."

"What rumors?" Gareth asked.

Thor looked Jane in the eye. "That the Queen of Hell is here to strengthen the army of her king. Lucifer. That she is the reason for the apocalypse—and, worst of all—she has been unfaithful to her mate by laying with Lucifer and Lancelot."

No one moved. Jane couldn't breathe. David didn't speak.

Death, however, laughed. He threw his head back and laughed.

Thor looked aghast. "Do you find these accusations amusing?"

Death stopped laughing and focused on Thor as he spoke in that emotionless tone that always shattered Jane. "What amuses me, Son of Odin, is you believe turning David on his mate will result in you banishing her and keeping him, the knights, and myself in your favor. What amuses me is you filled this room with subpar pussy to tempt me, along with her mate. What amuses me is you think I won't kill you because they could use your army in this war. Trust me, I alone can scare the fuck out of your men enough for them to fight alongside Jane. And I suggest you understand this —if Jane is your enemy, so am I."

Tingles trailed down Jane's arm until they encircled her hand.

Death slid his fingers between hers and chuckled. "If you must know, Jane does not spread her legs for anyone other than David. Is it your business if she chooses to do so for me or another? No. Is it your business if Lucifer took her and she did what she had to do to keep every soul she loved safe? Again, no. David and I could make love to her on your father's bed, and it would not be your business."

His eyes glowed brightly, making the angles of his face more prominent and as terrifying as they were beautiful. "What is your business is that the knights sought refuge here because they needed it. However, they also knew threats were coming to your gates, and you would need each other. You agreed and offered refuge without the stipulations that Jane's relationships would become an issue. Not to mention a topic of interest in battle strategies.

"She is a warrior. She has her very own legions that can crush yours in hours. I would think long and hard before speaking again, Asgardian. She is not the only one who defends what is hers. I am hers." He pointed to Thanatos. "He is her general." He smirked at David. "And he is the bastard who gets to claim her above the Angel of Death and King of Hell. Do you really want to piss us off?"

It was quiet for a few moments before Arthur spoke. "I had hoped you would keep your opinions to yourselves, but I see now your fear of Jane's following has outweighed your trust and ability to think rationally."

A vampire, sitting a few spaces from Thor, said, "We don't wish to go into battle with an unstable immortal who leads forces that can annihilate or enslave us all."

"Who is we, Nameless Joe?" Gareth spat. "My dead grandmother could enslave you."

Jane relaxed and squeezed David's and Death's hands as various arguments broke out.

Thor spoke over them. "She is going to cause division we cannot afford, Arthur. The rumors spreading through the fortress are causing panic. Do you honestly expect me to ask my men to fight alongside the Queen of Hell?"

Death chuckled. "I am positive the majority would fight beside her over you." His eyes flashed. "Ah, I see. You fear she will steal your army, destroy you, and take your father's mighty fortress. Those little legends about a Queen of Hell have you nervous, don't they?"

Thanatos scoffed. "She does not need your army. Hers is far greater without a bunch of blood-sucking sinners."

"Says the Fallen," Thor said before glancing at the men beside him again. "Am I the only leader who is against her joining us?"

Gawain let out a sharp laugh. "You haven't even told us where you are going, dipshit."

King Finvarra was the one to reply, "The Nereids and Rusalka are arriving tomorrow. A small party was going to receive them, but after the recent battle, we believe they should be escorted in. The Valkyrie are still away, harvesting and escorting smaller clans."

"More pussy," Death muttered as he cast David a glance. "There is no point in attempting to seduce him away from her. I have witnessed his commitment to her, and it is the greatest I have seen in my entire existence. You will not succeed. Your finest concubine cannot compare to her in his eyes—or mine. You will make enemies of your greatest allies and die. Painfully."

"The Nereids and Rusalka are invaluable to our cause," Thor said.

"You mean they are easy to get on their backs," Death snapped.

"You would know," Thor said with a blank look. "You would also know what it's like to bed fairies and elves, especially fairy queens. Wouldn't you?"

Death shrugged. "Say more to anger and hurt Jane. I will take my time skinning you alive."

Thor sat back in his chair as he focused on her. "You come into my home, parading around as though you are superior to all who exist here, yet, you and your filthy angels are worse than any of us can fathom."

Even with Jane's heart bleeding in David's hands, she lifted her chin and steadied her trembling lips before speaking. "I am superior to every one of you. Not because I am David's Other—not because I was chosen to carry the title of Horsemen Bringer, and not because I am the Queen of Hell. I am superior because, despite your choice to hurt me, to rip all I hold dear from my hands, I will still fight to save all of you. I may not have the power I once held, but I have enough to wipe the motherfucking floor with you, you spoiled, backstabbing oaf!"

She glared at every face she didn't recognize. "You want to turn them on me? Try. Try and fail, and then watch me still fight for you. Watch me ask my men to die for you. Watch as I bleed for you. And when you stand before God, you better have a good speech ready to go, so you can explain to him why I was unworthy of the man He chose to be mine. Explain to God why you would cause the greatest of you to fall because you wanted to secure your own lives—why you would seek to lure a man away from the woman he stayed true to before ever setting eyes on her." She glanced at Death. "Tell God why you would try to pry her oldest and most beloved companion from her bleeding hands after you stole her heart."

A tear fell on her lap, but she continued staring at them. "Shame on each of you. If you think I have failed to realize these women present are not all warriors, you are damned fools. I went to high school, you stupid fucks. These women are nothing compared to teenage girls." She made eye contact with the women she'd seen standing near Death. "You may think

I'm the Queen of Whores, but I know I am loved by the men I share my heart with. I am the only woman they see. Judge me all you like, but I know, and they know, our love is greater than any of you will ever come close to touching. Think about that before you offer yourself to him or any other man on behalf of your leaders."

Several women walked out of the room with tears streaming down their faces. Jane hadn't wanted to hurt them, but she wouldn't take this shit.

Death stood, tugging Jane's hand, which he still held. "She will not join your escort party. David will. He will leave his mate during her first cycle to partake in your desperate plan to turn him against her, and you will return here, humbled by the strength you witness as he stays true."

Jane wanted to argue. She didn't like Death speaking for David or the idea of David and the knights fighting without her, but she stayed quiet, trusting him.

David rose and nodded to Death, who released her hand.

"We have matters to discuss, Sir David," Thor said as David pulled Jane toward the door.

"Then discuss them without my input." David paused. "Knights?"

She watched as they all replied without tearing their menacing gazes from Thor.

"Brother," they said.

David nodded once as he spoke without looking back. "Death, Thanatos, we will see you in my quarters shortly."

Jane peered over her shoulder at Death.

He winked, sitting again as his voice caressed her mind sadly, *"Forgive me, angel. I simply love you more than the night sky loves the stars. Go. I will come and grovel after I scare the fuck out of these bastards."*

"We will arrive after we handle a few extra issues," Thanatos said calmly.

Death chuckled. "Did you know I was in the mood for dessert?"

"I recall you enjoyed Cursed and Damned," Thanatos said. "Old habits and all."

Death's laughter was the last thing Jane heard before David lifted her into his arms and carried her out of the room.

Jane watched Natalie playing with a little girl. They seemed to be the same age, and War had assured David they'd been getting along just fine.

JANIE MARIE

Her sad heart squeezed as her eyes drifted to where Nathan sat alone. He was playing, but none of the fifty or so kids were coming near him. She wiped a tear quickly and smiled at David as he spoke to his sister across the room. Jane wasn't ready to deal with family drama, so she'd told him to go over without her. She knew Guinevere still held strong feelings about her relationships with Death and Lucifer, and David's recent instability was likely the result in Guinevere's mind.

Tingles slid over her cheek as Death's presence engulfed the room.

"I thought we were meeting in your room." He sat beside her.

"I feel bad for not being with my kids, and I don't want others to act as parents because I'm parading around with multiple men."

Death sighed, putting his arm over her shoulder. "If you were parading around in the sense you and these dumb fucks are implying, I would not yearn to have you as I do."

Jane glanced at David, but he didn't look up.

"He can't hear us," Death said as he twirled a lock of her hair. "I only meant you shouldn't listen to other people who don't know what the fuck we do."

She shrugged. "It's easy to say that. But, even if I can ignore it, David, you, my children, and the knights are affected. And it seems the war may depend on whether I fucked you and Lucifer." Jane watched David as he continuously darted his eyes over to Nathan. She almost felt his anxiousness matching hers, fearing Nathan was lonely or hurt.

"It is human nature to concern yourself with others," Death said quietly. "You are not the one responsible for each of these immortals disobeying God's law. Your presence impacts the war, but you are not responsible for their sins. They will remain damned until they accept their wrongdoings and ask for forgiveness. Genuinely."

"Still," she said, "I have to think about crawling on your lap or yelling at some bitch like you're my boyfriend. I can't even imagine what Guinevere heard already. Let alone you and David talking about me like I'm a fucking whore you no longer want to share."

"You're not mine or David's whore."

She kept her eyes on Nathan and fought whimpering when a ball rolled his way. He picked up the ball and smiled at the boy, but the little boy snatched the ball before running away, laughing. Nathan watched him for a few seconds before looking back at his dinosaurs. She had no idea if he was sad, but she was, so she covered her sob when David stood and walked past all the little boys who stared at him in awe to sit with her son. He smiled at

236

Nathan, giving him a little pat on the back as he spoke to him. Nathan handed him a dinosaur, and David joined in as the other boys watched with their mouths hanging open.

"Nathan is not sad if that is what you worry over," Death said, pulling her closer.

Jane wiped another tear. She felt so out of control.

Death caressed her arm. "Your son is not sad when he is left out. He is confused when he sees other children playing without him, but he has no interest in their games. He is content to play in his own way, and he believes any child who does talk to him is his friend. He does not differentiate acquaintances from true friends."

"Do you mean just now or all the time?" She smiled as David laughed when Nathan corrected him on a dinosaur's diet. He'd tried to feed a carnivore a toy tree.

"I mean all the time," Death said. "I've sat beside you many times, and I've watched you worry over him. He is fine."

She nodded, calming a little. "It would still be great to see him with real friends."

"He has the Knights of the Round Table doting on his every need, Jane."

"It's not the same."

"Would you rather he have children who do not care to be around him?"

"No. I just think it would benefit him to have at least one true friend."

"I am sure the right friend will come along one day. Until then, he has an adoptive father who is causing every little bastard watching to be filled with jealousy at the attention he is receiving."

She laughed sadly as she continued watching David give all his focus to Nathan. "He's really good with him—with both of them." Then she almost cried as War walked up to Nathan and dropped various dinosaurs on the ground before sitting beside David, laughing loudly as Nathan took a toy David had grabbed.

Death chuckled. "My brother does not get to witness mankind in these peaceful moments. He has been curious for most of his existence. He often approached me when I needed to reap children. Just curious to see a human not yet corrupted by humanity's hate. Nathan is most intriguing to immortals like us. He is pure in ways even other children are not."

Jane glanced at the shocked children staring at Nathan in the center of two of the most powerful immortals they had ever seen.

"I think War likes Natalie," she said softly.

"He is drawn to them because of you. Your blood runs through their veins, and your heart is split among them. You call to us. Well, to me, which extends to my brothers."

"So it's just me that he is being kind for?" She frowned, watching War stand several dinosaurs up for Nathan as he seemed to be preparing the carnivores to fight. "Is he making a dinosaur war?"

"War is not doing it simply because of you," Death said. "He is drawn to them over others here. He sensed I would upset you earlier, and he is giving me the opportunity to do right by you." He kissed her head. "And, yes, he is preparing to pit a smaller army of Tyrannosaurus dinosaurs against the other carnivores. He favors the dinosaur king, apparently."

Jane chuckled, leaning her head against his side. "You are trying to do right by me?"

Sadness flickered over Death's face, and he looked much younger when his gaze fell on her. "It is probably best to discuss this privately."

She swallowed. "If it's about the fairy queen, I shouldn't have said anything. I can't watch it, though. I know you've been with other women, even with me in your life, but I felt like I would die if you went off with her."

"I know."

Her eyes stung. "Were you trying to hurt me?"

"Yes."

Jane's lungs seemed to freeze, and she tore her eyes from his to stare at a spot on the floor.

"I did not call her to me," he added. "She approached me on her own—but I did not push her away as I normally would have done in your presence. I needed to know what you felt watching me with another as I have to watch and feel you with David."

"I'm not with David to hurt you."

"I know." He exhaled as he rubbed her arm. "I am happy for you. He's a good man, and he loves you the way a man should love a woman. I know he will always do his best to treat you right, make you happy, and help you have the family you desire for your children. I have no objection to him. I can even tolerate you kissing him in front of me, but I have limits. I need breaks. With our bond and your current condition, I am overwhelmed with emotions I have never felt before. My desire to be with you physically is too great. I said I could control it, but I am slipping. I feel possessive when I should not. I want to do things to you I should not, given my acceptance of your relationship with David, and I want to hurt you for making me stand by to watch you with him. I want to make you feel what I feel every damn time you think of how great he is."

Jane couldn't stop her tears and didn't bother wiping them away. She merely watched as they collected on her lap.

"There are things you do not know of. Things that will destroy your heart if you ever find out, and I do not know how to cope. My urge to protect you is above any concern in the universe, and to watch my only desire love another is difficult. Before I could simply leave your side, satisfy the urges I have for you with another, and return to you to watch another man have my—" He sighed. "Thanatos and David are right, is all I'm getting at. I must sever our bond."

If Jane had ever been unlucky enough to experience a breakup, the excruciating agony she suddenly felt topped all heartbreaks.

Death rubbed his chest and turned his face away. "I will break your heart more if I do not, angel."

Her lips parted as she tried to find her voice, but she couldn't even figure out what to say.

David made eye contact with her, and she knew by his worried expression that she must look as pathetic and broken as she felt. War stopped him from standing, muttering something she didn't even care to ponder over.

"I don't want to," he added quietly. "But I fear my current state and yours will result in damage neither of us would be able to repair. I could kill David or injure him so he would never be the same. I could take you by force without once caring about the pain it would cause you after I satisfy my urges. This is not normal for us, which is why I am suggesting we break our bond."

Finally, Jane found the ability to speak. "Is this so you can go fuck whoever you want without feeling guilty? So you don't have to feel my pain?"

"Partly," he said without hesitation. "It is not the same for me as it is for other men. I feel nothing but release from the possibility that I might transform into destruction regardless of the consequences."

"That's such a pathetic response." She didn't look at him. "I very much doubt God added fuck allowances to your list of acceptable activities."

"Angels are not given desires. We develop them, and it often results in falling from Heaven. I cannot fall because I am neutral. The reason for my desire is not one I can share with you."

"Of course not." She smiled sadly at David. He looked so worried about whatever War was telling him.

"You chose David, Jane." Death raised his arm off her shoulders but took her hand. She sobbed at the tingles that darted up her arm. "This is our magic, and it is destroying both of us. We will destroy everything if we do not stop the pain building between us."

"I thought you chose me, too," she whimpered.

"I did. I choose you every second of my existence, and I choose to let you live with the man you gave your heart to. To do that, I cannot continue to subject myself to your lovemaking and emotions for both of our sakes. Do you realize I can feel your desire for him—that I basically feel your ecstasy when he touches you and brings you to an orgasm? I want to give you that. I want to consume you in a way even he cannot. I want to steal you from everyone you love and possess your entire being. Fuck, I even desire to impregnate you simply because I would have you in yet another way. It would not be the way David desires a child with you. I wouldn't give a fuck about a child we make, but I would do it simply to have the knowledge I touched you, tied you to me in another way that could not be broken."

"I can't lose you." She covered her eyes as David continued watching her. "No . . ."

"Jane, we have—"

She shook her head and lowered her hand to stare at David. *Home.* "Do what has to be done. I choose him." She wiped her tears, and even though she felt the light in her dying, she smiled at her vampire. "I choose David and to let you go."

18

BLOOD & HEAVEN

David squeezed her hand. "Baby, you don't have to do this."

"Yes, I do." She did. She had to do something. She had to protect Death and prove to David and herself that he was above all others. No matter how badly it hurt Death or her, she had to remain faithful to David and put him first.

But David seemed to be having the most negative reaction. He glared at Death for probably the twentieth time since they'd made it back to their room. "Can't you ride this out for a few days? You told me you could control your desire for her."

"I lied," Death said dryly. "Do you know I came and put her to sleep while you showered?"

"What?" David glanced at her.

"Don't get upset with her—she thought it was a dream, so she didn't say anything," Death said, waving his hand. "My point is I felt her lust building because of her feelings for you—that is nothing new. But I felt her desire to be claimed. Just as you do, she has instincts trying to take over. Her hormones went through the roof, and I felt them like they were my own."

"You wanted me to claim you?" David frowned.

"Seriously?" Death shook his head. "No, dumb fuck. I wanted to fuck her brains out."

David's eyes paled before almost turning black.

Death smirked. "Imagine if I were a weaker angel . . . I would have

241

killed you, fucked her, and then taken her to my realm, never to be seen again. Do you want to chance any of those outcomes? I assure you, I tried to get far away. Distance is no longer affecting my bond with her, though. I feel her as though she is a part of me. I hear her, smell her, taste her. This is the only way to keep from destroying her. Even if you were fine with me partaking in such a desire, I would slaughter everyone because of the pain she would feel afterward. I'm dramatic, I know. That is also the issue—I am feeling more than I should because of her heightened emotions and our strengthening bond."

Jane smiled sadly. "You realize you're calling me dramatic."

Death winked. "I love your dramatics. You get all sweaty and like to be touched."

David shot Death a dirty look. "There has to be another way, though."

"There isn't." Death stared at her. "Angel, I don't know what else to do. I'm not stable, and I fear what will happen between us when David leaves tomorrow. I refuse to leave you alone, but you will be in a delicate condition—one I will have the urge to satisfy. I may not fight it if we allow our bond to grow more than it already has."

Thanatos pushed off the wall. "It's for the best, my queen."

Jane nodded. "I know."

David looked between them. "You said it will hurt."

Thanatos folded his arms. "I am merely speculating—I've never seen it done."

"Have you?" she asked Death.

"No."

Jane stared at him, confused. "Then how do you know it will hurt?"

"Because, angel, bonds like ours are never meant to be broken. This is not the link I created when you were a girl."

"But you can't tell me where this bond came from," she guessed.

"Correct." He sat on the bed beside her. "I want nothing more than to tell you the truth, but it will cause too much damage."

David stared between her and Death before looking away. "I don't want you to sever your bond. We can think of something else to make sure you both get along without hurting one another." He stared at Death. "Don't do this to her. She loves you. You love her. I know you would stop yourself before hurting her."

"I'm not you." Death chuckled. "Father made sure of that."

A heartbroken look flashed across David's face. "Then he also made you bond with her this way. Don't go against it."

"Be careful what you say, Prince." Death's eyes glowed brightly. "I may change my mind and do something I shouldn't."

Jane turned to Death and grabbed his hands. "I love you. I won't stop. Ever." Her eyes watered as her world felt like it was about to end. "But I choose him. So sever the bond to keep us from destroying my choice."

"Baby," David said, but she shook her head.

"If I betray you, I might as well stab myself in the heart. Don't make me risk it. Because I'm not sure I'd be able to tell him no while you're gone. Not with the way I feel inside. My body is on fire, and I won't be able to stop myself if so much as an accidental slip happens. And if he feels it, too, we are in trouble. He's just being honest. I'm being honest. I can't betray you again."

"No, my love, you will be able to tell him no. I know you. I believe in you, and you are showing me right now how much I mean to you. Don't torture yourself for my sake. And Death will always do what is necessary to keep you safe and happy."

"That's why I am doing this," Death said. "You make her happy. She is safe with you, and you are giving her the life she wants—the life I've always wanted for her. This is the only way. I want to make love to her right now, and I am imagining a hundred different ways to do it with or without you present. I know exactly how I would kill you so she wouldn't see, and I have plans on how to keep her. I even know what to tell her—what to do to her —that would make her mine alone."

"You could keep that shit to yourself," David growled.

Death chuckled. "I'm just telling you the truth so you understand what's at stake. No one will be able to stop me. Not even her. I love her, so I am forfeiting what I might as well have never been given."

"Don't say that." She smiled sadly at Death as he caressed her cheek. She turned her face toward his palm. "Don't dismiss our past. Will the tingles go away?"

"I think so, angel."

His beautiful face became a blur as she whimpered. "And our mental conversations? It all goes away? Nothing?"

He held her chin and rubbed his thumb over her trembling lips. "Yes. It all goes away. I believe I can keep the Horsemen's Bond intact because you properly bonded with War, but that doesn't connect us beyond summoning your gifts from us and sensing you more clearly than a normal soul."

"When was this bond made?" She searched his eyes, looking for any clues. "Is it what you made when I had my birthday? Or was it when I got attacked by the wolves the first time?"

"No." He dropped his gaze. "Don't dwell on it. The truth is destroying me, and it will do the same to you should you find out."

She pressed her lips together when she choked out another cry. "Will you still love me?"

"I will never stop loving you." He leaned forward and kissed her softly. "It's okay. It's going to be okay."

"Death," David said, pacing the room. "Don't do this. She's already fading. I see it. I see it in both of you. Separating like this cannot be the solution. You promised to be strong for her—be the fucking Angel of Death."

Death closed his eyes as he rested his forehead on hers. "She wants a life with you. I will stop her from having it if I give in, and I will give in."

"Not if you think of her," David retorted. "I know you do everything for her—remember that when you are close to doing something that would hurt her."

"I'm too weak," Death said quietly. "She knows I am not the same. Even with the part of my soul that was with Lucifer returned, I'm growing weaker. If given a chance, I will give in to her. And because she chooses you, she will never consent, but I'm afraid that won't stop me."

Jane touched his cheek. "Will you get stronger without me? Whatever has been happening—will this fix it?"

He opened his eyes. "I think so."

"How do we sever the bond, then?" She pretended David and Thanatos weren't even there.

The smile that even beat David's spread over Death's lips. "The Kiss of Death, babe."

She grinned even though she felt them slipping apart. "Is that really how you do it?"

He pulled her onto his lap so that she straddled him before he copied how she held his cheek. "I 'do it' with a lot of thrusting—some growling, lots of biting and licking—definitely groping—but if you're only speaking about the bond, yes, just a kiss. I have to use tongue, though."

"Pervert," she said, sniffling as a quiet whimper slipped past her lips.

"I'll still love you," he said. "We will just be—less."

She tried not to let it show how much that little word devastated her, but her burning eyes welled up with tears, and her entire body tensed so painfully she thought she would shatter.

"*Shh* . . ." He rubbed his thumb over her cheek. "I know, angel. It's hurting me, too."

"Will you still find me?" She felt frantic but tried her very best to stay strong. It was time to let him go.

His expression crumpled, but he nodded. "Always, Sweet Jane. It may just take me a while now."

"Death," David said, but Jane held her hand up.

"It has to be this way," she whispered. "Thank you for not asking me to do this."

"You don't have to," David said. "We can figure something out. You can come with me, and he can stay here. Or I can stay. Something."

"*He really loves you,*" Death whispered to her mind.

Her tears finally broke free. *He does. I love him.*

"*I know.*"

I don't want to lose you.

"*You won't.*"

She nodded, staring into his eyes as if she wouldn't see them again. *I love you.*

"*And I love you.*"

David growled. "Death, you don't have to do this."

Death smirked as his eyes began to glow. "Just take care of her, Prince. Now let me make out with my girl in peace." Then he pressed his lips to hers.

Jane didn't hesitate to meet his kiss. She knew everything would change. This would be the last moment of *them*. It didn't matter that he would still be beside her when this kiss ended. What mattered was they would never be the same. They'd never be tied together in a way she believed they were meant to be.

"*Shh . . . It's going to be okay,*" he whispered to her mind as his tongue touched hers.

He kept it tender, guiding her slowly, but she already knew to follow him. Following him was instant—almost instinct. Her heartbeat sped up as her fear of losing him took over. He would go somewhere, and there would no longer be that thread connecting them.

"Shh, baby girl."

She gripped his hair, wrapping her arms around his neck as she hugged herself closer to him. If she held on, maybe they'd still feel something. Anything. This wasn't right. *Don't!*

"It's okay," he murmured against her lips before kissing her again. "Breathe with me one more time."

Jane saw her soul screaming and released a heart-wrenching gasp as her body shook.

He held her tighter, sliding a hand down her back. "Feel me one more time," he whispered, opening his eyes to stare into hers. "Never forget this. Us. We are magic and beauty. We are Heaven."

"Death," she whimpered.

"Smile for me. Show me everything, and you will see me. Show me so I never lose this part of us. Keep me." He waited, still keeping his lips just a breadth away from hers.

It hurt. It hurt so badly, but she smiled as she held his cheek.

Death smiled against her mouth. "That's my girl. Now live for me, Sweet Jane."

The tingles teasing her lips bloomed across her entire body, and she sighed against his smile before he deepened their kiss. Every sound except for their heartbeats and breathing slipped away. Everything faded, and it was only them. The thought of that being exactly what they were meant to be surfaced, but Death tugged her to him and flexed his fingers on the back of her neck as if he were making sure she didn't move.

Warmth, ice, fire, liquid—breath—sparks, and sweet tingles—swirled around them. She could feel him everywhere. The best part was when his presence touched that little spot near her heart—below it and to the side. It was home there, and she wanted him to stay. Those tingles finally kissed her heart as her entire being filled with that beautiful warmth she could only describe as Death.

He grunted and squeezed her as his body tensed up. *"I'm sorry."*

A deep stabbing sensation pierced her heart.

Jane gasped and tried to jerk away, but the searing pain grew too intense. "Ow," she cried, but Death held her to him.

He let out a strained growl as his weakened voice caressed her mind. *"It's almost over, my love."*

Her hot tears burned as they slid over their lips. *No, Death.*

"I love you, angel. Don't forget me."

DEATH! Her throat was being crushed. She couldn't breathe.

"Don't let me forget us."

She sobbed, gasping as a slicing motion cut between her heart and the spot that was his. *No! Death, don't leave me!*

"I won't, baby girl. I love you."

Then he was gone. That cruel blade was forced between them, severing the beautiful glowing thread that held them together. The harsh metal licked at her wound, grinning wickedly at the sight of the throbbing cut as it sizzled and bled.

She screamed, weak and trembling, and Death reached up to hold her face, cradling her cheeks like a delicate piece of glass.

"Come back," she cried, squeezing her eyes shut as the most unbearable loneliness seeped through her. Her soul fell to her knees, shocked, with her mouth open as her cries never found the strength to leave her lips.

"I'm still here," he whispered. His lips brushed hers, but there were no tingles. No magic. No him.

Jane sobbed, clutching his jacket as he wiped away her tears. She cried louder. It was all gone. They were gone. "Gone." She took panicked breaths as she searched everywhere inside herself for him. "Come back." She breathed faster and faster, searching, falling, and bleeding. "Come back." She gasped—she had to be dying. The pain. It wouldn't stop, and she couldn't find him. She needed him. "Come back!" Her body was wracked with sobs as she tried to open her eyes.

He made an anguished noise before pressing a soft kiss to her lips. "I'm here. I haven't left. It's okay." His deep voice soothed her for only a moment but slipped away as his voice faded.

"Jane," he murmured. "Open your eyes. Look at me."

Somehow, she managed to open her eyes. They burned, but those emerald jewels silenced the scream she was about to release. "Come back." That was the only thing that made sense. Nothing else mattered. She didn't exist anymore.

"Listen to me," he said, his voice growing rougher. "I'm holding you."

Her lip trembled as she shook her head. "They're gone." She meant the tingles. She meant him.

"I know." He kissed her again.

Like an inconsolable little girl, she stared at his beautiful face, clinging to him as sobs that should never be heard tore out of her mouth. She couldn't stop. He was right in front of her, but he was gone.

"Death." It was David, and he sounded broken. "Please."

She couldn't look for him. She wasn't there. She couldn't see.

Death smiled at her as he smoothed her hair back. "My Sweet Jane."

Gasping, she reached up for his face. If she touched his smile, she would see. Feel. Live.

He guided her hand to his lips as painful, shuddering cries continued to crack open her empty chest.

His eyes glowed when her fingers slid across his smile, lighting up his face. The face she always saw in her dreams. The face that came to her in the dark. The face she needed to see to live and breathe. "Death," she whimpered. "You're him."

His smile stretched wider. "I am."

Him. She knew deep down what she was trying to say but couldn't grasp it yet.

"Jane," David called. She turned her head, locking eyes with him. He tried to smile, but it never fully formed. "What can I do?"

"Hurts." She didn't know why she couldn't respond properly. "Gone."

"I know, baby." He lowered his head to his hands.

Her mouth was still slightly open as she searched for Death. Only when he moved did she remember he held her, and she looked toward him again and took a deep breath. "Death."

"She may be confused for a while. What he did isn't something that should ever be done."

Jane turned toward the voice. Thanatos.

David lowered his hands with a growl. "Then why the fuck did you all suggest it?"

Jane touched the empty spot, just below her heart and to the side. She expected to find a hole. Blood.

Death grabbed her hand. "It's okay."

Again, she stirred at the sound of his voice. She didn't know why he kept leaving. "Death."

David sighed and walked to sit beside them. He made eye contact with her before he looked where she had been searching. "Baby, he's right here. We're all right here."

"Gone."

"It's shock." Death squeezed her hand. She felt a spurt of warmth, but it left quickly. "Just give her a few minutes."

"What is going to happen after that?" David asked before reaching for her other hand. "Can you feel me?"

Heat. It wasn't quite what she remembered, but she knew he was her vampire. "Hot. David."

He smiled and leaned forward to kiss her hand. "That's right. Don't worry—I'm not leaving, and I swear Death is right here, okay?"

She lowered her head, looking at that same spot, waiting for blood to gush or smoke from her burning flesh.

"Is she hallucinating?" David asked quietly.

"I don't know," Death responded. "I don't feel—"

"Blood," she said, still waiting for it. "Where's the blood?"

"Are you thirsty?" David asked.

She lifted her gaze to him. "I'm bleeding. Where's the blood?"

David stared at her quietly, then whispered, "You feel like you've been cut?"

Jane pulled her hand from his and began searching for her wound. "I'm bleeding. He's gone."

David didn't say anything to whoever held her as he lifted her. He cupped her cheek before giving her a quick kiss and then covered her wound with his hand. "I've got it, okay? I'll help it."

She stared at his hands. He was shaking. There was no blood. There should be blood.

"Death, perhaps you should go to your realm, harvest as you rest for a while," Thanatos said.

"Death's gone." Jane looked at Thanatos. "I can't find him."

"He'll find you, my queen." Thanatos bowed his head before turning away.

David rocked her. The motion reminded her of Death, and she smiled.

"I don't think this is normal." David kissed her head. "Death, are you coherent?"

"Yes."

Jane looked toward his voice. "Death? You came back." She didn't see him clearly until two emerald eyes met hers. She smiled, stuck in that moment of just him and her as they watched each other.

David ran his fingers through her hair, distracting her a little, but she had found Death. He could come back now.

"Death," David said, "put it back for her."

"Give it time, Sir David," Thanatos said as a door opened.

Jane kept staring at Death. He was silent, and she didn't feel him like she should, but he was there.

"Well, this did not go well." It was War, but Jane kept her stare focused on Death.

"She's not right," David said, still caressing her. "He is off, too."

"She softened him and, well—" War said, walking toward Death. "Brother?"

Death blinked, breaking the connection he'd had with her.

She panicked, reaching out for him as he looked away. "Come back," she screamed, gasping as she looked for him.

David held her as Death grabbed his head. War observed her as she searched for Death. She looked at her wound. Where was her wound? Where was the blood?

"I think they are merely disoriented." War grabbed her chin and forced her face upward. "Oh, I see."

"What is it?" David asked, turning her face toward his. He quieted and stared at her, heartbroken. "What does this mean? I saw—"

Thanatos approached, sighing as he stared at her face for a few moments. "Excuse me." He vanished.

David watched her cry again. "It's okay, my love. We're going to fix this."

She didn't know what *this* was. "Gone."

"That's all she says," David muttered. "And for him to come back."

Jane touched her sternum, feeling around for the hole.

"She thinks she's been cut or something," David added, pressing his hand over her wound. "She's searching for it. I saw—"

"I would imagine it feels like someone cut her open and ripped out—" War turned toward Death. "Brother, what does she need?"

"Me," he whispered.

Jane lifted her head again.

"Restore the fucking bond then," David said, anger thick in his words. "I told you to wait."

"He can't restore it," War said. "Not on his own. He wasn't the one who put it there."

"Who did?" David asked, holding her as she sobbed into his chest.

War sighed. "I've said too much. Strip her down."

"What?" David wrapped his arms around her.

"Strip her down. She needs to feel him. When they touch, neither one is really aware. The magic of what they are is gone. They will remain in this confused, deteriorating state until they accept their new fate."

"And stripping her does what exactly?"

War chuckled. "He was right when he said she would feel him. Let her feel him. You have no idea what they have just done to each other."

"I think I do," David muttered, grabbing her shirt. "Baby, I'm going to take off your shirt and pants. If you summon the suit Death gave you, you'll find each other a little easier." He glanced at War. "Right?"

"He will find her. Just give him time." War patted Death's shoulder. "Brother, are you still you?"

Death shoved him away. "Close your eyes if she is undressing."

War chuckled and turned his back to them. "He's aware enough. Hurry, Sir David. I have news to deliver as well."

Jane stared up at David. She didn't feel him the way she knew she should.

"Stand for just a moment, Jane," he said, reaching for her pants.

"Death?" She looked around, touching where the hole should be.

A hand grabbed hers. It was big and strong, but she didn't recognize it. "I'm here."

Death. It was Death!

David sighed, standing after he got her pants off, and gently forced her to look at him instead of the green eyes. "Jane, I'm going to take your top off. Summon your suit once I do."

"Yes. He'll come back then." She nodded, clutching her injury.

David glanced at her hands and rubbed them. "This will help, okay?" He lifted her shirt off and smiled. "Summon it now."

Jane stared at her naked arms, but she could only focus on the pain and wonder where the blood had gone.

"Sweet Jane." Death stood and caressed her cheek.

"Death," she whispered, tilting her face toward his hand.

"Summon the suit I gave you, angel. You may feel me more."

"I can't."

"You can," he said softly. "Listen to my voice and think of me—then envision yourself wearing the suit."

Jane felt the fabric over her naked body and sighed upon feeling a faint tingling sensation swimming over every inch of skin. "Death," she whispered, focusing on him.

He smiled. "The one and only, babe."

War turned around. "Ah, there's a little spark. This is good."

David turned her face toward his and smiled. "Hi, baby."

"David," she said, touching his smile.

He kissed her fingers before pushing her mask down. "How do you feel now?"

She stared down, her eyes going to the wound she knew was there. "I feel."

Death sat down, patting the spot next to him. "You need to rest, Jane."

She sat as she stared around the room. The pain wasn't so present, but then again, it was. She lifted her hand to see how much blood was coming out and frowned when she saw a clean glove.

David sat on the other side of her. "Maybe you should rest together. Just for a while."

War chuckled. "Just because he removed their bond does not mean he is not a man anymore."

"I thought the whole point was to keep him in control." David held her hand.

"Does he look in control yet?" War leaned against the wall. "Brother?"

Death snarled. "I just can't feel her."

She grabbed his hand and was surprised when he lifted her onto his lap. He pressed his lips to her forehead and sighed.

David stood, pacing again.

"You could enjoy a three-way." War laughed when Death and David growled.

"How long are they going to be this way?" David asked. "I leave in less than twenty-four hours."

War shrugged. "He could go kill something to blow off some steam, but it will further distance them. If they stay like this, they will be calmer, but then they may grow dependent on each other. It's different than before. They feel lost inside themselves, and she seems to believe he is truly gone at times."

Jane heard them, but she tried to focus on Death. He was back. He was holding her. *Don't leave me.*

"She's tired." Death kissed her head. "I will rest with her. I cannot leave in my condition just yet, and I want her to be stable before I try to go."

"Okay," David said.

Death pulled the blanket back and gestured for her to lie down. "I will rest with you." He stood, walked to the far side, and lay on his back.

She crawled to him just like she had when she was growing up. He held out his arm, and she curled up, resting her head and hand over his heart.

War leaned over and touched her forehead as he said something to Death in a different language.

Death put his hand over hers as he replied in the same language.

The Red Horseman sighed. "Jane, if you need me, scream for me in your mind as loud as you can."

She peered over her shoulder. "Are you leaving?"

He nodded. "It's time for me to move on. We will see each other again, Horsemen Bringer." He kissed her head and turned to David. "He is in enough control, but you should stay close for the night. If anything, let her fall asleep and give him a chance to recoup alone."

David shook War's hand. "Thank you."

"Try not to worry over her while you are gone. You have your duty—all of us do."

War gave a nod toward Death, then vanished.

"She's going to sleep soon," Death muttered, caressing her hair. "Get behind her and rest. She needs us both, but I will leave again."

"Will you come back before I leave tomorrow?" David asked, rubbing her back when she whimpered.

"Yes. I need to sort some things out, but I will be here. Rest now. You both need rest."

"Death," she whispered, lifting her head. "Don't go."

He peeked down at her. "I'll wait until you fall asleep, babe. Your vampire is with you—he will keep you together. You will feel better after you rest. I promise."

David sat beside her, still rubbing her back. The heat was soothing, and she sighed, happy she finally felt it seeping in.

"You know this is one of her fantasies." Death chuckled. "She calls it the J & Ds sandwich."

David laughed, sliding down to hold her better. "I think we can allow her to have this fantasy."

"Kinky," Death said, but he didn't sound as playful as usual. "You realize she imagined both of us naked, don't you?"

Jane's eyelids became impossible to keep open, but she felt the bed shift and what felt like David hitting Death.

"Just fucking cuddle with her," David growled. "Be thankful I'm in better control than I expected to be because I think I know what you did to her. I won't lose her. Give her this."

Death sighed and rolled onto his side so he faced her. He caressed her cheek. "Look at me, Jane."

"Death," she whispered.

He stared into her eyes and smiled sadly. "This is why he is the better man, angel."

David nuzzled her hair. "We love you. I know you're trying to prove I am your choice, and you have." He leaned forward, whispering in her ear, "And I choose to share you with your angel. As long as we keep our lovemaking to just us."

Death chuckled. "And I was about to snap my fingers and lose my clothes."

David flipped him off. "Don't get greedy or out of control, but I want you to be close to her."

She touched the center of her chest. "Gone."

Death put his hand over hers. "I will find you—I'll come back. I promise. David—"

"You deserve to kiss her whenever you like. I'll touch her for both of us. Just put her to sleep or leave before we get too carried away." David moved her hair away from her neck. "And be back before I leave. With a level head."

"Thank you." Death leaned forward and kissed her softly as David pressed his lips to her neck.

At that moment, Jane saw her sad soul glow in utter darkness, and a sad smile spread over her soul's lips as both of her men continued kissing her.

No one spoke. Death caressed her cheek and hair as David kissed, sucked, nipped her neck and shoulders, and touched her everywhere. His heat seeped through her suit, allowing her to feel both of them, and somehow, those faint tingles came alive under David's touch.

She and Death gasped when David moved his hand over her heart and bit into her neck.

"Heaven," they whispered together as David sucked her blood.

In her mind, a faint gold thread shimmered into existence and surrounded them.

"Next time," Death whispered as if he knew what she was seeing.

Jane covered David's hand but pulled Death's with hers, all over her heart as David continued to drink and Death continued to kiss her.

David withdrew his fangs. "This is what we are meant to be, my love. One day, you will be whole again, and I will make sure you have us with you when you are." He turned her lips toward him and captured them with his.

Death kissed across her cheek and whispered into her ear. "I love you."

"I love you," she gasped against David's mouth.

Death removed his hand from hers and David's, but he pulled a box from his pocket and handed it to David. "Be careful."

David eyed him but nodded and allowed her to turn back to Death.

He smiled, cupping her cheek. "I'll see you tomorrow. Good night, my moon."

She felt panicked, but he pressed a long kiss to her lips, and when he pulled away, he was gone. "Death?"

David hugged her tightly. "He needs time, my love."

She trembled, touching her wound. "I'm empty."

Her vampire leaned down and kissed it as he moved over her. "You're just missing. I promise you will glow again. You'll be whole again. I swear it."

The empty feeling began to spread. "Please touch me. I don't feel."

He glanced at the box Death had tossed him: condoms. "It might be his way of saying this is how you can feel. It's up to you, Jane."

Jane ordered her suit away and welcomed her prince as he held on to what was left of her, cherishing and worshiping her as though she were still whole.

19

BEYOND FOREVER

Jane raised her hand, inspecting her fingers for blood. Nothing. Her mind had already accepted nothing had happened, but she'd been cut none-theless by a wicked blade, more devastating than any weapon forged by Heaven or Hell.

What that blade had cut out wasn't exactly clear, but she had been gutted. She was empty.

David's hand on her stomach startled her.

She jumped, gripping his hand and turning her head toward him.

"It's okay," he murmured, curling his fingers around hers as he kissed her shoulder. He was behind her, slowly pulling their naked bodies together. "Relax, sweetheart. It's me."

She nodded, trying to unclench in his hold, but it felt like she was with a stranger. All the heat was gone. There was no fire. It had gone out some-time during the night. She felt him, yet she didn't.

David kissed her shoulder, and she whimpered because she only felt the slight pressure of his lips on her skin.

"Do you remember who I am, Jane?"

A pang resonated through her chest. "Yes."

"Why do you seem afraid of me, then?" He moved away a bit. "Do you feel like I took advantage of you?"

"No." She peered over her shoulder. "No, I knew who you were. You just feel different. Like you are a stranger."

He rolled onto his back and dragged both hands down his face. "You need him."

Instinctively, she touched her wound.

"Baby, there's nothing there."

She trembled as she stared at her clean hand. "I know. That's the problem."

"Oh, baby." He rolled onto his side again. "He'll be here in a few hours, okay? We can talk with him and find out how to help the pain."

"Okay." She peeked at her fingers again. Nothing.

David kissed her hair. "Summon your suit. Maybe it will feel like he is with you again. I'll hold you."

Jane imagined Death's eyes and his smile before finally seeing his face. The fabric of the suit shifted over her skin, and she gasped as David pressed down on the spot where she'd been ripped open.

"Does this hurt?" he asked, sliding his hand back and forth.

Faint sparks erupted under his touch, and she smiled when tingles bloomed. They quickly faded, but she kept her smile in place for him.

David gently pushed her onto her back and smiled down at her. "That feels better?"

She nodded, reaching up and touching his lips. A surge of heat seeped into her fingers. "My David."

He kissed her hand, but his heat had already cooled. "I'll help you find each other again, my love. Just stay with me."

"Beyond forever," she whispered.

David glanced up from lacing his boots and watched Jane touch the same spot—below her heart and to the side. Just like she'd done throughout the night, she checked her fingers, expecting to find blood. Only, there wasn't any. There never was. It was all in her head, but that was worse than if it had been an actual injury.

He sighed, tugging his pants into place before walking toward her. She was too consumed trying to find her non-existent cut to notice him.

"Jane?" he called, pushing her hair back.

She lifted her head. "Is he back yet?"

"No, baby." He caressed her cheek, trying to ignore that the pull she usually emitted was absent. A lot had gone missing in the night, and he had no idea how to find and return what she'd lost.

"Oh," she said, lowering her gaze and hiding the dull gold eyes she had yet to see. "He's coming, though?"

"Yes, he will be here." He squatted, resting his hands on her legs. "I can stay with you."

"I don't want to deal with any drama from Thor or the others who think I'm here to steal the army. If everyone sees you babying me, I'll be blamed for all the lives lost when you don't fight."

"I don't care about what others think."

"I do," she snapped.

David sighed as he rubbed her thighs. His baby was always all or nothing. Her inability to find a happy medium meant she usually chose to let go of greatness.

"I'm sorry," she muttered. "I just don't feel like me anymore." Her trembling lips pressed together, her eyes watering. "I thought cutting our bond would be easier."

He grabbed her hand, kissing it. "Baby, I don't think our lives are meant to be easy, especially yours."

"I just wanted you both to be happy," she whimpered, wiping a tear. "Fuck. I can't do this."

He stood, lifting her into his arms. "Oh, my love." He shifted her so her legs went around his waist as she cried. She would never be the same again, and it was his fault. His throat tightened as he listened to her cry. She sounded like a broken little girl, and she was. She was his broken Jane, and he couldn't fix her. She had come so far—was on her way to becoming the greatest warrior there ever was—but she went and tore herself up —for him.

Knock, knock.

David knew who was there. "Come in."

"Sir David." Thanatos bowed. "My queen."

"Do you know where he is?" David asked, not putting Jane down.

"He should return soon. If he does not, I will stay with her."

"No." Jane lifted her head and glared at Thanatos. "You will find him and bring him here. You put this idea in his head—in my head. We did this because you said it would be for the best."

"Forgive me, my queen." He lowered his head. "My suggestion was made with your best interest in mind. I did not realize—"

David held his hand up to stop him. "Jane, he didn't mean to hurt you."

She glared at him. "No one means to." She wiggled out of his arms and marched toward the bath suite. "That's the fucking problem. Fuck all of you!" She slammed the door.

Thanatos shifted awkwardly and met his gaze as he muttered, "Female immortals are most volatile during their first cycle."

David chuckled and sat on the bed. "I know. I can handle her hormones. That isn't the problem, though. Is it?"

Thanatos eyed him quietly. "No, it isn't."

"I'm going to arrange for me to stay behind." David glanced at his bag and sword. "I don't care what the others think. She needs me."

Arthur walked into the room. "You can't stay behind."

David glared at him. "Stop reading my mind."

"Calm yourself." Arthur glanced toward the bathroom as he rubbed his chest, frowning. "David—"

David interrupted him. "I'm staying. Make the announcement. I don't care what you have to say or what the others think. I will take her to patrol the perimeter so we are still contributing."

Arthur sat beside him, staring at the door with the same lost expression Jane had been wearing as he spoke. "You can't stay, brother. Something has happened. Thor's behavior was not because he believed Jane to be evil. Well, it is, but it is unnatural."

Thanatos nodded. "Death sensed magic in the air. I suggested it might be Luc, but he felt it was someone else. Perhaps the Nephilim are not all true. They are powerful enough to conjure spells."

David stared at Arthur. He didn't care about anything but Jane. "Is she okay?"

Arthur shook his head. "Leave her be, but she is not okay, brother. I have nothing to suggest, either."

"Then I'm staying." He prepared to go to Jane, but Arthur spoke again.

"If you stay, the threat toward her will increase. Whatever—whoever—is influencing Thor and the others wants you separated from each other. They wanted Death separated first, though. They sought to recruit him with the fairy queen and will try again. I think, because of the attempt made by the fairy, they prefer to get Death away more than you. With Jane's cycle arriving, they likely assumed you would stay with her. Getting him away should have been easy—perhaps because he would be unstoppable, and you risk damnation if you give in to your desire. That could've been a backup plan. Jane should be near him anyway. It may help her."

Jane walked out of the bath suite, and Arthur stood, smiling sadly at her when she stopped in the middle of the room.

"Baby," David said, "I was telling Arthur I wanted to stay with you, but—"

"I heard him." She slowly turned away from Arthur so she could stare at him instead. "Why didn't you tell me my eyes are like this? How long have they been this way?"

David swallowed and went to her. "Your eyes are fine. They're as beautiful as they've always been."

She watched him with those glassy, dull gold eyes. "I want you to leave with everyone."

His heart ached. "I'll wait until Death gets back."

"I'm back." Death stepped away from a wall. His eyes never left Jane's. "Hi, baby girl."

She walked to her angel, reaching up immediately to touch his cheek, but she whimpered after she did so.

Death held her hand in place. "I'm here."

Arthur left without saying anything, and Thanatos followed, shutting the door behind himself.

"How are you feeling?" Death tilted Jane's face up.

"It would be better if you already knew." She moved to hug him. "I don't feel, yet I do."

Death cradled her head as he met David's stare. "It will get easier."

"Should I stay?" David asked him.

Death shook his head. "Draw out who seeks to destroy her. If I discover their identity while you are away, I will take care of them."

Jane looked up. "Might as well let them destroy me. I'm still fucking everything up."

Death stared at her—his face seemed emptier of emotion than ever before, especially considering he was looking at Jane. "You haven't fucked anything up," Death said. "Don't say that shit ever again."

She pushed out of his arms and walked toward a dresser. "Maybe you should leave, too. Asshole."

Death glowered at her. "Calm your tits. You're just fucking hormonal."

She slammed the drawer. "Fuck you!"

"I can't," he roared. "Why don't you just stab a fucking dagger in my heart?"

Her eyes welled up with tears. "You asshole."

Death glared at her through the mirror. "I've already suffered the way you are. I'm trying to help. Just let me fucking help you."

"Death." David walked up behind Jane. "What the fuck is wrong with you? Don't talk to her that way." He rubbed her back, watching her shut her eyes as she dug her fingernails into the wood.

"Just go, David," she whispered. "I'll be fine."

"No." He wrapped his arms around her. "Look at me. Please."

Those haunted golden eyes stared at his reflection. "What?"

"Breathe, okay?" His heart ached, but he knew it was nowhere close to what she felt. "You're still with each other—I'm still here. I know it hurts, but we will fix it. Just try to be calm. You need to comfort each other, not fight because you're both hurting. And don't use me as an excuse to push him away—I'm pushing you toward him. Don't worry about me."

Her face softened. "I don't mean to be angry with you. Or him. I feel like such a jerk for snapping, but I can't control myself."

"I know." He smiled, turning her around. "You can be angry. Just remember that you love him, and he loves you. You both promised not to forget each other—so I'm reminding you. Keep the promises you made. That will make me happy."

Jane glanced at Death but didn't say anything.

Death spoke, though. "Forgive me. I haven't forgotten our love. Please try to hold on to me. I swear I will keep you safe."

David kissed her forehead before nudging her to her angel and smiling when she hugged Death, mumbling she was sorry.

Death chuckled as he ran his fingers through her hair. "Do you remember how bitchy you would get with Jason? He stood no chance against your hormones."

She smiled as she touched Jason's ring. She'd put it on a string around her neck sometime that morning. "I was so mean."

Death shrugged. "Those are hormones, babe. Now I know what they feel like. He's lucky you never knifed his ass for the shit he said."

Jane sighed, leaning against Death's chest as she rubbed her hand over his heart. "It's not the same. Both of you feel different. Even with the suit. It's fading."

"I know, angel." Death lifted her, hugging her, and David wondered how many times Death had carried her around this way.

Turning away from them, David checked his bag before going through her supplies for the children. She had a bag ready to go in case they had to flee, and he wanted to ensure she had her photo album and personal items. He felt something brush his leg and looked down at the cats rubbing against him.

"Are you hungry?" he asked them, chuckling when they both meowed.

He glanced over his shoulder and saw Death whispering to Jane as he rubbed her back. When the cats got louder, he went to find the cans of food someone had found. "All right, calm down." He put the plates down, watching as they instantly began scarfing down the minced meat.

"Jason didn't feed them until he thought I had died."

David shrugged and went to clean the litter box. "And I think he regretted not helping you take care of them. I'm not Jason, my love. And I promised him I would not make the mistakes he did."

"I'm not changing that shit box," Death said.

David chuckled as he tied the bag up. "If you want to help her, you will. And don't forget they are the only kitties you get for the next few days."

Death's eyes flashed as Jane tensed.

"I trust you both." David wished he had kept his mouth shut. "I will say this now, though. I don't mind you holding each other as you need to, and I don't mind the occasional comforting kisses, but I don't want her condition to be an excuse to do more. You both chose to do what you did so you would not hurt me or each other that way. Remember that while I am gone. Remember others will try to upset you by making remarks about your closeness. I am fine with it, but I don't want you doing more than what I've said." He hesitated, watching Death. The angel looked frozen, but David went on after focusing on Jane again. "What we did last night—between the three of us—was ours. I swear we will have more moments like that. But we do it together."

"Do we call him Daddy now?" Death whispered to her. "Next time, if I can squeeze her ass without you throwing a fit, I'll let you grab mine."

David flipped him off. "Her ass prefers me. And, no, you do not call me Daddy. Nor do I desire to grab your ass. What the fuck is wrong with you?"

"Don't start the ass talk again. And no one is saying Daddy in a perverted way. Gross," Jane said, smiling at last.

"What about Papi?" Death grinned down at her.

She laughed. "No."

"Ay, Papi!" Death snickered, pinching her side.

"Stop." She giggled but closed her eyes suddenly and rested her head on Death's shoulder. "I feel so tired."

Death shot him a quick look before lifting and kissing her.

David watched as a green glow surrounded both of them. Almost instantly, her face regained some of its color.

Although Death appeared worried, he gave her a teasing smile. "Who's the better kisser, Sweet Jane?"

She shoved his face away from hers. "Me."

David laughed as he walked to them. "What did you do to her?"

"Just gave her some vitamin D." Death pushed her to David. "Spend some time with Papi. Let me check on some things with Than."

David shook his head as he took her hand. "I'm beating your ass if you continue calling me that."

"Is that a promise?" Death winked at her. "I'll be back, babe."

"Okay." She stared after Death, looking lost again. So lost that Death didn't leave like he'd said he would.

David sighed as he tilted her face up. "Are you going to be okay?"

Jane's fangs extended.

"Baby?"

She closed her eyes, exhaling as she squeezed her thighs together. "I-I."

"She's likely able to focus on her sexual needs again." Death tilted his head as his eyes began to glow. "Perhaps you can spend a few moments with her before leaving so she does not need release right away."

"Stop talking about me like I can't hear you," she said, breathing out.

David chuckled and watched her squeeze her legs together tighter.

"Oh." She opened her eyes, locking them with his.

"Feeling needy?" David asked.

"I'm fine."

Death leaned down and whispered in her ear, "Don't deprive yourself—it will end badly. Your hormones demand that you be conquered."

Her face scrunched up, confused. It lasted mere seconds before turning sad and then blank. "I said I'm fine. We should go let the kids say goodbye."

David watched her, his eyes drifting toward Death briefly. He couldn't get her pregnant like her body wanted, but "I have time to spend with you, Jane. And I can catch up to the others if they leave."

"What the fuck don't you understand about 'I'm fine?'" Her chest heaved as she glared at him before her eyes watered, and she whimpered, walking away from both of them.

He went to her quickly, wrapping his arms around her. The way she jumped and looked down at his arms, he knew she'd had no idea if it was him or Death grabbing her. Death had done more than sever a bond—he'd destroyed and stolen something she needed to be whole.

"Jane." He pulled her against him, hoping she would feel him if he just surrounded her in his presence. "I understand you tend to say you're fine when you are the opposite. I understand I am about to leave you while you try to cope with things I did not want you to go through. Your upcoming cycle only increases my worry."

"The whole point was to stop you from worrying." She tried to shove him off.

He didn't let her go. "Tell me what is bothering you most right now."

She whimpered, staring down at his hands on her stomach. "I can't feel you, and it makes me angry and sad. I don't know what the fuck to do. I don't want you to leave, but I also want you to go take care of things and get these assholes off my back. I want to be happy he's with me, but I know he doesn't want to be here."

Death let out a loud sigh. "What the fuck do you want me to say, Jane? I'm trying to be here for you. I want to take care of you. You're all I want to take care of and love. I can't, though. That is why we did this."

She took heavy breaths. "Then why don't you leave? Go fulfill your needs."

"Death, would you excuse us?" David asked.

The door slammed, and Jane covered her face, mumbling, "David, I don't know what's wrong with me."

He walked her to the bed and sat, pulling her onto his lap. "Baby, there's a lot wrong right now. It's not your fault, though."

She lowered her hands, whispering, "I thought this would help him. He's been so off, and I know he's wanted to be closer to me because I've wanted to be closer to him. I shouldn't, though. I chose you. I'm not regretting it, but I feel so lost without him. And now I feel nothing between any of us. I don't feel him." Her eyes burned as she touched the invisible wound in her chest. "I feel like a part of me died."

He pressed a kiss to her head and held his hand over hers. "You don't feel me, either. Do you?"

She shook her head. "I only felt you when you were both with me."

David hugged her to him tightly and kissed the back of her neck. "Do you feel that?"

"Yes and no."

"Try to describe it for me." He kissed her again.

Wiping her tears, she began explaining. "I feel your lips. I feel the pressure of the kiss, but it feels empty—like you don't really want to kiss me. Or like you don't mean more behind it. Like I'm not me, so the kiss isn't even meant for me. And the heat is barely there. It's still more than I feel without touching you, though. I think that has to do more with my hormones. It's less loving and more of just a need. I know you're not out to satisfy your urges with me, but that's how it feels. Then, worst of all, I slip into not feeling anything again. I don't even make sense right now. I think I've gone crazy."

"Hm." He sighed, brushing his lips back and forth against her skin. "You are overwhelmed. Your mind, heart, and soul have been split from each other on your quest to do right by everyone you love. And you're trying to cope with this during a time when your hormones are amplified to heights they've never been before." He chuckled. "Baby, you don't have to make sense. If you think you are overreacting, consider that my brothers often retreat from the castle or leave with their wives to help them cope with each cycle. And none of them have children or angels to concern themselves with. They get frustrated, violent, and even depressed. So don't linger on not making sense of your feelings. Let's focus on you and Death for now. I can control my mating urges."

Jane smiled sadly. "I should be used to hormones, but I want to fight him. I want him to undo this. I'm angry he couldn't be stronger, even if I know he had something affecting him that I could not relieve."

"You could relieve anything for him, my love. But your commitment to me stops you." He kissed her head. "I love you. I love that you want to make me happy. I'm thankful for every second you grant me by your side—and I am sorry I was not a strong enough man from the start."

"How were you not strong?"

"I saw magic when you two kissed," he whispered in her ear. "It was the most beautiful sight I have ever witnessed. The most incredible warmth washed over me as I watched you both glow in gold and emerald light. I witnessed God's work—one of his finest miracles—and watched it die. I will never forget the emptiness that filled me when you screamed." He rubbed her *wound*. "I never wanted you to experience that. I swear I will find a way to reunite you two. You should not have parted from each other."

Jane stared straight ahead, her mouth slightly agape.

"I can still stay with you two," he murmured.

"No." She turned toward him and smiled. "You need to go keep the others safe."

David held her cheek as he kissed her softly. "Then you need to make up with your angel." He brushed his lips over hers. "Both of you are trying to do what you think is best for the other, but you fail to see that just you loving each other is best. You—us—we are not destined to be like other couples. I see that now."

"What are you saying?"

He kissed her long before squeezing his eyes shut and saying, "I'm saying I love you. And I want you to keep your angel as close to your heart as possible. I want you to forgive and love each other—and if you ever feel you should follow him instead of me, I want you to go with him. I want you to be happy."

Her heart pounded faster.

David opened his eyes and smiled. "Don't panic. I love you and want to spend the rest of our lives together. I want you beyond forever. But never choose me just because you think you are supposed to. Choose me because you want to be by my side, but never feel I want you to give up your other great love. I swear I will make room in our bed for the bastard if I have to." He chuckled, giving her a quick kiss. "I am not meant to have you all to myself, okay? And I am no longer conflicted by that truth. I want you shining and laughing, and he is the one who does that for you."

"Okay," she said, getting that faraway look in her eye.

"Jane." His serious tone made her heartbeat speed up again. "Baby, I can see you thinking the complete opposite of what I'm trying to steer you toward."

"Maybe you should just spit out what you're trying to get at," she said, barely keeping her voice even.

David sighed as he turned away. "I'm not sure I can say what I'm getting at." He couldn't—it would destroy her. "I know that frustrates you, and I apologize, but I am nervous about leaving you, especially since you are not getting along with him."

"The way you're talking seems like you want me to have make-up sex with him."

He clenched his jaw shut before relaxing. "I don't want you to have make-up sex with him. I simply accept that your physical contact with each other will extend beyond what I expected to be okay with."

"Like you were really okay with all of us kissing in bed last night?"

"I never thought I would be, but I was more than fine with it." He smiled because it was the truth. "It's not like I want to kiss him if that is what you're thinking, but I think the three of us are meant to be closer than I originally believed when you came into my life. I do not want you to get out of hand. I think you know what I am okay with, but together, we are meant to be more. You felt it, didn't you?"

She bit her lip, nodding.

David nuzzled her neck, inhaling her scent. "Yes, you felt it—just like you are tasting it right now."

266

Jane closed her eyes, shivering as he dragged his hands across her stomach before bringing a hand up to the edge of her top.

He shoved his hand down, massaging her breasts as his other hand dropped between her legs. "You felt both of us, didn't you?"

"Yes," she whispered, tilting her head back so he could kiss her neck.

He did.

"Yes," she breathed, "I felt both of you wherever you touched me."

David smiled against her skin. "What do we feel like?"

"Heat and tingles. Strength. Love. So much love. Complete."

He kissed her neck as he made teasing circles between her legs. "And with just me—after he left—some of that magic left, didn't it?"

She stayed quiet.

"It's okay. I noticed it, too."

"So you're saying we should all be together like that?"

"I'm saying make up with your angel. That fucker loves you more than you can imagine, and I love you just as deeply. Together, the three of us will find our paths and help each other become what we are destined to be." He smiled against her skin and pressed his fingers down between her legs. "Order your suit away so I can relieve the ache you have."

Jane took several nervous breaths before her suit vanished.

He was about to tell her maybe it wasn't a good idea, but she put her hand over his and showed him where she wanted him to touch her.

She was trembling in his hands in no time, and thanks to the small box on the nightstand, David conquered her one more time before he had to leave.

Jane bit her lip as she sat beside Death. He didn't look at her or acknowledge her in any way. He just kept his gaze fixed on the gathering of soldiers preparing to leave. So, she sighed and watched the group load crates.

"Jane?"

She turned her head and smiled awkwardly at Artemis. "Hey."

Artemis pushed some of her hair behind her ear as she nervously darted her eyes between Jane and Death. "I wondered if I could speak with you before I leave?"

Death stood, walking toward Thanatos and David, who seemed to be arguing.

"Uh, yeah." She scooted over to make room for Artemis. "What's up?"

Artemis gestured to the few Norse female soldiers and fairy women among the group preparing to leave. "I wanted to assure you that there is no need to worry about David's faithfulness to you. I know now that he was never meant to be mine, and I was a foolish, infatuated girl. I should not have behaved as if I had a claim over him. He never expressed interest and clarified his feelings on more than one occasion."

"It's kinda hard not to be infatuated with him." Jane watched David glance their way.

"He never looked at a single female of any kind the way he does you," Artemis whispered. "Whatever their plan is to lure him from you—it will fail. I wish to earn your forgiveness for my wrongdoings toward you by eliminating anyone attempting to pursue him. Perhaps we might even become friends one day."

Jane chuckled. "You don't have to kill anyone, but thank you. Maybe just glare at him if he fails to push one of his fangirls away. And, yes, maybe we will be friends one day—you were one of my favorites of mythology."

Artemis smiled. "All right."

"Have you seen Adam?" Jane asked.

Artemis lowered her head. "No. He refuses to speak to me."

"I'll talk to him." Jane sighed, hating she'd not been there for Adam. "I shouldn't have reacted the way I did before—it wasn't like you knew he was my cousin. I was jealous. I'd only just gotten him back. I missed out on having him in my life the way he was meant to be, and then he's back and giving my rival heart eyes while my boyfriend smiles at her too."

Artemis peeked up at her guiltily. "I did not expect David to be friendly. A very pathetic part of me reveled in his attention, but I had no intention of pursuing him. It was merely a giddy moment to have him acknowledge me that kept me engaging with him."

Jane didn't blame her. Realizing how controlled David had been as an immortal meant that he had rejected thousands, including a woman considered a goddess. Having his smile and laugh would be hard to ignore. "He was trying to keep the peace and do what was best for our kids."

A faint smile touched Artemis' lips. "He is a good father figure. I had not expected that either. I apologize for what I said about them. They are wonderful children, and I am happy David and the knights have the joy of helping you raise them. Immortals envy humans for their gift to have children."

Jane grinned. "I forgive you. But back to Adam, I had no right to expect him to stop seeing you. He's a grown man. And weirdly attractive." She shook the thought from her mind. "I'm just saying he could easily have any woman, but he was completely caught up with you. I don't know if he realizes your relationship would only be temporary, but it's not my place to decide how he lives. Just don't damn each other."

"I would never." Artemis turned as someone approached them.

Apollo walked over, patting Artemis on the back. "Ready?" he asked before winking at Jane. "Where is David? I thought he would be all over you."

David bumped shoulders with him as he passed. "Stop contemplating courting my woman."

Apollo held his hands up, laughing. "Don't leave your baby sitting here while she smells like that." He inhaled. "Lucky bastard."

David glared at him. "If you must, go scent her discreetly from across the room. I might be able to restrain myself from killing you, but they may not."

Apollo cringed as Death and Thanatos walked up behind him. "Let's go, sister."

Artemis stood, bowing to Jane. "I swear I want the best for him, and I will keep an eye on this one while you are stuck here."

David raised an eyebrow as Jane stood and hugged Artemis.

"I'll talk to him," she said. "And don't forget—only kill these bitches if they try to take his clothes off—or if they fall on him while they're naked."

Artemis blushed before lowering her head. "Thank you, Jane. You have a lovely heart, by the way. I see why it was meant for them."

Death nudged Artemis. "Go."

Jane watched Artemis and Apollo leave. "She was being nice for once."

Death stared at Jane but said nothing, which had Thanatos rolling his eyes and walking away after giving David a nod.

"All right," David said as he put his hand behind her back. "Make up right now."

Death shot David a dirty look as he hissed, "We're not children."

David smirked. "I believe you asked to call me Daddy and then decided on Papi."

Jane leaned her head against David as she forced a smile on her face. "We'll be fine."

David grinned down at her. "If I come back, and you are at each other's throats, I will be disappointed."

"Whatever, Dad." Death took her in quickly. "Do you still feel me with the suit?"

Her eyes burned. "Only if you or David are touching me."

Death glanced at David. "You already had a quickie with her—I don't know what you want from me."

Jane's face heated up. "Shut up!"

Death's eyes flashed. "What?"

David rubbed his face before grabbing Death's upper arm and guiding them to a hallway. Once there, he glared at the vampires lingering there until they all ran away, then glared at her and Death. "Stop acting like brats."

Jane's eyes widened. "I'm not a brat. I'm trying to cope with everything and don't know what to do."

"I did not say you were a brat," David said. "I said you are acting like brats by the way you are behaving toward each other. I'm about to leave you while your body is screaming to be thoroughly fucked, and I'm trusting him to keep away or kill anyone who dares to claim you. Yet you are acting like neither of you cares about that. I told you we would work on getting you both what you need, but I need you to promise to get along while I'm away. I don't want to return and find you worse off than you are.

"But, baby, you are still peeking at your fingers after feeling your chest, so I need to know if you're okay with me leaving. Neither of us knows the long-term effects, but I see more and more light leaving your eyes."

"She'll be fine," Death said. "I will do whatever is necessary to keep her strong." His gaze fell to Jane. "I'm sorry. I feel empty without you, and it is painful? I am not sure how to describe it. But I swear I will protect you. You are still my only concern."

David unfolded his arms as he watched them. "Come here, Jane."

She tore her eyes from Death and took David's outstretched hand. Her heart throbbed because it was barely warm, but he smiled and pulled her to him.

"I want you to have each other the way you are meant to be." He tilted her face up and caressed her lips with his thumb. "That means he does no wrong in your eyes, my love. And if he does, you forgive his ass before he ever says sorry. Just like you always have, all right?" David glanced up at Death and inclined his head toward her. "Let her feel you."

Death didn't move. "You're entering dangerous territory, Prince."

A determined gleam sparked in David's eyes as he shook his head. "I'm trusting my instincts, faith, and heart. Get behind her."

"David." She shivered as Death's presence came to life behind her.

"See?" David turned her face for Death to see.

Death's eyes glowed, and he darted them back to David.

"What?" Jane asked as the two men stared at her.

Neither answered, but Death moved her hair aside and grabbed her waist, asking David, "You're sure about this?"

David nodded. "Only when I am here for now. We will discuss it more after I have time to accept it on my own."

Death flexed his fingers on her waist, and she shivered as heat and warmth pressed against her from each side. Heat and electricity prickled every inch of her skin.

"He wants us to share our kiss again, Sweet Jane."

"You do?" She stared at David, shocked.

David lifted her, pulling her legs around him as he pressed her against Death's chest. "I think there is a reason Death and I are similar in height and build." He grinned when Death pressed his lips against her neck, pulling a soft moan from her.

While Death sucked her earlobe into his mouth, David pressed a searing kiss to her lips. Fire sparked for mere seconds, but it had her trembling.

Death kept his mouth close to her ear and slid his hand to where his tingles had been stolen. "Forgive me."

"I forgive you," she whispered against David's mouth.

David kissed her jaw and turned her face toward Death's. Again, he bit her just as Death pressed his lips to hers. And just like before, a faint glowing thread loosely encircled the three of them.

Both men suddenly ripped their mouths away and turned their heads as David yelled, "Get the fuck out of here."

Jane blinked, realizing they were looking at someone behind them and the gold thread had vanished.

Death summoned his gun, aiming it at the fairy queen's frightened face. His wings unfolded to block Jane's view of her, and he said in the emptiest tone, "Leave."

David turned Jane's face toward his. "Sorry, sweetheart."

She wiped a tear that fell. "I'm sorry. To both of you. Fuck, I can't stop crying."

Death's wings disappeared, and he kissed the back of her head. "We'll kiss those hormones away. And David is right—we will find a way to make this work. Now tell Papi goodbye. I'll go scare everyone for a few minutes."

David chuckled, shoving him away. "Take care of our girl."

Death smacked her butt and walked away. "Don't tell me what to do."

"He is a child." David hugged her until Death was out of sight.

"David, I will never be able to express how much I love you," she said, touching his smile.

"When you glow for me, I'll know." He kissed her fingers. "The fact you are brightest between that bastard and me is proof I am right."

"Right about what?"

He pressed his lips to hers, murmuring, "You will know when you're ready." Jane frowned, but he continued, "Be happy while I'm gone. You should be completely over your ovulation period when I return."

"And you can go raw?"

His eyes shifted to ice blue, then back to sapphire. "I have never heard that term, but yes, my love. And you will smell of me but still have your angel's love radiating out of you."

"Thank you." She hugged him. "Be safe."

"You too." He rubbed her back. "He seriously gets to kill whoever tries to touch you, okay?"

She smiled, caressing his hair. "Let Artemis do the same with you, then."

He laughed, kissing her shoulder. "It is strange to see you comfortable with her, but I am glad you both are making an effort. It will please Adam, even if things do not work out for them."

Her chest ached, remembering she would outlive Adam and her children.

David squeezed her tight. "I will never stop fighting for them to have the greatest life possible."

"I know."

"David?" Arthur called out.

He sighed, turning her toward him. "I have to go."

Jane gave him a firm kiss. "Go and then bring your sexy ass back to me."

David smacked her butt. "I remember the days I dreamed about getting lucky enough to brush up against your pretty ass. All the way back in Texas." He squeezed both cheeks and carried her toward the gates where he would leave.

"Give me my girl and scram, Knight." Death smirked from his spot against the wall.

"Behave. None of that unless I'm around." David kissed Jane's cheek before lowering her to her feet. "We will figure something out."

Death rolled his eyes. "If you continue speaking like she can't make decisions for herself, you will wind up in the doghouse. And I know naughty time is only with you present, Papi. Now beat it."

"I think I'm going to have nightmares of you saying that," David muttered, cupping her cheeks and giving her a long kiss. "See you soon, my love."

"See you soon," she said as the magic of the three of them faded again. "Try to stay you, and I will try to stay me."

"I promise." David shifted his gaze between her eyes before kissing her forehead. "I love you."

"I love you." She pushed his stomach because she could sense people watching them. "Go before someone throws a fit."

He gave her one more kiss as he walked her backward into Death and then winked, walking away.

Death put his arms around her chest. "Already fading, Sweet Jane?"

"Yes." She watched David take his mask from Gawain and pull it over his head.

He sighed. "If I trusted I could keep you safe, I would not have done this."

Jane tilted her head back to look up at him. "You don't trust you can keep me safe—even now?"

He didn't respond, so she turned back, waving as the others waved to the men and women leaving.

David's blue eyes stood out, and she whispered, "I love you," when he exited the massive doors.

"Let's get you away from everyone. Your aroused scent still clings to you." Death took her hand and led her out through the halls. "And stop touching that."

Jane looked down, only then realizing she was rubbing her *wound*. "Do you know why it feels this way?"

He squeezed her hand. "Don't ask me. I am not coping with it as well as I appear to be. I swear I would tell you if I knew how to fix it."

She eyed the others who watched them as they walked. "Do you have our conversation shielded?"

"Yes." He glanced down at her. "Why?"

"I wanted to ask about something . . . I'm just curious about David's behavior. He has always wanted me to himself, even if he has said not to let you go. I know, for a fact, he did not intend for us to be intimate the way we were. So why did he change? Even last night, he said our lovemaking was only for us, but now it's almost like he's okay with having a three-way."

Death's expression gave nothing away. "Maybe he is."

She felt her cheeks heat up. "It's weird. I mean, I've never thought of that. Maybe the sandwich thing, but that's just me being stupid."

"Was it weird when we kissed you?"

"No." She frowned. "It felt perfect."

"Then how is it weird if we all agree to be more?"

She stared up at him. "Is that what you want?"

"I want you for myself," he said, shrugging, "but it felt natural. I did not feel he was intruding, and I did not feel as though I was either. It was more than simple lust as well."

Jane rubbed her forehead as images of the three of them on the bed flickered in her mind. "Yeah."

"You're thinking about it, aren't you?" He inhaled deeply. "It's a good thing I cannot read your mind, but don't get worked up. I still desire you. Without him present, there is not that sense of sharing you. I suppose that is a plus side from severing the bond—I can't teleport with you and steal you when you turn me on." He stopped and opened the door to her room. "We can call for your children to be brought back. Do you require anything before they come?"

She rubbed her throbbing chest, dropping her hand when he focused on the movement. "Just come here for a second."

He hesitated but walked to her. "What is it?"

"I hate that we are so awkward with each other now." Jane reached up, caressing his cheek. "It didn't fix you."

Death lifted her without warning and pulled her legs around him. "I cannot be fixed. Not without you."

She cupped his cheeks. "Then why did you agree to do this?"

"Because I didn't want to hurt you anymore. I feared I would rape you and take you away from the man you chose—maybe even kill him. And there are things I cannot say without breaking your heart. I thought it would help. It has helped, but we have created bigger problems by going through with it. I was not thinking clearly."

"If I had chosen you but still longed for David, what would you have done?"

"If you had chosen me—if you ever choose just me—we would forget the world." He cupped her cheek as he pressed his forehead to hers. "I am not David, Jane. I am only good enough to stand back for your choice. Now,

274

at least. Being connected was Heaven and Hell, but this just feels like Hell. To not feel our connection that we have had for so long, knowing you are there—existing but not tied to me—terrifies me. Then, when I left you, I almost forgot you. I know you and almost everything about you and remember us, but you stopped being that constant presence that anchored me. I think David figured this out, and he is pushing us together for that reason."

Jane frowned. "I feel that, too. Is there no way to put us back?"

"I can't undo it." He ran his hands through her hair. "Maybe David is on the right path. Maybe it is not just you and me—but all three of us who are to be tied together. Maybe it will not be the bond we shared, but a new bond."

"How would we make it?" Hope began to build in her heart.

He shrugged. "That I do not know. I am merely considering the line of thought I believe David is taking. I never expected this from him."

"A three-way?" She felt her face heat up when he focused on her. "Death!"

"Do not use that tone with me—your vampire started this."

"Wouldn't that be wrong? Like a sin or just a wrong toward David?"

His brows drew down as the cutest confused look flitted over his face. "Why would it be a sin, or even a wrong against David if he initiates it?"

"I don't know." She pressed her hand over her non-existent wound. "I mean, everyone says it's supposed to be one man and one woman."

Death stared at her hand. "Jane, you have always been right to think deeper than what religious leaders spout Sunday. Even the Bible had editors and publishers influencing what was published. Not to mention the church and how each man interprets ancient texts."

"What are you saying? The Bible is wrong?"

He stared at her for a few seconds in silence before he said, "I am saying that you should consider that each written religious text had someone or multiple people influencing it—just as any author does now. They are told by agents, editors, publishers, and even fans what they should put in, and if they have the power—the ability to cut or alter something to their best interest or what they believe is more suitable for readers—they do. And do not forget many translations are inaccurate because of language and time periods."

Jane shook her head. "Okay, I don't want to get into the Bible being . . . whatever you're saying, but are you suggesting God would be fine with the three of us together?"

His eyes began to glow. "I am not sure what Father's intentions were when he created us. Besides my duty, I am lost on the truths I have discovered."

A stabbing pain pierced Jane's chest, and she gasped, grabbing at it as tears sprang to her eyes. "Death, something's wrong."

His eyes widened as he covered her hand and pulled her close. "Kiss me, Jane. Now."

A sheen of sweat broke across her forehead as she clung to him, crying. "Help me."

His mouth crashed into hers. The warm sensation was weak, but it still raced to her chest, right where the tingles had been torn from, and it bubbled, trying to spread.

He growled, kissing her more frantically as she sobbed before screaming as black spots dotted her vision.

"Death." She tried to hold him. "Help."

"*Shh* . . ." He kept kissing her, sitting as he moved her hand aside and pressed his where it hurt. "Stay with me, angel. Don't leave me."

Slowly, the warm sensation spread, touching the edges of where she felt she'd been cut open. She gasped as oxygen she hadn't realized was absent rushed back into her lungs.

Someone cleared their throat, and Death snarled, summoning his gun.

Jane lazily peered over her shoulder, blinking away her tears as she noticed Adam, Guinevere, and Thanatos.

"It's not what you think," Jane whispered. Then everything went dark.

20

EVERYONE DIES

"I don't have to answer to any of you," Death snarled.

Jane heard him—felt him holding her—but she couldn't open her eyes or speak.

"She's my cousin," Adam spat, his voice just as violent as Death's. "Her boyfriend just left, and you're fucking kissing her while she's clearly sick."

"She's not sick," Death growled. "Back up."

"I just want to check her vitals." It was Guinevere.

"Death, she means no harm." Now it was Thanatos. "Perhaps she requires a blood transfusion."

"You know she needs more than that," Death said.

Jane felt the surface below her shift and realized Death was laying her on a bed.

"What is it she needs then?" Guinevere asked as delicate hands slid over Jane's forehead. "She has a fever. That should not be possible."

Another pair of hands, rougher, touched her forehead. "Ryder, what the fuck is wrong with her? She's burning up."

"She's dying," Thanatos said with finality.

"I won't let her die," Death roared. "No, this was meant to fix her."

"I will send for David's blood type and a messenger to retrieve him," Guinevere said. "Or perhaps one of you can go to him."

"He must stay to reveal the one who is after Jane," Thanatos said quietly. "And he cannot save her, so there is no point."

"Who can save her?" Adam asked.

Jane tried to open her mouth, but she still couldn't move.

Thanatos answered when Death stayed quiet. "Lucifer."

"He is not to come near her," Death said, his energy pulsing. "If you summon him, I will ensure you burn for all eternity, Fallen. I will slaughter your entire family!"

Thanatos remained calm. "Would you rather she cease to exist?"

"I won't lose her."

"I don't understand," Adam said. "What has happened? Gawain said I needed to stay away from her because she was ovulating, and David would be aggressive toward any male close by. No one said she would die from that."

"She's been dying since she was retrieved from Lucifer," Thanatos said.

Death growled loudly. "Than, I swear, if you don't shut your goddamn mouth—"

"Calm, both of you." Guinevere put a cold cloth on Jane's head.

Jane tried to cry—it was too cold. It felt like she was being stabbed with icy needles, but she couldn't make a sound.

Guinevere sighed. "We must get David. He can bring Bedivere, and they can come up with a solution. Or perhaps we should consult one of the fairies. They are powerful."

"No one is to know of her condition," Death said quickly. "Not even David."

"I will not keep this from my brother."

"She will die regardless of if he returns," Thanatos said. "Unless Lucifer saves her. This happened far sooner than we expected."

"If Lucifer shows his face, I will kill him." Death's voice was closer, and she felt lips touch hers as a weak warmth traveled down her throat.

"What are you doing to her?" Adam asked.

"He is supplementing her life force with his. He has been doing it since he revived her with Lucifer. Every kiss and touch he gives, he has been pushing his life force into her."

"She has been this way for that long?" Guinevere asked as Death murmured words Jane didn't know against her mouth. "Oh, goodness, and I made her feel bad for receiving his touch."

"Lucifer took half of Jane's soul." Thanatos sighed. "Half souls cannot survive on their own."

"Stop letting every fucking secret about her out! And you know there is more to it than that." Death growled against her mouth before he kissed her cheek and whispered in her ear, "Please don't leave me."

"No one will know," Guinevere whispered. "Adam, this stays within these walls."

"Fuck this," Adam said. "Call Lucifer."

Death lifted his head. "I will slaughter all of you if he is summoned. He will take her from me. None of us will see her again!"

"But she would live," Thanatos said. "Is that not what matters to you most?"

"I will find a way to keep her. I thought this would work." Death's hands cradled her cheeks as his lips touched hers again, and warmth entered from his kiss just as before. "Live, Sweet Jane."

"How long does she have?" Adam asked.

"As long as he can supplement her life force," Thanatos answered.

"How long can he?"

"As long as I fucking have to," Death snarled. "Get the fuck out of here. She may fucking hear us, and I have no clue what to tell her when she wakes. Now go. Do not utter his name or speak of this to anyone."

"I thought you controlled who lives and dies," Adam yelled.

"Not her," Thanatos said.

There was the sound of something getting hit and a grunt.

Death growled. "Say one more word about her . . ."

Guinevere replaced the cloth on her head. "Calm yourselves. She needs to overcome this fever. I have never seen an ill immortal, so this is serious."

Death released a breath and spoke in a less threatening tone. "She'll be fine. She's just recovering from—nothing."

"Should I bring the children back?" she asked.

"No. She would not want them to see her this way," he said. "And if she does happen to have a virus, it could be contagious."

"You don't know where her fever is coming from?" she asked.

"No."

"Queen Guinevere," Thanatos said, "can you perform a blood transfusion?"

"Yes. Let me gather what I need. I will be quick." There was shuffling. "Come, Adam. It is unsafe to be here. We do not know what is causing her fever, and the children will need you should her condition worsen."

Adam sighed, and a door shut, signaling their departure.

"You know what needs to be done," Thanatos said.

"He will take her," Death replied, utterly defeated and lost.

"But she will live."

"She can live with David and me. He needs to eliminate the threat and learn to control what is coming for him before then, but we can sustain her together."

Thanatos sighed, then said, "You know what you were supposed to do when that half was removed from her."

"She chose David."

"If he learns the truth—"

Death cut him off, "He figured it out."

"Are you certain?"

"Let it go, Than. I won't let Lucifer take her. I can keep her safe and supplement her. I thought I could do it this way, but I was wrong. It's okay, though. David will be able to help once he finishes his duties."

"And what will you do when Belial comes for her?" Thanatos asked. "He will come. And he is stronger than you are letting the others know. If he aligns with Lucifer, which they will once they realize what is happening to you, they will unite and take her. Then it will simply become a fight between them for who gets control over her. Summon Lucifer. Make a bargain, and then let him fix her. He cares for her."

"I will not bargain with Luc again."

A shift in the atmosphere made Jane's heart pound.

"Death, I have—" It was a woman. "Than?"

"Sister," Than said, shocked. "What are you doing here?"

The woman, Thanatos' sister, let out a laugh. "Brother, I cannot believe you are here. I knew you would redeem yourself. I told Mother not to lose hope. I never listened to our brothers."

"Nemesis." Death's voice was low but violent. "I told you not to find me."

"You said to come if I had news, and I have news." She laughed. "You could have told me about him last night, though. You know I have longed for a chance to visit him."

"Last night?" Thanatos asked. "You still use her?"

Death sighed as Jane felt a tear slide into her hair.

No. Jane's heartbeat slowed, beating irregularly and painfully.

"It meant nothing, brother," Nemesis said. "You know he must sate his urges or—"

"You know damn well I told you to stop," Thanatos roared.

"Brother, you left a long time ago."

"I didn't leave," Thanatos snapped. "I was fucking hurled out of Heaven!

And you whoring yourself to him was part of the reason I chose to do what I did."

"Leave, Nemesis," Death said, not sounding angry. He sounded broken. Weak. "Both of you leave."

"Her heartbeat sounds strange," Thanatos said. There was movement around Jane. "Death."

"Leave!"

"She's dying," Thanatos shouted as a finger slid down the path of Jane's tears. "She's fucking crying—she hears us. Nemesis, get the fuck out of here. Look at what you've done!"

"I meant no harm."

Death's lips brushed against Jane's. "Forgive me."

"Give her energy and leave," Thanatos said. "I swear I will call him. I will join him in the fight against you, Death, and we will ensure she survives."

Death pressed his lips to Jane's while she continued to cry silently. Her heart was turning black and dying. Her soul no longer glowed. She was lifeless and pale, gasping for breath as she stared upward.

"Come on, baby girl." Death pressed his hand over Jane's chest. "If not for me, live for David and your children."

She couldn't respond. She didn't think she was breathing anymore. She heard them arguing as Death kept pushing a soft warmth into her mouth. It gathered around her soul, but nothing was happening. Her soul wanted nothing to do with him.

"Please, my love," he murmured. "I did not mean to hurt you." He kissed her cheeks. "Live for them."

"Oh, goodness," a female voice whispered.

"Who the hell are you?" Thanatos yelled. "Get out of here."

"I was bringing fresh linens."

"Hela," Guinevere said, panicked. "Do not speak of what you saw. Go! You are relieved of your duties to my brother's quarters."

"Get her the fuck out of here," Death shouted. "Come on, Jane. Wake up for me. You can shout at me all you want. Just wake up."

"What happened?" Guinevere whispered, grabbing Jane's arm. "She's fading."

"Get the transfusion started," Death said. "She isn't fading. I can save her."

"Who are you?" Guinevere asked.

"I am—"

Death cut Nemesis off. "She is no one. Keep going."

A sad cry filled the room as the air shifted.

"If I could, I would kill you," Thanatos said.

"You can't, so fuck off. Go guard her children." Death pressed his mouth to hers again. "Breathe, Sweet Jane."

Jane felt a cold finger follow her tears and then nothing.

———

Jane pried her sore eyes open but could not move her head. Still, she saw Death holding her hand, his eyes closed. He wasn't asleep. He was mumbling under his breath in a language she assumed must be angelic. It almost seemed like he was praying. She didn't know why he would pray. He had done this. He'd destroyed her. Again.

"Go," she rasped.

His eyes flew open. "Jane!" He began to lean down, but she glared at him as best she could.

"Get away from me."

He stared at her, his expression giving away his pain. "Baby girl, she meant nothing to me."

She looked away from him and focused on the ceiling. "Leave. If I am dying, I want to die without you."

"Jane—"

"Just go." A tear slid into her hair.

"What about David?"

Her throat felt like it was closing, but she still choked out a response. "Tell him I will love him beyond forever and to take care of our children."

"I won't let you die." He rubbed her tears. "I have been trying to find out how to keep you, and you were getting worse—I was getting worse."

"So you ripped me apart and then called your fuck buddy once you were free of me?"

"Jane, you fucked David to feel, too."

She whimpered. She had asked David to make love to her because she couldn't feel anything but pain.

"That is how it is for me all the time," he said. "A few hours of sex is the only relief I can give myself. I always hate that I do it, but you are not mine the way you are David's. We are more. And I don't have you to myself. I have to watch you with him. Then, when I must leave you to him, I become nothing. It confuses me. I begin searching for you and only realize it until I am reunited with you. What I do with other women is what I desire with you. If I do not fulfill that desire, the outcome would cause you to weep for all eternity."

He raised her hand, kissing it. "I know you love me, angel. I know you are confused because you still desire to be near me as I do you, but no matter what, you chose another man. I am ensuring you get to have him. She was simply the one who was there. She gave me enough distraction from my pain and the knowledge you were in his bed. She was the distraction I needed to not destroy everything because I already knew I had failed you. All I could do was give you that moment with him."

She didn't know how to respond. What he said made sense, and she had no right to be angry, but she was dying this whole time, and he went off to fuck Thanatos' sister to forget about her for a few hours. He chose to please and distract himself instead of telling her the truth. "Just leave." Her eyes watered. "All I see is you and other women when I needed you. You lied to me, and now my David is gone, and I'm going to die without seeing him."

"Had I known David would permit me to be with you more, I would have stayed by your side."

"That's disgusting." She made a face since she couldn't smack him. "All you care about is fucking."

"You don't understand." He held her hand to his cheek—no more tingles. "Everything I do, I do for you—so you have what you desire. I weaken myself every time I give you life."

"Then stop. Let me go."

He shook his head. "I can't. I won't."

Jane tried to swallow the lump in her throat but could only croak, "Bring David back. I want to see him before I die."

"I'll keep you alive. I need him to find the other threat to you. Too many seek to destroy or use you, and it is vital to lure them out. This threat is possibly more dangerous than Lucifer and Belial, and I have no clue who it is."

"What does it matter if someone wants me? I'm fucking dying, dumbass. No one can use me or destroy me."

He chuckled, kissing her hand. "I know I've been a dumbass. But I'm not lying: Lucifer would be able to save and use you."

"I'm useless without my powers—he wouldn't use me. He hasn't even come after me since leaving with you. He's probably searching for a way to use that bitch he tore out of me."

"He can't use her." Death ran his fingers through her hair. "I know I hurt you, angel. That is always why I concede to David. But I am still more powerful than your knight. I can keep you alive and protect you. I want to be with you however I can, and if David is understanding, together we can make you strong again."

"David will not forgive you for this."

"No. He will fight me, I am certain." He chuckled. "But he will see what you cannot—that I simply love you too much to see anything but you. That I cannot have you, so I do everything for you to have the best."

She finally turned her head toward him. "My best would be you not breaking me every time you get a free day." He lowered his head, but she went on. "I know I'm with David, Death. But you're still mine."

A smile teased his lips when he looked up. "I will always be yours."

"I just wish I didn't have to know about it. I wish you didn't choose to forget me when I need you most. I'm selfish—I know—but I still need you for as long as I exist. I hate that I do and that you hurt me, yet I still love you. I feel so pathetic. I'm such a lousy girlfriend. I have the best boyfriend and can't let go of the one who continuously wrongs me. Then I make the step toward him, and I basically sign my Death Certificate. If I had girl-friends, they'd tell me to forget you or throw it in your face that David is the man I chose. And the stupid thing is I would tell them to fuck off. I would tell them they don't understand our love—that David understands, and that's all that matters. I will stupidly take you back every time you break my heart." She focused on the ceiling again. "Which is why I want you to kill me."

He stopped breathing.

She went on. "Do it yourself because you were the one who kept me here in the first place. So take responsibility for your mistake. Just maybe let me see David and my family one more time—if it's safe. I want you to tell them I will be okay and then do it. Let them live their lives without the shit that comes with being a part of me. If I don't exist, there is no reason for anyone to harm them. No reason for you to do half the shit you do. Fuck, maybe everything would become balanced again. Lucifer would regain control because I'm no longer a distraction to him—no longer a burden to protect or a pawn to use. You would have no reason to hold back. You could eliminate all threats because I wouldn't be a concern. There would be no reason to weaken yourself and no reason you could not fix the fact the apocalypse started earlier than it was meant to. No Horsemen

Bringer—no apocalypse. No me . . . everything is better. Everything is right."

A white light filled the room. "Not quite, my queen."

"Luc," she whispered as he shimmered into view.

He didn't look at her. He summoned a shining, silver gun, aimed it at Death's shocked face, and sighed. "Goodbye, little brother."

He lowered the gun a bit and fired.

Jane screamed, reaching for Death as he took the shot to his chest. He fell and didn't get up.

"Death!" She tried to crawl off the bed to get to him, but Lucifer stopped her. "Let me go."

"He will not die," he said, lifting her into his arms as he used a hand to wipe her tears. "I cannot kill Death, Jane."

She whimpered, staring down at Death's body. Blood was filling the space around him, and he wasn't moving. "How could you?"

Lucifer turned her face toward his. "To save you, my queen. He was killing you and himself."

"What?" She searched his face, always startled but awed by his darker hair color.

"I will explain everything you need to know," he said, "but I must bond with you and get you to a safe place. He will regain consciousness soon, and there will be no hope for you or the others."

Several loud bangs sounded, and the doors shook.

"What's happening?"

He glanced at the door. "Belial found out Death was too weak to fight him. He has come for you."

Jane took panicked breaths before staring down at Death. "Bring him with us."

"He will come for you." Lucifer looked into her eyes and sighed. "I swear it, my queen, but you must come with me now. You do not have much time. If you die, everyone dies."

Her head throbbed as more bangs and shouts thundered through the halls. "I don't understand."

Lucifer pulled her closer. "I need your consent to establish a bond. I must get you to safety. Now."

Jane darted her eyes down to Death and then the door. "My kids. My cousin."

"They are guarded. I made sure of it before I came." He smiled that genuine smile she'd only seen a few times. "Anything for you, my queen. I swear you will see them again. But you, and everyone you love, will perish if you do not bond with me this instant."

She glanced down at Death. "He'll be all right?"

Lucifer held out a hand, and she watched as it began to glow before shooting a beam at Death's wound. "He will be fine a lot sooner now. We must go."

Jane eyed Death. She ensured he was breathing before she leaned forward and kissed the King of Hell.

He smiled against her mouth and murmured, "Good girl. Take a deep breath—this is going to hurt."

"I trust you," she whispered, holding his cheek as she took a deep breath.

"I know." He gave her a soft kiss as white fire filled her vision. "Now, hold on to me." Then he gave her a firmer kiss as Death roared her name, and the world around them fell away.

21

LOYALTY

There had been very few times when David had felt the urge to smack a woman across the face, but he was experiencing it right now.

"Fuck off, Rahela." Gawain stomped toward the firepit, where David sat with Gareth. "He's not interested."

"I do not see a female by his side, Sir Knight," Rahela replied in a thick Russian accent.

David met the black eyes of the green-haired Rusalka woman. He didn't know if it was the fact this was the second night he would be away from Jane or if he'd really lost all patience with women, but he was in no mood to deal with this. "My *female* is my girlfriend and Other. One day she will be my wife." He knew his eyes had changed color when she took a step back. "She does not have to be at my fucking side to be my entire world. I suggest you get out of my sight because I would much rather go back to her than escort you when wolf stench is thick in the air."

The woman stood there. He knew she was shocked by his dismissal. Rusalka were not used to being told no. They were beautiful creatures, just like the Nereids, who were also camped around them, but they were nothing compared to Jane.

An arrow shot into the ground. Rahela snarled, as did many of her friends, and Artemis dropped down from the trees a few yards away with another arrow drawn. "Back off."

Rahela scented the air and laughed. "You do not smell of him."

Artemis raised an eyebrow. "No, I wouldn't. His mate would skin me alive if I did." She pointed to her neck where Jane's darker soul had burned her handprints into her skin. "I learned from my mistake that you do not get close to this knight."

Several green-haired women stood from their spots around various campfires, observing a wound none of them had seen before.

"Now leave him in peace," Artemis said. "I have promised to kill any who do not cease their pursuit after he has dismissed them because I wish to make amends for my transgressions against Jane. I will not disappoint her. Not again."

Gareth nudged David. "Has Hell frozen over?"

David chuckled, shaking his head before he glared at the woman still standing there. He knew she was offended. It was a disgrace not to succeed in capturing a male for the clan. He didn't care, though. He was tired and angry that the trip had taken them farther from Valhalla. "She's not joking," he said. "Find another to trap with your charms. There are plenty interested in company from your clan."

Several of the Nereids laughed at Rahela's misadventure as she flung her long green hair over her pale shoulder and marched away.

"I wonder how Jane would have reacted." Gareth laughed as David stared at Artemis, glaring at the other women nearby. "I bet she would love to see the Nereids."

David glanced at the closest group of Nereids. Gareth was right—Jane would have been giddy had she come. Like the fairies and elves, the Nereids were Nephilim, but these sisters were even more unique. Instead of near-useless wings, the Nereids had fin-like appendages along their arms and legs. Some even held an iridescent skin coloring that shimmered in the moonlight, much like a fish's scales.

There were fifty, all daughters of the angel, Nereus, who had fallen in love with one of his creations. After breeding with her, the angel became a Fallen, but his daughters devoted their immortal lives to God. They thanked Him for not damning them and other Nephilim children of angels and prayed daily for their parents' redemption while saving many men and women who would likely die at sea. David preferred them over the Rusalka, who were not so devoted to aiding humanity. In fact, had it not been for their leader negotiating with Arthur, vowing to discontinue killing humans, and their promise to destroy any who broke Heaven's law, they would have killed them all long ago.

"What do you think of Artemis trying to impress you?" Gawain whispered once the goddess retreated to her tree again.

"It's not me she's trying to impress. She said she was trying to earn Jane's forgiveness. I think she is enamored with Adam, and he hasn't talked to her since finding out what happened between them."

"Well, Jane has every right to dislike her, but she did get her back." Gareth rubbed his neck.

"That wasn't Jane." David glared at him, more angry at himself for the pain he caused Jane when the incident happened.

Gareth nodded. "I meant, as far as Artemis and everyone who saw is concerned."

David sighed as he leaned against the boulder. "As long as she does not bother me, I don't care what she does to these women. It is exhausting to keep them away."

"It hasn't even been a year with Jane, and you act like this is new for you." Gareth turned his meat as it cooked.

Gawain laughed. "Jane doesn't realize how intimidating she is. The fact she has only had to put up with Melody, Artemis, and a few chambermaids looking your way says a lot."

David smiled as he thought of his baby. "She radiates power when she's feeling territorial."

"David?" Gareth scratched his head, cringing as he seemed to try to figure out what to say.

"Spit it out," David said, not in the mood for games.

"Fine." Gareth removed a piece of meat he'd been cooking from the fire. "We were wondering why Jane no longer emits the pull. It vanished the last night we were at Valhalla. It was already weak, though."

Gawain threw a rock at Gareth. "We were going to wait to ask him."

Gareth threw the rock back. "No one is listening to us."

"Everyone is listening." Apollo sat next to David. "Whatever happened, wait until you return to the fortress to discuss it."

"But we can't feel her at all," Gareth muttered before looking at David. "Do you?"

David looked down at his chest. "No. It was weak when Death brought her back. Then it returned when she was in the room with Death and Lucifer."

"Why the fuck would Lucifer have any inclusion in her pull?" Gawain asked.

"I think it's her soul," he whispered. "We should stop talking now."

"Fine." Gawain glanced around the camp. "Apollo, do you think you will be able to achieve Tristan's level with your power?"

Anger flashed over Apollo's face, but he spoke calmly. "Hades spoke to me about it. War unlocked his potential by opening a mental barrier that we all have. All he said was mine is not meant to be unlocked yet. I think it is because I am damned."

"That's too bad," Gareth said. "It would be nice to have two fire wielders with that power at their fingertips. I wonder how angels select who to gift . . . It seems they all have some knowledge or even orders when they do these things. Jane, for instance, truly is destined for greatness. I always knew whoever David chose would be impressive, but it has been an incredible experience to see how many are drawn to her—how much power she can possess and wield. Her power goes beyond what she had with her other half and what the angels have given her. She, alone, can make all of us stronger. Good. It is awing to be in her presence, especially when she is just happy."

David closed his eyes. It had only been two nights, and already he missed her so much. Her presence was both beautiful and powerful. It destroyed him to know she wasn't the same.

Gareth spoke again. "She glowed when she stood between you two, brother."

David looked at him. "I know."

"Why?" Gawain turned toward him.

The image of Death and Jane surrounded in gold and emerald light as they kissed flickered in his mind. "I don't know," he said, remembering her scream as the gold light seemed to look at him and let go of the emerald light.

"I wonder what the other horsemen will give her," Gareth said. "I'd kiss Death if he gave me a gun like hers."

David forced out a laugh, but he was picturing Death's furious expression if Gareth were to ask for such a thing.

"I have wondered something," Gareth said. "What does he look like?"

"I forget you see him as the Grim Reaper." David frowned but was thankful he did not have to think about what he'd seen with Jane. "I guess he somewhat resembles—"

"You," Arthur said, walking over. "From your thoughts and those among us who have no heartbeat, your faces are very similar. He is of divine origins, obviously, with more defined features than you, but you almost look related. Like brothers or cousins." Arthur chuckled. "He's also quite tanned, so how David looked when he used to spend more time in the sun. The eyes are different, though."

David slowly glanced around. Everyone within earshot was staring at him.

"Well, that explains why Jane blushes when you two are next to each other." Gareth grinned. "Isn't Death supposed to be God's most perfect creation? Fuck, David's ego just went to new heights, Arthur."

Arthur shrugged. "She doesn't consciously pick up on the similarities, which is amusing. You have slightly different smiles, and she focuses on that and your eyes. Perhaps she sees something more than just physical appearance, though."

This revelation caused David to think about what he'd been considering with the three of them. It made more sense now.

"I am still not sure that is wise, brother." Arthur shot him a dark look. "Even if what you are thinking is true, it is wrong."

"Stay out of my head." David's anger rose. "I never considered it before, but I know what I'm doing. And you have no idea what this truly feels like, so do not provide input for what you have never had to fathom."

"What are you talking about?" Gawain frowned as he looked between them.

"Many of the others are whispering already," Apollo whispered.

"What?" David snapped.

"They think you and Death are sharing Jane," Arthur said quietly.

"What?" Gawain exclaimed as David glared at Arthur.

"Why do you think I came to speak to you?" Arthur shook his head. "The fairy queen saw you three together and was very upset. Nearly everyone knows, and they speculate what is happening while she is there with him."

"They should mind their own business. What happens between the three of us is none of their concern." David had spoken calmly, but he was pissed. He had tried to keep it from his thoughts on how it would come across to others—how he would be viewed from now on. It was his love for Jane and acceptance of the truth that had him willing to do this. And he wanted to—it felt right. But it was easy to begin thinking he was a weak man who couldn't please his woman or destroy a rival male. Not that anyone could take out Death, but still, David had to realize he wasn't enough.

"That is untrue," Arthur said. "If it were true, he wasn't either . . . And do not forget, she chose you and asked him to do this. I do not think even he anticipated what it would cause her to suffer, and it was unfortunate that it took doing that for all of you to see. You are always the man she will choose, and it says a lot about your strength that you are confident enough to leave her with him. A weak man who did not trust in his mate's love wouldn't leave as you did. You took complete charge of the situation because you saw what none of us could see. Your love is powerful, brother. She needs it. I think God knew this when he created you. She needs you to stay strong because she is weaker than any of us realize."

"She's weak?" Gareth asked.

Apollo smacked him. "Quiet."

David lowered his gaze. "I trust them. I trust he is doing everything he can to keep her safe, and I trust in my decision to be with her this way."

"Wait," Gareth whispered, leaning closer. "You and Death . . ." He made a back-and-forth hand gesture.

Arthur threw a rock at him. "Mind your manners."

David glowered at the ground. "It hasn't gotten that far, and I have no plans to be with him, buffoon. He does not, either. It's all for her and will help him remain loyal to her. She cannot cope with his lifestyle, and it is too complicated to understand why she cannot be expected to accept they are not together. Before, I was selfish and ignorant, but I see now. This way, though, he has what he desires and deserves, and he can go on without having meaningless relations for the sake of sating his need for her. It is not what you think between them."

Gawain frowned, scratching his head. "Brother, you know I love her very much, but I am not sure—"

David cut him off. "I have not come to this decision lightly. It is important they both have each other, and I only just realized how much they truly need one another. It isn't her being unfaithful or that she's being selfish and unfair to me. I must take this step to assure her she is not betraying me. That is why we will only engage in this when all three of us are present. He knows I do not wish him to take her whenever he likes. It's not passing her between us. She is with me. But he is with her, too. He was there first anyway."

Gareth began to speak, but Arthur pushed his arm up to shove his food into his mouth.

"Do not make this harder on him," Arthur said. "She is not the same. Nor is Death. They have been growing weaker but only appearing strong because of how close they were allowed to be. It is wearing off, though. Something was not right with him."

"Death isn't fulfilling his duty," came Hades' quiet voice.

David jerked his head up, meeting Hades' stare. "What do you mean? Is that why he is weak?"

Hades nodded. "What he has learned since her time with Lucifer has changed everything. He cannot sense her death anymore. She, like you, lives on borrowed time. Your souls make it harder to determine when you will finally pass, but he knows as soon as your body is fatally wounded. So, in her case, it changed because he always stopped it. Now, she is absent from him. He is terrified. Reckless."

"Why is she absent?" Gawain asked.

"Because he chose her over his duty." Hades sighed, rubbing his face. "Once he found out the truth about her, he was forced to choose, and he chose her. But he chose for her to have the life she wanted . . . with David. So, instead of claiming her to keep her safe as one would expect, he vowed to protect her at whatever cost. That is why he has been so attached to her. He is in a constant state of fear. And she is also relying on him to live every single day."

"What?" David almost jumped up.

Hades gave him a sad smile. "You know what you saw, David . . . The thing is, she cannot live without him. And the longer they keep this up, the more he will begin to deteriorate, and it will eventually destroy both of them. That is why Thanatos suggested what he did. He believed reducing how entwined they were would allow Death to return to his duty. It didn't. If he were to have stayed away—maybe he would have forgotten her to a degree and gone about his duties, but then she would grow worse off, and he still would not sense her death. So, he returned. It is because of you allowing him in that they are even functioning. It might last for a while. Thanatos warned me to watch them, but Death sent me here because he did not want anyone to mention that he must leave her. Not when you have given him what he already believed he would never have. She is even more precious than before.

"He has chosen her. War chose her, and the other Horsemen will as well. Keeping her safe is Death's only concern, and that is the worst thing that can happen to our universe. We need Death to live. But Death needs his Sweet Jane. We are doomed."

"I have to get back," David said, standing.

Gareth and Gawain jumped to their feet. "We're coming with you."

David didn't care who came with him. He was leaving. He turned to grab his things as Gareth and Gawain did the same, but they all froze when a powerful tug at their hearts nearly brought them to their knees.

"Jane," David whispered, touching his chest.

The others all had their hands over their hearts as they looked to the south. There was nothing visible, but they felt her. And Valhalla was north. She should not be down there.

"Arthur?" David asked, unable to move as he watched the knights stand, looking in the same direction as other immortals who seemed to be feeling the same disturbance.

"Lucifer," Arthur whispered. "She's with Lucifer. Death isn't with them. She left."

"What?" David's fangs cut his lip, and his eyes widened as her presence vanished. The emptiness made several immortals collapse. David panted, clutching his chest as he tried to feel her again.

Arthur grabbed his head. "She was teleporting with Lucifer. He's fleeing from someone to keep her safe. It's not just Death chasing them—there are many others. Death was wounded, and she chose to go with Lucifer for reasons I could not decipher. All I know is she was heartbroken over something Death had done."

"He was with Thanatos' sister the night he removed . . ." Hades whispered but didn't say more.

David squeezed his eyes shut. He hadn't made his choice vocal that night, and now she was heartbroken.

Arthur nodded. "Something happened to her. Her body was too weak. She was sick."

"Dying," Hades said.

David's heart was beating too fast. He gathered his things. "Where was he taking her?"

"I don't know, brother," Arthur said. "He bonded with her. He is traveling frantically to keep the others away. He must be afraid to fight because of her current condition. I sensed his feelings, but I couldn't read his thoughts. He was conflicted. Worried. But he was the one who shot Death."

David growled, strapping on his belts. "Hades, do you have any idea where Lucifer would take her?"

"If they are bonded, he can take her anywhere, even Hell. But I do not think he would do that with the alliances shifting the way they are. He needs to fully bond with her to show all of Hell his queen is truly his. He will not enter Hell's gates until he is certain she is safe."

"Fuck." David pulled at his hair. "I'm going back to the fortress.

Someone has to know where he would go." His heart rate spiked. "The children. You said they were under attack."

"She believed them to be guarded," Arthur said, gesturing for the knights to prepare for departure. "The fortress is under attack. Ready to leave."

The entire camp jumped into action, breaking down their tents and arming themselves.

"David," Arthur whispered. "Thanatos attacked Death to stop him from going after Jane. He must be helping Lucifer."

"What? No, he's loyal to Jane."

Arthur shook his head. "Death's thoughts were present for a short moment. He's chasing after them. He was furious and injured. Lucifer shot him, then Thanatos prevented him from immediately giving chase. This happened within hours of us leaving. They've been running ever since. Death only just caught up with them, and that is why they accidentally came this way. Lucifer is jumping from one destination to the next with her, trying to find somewhere to hide. Thanatos is not on Jane's side. Death injured him. Severely. He's imprisoned by some of the Fallen who have sided with Jane. If we can get him to talk, I believe he will know where Lucifer might be taking her."

"Then we will start there." David grabbed his pack, his mind and heart torn between going after Jane and getting to the babies. "Fuck. Why the fuck would she leave?"

"David, lower your voice," Arthur said, also packing.

He nodded, trying to breathe steadier. The cold air was cruel to his burning lungs and hot skin. It felt like fire was burning inside him. He'd felt it before when he'd given in to his instincts to kill for blood, and it was there again. It was from fear of losing her—losing her in any way. *She left us.*

"There has to be a good reason for her to leave," Arthur said. "She was hysterical, but she wasn't afraid of Lucifer. She trusted whatever plan he had given her. Just remain calm. Death will not stop searching for her. Our priority must be the children and the fortress. Jane would want her family safe. She knows we will go back for them because she has Death. Stay strong, brother. She will not betray you."

"I wouldn't say that," said a voice that had every vampire hissing. "After all, she's asked me to fuck her, and I have. Twice."

David raised his head, instantly locking eyes with Lancelot.

"Hello, brothers." Lancelot grinned as the forest surrounding them lit up with too many glowing eyes to count.

Arthur stepped forward. "Think carefully about what you do right now. I see inside your mind and know you are conflicted about what she did to you."

Fury flashed across Lancelot's face. "What she did to me was murder my son and daughter," he roared. "She slaughtered my entire family!"

"She had no choice," Arthur said sadly. "You know this. You keep arguing with yourself because you saw her. You saw her trying to help you and save them. You know that wasn't her."

Lancelot shook his head. "I saw her give up. She made me submit, and then she killed them anyway. Consider it a mercy that I kill you now. She will destroy all of you, just as she did me. All I had left were those she brutally slaughtered, and she laughed as she bathed in their blood. She will regain her darkness—they promised she would. But I will not let her go this time. I will find her, and I will destroy her."

Arthur cast David a glance before turning back to Lancelot. "Join us, brother. Together we can defeat them. We can keep her pure."

"Don't call me that," Lancelot roared. "And she will never be pure."

David's heart burned.

"You know that is a lie," Arthur said, holding his hands up in surrender. The forest hissed and growled. "You saw her, Lance. That is Jane. She didn't want to hurt you. And she died inside the moment she saw what that thing had done to you and your family. That wasn't her."

"No, just half of her disgusting soul," Lancelot spat. "Do you see what she did?" He pointed to the name carved into his stomach. "That was your mate. The hazel-eyed girl."

"You deserve worse," Gareth shouted.

Lancelot laughed. "You're awfully quiet, Prince David. Why is that, I wonder? Are you as destroyed as I was when the woman I loved betrayed me?" He turned to Arthur. "Did he ever tell you? Did she ever tell you?"

"Shut up!" David pulled his sword.

A wicked grin formed on Lancelot's face. "You buried it deep, didn't you? So deep he wouldn't find it because you couldn't stand the truth."

A look of betrayal flitted over Arthur's face, and he pulled his sword.

Lancelot laughed, clapping his hands together as several vampire leaders came to his side. Ares was there, with Zeus and Mictlantecuhtli at his side. None of them had heard any news about the Aztec 'god of death' in centuries, but he was there, which meant Lancelot had combined his forces with Greece's strongest army and the most powerful clan of the South. They had last rumored to outnumber Valhalla. They were screwed.

"Looks like our reunion is cut short," Lancelot said. "It is time we end our feud. I will make you all this promise before we slaughter you. Jane will die a slow, humiliating, and painful death. And when it is only her dark twin staring out of those once pretty eyes of hers, I will cut out her heart. Even the King of Hell cannot stop me. Because someone stronger than all of them is unhappy with the Fallen Prince. So trust me, that bitch will pay. And Jane will suffer because she was too fucking weak to fight her."

David's heart pounded. His pulse was so loud in his ears that he could no longer hear the growls of the werewolf army. He stared into Lancelot's eyes, and he saw Jane's sorrow. She had been devastated because of what she'd done to Lancelot. And she had yet to atone for it within herself. "She was sorry."

Lancelot's expression crumpled but hardened quickly. "I know she was, brother. But sorry isn't enough."

Suddenly, fire wielders within Lancelot's command sent flames and balls of red, orange, and blue fire at them. Tristan roared, racing out ahead of everyone as a wall of fire erupted from his hands and mouth. His fire absorbed the attack, but the dying flames revealed a wave of werewolves and vampires.

"FORMATIONS," Thor roared.

David snatched up his sword, his eyes still locked on Lancelot as Akakios and his pack charged into the front line, ripping everyone apart and tossing them into the air.

Lancelot smiled at David as he spoke. It was too loud to hear, but David read his lips clearly: We end this.

David nodded. He was going to silence the monster who raped and killed for pleasure. There were no excuses this time—they would fight to the death, and David knew it would not be him who lay ripped to pieces when it was over.

2 2

HAZEL

It was a rare moment for David to feel pain assault every inch of his body, and it should have been impossible for no sound to reach his immortal ears as the world seemed to carry on around him in slow motion.

He lifted his head off the icy rocks and watched the silent battle ensue. Utter silence.

Flashes of light surrounded him as bodies collapsed on one another and blood sprayed through the air, but David could not hear a single cry of death—a single shout of victory.

"Fuck," he said, but even then, he could not hear his own voice. There was no time to panic over this, though. A blast had hit him, and it had done its damage, but he was breathing. And he was pissed.

Grunting, he dug his fingers into the blood-soaked dirt and pushed himself up. He stood, spitting the bitter blood of his enemies from his mouth before scanning his surroundings.

Time had yet to catch up to him as he took in the muted battle. David scanned countless faces, searching for his brothers. It was difficult without any sound to guide him, but he luckily found Gawain and Arthur fighting close by as the others ran toward him. They must've witnessed the attack he'd suffered and knew he needed protection. The blast had taken him by surprise, and it had been aimed directly at him. It wasn't a standard explosive. Silver ground into fine powder had been released like a gas, weakening him so that he'd stood no chance when a second and third blast came right for him. The first exploded near his head while the other hit him in the chest, sending him through the air and away from Lancelot.

Humiliation washed through David, but anger flushed it out as he stomped through the piles of bodies to retrieve his sword. His body was already mending, but the deafness had not left him.

He was massaging his ear, hoping for some improvement, when someone approached. David drew his sword, snarling as he spun around. The Rusalka female glared at him before raising a bag of blood to his face. He took the offering as she began providing him cover by firing her gun.

Finally, muffled sound touched his ears, and he tossed the empty bag. "Do you have more?"

"No," she shouted, but he only made out her lip movement. "You may feed from me if you like."

Even though the urge to feed from her was great, he shook his head and reloaded his gun. He knew his reasons for desiring a donor were from Jane's betrayal. He was trying to hold on to his love for her and not let Lancelot's taunts get to him, but it wasn't easy. Lance knew what to say to him to break his heart, soul, and mind.

David covered his ears when an immense collection of noise bombarded him.

"David." Artemis ran to him. "Here." She tossed him another bag. "Drink quickly."

Thankful, he drank the next ration while watching Artemis fight beside the Rusalka.

The pain from the return of his hearing eased, and he breathed in the smell of fire and smoke as he joined Artemis. "Lancelot?"

She pointed ahead. "He is beyond the tree line to the east. Tristan destroyed the cannons they used on you. Are you going to be all right?"

"I'm fine." David glanced around and watched a third wave of the massive force getting ready to attack.

"Brother?" Arthur called, rushing toward him.

"I'm fine," David repeated as he squinted, searching for his rival.

"He's waiting for you," Arthur said.

David sensed Arthur wanted to argue about who would face Lancelot, but neither said anything. He knew Arthur would not step between him and a threat to Jane, and it was her that Lancelot held responsible for his new suffering. It didn't matter if Jane was no longer trustworthy.

"David." Arthur shook his head.

"Stay out of my head." David bared his fangs.

"You are not thinking clearly." Arthur grabbed his arm when he nearly rushed into a pack of wolves.

David paused, but fury surged through his heart as he recalled Lancelot's words before he'd shot the canon at him: *"She moaned like a whore. She trembled in ecstasy as I filled her with my seed. My seed, brother. She tasted it. All the while, she was still full of Lucifer's. She covered your scent with ours. You were not enough. Where is she now, my prince? With him."*

He was never enough for her. Even with Death at his side, she still abandoned them for that Fallen bastard.

"David, you know that's not what she's done." Arthur grabbed his face as his rage soared. He was ready to give in to the beast within. Maybe then he'd be enough. After all, Jane trusted in Lucifer. Was it the power he held? Lucifer could do what he and Death could not. Maybe she desired darkness because that is where true power waited.

Arthur shook him. "Focus. Jane left for reasons we cannot fully grasp. She was thinking about you, though. She was frantic, but she was aware of her decision, and it had nothing to do with that Fallen other than her trusting in the plan he presented. She was doing what she thought was best. Set aside your anger regarding Lucifer. She loves you. She loved you and thought only of you and your children when she allowed him to touch her before. When she submitted to him, she did it for you. For all of us. Her love for him is nothing compared to what she feels for you. Don't let Lancelot get to you."

David squeezed his eyes shut. Jane was everything to him, but she was never really his.

Arthur slapped him across the face. "Focus! She is yours. Her heart chose you. Don't let Lance destroy yours. He knows that it was not Jane who murdered his family and . . ."

David opened his eyes as his soul roared. "Fucked him?"

Arthur glared at him. "Jane is not the darker half, brother. I know I said things that confused you in the past, but you were right—Jane is good. She is the woman who smiles at you and calls you her David. She places you on such an incredible pedestal above the others. She is the girl who makes all of us laugh because of her innocence and charm. She is the woman who willingly throws herself into fire so you never have to burn.

"You were the greatest threat to her darker soul because your Jane loved you so dearly—because she considered you the best. That terrified her darker half. So Jane saved you from herself."

"She left," he growled. "She left me then, and she's left me again. Even when I was willing to let Death stand beside me. Neither of us is good enough for her."

Arthur held his face tighter. "Brother, she has a plan. She's following her heart, and it told her to follow Lucifer to protect her family. Something is wrong with her and with Death. She was devastated and fading, but Lucifer can give her something. You know her main goal is always you and her children. She was thinking of you, and she took the threats away from everyone. You are who she wants. You are more than enough—but she, David, she is only half. You saw it. She has yet to see, but, brother. Oh, how she will adore you when she does."

David felt like he was breathing fire. He wanted to believe this and in their love, but he kept imagining Jane at Lucifer's side and how she had smelled of Lucifer and Lancelot upon returning.

"She wanted to die for it, brother." Arthur shook his head. "Don't let this destroy you. She is your strength and why you have stayed good all these years. None of us could have done what you have. You did it because she was out there."

"But she's not—"

Arthur cut him off. "She is. Have faith in her. She has faith in you—in your life together. She may be Death's Sweet Jane, but she is *your* Jane as well. And your girl needs you because she still has battles to fight. What you saw—what we all saw with her and the Horsemen—is nothing compared to what we will see when you fully take her side with them. You are more than her Other, and she is so proud to be your Jane. Stay strong for her. You are the one who will help her become what we all need her to be."

"My Jane," he said, breathing in deeply. The freezing air swirled within his lungs, mixing with the fire he was ready to unleash. "It's her. It's always been her."

"There you go. Don't lose yourself to the beast waiting inside you. Jane trusted you to return to her as the man you are, not the monster you fear becoming. I swear, brother, she has every intention of returning. Have faith in her."

David released the breath he'd held in. "You are certain she was thinking of me?"

Arthur smiled. "Do you really have to ask?"

"No," he said, relaxing the muscles in his body. *She loves me.*

"She does. Keep her smile in your mind. She keeps yours in hers whenever she is surrounded by darkness. Lancelot is making you remember the twisted smile her darker soul wore. Jane hated and feared that smile. Don't associate it with her. And remember, the children are waiting for you to return to them."

"My children." David nodded, relaxing even more.

"That's right." Arthur patted his shoulder. "They're yours. Jane loves that you consider them yours. One day, that darling little girl and amazing little boy will call you their father. Their father will not be a monster. Their father will be their hero. Their father will be the man who was so great, he gave their mother everything that would make her whole, and he helped her glow for all of us."

David further relaxed, picturing Nathan's and Natalie's faces. They had been through so much. They'd watched Jane fade until she was a mere shell of herself, and they'd watched Jason sacrifice himself to save them. They loved Jason despite his faults, just like Jane did. Jason had trusted David to keep his family together and love them—to be strong for them. *My family.*

Arthur spoke again. "God made no mistake when he placed your soul next to hers. Don't linger on what you've discovered. Trust in your heart and soul. Trust in God. They all chose her, and she most definitely has chosen you. Even with him, she still seeks you."

Jane's face appeared in David's mind. He saw her through the red haze that had consumed him when he'd fought beside Death. After she had summoned the power of her suit, he and Death lost their connection to her. The pull she constantly emitted had vanished, and they lost their minds. She'd left them.

"She came back for you," Arthur said. "Remember what you saw when there was only blood."

Just as David had envisioned her long ago, his warrior goddess came roaring out of the darkness, and she'd brought an army with her to fight for him. And when she realized he'd lost control of himself, she didn't flee or go to Death. She challenged him.

He'd known who she was right away, and he'd wanted to conquer her. She was his, and all he could focus on was the fire roaring in her hazel eyes as she demanded he come back to her. She refused to leave him. She would have died for him—at his very hand. She had never looked more beautiful than she did at that moment, and it had terrified him.

She was too precious and powerful—too lovely and great to be his. If he did one thing wrong, touched her, tasted her as he had desired, David believed he would have destroyed her. So he tried to get away from her. But Jane refused to turn her back on him.

Her face suddenly changed in his mind. They were no longer full of roaring gold and emerald flames. He stared into dim golden orbs as she checked her clean fingers, searching for blood because she'd been cut and left with a bleeding soul. His baby had asked to be torn apart for him because she loved him and wanted to prove he was her choice.

"See," Arthur said. "You. She does it all for you. And you have decided to do the same for her. It truly is lovely, brother. No matter how hard it is to swallow, what you are doing for her, what all of you are doing, it is incredible. I am in awe."

Sadness rose and made breathing difficult until he remembered how beautiful she'd looked between him and Death. He'd made that possible. Not Death. Not Lucifer. Him. He'd been strong enough to light a new path for her. It was an unexpected path, but David had been the one to find and offer it to her.

He smiled. His hazel-eyed girl would be back someday, and she'd shine brighter than ever before. He'd weakened because he could not see the truth and believe in her love, but knowing what he knew now, he realized her love and choosing him meant even more. He wasn't less compared to Death and Lucifer. He was the man she needed—the man she chose again and again. And he chose her.

"You're ready, brother." Arthur held his face, staring him in the eyes. "And I saw what you have buried deep inside you—I do not blame you. When you see all you've kept hidden, know I am still your brother." He smiled, releasing him. "Fight well."

David nodded, tightening his hand on his sword before quickly snatching a brunette by her braid as she tried to rush forward.

Artemis screamed, trying to pull free as he yanked her close.

"You're going to get yourself killed," he growled. "Stay here."

She punched his chest as her green eyes glistened with tears. "Let me go."

Arthur turned, seeing what David had already witnessed, what Artemis was rushing toward. Hades and Zeus. Her father and uncle were in a brutal match with each other.

David grabbed Artemis by the chin, squeezing hard. "Stop! If you run out there, you kill Hades and your father. Stay here. You will not choose between them."

"Is Jane rubbing off on you, brother?" Gareth asked, grabbing hold of

Artemis as she cried, watching Hades take a hit before he delivered his own devastating blow to Zeus' side. "I have her."

David motioned for Tristan, his gaze shifting to the fight between the god of the underworld and the god of lightning. It was a battle between brothers who'd fallen so far from each other that they no longer remembered when their quarrel truly started.

Tristan ran close, patting his shoulder. "You ready? I have one big attack left in me. I need my wife before I can do more."

David smiled. He needed Jane, too. "I'm ready."

"I can't decide which fight I want to watch more." Gareth held Artemis in such a way she could not see her father and uncle destroy one another.

Blasts continued to go off around them, but David briefly caught sight of the moon above him. Only half. He smiled. *Hi, baby.* He'd make her whole again.

Gawain ran forward, ducking and yelping as a bolt of lightning ricocheted their way. "Fuck!"

Hades roared, his pale blue eyes nearly white as he swung his weapon. The claw missed Zeus but grabbed a werewolf off Akakios' mate. Hades swung the chains at Zeus, hitting him with the werewolf.

It landed on Zeus but exploded instantly from a blast of lightning.

"Damn." Gareth whistled, patting Artemis awkwardly. "I mean, they're fine."

David looked away as they began battling again. "How close can you get me?"

Tristan pointed at a boulder in the distance. "I think that's a good spot. Arthur will call the others in, and we'll be alone. Gawain will carry me back."

"I'll get him back," Gawain said before David could ask him.

David didn't like leaving Tristan vulnerable, but the knights were too engaged. Arthur was shouting commands alongside the fairy king and queen, and Bedivere treated some of the more severely injured men and women while Kay and Percivale's team dragged back more wounded. The Rusalka and Nereids led most of the offense, and David chuckled, knowing Jane would love to be leading her army alongside them right now.

A flash of green light made him squint. David expected Death, but he wasn't too surprised to see Hades wearing a cloak, shielding himself from lightning. Pulling the cloak down, he swung his chains, wrapping them around Zeus, then raised his sword high but faltered when Artemis screamed.

A bolt of lightning shot right into Hades' chest. The chains fell from around Zeus, and Hades collapsed.

"Dammit," Apollo yelled and took off to aid his uncle.

David growled, glaring at Gareth as he struggled to hold on to Artemis.

"I didn't mean to let her see," Gareth said, pulling Artemis' head against his chest.

"No, Apollo," Artemis wailed. "Father!"

David walked toward Gareth as he watched Apollo move between Hades and Zeus. This wasn't a fight he expected to witness. David caught sight of Artemis' agony-filled eyes as she tried to free herself.

"David, don't," she said, fighting harder.

He raised his hand. "You don't have to watch. We'll be here for you afterward."

"No," she screamed, and he quickly hit her on the back of the head with the hilt of his sword, knocking her unconscious.

"Get her out of the way." David turned toward the fight again.

Apollo roared as Zeus hesitated. Then, instead of attacking his son with lightning, he sent flames, which Apollo blocked using his fire.

"Oh, damn," Gareth whispered as he returned after leaving Artemis with the injured to be watched over.

David watched Apollo's arms become engulfed in flames until his entire body was ablaze, just as Tristan had accomplished with the help of War.

"Atta boy." Tristan nudged David when Zeus surrounded his body in sparking bolts of electricity.

"Come, David," Gawain said. "We'll use the distraction to get you closer."

David followed, meeting Arthur's gaze briefly. He knew Arthur was worried, but he smiled and turned away. He'd end this fight with Lance tonight.

Tristan pushed through the front line. David breathed deeply, glancing at the moon as Gawain patted his shoulder.

"She'll be back," Gawain said.

"I know." He looked away from the first quarter moon, praying she was okay and that she would indeed return to him. "Gawain, if I fall—"

Gawain shook his head. "You won't. And whatever has been plaguing you, remember how she looked the night we first found her. When she looked up, she had eyes only for you. Her heart told her one thing, brother: *he's the one.* Don't doubt her love. Now finish this fight before we all die."

David nodded as that memory of first setting eyes on Jane became all he could see through the chaos around him. She'd been so brave to run out there alone. She hadn't even screamed when they unleashed a hail of bullets around her, and she hadn't flinched as she raised her gun and shot the zombie about to attack him. Her pretty eyes had stayed glued to his, at peace. Just like they had when she almost turned into one of the undead. Dying in his arms, she felt peace looking into his eyes and thought he was an angel. Those hazel eyes were his whole world for so long, and though they were no longer hazel, they still looked at him with hope and love.

"Ready?" Tristan shouted, stopping beside a boulder.

They all looked behind them. Lightning and fire crashed into each other, holding the attention of the entire battlefield.

"Let's go." David scanned the tree line.

"Kick his ass, brother," Tristan said as his entire body lit in flames.

David grinned as the fiery face smiled before running into a pack of wolves fighting Akakios.

Whistles rang out, and their lines began withdrawing as Tristan set everything ablaze. The howls and stench of burning fur and flesh reached David's nose, but he breathed in the smell of death and watched his brother annihilate a large section of Mictlantecuhtli's forces. A sad smile touched David's lips, though. Jane had expressed interest in Indigenous gods, and Death had privately confirmed David's suspicion of Jane's Indigenous ancestry with him. She would've adored meeting the *Aztec god*. The immortal was strong and talented; maybe he'd and others would survive.

Akakios stopped beside David.

"Go protect Artemis," David said.

Akakios lifted his massive head, staring at the moon.

"I'll get her back," David said, smiling as the alpha wolf howled and ran toward his mistress.

"Jane will ask if he can sleep in bed with you." Gawain laughed.

David shook his head. "I already have Death in our bed. I am not adding a wolf."

"Well, maybe she'll pick him over Death." Gawain grinned, pushing a soldier in the right direction.

"No." David swallowed, glancing at the moon again. His eyes drifted to the dark side before shifting to the glowing half. "Death stays."

"My, how your tremendous heart has grown even greater, brother." Gawain checked David's weapons. "Tristan is about spent. Fight well. We will not leave without you."

"Just get Tristan home to Iseult." David breathed out, closing his eyes once more to see his girl. She was there, of course. She smiled in the dark, slowly lighting up more of her face as she stared at him, and his heart pounded as every moment between them came forward.

There were tears but also breathtakingly beautiful smiles. Cruel words were unleashed during moments of hurt, but they were always soothed with sweet and honest words. David remembered every caress, from the very innocent to the not-so-innocent. Every moan and gasp—every kiss from their first to the moment he left her was at his fingertips and on his lips. He sighed, remembering the taste of every drop of her blood on his tongue, how much she craved his, and how she thirsted for him in every way possible. They were so in tune with each other, without any bond to make them so.

She'd grown so much in such a short time. Not everyone would give her the credit she deserved, but he did. He was in awe of her strength and bravery. Of course, she could be foolish and rash, but she only followed her heart and tried to be everything she thought everyone expected her to be. All he wanted was for his girl to be happy and whole, and he knew now how to get her and keep her as lovely as she was meant to be.

Again, Jane came into view. Every emotion flickered on her face—every bruise and cut she'd endured when he was meant to protect her, but one thing always remained. Those eyes. Those pretty eyes, whether sad, hurt, empty, or filled with horror, a gold glint always stayed near the center.

David watched her smile at him. She was trying to glow, smiling even though her soul was dimming.

"It's time, David." Gawain squeezed his shoulder.

He waited, trying to see more of her before she slipped into the darkness again. Before she disappeared, he whispered, "Come back to me, Jane."

A smile lit up her face. *"I'll come back."*

Tristan let out an earth-shattering roar, and David finally opened his eyes, leaving his girl to find himself in the center of a firestorm.

"Get ready," Tristan hollered as the flames he'd created grew so intense that David had to shield his face.

Cries broke through the inferno as Tristan released another yell before an enormous wave of fire shot out of his hands and ravaged the forest.

Just as Tristan collapsed, exhausted, David caught sight of Lancelot stepping out from behind a boulder he'd used to shield himself from the flames.

307

Gawain patted David's shoulder once more before dragging Tristan out of harm's way.

"Brother." Lancelot walked out into the open.

David started at him. "We are not brothers."

Lancelot smirked, twirling a sword. "Have you truly forgotten, or do you simply hate me that much?"

"I haven't forgotten your evil acts." David crossed the charred earth until they were only twenty feet apart.

"So, we fight to the death right now without closure before one of us meets our end?"

"Closure?" David frowned. "Your death is the closure I seek. You nearly raped Gwen; you have done so to countless women. You've tortured and mutilated them, and you are responsible for the lives of your men and those they have slain. There is nothing else to have closure for. If anything, my only regret is not doing this sooner."

"Do you even remember I once had green eyes?"

David glanced around him. The forces had re-engaged, but the lines were holding better. It seemed Lancelot had ensured they wouldn't be interrupted this time.

Lancelot sighed as he cast a glance up at the moon. "She no longer calls to you, does she?"

"Do not speak of Jane again." David tightened his hand around his sword.

"I heard she no longer has hazel eyes." Lance lowered his gaze to him. "I have not seen it, but even my heart aches at that truth. Do you know yet what it means? The others think I have no idea—many of them do not. Actually, only one knows all, and he did not know I listened to him as he warred with himself."

David's heart beat faster. "You don't know anything about her. Let's get this over with. I have every intention of killing you so she feels safe. You will not harm another woman, especially Jane."

Lancelot rubbed his chest. "Such a perfect name for her, isn't it? Simple but powerful. Like David—God's most beloved. How it must have hurt to learn the truth. I see now that you have. Yet, I am confused. You do not seem as unstable as I expected."

"I'm done with this. Fight me."

Lancelot chuckled. "Very well—I never could refuse you, my prince. However, should I fall, send word to Galahad that I thought of him often.

Tell him I was proud to say he was of my line, and I would not have raised my sword against him."

"Fine," David said, unsure why Lancelot's stalling affected him so much.

"I would have raised him, you know? He would be far more skilled than a knight amongst legends."

"He is noble and a worthy knight," David said, closing the gap between them.

"But he stands no chance against you. None of them do. Who trained at your side, my prince?" Lancelot's smile turned wicked. "Do you remember anything? Or do you like to believe Arthur and Gawain have always been your closest companions?"

A much younger version of himself laughing as he sparred with a younger Lancelot flickered within David's mind. He always shoved these images down, but he had not truly spoken with Lancelot for many years, and now they would not stay hidden.

"So you do remember," Lancelot said, smirking and stepping closer. "Good. This way, you can remember your faults and how they led to me becoming your greatest enemy. Now let's start, shall we? I would hate to keep Jane waiting for either of us. She is quite a needy little thing, isn't she? I do hope the King of Hell leaves her unsatisfied."

David roared, swinging his sword at Lancelot's neck. The strike was blocked, and they exchanged several attacks before he landed a hard punch to Lancelot's chest.

For a moment, the battle roared around him again. Guns blasted and swords clashed as growls and screams echoed through the skies.

Then, as if someone sucked up all the noise with a straw, the world quieted again.

"Right in the heart." Lancelot laughed. "So like you, Sir David."

"Stop stalling," David roared.

His opponent grinned and charged him. David met his attacks, blocking each powerful swing aimed at him. He wouldn't let this fight end until one of them was dead.

Lancelot growled and sped his attack up, catching him across the arm with his blade. David hissed, but his sword found its mark across Lancelot's chest before David landed yet another punch.

It sent Lancelot back a step, but he immediately swung for him again.

They were even, which only enraged David because he knew why. He could see every moment of their youth replaying in his mind. Every spar, every scrap they fought out with each other, and how they laughed off their troubles after a good fight. He saw Lancelot getting teased for not having decent clothes and how the smaller peasant boy fought like a lion when the wolves circled him. That boy always had David's back. No matter the status of another, Lancelot was loyal through and through.

Lancelot landed a devastating punch to David's jaw. He fell back, but Lancelot didn't jump in for the kill.

"You are distracted." Lancelot placed his hands on his waist, breathing hard as David sat up, wiping the blood from his lip. "Thinking about your girl, or is there something else more important right now?"

David chuckled. "I was just remembering a boy who had no place amongst princes, yet he befriended the outcast prince who wanted to be a knight instead of a king."

Lancelot grinned. "And I thought you had truly forgotten me."

"I keep these memories hidden from myself." David stood, rubbing his jaw. "It's easier."

Lancelot glanced at the moon. "It is. I think that is why I respect your woman so much. I hate her, but I admire that she never lets a day pass when she does not face her demons. To remember and constantly face your torment and sorrow takes a great deal of strength. So does hiding it, I suppose. I have waited a long time for you to remember us."

David chuckled. "They thought we were lovers."

Lancelot nodded, grinning. "And I beat the shit out of them when your father told you not to engage the others over it. He thought you loved me as well."

"I did." David breathed out as more memories came forward. "But not as a lover."

"Yes, I loved you as a brother, too," Lance admitted. "You changed, though. My loyalty and friendship meant nothing when I told you about my feelings for Gwen."

David shook his head. He didn't want to remember, but Lancelot continued.

"I suppose you know a bit what it feels like to watch your beloved in the arms of a more powerful man. Well, in Jane's case, two of God's most powerful angels."

"It's not the same," David muttered as the fire returned to his lungs.

"Isn't it, though?" Lancelot asked. "Does it hurt? To watch her smile at him? I know I felt rage on your behalf when she smiled at Lucifer. I could always tell when she was smiling because he forced her to, but there was one moment she looked at him and smiled just for him."

David swallowed his roar. "Her feelings for him stem from him saving her in a way no one else could."

Lancelot smiled. "Perhaps. She is unique, isn't she? Gwen, though, she is no Jane. Yet, I still love her as deeply now as I did when I told you how I felt."

"Don't." David's fangs cut his lips.

The memory crushed him anyway.

David was only a boy of sixteen years; Lancelot was a year older.

"I love her, David," Lancelot had told him.

David glared at his adolescent friend, who had started to show interest in maidens. He had found himself attracted to them as well, but he wanted to focus on learning his sword and was not pleased to have his closest friend declare love for his older sister.

"You do not even know her." David felt betrayed and vulnerable because he had hoped they would go off to battle together like they always said they would. Lance was his only friend. The other knights and squires looked down on him, telling him to return to the palace. But Lance was there, telling everyone to fuck off. Still, David could not bear the betrayal he felt. "She is my sister. Has this been the only reason for our friendship?"

Lancelot's eyes went ablaze. "You dare accuse me of such a thing? You are my friend, my brother. I cannot help that I love her. I love you as well. I would die to protect you. I have always accepted the blame for our misadventures, David. For you!" His breaths came out hard. "But I have always adored her—even as a child. Still, you are my friend first. I am telling you before I make my desires known to all. Does that not prove how much I value our friendship?"

"You will not have my sister," David yelled. "She is a princess—not some whore who smiles at you when we walk past. I have seen how you look at her, and I have ignored it." He quickly recalled the moments he had caught Lancelot giving Guinevere flowers or going out of his way to offer her escort. "I never thought you would betray me this way."

"I am not betraying you, you spoiled fool," Lancelot roared. "You are so consumed with becoming a great warrior and having me follow you that you do not care for my feelings. I do not see how we were ever friends now. You are just like them."

"Take it back," David yelled.

Lancelot shook his head. "I will not."

David growled. "Stay away from her, or our friendship is done."

Lancelot stared at him, shocked. "You would have me choose between the two of you?"

"It remains your decision, but if you choose her, you betray me. I know you will grow tired of her—you grow tired of everything except for fighting. I will not let my sister suffer heartache because numerous women desire you. Pick another."

There was an understanding look in Lancelot's green eyes. "I will not grow tired of her. It is more than an infatuation."

"No, it is not, Lance," David said. "You do this with everything and everyone. I am the only person you have stayed with longer than a month's time. Every craft you have decided to study, you have given up for something more adventurous. I will not allow my sister to know this sort of pain. She is the only one I have, and you are the only friend I trust."

Lancelot sighed and rubbed his chest before looking him in the eye. "I choose her. I hope you understand one day. You are always my brother."

David had never felt more betrayed. He was losing his only real friend. "Then we are done. I will not let this go, and I will always be there to stop you from breaking her heart."

"I will not break her heart. Goodbye, brother." With those final words, Lancelot turned and left him standing there, fuming in the empty courtyard.

"I don't like remembering it either, brother," Lancelot said when the memory receded. "But that day in the courtyard haunts me every single night. You turned into a real dick after that. You laughed when she refused me in front of the entire court. I truly believed she would choose me, but, as I said, she is no Jane. She could not choose her heart over having the absolute best.

"Do not get me wrong, my prince, you are most worthy and the best in many areas, but you are not an all-powerful angel. You are not a king. You are a second son, an immortal created only when he was ruined in a deadly draw. You are not him . . . But she chooses you. Gwen could not."

David's eyes burned as his throat ached, but Lancelot continued.

"Did you even keep count of the many fucks you had throughout the palace? Does your precious Jane know how dark a past you have?"

"She knows I was foolish." He hated that Lancelot was right. "I will never live down my past behavior. It was a thoughtless way to deal with our falling out."

Lancelot nodded. "Yes, I do not even recall how we started that little charade. But, I suppose it matters little. It ruined both of us, didn't it?"

David growled as his fury rose. Jane's face became harder to keep in the front of his mind, but he grasped her when she reached for him. "At least I discontinued my sins," he spat. "You turned into a monster." His mind was at war with him. All of his buried emotions and memories were beating him down. But, *Jane*, he kept repeating. *Stay with me, baby.*

"Well, you are right there," Lancelot admitted. "I am curious, though, about how you would have reacted had your love chosen another over you and had your ex-best mate become friendly and accepting of a newcomer who stole her heart with his unnatural abilities and charm. Would you really keep your sanity if she chose one of them?"

David's heart nearly exploded. "She would never choose someone else!"

Lancelot smirked at him, and David saw the mistake he had made. He had betrayed his friend because he was a selfish youth, and he ignored the power of love. Then, out of pain or pride, he forced himself to forget everything they were before. As a result, the others never knew that the two of them had been the best of friends. Arthur didn't arrive until he was in his twenties. By then, they were hated rivals, and he had new friendships.

Lancelot chuckled with a consenting nod. "No, you are fortunate she is such a devoted soul. Perhaps that is the real reason I wish to destroy her. I envy that you have the best when my best turned her back on me when she saw Arthur's incredible power."

"Enough of this," David shouted. He was afraid. He feared Jane would do the same. *"No, David,"* her voice was soft as it caressed his hot skin. *"No, my love."* His mind attacked him. He remembered the horrible things Lancelot had carried out once Arthur arrived with Kay and Bedivere. It was clear that pain had caused Lancelot to grow more aggressive with women and other soldiers. David and his sister had destroyed all good that was in Lance. But one thing always confused David—Arthur's sudden friendship with Lancelot. It had been so abrupt, and Arthur had cast David aside, choosing more and more for Lance to accompany him. "Why did he befriend you?"

Lancelot smiled and tapped his head. "I knew he was not normal. Of course, I did not think him immortal, but I knew he had been gifted with unnatural abilities when I caught him carrying on a conversation with Kay without Kay ever uttering a word. So, I focused on your wrongdoings whenever I was in his presence. I focused on how cruel you were when we saw each other. He must've taken pity on me, not once, considering I was worse."

David sighed. "He was searching for other companions and saw I was full of darkness."

"Yes, I nearly had him fooled. I learned later that only Gabriel's instruction prevented him from changing me. I, of course, didn't know he had hoped to turn me, but I was only concerned with removing you from greatness with the powerful king."

"I did not see." David stopped walking when he realized how hurt his old friend was. Lancelot followed his action and waited for him to finish speaking. "I was foolish and young. You were my friend, and because I did not know the love of a woman, I disregarded yours. Still, I cannot forgive your attack on Guinevere. Or Jane."

Lancelot's dark eyes darted to his. "I would not either. I had already become the monster I am long before I became immortal. All it took was stumbling past their door and hearing her moaning his name for me to set it free."

David's heart cracked for his old friend.

"Will you let it take you, brother?" Lance asked. "When you find out, she let them consume her mind, body, and soul."

David roared, unable to prevent the images from forming of such an event with Jane. He saw her under Lucifer, under Lancelot—but instead of crying for him to save her, he saw her moaning with a smile on her lips.

Jane's voice whispered, and he tried to focus on it. *"No, my love."*

"Ah, I see your beast surfacing. Is she not enough, after all?"

"She's everything," David growled. "I will destroy you for her. She is haunted by what happened between you. I watched her scrub her skin off because she still felt you. I will save her. I should have made sure you were dead when we fought before. That is my only regret."

"Is that why I still breathe?" Lancelot laughed. "You cannot see how good you really are. You will lose yourself, David. Then you will be forced to sacrifice yourself or let her perish."

David's heart burned at the thought of losing Jane. "I'm tired of this conversation. You tried to rape my sister. You did so with hundreds of innocent girls and tortured millions. Thousands have died because of the monster you became. You tormented the love of my life, and my sister still has nightmares about you. I will end their suffering with your heart in my hands." He took a deep breath. "I will always carry the burden that I failed you. I should not have betrayed you, but I cannot let you leave here alive. This ends here."

Lancelot nodded and jabbed his sword into the ground. "If I die with you imagining me as a monster, I might as well make your tale great and accurate. Do me one favor, brother. Tell Gwen I never stopped loving her. If I had only been able to prove myself, I would have done every noble deed to earn her love."

David didn't respond at first but finally nodded and stabbed his sword into the earth.

"Thank you, brother. Now, enough of this reminiscent conversation—I feel like a pussy." He smiled evilly. "I want this as well. What will it take to break that nobility of yours? I just can't help myself. I still desire to watch you suffer for making me do so for so long."

David pushed his hair out of his eyes, his focus barely shifting to the war before resuming his calculations for the fight.

"Ah, I have it," Lancelot announced. "You said she felt me—did you fear I had succeeded in breeding with her?"

Fire blazed around David's heart. "I did. But I knew, even if she had, Jane loved me through it all. She still wore my scent, even then. I know you caught it clinging to her."

"Yes." Lancelot laughed, his wicked smile sharpening for mere seconds. "I could see how it vexed Lucifer to smell you. The entire camp expected you to leap out because she reeked of you."

David smiled. "You won't ruin me by trying to turn me against her."

"No?" Lancelot grinned. "Did she tell you how long she stayed with him? Alone in his cave? He may not have been able to cover your scent, but she certainly bathed in his. And she had no tears in her eyes when I saw her at his side, holding his hand, calling him her king."

David's heart cracked, and he roared, tackling Lancelot to the ground.

Lancelot was quick to brace himself and swiftly dealt a painful blow to David's jaw, then to his side.

Blood sprayed out of David's mouth as he threw his fist down.

Lancelot blocked the punch and knocked David away. David roared and taunted the beast he knew was waiting. His mind had completely pushed away all that he had just accepted and was only filled with destroying the monster who had lain with his Jane the way no other should.

"All right, brother." Lancelot chuckled. "I'll let you fight the monster. I did always give in to you." Without waiting, he morphed into his werewolf form, roaring across the small space separating them.

David roared back and felt his features morphing to reveal the beast he was. He no longer saw his young friend. All he could see was the monster he'd unsuccessfully fought for centuries.

When Lancelot charged, David was ready. He sidestepped the slide, Lancelot's wolf form expended, and landed a terrible punch to the ribs of the monster. The werewolf howled and turned to attack again, clawing David across his abdomen.

David roared, feeling fire in his lungs, and grabbed Lancelot's arm. He body-slammed him onto the rocks. Lancelot growled, quickly tackling him to the ground in return. David fought, letting his unsparing hits to the misshapen body above him weaken his opponent.

The violent attacks caused crippling devastation to Lancelot, and David rolled them so that he hovered over the beast.

Lancelot snarled before biting the arm headed toward his face. David hollered out in pain as his flesh tore away, and Lancelot freed himself from the dangerous position he had ended up in, knocking David across the face.

David felt his cheek split open, but it and his hand were healing.

Lancelot snarled, moving back.

David shook away his pain and used his speed to get in front of Lancelot. Again, he delivered a damaging series of punches, not letting Lancelot catch a breath.

Lancelot tried to keep up and returned swings, but David was crazed.

With a destroying blow to Lancelot's face, he watched his rival fall to the ground and shimmer into a man again. David was on him in a heartbeat, pummeling the human face of his old friend until he was an unrecognizable mess.

Lights began dropping out of the sky. They were so bright that even in his rage, David glanced up to see the balls of fire landing in the surrounding trees. There were a variety of colors, but most were red and white.

Lancelot coughed below him. David growled, looking down at his enemy. Only now, he stared in shock at the mess he'd made of his old friend.

"Fuck," David shouted, pulling back his fist that dripped with Lancelot's blood.

"Don't stop," Lancelot sputtered out in a choked taunt. "I won't stop. You can't stop."

David let him go. "Lance," he whispered and tried to look for help. He didn't know what to do. A raging desire to kill the monster beneath him consumed him, but he knew he'd helped create that monster. "What have I done?"

A bright series of flashes began exploding around them, but he couldn't look away from Lancelot.

"What you wanted to do all these years, brother." Lancelot groaned. "Kill me."

David shook his head. "No, I'm sorry. I can make this right. Just hang on. You will heal."

"They will kill her, David," Lancelot told him. He froze and watched Lancelot struggle to speak. "You cannot help me. If you want to save her, kill me. They want her dead. I won't stop."

"I'm not going to kill you. I know you have some good left in you. I will help you see it again."

Lancelot gave a twisted laugh that sounded more like a monstrous cackle. "I am the villain, and you are the hero. The hero does not bring the monster home to his beloved."

"Shut up, Lance." A brighter flash illuminated the tree line. David looked up and let out a ragged breath. Time seemed to slow as the battle resumed. Warmth embraced him and pushed away any hate that once clouded his mind. "You don't know my woman," he whispered. "She will understand."

"No," Lancelot said, making David look away from the figures exiting the trees, and time resumed once again. "I know she has pulled the darkest of hearts to her side, but I am not one of those. You are not meant to save me. No one can save me."

David shook his head. "You can fight the beast that lives within you. I saw my baby harboring the worst of them, and she is my heart. I will help you find yours again. Forgive me, brother."

A pained smile formed on Lancelot's face before his dark eyes looked into the distance and then back at him. "I guess it is up to me to keep your ass in God's good graces, then. I never could help myself when it came to keeping you out of trouble." He coughed weakly. "I will kill her, David. I will hunt her until her body is broken beneath me. I will rape her and cut

317

her into pieces. I cannot stop myself—I am the monster they wanted me to be. Will you let me leave here with that in your mind? You know I will find a way. She is too forgiving and trusting. How do you think I ever got the upper hand with her? She believes in people when she shouldn't."

He started to shake but tried to control his breathing. He looked back up and tried to hold onto the light he saw there in the center of the chaos.

"Don't let her go," Lancelot whispered, and David's side erupted in excruciating pain.

David roared as Lancelot's hand fell away, revealing the handle of a blade sticking out of his side. Screams mixed with his thunderous roar as he yanked it out, but David ignored everything, even when he swore he heard Jane screaming his name, and instinctively raised the dagger over his head.

"I will kill her," Lancelot roared as he yanked the gun from David's holster, aiming at David's heart.

As they roared through the chaos of battle, incredible pain exploded through David's body, and all he could see was white.

Just white.

23

ETERNITY

Lucifer held his hand over his bleeding leg. The light he emitted faded, and Jane pushed his hand away to inspect the wound.

"I'm sorry," she whispered, lightly trailing her finger over the edge of his cut.

He stood, lifting her. "It wasn't your fault. I should have reminded you to use your cloak to hide your presence from him." Lucifer carried her to a bed in the house he'd taken them to. It wasn't fit for his queen, but he needed a break after Death had surprised him. Lucifer had barely gotten Jane away, and he'd almost taken her right to David in the process. At least she was unaware of how close she'd gotten to her vampire.

Jane closed her eyes when her head hit the pillow. "I don't like using my cloak this way. I feel lost, and he gets so out of control when he doesn't feel me. I don't like hurting him, even if he has been a prick."

Lucifer sat beside her, his gaze momentarily sliding to her sides where Death's wings were visible to him and other angels before focusing on her face again. "You are doing great. And do not worry about Death—he brought this upon himself."

Jane opened her eyes, and he felt pain surge through his body at the sight of her gold eyes. "How long will we continue to run?"

"Not much longer."

"Good." She took a deep breath. "I feel weak. I thought you said I'd be okay after the bond."

"You are merely in need of blood. Our bond wasn't the full one you need to survive. I created a guardian bond to transport you, but you need something more to live without a constant supply of energy. The energy I gave you earlier is nearing its end."

She licked her lips, nodding. "Right. I forgot you told me it wasn't strong. Do I already have a guardian? Is that why?"

He remained quiet.

She rolled her eyes. "Fine, don't tell me. Will we be able to go to David soon?"

Lucifer kept his face empty of the rage he felt. "You will not return to your vampire. I believe he is engaged in battle anyway."

Her eyes flew open. "What the fuck do you mean I can't go back to him? And what battle? It was supposed to be an escort."

Lucifer sighed. "My queen, your vampire cannot protect you, and he cannot keep your life sustained with just his blood. Your soul has been torn in half. Death's choices could only result in him supplying you with his life force or me saving you. However, the fool that he is, he is so consumed with his lack of knowledge of your next fatal incident he refuses to resume his duty. Instead of separating his soul to do his job, he is staying with you in his full form because he is growing weaker by the day. If he does not fulfill his purpose, he ceases to exist. He cannot save you if he does not exist, Jane. Had he chosen you completely, it would be different, but he didn't."

Her mouth was agape.

"Close your mouth. You are still a queen—present yourself like one."

She obeyed but glared at him. "Don't give me the queen shit right now. I want answers."

"So vulgar. Fine, I will answer some. What is it you'd like to know?"

"What do you mean: if Death had chosen me completely?"

"That I cannot explain to you. Ask another question quickly, or we will be done with this conversation."

She took a deep breath. "I've been dying since you took her out of me?"

"Yes. She is half of your soul. I removed her to save you from suffering the torment she subjected you to and the risk of her gaining absolute control. A soul is not meant to be separated, though."

She nodded slowly, soaking everything in. "And Death has been giving me his life force with every kiss since getting me back?"

"There is more to it, but yes, he revived you enough to get you back to the vampire since I had taken your blood. And every kiss he's stolen has pushed more energy into you."

"And the bond I had with him? What do you know?"

"I have no answers I can extend to you for that question. It grew stronger, but now it is gone. That is all I will say."

"Dammit, Luc!"

He fought the desire to smile at her words, but the severity of her situation stopped him. "You are both dying, Jane. There is no reason to ponder why–we don't have time to. What you overheard is correct, though. I can save you, and he is too foolish to figure out how."

"Wait, Death can save me?"

"You would have to choose him over your vampire. He did not ask you to do that. I assume he was either afraid of being refused, or this is his way of being noble. Fool."

She had that faraway look in her eye. "Is Death my guardian?"

Lucifer sighed. "There is no point discovering why you and Death have crossed paths. Your focus should only be on the fact you must bond with me to live. That is the only way you save him."

"Fuck you, Luc. Take me back. Now. I'll figure out how to help Death. If I can talk to him—get him to relax—he will resume his duties and get stronger. I heard Death—he believes he and David can keep me strong." She sat up. "If you're afraid to face Death, take me to David. If you don't, I will drop this fucking veil and let Death kick your ass."

Lucifer smiled at her sass. "My queen, he is not strong enough to defeat me now."

She stared at him in shock. "Death is stronger than any angel."

"Not anymore." He tilted his head, watching her eyes dim. "You must feed now."

"No, I have more questions."

"Save them for another time. However, I will tell you we will not discuss the threesome you have been entertaining with each other. Do not bring it up unless you wish to see them both destroyed."

She balled her fists in the sheets. "What happens between the three of us was—is—our business. Don't act jealous because it's not a foursome, David hinted at."

He glared at her. "You have no idea why he desires to give you such a thing."

Jane swallowed, her confidence slipping. "He'll tell me when he's ready. And none of that would have happened if you hadn't betrayed Death. Just let me talk to him. He'll listen to me, and then we can return to David. Oh, God, who was David fighting? Are we close enough to help him?"

Lucifer stood, turning his back to her. "My queen, if you summon Death, I will wound him again and take you anyway. Do not call for him or War unless you desire to watch them receive my wrath. I am more powerful than you realize. Right now, neither of them stands a chance of defeating me. And, as charming as you can be, Death will not listen. He will attack and lose. It will cost you your life, and if you die, everyone dies."

"Why does my life mean so much?"

"We have no time for this, Jane." He turned to face her again. "I have answered some of your questions. Let me feed you before you slip into a coma or worse. Either way, Death will not find you until it is too late. He won't even know how close you are to having your heart stop."

Her eyes watered. "Why can't he feel me like he should?"

Lucifer rubbed his face, frustrated. "It is part of the bargain he was presented. He chose the option that did not allow him to know your fate."

"Does anyone know? Like they could tell him, and he'd be better. And who is it who makes these freaking deals anyway?"

"I know your fate," he said before she could rant further. "I will not tell him. As far as knowing who offered Death, Belial, and me deals regarding your soul—you will find out when you are meant to."

Jane gritted her teeth. "I'm leaving. I fucking trusted you, and you're doing nothing but running from them and keeping secrets. I'll fight by myself if I have to. I'll get back to David—you still haven't even told me who he's fighting. But with him, we'll figure something out. I should have fucking gone with him or made him stay. There's probably not even a secret threat out there. It was probably all your doing."

"There is an unknown threat, my queen," he admitted. "David has the opportunity to learn their identity, but he is being strengthened. That is why Death insisted he go and not stay. But I did not create a threat or rumor to lure them away. My spies are everywhere, and none have learned of this individual who seeks to destroy you. Just as Thanatos fed me information about you, others are near David and coming up empty on the enemy's identity."

"What does David have to be strengthened for?"

"You will know soon."

She growled. "Fine! Tell me how long Thanatos has been working for you."

"Who said he stopped?" He smirked at her fury. "It hardly matters who Thanatos works for. He is a complicated and wise angel—I barely trust him. Now that he has learned about his sister falling and that she has been spying on Death, it will likely cause him to lose any ties he has to anyone."

Jane's hand began to shake. "Nemesis? The angel who fucked Death? She's been banging him to get information for someone?"

He chuckled. "Yes. She fell some time ago, but she has always desired to save her brother. Thanatos never agreed with Death using women to stay in control of himself, but Death had few options. He needed a release reaping did not offer. Nemesis possibly felt it would allow her to get under his skin because she is vain, but Death feels for no one but you."

She swallowed hard. "How long has he been sleeping with her?"

"That, I did not bother to obtain. And stop being dramatic. Death is not your boyfriend, and he was fucking her, not carrying on a relationship with her."

She breathed harshly. "How long?"

"How should I know?" He didn't like she had not guessed the truth. "She is not my spy."

Jane frowned. "Then who is she working for?"

"There are others who seek to gain control over Death. Using his team of guards is ideal. I doubt she will talk, but he could always torture her. Or Than, for that matter. She might reveal her true master if she fears further punishment for him."

"So, she seduced him just to give someone information?"

"Death can only be seduced by you, my queen. You are his only desire." He caressed her hair. "He meant it when he said she was nothing but a distraction. Had he not distracted himself, he would have risked attacking your knight and taking you whether you chose him or not. At least, that is how it must feel for him. Do not let this distract you from what is important. Nemesis is the least of your concerns."

She sighed, turning her head to see the moon. "Who are your spies?"

"I have many. I will not disclose them to you."

She gave him a sour look. "Whatever. What about David, then? How do you know he was in battle?"

Lucifer chuckled. As much as her questions annoyed him, he welcomed her persistence to obtain what she desired. "Had you paid attention while we were fleeing Death," he said, "you would know we paused in the wilderness near your knight's camp. How on earth you could miss the vast collection of werewolves, vampires, and undead eludes me."

"Lancelot . . . That's okay. David can beat him." She chewed her lip. "Or Lance will get away."

"Is it merely Lance now, my queen?" He smirked as she glared at him. "Does your knight know?"

"Shut up, Luc."

He chuckled. "My queen, your forgiving heart will get you killed."

"I guess you would know," she muttered. Her breathing became shallow and weak.

"Do not argue with me again, Jane." He unbuttoned his sleeve. "It's time to feed."

She stared at his arm with wide eyes. "Feed from you?"

"That would be why I am preparing my arm for you." He rolled the sleeve higher, revealing more enchantments that created his prison. "Ready? You cannot take a huge amount without harming yourself, so I will tell you when to stop. Do not worry about me, though. My blood is merely more powerful than your vampire's."

"Do you have to always blurt out how superior you are?" She lightly trailed her fingers over his curse, unaware of the horror he'd done to earn such marks.

"I am superior to your knight, Jane. That is a simple truth."

She gave him a fierce look as the gold in her eyes burned brightly momentarily. "David is greatness in my eyes and in my heart. You will never be as good and beautiful as him. Those are simple truths, my king." She smiled sweetly but might as well have thrown him into hellfire.

He grabbed her by the chin with his free hand. "Did he stop your monster? Did he extinguish the fire constantly burning you?" He glared into her defiant eyes. "Did he slay his own army for you? Lose his throne for you?" He struggled not to break her jaw. "Do not insult me by comparing me to your knight. I burn more every second because I chose to save you from that bitch, who would have easily been at my mercy had I not decided I loved you more than my desires. I gave up power and ruling, all for you." He closed his eyes when she whimpered. He spoke softer as he looked at her again. "Do not speak to me this way again. I have no way to change my past, but my actions now should prove I am doing everything for you.

"Your knight was promised a gift long ago. He was told his gift would love him so greatly that he changed his entire view on life to become great for her. No other has ever received such a wonderful promise. To know beauty and love equal to God's awaits is more precious than any promise of power. Your knight was blessed while he led a life of sin, Jane. While I admit his love and devotion are greater than any human I have ever

324

witnessed, he became great because he was promised and saw you through the darkness. He would be another sinner burning in my kingdom had it not been for you."

He took a breath and continued, keeping his tone gentle, "I was told I would not have such a gift, my queen. As I witnessed others with little to no love for my father gifted more than their pitiful minds could fathom, I was told I would never have what they would eventually receive because they were simply picked at random. Now, tell me, does the fact I chose to set aside a great weapon because I love you so—because I would rather see you happy than full of darkness and suffering while he was sinning day and night but promised beauty beyond comprehension—still make me less than your knight in your eyes?"

A tear slipped free from her pretty eyes, and she reached up to hold his cheek. "Forgive me."

Lucifer leaned down, sighing, when she pressed her lips together so he couldn't kiss her. "I already have, my queen. I would not be here if I did not." He kissed the corner of her mouth, taking at least the tear shed for him onto his tongue.

"Thank you, Luc," she whispered, kissing his wrist as she turned her face toward his hand.

"You are lucky I cherish you." He released his hold and held his wrist up. "Feed now. I sense your angel locking onto our location. We will flee no more, and I will finish this. Once it is done, you will be reunited with your angel and prince." He smirked. "I lied. You will return to them sooner than I had hoped. Now hurry. Death is getting closer, and David is not far from us. I am sure he is still in battle. I would not worry. Your knight is considered the best for a reason. If you are lucky, you will reach him before the battle ends."

She stared up at him, lightly holding his arm but not moving to feed.

"Do not look at me as though you are finally seeing me," he said coldly. "I assure you I am still evil. I still tortured, raped, and ruined you and haven't the slightest concern for any human on Earth, with the exception of your family. And that is only because their demise would destroy you when I desire to see you full of light."

A faint smile teased her lips. "Of course, my king."

He pushed her hair behind her ear. "Feed. You are fading. I need you to have my blood before we form the bond that will save your precious life, and we are running out of time."

Jane sighed, tilting her face toward his hand before lowering her eyes to the marks on his skin. Her hunger increased, and she didn't seem aware her fangs were cutting her lips. "I have had your blood before. Will I become evil again?"

"You already harbored the monster before I gave you my blood. I merely unlocked the door for her."

Her head bobbed as she trailed her fingers over his cage. "You always tense up when I kiss them. Does my kiss hurt?"

"The opposite, my queen." He held her curious stare as he caressed her cheek. "Your kiss allows me to glimpse my home again. Now drink and stop staring at me misty-eyed."

A sad smile spread over her lips before she sank her teeth into his flesh.

He shivered, closing his eyes as her presence came so close to his. Lucifer opened his eyes and pushed some of his essence into her, smiling when she sighed. Her skin began to glow with white light, and she sucked harder, pulling him closer but not losing herself as she usually did with her prince.

Thinking of her knight, he increased his body temperature and watched her smile, unaware of how much she reacted to anything that resembled the vampire.

"That's enough," he said, exhaling as she withdrew her fangs.

Before he could pull his arm back, she looked at him as silver quickly hid in the depths of her gold eyes.

She smiled the lovely smile that she only gave him before pressing a long kiss onto one of his inscriptions. The relief was instant, and he closed his eyes, breathing in the sweet scent she emitted as it mixed with that of Heaven's.

Instead of pulling away, she kissed along his arm, turning it so she encircled his forearm three times before returning to his wrist and kissing it deeply. She sighed as a tear fell on his skin, increasing the power of her gift to him. "Thank you, Luc." She kissed his wrist again. "My king." Her gaze connected with his, but she kept her sweet mouth against his fiery prison, extinguishing the flames in a way he'd never felt. "I hope this shows you that you never needed a promise . . . You earned my love all on your own."

Warmth spread through his body, but he did not let her see how he felt. "Enough of your silly fantasies. You know I am not affected by that nonsense the way your mate is."

She pouted her lips.

"That does not work on me either."

"Of course," she whispered, smiling.

"That smile, however, works on me every time." He chuckled as she grinned wider.

"One for the road." She kissed his wrist before pulling him down as she leaned forward and kissed the corner of his mouth. "Only this much, my king."

He closed his eyes. "Yes," he said, kissing the corner of hers. "Only this."

She sighed, lowering her head as she wiped her tears. He knew she felt guilty for extending him this affection, but he was awed that she had done it anyway.

"Our time is drawing to an end, my queen." He sat and pulled her so she sat across his lap and watched her entwine their fingers. He squeezed her hand, touched by the comfort the small action gave her. "I will establish the bond between king and queen now. It will grant you what you need to survive the breaking of your soul. It will also allow you to once again hold power over my light."

She lifted her face. "Really?"

He smirked. "I know you enjoyed wielding it. It has always been yours to command. You will master it without my help, as you and I will separate very soon. Still, we will hold this bond, and not even Death will be able to destroy it."

"If it saves me, why would he want to destroy it?"

"Because the bond you shared with him will never be able to form again while my light is within you."

"I thought he said he couldn't put his bond back." She frowned, looking down where he knew she still felt the cut Death had made.

"He can't, but there are ways to re-establish what you shared with him. It simply will not take unless you are free of light. After all, Death is neutral. Too much light, and he does not belong there. You had achieved neutrality when he made his choices, which is why you began seeing the strength of your bond surge."

"Your light is pure?"

He shook his head. "Not anymore, but there was a time when it was. Now it is unique to me, and so it will be for you as well."

"Okay." She chewed on her lip. "But what if I want to be with him again? I loved how it felt to be that close to him. Minus him being pissy with me because of my hormones."

"Had he not been so unstable because of what he learned, he would have been able to bear your hormones, but he is a foolish child. To answer your question, I would have to free you of my light, and you would have to choose him over the knight. Is that what you desire? You die again without one of us there."

She shook her head. "No, I choose David. So, you and I can bond as king and queen—is this more than us being crowned?"

"Yes, Jane."

"I guess that's not a big deal. You already said I am always queen. All right, so I get your light so I can kick ass again, and Death will still be separated from me—but he'll get strong again? Because that is my main concern. If Death is fine, I will be fine."

"You have the Horsemen bond with Death and War. It is something only the Horsemen Bringer can have, and that is you. But, yes, you will get my light. It is what will save you from death. It is more powerful than any force in all realms, and you will learn to wield it as you did your previous powers. In the meantime, it will mimic half of your soul, feeding her so she can glow once more. As long as my light stays, your soul will latch on to it."

Jane smiled, touching her heart. "This will wake her up?"

His soul rammed against its cage. "Yes, my queen. She stirs now because she senses I am with you. The darker half within me is still a part of her, and though they loathe one another, they crave to unite as any soul does. Your darkness is calling her while she awaits your decision. After all, she is you."

"But you're not uniting them, right?"

"No. I will not release her into you unless you ask me to. Even then, I would not do so lightly. Do not linger on that. Let us simply agree that you will accept the King and Queen Bond I will forge, and you agree to harbor my light within to keep you whole."

She stared at the moon outside, her voice a whisper full of hope. "And Death? He'll be okay? This will fix what has been weakening him?"

"You are stalling." He glared at her because she cared more about fixing Death than herself. "He will resume his duty once you are safe. He will stop fading and take his place in the universe, just as he has always been destined. He will be more powerful than ever, but only if we do this just right. Then, between us, you will be protected from Belial and his forces." He couldn't stop himself from smiling at the relief in her eyes. "Death will see you again, Jane. I swear it. Your angel will be who he has always been destined to be, your children will have their mother, and your knight will still have what Death and I do not: you."

There was happiness in her watery eyes as she smiled. "Well, thanks for making me feel like a bitch."

He rubbed his thumb across her lip. "Do you consent?"

She stared into his eyes. Sometimes she'd scan his face, and other times she'd glance at his hair, smiling sadly. Then she finally took a deep breath and smiled wider. "I told everyone you were good." He didn't respond, but she didn't care. "I consent. Form the bond that ties us together as king and queen."

"For eternity," he finished.

Her breath hitched, but she nodded after searching his eyes. "For eternity."

Lucifer cupped her cheeks and kissed her forehead. Images of them embracing one another, naked and in ecstasy, flickered in his mind.

"Luc," she gasped, but he held her to him.

He was sitting up with her then and knew he was close to his climax. He could only grunt in response, rocking her to him faster and harder.

"Luc!"

He opened his eyes that time. There was pain in her whimper. He had been looking down and was immediately greeted with blood dripping down her body.

Panic filled him, and he lifted his gaze to her face to see the source of her blood across her neck. The agony in her crying eyes made his own tear slip down his cheek.

"Jane," he said in complete heartache as he tried to put pressure against the wound that was cut across her neck, but she only made a strangled sound while her terrified eyes begged him to help her, and she grabbed at him wildly.

"Forgive me," he said, watching her tears slide over his hands. "Forgive me," he repeated when she stopped fighting and stared at him for what felt like an eternity.

One more tear fell from her beautiful eyes before she went completely limp in his arms.

"No, my queen," he whispered as his heart shattered. He tried to wake her, but her empty gaze was all he received. "No," he roared into her hair.

Lucifer opened his eyes, pressing a firmer kiss to her head as the vision he'd been given faded. "I love you, Jane."

She tilted her face up, smiling the lovely smile that was only for him. "I love you as well. So much, Luc." She held her hand over his and turned it, kissing his palm. "Thank you. For everything, my king."

"Never thank me for this, my queen."

She rolled her eyes. "I do what I want, Luc." She motioned to her head as though she truly wore a crown. "Queen."

"Mind your sass." He pushed her hair away from her neck.

"Wait, I have one more question." She touched his cheek. "You said you would keep me safe from Belial. Thanatos said Death wasn't strong enough. Just how strong is he?"

"Belial is second strongest, but his followers outnumber mine and Death's, which is why it is so important to strengthen your angel. It will be at a great cost, but I will defeat him." Lucifer didn't want to pay the price, but he knew he would. No one knew his arrangements, and it would stay that way.

"What if Death comes?" She watched him move her hair back.

"I told you he is near. You will witness us fight for you."

"What?"

"How did you think your angel would find his path again? He has to lose you to become the Pale Horseman. Do not worry. This is part of the plan."

"You did this to strengthen him?"

"It is for my benefit, not his." He pulled her to him by the back of her neck. "Although he does make you smile, and that is always a gift to all of us. Now, close your eyes."

"Why?"

He smiled to reveal his razor-sharp teeth. "My bond needs more force than the gentle Kiss of Death. Think of it as a love bite, my queen. I promise you will enjoy it."

"Will you be able to read my thoughts and communicate telepathically with me?"

"No. I will only have the ability to influence you like I already have. You will hear me from time to time, but only your previous connection with Death allowed full telepathic communication." She frowned at him, but he continued. "Jane." He searched her eyes, not sure why he was telling her this but unable to keep the words back. "After this, everything will change. Show no fear."

Now, he took the kiss he had been craving. She didn't shove him away, but she didn't return it either. Lucifer sighed before he whispered against her mouth, "Promise me you will go when your heart tells you to. Even if you must injure me, find a way to return to Death. When you realize you have to betray me, stay with him. He will be ready for you, and he will not leave your side until it is safe to do so."

330

"Betray you? What are you going to do?"

He kissed the corner of her mouth. "What I must. Forgive me, my queen."

Her eyes glistened with tears as she copied the kiss he'd given her. "I already have," she whispered before offering him her neck.

"Thank you, Jane." His soul quieted. "Do not worry, this will barely hurt," he whispered, kissing her neck before biting down to cement their bond.

She dug her fingers into his shoulders as he closed his eyes and thought one word.

Eternity.

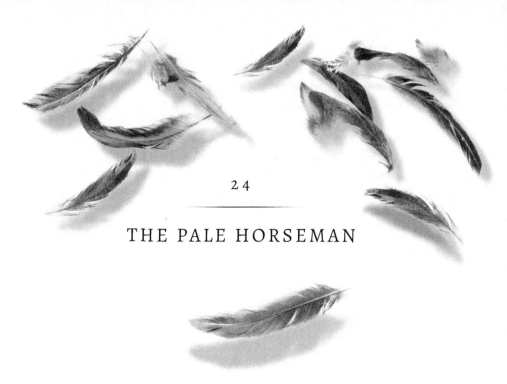

2 4

THE PALE HORSEMAN

Jane gasped as the spinning sensation from teleporting faded.

"*Shh*," Lucifer whispered into her ear. He held her in his arms and cautiously scanned their new surroundings. They were in a clearing, and she knew they were only moments away from having everything change between them. "Remember my words."

She turned to stare at his torn expression, but twigs snapping had her jerking her head in the other direction.

"I knew you were a disgrace, Luc." Death walked out of the tree line. "I just did not realize how far one could truly fall. You are by far the biggest disappointment our father must have."

"Death," she whispered, her eyes watering at how wild he looked. His eyes were almost black, and he still bled from where Lucifer had shot him.

His dark eyes settled on her, his voice rougher than she was used to when he said, "Did he hurt you?"

Jane could feel the tension in Lucifer's posture and his desire to flee again, but he was forcing himself to stay. "No."

Death gave her a stiff nod before returning his focus to Lucifer. "I had not anticipated you luring both of them. I must say, I am still surprised by your abilities to corrupt."

Lucifer smirked. "Did Thanatos make it out? And I already told Jane Nemesis is not one of mine. If I were you, I would torture her to find out who her master is."

"She escaped after stabbing Thanatos," Death said. "Unfortunately, neither was on my list, so I didn't give chase after her. Than is wishing he had been on my list, though."

Jane wasn't sure if she should feel relieved that Thanatos was alive, but she still had some hope he was on her side. She honestly didn't know who to trust, but her heart still whispered *Lucifer*.

"Were you going to tell her why you were so weak—why you have been so reckless?" Lucifer asked.

Death's face flashed with anger. "She is my business, not yours."

"I think you will find that is no longer true." He slid his hand down her back.

Death's gaze darted to the movement, and his nostrils flared as he looked back at Lucifer. "What have you done?"

"What I needed to do. It only took a few sweet words and revealing some of your secrets for her to willingly bind her soul to mine."

Jane's breathing quickened at the absolute fury that radiated out of Death as he spoke in the most detached tone, "You bonded with him?"

Her eyes watered, and she croaked, "He said it would make you better."

"You replaced my wings with his." Death's own wings unfolded as he roared, "Do you realize what you've done?"

"I was trying to make everyone safe," she cried. "I'm sorry." She couldn't see her wings, but she had no idea they would change to Lucifer's color. Her heart broke even more. "We were dying."

Lucifer chuckled. "She does believe almost anything I tell her."

Her eyes stayed on Death's furious pair. She watched his body grow larger, but the frightening thing was that his face held no other emotion.

"You lied," she whispered to Lucifer without looking at him.

"I wanted you, my queen. Do not feel too upset with yourself. Everything I told you was true. I did him a favor. His sacrifice would be for nothing if he lost you. Isn't that right, Death?"

"Break the bond and give her back," Death ordered, but it didn't come out in an uncontrollable rage-filled demand as she expected. It was just a simple uttering of words, but it proved Lucifer's accusation of Death being weak.

"I rather like where she is," Lucifer refused. "It is where she will sit for the rest of eternity when this is finished."

"You won't succeed," Death said. "I will take your life even if it isn't your fucking time, Fallen."

Lucifer's eyes flashed. "That is not how it will play out, and you know it.

You know what happens to a soul willingly bound to one that resides in Hell. She will not reach Heaven's Gates. And you know what happens to a child of God whose soul is bound to one that burns. Will you submit her to that torture? For now, she has my light protecting her from the flames burning within me. If I die, she burns."

"She will not remain chained to you. She will not die," Death yelled. "Every last puny soul, including yours, will be crushed under my boot. I will find a way and make it so. Every single one of you will burn for this."

"Death," she whispered, shivering from the icy wind that brushed her skin. He didn't look at her and kept his eyes trained on Lucifer.

"It looks like we have a bit of a problem that needs to be addressed then," said Lucifer. "I will not be giving her over. You cannot break the bond I have made—only I can. You are no longer bound to her."

"I will always be bound to her," Death roared, summoning his scythe. "I will destroy you, even if that means destroying Heaven and Hell. The entire universe will cease if I will it so."

Lucifer chuckled and set her down on her feet as his gray wings emerged from his back. "Destroying me and the universe only destroys her. And only I know when that will happen, don't I? How easy it would have been to have all the control over her, but you had to let her heart choose. Pity she didn't choose you."

Death roared as green flames ignited around him. "She is mine! She will always be mine."

Breathing became difficult as Jane watched Lucifer summon the most breathtaking sword she'd ever seen.

"Please don't, Luc," she begged. "I trusted you."

His silver eyes pierced her soul. "I told you I was evil. You never listen."

Her heart throbbed. "Please!"

His eyes began to glow. "Remember my words."

Betray me.

She didn't want this to be true. She wanted to see him be good so badly. It broke her heart that he had tricked her again, and now he had manipulated everything to keep her soul with him. For eternity. Why he wanted Death to gain power didn't make sense, but she knew there must have been some gain for him. He had even told her that, but she was stupid and didn't question it.

"But you said you loved me," she whispered. His face softened for the tiniest of moments but hardened again. "You do."

"Are you sure?" His liquid eyes silenced her, and she watched a dangerous smirk form on his handsome face.

A tear fell from her eye, and he watched it splatter at her feet on the rocky ground. "Yes," she choked out.

He just chuckled and took a step away. "So naive and innocent. I don't think I will ever grow tired of watching the mistakes you fall into because of your sweet heart." He gave a sadistic laugh when she cried that time, and then he looked at Death. "It's a shame you love her so much you couldn't take her for yourself. You wanted her to be happy, even if that was with him. Wishing you had taken her at least once? You should have taken advantage of their broken hearts instead of fucking that whore."

Death growled as his wings twitched.

Lucifer smirked. "Perhaps I will express to you in writing what it's like to fuck her."

A hood formed over Death's head before his clothing was replaced with his black reaper suit. All she could see were two green orbs burning brightly in the darkness.

Lucifer went on, not sounding alarmed in the slightest. "It amazes me that she actually believed I would reunite you with her. Women, always hopeful they will be the ones to change the bad boys."

Jane's eyes widened further as Death's arms were wrapped in skeletal armor, and his wicked skull mask reflected the eerie green glow of his eyes.

"Have you dreamed of her as I have?" Lucifer asked. "That is all you will ever have, little brother. I think you must fantasize about having a life with her, just the two of you. It will never happen."

"Stop," she screamed at Lucifer as fiery jolts of energy began surging up her arms.

"What will you tell David, Death?" The cruelty in Lucifer's smile choked her. "When you go back empty-handed and reveal your failure. When you tell him you are not all-powerful and how she fell right through your fingers and into mine. To think he was considering sharing his bed with you."

"Stop this, Luc," she whispered, watching Death breathe harder. He wasn't moving beyond that, and it was terrifying.

"Do you ever look at her daughter and see the same face you did all those years ago?" Lucifer asked, giving Death the evilest smile. "I wonder if your heart will feel anything when you see such a similar face crumple because you were not strong enough to save her mother. How it must infuriate you to care for one soul, and you can't even protect her."

Death's muscles flexed, and she could see them growing denser with every word Lucifer spoke.

"Will it bother you when Jane's efforts to shield her children from horror finally fail? Do you think Natalie will follow Jane's same fragile path? Or will she fall into darkness without seeing there is always light? Perhaps it is a waste to wonder how you will feel about her children. I suppose knowing it destroys what is left of Jane's heart matters, though. Will you blame Death, my queen? When he fails to protect your children?" Lucifer chuckled as his massive wings flapped. "It must be devastating to know all Death's power was nothing compared to mine."

"Death, please calm down," she pleaded. "He's only trying to anger you."

"Hm." Lucifer hummed. "I think you both underestimate me. Perhaps chaining her children to my bed as they watch their mother please her king will do the trick? I am patient. What are a few years to wait for the experience of having both mother and daughter writhing under my hands."

Jane screamed at the same time Death did. She squeezed her eyes shut from the bright light that exploded out of her and the green fire that roared around Death.

"Finally." Lucifer's whisper barely reached her ears before she ran at him.

He expended no effort and grabbed her by the throat, then pulled her back against his chest. The sharp pain that jolted her spine made her realize he was now in his shiny armor.

Death quieted but huffed in place as the emerald flames pulsed with his every breath.

Lucifer tightened his grip around her neck and kissed her cheek. "You have no power over me, my queen. Your precious gift to me, remember?"

"Fuck you!" She pulled at his wrist, but he was indeed still stronger.

"Not yet, Jane. Just a little more . . ."

Death's wings flapped as though he was preparing to fly at them.

"Ah, ah," Lucifer tutted. "Will you risk me crushing her pretty throat?"

Death roared in response.

"I rather like having the upper hand with you, little brother."

She squirmed, but it was useless. Looking at Death's terrifying figure, she realized he was not the same Death he had been, not even when he transformed at Camelot. The real Horseman of the Apocalypse was staring at her.

Lucifer's words replayed in her head, 'He has to lose you to become the Pale Horseman.'

Her rage stalled at remembering their conversation, and she scanned the horrifying image of Death in front of her. *He made him stronger.*

Jane tried to turn her head toward Lucifer, but he squeezed her throat to prevent her from moving. She was still able to catch his side gaze. There were no emotions on his face. He had also morphed his features and was the stunning angel she had caught glimpses of before.

He smirked at Death. "Do you envy that I have tasted her while you have only sampled her kiss?"

Death's scythe ignited before it transformed into the enormous weapon he had wielded in front of her once—*the Collector.*

Lucifer's fingers rubbed her gently again, and his smiling lips pressed against her cheek as she watched Death struggle not to fly at them.

Blue balls of light appeared over Death before shooting into his chest.

"Tell him to save you, my queen," Lucifer whispered. "But remind him that you are mine." He nipped her ear when the last glowing orb shot into Death's chest.

"Don't do this," she begged, feeling the coals raked across her skin.

"Tell him how you chose me," said Lucifer. "That even with the prince, you did not want him."

"No," she said, staring at her angel. "That's not true, Death. I love you. I did this for you. For you and David."

He growled, but before he could speak, numerous black masses landed around them.

Lucifer let out a sigh before he pressed his lips against her cheek. "Pray that was enough."

"Well done, King Lucifer." Belial walked toward the side of a wide arc forming around them.

Death snarled, shifting his stance so he could see both Fallen.

Belial observed Death but addressed Lucifer. "You promised he would be reduced in strength. Why does he appear stronger?"

Lucifer chuckled. "Were you foolish enough to believe me?"

Surprisingly, Belial smiled. "Certainly not. Did you really believe I would keep this bitch alive? You know what has been promised to me. Release her demon, and I will let you fuck her once before her beautiful duplicate crushes her pure heart."

Lucifer's body tensed, and his temperature rose. "Do you honestly believe I care for this woman? I am aware she so foolishly did, but are you that ignorant?"

"Oh, he loves her," said a familiar female voice.

Jane stared wide-eyed at Nemesis as she walked toward Belial.

Lucifer stiffened, and he gripped Jane tighter.

"He dreams of her. They both do," Nemesis said. There were twisted cackles of laughter all around them. "She is all they are concerned with. They are nothing without her, and she is dying."

Belial caressed Nemesis' cheek with the back of his fingers. "Thank you, my dear. Did you enjoy breaking her heart as much as you enjoyed stabbing your brother's?"

The angel nodded before settling her gaze on Jane. "No one can make me scream like Death can. Not even Prince David."

Jane held her breath when Nemesis hid her wings and shed her angelic beauty to reveal a simple peasant girl from medieval times. She was still lovely, just a diluted version of her true self.

"Even as a mortal," Nemesis continued, "David was beautiful to behold. All of Heaven whispered about the handsome young knight who slayed monsters all on his own. I had to find out after I was ordered to shatter his friendship with Lancelot. All I knew was Arthur planned to choose the two friends, and my master did not want the best in God's favor. I might have failed at damning David, but Lancelot was a lovely consolation prize for my master."

It became hard to see. Hard to breathe. Jane gasped as tremendous heat shot to the surface of her skin.

"There you go," Lucifer whispered in her ear. "Release it now."

Jane didn't hesitate and summoned her gun just as she let his light burst out of her. It caused screeches, and many demons fell to their knees, disintegrating into piles of burning ash.

She roared along with Death and fired her gun at Nemesis.

Belial yanked the angel from meeting her end and growled at Jane. "Prepare for your end, Queen Jane."

Lucifer lifted Jane, and she didn't pause before wrapping her legs around his waist as she fired over his shoulder.

Death landed just feet in front of them and held out his hand when a swarm of black beasts flew at them. They were not the same as the demons she had fought before. They still had bat-like wings, but their bodies were covered in scales and spikes.

Death was silent as his hand began to glow in the pulsing green fire that had consumed him. She continued firing her gun, grinning as demon after demon disintegrated or dropped dead to the rocky ground.

She squeezed her arms around Lucifer when he took a few steps toward Death. She feared he would fight him, but she was surprised when a silver gun appeared in his hand. He aimed it at a demon that had landed behind Death.

Her eyes widened when his gun fired, and the demon burst into white flames on impact.

Death lowered his hand and turned his head. His emerald eyes were ablaze as they met Lucifer's equally furious glare.

Neither of them spoke, and then they turned away from each other.

"Hang on to me, Jane," Lucifer said.

She nodded and squeezed her arm around him tightly. Resembling a knight instead of the sophisticated King of Hell she was used to, Luc's silver battle armor heated before glowing, revealing white markings similar to those covering his body. He noticed her looking and grinned, exposing a set of sharp teeth.

She was pissed at him but smiled back before they both turned toward Belial.

Belial unfolded his wings. "I never thought I would see the day a pathetic little whore would bring the Angel of Death and the King of Hell to their knees."

Lucifer didn't respond, but Death moved closer to them, seeming to guard her and Lucifer.

Belial chuckled as more black figures poured out of the trees. "You can't stop all of them."

"Watch me," Death said as his muscles flexed under his suit.

Lucifer's hold tightened. "Don't forget your weapons, my queen. You will fight as well."

"If you try to flee with her again," Death said but didn't finish his sentence.

"Focus on the situation at hand, little brother," Lucifer said. "I didn't provoke you into embracing your role so the two of us could fight today."

"I should have known." Death shook his head. "Pray I can control myself before it takes me."

"I'm sure you will find the will to fight it." Lucifer chuckled again. "Be ready to receive her, and for fuck's sake, stop holding back. She is strong now."

Death growled.

"Get the girl," Belial told his army. "Our king will come to his senses when he finds her chained to my bed, crying for him."

Jane snapped before either one of her enraged angels could reply. "Try to take me to your bed, and I'll skin you alive."

Belial threw his head back and laughed. "Perhaps there is still fight in you, little girl."

"That's Queen to you, bitch." Jane aimed her gun at him and fired.

He dodged the shot as an onslaught of gunfire roared around them, and Lucifer snarled, squeezing her tightly as the air left her lungs. He'd teleported them out of the way, and together, they delivered an attack with their guns.

Death flew at Belial, and they disappeared into the trees; only blasts of green and red flames revealed their location.

Lucifer never stopped firing. His blasts emitted white light while hers burst with green flames.

He muttered a curse, tightening his hold once more as the air left her lungs again. Jane tried to keep her eyes open, and she realized they were not fully vanishing. Instead, it was like looking through an opaque wall as Lucifer flew at tremendous speed.

"He's used an enchantment to keep me from teleporting with you," he said, landing but leaping into the air again.

"You said we wouldn't flee." She held the trigger of her gun down, smiling when the automatic fire took over. "Holy shit!"

Lucifer roared as he landed, kicking a demon down before shooting it in the head. "We are not fleeing, but it makes it easier to keep you safe. Now keep fighting. He's lost Belial already."

Jane laid down a wave of blasts as a green cloud hurtled through the sky.

Death landed beside them, holding out his hand as what looked like black fire shot from his palm. Demons screeched, igniting into flames as Death held his other hand toward her.

"I have her." Lucifer shifted her away from Death.

Her angel snarled. "I want her back!"

"Destroy the threat first." Lucifer smirked. "She likes where she is."

Jane kept firing, only realizing what she was saying as the words left her mouth. "I'm fine, my love. Keep fighting. I will be with you soon."

Death's skeletal mask glowed, and he tilted his head as he lowered his hand. "My love."

She smiled before lifting her mask. "Behind you."

He turned, swinging his scythe, cutting four demons in half.

When she turned to Lucifer, she found him glaring at her.

"Shut up, my king. If I didn't need you, I would let him break your arms and legs."

"Stop flirting with me." He exchanged his gun for his sword.

A sudden jolt brought the flickering jumps to a halt. Lucifer roared, kicking down a fallen angel in their way.

Her arm shook as each powerful bang shot out of her weapon. From the corner of her eye, she watched Death land and swing his scythe in a wide circle while he growled out a low, spine-tingling, inhuman sound. His deadly gaze settled on her momentarily before he vanished and reappeared yards ahead to intercept the endless wave of monsters thirsting for her as their captive.

Jane felt the impact of each attack Lucifer delivered. A part of her wished she could see him fight to his fullest abilities, but she was too overwhelmed with shooting demons she'd never seen before.

Death roared, encouraging them to leave. Jane squeezed her legs around Lucifer and let off several rounds before a bright flame ignited behind her. She winced but looked to see Lucifer had let out type sort of blaze in front of him. She marveled at the bright flames as they sparked and crackled in white and blue fire.

Her fascination quickly ceased when he jumped into the air. Again, he was landing from one place to the next. She could feel Lucifer trying to teleport, but he couldn't break the enchantment.

Jane's eyes widened when a giant winged hairless griffin-type creature crashed into them, and she was yanked from Lucifer's hold.

"Luc," she screamed, but dozens of fallen angels swarmed him. She felt the wind rushing over her head and looked down toward the ground as it streamed past her. The beast was holding her by her hood, and she was hanging upside down and flying toward Belial. "No!" She turned her head to see the creature as Death yelled her name.

Jane didn't scream for him. She summoned her gun again and aimed over her head, firing at the monster's underside.

The shot hit her mark, and she hurtled from well over a hundred feet toward the ground.

"My Queen." Lucifer's yell made her heart pound. It wasn't worried — he was scolding her for being momentarily afraid. She slammed her lips together and tried to swing her body around since she was spinning wildly out of control.

Her heart pounded when she was nearly on the unforgiving ground, but she managed to get her feet under her and landed, letting out a roar of victory at her accomplishment when she pushed up to stand straighter.

She didn't get to celebrate her first landing with cheers, but that didn't stop a dangerous smile stretching over her lips as she immediately summoned her sword to engage the handful of demons charging her.

They snarled at her with mouths full of razor-sharp fangs that dripped with venom, but Jane showed no fear. She roared again and attacked. Her steel clashed with theirs before she spun, slicing them across their stomachs, and smiled as she was aware of the glowing white light racing toward her.

She didn't stop to wait for him. Jane punched the monster in front of her and kicked the next. Her blade sliced off heads and limbs, and she growled when the inky blood sprayed across her face.

Her attacks increased when she felt Lucifer drawing closer. He was furious, and she almost shook from the dangerous feeling shifting around her. Death's roar only excited her, though. She wanted them to fight beside her.

Unfortunately, more demons and Fallen landed around her. With a swift punch, she knocked back a male angel and quickly exchanged her sword for her gun. She squeezed the trigger without hesitation, ending the fallen before he could spew curses at her.

Jane switched her gun for her blade again, waiting for the ball of white light to get closer. She cut down one, then another. She was pulling her sword free when claws dug into her back. She screamed, her eyes watering, as Death and Lucifer howled with her when the creature dragged its claws downward.

Shaking, Jane roared, yanking free and feeling her skin rip away. She turned and fired at the slimy creature until it slumped to the ground.

She tried to keep upright, firing wildly as tears blurred her sight.

Finally, white engulfed her vision, and a pair of strong arms wrapped around her before he took flight.

Again, Lucifer darted from one point to the next as she weakly clung to him. He growled, touching her mutilated back.

"I'm okay." She gasped when she finally pried her eyes open, and a burning sensation spread through her wound. "Ah, stop!"

"*Shh*," Lucifer whispered, leaving his fingers on the blistering cut. The pain sliced across her skin again, and Jane screamed, digging her fingers into his neck and biting down where his neck met his shoulder.

"Hang on, my queen," he said with a grunt as she pulled her teeth from his flesh.

She felt bad for hurting him, but his skin was healing already. The blinding pain ebbed away, and she could see the speed he was traveling at. He held her tight and never let a single blade or shot ring out by her.

The constant green glow at the center of the massive field told her Death was unleashing his own hell. She was proud to see the crater of disintegrating corpses that surrounded him.

"Be ready, Jane," Lucifer whispered, kissing her temple. "Remember my words."

"Luc," she whimpered, turning her face toward his.

He sighed before pressing a hard kiss to her lips. "He is almost ready for you."

Jane opened her eyes and realized he was still constantly transporting them across the battlefield, but he had a wing shielding her.

She shook her head. It felt like he was saying goodbye.

"Focus on your fight, my queen. I will keep them from landing a hit on your skin again."

"I know you will."

He stole another kiss just as she squinted from the green flash lighting up the entire field. "He does not like my lips on yours," he said when Death's roar greeted her ears. "Too bad they will be mine for eternity." Her heart stopped, and she pulled away from his lips. He gave her a deadly look. "Fight, my queen."

He tossed her off him before turning and immediately engaging several fallen angels.

Jane followed his lead and tried to press her back against Lucifer's, but his wings kept her from getting too close. He was more lethal than she imagined—and far more skilled than any other she had seen fight, except Death.

His blade glowed white, and his victims burned from the contact even if he didn't get a fatal strike.

She pulled her focus away when he cut into one angel and then slammed another to the ground. He almost moved too fast for her to keep up, and she needed to focus on her fight. Her attention returned to the attackers in front of her, and she fired quickly, blasting holes into those unfortunate enough to step in her line of sight.

She yelled when two demons dropped into her path and switched her gun for her sword. She blocked their attacks. They weren't as good as her, and she fended off their advances before slicing through the first, then spun to use her gun when the second grabbed her from behind.

Her yell must have alerted Lucifer, but she was already aiming her gun at the chin of the demon holding her. She fired, shouting when its blood sprayed across the back of her head.

There was no time to relax as the grip on her fell away because more landed right in front of her. She fired three quick shots to level the onslaught, but it was no match for the sheer number of angels and demons coming at her. Her skill kept them away with quick kills, but she didn't know how long she could keep it up.

Angels were more challenging to take out than vampires. The demons were equally demanding, but the speed of the fallen overwhelmed her.

"Luc," she yelled when she was pushed away from him. She managed to block their attacks but was thankful when she saw white light cut through to her, and once again, she was yanked against an armored chest.

He didn't speak. He slaughtered everyone close to them. Still, despite having Death and Lucifer on her side, she didn't see how they would escape this. There were too many, and Lucifer couldn't flee with her.

The mob grew thick, and she yelped when Lucifer leapt into the air with her. He landed quickly, kicking someone down, then threw her like a rag doll without warning.

Jane didn't have time to scream as another set of hands caught her.

"Jane." Death lifted her as he pulled her against his chest.

She smiled and tightened her legs around his waist. He was still attacking those around him, but she didn't look over her shoulder to see his destruction. She was too happy to have him holding her and couldn't stop herself from pressing her face under his hood. A bony mask greeted her, but it shimmered away in seconds to reveal his perfect face.

His lips claimed hers, but he growled almost instantly. She could feel him trying to form a bond, and as it felt like a fiery rope had tightened around her, she cried out.

"Bastard." He looked over her shoulder as he returned to his fight.

"Death," she breathed out, relieved and full of peace anyway.

His muscles flexed against her body with each powerful swing. The realization that he was still fighting rushed back into her mind and ripped her from enjoying their embrace.

"Fire behind me. Keep them off my back," he said before quickly pecking her lips.

She nodded as his mask appeared, then aimed at his shoulder, shooting without mercy.

Death's heavy breathing tickled her skin, and she squeezed him tight, keeping her face pressed close to his.

Death began moving forward, allowing Jane to see the carnage her angel had unleashed behind her. Bodies were barely recognizable. Flesh and bone—blood and ash. He left none breathing.

"Shit," he grunted. Her eyes instantly caught his distress and widened. Hellhounds were streaming out of the trees with behemoths following them.

"Luc," he roared before throwing her into the sky.

The air rushed out of her lungs when her back again met Lucifer's armored chest. He didn't bother turning her, so she was in the midst of his fight and tried to aid him as best she could.

Death's massive figure landed several feet ahead, swinging his scythe in ruinous circles. She shot around him until he took flight.

Lucifer followed, flying incredibly fast before landing hard. He shoved her back before turning away to block an attack. "Behind you!"

Jane spun around, hollering and swinging her sword at several demons. The four demons stood no chance against her. She blocked their attacks, kicking one in the leg before bringing the hilt of her sword down on its collarbone. A nasty crack sounded, and she knew she had broken the monster's bones.

Her angels let out yells, praising her when she switched her sword to fire at the knees of the next set of demons, then swung her blade at their necks after they dropped down on their destroyed limbs.

She took several more shots before Lucifer pulled her against him and folded his wings around her. He grunted, squeezing her tight.

"Luc," she yelled, knowing he was getting hit by some sort of attack but was keeping his promise not to let her receive another wound.

"*Shh*," he hushed her, taking flight again. Fiery blasts exploded around them, but he dodged each explosion.

Her fingers dug into his neck, and her nails scraped his armored back. The speed at which they were traveling was unbelievable. Her eyes watered when she felt liquid spilling out of a couple of holes in his armor.

"No, Luc," she cried, hugging him when she saw his blood falling behind them.

"I'm fine." His fingers gently massaged her head as he nuzzled her cheek with his.

She whimpered and hugged him more when he sped up.

"This won't hurt you but shield your eyes, Jane."

She squeezed her eyes shut, knowing he would use his light. The metal from his armor heated, but she let it burn her and buried her face against his neck when the white light flashed around him.

It caused screeches to erupt around them. His armor cooled quickly, though, and Jane opened her eyes. They were still flying, but the black flock chasing them was no longer on their tail.

"You're draining yourself," she yelled. "Fly us away!"

"They will follow, and I need to keep you near him," he replied before cursing. "Fuck."

Jane gasped upon seeing Belial and several other fallen angels following them.

Lucifer sped up. "Go with Death when you see . . ."

Tears spilled down her face when she saw the red smoke coming closer. "I love you," she cried, kissing his jaw repeatedly.

He sighed and hugged her in response. It made her cry more, but she prepared herself and kissed him one more time to show him she did love him.

His eyes met hers, and she smiled through her tears.

It gave her the reaction she craved, and her heart sped at the smile on his lips. "So beautiful, my queen." He sighed loudly and turned his lips to her hand. "Stay with Death. Never leave him, or you will both be lost." He then landed with a hard thud.

The impact caused her to loosen her grip, but he pulled her to him to keep her from falling.

Lucifer growled when several other figures smashed into the earth around them.

"That was impressive, my king and queen," said Belial. "You truly do make a stunning couple. I am certain the kingdom would be proud to witness your abilities to destroy, but you fall short without the aid of her demon."

Lucifer gripped her tighter and spoke calmly, "I am more than capable of destroying all of you without that bitch looking at me. Pity you cannot say the same."

Belial growled, and Jane shook when Death's roar drew closer.

Lucifer continued, standing tall and proud even though a puddle of his blood reached her feet, "You require that evil whore, isn't that right?"

"Hand her over," Belial ordered, sounding bored. "Or I will rip the soft flesh from her bones until you release my prize. You have my word this weak little girl will stay intact if you do. Whatever you find appealing in her eludes me, but I will honor our deal."

"I don't recall shaking on it," said Lucifer.

Belial roared and unfolded his wings. Lucifer braced himself when they rushed him. He kept them back, wielding his sword with masterful precision. It was a tremendous effort, and it seemed he would keep them away, but arms wrapped around his throat from behind, putting him in a chokehold.

She screamed when he almost dropped her but brought her gun up and fired right in the face of his attacker. His tight hold resumed, and he fought again, but the black blood burned her eyes. "Fuck," she cried, rubbing them, but it worsened. She started shooting at the dozens of blurry figures behind them anyway. Her heart told her none were friendly, so she fired into the shadowy mass that bubbled in and out of focus.

She blinked away her tears, relieved they were slowly helping her recover her sight so she could at least make out some facial features.

"Jane?" Lucifer called, but his body jolted from the constant blocks of his sword.

"I'm fine," she yelled, never stopping her assault. "It's just blurry."

"No," he roared when several blasts erupted behind her. She screamed and tightened her hold, but they were pulled apart. "Jane!"

She tried to hold on, but she was ripped away and flying in the opposite direction.

"Death," she screamed as she watched Belial and many fallen angels swarm Lucifer.

"He can't help you, Sweet Jane," came a female voice.

"Nemesis, you fucking bitch," Jane screamed before yanking the angel's hair enough to rear back and land a hard punch to her face.

Nemesis yelled and threw her toward the ground. Jane was startled by the quick reaction and wasn't nearly as high up as she thought because she smacked the ground almost immediately.

She groaned and started to push herself up, but a painful kick slamming into her side made her scream out in agony; something was definitely broken.

Jane summoned her sword and darted her head around. The tears from her pain mixed with her still blurred sight made it impossible to have a fair chance of defending herself. "Death," she cried, unable to make out anything useful.

Nemesis laughed off to her right, so she immediately switched to her gun and fired several shots. More laughter greeted Jane, so she knew her attempts were ineffective.

"How could you betray him?" Jane yelled, rubbing her burning eyes. She finally saw a silhouette form a short distance away and shot, but only a low laugh resulted.

"I wanted my brother back," Nemesis said behind her.

Jane spun around, arm raised her, but didn't shoot.

Nemesis spoke bitterly, "Thanatos should not have been punished as he was."

"So you joined a man he hates?" Jane couldn't believe the stupidity of some people. Although she quickly remembered she was just as stupid for trusting Lucifer and Thanatos.

"He promised me my brother's safety," Nemesis said. "Surely, you understand my decision. You are a foolish, self-sacrificing soul—this should appear routine for you."

More figures landed around them. Jane's heart pounded, breathing heavily and switching aim at each blurry figure. She knew she'd receive their attack once she fired, so she waited, hoping that if she could keep Nemesis talking, Death and Lucifer could get to her.

"Don't do this, Nemesis." Jane held her side when her broken bones snapped into place. "Your brother doesn't want this for you. I don't care if he betrayed Death. I know he didn't want anything to happen to you. You'll be sorry when this is over."

Nemesis laughed. "You are so naive. Do you even know the bargain Lucifer has made?"

"It doesn't matter." Her vision cleared, and she stood straighter. "My feelings for him will remain. I won't give up on him."

A chorus of cackles made Jane's muscles twitch. She wanted to fight, but she knew that even with all of David's skill and strength, the vast numbers of the army would overwhelm her. It didn't help that the injury she'd sustained earlier ached severely.

Jane noted where Lucifer and Death were, then the group around her as she formed a plan. She exchanged her gun for her sword. The wings of her enemies flapped.

Nemesis' black eyes locked on her. "Are you under the assumption you stand a chance against us?"

She let out a slow breath and pushed out all the noise around her. *Focus.*

Nemesis glared at her, but Jane found what her heart needed. *David.* She blinked and saw his face flash in her mind. He was where she had to get back to. *"Be brave, my love,"* his voice whispered.

She looked ahead and watched Nemesis reveal her sword.

"Remember, he wants her alive," Nemesis told the large group.

Jane wasn't going to let them take her. They wouldn't be taking her back to Belial breathing if they did.

Jane's eyes went to Nemesis and then the crowd. She felt it building when they roared for her. *Now,* Lucifer's voice kissed her thoughts.

She didn't let them take a single step. Roaring like a lion, she let the building light rise to the surface and consume her. They screamed from the flashing light bursting out of her, and Jane attacked.

In an instant, she was in front of them and swinging her sword at their throats. Her kills earned vicious yells and immediate retaliation from the survivors. While her light damaged the demons, it only momentarily impaired the Fallen.

Blades cut through the air, but she blocked them and shut off her light abruptly. It confused and disoriented those that had grown accustomed to her bright glow. But she wasn't hindered. She had embraced Lucifer's gift and looked on with bright eyes.

She dashed from one confused victim to the next. Their headless torsos swayed in her wake. The daze seemed to wear off for her hopeful kidnappers, and they attacked again. But she met them bravely.

A tug on her hair only made her yell and summon her gun to aim behind her. She fired once, not pausing to see if her target was met—she knew it was. More arrived, and Jane's fist balled when she ordered her gun away and slammed into the face closest to hers before she called her blade again, swinging out as she spun away.

It gave her two more satisfying kills, and when a set of arms wrapped her up, she didn't scream in fear. Instead, she let them drag her for a few feet before summoning her gun and firing down at their foot. Her captor's arms fell away from around her, and pained screams erupted from her victim's lips.

Jane lifted her gun and took five more shots before aiming at the one who had dragged her off. His black eyes widened, horrified, but she aimed at his head and fired once.

When Jane spun around with her gun, she paused on Nemesis. Her finger relaxed, and she ordered her weapon away. She did not want the angel to have a quick death if it happened at her hands.

"Well, it looks like you found some guts after all." Nemesis glared at the Fallen who remained. "Leave her to me."

She knew Nemesis was a part of Death's select team; she would be a difficult opponent. In truth, she had mixed feelings about fighting her.

"I am curious," Nemesis said. "What did you find inside that little mind of yours? You certainly surprised me with your sudden discontinuation of crying for help."

Jane darted her eyes to where her two men fought.

Nemesis also looked over and grinned. "Does it hurt knowing I have had him so many times? That I took your lovely David's virginity?"

Jane summoned her sword as the fire sparked inside her again.

"He was a sex god before he was even immortal," Nemesis continued.

Jane's heart pounded when images flashed in her mind of David holding Nemesis in his arms and Death taking her to his realm to do what he wished to her. Instead of crying, she fixed a mean smile on her lips and said, "Does it hurt to know they were never thinking of you when you gave yourself to them?" Nemesis clenched her jaw, and Jane continued, her smile stretching wider. "I am their only thought and desire. What were you?"

Nemesis didn't respond, but Jane wasn't done with her.

"I love all of my men," she said, "and even though I don't make love to each of them, they are mine. There isn't a single woman who can take them from me. You're just the tissue they tossed into the trash when they were done with you. I am the woman who holds their hearts. At least when I offered myself to Death, I knew he loved me above any being ever to exist. Even Lucifer, the bastard that he is, loves me. And don't even get me started on David's love for me. I doubt he would even recognize your face."

Nemesis growled and unfolded her wings, pacing.

Jane knew her stalling was up. "You had at least one man's love, your brother's, and you gave it up."

"It was to save him," Nemesis screamed. "No one believed in him. I did. I never stopped believing in him."

"And he knew that." Jane tightened her hand around her sword. "It doesn't matter now, does it? You betrayed him. Now you will suffer for it."

Nemesis roared at her.

"I'm sorry, Nemesis." Jane made a decision that would probably cost her her life, but she switched to her gun when the angel's wings twitched and fired twice, destroying Nemesis' knees.

Jane looked up as the others charged. She couldn't take all of them, but she could kill as many as her gun would claim for her.

Death and Lucifer roared. She felt awful for worrying them, but she couldn't cry about it. She roared out as a sign that, at least for the moment, she was still fighting. Her gun went off in bright, loud bangs. The demons she hit exploded in green and black flames, but there were so many.

She yelled and kicked out when arms secured her from behind. Her feet did enough damage to keep the blades of those in front of her from meeting her flesh. The being holding her from behind tried to drag her flailing body before trying to choke her, but she moved quickly and bit into their forearm. They yelled, tossing her through the air. Jane smacked the ground right near Nemesis.

She coughed and started to push herself up. That was when she realized Nemesis already aimed her gun at her face. There was no way she would be able to move in time.

"You don't deserve them," Nemesis said as tears spilled down her cheeks. "You don't deserve him."

Jane didn't move and didn't ask which him she was speaking about, but Nemesis answered her internal question.

"He's my brother," she screamed. "He won't have his queen anymore."

Death yelled for her, and Jane silently said she loved each of them when Nemesis' finger squeezed.

The bang sounded, but a colossal figure landed in front of Jane, roaring louder than any sound she had ever heard.

Fire flew all around the sky, and she screeched when big hands yanked her up off the ground.

Jane finally saw what was blocking her attack from Nemesis and screamed with happiness at seeing a black-and-red dragon.

When she thrashed, unsure of who had her, an amused but familiar voice spoke, "Calm yourself."

Jane almost cried and felt her body being turned. "War, you big bastard!"

He smiled. "Tex, I told you, you need only call."

"I forgot." She hugged him, laughing as she turned to see Asmodeus in his dragon form, spewing fire. "That's my fucking general!"

War laughed as someone else spoke beside him.

"Show-off," he said. He had white hair and white eyes, and somehow, he was sexy as hell.

He smirked at her as her eyes trailed over the white and gray leather archer's armor he wore. Then she saw the bow he wore across his back and the angelic symbols glowing along its grip and limbs. They matched the glowing white patterns on his gray arm guards.

"Jane," War said, "meet Pestilence, our brother. Pest, meet the Horsemen Bringer."

The White Horseman gave her a tilt of his head, then pushed back his white hair as it spilled across his eyes. "Pleasure to officially meet you, Jane."

Every girly thought over his looks vanished as she realized he was the plague. He was the reason everything had started.

His smile vanished, and he moved closer to her.

She summoned her gun and aimed it at his chest.

"Jane," War said, "he is free of his enchantments. I would not bring him with me, and your general would not let him out of his chains if this were untrue. He is here for you."

Her hand shook as she studied the boyish face looking back at her. He looked younger than Death and War. While they looked to be in their late twenties or early thirties, Pestilence looked only twenty or so.

"Don't betray your brother again," she said between clenched teeth as she lowered her arm.

War chuckled and pulled her to his side. "He has learned his lesson, Jane. Though I am sure a woman of your status can help it sink in a bit deeper."

"Shall I assist my big brother for you then?" Pestilence grinned as he pulled his bow over his head.

Jane nodded. "Destroy these fuckers."

"As you wish." He winked.

"My queen," Asmodeus called from behind them.

Jane extracted herself from War to run toward the King of Demons, who now stood on two legs rather than four.

"I knew you would come back." She smiled, hugging him.

"I told Lucifer I would side with you, my queen," he replied, his gaze sliding to her side.

She rubbed her arm. "I didn't know they'd turn gray."

He smiled, caressing her head. "You look beautiful. I know Death believes so. But it must be a painful sight for him." He turned her around, guiding her toward War. "Where is your king?"

War pointed off in the distance, making them all turn.

Two balls of emerald and white light flickered amongst the flashes of gunfire and smoke.

"Luc," she whispered when his roar broke through the clouds of death. "He was hurt," she told Asmodeus.

War nodded to Pestilence and watched two giant horses erupt from the earth. One was covered in fiery red flames, and the other in ghostly white. She smiled when a third emerged from emerald flames.

"Those boys are having too much fun." War mounted Ravage.

Pestilence followed his lead and affectionately rubbed the muzzle of his white horse.

"Sorrow," Jane whispered and beamed when he walked right to her and lowered his head for her to climb up.

"You are making Ravage and Perish jealous, Jane." War nodded toward the white horse.

"Hello, Perish." She smiled when he bobbed his massive head. "Hello again, Ravage."

Ravage snorted, stomping his hooves, kicking up dust.

"You are forbidden from being here, Moros." War glared at an angel who appeared next to another, almost identical to Thanatos. Only he was blond and had blue eyes.

"Than?" Jane stared at him in shock.

"I am his twin, Hypnos," he said, focusing on War again. "We have come for our sister."

War grunted and glanced at Asmodeus briefly before addressing her, "Jane, do you wish her to return home for judgment, or should we send her now?"

Jane watched as Asmodeus tied Nemesis up with his chains. She was unconscious, though.

She turned to face Hypnos and Moros. "Take her home."

Asmodeus undid his chains as he stared at Nemesis in disappointment.

"Thank you, Jane," Hypnos said as Moros lifted Nemesis into his arms. They then bowed before shooting upward in beams of white light.

"Grimm," War yelled, and an angel with black armor dropped beside him. Jane scanned his muscled body and received a wink from his brown eyes when she finally got to his face. "Watch it, Lykos," War said in a humorous tone. "Tex does not need another admirer."

"Just looking." Lykos smirked as he produced a helmet identical to War's. Instead of a red plume forming through the slit, a black one formed as his long black hair was pulled through.

War pointed off to the edge of the field. "Take out the behemoths. And find the bastard who did that to her. Leave them for the Demon King. I am sure he will enjoy punishing them for marking her skin."

Jane noticed he was pointing to her exposed back.

They observed her briefly.

"Lucifer sealed the venom with light." Asmodeus shook his head. "That's going to hurt to heal."

"She's tough," War said.

Pestilence spoke up, "Brother, I believe we should hurry this if you desire to join the other battle as well."

"You mean David?" Jane whipped her head around.

War nodded, waving Lykos away. "They have been in battle for an entire night. Go ahead, brother. Make sure they feel it."

"Of course." Pestilence raised his bow toward the sky. An arrow formed out of nowhere as he aimed at the moon. "Falling stars for the little moon." He released the arrow, and Jane watched it explode as it peaked; then, it rained down streams of white fire. They seemed to come to life, splitting and turning in thousands of directions. Each arrow sought its victim, hitting the fallen angels who fought against them and knocking them onto their backs.

They cried in agony while their bodies arched and contorted into unnatural positions. Each of the horses reared back, letting out wild cries of excitement, and when Sorrow settled, the punishment of Pestilence's attack was revealed.

Every fallen was replaced with a grotesque demon. The arrows had transformed them, leaving their bloody feathers shed around them as if they had been forcefully plucked from their wings.

"Let's get you back to Death, Jane," War said. "Be prepared to meet a very pissed-off Pale Horseman."

Pestilence took off first, pulling his arm back to unleash another arrow targeting the demons and hellhounds.

Jane glanced at Asmodeus. "David better be safe."

Asmodeus let out a whistle. "I'll see you there, my queen." Then he morphed into a dragon, flapping his wings and disappearing into the clouds as smaller dragons flew after him.

"Get a move on, Tex," War said as Sorrow reared back before galloping toward the roaring emerald inferno, fighting beside flames so bright, she had to squint to see the armored king inside them.

"Betray me," she whispered as War and Ravage raced alongside her and Sorrow.

"Yes," War said, catching her eye. "Choose Death tonight, Jane. He needs you now, as does your knight. It's time to side against your king."

She tightened her hold on Sorrow's reins. "I choose Death. I choose David."

"Tell them," War yelled, speeding up as Sorrow kept up with them.

"Forgive me, my king."

25

THE MAN IN BLACK

Jane climbed down from Sorrow, but her eyes were glued to War's general, Lykos. He and dozens of other angels dressed in Spartan-style combat attire were attacking the last of the behemoths. They were like a pack of wolves, and she was awed by their skill.

Thanks to Pestilence's arrows destroying the hellhounds and demons, the others were making quick work of the Fallen, now demons.

"Jane," Lucifer whispered, yanking her away from Sorrow.

"Hey," she snapped, shoving him as Sorrow stomped.

Lucifer gave Sorrow a dark look. "Get your master. Now."

Sorrow snorted but galloped away.

"Luc, what are you doing?" she asked.

He turned her around, running his fingers along the wound on her back. "Death will have to break through my light to remove the venom. It will hold for a day or so before releasing the toxins into your body."

"Okay." She glanced around. She didn't see War, Pestilence, or Death.

He also looked around. The other angels were binding the fallen, well, the new demons, in gold chains. "Do not forget what I said."

She noticed him tensing as he yanked her closer. "You said a lot of things, Luc. And you broke my freaking heart because of the shit you pulled with Death."

Lucifer shifted his gaze away as his body grew unbearably hot. He growled and quickly lifted her into his arms before walking in the direction Sorrow had gone.

"Put me down, asshole," she said, preparing to yell for Death when she realized every angel was looking in the same direction Lucifer had been.

"Luc," she whispered, tearing up when his hands started to tremble beneath her. "What's wrong?"

"Well, King Lucifer," a deep, menacing voice spoke.

Lucifer stopped walking as every angel froze.

The voice sounded familiar, and the speaker continued, "Are you ready to give me your decision? Though, it seems you have already chosen."

Death landed in front of her and Lucifer. He kept his back to her as Pestilence and War landed beside him.

Jane twisted around to see better and gasped at a colossal man who shimmered into view as he walked toward them. He was handsome in a black suit with his black, slicked-back hair. He had dark red eyes, much darker than any of the Fallen she'd seen. He radiated power, and Jane knew this would be the moment everything truly changed.

"Well?" He stopped nearly twenty feet ahead of Death, still only staring at Lucifer. He smiled, and it was breathtaking. "Did you tell her about the offer you accepted?"

Lucifer's fingers dug into her leg, but he stayed quiet.

The man in black chuckled, clearly eying her wings. "No, I see now you've tricked her into accepting you. Clever boy."

"What did you do?" she whispered when Belial landed beside the dark man. His skin wasn't dark; no, the mystery man's skin was a flawless creamy color that rivaled David's. Only the aura around him made her insides clench and her heart pound. "Luc?" She watched him through the tears building in her eyes. She knew something terrible was about to happen.

Slowly, Lucifer lowered his eyes to hers. No emotion. Nothing that made her think of her king.

"Luc," she repeated, searching his handsome face before she flinched at the sound of more figures landing behind the man in black.

Every angel, including the Horsemen, tensed and summoned their weapons. The newcomers' identities were hidden in shadow, but they were clearly beings to be feared.

Jane tore her eyes away from them and back to Lucifer. "What did you do?"

"What was necessary to obtain control of your soul," he answered.

Her eyes burned, but she didn't say a word.

"You are too desirable, Queen Jane," said the man in black. "He could not resist my proposal."

Death growled and shifted his stance to view them. "You piece of shit," he roared at Lucifer.

Lucifer chuckled and walked forward. Death went to lunge for them, but the man in black held his hand up, and Death froze in place.

"What a shame," the man in black muttered. "You had your chance, Horseman. Did you think he would pass up having her? I warned you that choosing her the way you have would not end well for you."

She breathed faster when the Fallen from her army fell to their knees, and the others who had come with War and Pestilence bowed their heads.

"Luc, what have you done?" she asked.

He smirked, stopping halfway from Belial and the man who seemed to hold more power than Death.

"I told you I was evil, my queen," Lucifer said, his tone amused. "So naive. You never listen."

Belial growled and looked at the other man. "What of my deal?"

The man still held his hand toward Death but turned his head to Belial and shrugged. "His deal with you remains. Be patient."

"Luc," she whispered, gripping his face to make him look at her. His eyes flashed, but his face held no emotion. "What's happening?"

"Oh, my dear," said the man, making her look back at him. "He has claimed his prize—you—for all eternity. All he needed was for you to willingly consent to an eternity bond. You gave yourself over to him, don't you remember?"

A tear rolled down her cheek.

The man gave her a charming smile. "After your death, the time, place, and method of which only he is aware, he will retrieve and keep you. There will be no Heaven for you, my queen. You belong to King Lucifer for the rest of your existence."

"She does not," Death roared. The green flames around him ignited, and he tried to move but remained in place. He yelled again when he was unable to break free. "Luc, don't you fucking do this. She doesn't deserve this."

"She agreed to be mine," Lucy said, almost bored. "She chose to do this for you."

Death roared up at the sky as green lightning began crackling around him.

"Don't cry over this, my queen," Lucifer said, not smiling or showing any of the love he had before. "I swear you will still be the only woman I take to my bed. Our bed. I will even be gentle the first time I fuck you."

She dropped her head and cried. Her heart couldn't take this betrayal. *Betrayal.* She snapped her head up to stare at him through her tears.

His eyes flashed, but he spoke poisonous words again. "Because after I take you, I will release your demon and reclaim my light. If you behave, I may let you view the kingdom we rule from time to time. Of course, only if you behave. I have grown tired of your dramatics."

Her heart was stabbed, but she hardened her gaze when Belial spoke. "I want my promise, Lucifer. You know the consequence should you choose his offer. Mine is the only one that allows you to keep this little whore. There will be no keeping her intact without me."

Lucifer tore his eyes from hers to look at Belial. "Oh, yes, I forgot the little catch. How foolish of me." He sighed, returning his gaze to hers. "Like I said, though, I'm not sure I want to deal with her tears anymore. I think I will be satisfied with my thirst for her pure soul once I've had my way with her."

Belial growled and summoned his sword when the man in black chuckled and crossed his arms over his broad chest.

Lucifer smiled, and it was the cruelest thing she'd ever seen on his face. "Did you really believe I would hand my greatest weapon over to you, Belial? Did you believe I loved this pathetic girl? My only desire is to see her burn as her loves watch, helpless."

"We had a deal," Belial said. "I will still succeed. We will crush you now if you do not reconsider. You know you are not ready. Even three of the Horsemen stand no chance against the Destroyers."

Jane glanced at the shadowed figures before looking back at Lucifer.
Betray me.

"Perhaps you are right," said Lucifer as he observed her. "This would allow me to sit back and enjoy my prize while you take care of this little problem up here. What do you think, my queen? Are you ready to see your new home? I have grown tired of playing this little game with you. Pathetic or not, you are an irresistible fuck I cannot get out of my head. The taste of you was not enough, it seems."

Without a breath of hesitation, Jane slapped him across the face.

There was a cackling of dark laughter in the distance.

Lucifer slowly turned his face back to hers. His eyes were ablaze with fury, and she screamed when he reached out to grip her face with his hand that did not hold her. "You will pay for that, little queen."

Death roared as he thrashed in place.

Jane whimpered in his painful hold and cried at the evil she saw flickering inside his steel eyes. *Betray me.*

Lucifer chuckled and forcefully let go of her before walking toward the man in black. Death continued to fight the invisible hold on him, but the others didn't even try to get away. Sorrow and the other horses, however, fought as hard as Death, their flames and armor constantly shifting as they neighed and snorted.

Jane closed her eyes and saw Lucifer's smile in her mind. *Betray me.*

Lucifer halted in his stride. Death's Angel was in her hand, and she pressed it to his chest before slowly opening her eyes.

Lucifer looked at her gun and smirked.

"Put me down," she said. "I will kill you right now."

"This is interesting," said the man in black.

Jane kept her shaking hand in place and challenged him to try her.

"Do you think you have the guts to kill me, Jane?" Lucifer laughed when she nodded. "My sweet little queen, you are defenseless against me. That includes your forgiving little heart."

"Put me down, you bastard," she screamed, pressing her gun harder against him. For some reason, she knew Death's gift would be able to inflict harm on him. The tears that fell from her eyes could not be stopped. *Betray me.*

Lucifer studied her face for a long moment before lowering her to the ground. Death thrashed harder, and she saw him slowly breaking the invisible restraint that had prevented him from moving.

A whimper fell from her lips as she took a tiny step back, but she kept her aim steady.

Lucifer gave her a wicked grin before speaking. "You have your bargain, Belial. Finish them, and when the war is done, I will be through with this sniveling girl. If you can acquire her now, I may throw in her daughter for your collection."

Betray me.

Jane screamed and squeezed her trigger. Her loud sobs shook her body, and she watched Lucifer look down at his chest.

He reached up to touch the hole in his shiny armor when blood dripped down his waist. "You missed," he whispered, clutching his chest before growling, "Destroy them."

Belial and Lucifer lunged for her, but a figure landed inches in front of her and knocked her back into Death's arms.

"Not today, my king," said a familiar voice.

Jane opened her eyes to see Beelzebub land a devastating punch to Lucifer's face that sent him flying back.

The man in black merely laughed as he vanished while more dark figures landed beside the other High Prince of Hell.

Death lifted her into his arms and roared as the green flames completely engulfed them, and bolts of green lightning exploded outward, sending a massive wave of energy out. Every one of the angels who had been frozen cried out in relief and aimed their various weapons at Lucifer and Belial.

They hesitated, though. The shadowy figures were in front of Lucifer as he slowly got to his feet. He held his chest and glared at Beelzebub and the other Princes of Hell he'd brought with him: Astaroth and Sonneillon.

Jane gasped, holding her chest as Death tightened his grip.

"This isn't over," Belial said, disappearing with his remaining forces.

Lucifer grunted, standing straighter, but his eyes were on her hand holding her chest. She could feel his wound, but she also felt betrayal that wasn't her own.

"What have I done?" she cried when the pain spread and her mind slipped.

"Hang on, angel." Death put his hand over hers before throwing a glare at Lucifer. "You fucking bastard. How dare you use her to protect yourself?"

Lucifer let out a pained laugh. "I may be a bastard, but I got what I wanted. Enjoy what time you have left with her, little brother, and enjoy the reminder she is mine every time she summons your suit."

Death growled, but he was more focused on her.

"Death," she said, staring at his hand. "I'm shot. I shot myself. I shot her."

"No, baby." He hugged her to him. "*Shh*. I'll fix this."

"I will not be taking my prize just yet," Lucifer said to the beings still hiding in the strange darkness. It was as if they were not entirely in the same plane of existence.

They bowed before fading away.

Lucifer scanned her face before dropping his gaze to where she held herself. "Quite the betrayal to wound your soul and savior."

Death snarled, hugging her as his aura pulsed with a pale light.

"Careful, little brother." Lucifer smirked. "You still remember, don't you? If I go, she burns. You can't touch me."

"We'll see about that," Death said, flapping his wings.

Lucifer rubbed his chest as hers throbbed. "I will be there when your heart prepares to stop, Jane. Then you will see my cruelty at its greatest as you watch your loved ones perish. That will be my last gift to you. You can at least say goodbye."

"Please, Luc," she cried.

He ignored her cries and looked at Death. "When the time comes, enjoy holding her lifeless body in your arms. It will be the last time you ever see her. Sweet Jane is arriving at her end, and you cannot stop it."

The entire army roared with Death as she cried, digging her fingers into her skin.

"Goodbye, my queen," Lucifer whispered, then he was gone.

A crushing sensation squeezed her heart. Jane whimpered, peeking at her fingers. "Death?"

He kissed her forehead. "I know. I will find out how to help it."

Pestilence approached, taking her hand as he pressed his lips to her wrist. "She hit her soul." A cooling sensation began to seep into her skin. "And his."

"I know." Death pulled her shaking body closer. "Jane, you need to look at me. You're not hurt. Your body is intact. You're feeling what's happened to him. Fight it. Push the connection from your mind and heart. Your soul does not want him. She will help you."

Pestilence smirked as he chanted under his breath. He shook his head. "The light is already fusing. I can't numb her enough."

War touched her head. "She's going into shock." He turned to Beelzebub. "Summon Asmodeus."

Astaroth, Sonneillon, and Beelzebub walked closer.

Death growled. "Back off!"

Asmodeus shimmered into view. He took one look at her and glared at Death. "What have you done?"

Beelzebub crossed his arms. "She shot Lucifer when he threatened her. She saw *him*."

Asmodeus glanced at Death and sighed. "We can help. We'll bond with her. She is our queen, not yours."

Pestilence stepped away, but Death hugged her, growling.

"Brother, let them bond," War said. "It will happen sooner or later."

Jane squeezed her eyes shut as blinding pain shot through her. "Let them help. I need to get to David."

"At least she's coherent," Pestilence said. "But she's right. If you desire to aid the immortals, we must go."

"Death," she whispered, touching his face. His mask had formed again, and it caused her soul to scream inside her. Jane opened her eyes and stared into his as her soul spoke with her. "Not yet, my love. Stay with me."

Death stopped snarling and nuzzled her hand as the mask disappeared. "I'm still here. You'll wear my wings again—I swear it."

She smiled, feeling her soul do the same. "Let them help me. They are true."

He grunted, and the mask formed yet again.

"Not yet," she whispered, trailing her fingers along the sharp jawline of his mask.

"Not yet," he muttered as his face appeared once more.

Asmodeus came forward, holding out his arms. "The knights are heavily engaged. There are Fallen around them that my men are breaking through as we speak. Let's do this quickly, my queen."

"Can she shut that off?" War asked, shielding his eyes. The light was pulsing all around her.

"She may if we can soothe the light. It is unstable and confused because she attacked it. If we add more negative energy, it will stop attacking her pure soul and resume fusing."

"I don't want it to fuse with her," Death snapped.

"You have no choice," Pestilence said. "She welcomed the light, brother. Only Lucifer can remove it. But if she can wield it, she will be unstoppable."

The others nodded.

"Just make it stop." She reached for Asmodeus. "Dragon. Let me go to my fucking dragon, Death."

Asmodeus chuckled and pulled her into his arms. "I must stay in this form, my queen. Let's fix you now."

Astaroth, Beelzebub, and Sonneillon surrounded her. "My queen." They bowed.

"Hi, boys." She clutched her chest, ignoring their amused smiles. "Get to work. I need my David, and I doubt he wants to see me looking like a broken Christmas tree."

Asmodeus nodded to the others as he spoke. "The light looks lovely, my queen. You will have time to harness it soon."

Jane darted her eyes to Death. War was holding onto his shoulder as Pestilence stood in front of him. They didn't look happy, but they were there, at least.

"I'll be okay," she whispered, gritting her teeth as she looked down again. "It's getting empty."

"She's reacting to him leaving." Astaroth caressed her hair. "My queen, take a deep breath and close your eyes."

She whimpered, knowing she shouldn't trust anyone after Lucifer, but she trusted the Horsemen. It had to be okay if they let her go through with this.

"Close your eyes." Death balled his fist. Green fire still raged around him, but it didn't threaten her. "I'm here. I'm not leaving again."

"David," she said, looking off.

"We'll get to him." Death nodded to Asmodeus. "Hurry."

Jane kept her eyes on Death as the others got in place. Something inside her longed to join with him, but something kept pulling her away. It felt like she was constantly moving in one direction, only to be dragged backward before trying another. She was trying to find something but didn't know where to go or what she was looking for.

Death growled, and she felt as if he knew she was trying to connect with him but was being restrained. "I'll find a way. I'll find you. Close your eyes now."

She followed his command, soothed by the confidence in his declaration.

"This will not hurt, my queen," Asmodeus promised before various whispers penetrated her mind.

She recognized each voice as one of the princes. They spoke in a language she didn't know, but it sounded more like a haunting melody sung to her thoughts than a prayer.

Each voice seemed to wrap around and hold her to them momentarily before passing her to the next. Then she settled on Asmodeus' deep voice when each of the princes took turns placing a kiss on her temple.

Each kiss spread a delightful warmth into her mind and grabbed her chaotic thoughts to steady them.

"*Eternity.*" His voice wrapped around her mind.

Without questioning herself, she responded, "Eternity."

The King of Demons smiled and kissed her forehead when the others chorused in her mind. "*Eternity.*"

The tumultuous thoughts stilled, and her insides relaxed. It was such a calm feeling that it made her aware of how out of control her mind had been.

"We are yours, my queen," said Asmodeus with a small smile. "For eternity."

"Y'all can leave me whenever." She took a calming breath as Death came closer.

"They can't." He lifted her out of Asmodeus' arms. "Eternity is for all time, Jane."

She sighed, knowing he was hurting because he wasn't bonded this way. "Take me to David."

Death kissed her forehead as he waved his hand. "Half of you join my reapers at Valhalla. The rest join the battle with the immortals. War, go to the family. Pest, stay with me."

Various flashes of light signaled the angels and Fallen vanishing.

Pestilence chuckled as his white wings unfolded. "You were the one who told me not to trust Fallen, big brother. At least you and I are the fastest by air."

Death flapped his wings after tucking her head under his chin. "She'd already be dead if I hadn't listened. Their plan is to keep her intact for as long as possible."

Pestilence caught her eye. "Close your eyes, angel. We fly too fast for even your immortal eyes."

Death kissed her head and flew up. "Next time, we will fly for us, my love."

She smiled, wrapping her arms around him as pale light began to glow around both angels. "Don't let David hear you call me that. That's his thing."

"David can suck my left nut. You were my love well before his." He kissed her hair. "Close your eyes. The battle he fights is drawing to an end."

She closed her eyes and hugged him tight. "Death?"

He started off slow. "Yeah?"

"The man in black . . . Was he the Devil?"

"Yes." He kissed her and started flying faster. "He is the one who corrupted half of your soul, baby. He wants her back. He wants her with the king he's chosen."

She let out a breath as the image of her darker soul smiling came forward.

Pestilence's voice whipped through the wind. "He did not expect this half of her soul to be the Horsemen Bringer."

"He didn't expect her to be many things." Death tightened his hold when the wind gusts became unbearably cold and strong.

Pestilence chuckled. "True. I suppose the best secrets are left for last."

The muscles in Death's body flexed as he went even faster. She lifted her head and tried to open her eyes, but they were right—it was too fast. The wind felt like razorblades, and she could barely close her eyes.

Death turned his face and pressed kisses to her eyelids. "You're still glowing."

"Sorry." She smiled though her heart pounded and her thoughts raced. She couldn't stop thinking of Lucifer and everything he'd said to her before and after. She was worried about David, and now she was learning her thoughts about Lucifer being different from the Devil was true. And that he was the reason her soul had been evil. "I am evil."

"No. You are everything bright. You were only submerged in darkness."

"What does this mean? What am I?"

"You are Sweet Jane, I am your Death, and David is your knight—your prince. We are going to him, and we will find a way to keep us together."

"You're changing into the Pale Horseman," she whispered, rubbing his cheek.

"I am him. Keep me. Keep me with you, and I will stay."

She knew he could lose control any moment, and that would mean . . . "I won't let you go. Ever."

The wind howled, but he nuzzled her as though they were standing still, preparing to put her to sleep. "Imagine our kiss," he murmured. "Imagine you are between us again. That is home, yes?"

She nodded, remembering how Death kissed her as David bit into her. "David is home. You are with me. With us."

"There you go." He kissed her temple. "Keep your light like this. David will need to see you."

"What's happened?" Her heartbeat sped up, and she pried her eyes open to see she'd managed to dim the bright, flashing light she'd been emitting. "Death?"

"See for yourself." He landed, lowering her to the ground.

Jane turned, gasping at the absolute carnage—smoke and ash—blood and death.

And David.

David was fighting Lancelot. No, he'd already beaten him.

Death took her hand. "Wait."

She covered her mouth at the sight of the sadness in David's eyes when he looked up from how he was leaning over Lancelot. Angels were still arriving, falling around the battle as balls of light, but he was staring at her.

All Jane could think of as she watched David look back down was what she'd heard from Lucifer and Nemesis. Lancelot was David's best friend. They'd been torn apart because someone didn't want Arthur to have two of the best knights.

"David," Jane screamed as David was stabbed in his side.

He yanked the blade free, raising his arm high.

"I will kill her," Lancelot roared, aiming a gun at David's heart.

"No," she shouted, breaking out of Death's hold and running to David as white light filled her vision.

26

FORGIVENESS IS GREATNESS

White.

Just white.

"Open your eyes, David." It was Jane.

Even though he was sure they already were, he followed her command. And there she was. His Jane was leaning over him, surrounded by a silvery white light, brighter than her usual lovely glow, smiling just as he'd dreamed of her so many nights in his long life. His baby—his goddess. She'd come back to him.

"Baby," he said softly, afraid the vision of her would shatter if he spoke too loud, "are you dead with me?"

Her beautiful smile stretched wider as someone else responded behind her.

"If you were dead, you would see my face, dumbass. Not hers." Death came into view over Jane's shoulder. "Well, I guess you're seeing me now. Shall I kill him, angel? We can run off and make Jane and Death babies without Mr. Perfect now."

She wiped a tear from her cheek and leaned close to David as he lay there confused.

"We're not dead." She kissed him softly, breathing him in. "I knocked you out of the way."

Before David could return the kiss, Death lifted her away.

"All right, he woke up. Now let me see your fucking gunshot wound." Death threw a glare at David.

"What?" David tried to move but instead groaned in pain as he heard cries and cheers.

"Ah, so this is brother's competition," said an angel in white.

"Who the fuck are you?" David asked, staring at his strange white eyes. "Where's Lance?"

"He's there," said the angel in white. "And I am Pestilence. Death is my brother." He held out his hand. "Need help? She hit you hard enough to kill a hundred mortals."

"I didn't mean to," Jane said. "David, let him help you." She then glared at someone in the distance. "Back off. He is not to be harmed."

Death motioned for someone to follow some silent order as Pestilence grabbed David's arm and pulled him upright.

Once David was standing, he limped toward Jane.

"David, you can relax for a bit," she said, slumping against Death's chest.

"Baby, what's happened to you?" David tried to pull her away but swayed.

"Easy," Pestilence said, holding him still. "She's just drained, and you basically got hit by a five-foot missile."

David watched a fallen angel kneel behind Jane. "Jane?"

She closed her eyes. "I love you."

Death rolled his eyes and glanced at David. "She was already injured, and then she got hit by the bullet meant for your heart."

David watched Jane's face. She was asleep.

"I don't understand," he said, unable to move. "She took a bullet for me?"

Death cradled her head and didn't answer.

"He's moody," Pestilence said as he pointed across the field. "We were there when you and your boy tried to kill each other. You might have seen some flashing light." He pointed to Jane's shimmering skin. "Like this but brighter. That was her. She ran to you when you were about to be shot."

"She got to me before I was shot? Baby?"

"She's fine," Pestilence said. "It's just that she was already hurt. Beelzebub is getting the slug out, though."

"Jane?"

"Let her rest," Death said, lifting her so she could put her head on his shoulder. "She used Light to get to you. I tried to hold her back, but I knew she'd give me shit if I let you die. She knocked you out of the way, but the gun had already gone off. The bullet is in her side. Nothing serious was hit, but a manticore had already scratched her—they're poisonous. The venom has been trapped within a light cocoon that Lucifer made. The bullet grazed the cocoon. Beelzebub is trying to mend it."

David stared at Jane's face. She looked at peace. Dirty and bloody, yes, but she didn't seem to be in pain. Every bad thought he'd had about her came rushing back, and he wanted to ask one of these angels to beat the shit out of him. She'd been severely injured and still risked her life to save him.

He focused on Death, noticing a pained look every time his eyes fell on her back.

"Her wings are gray now—Lucifer's colors," Pestilence said quietly.

"What?" David watched Death clench his jaw.

"He can't hear us." Pestilence waved his hand toward Jane. "You realize she had his wings from the cloak. It was more than just a cloak. He was protecting her and showing all who she was to him. Not that the secret can be kept for much longer."

David sighed. "I don't think I can handle knowing why she's wearing Lucifer's colors. What else happened?"

Pestilence smiled. "She traveled at the speed of light—that will drain any soul."

"How did she move at light speed?" David held his side as he stepped closer.

"Lucifer gave her his light." Pestilence chuckled. "That's why it feels like a Jane-sized missile struck you and why she glows. She somehow chan-neled the light into speeding up and knocked you out of the way before you could receive the hit. She wasn't quite fast enough to avoid the bullet, but she wasn't thinking about herself."

"I have it." The fallen angel, identified as Beelzebub, stood, holding a silver slug. He grinned at David. "Would you like to keep it? It had your heart written all over it."

David held his hand out as the angel handed him the small object destined to be lodged in his heart. "My baby almost died for me."

"Stop being a sappy fool." Death kissed Jane's cheek as he shifted her so David could hold her. "Drop her, and I'll break your legs."

David flipped him off but carefully took her, using one of his forearms to support her ass as he held her head with his free hand. Death was now inspecting the wounds on her back.

"She wants Lancelot to be kept safe," Death muttered, holding his hand over her wound as a pale light radiated from his palm. "She found out you two were friends and that one of my guards seduced you as a human."

"What?" David peeked at Jane, worried she'd hear something he wasn't ready to deal with. He could barely keep himself from killing Lancelot for shooting Jane.

Death chuckled. "You lost your virginity to a fallen angel because someone didn't want you or Lancelot chosen to become immortal. The angel was one of my guards, a traitor. A very powerful immortal put a glamour over her to shield us from knowing she'd already fallen from Heaven."

Pestilence and Beelzebub laughed.

"I don't even remember my first time," David admitted.

Death smirked. "That is probably because she's a lousy fuck. She's Than's sister, though. Jane showed mercy because of that, I suppose. The bitch was taken away for imprisonment, so Jane doesn't have to see her again."

David looked at him as his mind spun out of control. "I lost my virginity to Thanatos' sister? And Jane found out?"

Pestilence laughed again. "Nemesis tried to kill her after bragging about how she'd taken your virginity and that she was one of Death's frequent distractions. So your woman shot the bitch's kneecaps out. Feisty girl."

"What are you doing to her?" David asked, refusing to turn when he heard Lancelot yelling.

Death glanced at the commotion but answered. "I'm adding an enchantment so the venom doesn't spread. When we return to Valhalla, I will have to break through and remove all of the poison. I would do it now, but it's extremely painful, and she's too weak." He sighed, standing straighter. "We have much to discuss. I apologize for keeping her condition from both of you—I was doing what I thought was best."

"You have that in common with her," David said.

Death's lips twitched with a faint smile. "I will have Lancelot locked away. My reapers already hold Thanatos and various immortals who fought to reach her. You can decide what you'd like to do with him, but she's still hormonal and wants you to make up with your old friend rather than kill him. Although, it seems you already found some reason to hold back. I am only holding back for her sake—don't forget what he did to her."

"Eat ass, Death," she mumbled without opening her eyes. "My evil ass tortured Lancelot. I am seeking forgiveness as well."

371

"I knew you were awake. You kept him from killing his friend. You are redeemed." Death smacked her ass before kissing the back of her head. "Now stay with David while I handle some things. Then we will fly you ahead of the others as they make their way back with survivors."

"Fly the survivors," she mumbled before kissing David's neck. "Hi, my love. Are you okay? I didn't mean to hit you so hard."

David couldn't respond. He loved this woman so much.

Death shook his head at him. "Pussy."

Jane weakly kicked her leg out at him. "Go. Wait. Are you still you? Do you need me?"

Death gave her a dark look but kissed her head as he whispered, "Keep quiet about what's happened. We will talk to David and the others later. But I am fine for now. If you are with David or me, I will be fine."

She opened her eyes and turned her face. "Okay. Get me if you need me, though. Not yet."

"I know." Death kissed her forehead before turning away.

Pestilence motioned for Beelzebub to leave. "I will stay with them."

Beelzebub smirked as he bowed to Jane. "I will find the most injured and see they are transported, my queen."

"Thank you." Jane sighed as she turned to him again. "David, are you okay?"

He carried her toward a boulder with Pestilence quietly following behind them.

"David?" She kissed his neck.

After situating himself against the rock, he tilted her face toward his. "Baby, I am holding you. Therefore I am happy and well."

"Okay, good." A sleepy smile formed on her lips. "So can you kiss me now?"

He smiled and lowered his lips to hers. His beautiful girl tasted sweeter than ever, but she was exhausted and struggled to keep her head up. He ended their kiss with a laugh, supporting her head when she struggled to keep it up. "Do you want to feed?"

"Yes, but I will wait." She winced but pointed to her lips. "More."

Ignoring the chuckling White Horseman, he smiled and kissed her, though he kept it brief. "Rest now. I'll thank you properly for saving me when we are alone."

"Don't expect Death to leave you two alone," Pestilence muttered. "He is hiding his stress."

David stared into her dull gold eyes, noticing a silver flash every few seconds. "Death is part of the package with us."

She smiled tiredly before resting her head on his shoulder, murmuring, "I will help you fix Lance."

David tensed but lightly ran his fingers through her hair as he felt the bones mending inside him. His stab wound felt worse, but he could handle it.

She spoke again when he stayed quiet. "If we give him a chance, I feel he can be redeemed."

"Don't worry about Lance." He watched Arthur issuing commands. Then, he quickly counted all his brothers—they were all in good health.

"Did you know I was gone?" she mumbled.

David caressed her hair. "I felt you for a moment. Arthur was able to pick up some of your thoughts and knew what had happened—that you'd gone with Lucifer, and Death had given chase. We were preparing to return to Valhalla when Lancelot showed up."

"Oh." She took a ragged breath, whimpering. "He was the only one who could save me. Forgive me."

Pestilence gave him a slight nod and left them, heading toward Lancelot.

"You came back to me," David whispered, rocking her when she began to shake. "I began to doubt us, but I see clearer than ever now."

"I won't leave again."

"I know." He smiled but frowned when she kept jerking in his hold. "We need to get you to the fortress so he can mend you."

"I'm fine. It just shocks me. I have to figure out how to control it." She began playing with his hair as she stared over his shoulder. "Do I look weird?"

"I thought you were a goddess, my love. You look beautiful."

"David?"

"Yes, baby?"

"I met the Devil today." She sounded so lost.

"I'm not sure I understand." He kept rocking her.

She sighed. "You're going to be angry when you find out what I've done. I think I broke Death."

David glanced out to see Death speaking to the demon who held Lancelot. He looked colder than usual, which threw David off because he'd just been joking with Jane. "I'll help you keep him. He's my wingman when it comes to you."

She smiled sadly as she whispered, "I eternally bonded my soul to Lucifer to save Death and myself. So you and I could still be together."

David closed his eyes and felt he had to force his heart to keep beating. *That's why she has his colors.*

"I trusted Luc," she continued, "and thought I could find a way to fix things, but I don't think I can. I want my life with you and my bond with Death. Now I'm afraid I've lost both of you because I think I'm still going to die."

He swallowed, keeping his eyes on Death. He was ready to save both of them. "You will never lose us. I'll find a way for you to bond with Death again, and together, we'll keep you safe."

"Are you angry with me for bonding with Lucifer?"

"Yes, my love." He smiled and kissed her anyway. "But I trust you believed he was the only one who could save you, and I know he desires you to live. His love for you was visible when he watched you smile. But you and I are beyond forever without any bond. No one will separate us. Not Lucifer, not God, and Death will always bring you back to me."

Death shimmered into view just a few feet away. His gaze was empty, even when it settled on Jane. David knew it was up to him to keep them from falling apart.

"Will you take her?" David watched Death snap his eyes over to him and explained, "My side is killing me. I should probably stop the bleeding."

Jane lifted her head. "You're still hurt?"

Death carefully took her, but he showed concern as his eyes lowered to David's wound.

"Oh, God, I forgot he stabbed you," she whispered, trying to pull free. "And you're holding my fat ass after I hit you like a fucking semi."

David laughed, kissing her head. "Don't talk like that about yourself. You saved my life. Plus, I'm fine, and I wanted to hold you. It's just that it was my silver blade. I need to give it an hour or so to seal up properly. Stay with him while I go see Bed."

"Okay," she mumbled, shaking her head from what seemed like dizziness.

Death motioned for him to go and lifted her again.

As David walked away, he heard her whispering, "Can you fix him for me?"

Death answered immediately, "Fuck no. I let you save him. That's enough."

"Wait! You knew his time had come again, and you were just gonna let him die? You asshole."

"I knew you would save him," Death argued. "That's why I got you here in time. I just didn't plan on you getting shot. I thought you'd throw your shield again."

"Aw, Death. You do care about David."

"Shut up."

She laughed.

"Let's go make out before he gets back."

Her sweet voice held a smile even though she scolded her angel, "Death."

"I would tell you to scream it," Death said, "but I think he's listening to us."

"You asshole. Is he really?"

David turned, smiling in their direction. "You're not talking quietly, my love. And no making out."

Jane smacked Death, but she looked pale and tired as Death situated her better, swaying with her like David had seen him do.

"Take her sooner if she needs warmth." David patted Bedivere on the back as his brothers cheered at his arrival.

"You just told me to take her," Death hollered. "You must be suffering from blood loss."

David shook his head. "Take care of her."

Jane seemed to have fallen asleep, so David turned away and smiled at his brothers.

"Is she all right?" Gawain asked.

Bedivere lifted David's shirt as Kay handed him gauze and tape.

"She's been wounded. She already had a poisoned scratch on her back, and the bullet hit her where she's torn open."

They all cringed and tried to look in her direction.

"I can see her cuts from here." Bedivere shook his head. "I will examine her as soon as I'm done."

David shook his head. "The angel removed the bullet." He held it up.

"Damn, that had your name on it, brother," Gareth said.

"I know." He pocketed it. "Their main concern is the original wound. The creature that did it is poisonous, but they did something to keep it from spreading. When we return, Death will remove the venom. He said it would be painful, and she seems too weak to do more."

"Did you see how fast she fucking moved?" Gareth laughed. "Jane's a superhero."

David chuckled. "I only felt it. I think she broke at least four of my ribs."

"Five," Bedivere corrected. "And none of us saw her, Gareth. That would be what happens when one travels at the speed of light."

"I saw a white streak, and then she was on top of him."

"Why is she letting him live?" Tristan cut in. He was chugging ration after ration. "Why did you hesitate?"

"He has his reasons." Arthur rubbed David's shoulder as he passed him. "Apollo thanked you for knocking Artemis out."

"He's all right?" David asked, scanning the sea of soldiers.

"He is. He subdued his father. We have him in chains for transport. Hades is alive as well." Arthur glanced at Lancelot. "You should go talk to Lance. He is very confused and angry. He wanted you to kill him."

David nodded as he lowered his shirt. "I'm going now."

"Be careful, brother." Gawain patted his back.

"I will." David passed the crowds preparing to leave until he stood before a demon. "I wish to speak to him."

Pestilence was casually sitting beside Lancelot, and he motioned for the demon to release him. "If he runs, Asmodeus, I'll shoot him."

Asmodeus undid the chains before they completely disappeared. "When you are ready, we will transport you, the queen, and Lancelot to the fortress."

"All right." David made eye contact with Lancelot before sitting beside him.

"How bad is she?" Lancelot asked.

"She seems weak," David said casually as his heart sped up. "It's not so much the gunshot—she's been poisoned."

"I heard," Lance muttered. "So she has power again. You must know that is not a good thing."

David watched Death speaking to the demon who had just been holding Lancelot captive. "It suits her, but I know there will be consequences."

"Lucifer knows how and when she will die." Lancelot tossed a rock away. "Death does not. He chose for her to live her life with you instead of bonding the way Lucifer did."

"There is more to it than that," Pestilence cut in. "Shouldn't you two be speaking about your own quarrel?"

Lancelot threw a glare at Pestilence. "When did they free you?"

"I'm not sure." Pestilence laughed. "Asmodeus is unforgiving, and my brother wanted me to suffer by staying conscious during the cleansing. I still do not know how much time has passed. It's a blur."

Lancelot nodded. "I did not want to unleash them onto humanity. I only desired a weapon."

"I know," Pestilence said softly. "That is why I told my brother to allow her this chance at letting you live."

A scoff left Lancelot's lips. "You should all kill me. I cannot forgive her."

"You will." David rubbed his side. "I think you already have, just as she has you. My heart aches for your loss. I swear she didn't mean it. She was devastated."

"I know she was," Lancelot said. "It nearly killed her. It knew exactly what to do. Betray you and kill innocent children. Lucifer couldn't do it himself because she is too forgiving, so he let that monster out. I should have kept my family away from the camp, but I was confident I was untouchable. There are many secrets, David. Lucifer is not the greatest threat in Hell."

David kept his eyes on Jane's sleepy face as Death again cast a glow over her wound. "I realize that. What were your children's names?"

Lancelot tossed another rock. "The girl was Arianna. She was four. Very wild. Her mother, Maren, had a difficult time with her, but Arianna always listened to me. I found Maren when she was only sixteen. She was homeless. I do not know why I didn't hurt her. I did not necessarily like her. She was boring, but she was lovely to look at. Very lovely. I think she had been abused by men, but she trusted me to keep her safe. So I kept her close, away from the others, to see if she would produce. She gave me the boy first. He was strong and could shift at will, but I ordered him not to. I only allowed him to shift if I was there and kept him away from the others. The girl never shifted. I have no idea why."

"You didn't want him to damn himself further," David muttered, his heart breaking at the knowledge that his friend tried to protect his son from becoming the monster he had turned into.

Lancelot shrugged.

"What was his name?"

Lancelot sighed. "David. I never called him that, but that was his name. He was just 'boy' because I didn't want the others to know I had named him after you. He was six."

David's eyes burned, and he held his head to avoid letting too many emotions out.

377

"He would ask about you." Lance chuckled sadly. "He had heard the stories of who I was fighting, and he wanted to grow strong so he could fight you for me. He was upset I named him after you, which is another reason he was just 'boy' to me. He was the only one I ever told about our friendship. I had no one else, and I could not help but see you whenever he increased in skill."

David laughed, rubbing his face to keep from crying. It felt like Jane was dying again or when he'd learned Nathan had been attacked.

"If you want her to stay sane, don't tell her his name," Lancelot whispered. "She seems a lot stronger now. Almost peaceful despite the situation around her. You know she is only half, and what that means, don't you?"

David nodded. "I know, and I won't tell her. I am sorry, Lance. If I could do anything to change what happened . . ."

"I know." Lancelot sighed. "Your heart is strong and good, but I cannot be saved, brother. I may sit here now, calmly speaking about my family—as if we are friends again—but if I get the chance, I will kill her or anyone I get my hands on. I might even kill you."

"You will be imprisoned," David said quickly, not rising to the fight Lance was trying to get. "I don't expect us to be the same. I don't expect there ever truly to be a friendship between us again. I will not forget the crimes you have committed or what you did to Gwen. None of what happened between us should have led you to become what you have. I see, though, we were targeted by darkness. Had I been a true friend, I may have been able to protect you as you always did me. I didn't. I let my pride and the betrayal consume me so greatly that I forgot you were my dearest companion—my brother. I should not have turned my back on you when you needed me. I will not again. If my baby has taught me anything in the short span of our relationship, it is that good can be found in the darkest people, and it is worth fighting for. It's never too late. Forgiveness is greatness."

David smiled as he watched Death kiss her forehead when she whimpered in her sleep. "Love is God's gift to us. And I am grateful to have been gifted with the love of a brother as I was with you. I will try to earn your forgiveness by helping you on your path to redemption. I know you seek it —I see it. And while I forgive you, I will never forget or let my guard down around you. I have children with Jane, and I have my new brothers. I will not let you hurt them or their wives—or any other. But I will stand by you in whatever way I can. I will not let the others attack you, and I will honor the memory of your son, daughter, and woman when we establish a new home."

Lancelot shook his head. "Your woman has made you soft. There is no helping me. They wanted a monster, and they got one."

"They wanted a monster with Jane as well," he pointed out. "And she did not make me soft. She has opened my eyes and shown me strength I did not think existed."

Lancelot rubbed his swollen jaw. "I am not her, though. She was an innocent that the Devil had countless years to corrupt before she was born."

"What do you truly know about her?" David asked.

Pestilence cast Lancelot a dark look.

"No, I want to know," David said. "I deserve to know, as does she."

"Telling you more than you have figured out is forbidden," Pestilence said before glaring at Lancelot. "If your old friendship with him is important, keep what you know to yourself. She will tell him what she has discovered today, just as he will eventually disclose what he has figured out. Although, I should warn you some of your conclusions may be incorrect or incomplete. So, until you are certain they are truth, perhaps wait to discuss them. Her existence is vital to all worlds. And I mean, all worlds. Your puny minds cannot yet fathom the greatness that my father is capable of. Nor do you realize just how truly powerful Jane is."

Lancelot chuckled as he crushed a rock in his palm. "She is great, that is true, but the secrets your brother has held, as well as my former master and his master—they all deserve to burn. That I do not understand. How are any of you considered divine?"

"We are created by God, fool." Pestilence shook his head. "And divine does not mean good. The Accuser is also of divine origins. I made mistakes because of the role I was given. I allowed myself to be manipulated because, years ago, I discovered my brother with Jane. So, I say again, keep what you think you know to yourselves. There is darkness still present, and it seeks to destroy her. She will try to help both of you because you have shadows clinging to your souls."

He glanced at Lancelot. "Well, your soul is barely lit, but as I said, she is powerful—more than you can comprehend, and she will fight for all of you. Keep her safe. And for fuck's sake, Lance, you did not want the damage you caused. If you seek redemption, seek it with the help of those who care to help you. You need their support, and you know very well you do not wish to burn. Do not forget what you have seen. That was only the highest level of Hell, boy. You are set for the deepest. Your nightmares cannot produce the horror and suffering that awaits you there."

Pestilence stood. "Let's get moving. David, come with me. They will tell you where he is later. She needs to be treated now."

David glanced at Lancelot and smiled. "I have faith in you. I am sorry I lost it before, but I swear, I am with you until the end."

"Fool." Lancelot stood, holding out his arms for the chains Asmodeus held as he walked closer.

David started to get up, but Lancelot spoke again, stopping him.

"David, I did not really desire to fuck her. I knew you were listening when I said what I did. I wanted to hurt you and provoke her. I was in agony when I did what I did to her. My woman and children were watching, but I had hoped doing as I was told might save them. It destroyed me, though—knowing what I was doing to your heart and to my family. They never saw me that way. I do not see how Jane can see me differently. I swear I didn't want her that way. Not really. And when I fought the real her, I was furious that she wore his scent. I thought she willingly betrayed you until I saw her the next day. She was already dying for what she'd allowed him to do, but she was doing it for you and her family. She doesn't love him as she does you. Forgive me for saying the things I said before."

David stood. His heart was pounding, and he didn't know what to say. He had avoided thinking about what had happened between them.

Lancelot smirked at him, looking like the boy David once knew. "Beat my ass later, you lucky bastard. I only had the evil twin—you have the angel, who I am sure is a feisty kitten. But I'll look forward to you making me pay for having her."

Pestilence gestured for David to come.

"See you soon, brother," David said. "I expect a better fight next time."

Lancelot nodded, wincing as the chains embedded into his skin. "I learned a lot this round. I will be ready. Go so they can get on with the torture they have planned for me. I feel like a pussy."

David rubbed his heart as he turned away.

"I see why Father chose you," Pestilence said as they walked toward Death. "Your love is endless."

"Was I really chosen?"

Pestilence smirked. "I was not there, but I have seen things through others. You were chosen to stand at her side—that I am certain."

"That's all I need," he said as they reached Jane and Death. "How is she?"

"She's in for a world of pain," Pestilence said, staring at Death's blank expression. "Not yet, brother. She will be fine."

Death barely nodded to his brother before his wings unfolded. "See you there. As soon as you arrive, we are treating her."

"We?" David asked as Sorrow and a white horse erupted out of flames.

Death flapped his wings. "My brothers will help me. She is about to be burned from the inside."

"We will hold her, and you and I will soothe her after." David kissed her cheek. "Do whatever you can to keep her comfortable. I will be there soon."

Death seemed to soften a bit, but he simply grunted and shot up into the air.

Pestilence took David's arm. "He forgot to bond you to Sorrow. You may bond with Perish, and we will ride much faster."

David glanced at the horse. "You mean he will get the flames Sorrow does?"

Pestilence nodded as he summoned a blade. "Yes, they are faster in that form. Perish's flames will inflict disease unless I bond you. I know things you do not about yourself and them, so I do not mind allowing you this bond. Ready?"

David held his arm out. The cut felt like fire and burned more as the horse licked his blood. White flames swirled around his forearm as Pestilence exhaled white smoke, then Perish became engulfed in flames as armor formed on him.

"You're ready. Get on. I will ride Sorrow. We should arrive in forty minutes or so. He is likely already there."

David mounted the white horse, patting his neck as he heard Gareth groaning about needing an angel to give him gifts.

"Hang on, knight," Pestilence said before Perish reared up and took off.

27

PESTILENCE

"Mommy's fine." Jane smiled at Nathan. She was lying on her stomach as Death held his hand over her wound to hide the more gruesome parts. Nathan and Natalie were sitting on the bed by her face.

"What's Ryder doing to you?" Natalie whispered.

"He's giving me a special kind of medicine." She held Nathan's hand. She felt weak and knew she looked horrid, but she was happy to see them.

"Yeah, Ryder is all about medicine." Adam gave Death a dirty look. "I thought you were supposed to be the biggest and baddest. You let her get taken, and then this?"

Jane sighed as she kept hold of Death's free hand. "Relax. He is the awesomest, but we all have our weaknesses. Stop being a prick to him— you know very little of what's happened to all of us."

"When's David coming?" Natalie asked.

"He'll be here soon, baby. I was asleep, but he's coming with one of Ryder's other brothers."

War said something to Death in a language Jane didn't recognize.

Death replied the same way.

"Why do y'all do that?" Jane tilted her head up toward Death. She hated that he seemed to be shutting down still.

"It's Horsemen business," he said.

She pouted but quickly smiled when his lips twitched. "I'm gonna learn your language so I can be in on the fun. David knows different languages, too. It's not fair."

"You can't learn Angel Speak." Death chuckled. "What you hear is not even how it sounds to us."

"Mommy, do we have to stay with Uncle Adam again?" Natalie asked.

"Yes," Death answered before she could. "She needs to have medicine from me. And unlike David's, mine will hurt her. She will need to rest with David afterward."

"Hurt Mommy?" Nathan looked at Death.

"I don't want to," Death said quietly.

Jane almost cried. He looked so upset over what he was about to do to her, and she grew fearful she wouldn't be able to take the pain she was about to experience.

"Ryder loves Mommy. He would never hurt her." David entered the room, smiling as her kids jumped and ran to him. He picked them up, kissing their heads as he walked toward the bed. "But sometimes getting better hurts. She has her men and these big fellows to help her feel better, though." He leaned close to her, somehow still holding the kids, and kissed her. "Hi, sweetheart."

"Hi." She smiled, sighing when he gave her one more kiss before straightening.

"Did you behave for Uncle Adam?" David asked the kids.

"They were fine." Adam crossed his arms. "The reaper guys were able to keep them from seeing anything disturbing . . . Um, do you have any word on Artemis?"

David smiled, nodding. "She is fine. Unfortunately, I had to render her unconscious so she wouldn't do something foolish, but she awoke to find all of her kin alive. If you wish to see her, she's at the infirmary with Hades. She refuses to leave his side. Seeing a friendly face might do her some good, so perhaps you might encourage her to feed—she feels guilty for the injury he sustained."

Adam glanced at Jane.

She smiled. "Go. Maybe wait to be her donor, though. But I think you would be the best person to persuade her to care for herself."

"Jane." Death caressed her cheek. "We must hurry."

She sighed, waving Adam away. "Go. I will see you tomorrow."

"Do you want me to stay with them?" Adam asked.

David patted his shoulder. "My sister is here, but thank you."

Natalie hugged David around the neck. "I want to stay with you and Mommy."

David kissed her head. "Soon, princess. Tonight, Mommy needs to recover after Ryder treats her owie."

Natalie frowned as she glanced at Death. "I thought you fixed Mommy's owies."

"I fix many of them, but he was Mommy's first owie-fixer, and he's the one who can fix big owies like this one."

"David." Death leaned over her when she began to shake.

"Okay, it's time for dinner and then to bed." He kept his tone calm even though she saw the worry in his eyes. "Mommy and I will see you tomorrow. And she'll be all better." He kissed their cheeks as he handed them to Guinevere and Ragnelle. "Thank you."

"Of course, brother. See to Jane now." Guinevere kissed David's cheek and carried the children away when Jane began to tear up. Pestilence sat beside her and took one of her hands as David ushered Adam out.

"The barriers are breaking." Death moved her hair away from her back.

"Jane," Pestilence said, rubbing her hand. "I would like to bond with you."

"Now?" Her muscles began to spasm.

He smiled as War instructed David how to hold her down.

"Yes, Jane." Pestilence turned her palm over. "I am disease and pain. For those suffering, the best relief can often be found in memories and dreams. I will gift you Vision. This is more than a normal dream or memory. Embrace it as you are ready. For now, I will guide you through a journey I believe you need to see. There will be moments when you wake and feel yourself burning inside, but I will pull you back as quickly as possible. You just have to follow me."

David sat beside her as he patted Death's shoulder. "You can do this."

Death glared at him. "You never have to hurt her."

David smiled at him. "I promise you will have the chance to make it up to her."

"It's okay, Death." She squeezed her eyes shut as a piercing sting started to spread. "I know it's going to hurt."

He leaned down and kissed her forehead. "I love you."

"I love you." She smiled, cupping his cheek as her eyes watered. "Hurry now."

War's big hands clamped down on the back of her calves. "We will be here when you wake, Horsemen Bringer."

Death kissed her quickly before moving back for David to take his spot. "Hi, baby." He kissed her cheek as Pestilence took her hand again.

"Hold her tight." Death kissed the edge of her wound. "I'm sorry, angel."

"It's okay." She whimpered as Pestilence leaned closer.

He smiled, kissing her hand before caressing her cheek. "Ready?"

"Yes."

Pestilence's white eyes began to glow. "When pain, suffering, or the end finds you, let my visions carry you far away, where only your loves will find you and bring you home." He leaned down, his eyes glowing brighter as he kissed her lips. A coolness seeped inside her. Instead of traveling down near her heart, it moved to her head, behind her eyes. "Now, follow me, Sweet Jane. I am yours to bring."

As soon as his lips left her skin, she screamed and thrashed in their hands. White light danced behind her eyes as though they'd thrown her into Hell's inferno.

"Let me in, Jane," Pestilence whispered, kissing her eyelids.

She screamed, sobbing.

David's hot lips touched her temple. "Follow him, my love. I'll call you back when it's time." He kissed her again. "Go."

Jane pried her eyes open, gasping when she saw Pestilence before the whole world turned white.

Everything settled, and she opened her eyes again. No longer was she in their room, but she recognized it immediately; she'd been taken to Death's realm.

Her angel lay on his bed, staring up at the ceiling. He was talking, and it took a moment before his smooth voice greeted her ears. "It is her time." He sounded different from the man she knew and loved—detached—a Death without his Sweet Jane.

She opened her mouth but did not speak words of her own. A male voice left her lips, and she had no control over what he said. "They are coming for her. You know I have been involved with her—all I ask is for you to spare her or extend her time."

Jane glanced down at her arms when she crossed them, and she knew right away she was in Pestilence's body.

"I spare no one," Death said. "And you are not permitted to interfere with the affairs of the Immortals. Try to save her, and I will place you in Tartarus myself."

Fury filled her while a faint whisper of a female's voice touched her thoughts. *"He hates you,"* she said. *"All he does is use you and step on your conquests to claim them as his. He owes you."*

Jane tried to shake the sinister voice from her mind. It was lovely, but she knew it to be evil. Pestilence's emotions were adoration, with doubt only surfacing briefly.

"You owe me," Pestilence growled.

Death slowly looked over at her. He didn't appear angry. There was really no show of emotion. He just waited.

Pestilence continued, "I have done everything you have asked of me. I cannot help that you hold no love for these creatures. Do you not even hold love for me, your brother?"

Death sat up, his body now cloaked in black as he studied her. It felt like he was looking at her, and Jane had to remind herself that this was Pestilence's memory. "You are my brother," he said. "That is the highest attachment I will have to any other." He stood up and took a few steps toward a mirror to look at his reflection.

She wanted to smile at how Death still looked the same as he did now.

"I will not spare your female," he told Pestilence. "She is one of the Furies, parading around as a Siren since she failed her duty. That, I do not care about, but no one is spared, not even for one of you. Say your good-byes and let this be a lesson that a human life, even an immortal one, is brief in comparison to our existence. If you desire a companion until our duty is called, choose one of the Divine and not an abomination the Immortals are ridding this world of."

Jane clenched her fist and looked down at Pestilence's pale arms pulsing with strength. She could feel his rage and betrayal.

Death turned toward him. There was no sympathy in his gaze. He was just—Death.

"What if she was someone you loved?" Pestilence asked.

Death tilted his head, appearing confused. "I do not love."

Explosions of light caused the scene to vanish. Jane briefly heard her own screams and David promising it was almost over, all while Death chanted in his angelic language.

She tried to beg them to stop, but her mind was yanked backward, and she opened her eyes to another memory within Pestilence.

Jane took in the empty hallway. She knew the house; it was the one she'd grown up in—the home she had lived in with her aunt, uncle, and cousins.

"It is not that funny, Jane."

Jane's eyes widened as she heard Death. He sounded like her Death, nothing like the emotionless angel she'd just seen talking to Pestilence. She had to look down to ensure she was still in the White Horseman's body because she was angry at hearing the soft laughter. It was her.

"Don't overlook my butt. I work out all the time." Her voice was younger, and she giggled as she tried to mimic Death's voice. "And reaping burns lots of calories."

"Jane," said Death without humor.

She continued in the different male voices. "Ted . . . What, dude? Don't fear the Reaper."

The sound of Death somewhat trying not to laugh when she made a stupid guitar riff sound made Pestilence scowl. Jane would have smiled, but she could only feel Pestilence's irritation. He fumed as he heard his brother sound so loving.

Younger Jane, whom she guessed was around sixteen, burst into a louder fit of giggles. "Damn right!" She squealed from what she knew was Death tickling her. She remembered this. She loved the *Bill and Ted's* movie because the Grim Reaper was in it, and she'd teased Death that the movie Grim Reaper was funnier than him.

Pestilence's fury grew as he took the chance to peer through the crack of the doorway. Death had her pinned as he covered her mouth with his hand.

"Are you going to stop?" Death fought smiling but chuckled when she shook her head. "You need to go to sleep. Your uncle will wake if you don't quiet down. I will not drain him again."

Jane remembered, nodding to him and getting a scrutinizing glance before he let her go.

"Catch ya later, Death," she blurted out, laughing loudly.

Death smiled, the beautiful smile he only gave her. "I cannot believe you are still quoting that movie. I am the only Death, baby girl."

The teenage version of her beamed at Death. "I know. You must always remind me, though."

"Why must I remind you?" Death motioned for her to lie down, but she crawled on his lap and pressed her ear against his chest.

She closed her eyes. "Because I always want the reminder you will be there when it's time for me to go."

Death hugged her as he kissed the top of her head. "I do not think I can part with you." She had already fallen asleep when he caressed her cheek and glanced at the moon outside her window. "You are mine," he whispered, rocking her. "I will never lose you. We are always."

Pestilence balled his fists as Death rolled her onto her back and covered her up.

Death kissed her forehead. "Good night, my moon." Then he vanished.

The scene quickly bubbled, and another room came into view.

It was her room, but this time, she was an adult. It was the home she had with Jason.

Jane saw her reflection—she was still Pestilence. He looked away, and that's when Jane saw herself sitting on the edge of the bed.

There were no lights or TV on. In fact, there was no noise at all. She was alone, just sitting there with her phone in her hand, staring at the screen as tears streamed down her face.

Jane wanted to cry. She remembered what the phone said and almost sobbed when Pestilence leaned over to view the messages written.

> Happy Thanksgiving! Hope you have a great holiday... I love you!

WENDY
> I love you too.

> What's wrong?

WENDY
> I don't want you to have a bad day.

> You can tell me.

WENDY
> I'll tell you tomorrow.

> Tell me now.

WENDY
> They called. My cancer is back. It spread.

Pestilence frowned and moved away to observe her more. Jane could feel his hate for her, but she was devastated and didn't care. She looked at the way her empty eyes stayed fixed on the phone. It was as if she was hoping the words written there would change, but she knew they wouldn't.

Jane tried to cry but could only continue watching herself slip away.

"Pathetic, isn't she?"

Pestilence snapped his head over to look at the man in the corner of the room.

The Devil smiled at him before he continued, "Surely, she understands by now she does not deserve happiness. Why your brother keeps her breathing eludes me."

"He has kept her alive?" Pestilence asked in shock and anger before returning his attention to Jane. Tears silently fell down her cheeks and landed on her arms and phone. There was a brief feeling of guilt, but he pushed it away when the Devil spoke again.

"Many times. Just look at her wrist." He walked to stand in front of Jane. He pointed to the faint scars there with disgust. "Those are her newer method. She used to take pills and would even consider driving off a cliffside. Your brother stops her each time. He will put her to sleep before she presses too deep, and he makes her nauseous when pills touch her tongue. Now she cannot even keep a few pills down without vomiting, so she thinks about dying and how to do it. She even prays to your father to erase her from existence."

"Does my brother not visit her as he used to?"

"He erased her memory when she declared her love to him. He wanted her to live a long, happy life. Strange, isn't it?" His smile was cruel but beautiful. "Death wants life for another. He does anything to ensure she has it, but her soul is doomed to suffer."

Pestilence wasn't sure what he felt as he watched her cry. "So, without him, she is suicidal?"

"She was before him as well. He has tried several times to leave her, but she always calls him back to her—a clever little witch. She will ruin him."

"Ruin him? She's just a girl. What could she possibly do to him?"

"It's just a thought," the Devil replied. "I am merely pointing out that your brother has let a female of the human race beat him. Never has he loved or even cared for these beings. Death is not supposed to feel. Yet, he goes against his duty to save a girl who does not even wish to live. You are looking at the destruction of humanity."

"She doesn't look bad," said Pestilence. A hazy feeling poured into his head. "What is happening to me?" He didn't seem aware he was speaking aloud.

"You are just experiencing betrayal. Your brother promised never to spare a soul. He lied to you. He let your beloved die and never gave a second thought to the misery you suffered from the loss. Does he even know you seek admittance to Tartarus to visit Megaera?"

"No."

Faint whispers started up again, and Pestilence thought of his old love. He'd honestly forgotten Megaera until a few years ago. Then he heard her voice calling him from Tartarus, and he took desperate measures to visit her in Hell's most impenetrable prison. It was only due to the powerful being standing before him that he managed to enter and exit Tartarus, and with each visit, Pestilence became more desperate to see Megaera free.

"I sometimes wonder how I came to love Megaera," Pestilence whispered when Past-Jane finally made an audible cry. He frowned as he watched her weep. "I just remember seeing her and wanting her to be mine. I don't know—"

"What if I were to say there was a way you could have Megaera in your arms again?" the Devil asked. "After all, your brother has allowed this mortal to live well beyond her time. She never contributed to humanity as Megaera once did. She does not even wish to live. Surely, Megaera deserves a second chance over this pathetic female."

When Pestilence didn't respond, the Devil patted him on the shoulder and spoke sympathetically, "I hear Megaera weeps so loudly for you that she is given extra punishment. I know of a way you can hold her again."

Jane's heart raced as she heard a woman's voice whispering again. Pestilence began to feel desperate and enraged as he watched the past version of Jane cry.

"How?" he asked.

———

Fiery pain seared across Jane's back. She screamed, briefly opening her eyes to see Pestilence and David's faces right next to hers. She screamed louder when she began to burn, but again, she was forcefully ripped from reality into memory.

———

Heavy. That was how Jane would have described Pestilence's current state. His head and mind felt weighed down. She blinked as he did and took in the beautiful woman before them. She had dark, luscious brown hair and ruby lips. *Megaera*, Pestilence thought.

"How will he help me?"

Jane nearly gasped at the sound of Lancelot's voice. Inside Pestilence's body, though, she merely tilted her head in Lancelot's direction and calmly took in the other vampires and demons around him. Mania was there, and so was the Devil.

"Have you not read any of the holy texts?" the Devil asked with an amused smile at Lancelot. "He can bring disease. Even one that would allow the dead to scour the earth."

Lancelot didn't look impressed as he gazed back at Pestilence. Jane realized Megaera was touching her arm, no, Pestilence's arm, and she was whispering endlessly. The words were foreign to Jane, but the haunting melody only clouded her mind.

"Zombies?" Lancelot laughed.

"You are a werewolf, Lancelot. Your greatest rivals are vampires." The Devil smiled. "Do not assume other horrors are fictitious."

"How will a plague of zombies help me? Arthur and the knights are the best. An animated corpse will do little against them."

The Devil shrugged. "Refuse my offer, then. I do not see your master jumping to offer you any upper hand against them."

Lancelot scowled, crossing his arms over his bare chest. "I did not say I wish to refuse. I simply want to understand how this is beneficial."

"A corpse has no weakness, save the destruction of the brain that still allows its nerves to fire off orders. Being dead also removes the hindrance God has placed on all other cursed immortals."

Lancelot's eyes widened. "You mean—"

"Yes, your creations would be immune to silver, and if successful, they could challenge a vampire during daylight. Of course, I do not expect the undead mutations to annihilate the knights. However, they will be forced to fight you day and night, and you will no longer have the hindrance of the others who seek redemption by aiding Arthur."

"The humans ... What of them?" Lancelot asked.

The Devil tilted his head, observing Lancelot quietly before he finally said, "Humans are the only beings capable of initially succumbing to this disease. We will use the men you select to transfer a mutated virus."

Lancelot seemed hesitant.

"Do not worry, Lance," said the Devil. "The human race will survive.

Yes, some will fall victim to the undead, but a few casualties will be worth sacrificing. You seek revenge, do you not?"

"I do," Lancelot said quickly. "I just—if the plague were to escape us—" He shifted his eyes toward Pestilence. "If the humans die, we all die."

The Devil placed a comforting hand on Lancelot's shoulder. "You will enjoy your new pets. The human race will bow to you, and when this is over, the lovely Queen Guinevere will stay chained to your side. That will be your prize for taking on this burden and going against your master's order."

"I get Gwen?" Lancelot asked. "But she doesn't love me."

Jane wanted to hug him for a moment. She could see that her evil enemy was a broken, desperate man who still completely loved a woman who would not be his.

The man in black smiled. "She loved you once—she will again. I can make it so you will her to love and obey you. She would be your queen, just as you had hoped so many years ago."

"My queen," Lancelot said softly.

The world spun, and Jane had to take a deep breath before she looked at a grim scene. She didn't recognize this new place. It was dark and damp, like an old castle dungeon.

A door opened, letting bright light flood into the dark cell.

"Bring him," said a male voice.

Jane looked down to see she was still Pestilence chained to the rocky wall.

"What did they do to him?" one of the men asked as they dragged Pestilence toward the doorway.

"No one is saying," the first replied.

Jane couldn't see them all that much. She was squinting at the sudden white hallway she was being pulled down.

"I heard one of his men talking," whispered the same man, sounding scared for even speaking on the subject. "They are using demons."

"Demons?"

"That's not all. You've heard those stories about vampires with abilities to bewitch?"

"Yeah."

Jane's head bobbed off to the side, and she could only see their feet and legs as they continued dragging Pestilence.

"Well, they've had some coming in and out of his cell. Sirens and Muses, I heard them say. I thought they were all dead or imprisoned with the knights."

"Do you know what they're going to make him do?"

"No. They won't say a word. I hope they can control him. If he goes berserk like he did when they first brought him here, we're all dead. They are not supposed to be able to harm made immortals, but he was able to when he was not aware."

They opened a series of doors, and Pestilence was dragged into a heavily occupied room. Jane looked around and was shocked to see Lancelot standing with Ares, Hermes, and other vampires.

"Stand him up," Lancelot said.

Someone lifted Pestilence to his feet as Lancelot walked closer. He seemed nervous or regretting what he was doing, but he emptied his expression of any emotion and ordered the men holding Pestilence up. "Put him over there." He pointed to a chair that was in the center of the room.

Then, Jane noticed the others all standing or tied to the opposite wall. She knew right away that some were human. A few others were vampires, and she thought the others might be werewolves still in human form. The humans cried and tried to pull at the restraining chains.

She was pushed into a chair and looked over lazily to see the door open again. Jane internally gasped when she watched the Devil enter, followed by Belial, Berith, and Thanatos. She wanted to yell at her general for being a traitor, but she could only stare at him because Pestilence did not react. He felt nothing.

"Are you ready to see your plans come to life, Lancelot?" The Devil chuckled softly with the others. He was making a joke.

Jane glanced at Lancelot as he quietly eyed the chained victims before staring at her for a moment.

"I told you he would back out," Belial said, glaring at Lancelot. "Coward."

"I am no coward," Lancelot said to him. "I even picked a human named Zev Knight to show Arthur it was me when his body is discovered."

Belial shook his head. "I still smell your hesitation, dog. Are you frightened of your master? He cannot even touch you, and you shake in fear."

"I do not fear Lucifer," Lancelot spat. "Proceed." He moved over to stand amongst Ares and Hermes.

Looking at the young vampire who had saved her life pained her heart, but she was forced to focus on Thanatos when he walked forward with the man in black. Thanatos reached behind him and pulled out a bow, Pestilence's bow, to be exact.

"Hello, Pestilence," the Devil greeted. She felt the White Horseman's mind stir at his name. "It is time for you to unleash the plague you promised."

There were cries and whimpers from the victims. Thanatos said nothing as he held the bow out to Pestilence.

Pestilence took it and quietly inspected the ethereal weapon.

The Devil continued, "These creatures have broken God's law. He wishes them to suffer your wrath. Let them grow sickly and crazed. Stop their beating hearts and let their rotting corpses spread your impressive creation."

"It is not time," Pestilence said automatically. This order was not ready to be issued. He was waiting to be called.

The Devil smiled and lowered his head. "It is time. Remember, Megaera awaits you. Do you not still wish for her new life? Your disease will allow the dead to rise again. She can return to the precious earth that she has missed."

"Megaera?" Pestilence asked.

"The woman you love," the Devil confirmed.

"No, I love no one. Only Father. My duty." He frowned, taking in his surroundings. "Where am I?" Pestilence panicked as he remembered fighting off and destroying several demon guards until Thanatos, Belial, and Berith finally subdued him. After that, he only recalled blurring images of being beaten and left in darkness. Occasionally, his strength returned, but female visitors were brought in, and everything dulled again.

Jane's rage grew with Pestilence's as Melody's face came to his mind, along with a few other vampire women with sparkling eyes.

Pestilence focused on Thanatos. "You traitor!"

The Devil spoke calmly at his outburst. "This would have been simpler had you continued your dislike for your brother's whore."

Jane's mind raced as she saw Pestilence remember sitting beside her and Wendy. He had been staring at Jane and told her he was sorry—that he had no choice.

"Have you remembered your hatred for the girl?" the Devil asked.

The others seemed confused, but they stayed quiet.

"I never hated her." Pestilence lifted his gaze to the Devil. "She was not what you said. She was innocent and pure."

"She bewitched you, then." The Devil shook his head. "Foolish boy."

Pestilence grew angrier, yelling, "She is a pure soul who does not deserve the horror you have inflicted upon her. I know what you have done to that child of God."

"Did you finally use your talents to peer into her memories?" The Devil chuckled. "A lovely creature, isn't she?"

Pestilence glared at him. "You have ruined Father's beautiful creation. She was special, and you poisoned her."

"I poisoned half. One will triumph over the other, and I believe my daughter will smile in the end."

Pestilence smirked. "Then you are not as knowledgeable as you think, Accuser. You picked the wrong soul to tamper with."

Thanatos frowned but said nothing.

"We will see." The Devil smiled.

"Whatever you do here today will bring Heaven down on you." It was then that Pestilence seemed to register he was holding his bow and tried to draw it back, but he was weak, and his movements slow.

Within a blink of an eye, Belial had restrained him in a chokehold.

She gasped as his muscular arms squeezed tightly against her neck.

Pestilence took in the bound victims and knew what was meant to happen. His heart pounded as he fought against the powerful Fallen, but it was no use; enchantments had weakened him.

"What will your brother say to you when he learns you have cost him his beloved human?" the Devil asked.

Pestilence struggled to breathe and looked around to see if the others understood who they were speaking about. Besides them, only the Devil and God were supposed to know who the Horsemen were. There were various angels and even demons of sickness. He would not embrace his role as the White Horseman until it was time.

The Devil smiled, making fear flood his veins. "They know your secret."

Jane wanted to cry at the overwhelming emotions assaulting the White Horseman. He was so scared for her and his brother.

The Devil smiled evilly and spoke softer, "Did you know I can block her soul from his sight?"

Pestilence's eyes widened in horror as he sputtered, "That's not possible."

"I assure you it is." The smile grew on the man in black's face. "Do you think he loves her?"

"You can't touch her." Pestilence gasped for air.

"No, I can't," he said, grinning nonetheless. "But her husband can. Just as her cousin did and the other boys your brother failed to protect her from."

Jane wanted to scream. The terror inside the horseman's heart was unbearable. Pestilence thrashed harder, but when the Devil put a single finger on him, he was instantly paralyzed. All he could do was blink while Belial loosened his grip.

"Don't," Pestilence rasped. It was almost impossible to speak, but he tried his hardest to fight the invisible hold on him.

Berith walked closer, tilting his head. "What girl do you speak of?"

The Devil just waved him off. "She's just a pretty face that makes weak men want to protect her." Pestilence breathed harder as the Devil continued. "But this pretty human has found herself a powerful immortal protector, has she not? We cannot allow that."

"She doesn't deserve to suffer." Pestilence's throat burned, but he kept going. "You've tortured her enough with your minions. Leave her in peace now." He darted his gaze toward Thanatos, holding onto a small bit of hope his brother's former general still had a heart.

Thanatos avoided his gaze, though, and Pestilence's hope slipped away. He tried to call out to Death or any of his other brothers, but there was nothing. His bond had been tampered with.

"Your brother should not have shown interest in her," said the Devil. "She was not his to claim."

Jane realized the Devil had intended for Lucifer to claim her. Death had just gotten there first, and he protected her without knowing what was happening.

"Unleash your plague on these beasts, and I will leave her in peace," the Devil offered.

Pestilence was torn. The entire human race was at stake, and once he let loose his plague, his brothers were sure to follow his path without question. He looked back to the victims, then to the Devil.

"I can force you under their spell again," he continued. "Wouldn't you rather spare at least one human from horror?"

Pestilence knew there was no way to win. He could already feel himself slipping into a new trance. He attempted to call his family once more, but again, no one could be felt.

All of Pestilence's hope faded. She could feel the effects of whatever was being forced on him. He was incredibly strong, but she had seen the power the Devil held.

"You will make them leave her alone?" Pestilence asked softly.

"You have my word." The Devil mockingly covered his heart. "I will not order another assault on her and pull those who torment her husband. I cannot prevent them from falling victim to your plague, but I know she has strength hidden in her. She will fight until the very end."

Pestilence thought everything over. He knew what the girl was, even if his brother did not. Jane couldn't figure out what Pestilence knew. He avoided thinking of it to protect her.

He quickly prayed for all of humankind. But, for now, he would try to protect the one person who might make Death hesitate to carry out his duty. *Jane.* After all, she was the key to everything.

"I accept your offer," Pestilence whispered. "Just leave the girl in peace. Remove your subjects and wipe their memory of her. No one is to go near her again."

"Fine." The Devil smiled meanly. "You have my word. I will not suggest any begin to torment her, and I will cleanse those who cling to her husband. She has isolated herself so much that he is the only one who can access her. I cannot stop any that find him on their own, though. And I cannot change what he has been shaped into. Perhaps he will find his path again."

Pestilence nodded and felt the break in the hold on him. He stood, watching as the humans begged for someone to release them.

His heart pounded, but he lifted his bow and drew back. "Come, for I am the White Horseman." As expected, his deadly arrow manifested between his fingers. Its white glow would be considered beautiful had it not represented something so terrible.

Pestilence noticed Thanatos staring at him, and since the others were watching the weeping people, he took the chance to mouth a last request to his brother's former guard: *Tell Lucifer.*

Thanatos nodded stiffly in response. It wasn't much to hope for, but Pestilence had no choice. Jane was the one being who might stop his brother from ending the world.

"Forgive me, Father," Pestilence whispered as he released his arrow.

Screams of panic and horror echoed throughout the room. Jane felt like she would cry, but she could only listen to the blood-curdling screams of death. The silence didn't last long. Groans and snarls she had heard for

397

months trapped in her home shortly followed it. The undead were unleashed.

"Please, Lancelot," a man yelled.

"Shouldn't they be changing?" Ares asked.

"It's coming," said Lancelot. He sounded unsure of himself but said nothing more.

"Stop this," shouted another man. There were clangs from their chains and cries as the snarling humans tried to break free.

"You promise they will be under my control?" Lancelot asked.

Seven bound men with emptiness in their eyes tugged at their chains to reach the chained werewolf and vampire prisoners. The cursed immortals looked just as terrified and began to fight against their restraints.

"You will have complete control," the Devil assured. "It is the blood drinkers I am unsure of."

Pestilence watched Ares and Hermes exchange worried glances. He already knew vampires would not fall to this disease, but he was unsure of the total goal with them here.

"Are they nearly ready for their change?" the Devil asked.

"Yes," Lancelot said.

"Do it now, then."

Again, Lancelot hesitated but finally moved toward the bound werewolves. They were still stuck in weak human forms. Pestilence realized these men had already been beaten. Lancelot had picked his prisoners.

Ares and Hermes joined him. They took the chains from the walls, each knocking the fighting vampire or werewolf unconscious and dragging them to be just within reach of the hungry humans.

It would have been funny to witness if it wasn't so terrible. But Jane could see the fear in her old enemies' eyes. They were scared of what they were doing.

"A single bite will do the trick," said the Devil. He watched with folded arms over his chest. There was no remorse or worry in him. He was just observing.

The infected humans began to feed just as brutally as she remembered. Luckily, Lancelot pulled them out of reach after each sustained a single bite. It didn't please the snarling corpses, and they growled for more.

Pestilence slumped in defeat when the Devil placed a comforting hand on his shoulder. "Well done, White Horseman."

The cracking of bones and mutating flesh reached his ears. He looked over when screams started erupting. The vampires knocked out were coming around, but the mutated wolves were already thrashing in their chains.

His eyes widened, and his mouth fell open.

The mutated wolves were wild, like when she'd first seen them. Decay had not set in, but their white eyes were the marker.

They began attacking the bound vampire victims, and the screams were sickening.

Lancelot rushed forward and roared, transforming into his wolf. He knocked his mutated beasts back with his destroying claws and growled before putting himself between the wounded vampires. The mutated wolves stilled, lowering their massive heads.

Pestilence was shocked he could issue commands to them, but it mattered little.

"Let the humans out," said Belial.

Pestilence snapped his eyes over to him.

Belial smirked and spoke again, "I will not repeat myself."

Lancelot growled and returned to his human form. "It worked," he said. "There is no need to test them further. Let me destroy these creatures. I have my weapon now."

"But we are not finished with our objective," Belial replied. "Do not make me repeat myself, dog."

Lancelot looked furious and darted his gaze to the Devil. "You said only my chosen. You can't let these things out. They will destroy the world."

The Devil did not respond.

Lancelot roared at his silence. "This was not our agreement!"

Belial spoke again, "Release the infected, or I will visit your beloved queen."

Lancelot seemed to stop breathing.

"He promised you would have a queen." Belial gestured toward the Devil. "He did not say when or what state she would be in."

Lancelot looked on with shock. "You will not touch her."

Belial grinned. "Release them, and I will avoid the fair queen."

Lancelot looked down at the monsters. His wicked beasts growled behind him, but he had complete control.

Jane actually admired his power and saw what David must have seen inside him. Lancelot still had some good in him. She wanted to smile but could only stare at the scene in front of her with sadness.

"Open the door," Lancelot whispered.

Ares unlocked the many locks that were in place before tapping on the door. She listened to locks coming open from the other side and looked away. Whoever was on the outside would likely fall victim to these new nightmares.

"Time to go home, Pestilence," the Devil whispered. "We cannot have you warning your brothers of what has happened or protecting the girl. You forgot about the pull she emits. They will continue coming for her, and your brother will be very busy from this day on, won't he?"

"You won't succeed."

"I already have. Lucifer will seek Lancelot out but will not reach him until he happens upon her home. Each half of her soul will call to him. The pure one will shine like a beacon, summoning darkness like a moth to a flame, then he will see what power she hides. He will set her free, and your brother's little human will be no more."

"Death will protect her," Pestilence promised. "You have no idea what you have done, and I will laugh when you all see. Light will prevail."

"I have your father's most cunning and beloved son at my disposal. He wishes to see the Kingdom of Heaven fall, and she is his weapon. He will rule all with her at his side."

Pestilence laughed. "You underestimate her."

The Devil smiled. "I created the darkest being out of half her soul. Once she breaks her pure half, she will be unstoppable."

"Like I said, you underestimate her."

The Devil merely chuckled.

She watched Lancelot glare hatefully at the stone floor before he ordered Hermes to undo the chains.

Pestilence rose to his feet. She felt him trying to fight, but the hand on his shoulder kept him from achieving any freedom.

"Make sure you are careful with your men, Lancelot," the Devil warned. "These beasts will not return to their original form, and should any change due to a rogue wolf attacking a human, you will hold no command over them."

Lancelot nodded. "I understand."

"Don't get bitten." The Devil smiled. "Make sure our new additions to the human race meet their family. And might I suggest traveling south? My son will soon follow, and I will be disappointed to find the two of you fighting amongst yourselves when you should be increasing your forces to fight Arthur. I hear Texas has lovely females. Perhaps one will catch your eye and entertain you on your journey?"

"Yes, Master," Lancelot said.

Pestilence made one last attempt to seek help. All she could see was Thanatos as Hermes and Ares carefully dragged out the infected humans. The vampires weren't changing as Pestilence had expected, but they were still wary.

Pestilence locked eyes with Thanatos and felt a small ounce of relief when he received a subtle wink from her general.

Then there was darkness.

Slowly, all that was black began to spark with warm light.

"Come on, Jane." David's voice caressed her ears. "Please, my love."

"I should have tried sooner." Death sounded broken, and she could faintly feel his hand holding hers. His lips and breath barely warmed her cold skin.

"Stop talking like she isn't going to wake," David snapped.

She wanted to tell them she was there, but her whole body protested. David pressed several kisses to her forehead as he ran his fingers through her hair.

"She will wake soon." It was Pestilence at that time.

"I should have fed her before we started," David whispered. "Wake up, Jane. I will feed you, and you will feel much better."

She didn't care about feeding, but she slowly felt pressure and a searing pain in her back; she didn't want to feel anything just yet. David's earlier statement that getting better sometimes hurt surfaced in her thoughts, halting her desire to seek refuge in more memories. He was right.

After a few moments of concentration, she finally let out a strangled breath.

"There you go," David cooed. "I know it hurts, but we're here. We will help."

"You can take this, Jane." Death's low voice moved closer when she heaved another painful breath. "Come back to us."

The light feeling was still there, but it was smothered by the excruciating torture burning her.

"Are you sure you got it all out?" David asked. His hand trembled against her cheek.

"I got all of it, but light is powerful, and I could not stop it from burning her."

"It's okay," David said. "She's strong."

"You boys baby her." War yawned. "How am I tired?"

"You just spent seven hours pinning down one of Earth's strongest immortals," Pestilence said, laughing.

"Ah, yes." War chuckled. "She kicks as hard as Ravage. Are you sure the two of you are enough for her?"

Death growled. "Suggest what I think you are joking about, and I will see that your balls rot and fall off the next time you bed a woman."

"She's our baby." David chuckled. "I am enough . . . He will be, too, if she wishes and accepts him."

It got so quiet. Jane would have rolled off the bed and right out of the room if she had been able to move.

Pestilence laughed softly. "You know, while she followed me through my memories, I saw some of her dreams. She is quite innocent, but a naughty kitten has been purring to be played with since you two joined forces."

War laughed loudly as David's warm, smiling lips pressed against her forehead.

"Shut the fuck up," Death said. "Keep her dreams to yourself."

"Yes, brother." Pestilence chuckled again. "But might I suggest you search for lube first?"

War laughed as two hits sounded.

"Baby," David murmured, "I do not think I can handle three Horsemen alone. Please wake up."

Jane whimpered. She wanted to smack all four of them, but she knew they only tried to cheer Death up and distract her from the pain.

"Jane." Death nuzzled her cheek. "You must feed, sweet girl. I swear we will let you rest afterward."

"Are you sure?" Pestilence asked. "How many times have you peeked at her breasts without releasing pheromones?"

"Get out," Death said sharply.

"I shall take him," War said.

Pestilence chuckled, adding, "I am merely saying what we all saw."

"I will have you back in chains if you do not shut your mouth," Death snarled.

"We will inform the others you are not to be disturbed," War said. "Her eyelids are fluttering, by the way. She probably heard everything."

A door shut as two pairs of lips pressed against her skin. Death had kissed her shoulder as David did her cheek.

"They were trying to keep you relaxed," David said after a few seconds.

"I know what they were doing," Death said, kissing her again. "Come on, angel."

"Do you think I should give her a transfusion?"

Death seemed to shrug. "You know her blood requirements more than I do. But I don't know how much she will need now that she holds Lucifer's light."

The fire sent jolts of electricity into her limbs—each painful and debilitating.

"I think she is still being burned," David said seriously.

Before Death could respond, she gasped and tried to speak. "Da—" she broke off in a strangled sound.

"I'm here," he quickly cooed. "It's okay."

"Death," she cried as he kissed her cheek.

"Breathe, baby girl," he said, caressing her fingers as they squeezed his hand. "David, pull her against you."

David obeyed, and the movement caused her to scream out in agony.

"Stop," she sobbed.

Death caught her flailing arms as it felt like acid was shot through her veins.

"It's okay." David pulled her close. His strong arms wrapped around her shaking frame. The heat and pressure he provided kept her from feeling like she was going to break apart.

"David, please make it stop," she cried.

"I'm trying." His blood was there. "Drink."

Sparks of silvery light overwhelmed her sight as more flames consumed her.

"Fuck." David struggled to hold her. "Open her mouth for me."

"It's just spilling out. She's not swallowing," Death said. "Please drink, Jane. I can't bear to see you like this."

Jane managed to swallow what had made it into her mouth.

"Good girl." David pressed his wrist to her mouth. "Suck, Jane."

"This sounds like we're in a horrible porno," Jane stuttered.

Death chuckled, kissing her hand. "Sweet Jane, you have never watched a porno."

"Jason's," she mumbled.

Death pushed David's arm away, cupping her cheeks and kissing her as David kissed her neck.

"Follow me," Death murmured against her mouth.

She felt faint tingles caress her lips, but every time they tried to travel down her throat, fire rose, blocking them.

"Fuck," he growled, kissing her over and over again. "I can't get to her."

David pushed Death away. "Hold her. Let me send for a transfusion kit. I should have fucking had one prepared."

Death lifted her and put her in the same position David had, just as her vampire got off the bed.

"Hurry!" Death sounded panicked, and Jane felt her entire body convulsing as he threw his leg over hers.

A sudden icy sensation shot through her body, and she stopped everything. It jolted her again. Death's hand covered her arm where the intense blast of cold came, but he hissed, ripping his hand away as if it had burned him.

Jane gasped, opening her eyes and looking right at David.

"Baby?" He lowered the phone. "Can you hear me?"

Numbness spread over the internal flames.

"Blood." She sighed as the chill spread through her body.

Death snarled but kissed her. "Feed her now."

David bit into his wrist and held it against her lips.

This time, she drank without difficulty and sighed as she felt the skin on her back sealing.

"What did you do to her?" David asked.

"Nothing." Death smoothed her hair back. "I did nothing."

Jane released David and closed her eyes, feeling incredibly tired.

"You will," David said quietly. "I promise."

28

THE SECRET

"You should have told me. And her." David's angry whisper stirred Jane from her slumber, but she was too tired to bother with him yet. She just wanted to sleep, so she nuzzled his chest, smiling because he was there. He was safe.

"You're going to wake her up," Death said behind her.

"Don't change the subject." David held her head in place.

"What should I have said?" His tone started serious, then suddenly dripped with sarcasm. "Sorry, Jane, you're dying. For you to live, you have to choose me instead of David, or let Lucifer bond with you for all eternity . . . I was giving her a chance to have a life with you."

"We still should have been told," David said fiercely. "If we had known, we could have come up with a solution together. She should have been allowed to choose as well."

"She would've picked the same, and I didn't want to admit I was power-less when it came to keeping her safe."

"You were keeping her alive," David reminded, then scolded, "by slowly killing yourself, which extended to her after a while. But you were trying. You still let her go for a chance to be without you. You make her shine . . . And—"

Death cut him off. "Don't say it. It's difficult for me to know this and not—"

"I would imagine it is." David sighed. "What's happening to you? Did Lucifer giving her light help you? You are different."

Death sounded lost. "When I found her with him and realized she is now eternally bound to him, I thought I had lost everything that made me the man she loves. He taunted me, and I could see she had willingly sacrificed herself to save me. I had nothing left to hold me back from what my brother started by unleashing the plague. I allowed my transformation to the Pale Horseman to unfold because I am nothing without her."

"But you're still you."

"That is her doing," Death said as his fingers caressed her back. "She is tethering me to her so I don't destroy everything. She shouldn't be able to do this to me anymore . . ." He kissed her head. "The bond she has been attempting when we kiss her—she is doing it. It's almost stronger than what I shared with her. Almost. It is why I am still *me*. I think if we allowed her to make it, it would be the most powerful bond ever created. Unbreakable by any."

"Should it even be possible?"

"How should I know?"

David was quiet for a few seconds, then he finally said, "Would you consent if she wanted to?"

"I'm not sure."

"I know it's not the same—"

"It's not that," Death said quickly. "It is more than I could have hoped for. But it changes everything. You risk losing your honor as well."

David chuckled. "I did not expect you to care."

"I don't." Death's mean but gorgeous smile was unmistakable in his tone. "I worry about how it will affect her, though. She might blame herself for you appearing less in anyone's eyes, and she would worry you do not want such a thing. Even if we tell her, she isn't ready for it."

"I realize you can't tell her, but she needs to know."

"No," Death said. "You can't tell her either. It's different if she figures it out, but we must stay quiet."

David growled, his grip on her momentarily tightening. "Not telling her leads to trouble. She might not react well or realize she knew all along. Maybe that's why she's doing this. She knows."

"How are you not upset?"

"I was for a while," David admitted. "I think it just came down to how she loves me—how much she is willing to do for me. I don't know why things are this way, but I know there is a reason behind everything that happens. I accept it."

"You say that now," Death said, "but if we continue, you will realize you still want her to yourself."

"I'll have her to myself. I already know your line of thought on how you desire to be with her, and it does not involve being a boyfriend, husband, or father to her children. That is why you desire her to be with me, right?"

"I can be a boyfriend if I want to," Death muttered. "And I can be a daddy."

David laughed quietly.

"Okay, fuck you, I can't."

"There you go, then. You know she will only be our Jane with you. You desire to see her glow, just as I do. She shines brightest between us, and you know why."

"It's because I'm sexy."

"I am being serious," David said.

"So am I. She glows because I'm sexy."

"Idiot." David seemed to shake his head. "I have no idea how I will put up with having a relationship with you, but I will."

"Aw, honey," Death cooed, "you say the sweetest things."

"Don't fucking touch me." David chuckled. "We are trying to have a serious discussion, and you are fucking around. I swear you can't be within five feet of her without turning into a juvenile. Behave."

"Going for the alpha position right away, I see. Don't I even get to fight for it?"

"No, you submitted the moment you called me Daddy."

"Fuck, that's right. I want a do-over."

"No," David said quickly.

"Just try calling me Daddy." Death's playful tone toward David had her stomach fluttering. "You might like it."

"I won't like it." David's serious tone had the same effect. "Stop acting like a child for five minutes so we can discuss this before she wakes up."

"Yes, Daddy."

There was a definite hit thrown from David.

"Ow." Death chuckled. "That might bruise."

David ignored his childishness. "I want her to form it if she wants to. It would mean so much to me."

"I know it would." Death sighed, his teasing absent.

"Do you not want it?"

"Surprisingly, I do. But I still don't know if it will end well. I never truly considered this option."

David went on. "Nor I."

"It really doesn't bother you knowing what I want with her? If she ends up wanting it as well?"

"It doesn't bother me anymore," David confirmed. "I don't think she has considered being intimate with you while she and I have been together—not really. She was hysterical when things happened with Jason, and I know she did what she did for the wrong reasons. It was not because she desired you over me."

"Ouch."

"Sorry."

"It's okay, Papi."

"Fucking moron. Focus. I'm trying to tell you I think she desires you, but she has buried it because it is not the norm and because she has—we all have—believed it's only her and me. But when I permitted you to kiss her, really kiss her, it surfaced. You know she wanted you—both of us. Don't be afraid."

"I'm not afraid." Death sighed loudly. "I know she hasn't truly considered being intimate with me for some time. Even when I restored her memories, she was only aroused with me, but she was always thinking of you. I couldn't even get past first base." Death paused. "Fuck, you really don't mind."

"I told you it is not the same." David sounded utterly confident. "I believe she will only desire you physically if we are together. It's not that you're not good enough, but she started a relationship with me. You two will never really have that option, and you know that. I am saying this is an option I want for her, which is why she needs to know."

"She asked me to go through with breaking our bond," Death reminded him. "Her reason was not the same as mine. She wanted to make it clear you were the only man she wanted. She was cutting me out."

"No," David said, definitely shaking his head, "she knew something was wrong with you, and I wasn't strong enough to accept she needed more than me. She was doing it for both of us. I know we could make things work without you, but she would not be my girl. I want her to be everything she is meant to be and be the happiest she can be, and you are part of her happiness. You are a part of her, and I fully accept that."

Death began playing with her hair. "It's still not the same. She doesn't desire any type of relationship like this with me. She has only had a few moments where she thought of us together, and you've wanted her to your-self. We've all been trying to accept that you're the one and I'm not."

"Stop going back to this," David said, growling. "I was selfish and didn't stop thinking about the two of you. She's been trying to make me happy and give me everything she thinks I deserve when it should have been the other way around. We're not normal, and that's okay."

"No one will understand," Death said.

"No one will understand unless they know the truth," David retorted, "but it is for us to know. Even if it comes out, some will feel their opinions matter, but they don't. What matters is that Jane is happy. She is who she is meant to be with both of us. So even if she chooses me alone, she is not choosing herself. If she were, you'd be right there. I think that is why we are always falling. I am meant to accept you, and you clearly accept me after what you have done. For her, I mean. You and I don't have romantic feel-ings toward each other. It's respect and, I suppose, love as well. We love what the other does for her and the part of her we hold. You are only fighting this because you're worried she will reject us. Both of us have wanted her to ourselves, and that tears her apart. You know why."

Jane was beginning to have trouble keeping her charade up. *What fucking secret do they have together?*

"I can't lose her," Death murmured. "Having you let me in as you have has been unexpected. I am grateful, but I have not allowed my hopes to build."

"You are so like her," David said.

"She's my baby—my moon," Death said. "I'm nothing without her."

"She is the same for me." David kissed the top of her head. "Let her form it if that's what she wants. If either of us tries to stop her, you lose who she's changed you into—you lose who you two are, and we both lose our Jane. It feels right for a reason. I swear I would not suggest it on a whim. My honor is reserved for Jane and God . . . And I extend it to you. We can make it work."

Death rested his head on hers. "I could kill this bond she's creating before it grows—and she'd be all yours. Until . . ."

"You need to stop whatever the fuck you are considering," David snapped. "You can barely look away from her, and it will destroy you to hurt her again. Both of you are watching each other slip away, and you're both still reaching out. I never want to see what I saw again. I'm trying to hold all of us together. Even I need you. You always bring her back to me. You open my eyes when I cannot see what is before me. I won't change my mind. I have the patience and understanding I need for what we are discussing.

"Anyway, she is doing it without us. Are you willing to remove her choice? That is, after all, what you desire most. You said you wanted her to live the life she chose. She's showing us what her choice is. She's choosing both, but she's afraid because she's committed to me. She tried to let you go and look at what happened. She needs us to assure her we are in this together. I will do my part, but you must also support her. If she senses either of us is uncomfortable or against it, she will lose that light in her and the incredible bond she has started. Do you want her to be without—"

"No," Death cut in. "It is the one thing I feared most when doing what I did. But I thought it would save her. That is all I was concerned with. That and not ripping her from you."

"I know," David said. "We have never been a traditional couple. You were always a presence, either in my face or lingering in the darkness. It might be awkward at first, but I think you and I are comfortable enough with each other now. She feels natural between us, and I see her at peace. Just look at her right now. Normally she is on me, trying to get closer. Yet with you right there, she is perfectly at ease. We won't always be able to be with her like this, but I will welcome your ass whenever you come home."

"So romantic, baby," Death snickered.

"Fucking hell." David released a breath. "Did you know those who can see you think we look related?"

"I'm sexier," Death said without hesitating. "And it explains why she thinks you're hot. But green is still her favorite color."

"Do not use that term."

"What term? Hot?"

"Yes."

"I'm hot, though. I wish I could read her mind again. I feel lost."

"Maybe it will come back with the bond she's making. You said you couldn't put it back, but anything is possible if she makes her own."

"That's true. It would still be easier to know if she wants us like this."

"She will have a chance to say, and we will respect it," David said. "I will still accept whatever she wants. If it's us at the same time, I think that is best. Are you content with me alone with her if we do this?"

"Yes. I would not ask to have her to myself. I understand you two are still together. It just pains me that I no longer have a single part of my bond with her. I only have the Horsemen's Bond."

"I think you will find peace this way," David said. "So will she. She's going to be just as lost with the complete separation. Without a physical relationship, I do not see her glowing like she did between us. Like you said, you grow unstable watching or knowing she is with just me, and you seek distraction. Now that you're separated, I think it will be worse. You're craving contact without the connection, and she is trying to keep you together. I wonder if War and Pestilence would be so *normal* without her?"

Death seemed to have shaken his head. "She changes everyone she draws in. She is changing the entire war between Heaven and Hell, all because she is our Jane."

"What will Lucifer do now?"

"He knows her fate." Death's words sounded like they caused him physical pain. "He does not wish to risk harming her, it seems. Perhaps he saw staying close to her would cause her death, and he doesn't want that yet. It's possible to adjust her fate this way. It is what I have done in the past. I always ensured she was protected, which results in a reset, basically, and a new death awaits."

"Her death will destroy you," David whispered. "Is there anything the two of us could do so you control her fate?"

"No, because I chose her."

"It's okay. I would have too." David let out a frustrated breath. "Let's see if she can figure it out. I think that is best. If she wants to do this with us, we prove we want it."

"Her bond might not work with his light. Perhaps it will work with you, but it's fighting me off."

"Do you not want me to have it without you?" For the first time, David sounded vulnerable. "Even if I agree to welcome you once it's possible? You are stronger than him, Death. You are devoted to her—you will find a way."

"I want her to have it with you," Death said softly. "I enjoy watching her happy with you, even when I am left out."

"You won't be left out this way. She is simply changing her whole. Even without the bond, you will feel some peace until we get it right."

"I suppose." Death huffed. "You are certain about this? It could be disastrous if one of us changes our mind or breaks what we complete together. Fuck, now that I'm truly considering this, I don't think it will work, and I desire it more."

"We will find out together then. If we hit that barrier, you will see that sometimes no bond is necessary to be everything to her. I believe in this, and she wants you back with her. She told me so, and I promised I'd find a way."

Her hair moved, and she felt warm lips press against her neck.

"I didn't say you could kiss her yet," David said with a light laugh.

"You didn't have to." Death chuckled as a finger left a trail of faint tingles down her spine. "Once you told me to stay, I knew you would permit me this affection with her. She's healing fast."

"She needs to forgive you for the shit you did before you assume you can kiss her whenever you want."

"Ask her then," Death said. "She's been awake, faking sleep, for at least a minute."

"Jane?" David tilted her face up. "Hi, baby."

"Y'all are annoying." She peeked at them before shutting her eyes again. "Never letting me sleep and leaving out all the important secrets when you talk."

"Jane?" Death whispered as he caressed her arm. "How much did you hear?"

"Not much."

"Liar," he said.

She sighed and raised a hand for him to come to her.

He grabbed it and held it to his cheek as he pressed kisses to hers. "I'm sorry for hurting you and keeping secrets."

Her tears had dried out. "I already forgave you."

David chuckled as he said, "You could make him work a bit harder for your forgiveness, my love."

Death had yet to move his lips from her skin, and he gently turned her head so their lips almost touched. "I just wanted you to be happy. I wanted you to live the life you wanted."

She smiled at him. He looked so beautiful. So conflicted. So sad. David was right—Death was still breaking, just as she had feared.

David kissed her hair again. "You heard us. I swear it's okay, but I want you to figure out what I learned. He can't tell you, and I am not allowed to, either. But I know if you can see what I saw, you will know."

"You want me to use Vision to find out?"

David smiled. "She was listening for longer than a minute."

Death nudged her nose with his. "I want you to know, but I fear you will not react well."

She stared into his eyes before looking at David. "Will this tear us all apart?"

He smiled sadly. "It might, but it might also change everything between us for the better. I choose to have faith in our love."

Jane sighed as she turned toward Death again. "You're afraid."

"If anything involves losing you, I am afraid. But I want you happy."

"I am happiest between the two of you. When you are both getting along, when you seem happy, and especially when you touch me together —that is heaven."

"Then make your choice," David told her. "You know what we are considering. I still want what we have, but I want to include Death. Not romantically between him and me, but the three of us. Of course, you will decide, but I want him to be a part of our relationship."

"You're not like crushing on each other, right?" She peeked between the two of them. "This isn't some trick because you realized you like each other? I mean, I guess that's okay, but I think I'd be jealous. Yeah."

Death dropped his head to her shoulder, shaking with silent laughter.

"No, baby," David said, amused. "Death and I only crush on you."

Death laughed aloud at last and lifted his head. "Baby girl, try to use your gift. If you still love us after, and you want this, we want it too. If not, well, that sucks. I still love you. For longer than always. And he's about to say you're his baby beyond forever."

David scowled as she giggled.

"I'm nervous," she whispered.

Death leaned away. "We are, too. But this fucker thinks it's best, and I keep messing up. Do you want to know?"

"Yes," she said, shifting her eyes toward David. "Right?"

Her blue-eyed prince smiled, nodding. "I want you to know, and then I want you to consider both of us. I'll go into details later."

Jane hadn't expected to wake up and learn more truths, but she didn't think she could do anything else now. "How do I do it?"

"Like Pest told you." Death took her hand. "You think of him and let Vision take you. Imagine Pest is walking you through a hall, and you are choosing which door to look in. Find the door David is referring to, the door that shows our separation, and open it. We will know when you see and call you back."

David was on his side, cupping her cheek before kissing her softly. "I love you. We love you."

"And I love both of you," she whispered, taking him in before searching Death's worried face. "I do."

"I know, angel." He kissed her hand. "Focus now. When you come back, we will give you time to think. You can bathe or whatever."

413

Jane's eyes widened, and she breathed a sigh of relief when she noticed a towel covering her.

Death's grin was wicked. "Were you nervous that I saw your tits?"

David smiled. "Baby, I kept your breasts covered as much as possible, but your back needed to be accessible. We've both seen you."

She tugged the towel closer. "It's just being unaware. Like boobs flopping around in your faces. What if you fell asleep and woke up with my boob on your face?"

"I'd be in heaven," David said.

"I'd open my mouth," Death said in all seriousness.

Jane's face felt like fire. "Death."

"Hm?" His gaze dropped to the top of her towel.

David shoved him, laughing. "Behave. Let her find everything out before we start joking with her again."

"Fine." Death focused on her. "I love you. I didn't know until just before I got you back from Lucifer. I know that will matter very little, but I just wanted to let you know I didn't always know."

"Okay," she said, breathing out. "Make sure I wake up."

"We will." Death rubbed his thumb over her forehead. "See, Sweet Jane."

———

"So, they found a way to tell you," Pestilence said quietly.

Jane looked around a dark hallway. Everything was gray, black, or white. There were several halls lined with white doors, each with a narrow rectangular window.

"If you are ready, follow me," Pestilence said before turning and walking away.

"Pestilence?" she called, running after him. "Is this okay? Is it going to cause harm?"

He shrugged without stopping his stride. "I think you deserve to know, but it's what you do because of it that matters. I do not think your vampire can keep it to himself."

"Is it bad?"

"I don't think so," he said without looking at her. "It's limited knowledge, but obvious when you think about it." He stopped and pointed to the door across from them. "This is you. Open the door and enter if you are ready. They will not see you, and your presence will not affect the past. This is simply what David saw."

"Will you be here when I finish?" She turned to find he was gone. "Fuck."

Jane tried to see through the thin slit, but she couldn't. There was no way she could turn around and leave, though. So, sucking in a deep breath, she opened the door.

Just as she remembered that night from her own memories, she was in the room she and David shared in Valhalla and about to lose her bond with Death.

"It's okay," Death murmured against her lips before kissing her again. "Breathe with me one more time."

Jane's eyes watered as she felt David's panic and watched her body in Death's arms begin to shake as she gasped for air.

Death held her tighter, sliding a hand down her back. "Feel me one more time," he whispered, opening his eyes to stare into hers. "Never forget this. Us. We are magic and beauty. We are Heaven."

"Death," she whimpered as he smiled.

"Smile for me. Show me everything, and you will see me. Show me so I never lose this part of us. Keep me." He waited, still keeping his lips just a breadth away from hers.

Her past self gave him the saddest smile as she held his cheek.

Death smiled against her mouth. "That's my girl. Now live for me, Sweet Jane."

Jane almost looked away, but she couldn't. Not when both she and Death began to glow in green light. It was so beautiful as it swirled around both of them. It grew brighter, making a sphere as Death kissed her. It began to spin around them like the flames surrounding him and Sorrow, but the gold glow between their lips made Jane gasp with her past self.

It was just a flame at first, held by a larger, dark green flame. They danced in a circle as David and Thanatos looked on in just as much awe as she was.

The green flame pulled the gold flame out, but that's when Jane realized, for the tiniest moments before they'd spin into a circle with the gold flame in the middle, that each flame looked like a person. The gold was clearly female, small as she twirled daintily before flaring up into a bright inferno and spinning in a circle, and the green flame was a man.

Jane felt tears dripping from her chin as she watched him pull her close and kiss her before spinning around with her again. They'd mix, with the gold flaring out each time the green began to fade into a dull olive color, almost gone completely. The little gold flame would roar, pulling him back until he grew brighter and engulfed her.

"Death," Jane whispered, covering her mouth and unable to look away. "My eyes."

The couple appeared again. This time, it seemed he was whispering to her, and then Jane heard their whispers—the same words he'd spoken to her mind:

"I'm sorry."

Jane could barely see as the gold flame shook her head when her past self cried out.

"It's almost over, my love," the green flame said.

The gold flame clutched him around the neck. *"No, Death."*

"I love you, angel. Don't forget me."

The gold flame cried, *"Death!"*

"Don't let me forget us."

"No! Death, don't leave me!" The gold grew bright.

Then it seemed both flames looked right at her. No, they were looking at David.

The green flame kissed his gold flame, pulling a thread from just below her heart and to the side. It was connected directly to his heart.

The gold flame kept watching David.

He was in tears as he shook his head. "Don't do it."

It looked like the gold flame smiled at him before she stared at her green flame.

The green flame glanced at David before kissing his gold flame. *"I won't, baby girl. I love you."* Then he produced what looked like a blade and sliced through the gold thread, tying them together.

Past Jane screamed, "Come back."

"Wake up, Jane," David said.

Her eyes flew open. David and Death were leaning over her as she sobbed.

Death's eyes strained as David smiled and caressed her head.

"I saw," she cried, reaching up to touch each of their cheeks.

"I'm sorry," David whispered, holding her trembling hand.

She didn't know who she felt more agony for as she stared between them.

"Death." She tilted her face toward him.

He kissed her palm. "I didn't know."

"You were him." She sobbed as her heart felt like it was being crushed.

"I am. I will always be him." Death moved to kiss her forehead. "I'm so sorry, my love."

Jane cried as she turned to David. "Baby." She shook her head. "I didn't know."

"I know." He kissed her hand. "It's not your fault." David gave her a sad smile. "It just means you loved me on your own."

Death leaned away, but he didn't say anything.

"You're not my soul mate." She stared into sapphire eyes that still welcomed her home.

David shook his head. "I'm not."

"No, he's not." Death took a deep breath. "I am."

417

2 9

SOUL MATES

Jane stared at the shower wall as the hot water pounded her sore back. She was pretty sure she was either in shock or having a mental breakdown.

Death's my soul mate . . . Not David.

She squeezed her eyes shut tight as she remembered the heartbroken gold flame clinging to the green one. They hadn't wanted to part. He had tried to leave, but she'd fought for him. They'd swirled together just like she'd seen the colors of her eyes do so many times before. She did glow for him.

My eyes are only gold now—dull gold. My green is gone.

Tears mixed with the water cascading down her face. He was gone. He'd cut them apart, and she'd asked him to do it. No, she'd pushed him to do it.

A high-pitched sob left her mouth as she covered her face. She didn't know what was worse: that she'd cut bonds with her real soul mate or that David wasn't. He must've been devastated, yet she couldn't remember seeing him upset with her or Death. He'd only tried to keep them together since seeing the truth.

"Why?" Jane didn't know who she was asking or even which question she was asking—there were too many. She was heartbroken for both men. They'd lost her that same night. It had always lingered in the back of her mind that David wasn't her soul mate. She kept telling herself they weren't real, and that was because every time Gawain told her she and David were soul mates, she felt an automatic recoil. Now she knew why. Her soul knew he wasn't the one.

But she'd felt magic when she saw David that night. Knowing now that it meant nothing was truly devastating. She loved him. She had fought it for so long when everyone kept pushing him on her, but she'd fallen for him, and poor Death had stepped aside to watch it unfold.

Jane shook her head. How were either of them joking with each other? How was David not simply packing his bags to find his real soul mate?

"No," she cried harder. She would lose him all over again, and now Death was separated from her. "No." That's all she could say as her entire body ached from shaking so badly.

A pair of arms wrapped around her and pulled her against a firm chest. "It's going to be all right."

It was David.

She balled her fists into his wet shirt, shaking her head as he held her tight.

"It will, Jane," he murmured.

"I broke him," she whispered. "And you're not—" She wailed.

"You didn't break Death. He was trying to give you what he thought you wanted, and you were trying to save him while showing me how devoted you were to us."

She held his sides. He wasn't hers anymore. "But I'm not who you thought I was. I'm not the girl you were looking for. It's just like I told you in the beginning."

"You are the woman I was searching for." He tilted her face up and smiled. "Baby, I have dreamt of your face for centuries. When I saw you that night, everything stopped for me. My search was over because I saw my love. My heart agreed with me—it still does." He cupped her cheeks. "Remember when I said, 'You and I are beyond forever without any bond?'"

"Yes." She wiped under her nose. Her whole face hurt, but she didn't want him to feel bad.

He gave her that beautiful David smile. "I meant it, Jane. We chose each other on our own. Yes, I mistakenly assumed Michael meant a soul mate when he spoke of me finding my Other, but I realized he never used the term soul mate. It was an assumption on my part—on all our parts. It does not mean we are not meant to be."

She put her hands over his heart. "But what if you have a soul mate waiting for you? What if you see another woman, and she's the one? I've read soul mate books before, David. This shit happens in them all the time.

You'll drop me like an empty box of cookies and run away with your chocolate cake without a second thought."

He chuckled, shaking his head. "Jane, you are my woman. You are my sweetheart, my baby, my kitten—my Jane. You're my chocolate cake—my ice cream with gummy bears and berries. There is no other woman."

Her face scrunched up. How could he still be so perfect? "But I'm not your soul mate." There were so many things to think of. From being sad over Death and not choosing him when he was the one she was technically supposed to be with. Everyone had said she was meant to be with David. All of them had. And she'd turned her back on her true soul mate.

David kissed her head. "Baby, I love you. You love me and Death—that has always been the case with us. Your soul knew I was not the one it was destined for, but it still allowed you to love me. It still looked at me that night and smiled before it let Death separate them. I don't know what any of it means, but you are my girl, and I am your man. Your David. We are Others, and we fell in love and fall more in love with each other every day that passes. I may not have a soul mate, but I'm almost certain you're trying to make me yours."

Jane blinked away her tears. "What do you mean?"

He pushed his wet hair back. "Your gold thread . . . Twice now, you've put it around Death and me. I think your soul is choosing me, just like you have. To know your true soul mate has been with you all these years and you are still holding me is incredible. That gold thread would not be there if it was not meant to be. You're picking me all over again, my love. I'm in awe and thankful. And I'm so grateful your soul mate stood back when he could have just taken you. I know you wouldn't have turned your back on him if he had told you the truth, especially then. You were devastated over what had gone on between Lucifer and us. After hearing I was not your soul mate, you would have let me go. Your angel knew that, and he still saw our love. He believed it was worth the sacrifice to watch us live our life together. When I fucked up, he made me see my errors."

He caressed her cheek. "My heart would not have recovered if you had walked away with him, Jane. I wouldn't have understood at the time. But seeing your soul and his look at me that night—baby, they both chose for you to be with me. I am heartbroken for the pain it caused you both, but I am overwhelmed by the love you give me. Death doesn't love me, but he saw inside your mind and knew there was no way to take you from me. He wanted me to love you, and I want you to have him. And your gold thread, that beautiful connection you had with just him, you're showing us that it doesn't matter who you were selected to be with. It shows us you are still committed to him, which you have always been, but you're blessing me with something I was not given. It's not just you who will eventually get two soul mates. You are giving two men who were not supposed to have a soul mate the most beautiful one while we stand together for you. It takes a lot of power and strength to shine as you do. It makes sense that you would need more than one to tend to your flame. When one of us falls, the other holds all of us together."

Her lips parted, and she sputtered, "You really think this? You're not just being you by trying not to hurt me?"

"I never want to hurt you." He smiled, smoothing her hair back. "The first night away from you, I prayed for guidance and answers. I thought about my wrongdoings and wondered if this was a form of punishment. I questioned whether I should leave and let you two have each other as you were meant to. You know what I dreamt about that night?"

She shook her head.

"I dreamt of blue fire burning across from a beautiful gold flame as a larger emerald one held her. They were not swirling together as they were meant to. They were dull in color, longing for each other, but neither going to the other. In fact, they seemed to be preparing to be pulled away forever.

"Then the blue flame became an inferno and encircled the two until they danced together again. And the pretty gold flame reached out for the blue one as she wrapped part of herself around the green one." He grinned and kissed her forehead. "The green flame made space for the blue one on the outside, Jane. Together, they grew in strength around her, burning brightly as they begged her to glow. And she did. She began to glow. It was so bright I thought she might destroy them, but they gave each other strength until she mixed with both.

"I got the answer I needed with that dream." He cupped her cheeks. "And every time I see you smile between us, I know there was no mistake when my heart—and my soul—told me, there she is. I chose you. Every part of the man I am chooses you, and I will continue to, beyond forever."

Jane sniffed, smiling, when the image of her soul smiling flickered in her mind. She saw her standing, almost swaying with happiness at David's words.

"Did your soul fucking blush when it saw me?" came Death's voice from outside the shower.

Jane choked out a laugh but still cried as her vampire pulled her closer.

"Do you make a game of ruining my moments with her?" David asked, hugging her.

"It was a serious question." Death snickered. "That blue bastard turned pink—I know it."

Jane wrapped her arms around David, smiling as she stared up at him in awe. "I love you."

He cupped her cheeks and gave her a long kiss. "I love you, too."

She kissed him back, but her eyes drifted to the opening of the shower.

David lowered his mouth to her ear. "Do you want this?"

Jane closed her eyes. She had tried so hard to let Death go when he was the one she was supposed to hold tightest. All she could think of was how beautiful she felt between them—how comfortable they both seemed opposite but somehow together. For her.

"Yes," she said upon seeing her soul smile at her. Jane looked up, and David was smiling as well. He wanted to be her soul mate, he wanted her to reunite with her true soul mate, and he was ready to keep all three of them together. "All of us."

David gave her another kiss. "I think he needs you to tell him."

She nodded as David leaned away. He checked her back and her overall state. She was dirty, and the drain still swirled with blood. David was in the same state.

He smirked and pulled his shirt over his head before tossing it on the floor, and then he gestured toward the opening. "Shall I get him?"

Her eyes widened. "You're really sure?"

"Positive," David said, unbuttoning his pants. "And I need his help to hold you up."

"What?" She covered her cheeks, knowing they were red, as she looked down at her nakedness. Death had seen her plenty of times, but now he'd see her with David as both were ready to touch her. "I don't know if I'm ready for everything."

He kissed her head, still wearing a big smile. "I meant to clean your wound, my love. I'll keep my briefs on, and he'll do the same. He can hold you while you comfort him, and I'll cleanse the open parts of your cuts. It's healed a lot, but some deep cuts might have debris."

"Oh, gross."

He gave her another kiss. "We'll take things slow. You can tell us if it's not what you want or if you're not ready. I think we will be fine, though. It feels natural, doesn't it?"

"Yes." It really did.

He smiled wider and peeked around the shower, waving in a *come here* gesture. "Until she's ready, leave your briefs on. But come kiss our girl before she cries again. Or you do, for that matter."

"I don't cry," Death said, but he didn't immediately enter.

David gave him an encouraging smile and moved to her other side.

Death still didn't enter.

Jane's throat closed up. Now that she knew he was hers and she hadn't been wrong for wanting him, she wanted him beside her. But maybe it was too late.

David kissed the top of her head. "Give him a moment."

"You're sure?" Death still stayed out of view, but he was closer.

She smiled, rubbing her sore eyes. "I am. Please don't leave me now."

Finally, he entered. His huge size took up so much of the shower— both her men did—and she felt so small but so loved because of how they looked at her.

A gorgeous but slightly nervous smile spread over Death's lips. "I'll warn both of you—this has been a fantasy of mine for months. I might not be able to hide my erection. I'm hung like a—"

Jane laughed as he chuckled and held his hand out for her. She didn't care if she was naked anymore or if her men were standing in a shower with her, wearing only their underwear. She had two men who loved her, and she was so lucky David was the man he was. Because she'd lost her soul mate, and her David was ensuring she got him back.

She threw herself at Death, sobbing when he immediately lifted her and found her lips with his.

"I'm so sorry," she cried, holding his cheek. "I'm sorry I made you do it."

He held the back of her head, never pulling his mouth from hers. "You didn't know. I love you."

She sniffed, nodding. "And I love you."

He grinned, kissing her again, not deepening it, but still pouring all his feelings into every second.

Death situated his hold but kept pressing his lips to hers. When his fingers grazed her ass and thigh, he grinned and guided her legs around him. "I always wanted to hold you like this in a shower."

Jane smoothed his hair back as she stared into his eyes. He was hers, and so was the man behind her, moving her hair aside and pressing a fiery kiss on her shoulder.

"Just avoid her dimple." David kissed her shoulder again as he pushed Death's hand away.

"I've wanted to touch it, though." Death winked at her.

"I'm sure you have," David said, kissing her dimple.

Her eyes went wide as Death laughed and kissed her cheek.

David caressed her back. "I know, technically, this means I was the one to come between soul mates and not the other way around, like so many assumed, including myself, but I kind of have an attachment to this cutie."

Death squeezed her butt cheek. "Okay, I'll wait to touch it, Papi."

Jane smiled, peeking behind her as David glared at Death.

David pushed his hair back as he licked the water off his lips.

Oh, God, that was sexy.

"Don't call me that," he said, looking Death in the eye.

"Do you prefer Daddy?"

David shook his head but grinned as he grabbed the soap and a cloth. "I'm still hitting you if you annoy me."

Death pulled her hair over her shoulder as David's fingers slid down her spine.

She bit her lip as she glanced between them. They were either good actors, or they didn't mind each being with her, and they'd accepted each other in her life.

Jane cupped Death's cheek, smiling at the happiness she finally saw shining in his eyes.

He pulled her head close and kissed her nose before giving her another kiss. "Stop looking at me like that."

"Like what?"

He chuckled, squeezing her butt again. "Like I'm a puppy your daddy let you keep. I'm the fucking Angel of Death, babe."

"You're a child," David said, lightly prodding a tender spot. "Sorry. Let me rinse this spot free of dirt."

Flinching, Jane hugged Death tightly around his neck.

Death kissed her neck, murmuring, "Maybe don't make her do that. I'm not used to her pretty pussy and tits rubbing all over me."

David's response was instant. "Get used to it."

"David." She held her aching cheeks as she stared over Death's shoulder. She could feel Death grinning like a cat against her neck, but a sting on her wound made her shout, "Bitch ass!"

David chuckled. "Does her foul language weirdly turn you on like it does me?"

Death nodded, still grinning. "But so does everything else she does."

"True," David said.

The sting faded as David moved his hands, and she played with Death's hair as she said, "I don't turn either of you on."

"Tell that to our dicks, babe." Death nipped her neck. "If we didn't have our underwear on—which I had to create because I don't wear any—we'd be sword fighting right now."

Jane laughed, covering her face. "How do y'all make me smile when I should be crying?"

"Because we're your Ds," Death said. "Seriously, though, I'm getting hard from all your rubbing."

"I'm not rubbing." She couldn't believe what was happening. It was so easy to be like this.

"Jane, you rub on what's yours like a cute kitten," David said. "It's what you do. I'm sure you will start marking each other as the days pass now that you don't have to hold back. It's most likely why you always felt the need to touch. You were going against your souls, and they wanted to be joined."

"David?" She kept staring at the wall.

"Yes, baby?" He carefully ran a cloth around her cuts.

"You're really the bestest, you know that?"

"So you have said before."

"It is a bit annoying, but he kinda is," Death mumbled, lightly sucking the skin on her neck. She was slightly glad he couldn't read her mind and know that his mouth on her neck was making her throb between her legs.

"How do you know you don't have a soul mate out there?" she asked, clutching Death because there was still so much that could go wrong.

"I don't know—but my heart is telling me there's no one else." David moved on to the rest of her back. "As far as I'm concerned, you're still my soul mate. My soul chose you. It chooses you every day, even after I saw the truth. And the fact that both of yours chose mine by letting you pick me proves that we were still meant to come together this way. However, God tied you two. I will not question why."

"No angel has a soul mate," Death said.

"Well, I thought you were the fucking Angel of Death," David said. "I think you're in a different category."

"Are you flirting with me, Prince David?" Death snickered, massaging her ass.

"I will punch you before I flirt with you." David began working the shampoo into her hair.

"How did you know I like it rough?" Death turned them so David couldn't hit his shoulder. "Don't, I'm delicate."

"You're a fool." David squeezed her other butt cheek and asked her, "Are you okay, baby?"

"Yes." She turned, leaning over with Death supporting her so she could kiss him.

David smiled, holding her face between his hot hands. Just as it always did, his touch warmed her without burning her.

Her eyes shot open, and she gasped against David's mouth when Death kissed her neck.

"Are you good?" David asked as Death kissed down the column of her neck, lifting her to reach where he wanted to kiss. "He's been holding back for quite a while."

"I know." She sighed, struggling to keep her eyes open.

Death squeezed her ass, and David deepened his kiss, and at that moment, a gold shimmer of light danced behind her eyes. She gasped as it loosely wrapped around them.

They both tightened their holds on her.

Death sucked her skin into his mouth as his warm tongue flicked her pulse, and David sucked on her bottom lip.

She whimpered, nodding. She wanted it to tighten around them, but nothing happened.

David leaned away, but he still smiled as Death hugged her.

"I think it will take time." David kissed her forehead as he stepped under the shower spray. "Don't get discouraged. That was the first kiss of many to come."

Jane sighed as she tried to calm down. Her whole body hummed with sparks and faint tingles, and it was almost unbearable with how hot her skin felt where their lips had been.

Death nuzzled her cheek. "I'm not sure it will attach to me."

"I'll make it," she said, determined. She could tell from their conversation that Death was truly upset and afraid he'd never hold the bond he'd had with her. Just as badly as David seemed to want to be claimed as her soul mate, Death was desperate to have his place again. "I don't care what anyone says—I'll get you back with me. And I'm bringing David with us."

A tender smile touched his lips. "Okay."

"It's already beautiful," David said. "You started this on your own. You and our little gold flame. Our girls."

"Is she separate from me?"

"No." Death stepped closer to David as her vampire began rinsing her hair and body.

426

"She's you, Jane," David added. "I think we can each think of our soul as an extension of ourselves. They follow our lead, but we also listen to them. The same with our hearts and minds."

"Let's wash your front." David leaned close and pressed a kiss below her ear. "Me, him, or both?"

Death chuckled as he lowered her to her feet. He cupped her hot cheeks. "So pretty all shy."

"Y'all are so blunt." She kept her boobs pressed close to his stomach.

"Babe, your nipples are digging into my skin, and your hot little pussy was all over me—I think you're fine to let us wash you. He's done it plenty of times, and I've comforted you in the shower before." He pushed her hair back. "But I'll step out if you're overwhelmed or don't want me here."

"No, I don't want you to go," she said quickly, peeking back at David.

He nodded, tugging her arm so she wasn't clinging to Death. "We're blunt because you're ours, and you belong right here between us." He glanced at Death. "I have this thing with her that we make happy memories in bath suites, so one day there are so many she thinks of only them when she's alone in one."

"You want to make another happy memory now?" Death dropped his eyes down to her.

Jane held her breath as David pulled her back against him, almost like he was giving Death a chance to take her in. The craziest thing was she wasn't uncomfortable when those emerald eyes glowed and slid down her body. And holy fuck was he sexy, all wet with his black hair hanging slightly over his eyes. She almost fainted when he jerked his head to move the hair out of the way.

"I think now is a perfect time." David slid his thumb along her jaw. "It is, after all, the moment we are starting a relationship with her—with each other. Right?"

"If you both want to," she whispered, trembling as she felt the light pulsing. Then, she began to glow a bit as well.

Death watched her with a faint smile. "I want you, Sweet Jane. . . . With Mr. Blue Flame at my side. I want us. I know I am the Pale Horseman now, but I feel stronger, more me, than ever before."

Her heart beat incredibly fast. "What about your distractions?"

He shook his head. "No more. I won't push you to give all of yourself to me, but having even this is more than I ever hoped for. So, if you want me with you two, I commit to you, angel. I won't betray either of you. It's always been you, Jane."

Her eyes burned, and she couldn't quite speak yet.

David did. "Our relationship is not a normal one. We never really were with the amount of kisses this asshole stole."

Death smirked. "Most of them were for medicinal purposes."

David's fingers drew circles on her sides. "I still see it that you and I are together. This would be adding Death. He will always have his duty, and he will always leave. But we will welcome him back each time as if he had never left. While he is gone, he will remain devoted and know you and I are together in the way we have been."

"I expect nothing less," Death said with a nod. "I don't want the beautiful relationship you have with each other to weaken. I want it to grow stronger. I will be content knowing you are together, and I will have no desire to distract myself because I have this waiting for me."

Her body burned as she watched the light flicker across Death's face. "The light—does it bother either of you? And Lucifer?"

Death shook his head. "I see you are meant to have the light he gave you. It's not the same inside you as it was inside him. And there is nothing I want to say about your bond with him. You are alive, and he left you without too much of a fight. I won't let you go with him again, but what matters to me is you're alive."

"My wings?" She held her breath.

Surprisingly, Death smirked. "You're naked, angel. I see only you."

David responded next. "You will have his wings again. Perhaps you can remember to wear something else around him so he does not have to see, though. I'm sure this"—he slid his hands across her stomach—"is a welcome sight."

Jane couldn't believe him. He was perfection. They both were. They were the most beautiful creations in the universe.

"And I have nothing to say regarding Lucifer's bond with you," David added. "I don't like it, but I believe we are more powerful together than any bond he forges. I do think you look beautiful in this light, though. You are controlling it more than you were earlier, but I think you're getting excited or nervous with the way you are shimmering. Either way, you are our goddess. I look forward to watching you do great things with this power."

"Is it different from my normal glow?"

They looked at each other.

"Yes," Death said. "I'm not worried—I still see your light. So does David."

"Are you nervous about how physical things will get?" David asked.

"Yes." She wiped the water from her face. "It's not that I'm intimidated. I'm worried about the two of you watching the other with me. Everyone expects David to be the only one I am with, but knowing the truth, I don't want to fight the contact we've craved. And I want both of you there. It's like I can't even fathom having a relationship without either of you now. I want to see us tied together."

"There's my kitty." David tilted her head back. He held the front of her neck as he smiled at her. "We want you together, too. Like I said, you and I will resume our alone time when it's just us, but when he's here, you're meant to be between us."

"We can go slow, Jane," Death said. He'd moved closer.

David glanced at Death and held out his hand.

"I'm not holding your hand." Death smacked David's hand.

David snatched Death's forearm. "If you are going to be this difficult, you're cut off from shower time."

Death winked at her as he let David guide his hand to her side.

Jane sighed when David placed his on her other side. She saw the gold shimmer behind her eyes again, and this time she felt their touch the way she'd felt it in the beginning. One hand scorched with addicting heat, and the other warm as tingles seeped through her pores.

"I feel the tingles a little bit, and the heat is hotter."

"That's our girl," David said, squeezing a bottle of body wash into his palm and then Death's. "Tell us if we need to stop, but we're going to touch you now." He cupped her breast, kneading it gently. "Okay?"

Her mouth popped open, and she panted as she stared at Death, watching everything. He liked it, but he was hesitating.

"Yes," she whispered, tilting her head back as David slid his hand over her.

Slowly, while keeping his eyes on hers, Death teased her collarbone with his fingertips.

David chuckled, cupping both her breasts. He massaged them, building up a lather of bubbles as Death watched the movement.

"Are you going to help?" David asked.

Jane swallowed, covering Death's hand with hers. "You don't have to hold back anymore."

He pushed his hair back with his free hand before stepping closer.

David slid his hands down to her waist. He cupped her stomach, applying pressure on her lower abdomen. "When you're ready, we will fill your womb so you carry both our scents. We cannot give you children, but it will be a sign to all that you are our woman."

Jane could only moan when he slid a hand between her legs.

"I'm only washing you unless you want more." David didn't push his fingers inside, but he knew what he was doing to her.

"Oh." She tightened her hold on Death's hand.

Finally, her angel, her soul mate, touched her without worrying. His darker skin stood out against her pale skin, and it was absolutely beautiful.

Jane panted when they both started breathing faster. She held Death's waist but leaned against David.

Death muttered something in a foreign language, and David replied in the same tongue.

"What?" she asked, gasping when Death knelt in front of her.

He wiped away the suds and pressed his mouth against her stomach.

"Oh, gosh!"

He smiled against her skin as he kissed and licked until his mouth was around her nipple while his hand gave attention to the other breast. She really did fit with him.

When her legs buckled, David held her upright and gently pushed a finger inside her. "Purr for us, kitten."

"Oh fuck." She tangled her fingers in Death's hair with one hand as she used the other to pull David down by his neck.

He kissed her begging lips with a grin and flicked his thumb over her clit. "That's not purring. Are we doing this wrong?"

Death smirked, kissing her breast. "Do you have a good hold on her?"

David nodded to him and resumed kissing.

Death, however, nipped her skin as he lifted one of her legs.

Jane's eyes flew open.

"You okay?" He watched her as he kissed, sucked, and licked his way down.

"Mhm." She was shaking.

"Good girl." He hoisted her leg higher but turned his head to kiss the inside of her thigh.

"I think he's been waiting to taste you, my love." David chuckled at Death's glare. "I think he is intimidated."

"I'm taking my time."

"Well, the water will get cold soon, so satisfy her, or I will. You can take your time later."

Jane moaned. David was so sexy for taking charge. This entire thing had been his doing. He wasn't letting the fact he wasn't her soulmate bother him. In fact, he seemed more sure of their relationship and his dominance.

"She likes you being alpha." Death snickered, sucking her skin.

"I know she does." David gestured to Death's free hand. "Let her feel you first. Then she can tell you if using your mouth is okay."

Jane was pretty sure she was going to combust. Her stupid light was flickering along with the erratic beating of her heart, and she trembled as goosebumps erupted from where they touched.

Death squeezed her hip before moving his hand near David's.

She breathed so fast that she was sure she'd pass out.

David kissed her head, whispering, "Ready, my love? This is just a taste of us. I want you to have it."

Death kissed her stomach as his fingers grazed her skin. "Do you want to feel us both?"

A million questions raced through her mind, but only one answer left her lips. "Yes."

"Beautiful, brave girl." David pulled his finger out only to guide Death with him.

"Oh, God." She gasped, tightening her hold on both of them.

They grinned and continued sliding in their long fingers. It was too much. She saw sparkles as heat and tingles filled her core.

David guided Death's finger up, and she moaned.

"That's her spot," he said.

Death chuckled. "Obviously." He kissed her stomach and then flicked her G-spot while David slowly dragged his finger in and out, pressing his palm down.

"I can't see," she said, still seeing, but she didn't know what to say.

"Yes, you can." David cupped her breast and matched the rhythm between her legs. "Do you like how we feel?"

She licked her lips. "Yes. Oh, dammit, yes. Don't stop."

"We won't." He kissed her temple. "We're going to make you see stars now."

Her tummy tightened. "Okay."

Death chuckled, and she almost came from his breath kissing her tingling skin.

"I can't believe this is happening," she gasped, arching into their large hands. One was scorching hot while the other was warm—both calling to her: tingles and so much heat.

Death kissed her belly button, flicking his tongue out before dragging it up her stomach. He never stopped with his hand, not even when he latched onto her other breast as David tilted her face to cover her mouth with his.

She couldn't stay still. There were too many sensations: heat, pressure, warmth. She writhed in ecstasy in their arms.

"Do you want us inside you?" Death asked before biting her breast and becoming faster with his movements.

"Am I still ovulating?"

"No, you're ready for us." David grinned.

Her eyes widened, and she whimpered against David's mouth as he rejoined Death's hand.

"Then, yes," she said, panting and moaning. "Oh, please. I want both."

Death smiled against her skin. "Come first, angel. I promise you'll have what you are aching for, and I swear both of us are aching to be inside you."

David's breathing and hand became faster as he slightly thrust, the base of his shaft sliding between her ass cheeks. Death had made room for him and ensured her ass hugged David's dick.

Oh, God. Their confidence and how in sync they were was erotic but so loving at the same time.

The gold thread began to glow around them again.

"Yes," she whispered, her entire body tensing up more.

"Come, Jane," they said together.

She did, screaming out as David bit her neck and Death kissed her.

"Ours," they said, sending her into another orgasm as stars filled her vision.

"Oh, shit," she whispered, trembling and clinging to them both.

Death pushed a finger in with David's, massaging her together and getting her worked up all over again, but he removed his hand and raised it to his mouth. "Sweet Jane."

"Shall we let your soul mate quench his thirst?" David slid his hand up her stomach.

Jane tiredly glanced down at Death. "This isn't a dream?"

David shook his head. "This is the beautiful truth that is us."

Death gave her a gorgeous smile as he hoisted her leg higher, grabbed her ass, and tugged her a bit. "I've walked into your dreams many times." He lowered his eyes to her core, licking his lips. "This is no dream. Let me taste you, and if you're ready, we'll give you more."

"Everything." David licked the blood on her neck. "Just one at a time, though. We'll work up to you having us at the same time."

Oh, jeez.

Death smirked as he rocked back on his heels, positioning himself to feast on her.

She had to blink a few times. *They do look alike.* Jane turned to David. *Like fucking brothers!*

"I know you, babe." Death pressed his lips against her hip. "You don't do slow."

"She really doesn't." David chuckled.

Death glanced down before lightly teasing her with his tongue.

"Oh, fuck." Her eyes almost rolled back. It was like he'd shocked her and soothed her all at once.

"Mm." He got a nod from David. "Papi's okay with it. Are you?" He flicked his tongue over her clit, grinning when she bucked her hips. "I promise you won't last long. Then I can make love to you like I've wanted to for so long, and David will follow me, sealing my scent in with his because we're both going to love you tonight if you want us to. So tell me 'no' if you want to stop."

"You're ours, and we are yours." David kissed her hair as his erection ground against her lower back.

Jane swallowed.

"Sweet Jane, tell me—is this what you want?"

For once, there was no internal battle. "Yes."

A dangerously sexy smile formed on Death's lips, then he glanced at David. "You're ready for us to do this? I still respect your choice, and we can talk to her if you change your mind."

"I won't change my mind." David leaned down and gave her a long kiss. "I love you. I want you to know his love and for him to have it with you. I'm happy to be a part of it, and if you somehow make me your soul mate, too, I'll be the happiest man on Earth. Let him love you. He was always meant to love and be loved by you."

"Both of you," she whispered, kissing him back.

He smiled, nodding. "Both of us."

Death kissed her stomach once more. "Hang on to her. I know you're supposed to be amazing in bed, but I'm Death." He smirked. "I'll teach you, though."

Jane pressed her smiling lips together as David kissed her nose.

"Start already." David cupped her breast again. "And she's flexible, so don't hold back with her."

Oh my God.

"Ay, Papi." Death laughed before pressing his tingling lips against her.

Any giggles she'd been about to release vanished. "Oh." She stared down at him wide-eyed as he watched her, and he lifted her, closing his mouth around her.

"Oh!" She tried to clamp her mouth shut.

David supported her, raising her so Death didn't have to bend. He sucked her earlobe into his mouth just when Death became serious. She shook, pulling her leg around Death's neck—trying to be quiet.

"Scream for him," David whispered. "We want you to lose your voice."

Holy shit.

She screamed.

WINGMAN

Jane clenched her legs together as she watched David walk to the dresser. He was naked, and she still considered him to have the body of a god. So did her angel—her soul mate.

Her soul mate, who was brushing his lips along her neck. "We'll be together again soon," he murmured against her skin.

David looked over his shoulder and winked at her as Death rubbed her stomach. She was in David's shirt and nothing else. Death had summoned his pants, but she could feel the outline of his erection pressing against her core, and it was torturous.

She squeezed her legs together tighter.

"She's even more addicted to dick." Death chuckled. "How on Earth you can want more than what you just had while your ass hurts like it does, I have no idea."

David laughed at Jane's disappointment when he pulled on a pair of combat pants and a shirt.

Her beloved soul mate snickered at her before putting his hand between her legs.

"Don't just grab me." She covered his hand, ready to pull it away, until he curled his finger over her tender clit. "Oh, fuck." She sighed, peeking at David.

He stared at them through the mirror as Death slid his other hand under her shirt to massage her breast.

"Do you remember how I felt?" Death kissed the back of her neck.

Jane kept her eyes locked with David's. She worried he wouldn't react well to Death touching her when they weren't together, but he didn't look angry.

"Do you remember how it felt when he dominated you?" Death asked. She moaned as he applied more pressure. "You liked it, didn't you?"

Her mouth felt dry, too dry. She nodded as David turned and crossed his arms to watch.

Without warning, their final moments in the shower together popped into her head, and she could see and feel it like it was happening all over again.

Death had growled after she orgasmed and lifted her to carry her to the room. He laid her gently on the bed, kissing a path between her breasts as he spread her legs apart. He only paused to get David's approval before nudging her entrance with his dick.

David sat beside her head and leaned over, kissing her as he held her cheek. "Are you comfortable with this?"

"Yes," she whispered, throwing her arms around his neck. "If you are."

He kissed her sweetly. "I'm more than fine. I'll love you after him." He grinned, nipping her lips. "Roughly."

She nodded, her mouth popping open as Death groaned, pushing in just a little before pulling out.

Death slid the tip of his cock up and down her slit. "Can I?"

David nodded, kissing her as he lay on his side, giving Death a view of her face. "Be gentle with her. She's always tight no matter how ready she is."

Death locked gazes with her. "Love you, angel."

"And I love you."

He smiled. "Ready?"

She didn't feel uncomfortable at all. "Yes."

David kissed her temple as he placed a hand on her breast, massaging it. "Make love to our girl."

"I already feel like I'm gonna come." Death spread her wider and pushed in.

"Oh, gosh." She gasped, coming out of the memory.

She trembled, covering Death's hand as he rubbed beautiful slow circles that had her raising her hips, trying desperately to figure out how to get him inside her again.

David walked toward them, stopping in front of them as he watched

Death suck on her neck and work magic with his hand. Her vampire smirked, fisting her hair and tilting her head up. "Feel good?"

She licked her lips. "Yes. Kiss me, please. Oh, fuck." She was shaking as sparkles appeared in her vision.

He flicked his tongue over her lips. "Think of me now. Think of how it felt after he filled you, and then I conquered you."

Death brought his mouth to her ear. "He joined us, Sweet Jane. He flipped your sexy ass over and sealed my scent in with his."

David tugged her shirt and dropped his hand next to Death's.

"Oh, gosh, don't stop." She put one hand around the back of Death's head and pulled David by the neck until his lips were on hers.

They worked together, neither outdoing the other, as they brought her to a place she hadn't known existed.

David bit her lip as Death sucked her neck.

"Remember it now." David flicked her clit as Death slid two fingers inside her.

She did remember it. She remembered everything.

Jane had screamed, "Oh, fuck. Death." Her entire body spasmed underneath him. He had crushed her as if he was making sure every inch of her was covered in his touch.

He thrust his hips forward, kissed her temple, and grunted as he flooded her pussy with his cum.

Jane moaned—he was so deep. So heavy, but he wasn't destroying her.

He squeezed her ass, lifting her so he could go even deeper. "All of me. I'm yours. Take all of me."

"Yes." Jane felt a hot hand slide up her leg. She couldn't open her eyes, though. "Oh, I can't stop shaking."

"You'll stop in a second." Death turned, claiming her lips as he slowly thrust, ensuring she got every bit of what he wanted to give her. "Better than I ever dreamed it could be." He kissed her over and over. "My beautiful girl. I'm going to love you for eternity."

She smiled as the tightness of her muscles began to relax.

He kissed her once more, long and sweet. "Ready for your other love?"

Jane nodded tiredly, and Death eased out, hissing as she clenched up.

David kissed her softly when she whimpered and used her legs to keep Death in place. "Relax for him."

She panted, purring with delight as her vampire kissed down her neck and bit the top of her breast to distract her.

Jane and Death groaned when he was free and rolled to the side as he reached over to caress her cheek.

David, however, released her breast and wiped what spilled free with a sheet.

"Sorry." Death chuckled, rolling again so he could kiss her forehead. "I have a feeling you're about to get dominated."

"Good." She smiled at David.

He smiled back. "My feisty kitten is ready to play."

Death kissed her once more before leaning away.

David didn't hesitate to grab her hips and flip her onto her belly.

Jane got on all fours for him, moaning as Death gathered her hair and David palmed her ass.

"Are you going to start prepping her?" Death slid his hand along her spine. "Her wound looks good. Here."

David raised her hips and grabbed the ponytail Death had made with her hair. He tugged, keeping her right where he wanted her as he slid his dick between her ass cheeks. "If I think she can handle it. Hold her hand the entire time or touch her somewhere."

Death moved so he was in front of her. "Dominating me, too?" He cupped her cheeks, kissing her as she pushed against David's dick, begging him to enter her.

"Something like that," David said. "You and I are not fucking. Ever. But my instincts are demanding this. Just keep touching her. Your souls are linked, and I want all of her."

"Damn, Papi." Death flicked his tongue over her lips. "Ready, angel? He's going to love you like a mate. He's going to show your soul who he is."

"Oh, fuck, yes." She tried to look over her shoulder. "I love you."

David allowed her to, and he leaned down, kissing her quickly. "I love you, too." He grinned, kissing her again before leaning back. "Now scream it."

The memory faded, but her ecstasy still consumed her in the present.

"Oh, yes," Jane cried, her throat aching as she tried to squeeze her legs around their hands.

They held her apart, though, letting her tremble under their touch.

"Good girl." David kissed her softly as he slowed his movements and removed his hand. He sucked his fingers clean before kissing her again. "So beautiful."

She realized she was glowing again and sighed at the sight of Death lifting his hand to his mouth.

"I almost came in my pants," he said. "Fuck, I've never done that before."

David chuckled as he lifted Jane's limp body. "She's your dream girl, that's why. It's completely different when you love a woman." He hoisted her up, grabbing her ass as he kissed her.

"Thanks for the lesson, Dad." Death rearranged himself. "You both realize we may have to wait a while before we try this again."

David massaged her ass and said, "We'll sneak in what we can. We have to get back to the war and the children anyway, and we have to make sure you"—he glanced at Death—"don't lose your mind any time soon. I want us to have some peace together."

Jane nodded. They'd already discussed they should wait for a little to get used to the relationship, but they knew she was all or nothing, and they wanted her to have all. They needed it, too. The kids were the other issue. She felt awful about the time away from them. She was having sex with two men while they were probably worrying about her.

"I'll try." Death stood up. He smacked her ass as he passed them. "Summon your suit, babe. We're about to have visitors."

"Shit," David said, pecking her before lowering her to her feet.

Jane was completely alert, and she summoned her suit instantly. "Do I look okay?"

Death smirked. "You look like your men claimed you. Next time you can take both of us at the same time since he already destroyed your ass. Maybe then you won't scream 'Exit Only!'"

"I thought she could take it," David muttered.

She peeked at her vampire, murmuring, "I think it's already healing." She knew he felt bad for making her cry, but she'd asked for it, and he'd been as gentle as he could be.

David leaned down to kiss her head. "Good. I thought his fingers had done the trick."

Death laughed. "Papi is bigger than my fingers, babe."

"I know." She fanned her hot cheeks. "I'll be more prepared next time. I had no idea it would hurt that much. I mean, mortals do it, and I'm supposed to be a super-powerful immortal, and I couldn't even handle the tip."

Death snickered. "Little tight ass. That's going to be your new name."

"No!" She laughed as David pulled her against him. "Did it look weird?"

"It looked like you got anal." Death smirked. "Papi tore your pretty ass up. I think once you get used to him, you can take me."

"Stop calling me that." David shook his head. "And if you shout that out again as you fake an orgasm, I'm throwing your naked ass out the door."

He winked at her but asked David, "So you want me to have a real one when I shout it?"

"Get the fucking door," David snapped. "And you don't get her ass until I say."

Death waved him off. "If I get the lube, I want to have a chance to use it. Then I think that thread will tighten around us and never fade. It wants us together, not separate."

David sighed, taking in her no doubt red face. "Don't be embarrassed, my love. We enjoyed every second. And one day, that thread won't disappear after we make love to you. Some of it is working—you're feeling him more now."

Death was quiet as he stood there with his hand on the doorknob, then he said softly, "One day, Sweet Jane. It will happen one day, and it will be like I never left."

David hugged her, and she knew he was worried about what would happen.

"And let us do the talking." Death gestured to the walls, flickering with silver and white light. "Light is more powerful than you realize. It can bring great things, but you can also destroy on epic proportions you have yet to discover. It will take time for you to learn how to harness it. So let us handle any who judge you or us. We don't want you accidentally hurting people who don't know how to keep their opinions to themselves. You're our woman. If anyone gets killed because they can't stand the fact you have two men loving you, it will be by our hand. You stay as pure as possible, okay? That will help me. Kill your enemies, not fools with irrelevant opinions."

"Thank you, Death."

"Anytime, baby girl." Death took her in once more before sighing. "By the way, that was the best night of my long fucking existence—even watching him take you was beautiful." He glanced at David before turning and opening the door to reveal War, Pestilence, Arthur, and Thor.

Pestilence and War walked in.

War glanced at Death. "It smells like dick, ass, and—" He grinned but said nothing else.

"Dicks, brother." Pestilence winked at her. "Plural."

War laughed. "It is about time you three fucked."

Jane covered her cheeks as David wrapped one arm across her chest.

Arthur quickly shut the door.

"Does this make her a sister of sorts?" Pestilence glanced at the messy bed. "It is a good thing these Norsemen are fine craftsmen of sturdy furniture."

"Enough." Death shoved Pestilence as he turned, glaring at Arthur. "Stay out of his fucking head, or I will block you."

Arthur sighed, looking at David and then at her. "You're happy with this, Jane?"

"Yes." She lifted her chin but leaned against David for comfort. She didn't want Arthur to disapprove. He was David's family, and she didn't want him shunned.

Her vampire hugged her to him tighter. "It's our business, brother."

"I know. As long as she's comfortable, I have no objection. I already saw your thoughts before the battle—my apologies, but you were very loud. I understand, though. It makes sense on all accounts." Sorrow filled his eyes as he focused on David. "Forgive me for ever pushing my misinterpretation of what your Other should be on you. All I can say is trust in God. He will guide all of us, and I believe the love you all have for each other is meant to be."

Thor, who still stood by the door, shook his head. "You cannot seriously condone this immorality, Arthur."

Death moved in front of her. "Choose your words wisely, Asgardian."

Arthur pointed at Thor. "It is not your place to judge. You haven't the vaguest notion of what's unfolded between them, and you admitted your feelings before were unnatural."

Thor laughed. "They may have been unnatural, but I know Lucifer came and took her. I know she has bargained with him for him to gift her with power like this. And now she has returned with even more darkness disguised as allies. And now this." He gestured to the three of them.

"Do you truly believe her men are here for you?" Pestilence asked, no longer smiling; his boyish handsomeness became replaced by that of a killer. "Do you think they give a fuck what you think of them together?"

War butted in next, equally threatening with the look he gave Thor. "Jane's army arrived to fight for its queen. She is your ally—probably your greatest. I would tread carefully, Norseman. We are not delivering our father's wrath because of her. Be grateful she holds us back because there is no stopping us once we are unleashed. Summoned and invoked to transform is one thing, but you have yet to see our true forms. You have yet to see what will happen to our minds once we give over to our duty completely. She is your current protector. Casting her aside when your fortress teems with tainted souls is unwise. If you had the ability to see what we do, you would fall to your knees before her."

"And if she goes, we go," Pestilence added, his tone empty. "I am sure that also extends to David and most of Arthur's knights."

Thor hesitated, but he spoke again anyway. "This is my fortress, left to me by my father to command. Tainted or not, I am charged with protecting the souls who seek refuge here. I have voiced my disapproval over the demon and Fallen trash, yet you use your power to let them roam my halls. And regardless of her being shared between these two, she is, above all, Lucifer's concubine. She is a whore who bathes in sin."

David moved fast, and he had Thor slammed into the rocky wall before he could take another breath.

Arthur put a hand on David's shaking arm. "Calm, brother."

Thor roared, trying to break free, but David didn't budge.

Death held his hand behind him for her to take, but he kept his gaze on David and Thor.

Jane let him pull her to his side as David squeezed Thor's neck.

She covered her mouth, darting her eyes at Death and the other Horsemen. They had no emotion as they watched.

"David." Arthur pulled on David's shoulder. "Brother, if you kill him, you become that beast you have fought becoming. Think of Jane. Think of your children together. Think of your brothers and the innocents here. If they learn you killed the leader of this fortress, we will be at war amongst ourselves, and those who cannot fight will pay the price."

"David," she whispered.

He stopped squeezing but didn't turn.

She blinked away her tears. "Baby, please don't do this." She hated seeing him lose himself.

"Brother, you are stronger than this," Arthur said. "Lancelot sitting in a cell is proof of your strength. Do not allow any man's ridiculous accusations to blind you. We have so much ahead of us."

David gave a stiff nod, but he didn't release Thor. The muscles across his back flexed, and he took a deep breath as he pulled Thor out of the hole he'd made before speaking in that raw voice she'd heard him use when he was more monster than man. "Speak about Jane like this again, and no pleading from anyone—not even her—will save you. I would burn for her over lesser offenses. She is my Other, my woman, my goddess. I care not for what you think of her, but you will treat her with respect, or I will rip your Damned heart out and crush it beneath my boot."

Jane pressed her trembling lips together. He would have to face many people who looked down on them.

Death shook his head at her. "Stand beside him. Do not fall weak and whimper when he is standing there, roaring to all that you are worth fighting for."

Pestilence muttered to Death, "They do not know what she is, brother."

"Quiet," Death said.

"I have us blocked," Pestilence added.

"You mean I'm Death's soul mate, and I guess the Horsemen Bringer? No, they already know that one."

"Don't worry about it," Death said as David released Thor. "I would tell you if you needed to know."

Arthur pulled David back, putting himself between them again. "Brother, I came to discuss some things regarding our survivors and the food supplies after the attack."

David held a hand out for her, ignoring Thor's growls as he dusted himself off.

Jane went to her vampire right away.

"Are the children being cared for?" David hugged her, dropping a kiss on her head. His posture was surprisingly relaxed.

"Yes, Gwen will bring Natalie to the hall for breakfast. Natalie made a friend, though, so Gwen let her play for a while. Nathan is with Elle and Gawain—they will bring him."

David shook his head at Thor. "If you have more nonsense to spout, leave."

Thor pointed his hammer at Death. "You—"

Death cut him off and summoned his scythe, pointing it at Thor in the same way. "Do not point your pathetic hammer in my direction, Son of Odin. And do not ever voice your opinions regarding Jane or David. They are mine as I am theirs. Do not insult them. I can bring you to the edge of death and keep you there until I destroy everything you once held dear, including this whorehouse you call a fortress." He raised his scythe under Thor's chin, forcing him to look him in the eye. "Tell David why you insist on calling our Jane a whore."

Thor glared at him but stayed quiet and still.

Death smirked. "Tell him you caught your wife sucking your father's dick while he was drunk off his ass. Then, tell him your father wiped the floor with you in his stupor because you flew into a rage at her moaning as

443

your father's best mate fucked her while your father shoved his dick down her throat."

Jane watched the fury and sadness flash across Thor's face, but he stayed quiet.

Death continued coldly, "Do not let your anguish over your adulterous wife influence you in any way, especially regarding Jane. You have no idea who she is to me—or this universe, for that matter. But she is no whore. Now apologize and run along before I cut off your ugly fucking face." He made sure his scythe drew blood before allowing it to vanish.

Thor rubbed his bleeding chin before staring at her. He glared at David and then turned, leaving without a word.

Arthur held up his hands when Death growled.

"He has hidden that secret from everyone." Arthur glanced over his shoulder. "This is no time to fight. I came here to bring David to Lancelot."

"Why?" David glanced at Jane, tightening his hand around hers.

Arthur sighed. "Gwen went to see him—without my consent. She left the children with Elle before I could finish my duties, and she managed to find him."

"Is she all right?" Jane darted her gaze between David and Arthur, knowing David was relaying his thoughts to him.

"She lied to me when she said they had not been involved before I had come to your father's kingdom." Arthur's gaze hardened. "So did you."

David tightened his hand around hers again. "I didn't want to believe it, brother. It made everything that much harder to bear."

"Wait, what?" Jane looked at the Horsemen.

They shrugged.

David dragged his hand down his face. "Lance had already been visiting my sister when he spoke to me. He had come for my blessing to make her his bride. He thought if I supported him and we triumphed in our quests, he would win her hand. Since I didn't stand beside him, and my father laughed in his face, he grew desperate. She led him on, knowing she would not wed him, but she had promised they would run away together."

Jane covered her mouth as she watched Arthur's sadness rise with the strain in his eyes.

"He truly loved her," David continued, "and she merely fancied a handsome knight. She wanted to brag about him at tournaments because many other princesses had their knights. He thought she was genuine."

"She was." Arthur shook his head. "She only told you it meant nothing so you would not argue with your father or hate her. She knew you would

THE LIGHT BRINGER

apologize to him and do whatever you could to support him if you knew she returned his feelings. Then I arrived."

David dropped his head, and Jane hugged him as she watched him trying to control his emotions. She didn't know everything that had happened with Lancelot, but she was determined to see them at least make amends.

"Is this what mortals call a Soap Opera?" War whispered loudly.

"This is real life, brother." Pestilence chuckled, holding up a hand when David glared at them. "Forgive us. We are merely curious."

Death pointed to the door. "Out. Find her generals and have them gathered in the mess hall. And watch the children when they arrive."

"Where are you going?" War paused at the door.

Death nudged David out of the room. "I have to back up my wingman."

David smacked Death's hands when he began massaging his shoulders as they walked down the hall.

Jane laughed before grabbing Arthur's arm to follow her men. David was punching or shoving Death every time he got close to him.

"I swear, I will throw you." David glared at the others when they chuckled. "Baby, come between us so he stops touching me."

"I think she already did." Pestilence vanished when Death summoned a knife and threw it at his head. It became embedded in the wall.

War waved his hand over it, making it vanish. "I will warn him. He has been away for too long, brother. He must relax. He saw Tonia in the halls and ran."

Death smirked, throwing his arm over David's shoulder. "Well, that makes sense. Remind me to get back at his ass."

"Will do, brother." War vanished.

David elbowed Death. "Get the fuck off."

"Don't be like that, Papi."

Arthur stared at them, chuckling as they bickered. "You did this?"

She beamed up at him. "I'm the mature one."

"When you have him anywhere near her, they are a pair of mischievous teens." David plucked her up and held her against his chest, her legs dangling.

She turned her head, kissing his jaw. "Are you okay?"

He raised a hand to her cheek and kissed her on the lips. "Yes. Thank you."

Jane kissed him before pointing to the floor.

"No." He tightened his hold.

445

"Death." She turned her head, pouting.

"Babe, Papi said no."

David laughed, lowering her to the ground but kept hold of her hand and walked to Arthur's side. "Brother . . ."

Arthur held up his hand. "You protected your sister—I would expect nothing less from you. I am saddened for you and Lancelot and that you could not cope emotionally with the loss of your friendship. Had it not been for Michael telling you about your Other, I fear you would have fallen in one of the many battles we have engaged in with Lancelot."

David kissed her hand. "Still, I will make this up to you."

"Make it up to him." Arthur stopped at the door guarded by four men. "Don't let him provoke you. He has caused injury to twenty of their guards because he taunted each until they attacked him."

David ran his fingers through his hair as he asked Arthur, "Where are you going?"

"Away. I cannot cope just yet." Arthur gave him a sad smile. "To have my wife hide such things from an immortal who reads minds is quite devastating. She has become depressed as well, and I must figure out how to help."

"Arthur," David said quietly. "Did he even attempt to—"

Arthur shook his head. "No, brother. He did not."

David's hand tightened around hers as he stared at the floor, and she realized Arthur was saying Lancelot had not tried to rape Guinevere.

Jane's eyes burned, but she smiled sadly at Arthur and hugged David.

"Do not worry about them." Death motioned for Arthur to leave. "See to your wife."

Arthur turned away. "I will see you at noon, brother."

David didn't respond. He kept staring at the floor.

"Go inside, David." Death pulled Jane from David's side.

"Wait." She tightened her hold on David. "I think I should see him."

David shook his head. "No. Not after the things he did to you. I know it was her, but both of you are hurting from that."

She kissed his chest. "Sometimes getting better hurts, right?"

David cupped her cheeks. "I love you."

She told him with her eyes: *I love you.*

He chuckled, kissing her again before looking at Death. "If he gets out of line—"

Death waved him off. "Remember, Thanatos is in there as well. All the prisoners are. She is their enemy."

David held her hand tight. "All right."

Jane hadn't thought about Than. Too much had happened, but her general was a traitor. *No.*

"Baby, be cautious with your forgiving heart." David kissed her hand. "I know you're thinking about Than and even Lance. Your heart is too beautiful, my love. Please try to help me protect it."

Jane motioned to the guards. "Let us through."

Death chuckled before taking place beside her when the guards didn't move.

"Let us pass." David shifted his gaze between the four men.

One spoke up, "Our orders were to keep her out."

David glanced down at Jane before glaring at the guard. "Whose orders?"

"Thor's, Sir David."

David grabbed the guard by the neck. "You have two options: try to stop us from entering and face Death and me, or you can run to Thor and inform him that Prince David, his beautiful girlfriend, and the Angel of Death have entered his cells. If he still wishes to ban her from visiting her prisoners, he can tell us himself." David shoved the guard away and pushed past the other three.

Jane held his arm. She was slightly turned on but knew to stay close to him. Lancelot knew what to say to set anyone off.

"Ah, Prince David and the Queen of Hell," came Lancelot's mocking drawl. "Shall I stand and bow, or do you desire to feast on what's left of my heart?"

Jane locked eyes with two onyx orbs.

Lancelot smirked at her and gestured to his left. "Your former general, my queen."

Thanatos didn't even look at her.

Lancelot chuckled and waved his hand to his right. "And the great Zeus. You know, the father of the woman you tortured and murdered before losing your mind."

Jane swallowed as she met the glare of the vampire she once awed over as a child. He looked every bit of what she imagined but younger. He had dark blond hair that fell to his shoulders, and he wore gold and silver armor and a matching shimmery cape, just like she imagined he would.

She couldn't help it. "Oh, my gosh. My loves, it's Zeus!"

31

TEENAGERS

I am a complete and utter fool.

All eyes were on Jane. Hundreds of prisoners, all Damned, all men and women who saw her as the enemy, leered at her from behind glowing silver bars.

David lifted her hand, though, and kissed the back of it before staring at Zeus. "I am here to speak with Lancelot, but we extend our condolences."

Jane stopped smiling like an idiot and stood as tall as she could under the hundreds of Damned eyes glaring at her. "I won't ask for forgiveness," she said. "I don't deserve it. But I'll pray your daughter and family find peace."

Zeus glanced at David before shifting his gaze to her again. "Melpomene was one of my most vile daughters. It was only Arthur's foolishness that prevented her from being returned to my care. Many believe those who escape damnation are good, and that is not so. It is the same with mortals. They brag about their righteousness because they worship God, yet they live lives of sin, cast judgment on others, and commit crimes. You do not hate and get to say you follow the written word. My daughter attended the same celebrations of God as the knights. She bowed her head and declared she believed the same as them, but she had a black heart. However, she did not look wicked with her jeweled eyes. She was clever, and when she failed to achieve what she desired with Prince David, she sought the Devil's help."

THE LIGHT BRINGER

Jane peeked up at David. She knew he still believed Luc was the Devil, and she had yet to figure out how to tell him his belief was not accurate.

Zeus followed her eye movement and chuckled. "Yes, that is right—the knights do not know the truth. They also do not know I would have destroyed my daughter once she was returned to me."

Jane's mouth fell open.

He shrugged. "I agreed to join Arthur's alliance because I sought redemption, just as many immortals do."

"Like Dagonet." Jane hadn't meant to say that. When Zeus stared at her, she gave him an awkward smile. "I mean, you were saying that someone who isn't marked as Damned is not necessarily good. Dagonet was Damned, yet he was one of the best men I have come across. He died saving my son."

"Dagonet?" It was Lancelot.

David nodded. "In Texas. Your wolves were there, but I did not see you. He had been carrying the boy when he was hit with silver."

Lancelot lowered his dark eyes to the ground as several whispers broke out amongst the prisoners.

Jane looked between David and Lancelot, remembering Dagonet was one of David's oldest companions. He had served him at David's home, which meant Lancelot knew him.

Zeus' armor clinked as he moved on the stone bench he sat upon. "Yes, child. Dagonet was a Damned but good soul through and through. My daughter was dark for as long as my old mind can recall. Perhaps it is my curse to watch many of my children fall as I did.

"The alliance I made was to protect my children from the wrath of the knights, but I never once allowed them to believe they would not face mine. Manipulating a human to kill his own children is a horrendous crime I would not have allowed to go unpunished. Arthur did not know because he never questioned me and relied on his abilities too often. He assumed those who wound up dead were killed in battles when they were simply executed for their crimes."

"You've been punishing your own children?" she whispered.

"Every child of my line that has returned to my ranks has been punished according to their crime. It is the same with any immortal who follows under my order or seeks refuge with us. We stopped following the rules set forth by God once. We promised not to again. Killing a human and manipulating one to attack his children is punishable by death. She would have been executed in front of our family and ranks,

449

and the entire time, she would have cried out to the Devil instead of God."

David stared up at the ceiling. "Why did you join Lucifer after you heard Jane killed her, then?"

"Because I believed Arthur and the knights had lost their way. After all, you protected a demon." He waved his hand toward Jane. "I saw her from afar at Lucifer's camp. But she is not the creature I witnessed torturing and slaughtering Sir Lancelot's family."

Jane smiled sadly at him. "You joined the side opposing Arthur's because you thought they were no longer in the light."

"Yes. Lucifer is cunning, and his generals"—his gaze slid to Thanatos—"are just as clever. I believed I was joining the side to bring down the unholy knights. It did not matter that Melpomene deserved death. It mattered that the knights had the darkest creature within their castle, calling it family and letting it torture others. I had not expected to see the same demon when I arrived at their camp."

Jane lowered her eyes. "I stopped fighting her."

Zeus nodded. "You deserved justice for what she did, and you fell due to sorrow and the torment you had already suffered. Lucifer ensured you would go to him. You are not the same as the beast you once harbored, though. Even though I know her to be the other half of your soul, you—this half of you—was not groomed to be a monster by the Devil himself. I admire you for fighting her as well as you did."

"David, can we let him out?" She looked up at him.

Zeus chuckled, shaking his head. "Child, I am here for my crimes, which I committed by following the armies of Hell—I will answer for them. I failed Heaven many times before and did again by not continuing my alliance with Arthur. I should have sought him out on my own rather than believe they were preparing to unleash darkness and that the upcoming King of Hell sought to destroy her before she destroyed what was left of the world.

"I thought any world would be worth saving and willingly walked my frightened and vengeful children into Hell. So, here I will stay. Go now. I suggest you leave these cells quickly. Not all Damned seek redemption. Remember that, girl. And my condolences as well. From what I heard, it took very little persuasion from Lucifer to help your husband break the spell she cast upon him. You should be proud."

"I am. Thank you." Jane smiled sadly. "And I will do what I can for you. Oh, can I take a message to your son and daughter? Or your brother?"

450

"You are friendly with Artemis?" Zeus laughed, as did several others.

David answered, smiling, "They were not always tolerant of one another, but I believe Jane's cousin softened Artemis. She has been making attempts to get on Jane's good side."

Zeus laughed. "She was waiting for you, Prince David. God must have a sense of humor if he sent a soul to charm her now." Zeus smiled at David. "Do you remember when Sin and Nyctimus tried to persuade you to join them after you freed over sixty Nephilim females from that compound?"

David sighed, dropping his gaze to Jane's.

Lancelot laughed. "Were the tales of your celibacy false, my prince? Did you resume our game without me?"

"Oh, he did not go." Zeus grinned at her. "He told them he had a woman waiting. They asked him why he had not told them he had claimed an Other, and he told them he had not. He said his woman was still a dream, and this dream girl with hazel eyes of emerald and gold was the only woman he wanted to sleep with that night or any other."

Jane tilted her head back to see David smiling.

Zeus went on. "Sin told you to look for gold, and because I knew my daughter was listening, I suggested green-eyed goddesses, then Nyctimus—"

David finished the sentence "—said, 'Keep searching for the dream girl. You will find your goddess when the gold and emerald flames meet.'"

Zeus looked between Jane and Death. "I see you found what you were seeking. Beautiful. Good boy, David. Keep them safe."

"I will." David cleared his throat. "Sin and Nyc?"

Zeus pointed to Death. "Ask him. He has many who carry out duties for him. With Lycaon slain, there is chaos amongst the wolves, but he knows where to find those two."

"I see." David gave Death a dark look before returning his attention to Zeus. "I will speak to Arthur about transferring you."

"No." Zeus pointed upward. "All one has to do is pray and ask for guidance. I am to stay here."

"Very well." David nodded to him. "Send for us if there is anything you require. Thank you for showing restraint with Apollo."

"I did not." Zeus smiled. "He finally made me proud, fighting for his family."

Jane wanted to hug him so badly. She knew there was a reason he was her favorite.

David pulled Jane under his arm as he slowly looked at Lancelot.

"Don't you dare look at me with pity, my prince." Lancelot leaned back, a sneer on his handsome face. "I know you found out she was here."

"Why didn't you tell me?" David tightened his hold on her.

"What should I have said, brother?" Lancelot laughed. "That I was fucking your sister behind your back? Should I have let you think she was willing to have an affair because she still loved and pitied me after seeing what pain she had caused me? Should I have risked her life when she finally gave in? Even Queens are executed, my prince. She would have been ripped apart by both kingdoms. She would have had nowhere to go, and I would have failed at keeping her safe. I would have had to watch her sentenced for her crime, and I would have been executed alongside her. But it would be her they tortured. Even immortals are punished by Arthur, brother. He would not have spared an adulterous queen. At the time, at least."

David sighed as his body heated up. "I did not know she had feelings for you."

"You did not ask. It matters little—she is Arthur's soul mate. Not mine. Hard to go against that." He looked at her and Death. "It appears you got a lucky hand with her. This half of her, that is."

Jane bit her lip.

"You knew about her?" David glared at Lancelot.

"She glows differently with him, and I have heard things." Lancelot glanced at Thanatos. "Plus, you all smell of each other. I would never have thought you would do such a thing."

David's gaze moved around the cells.

"I will keep the secret, for old time's sake." Lancelot studied Death. "Taking me soon? I am getting rather tired of sitting in this cell."

Death said nothing.

David rubbed his face as he glanced around. "Thank you for keeping this private."

Lancelot shrugged. "Always brothers, right?"

A heartbroken look flitted across David's face. "Yes. Always brothers, Lance."

"Pussy." Lancelot smiled, shaking his head. "I will still cut out your heart if I get the chance."

Jane couldn't help but smile at him. He was all talk.

Lancelot glared at her. "Your smile does not work on all of us, my queen. Wipe it off your face."

"Don't talk to her like that. She is here for my sake." David pulled her closer.

"She is here to see what she did to me." Lancelot motioned to Death. "And because you are unsure how you feel about them alone together."

"Enough." David growled. "I would have supported you and Gwen however I could."

Lancelot laughed. "That is the point, isn't it?"

David stared at him. "What point?"

Jane kept her eyes on Lancelot. "He was protecting you, David. You are his brother."

Her vampire looked between Jane and Lancelot, and she wanted to hug them both.

Lancelot finally looked away. "You should go. Do not come back, and keep Gwen away. Keep her away, too, while you're at it." He threw a glare at Jane. "Your idiocy will not win all black hearts, and I will not hesitate to take your life."

Thanatos turned but did nothing else.

David was pissed, though. "You know that was not her."

"Wasn't it?" Lancelot stood. "She admitted she stopped fighting that monster. She did not look at my son and daughter and fight for them or flee as she did for you and her brats! She cowered like a child under Lucifer and spread her legs like a whore, forgetting she was making deals with the most clever Fallen. How foolish does one have to be to trust him not to have multiple motives for everything he does?"

"You bargained with him," David snapped. "Don't talk badly of her because you have no idea of the control he had over her. She fought that beast for so long on her own, and he was the only one to relieve her of it."

"She raped me and killed my family," Lancelot roared.

Jane gasped, closing her eyes for a moment. She saw everything her monster had allowed, the devastation on Lancelot's face as she took all he had left—the pain she'd felt when he howled at the sight of his children's blood on her hands.

"And how many innocents have you raped, tortured, and murdered?" Thanatos asked calmly. "You raped a woman like her right before her eyes. Lucifer gave you a choice when he showed you a girl with hazel eyes, begging him to spare you and your family. You chose revenge over your family. Blame yourself for their deaths. Not once have you risen above your beast to save others. Your thirst for vengeance has cost you everything. Not this girl. Nor the prince you call brother."

Jane opened her eyes and darted them between Lancelot and Thanatos. Her former general, she realized, was bound around his wrists and ankles with gold ropes, and there was a shimmering translucent wall around him. Why was he defending her?

Lancelot whirled around. "Do not speak to me, Fallen. You have told as many lies as Lucifer and corrupted just as many souls."

Thanatos chuckled. "Your soul seeks redemption. Seek it, or shut the fuck up. They came here to save you. None of the other bastards here care to be saved."

Snarls and hisses erupted from the cells.

"Hiss all you like, Damned." Thanatos glared at those in the cells, baring their fangs. "Do you really think Hell favors you? You will scream and beg for mercy under our wrath."

David stared at Thanatos before he said, "Which side are you on?"

"That is the question, isn't it?" Thanatos smiled as his ruby eyes began to glow. "My loyalty demands I not answer."

"You are loyal to no one." Lancelot spat at the edge of the barrier.

Thanatos slid his gaze to hers, then Death's. "His light will corrupt her if you are not careful."

"Than," she whispered as a dull ache spread through her chest.

"You are the enemy of many, my queen. You should not be here and be cautious of what you are attempting with the two of them. It will not work. Not while you are harboring his power. Lucifer will not allow it."

Rage flooded any sorrow she felt over his betrayal. "I will succeed. I will send each of you back to where you belong while I'm at it."

Thanatos glanced around at the light she was emitting with a faint smirk. "It's already starting."

Death grabbed her hand. "Be calm, angel."

The inmates began to growl and move about, kicking the gates holding them, which she realized were silver and surging with electricity. Someone yelled from a cell, "The King will come for his queen, and she stinks of two. We will all burn for her crimes."

David and Death growled.

"Ignore them," Jane whispered.

The prisoners threw objects against the cells and shouted in various languages.

Death tightened his grip. "Come, Jane. David must do this alone."

David let her go. "Take her to the children. I won't be long. Make sure you eat, Jane."

Before Death could drag her away, she looked over her shoulder at Lancelot. "Do you wish for my death?"Death and David froze, but she said, "Would that give you peace? I may not have done it, but like you said, I stopped fighting. I am responsible for their murder. If it's justice you seek, I will pay for her crimes. It doesn't matter that you're a monster. So was I. I still am at times. But your crimes have nothing to do with what I did to your family. I will pay for my crimes. Even if it hurts everyone around me, I will pay. So do not hesitate to request a sentence. Just know I would take it back if it were possible. If I could, I would go back and change it all. I can't, and I am so broken for what I did to them and you. So go on."

"Shut up, Jane." Death lifted her. "Handle your business, Prince. I will keep her with me." He then pointed at Lancelot. "If you so much as whisper a request for her death, you will regret it. It was their fucking time. And she is already suffering, just like you are, for what you have done to innocents. So keep your filthy mouth shut and be grateful I am not skinning you alive because you still chose to follow Lucifer when you saw this angel begging him to spare your entire damned family."

Death turned, marching to the exit before he kicked the door down and growled at the guards. "Move."

They backed up, lowering their heads as Death stomped past them.

"Why can't you keep your beautiful mouth shut?" He situated his hold on her so she was now over his shoulder. "I let you go with David because I knew he would need you, not so you could offer to toss yourself behind bars with a man who wishes to see you dead."

"But I deserve death."

"Yeah, me." He shook his head. "Not to actually die because you broke down against the most powerful being Darkness has ever created. Dammit, Jane. You cannot save every soul."

She stared over his shoulder. "I can try."

Death snarled, lifting her so he held her in front of him. "Stop! I will not lose you. You know I cannot see your fate. Now you have even more reason to fight for yourself, and you are throwing it away for a Damned! Who the fuck cares if Lancelot has reasons for the way he turned out? He, like every Damned, still chose to commit the crimes he did. Think about yourself. You have been subjected to horror for most of your life—you had your soul corrupted by an evil trying to destroy you—but you did not go molest little girls."

"But I did let a monster kill, torture, and rape. I stood by and did nothing when she beat me—when Luc broke my heart. Not doing anything makes me as guilty as those who commit the crimes."

He pulled her face close to his. "You are not guilty."

She caressed his cheek. "I am. Don't worry about me like this."

He squeezed his eyes shut. "Your soul is tied to Lucifer's, baby girl. He gets you if you die, and he is the only one who knows your fate. He wants you for all eternity, and you bonded with him as his queen."

A gasp sounded behind them, and they both looked over to see a group of maids.

Jane recognized the one she'd seen several times before. "Hello, Hela."

The frightened maid bowed her head. "My lady. Might we be of service?"

Death covered Jane's mouth and snapped at the poor group of women. "Get the fuck out of here and keep your traps shut about what you heard, or I will rip your tongue from your mouths."

They whimpered, running down the hall.

Jane sighed, turning his face toward hers. "Hey. Calm down." The glare he gave her should have made her shrink back, but she leaned forward and kissed him softly. "*Shh* . . . I know my end frightens you, but that is no reason to scare or hurt anyone else."

"You don't get it." He nuzzled her, kissing her cheek as he hugged her and situated her legs around him. "I have nothing without you."

"You'll have David now." She tried to smile. "I know not romantically, but you are adorable together."

He ran his fingers through her hair. "No, my love. It is still only you. I feel slightly protective of him, and I do love watching the two of you happy together, but if you are lost to me . . . I will not watch you burn."

"I will anyway if you don't let me atone for my sins."

Death let out a frustrated breath. "I know what you wish to atone for. What are you planning? Because I cannot lose you. You must know this."

"We are always."

"Yes." He pulled her in for a kiss. "We are always."

She grinned. "Let's go see the others. I feel so down for not taking care of my kids. I'm letting you love me, and they're with Gwen."

Death began walking. "And here you thought she was the better mother figure. When will you see it is you they benefit from most?"

Jane rested her cheek on his shoulder as she massaged his scalp. "I only have it in me to give small spurts of goodness."

"Because you have responsibilities." Death turned his head and kissed her neck. "Do you think he minds me loving you without him?"

"I think he does a little." She sighed as he kissed her again, this time sucking as he let out a low growl.

"Hm," he hummed. "We must discuss this further with him. I still want my kiss without having to ask."

"Let's wait for him, though." She hugged him and tried to steer their discussion to the previous one. "And my first responsibility should be my kids."

"Are they not?"

"I keep leaving them, Death."

He shrugged. "I thought trying to make the world a better place for them would be a top priority. If you had not started fighting, they would have starved. I would have kept you alive, but they would not have concerned me. You know I will not fight for them when it comes to keeping you safe. That is more the case now than ever before. When we were—" He sighed and shook his head. "When we were bonded—I could watch over them to a degree. It is different now. My only options are to keep you safe."

Her eyes watered. She knew he wasn't close to a human at all. He wasn't even like the other angels. He was unique, and for reasons she didn't understand, he could not care.

He tilted his head toward hers. "I am sorry. I am simply trying to express that you are a good mother. Not all mothers can dote on their child's every need. You did before, to the best of your ability, but now you have chosen to keep the world intact. That is a sacrifice all of you are making. And you sacrificing all that you have is for them when you look at your motives. It is never for you. Just as my sacrifices are only for you. David is the only one able to sacrifice for all of us."

Jane leaned away so she could stare at him. "Do you think that is why?"

"Why what? Fuck, you're beautiful." He pulled her in for a kiss.

She chuckled, holding his face to kiss him as well. "You're such a teenage boy sometimes."

"You make me this way." He dropped his gaze to her breasts. "It is because I walked away from you when you were seventeen. My heart stopped then, and I reserved every bit of a relationship I wanted with you until I got you back. Now, with David's consent, I get to release everything I held back for you. Hence, the horny and mischievous teenage boy I would have been for you had I been able to.

"I would have loved you so much, baby. I am trying to be a man, but you

457

still turn me into a boy who loved a girl he could not have. So I indulge in the dreams I had of us before while David is the man you need now."

She was speechless.

"Did I manage one of Mr. Perfect's panty-dropping moments just now?"

"Kinda." She teared up. He'd held back for so long, and for him, he was starting all over so she could have everything he'd always wanted to give her.

"Don't cry." Death chuckled. "Damn, I might need him to help me with my lines. He gets you horny, and I'm making you emotional. Perhaps I shall embrace the inner-bad boy I know gets you all dazed and tingly. Of course, I will still be sweet with you, but everyone else will hate me." He smiled and kissed her cheek before nibbling her ear and whispering, "I love you, angel."

Jane's heart fluttered like it had when she was a girl in love with her angel. "And I love you. Thank you for being you. You would have been the best boyfriend an emotional teenage girl could ever ask for."

He squeezed her ass. "Too bad I will always have my duty. I would have pampered the fuck out of you if you were just mine."

She grinned as she took in his face. "I wonder what you would look like as a teenager."

"Hot." He chuckled. "I have always looked like this, but as a mortal teen, I imagine I would be slightly shorter and less built. Still, I would have made every girl drool. But I'd only have my eyes on you. Jason would have had a fit because even if you were loyal to him, you would never be able to resist me, especially knowing what we know now. Our souls will always know each other, even if we do not. So you would have stared at all this, and he would have lost his mind."

"Yes, he would have." She frowned as she thought of Jason. He was really dreamy. All the girls loved him, and he would have hated Death.

"I know you miss that prick."

"Don't call him that, and I miss a lot of people."

"Sorry, babe. I just think you should focus on what you have now. That is what I want for you. Life." He glanced behind her. "We're here. Be ready for teasing from my brothers. They behave like teenagers because I am around you."

"Really?"

His head bobbed. "We are bonded, and they feel what I do. But also be ready for judgment from others present. Not even the knights will understand the love between us."

"I'll deal with it."

"I know you will." He lowered her to her feet. "Wanna hold hands like boyfriend and girlfriend and watch everyone stare as we enter?"

"Are you basing that on your knowledge of teen movies?" She took his hand.

"That is what you forced me to watch with you." He frowned. "Is that not correct? No, I remember Jason taking you to his campus for lunch once, and he stopped asking you to come because you were panicking about the stares."

"Ugh." She shook her head. "Don't remind me. At least now I'm the shit."

He smirked. "That's my girl. Just burn their eyes out if they stare for too long, and remember, I only have eyes for you. And occasionally David." He snickered when she blushed. "The boy has moves I didn't know about."

"Shush." She fanned her cheeks as they walked into the main banquet hall.

"Told you," Death muttered, dragging her past immortals scenting the air.

She held her head high as she approached Gawain, Ragnelle, Gareth, the Horsemen, and Asmodeus.

"They are precious." Pestilence grinned at her.

"Quite." War held up a dinosaur as he spoke to Nathan. "Which is this, boy?"

Nathan didn't look up but answered perfectly, "Ankylosaurus."

Asmodeus bowed his head as Beelzebub and Astaroth shimmered into view, bowing as well.

"My queen," they said in unison.

"Hi, boys." She beamed at them before bending to kiss Nathan. "Hey, bubby. Are you playing nice with War?"

Nathan nodded.

War gave him another toy as he pointed at Natalie. "She was not playing nice."

Natalie crossed her arms. "I didn't want to play with him. It's boring."

War looked Natalie dead in the eye. "He is your brother, little monster. You cherish every moment he wishes to share with you."

Her daughter turned away, huffing as Gawain rubbed her back.

Jane was in shock. War was disciplining her daughter.

Pestilence chuckled, kicking out a chair for Death as Astaroth placed one behind her.

"Oh, thank you." Jane sat.

Pestilence pointed across the room. "She wishes to play with the children there, but your knights explained you would be coming soon. She tried to keep playing when the boy offered her his toy, and she threw it down and said you would only care about seeing Nathan and Death."

Jane darted her eyes between her kids as her heart throbbed.

Pestilence waved his hand. "She cannot hear us. I was simply warning you because I know you must be upset over what happened in the cells."

"How do you know what happened?"

He tapped his head. "Vision. Offering your life to him was foolish. But for what you were hoping to accomplish by showing forgiveness and responsibility, it was wise and good. Sometimes that is all one needs to let go of even the most violent hate."

Death snarled, throwing an arm over her shoulder as he took the plate Gawain was trying to hand Jane. He put it on her lap. "Eat." He pointed at Pestilence. "Stay clear of her."

Astaroth spoke before Pestilence could. "The immortals are becoming more unstable, my queen."

Jane was about to go to Natalie instead of listening to this, but she needed to know what was happening. She noticed Arthur was missing, along with Thor and many of the knights. "What's going on?"

Asmodeus was the one to answer. "Besides our presence agitating them, they are beginning to fight over control of the donors. Several were lost, and many of their blood stores were depleted with the battles."

Pestilence and War looked at Death.

"I know." Death shook his head. "I already made arrangements. They are not ready, though."

"That is a pity." Pestilence glanced at something before quickly moving to sit beside Jane. He threw his arm over her shoulder too.

"What the fuck are you doing?" Death shoved him off.

War laughed and glanced behind him. "Tonia is here. I summoned her into duty."

Pestilence threw a piece of food from Jane's plate at him. "I told you not to. Send her away."

"No." War grinned before paling. "What the fuck is she doing here?"

Pestilence tried to put his arm over Jane again, flinching as Death punched him.

"Payback, brother." Pestilence blocked the toy thrown at his face.

"What are you two talking about?" Jane looked where War was and saw two female angels embracing.

"Are those your girlfriends?"

War laughed, shaking his head. "We do not have girlfriends."

"More like frequent ass." Death held up the fork for her to eat.

Again, Pestilence tried to put his arm over her shoulder. "Go along with it."

Death covered his face, groaning. "You are lucky I cannot kill you yet."

"Yet?" Jane whipped her head around.

He shrugged. "I kill everyone eventually."

"Why the fuck do they always find each other?" War muttered.

Jane peeked at the women. "Oh, shit. They saw me. Now they're looking at me."

"Be cool." Pestilence grabbed a roll off her plate and held it to her mouth. "Here. Eat from me. This is what lovers do."

Death smacked the roll away. "You're not her lover."

"Obviously," came a female voice. The tall brunette stared down at Jane before her eyes drifted to War. When War didn't acknowledge her, she scowled and turned to Jane again. "She does not reek of Pest, yet she smells of honey and earth. Sunlight." She glared at Death. "And you."

"Lovely to see you, Monica," Death greeted dryly. "What the fuck do you want? Have you gone through my ranks already?"

"Fuck you!" Monica snapped. "Sexy bastard."

Jane's mouth fell open.

"No thanks." Death shuddered. "I prefer my angel. Try one of my reapers if you must."

Monica summoned a knife and threw it at him.

Jane gasped as Death caught it and threw it between Monica's feet.

"Throw a weapon in my woman's direction again," he said, without any of his previous playfulness, "and I will rip your head off."

War looked up and motioned for Monica to come to him. He pulled her onto his lap and flipped Death off.

Death smirked, and every muscle in his body relaxed again.

Jane watched War whisper in Monica's ear before kissing her and focusing on Nathan. The angel, who had just had a sneer on her face and threatened Death himself, smiled at her son and began playing with him.

"No, we will not have a child." War shook his head as he smiled at the glare Monica gave him.

"This is bizarre." Asmodeus shook his head.

461

"Very," Beelzebub agreed. His eyes turned black, and he vanished, but no one seemed unsettled.

Pestilence tried to feed Jane a carrot.

She blocked his hand. "Stop."

He glared at her. "Eat."

Jane darted her eyes up to the other angel. She was awed by her beauty but noticed her sadness when the woman tried to hide her gaze from Pestilence. She was trying to find a way to leave without being noticed.

"Don't," Pestilence growled at Jane.

She winked at him and held her hand up to the other angel. "I'm Jane. I've never met a female angel who hasn't fallen."

"Tonia." She did not shake Jane's hand. Instead, she bowed to her as well as Death and War.

"It's nice to meet you." Jane ignored Pestilence's glare and continued smiling at Tonia as she lowered her hand. "Do you want to sit with us?"

Death smacked Pestilence's hand again. "Get Tonia a seat, moron."

Tonia darted her eyes to Pestilence and shook her head. "It is all right. I am relieved to see you have returned safely. I know you did not intend to start this."

Pestilence removed his arm from Jane and stood, bowing to Tonia. "My love."

Jane's lips parted, not expecting him to say that.

Death pushed her mouth shut and motioned for Tonia to sit. "Make amends so my girl can return to her meal."

Tonia embraced Pestilence when he walked closer. He murmured words Jane did not understand before kissing her softly.

Jane turned away and stared up at Death. "Did you just force them to make up?"

Death shrugged. "She was practically a wife to him until he became trapped by Megaera, one of the Erinyes. Or, as you may know them as Furies."

"You knew he had a wife and let him go off with one?" Jane watched Pestilence wipe the tears from Tonia's eyes. "Wait, are you keeping us private?"

Death held up her food. "Yes. And I do not care what they do. We are rarely together, especially more than just a pair. If we all come together, that is it. It's the end. And I use the term wife loosely. My brothers are only truly bonded to you."

Jane didn't know what to make of his comment and decided to eat. She always learned new things, but she was supposed to be focused on her kids and keeping the end of the world from happening. "Let me sit with Natalie."

Death removed his arm but smacked her ass when she walked past him.

"Does the other one she smells of know you touch her so without him?" Monica asked.

"Mind your fucking business." Death gestured for Asmodeus and Astaroth to come closer.

Jane ignored them and sat by her daughter. "Hi, baby."

Natalie didn't look at her.

Gawain gave her a sympathetic smile before talking to Natalie. "Mommy said hello to you."

"She doesn't care about me," Natalie mumbled. "She doesn't love me. She only loves Nathan, David, and Ryder."

Jane felt everyone staring at her, and she could only sit there. Numb.

David walked up to them quickly, lifting Natalie to hug her. "Princess, do not say such things."

"She doesn't love me anymore. All she cares about is you and Ryder."

Jane couldn't look up. She knew she'd failed as a mom, but there was no escaping it now.

Death came to David's side, but he reached out, touching Natalie's head. "Sleep."

She knew he'd just rendered her daughter unconscious.

Gawain kissed Jane's head before moving, allowing David to take his spot.

"Baby." David grabbed Jane's hand, lifting it to his lips for a kiss. "She did not mean it."

She did, Jane thought.

The light she emitted sparked, and the immortals in the room gasped.

"Sweet Jane?" Death tilted her chin up, sighing. "Stay with me."

She realized Natalie was asleep on David's shoulder. Nathan was watching her as Pestilence and War spoke to him quietly. They were comforting her children when it should have been her.

None of her efforts to protect them mattered. She'd still failed to be a mom. All the years she spent making sure they were never abused meant nothing. Not when she'd abandoned them because of her fear of harming them herself and because she knew every one of the knights' wives would be a better mother than her.

The walls lit up with bright flashes as more light rose to the surface. She wanted to let it destroy her. She deserved it. After all, she'd taken Lancelot's children from him, and he, even evil, had tried to be a father. His children loved him, and she'd killed them. Then she'd left her kids like they were nothing.

Astaroth and Asmodeus came to Death's side and observed her.

"It's becoming unstable," Astaroth muttered. "I hoped it would hold off longer."

A low boom shook the walls. There were screams, but the angels and Fallen merely glanced upward.

Death closed his eyes, sighing.

"This is unfortunate," Asmodeus said. "Death?"

"She's summoning him." Death opened his eyes and quickly focused on David. "I have arranged for a settlement to be cleared for you and the others. It has taken longer than expected, but we must figure out how to transfer everyone worth taking. War and Pestilence will have to leave soon."

Death turned toward Astaroth. "Find Arthur. Let him know what is happening. Have your men organize groups for us to take. Her family and Arthur's humans are your priority. We have some time, but not much."

Astaroth nodded before vanishing.

Another boom shook the walls, and it sent many fleeing.

Death focused on Asmodeus. "Do it."

Asmodeus bowed, vanishing without a word.

"One night, brother." Pestilence lifted Tonia's hands to his lips and kissed them. "I will hold him for as long as I can."

"Get me at least one more," Death said.

"Yes, brother." Pestilence smiled at Tonia. "Farewell, my love." Then he vanished.

"Death." David stood. "What is happening?"

"Those were seals being broken." Death cupped Jane's face. "She has summoned the third Horseman. Famine."

32

TO BE LOVED

Jane tried to keep her face relaxed as she followed David to their room, but an old pain rippled through her, burning her eyes, throat, and nose. How could she relax when a slow but devastating fire ate her heart and soul?

It was no one's fault but her own. She was the one who had put herself in this situation, and she was the only person who could mend it. She just didn't know how or if she should even try. It was probably too late anyway. And living felt pointless when your child hated you.

Her little girl, probably the best daughter anyone could ask for, believed she didn't love her. Everything Jane had done to protect Natalie felt like it meant nothing now. She supposed it did mean nothing, considering she had been so quick to dump her children with strangers—with monsters. She hadn't questioned if they would harm her kids or even questioned them at all. She'd repeatedly left her babies because she was consumed with herself. She'd done it because she feared she was their greatest threat, but that didn't matter. Not when she was cuddling with David or Death. Not when she left her family without ensuring they were safe. She'd lost Jason because she'd gone with the knights, and she'd been fucking David while Jason and Nathan fought for their lives. Now, she was fucking David *and* Death, and where were her kids?

No wonder she hates me.

"I don't understand." David opened the door to their room and quickly carried her sleeping daughter to the cot beside their bed. He covered her up before taking Nathan, who was asleep on Death's shoulder and laying him next to Natalie. "She didn't seem to be doing anything to summon anyone."

Jane stopped in the middle of the room, watching her two men care for her children without her.

David turned, running a hand through his hair. He was stressed, and that was her fault, too. "How did she summon Famine?" His gaze shifted to her. "Baby, are you okay? You know Natalie didn't mean what she said."

Death walked to where Jane stood, tilting her chin up. "Jane has been calling them since Pestilence released his arrow. There is nothing she can do to control it—it's fate. It simply coincided with everything that is happening."

"I didn't know," she whispered.

"I know, angel." He brushed away a tear from her cheek. "It's time for him to come. I know you will hold him back from completely transforming, but his presence will be felt. It has already been building to this point, which is why I have been trying to secure a large enough settlement for everyone here."

"Why haven't you brought this up?" David came to Death's side, wiping her other cheek. "Don't cry, sweetheart. You had no idea. At least we can try to get everyone out safely."

Death shook his head. "Not safely. There will be many lives lost. The time keeps shifting, though. So do the number of lives. There's a disturbance, and I can only assume it is Jane's doing. Still, what will happen is certain to be a great loss of life. And I didn't bring it up because we have been busy with other matters. There's a lot we all have to discuss, but we have no time."

David sighed as he took in her tears. "Thor and the other clan leaders are already in an uproar because Jane's men and your reapers protected our humans during the attack." He pulled Jane to him, hugging her as he kissed the top of her head. "Try not to stress, okay? Those who matter are not upset with you."

Death watched her face as she stared ahead, her thoughts drifting away from her heart. "Sweet Jane." He tilted her head. "Don't slip. David and I are both here beside you. You can reach for us or tell us to hold you up. I know what she said hurt you, but she is a child—an observant little girl who dearly loves and misses her mother. She has the most beautiful and important mother in the entire fortress, but the new friends she is making are causing her to question what she trusts: your love for her.

"No one knows about the burdens you carry, angel. Not Natalie, and especially not a group of small children who are jealous of the attention she and Nathan receive. Those children see your knights as superheroes. They see the wives and know one is a queen. Then everyone is always talking about you. You are the Other to the most powerful and famous immortal knight, the love of the Angel of Death, the Queen of Hell, and the Horsemen Bringer. There isn't a soul here who does not know your name. I would guess Natalie was proud to say you were her mom, but they could have asked why you were never with her."

David caressed her hair, adding, "Natalie loves you, and she knows you love her. But she's a baby. She misses you. She grew up with you responding to her every desire, and now you have so much pulling you away. Still, everything you do is for her and Nathan."

The words flew out hatefully before she could stop them. "Even fucking you both when they were worried about me?" She squeezed her eyes shut when his gaze darkened. "When you and I fucked while Melody was killing Jason?"

David held her arm's length away, his voice sharp as knives, "Open your eyes and look at me right now."

She shook her head. She hadn't meant to say that to him.

His lips touched hers very briefly before he spoke in a softer tone than she had expected. "Do not let your sadness take your thoughts there. We have been through this about Jason. I do not wish to open your healing wounds when you have just begun to recover from your loss, so I will not repeat what I said. You must know, though, there is nothing wrong with us making love. It was not wrong during our first time, and it wasn't this time —it never will be."

David cupped her cheeks when she finally opened her eyes. He smiled and turned her so she could see Death. "He is yours, and you were always his."

Jane's face scrunched up as she tried to hold back her tears.

David smiled. "You are no ordinary woman, Jane. He is not even a normal angel, and you both tore yourselves apart out of love for each other and for me. It was a terrible thing that should not have happened. Instead of falling further apart, we began forging a new path for the three of us, and that requires us to be alone. We took the chance while you were recovering."

David turned her toward him again. "You are allowed to be loved. Do not regret that we had a moment to ourselves after nearly losing you and that we tried to pull ourselves together in a new way to strengthen our love. Being loved by your men doesn't make you a bad mother.

"We will keep fighting, so there hopefully comes a day when she wakes, and she and Nathan are the only two you devote your time to. We can talk to her together if that helps you. She's a very smart little girl and has done nothing but hope for us to be together. I will never forget that she told me she and Nathan wanted you to be loved by me. This was just an overflow of built-up emotions. She has been worried about you being gone and then returning with a terrible injury."

Jane covered his hands, sniffing as she glanced between him, Death, and her children. Her eyes still stung, her lungs still ached, and her throat still felt like it was being crushed, but she smiled and nodded. "Okay. I'm okay. Let's focus on what we need to do to get out of here and save as many as we can."

"That's our girl." David kissed her forehead as he hugged her tight.

Jane reached for Death's hand and gasped when shocks sparked between them.

Death tightened his hold and smiled. "It's not what it should be, but there is still something there."

"Good." She sighed as David motioned for Death to get behind her.

They lifted her between them, but it wasn't sexual. They only held her, pressing their lips sweetly to her shoulders as they murmured, "I love you."

"And I love you," she whispered as that gold thread appeared. It hugged them but quickly faded.

"It's okay." Death kissed her tears, nuzzling her cheek.

"We will get there." David squeezed her a tiny bit tighter.

She wanted to stay between the heat and knowing she was alive with her Death holding her, but she knew it was time to move forward. David was right. They were fighting for the world—for Natalie and Nathan to have the chance to one day wake up and be her only focus.

Death kissed her cheek. "Our brave, beautiful girl is finally choosing to live."

She turned and received his kiss before spinning to meet David's kiss.

Her vampire grinned. "I'm so proud of you."

She gave him the best smile she could manage because even with their support, Natalie's words were a knife she couldn't pull out of her heart. The pain was so unbearable she wanted to give up. It brought forward every negative thought she'd ever had about herself, and she just wanted to crawl away. But she didn't. She'd leave the knife in instead of bleeding out just yet. "Tell me that when I actually do something worth praising."

David gave her another sweet kiss. "Every smile you give us when we know you're hurting inside is worth praise, my love. The fact she does not realize the magnitude of what you are constantly sacrificing for her means you are succeeding. And don't you dare start doubting how wonderful you are for ensuring she does not have the same horrific memories and night-mares you do. She has lived through horror, but you've protected her from the monsters people cannot see. She will never know the horror and sadness you do, and that is so precious."

Death kissed the back of her head before stepping away. "You're welcome to cry between us as much as you need to later, but it's time to work now."

"I love you." David lowered her to the ground. "Get your angel to help us pack."

Death collapsed on the bed. "Give me Jane's panties to pack; then I'll help."

She chuckled, wiping her tears away before grabbing her pack.

Surprisingly, David agreed to Death's request and removed the entire drawer for him to sort through. "She likes the cotton style, but get these with bows too. And that one."

Death dug through her clothes as though he had something he was searching for. "There it is." He pulled out a black thong and pocketed it instead of putting it in the pile David had started to make.

"What the fuck are you doing?" David tried to get it back.

Death shielded his pocket. "Prince David, if you reach for me again, you will be disappointed to find I don't have a boner. Big D is reserved for Sweet Jane, even if you have a nice ass."

Jane giggled as she began organizing the kids' things.

David shook his head. "Stop looking at my ass."

"Don't tell me what to do." Death kept going through her panties, putting pairs over his shoulder as David walked away. "You know, if I want, I can change her suit. We can practically play dress-up with her."

"Really?" David looked up, his eyes suddenly locked on her.

Death grinned at him. "We'll arm wrestle or fight to decide whose fantasy we get for the night."

She tried to keep her mind on the situation and figure out how to get Natalie to understand that she and Nathan were her top loves, but the way they stared at her made her squirm. It was like they were talking to each other telepathically.

Death chuckled as he put the drawer aside. "We'll share the fifty ideas we each just had later. Let's get shit packed. Hopefully, we can get you all a decent meal before he comes."

Jane hid her happiness over them behaving like this. She didn't know if they were doing it on purpose to cheer her up or if they genuinely were silly together. Either way, she loved that they had come so far and that Death seemed to develop a stronger urge to protect David and her family.

"I hope your brother is more mature than you," David said.

"I am mature." Death held a pair of her panties over himself.

"Jesus. Will you stop?" David snatched the panties away.

"Jesus wishes he looked like this."

David pinched the bridge of his nose and turned away.

Jane grinned as Death winked at her, but she got excited about meeting the third horseman. "Oh, what does Famine look like?"

"He looks just like me. So, sexy as far as you're concerned. You will probably drool like you do whenever you see me." Death snickered when David cut him a glare. "Actually, I suppose he looks very different because no one can achieve my beauty. Except for baby here."

"Stop complimenting yourself and respond to her question."

Death shrugged. "She'll see him when he comes. I don't really notice these things anyway. He has a wife, so you can stop panicking."

Jane stared at him wide-eyed. "He has a wife?"

"Well, not exactly—angels don't get married, but he is paired with another angel in the same way we are with our horses. We have just joked that she was his wife in the past because they fuck sometimes—she's never satisfied.

"She's actually the embodiment of hunger. She will follow him wherever he goes. If we are lucky, she will wait before coming. No one really stops how they work once they are set in motion. He will come, food will deplete, and once Hunger arrives and consumes everyone, hysteria will ensue. This is why we must leave as soon as possible. You are in an underground fortress filled with more immortals than humans and dwindling food and blood supplies. It's going to be disastrous for all present. No one will be able to fight the effects of Hunger, which always makes humans take drastic measures. Brothers will turn on each other, and parents will sacrifice their children to fill their stomachs. All humanity becomes lost. It mirrors Pestilence's plague. Only, it will be the living who kill and consume their kin."

"That's awful." Jane thought about all the parents she'd seen with their kids here. They were going to kill their babies.

"It will be difficult for you to witness," Death agreed. "The other issue is none of the light angels will be able to protect them from each other. They can only fight Hell's forces."

David looked up with a big smile. "But the Queen of Hell brought her army."

"Exactly." Death smiled, too. "She is their only hope."

Her soul lit up. "So, I can order my men to protect everyone?"

"They won't be able to stop everyone, but it will make a huge difference," Death said. "We will make sure the children, Adam, Arthur's humans, and the knights are a priority for your men."

Jane's pressed her lips together, then asked, "They'll fight each other, won't they?"

"Brother against brother, Sweet Jane." He smiled sadly. "We will have to keep the humans away from the strongest immortals. It will be easy to render a human unconscious, but then we must transport them. That's not a huge deal until you consider that hundreds or thousands of humans will rely on your army. They will have to choose which individuals to save if it comes down to protecting a warrior or an innocent. Since they are your men, they will follow your orders, which I know will be to protect the defenseless. Those who get away from Hunger will begin to restore order amongst themselves. The problem we face, though, is outside. The humans are susceptible to the elements, and Belial's men are circling the forest. We need a way to travel quickly while freeing up our warriors to fight them."

"But, even if we get the humans out and find a way to transport them, the immortals will be tearing each other apart inside," she whispered as she tried to steady her breathing.

David locked eyes with her. "Promise you will stay away from me. Let Death take the children and have him get all of you away. You know I'll survive because I'm the strongest. I will be your greatest threat, so don't stay behind for me."

Her eyes stung, and it felt like no oxygen was in her lungs, but she managed to whisper, "Okay."

He smiled sadly and turned away.

Jane slowly slid her gaze to Death. She wanted to tell him to protect David, even though she knew he'd live. And that was the problem. David would live, but how many lives would he be responsible for taking? What would that do to him? *I'll lose him anyway.*

Death's expression was blank when he said, "I'll stay with David."

"What?" David spun around. "No."

Death responded without tearing his eyes from hers. "I won't let her live without you. That includes keeping you the man you are for her. If you kill one of your brothers or the wives—anyone you come close to considering a friend or an innocent—it will change you forever. She knows that. We won't let that happen."

David immediately argued, "She might get attacked or hurt the children on her own."

Her angel shook his head. "She needs me to stay with you. I will make sure the children are guarded."

She gave her angel a teary smile. "Thank you, Death."

"Always, Sweet Jane."

David stayed quiet, and Jane forced herself not to look at him. She didn't want to break down crying at the thought of him doing something he couldn't forgive himself for. She wanted to make sure he believed she'd make it through this. Her men needed to believe she'd be okay, and that meant she had to find a way to keep her heart beating for them.

"Stop. I don't touch your weapons," David said before a smacking noise sounded.

She raised her gaze to see David smack Death's hand away from a knife he'd laid out on the bed.

"It sounds like you want to." Death smirked. "I'll pull mine out for you next time. Our baby is watching, and we don't want to make her jealous."

David sighed and handed him the knife he'd been trying to inspect.

"Thanks, babe." Death chuckled as David punched his shoulder.

"Grow up when serious matters are upon us." David handed him another drawer. "Select clothing ideal for where we are going."

"I know, Papi. I'll be serious now." Death held up a pair of David's battle-torn pants. "Are these assless chaps?"

"No." David glanced at her as a smile finally teased his lips. "Those are what's left of my pants when Jane is hungry for me."

Death tossed them at Jane. "Ay, Papi!"

Beelzebub crossed his arms as he glanced over the bed strewn with clothes. "Did you ask the children to pack your garments, my queen?"

"No, she let Death." David dropped a duffle bag on the floor. "So, never mind, basically a child."

"Jane doesn't think I'm a child." Death dodged the pillow rocketing toward his face.

"Behave," David said harshly, motioning for the knights to put their non-essential bags on the bed.

Death vanished without saying anything.

Jane looked up. "Where did he just go?"

Beelzebub tilted his head to the side as though he was listening to something. "Asmodeus has summoned him."

"Oh." Jane smiled at the two demons. "I'm sorry. Your names are so hard to say."

Succorbenoth and Sonneillon bowed their heads. "Apologies, my queen."

"Oh, don't apologize. Um, just forgive me if I mispronounce your names."

"Of course, my queen," they said.

"Right." Jane peeked at David. He didn't quite trust the room full of demons and fallen angels, but he was letting her do her thing. "So, we need to find someone to transport Arthur's blood rations before this goes. But if there's a way to salvage any of this, or for others to come back after we clear people—"

"We are awaiting Death's orders on where to take these items," Succorbenoth said. "Once he has a destination, we will begin immediately, my queen."

"Thank you." She smiled as they bowed before vanishing.

Gareth slung his arm over Jane's shoulder. "So, sis, who's alpha out of the Ds?"

She elbowed him, laughing. "Shut up."

He snickered, kissing her head. "As long as you're happy."

"I am." She gave him a side hug. "Thank you."

"Always, darling."

"Have you seen Adam? I sent a message for him to come here, but he hasn't shown up."

Gareth nodded. "He's with Artemis. She wants to stay close to Hades during the transport, but he's preparing just like the others."

"Okay." She chewed her lip as her eyes slid to Natalie and Nathan. They were still asleep.

"Have you heard from Arthur and Gwen?" She peeked at David, but he was busy with Gawain and Kay.

Gareth cringed. "Things are not looking so well."

"Oh, no." Jane pressed her lips together and waved David off when he looked at her.

When he returned to his conversation with Kay and Gawain, Gareth guided her outside.

He shut the door quietly and sighed, leaning against the wall. "He's not angry with David. In fact, David's pain is what he is most angry about—and Lancelot's. My memories are of Arthur and Lancelot being close, not David. So what has come out about David and Lancelot being best friends is difficult for us to accept.

"Try not to worry about it too much, though. You had nothing to do with what happened. Arthur is a wise immortal, and he will cope. Keep David's heart intact, though. Regardless of his sister's mistakes, she is still his sister, and Lance is the one who chose to turn into a monster. He knew David did not know the truth. Every one of them was responsible for the shit that happened, and it is up to them to figure out how they will mend their broken trust and relationships."

Jane looked up when a green glow flashed.

Death looked massive as he stood there, staring Gareth down. "Why is my girl out here?"

She frowned as Gareth tried to slide away.

Death put his hand on the wall, trapping Gareth, but he settled those emerald eyes on her. "Get in the room. Do not venture from David or me while we await Famine's arrival. Go."

"Don't leave me with him, Jane." Gareth clutched her hand.

Death bent down and glared at Gareth.

"Oh, fuck, this is the scariest sight." Gareth seemed to be trying to learn magic so he could vanish as he blinked over and over.

Jane threw her arms around Death's neck and jumped so he'd have to hold her. "Run, bro!"

Gareth dropped to the floor and almost broke the door to the room as he crawled inside and slammed it shut.

Death straightened as he dropped one hand to her ass to hold her up. "Next time, you will have to shove your tits in my face."

"Noted. Just promise you'll kiss them after biting." She laughed when his jaw dropped.

His eyes lowered to her breasts. "You realize I'm doing dirty things to you in my head right now, don't you?"

"I can tell."

His lips twitched with a smile. "That's not my dick, Jane. I snatched David's dagger when he wasn't looking."

"Give it back," came David's voice.

Jane yelped as her vampire plucked her from Death's hold and tucked her under his arm like a teddy bear. "And stop flirting with her out in the open."

Death gave David the knife. "She smells like both of us. I think they know she's mine too."

David carried her into the room. "Not the mortals."

Gareth was shielding himself with Nathan, who was finally awake. Natalie was with Gawain. And she looked at Jane with the same anger and sadness she had before.

David lowered Jane to her feet and took her hand as he walked them toward her daughter. "Princess, Mommy is going to give you a bath before we go eat. We are packing to move, and you will want to be nice and clean."

Natalie reached for David.

He took her from Gawain and carried her toward the bath while pulling Jane behind them.

When he put Natalie down and kissed her head to leave, she clutched his leg. "Not Mommy."

Jane's breath stilled in her chest, and she stared wide-eyed at her daughter.

David squatted down, holding Natalie by the shoulders. "Princess, Mommy is going to help you. I have matters I must take care of. Mommy wants to help you with your bath."

Natalie shook her head. "I want Aunt Gwen."

"No, princess." He managed to sound firm and caring. "Aunt Gwen is busy as well. Mommy has worked very hard to free up her duties while you slept so she could spend this time with you."

Her daughter wouldn't even look at her. "No. I hate her. I wish she were dead and Daddy were still here."

Jane couldn't take it that time. She walked out before David could stop her. Death was standing right outside the door, though. Instead of embracing her like she figured he would, he spun her around and marched her into the bathroom again.

His gaze and tone were fierce. "Do you know who I am, Natalie?"

David held his hand up for Death to stop. Jane was too paralyzed by his and Natalie's reactions to do anything.

Death ignored David and repeated his question. "Do you know who I am?"

Natalie flinched but nodded as her eyes welled up with tears.

"Do you know I heard every prayer you made for your mommy to come back to you?" Death's tone didn't soften even when Natalie shook her head, her eyes red. "Do you know how many times Mommy's time to go to the stars has happened?"

"No," Natalie cried.

Death glared at her. "Twenty-one times. That is because I kept her alive when she was supposed to go—when she was only five, just like you are right now. That means every year since then, I've had to push back her death. She's not supposed to be here!"

Natalie sobbed as David pulled her head to his shoulder.

Death pulled Jane in front of him and raised his voice. "Do you still want me to take her from you?"

"No," Natalie cried, reaching for Jane.

She tried to go to her, crying herself.

Death didn't let her. "Why? You hate her, don't you?"

"No," Natalie wailed.

"You screamed it just now," he was almost yelling. "Do you realize how much I love your mama? She's my soul. She gave me up for you, Nathan, and David. I gave her up for you to have her. Do you think she wants to hear this? Do you think I want to hear my sacrifice means nothing to you? Mommy's sacrifices?"

"No!" Natalie buried her face against David's shoulder.

"Death, that's enough," David said.

He ignored him. "Cherish these moments you have with her. I will not always be there to save her."

"I'm sorry, Momm-y." Natalie's chest heaved up and down as tears soaked David's shirt. "Don't take my mommy."

Death released Jane and turned away.

She went to Natalie, falling to her knees as she hugged her daughter. David pulled both of them onto his lap.

"I'm sorry, Mommy. Please don't leave."

"I won't. It's okay," Jane whispered, lifting her gaze in time to see Nathan rush to the doorway. He stared up at Death, and her angel picked him up without even a pause in his step and carried him out of the bathroom.

3 3

FAMINE

Jane smiled sadly when David pulled her against his side as they walked through the fortress. Death led the way with Gawain, Gareth, and their wives trailing behind him, while Jane carried Nathan and David toted Natalie.

She leaned her head against him for just a moment. He was trying to help, but she felt too disappointed in herself, and Natalie's feelings were still clear; she didn't want her to be her mom.

Yes, she had cried and said she didn't want her to die, but she still wanted nothing to do with Jane after her bath. It wasn't like Jane had expected things to be fixed right away, but she didn't think Natalie would immediately return to despising her.

Natalie had always been Daddy's girl, probably because Jane had to do so much for Nathan. Jason didn't know how to soothe Nathan or figure out what he needed, so he usually went for Natalie. It made sense she and her daughter wouldn't know how to be around each other, and now without Jason there for Natalie to turn to when someone else took up her time, she felt abandoned.

Jane frowned, hiding her whimper under a cough as pressure suddenly manifested in the center of her chest. The noise, unfortunately, pulled Natalie's gaze to Jane's for a moment, and when Jane tried to smile, her daughter whined and turned to hide her face against David's neck.

Jane looked forward, trying to ignore David soothing Natalie. But all that she could think of was how Natalie had run to Ragnelle when Jane had gone to pick her up to leave their room. No one seemed to know what to do, and Jane had been the most unsure of how to make things right.

Was she supposed to wrestle her out of Elle's arms—force her to stay when she didn't want to be near her? Jane didn't know where to begin or where she had messed up in the short period between the bath and reentering the room with the others.

She didn't know where to turn. There wasn't a single direction that would make things better. Failing and not being enough had always been her fear. But it seemed impossible to do the right thing. It seemed failing was all she could do.

Jane's eyes and nose burned as her throat ached and closed up. But it was like a dam had broken as tiny rivers flowed down her cheeks. She didn't wipe them away. She didn't allow Gawain to comfort her, or even Death, when he turned his head, catching sight of her scrunched-up face as she tried to regain her composure.

Her angel's empty expression made her feel worse. She knew his words were partly intended for her. He'd given her up for her family, so she could raise her kids and be with Jason at first and now David. He was telling her his sacrifice meant nothing if she gave up. It was a blurred reflection of how she felt about her shortcomings with Natalie. He suffered each time he watched her give up on being a mom—each time she thought about dying. So, like her angel, she could only do half the job. She kept Natalie safe from sexual predators, but she hadn't been there for her in the way Natalie wanted her to be.

That was always Jane's problem, though. She couldn't find a balance between being a mom, a girlfriend, a broken soul mate, a warrior, and a queen. It went right back to what she'd always believed: she wasn't enough. Everything she'd given Jason hadn't been enough to keep him loving her. Even staying home and ensuring she watched their kids every second hadn't brought them happiness or been enough to show them she loved them so dearly. So, she didn't know what options she had. Did she devote her every moment to her kids again, despite her not being the type of mom Natalie wanted? Did she fight for their chance to have a life? Did she let David and Death love her or push them away so she could be a mom?

Jane sniffled, shaking her head at Death as she finally wiped away her tears. He looked forward again, but his muscles twitched as he clenched his hands repeatedly.

Those thoughts of her kids finding a better mom in someone else came forward. The fear of David having a woman who loved only him—gave all of herself to him—and had no angels her soul needed to function—no angels that kept her alive in every way.

More hot tears escaped, and she squeezed her eyes shut for a few seconds when David took her hand.

When she opened them, Nathan lifted his head and watched her smile through the agony destroying everything good she had started to accept about herself.

Her little boy watched her for a moment longer before letting his gaze drift away and finally resting his head on her shoulder again.

Jane felt like such a failure. She felt weak. Greatness was not supposed to fall at the uttering of a few words. Yet, she was doing so right between her pillars of strength.

Death slowed until he finally stopped. He stared at the ground for a few seconds before turning and pulling Natalie from David and motioning for David to take Nathan from her.

Jane thought he was preparing to render Natalie unconscious, and she was about to stop him, but he didn't put Natalie to sleep. Instead, he held Natalie, meeting her stare before he reached out to wipe the tears from Jane's cheek.

His efforts were futile because she could not stop crying, but he smiled at Jane before holding Natalie out for her to take.

She hesitated but slowly pulled her daughter from him. Natalie's little face was just as scrunched up as her own, and her eyes were red from the strain of containing her tears. Her daughter had managed, but Jane had not. Natalie was stronger than she would ever be.

Death tilted Jane's chin up. "It's not that you are not good enough, angel. You are. Just like she is." He turned Natalie's face toward him. "You are just like your mama, little one. You are both enough. You are both worth loving, and you are loved by each other. These feelings exist inside you because you doubt yourself and are hurting. But you, Natalie, have what your mama didn't: a mother—a warrior goddess willing to suffer so you never have to. Even when she was supposed to go to the stars, even when it hurt so badly she wanted to go to them anyway, she stayed for you. When she was too lost to see how much she meant to you, I kept her here because I knew she would always find the strength to get back up for you."

Jane wanted to bawl at his words, but she could only stare through her tears as he continued in his beautiful, soothing voice.

"She is doing all of this for you," he said. "She is trying to be bigger—

better, but she had no mother to guide her. She does not know what it feels like to be protected by a mother and father, but she's giving you everything she did not have when she was a little girl.

"But you must know something about your mama. She only knows how to fight monsters—how to survive their attacks. How to stay aglow in the dark. What she knows no longer helps you.

"Mama can slay demons with her bare hands, but she cannot be like the other mommies you see. Those mommies know how to be mommies. Your mama is a warrior queen trying to save lives she will never know. But, most of all, she is the mama who wants to give her babies a chance to live a life she never got to.

"She may have walked away, but she was never going to leave you. She just didn't want you to see this." He turned her toward Jane. She was a mess, of course. Death wiped Jane's tears again. "It hurts to see her this way, doesn't it?"

Natalie nodded as her eyes watered.

"She's always protecting you, even when she leaves. Sometimes it's from this. She hides her pain because she is never better, Natalie. She has a lot of sadness that will never really go away, so she cannot always keep her tears in.

"The bravest warriors have the biggest hearts. They do not want to fail. They don't feel they deserve any support because everyone expects them to do it all alone—to lead. So they turn away.

"Her desire is for you to live. But, in your world, she has to fight, so you have that chance because the monsters are too many now. That is why she leaves with the other warriors.

"You must cherish the moments when she returns and remember that while she was away, she burned within, but she roared and slayed the monsters so they would not find you. Fighting monsters makes one strong. It makes one capable of cruelness others cannot withstand. And during those moments, she must remove or repair her armor, or that cruelness and weakness might escape. So she hides, walks away, and takes out her fury on one who is strong enough." He lifted Jane's free hand and pressed it to his chest. "She must let him absorb and soothe those flames that might burn you."

Jane's heart and soul cried.

Death smiled at Jane. "Mama is trying. She will learn how to be the mama she wants to be for you. I will shield and soothe her so she can have more days close to you, and she will learn how to be a warrior and mama.

"But know that Mama is only half. That is why she cannot be both. That is why she always chooses one love before switching to the next. When half is all she can give, she gives all of it. When she is full—whole— she will finally be able to divide herself."

Jane couldn't speak. She could barely think.

Natalie touched her cheek as she stared into her eyes. "Her green is gone."

Jane sobbed, covering her mouth.

Death nodded to Natalie as he pulled Jane's hand away and held it to his cheek. "Do you see?"

Natalie's little face scrunched up again as she looked between Death's eyes and Jane's. "Whole."

Death smiled at her daughter. "We will be again. For now, know that when I touch her—when she comes to me—she's remembering what it felt like when I was with her always. And when she sits between David and me, we try to make her whole and bring her home. That is why she glows so pretty when you see her between us. One day, I will find her again and protect and complete her the way I was meant to. Then she will be what she has always wanted to be for you and your brother."

He leaned down, tilting Jane's face up so he could kiss her softly. Jane pressed her lips against his, crying as he kissed her tears.

"Time," he said, pressing a final kiss to Jane's forehead. "Give us time. We are trying to find each other still."

Finally, Natalie hugged Jane. She did not cry as Jane did, but she trembled, tightening her arms around Jane's neck and only calming when David caressed her back.

Death nuzzled Jane's cheek before whispering in her ear, "This is the battle you fight alone, Sweet Jane. When we find each other, you will already have conquered the one who truly stopped you from being all you desired. Yourself." He kissed her jaw. "Now give her all you are capable of, my love. I will watch for monsters." He straightened and walked away before she could speak.

David chuckled, pulling her back against his chest. He tilted her face up and rubbed away her tears. "He does not know how to be whole without you. But he's doing a better job than he thinks. So are you."

A sniffling sound came from behind them.

David turned and shook his head. "Really?"

Gawain rubbed his red eyes. "What? I'm not crying because when he speaks of his love for Jane, it's the most beautiful thing I have ever heard. I just have dust in my eyes."

Jane squeezed her daughter, smiling when Gareth let out a cry.

"Oh, my dear husband." Lyonesse laughed sadly.

"It is only dust." Gareth blew his nose in the handkerchief his wife held up. "Dammit. I cannot believe I did not see it. Her eyes are gold. Her eyes are not supposed to be gold."

David smiled down at Jane again. "No, they are not. They are meant to dance with emerald fire."

"My blasted heart." Gawain stomped past them but turned and walked to Jane, hugging her and Natalie. "I see. I will help him find you, sissy."

Jane gave him the best teary grin she could. Gawain took in her eyes once more before making an anguished noise and leaving, pulling Elle with him.

"And to think we wanted to gang up on him when we first saw him," Gareth said, sniffling. "You're a good mom as you are, but I cannot wait to see you when you are truly whole and home. I will always help these two find you and help you fight the monsters so you don't always have to."

Jane kissed his cheek before he led his wife down the hall.

"Shall we go find Mommy's angel while we eat?" David asked.

Natalie sniffled. "I will be bigger, Mama. I'll help Nathan."

"No, baby." Jane kissed her forehead. "My wish for you is to stay small for as long as you can. I never got to. I grew up when I was five. Stay little, my loves."

David turned his head, and she knew he was hiding his emotions as he guided them to the banquet hall.

They stopped as soon as they turned the corner. Jane's breath hitched as she stared ahead.

There her angel stood in all his glory. His massive wings were outstretched as he stood across from a man dressed in a black suit. It wasn't the Devil, though. He was almost a mirror image of Death. Only, he had very pale skin, black eyes, and long black hair tied into a half topknot. He was not quite as tall as Death, and he was much leaner than him as well. When his dark eyes slowly shifted to her, and the corner of his mouth twitched with the faintest smile, she knew immediately who he was.

"Famine," she whispered, gasping as his suit transformed, revealing the black armor resembling a samurai's before returning to the black suit.

The entire hall gasped, some screaming in fear as it became clear they were staring at the rider of the black horse.

"Horsemen Bringer." He bowed his head. "I must admit, though, I prefer Sweet Jane."

Jane darted her eyes around, waiting for all hell to break loose.

"She is not with me," he said as his gaze slid down her body. "So small but so powerful."

Several flashes of light erupted around her, and Jane found herself surrounded by her general and the Princes of Hell.

Famine chuckled before glancing at Death. "Merely introducing myself, brother. And I came to bestow my gift."

Death flapped his wings. He was shaking, his aura pulsing with emerald light. "Jane?"

David tightened his hand on hers.

"Let her come, David. This must be done." Death held out a hand but kept his gaze on his brother.

Jane realized now that he would not be like Pestilence and War.

"Gawain," she whispered, kissing Natalie's cheek. "Stay with Gawain."

Natalie tried to cling to her, but she let go when Famine glanced her way. It was not a threatening look, more so curiosity as his dark eyes moved between Natalie, David, and Nathan.

David finally let her go, but he handed Nathan to Ragnelle and stood in front of them.

"She is lovely, brother." Famine studied Jane's face once she reached Death's side.

"Where is Pest? He was supposed to hold you." Death kept Jane slightly behind him.

A faint smirk formed on his lips. "Why do you think I am alone? He is providing a distraction."

War shimmered into view on Jane's other side.

"Hello, brother." Famine nodded to War. "You have kept me busy as of late."

"Time?" War asked.

"Tomorrow," Famine answered instantly.

"Which of us must go?" War asked next.

"You must move on." Famine tilted his head as he continued staring at her. "Make haste, and I will follow sooner rather than later."

War scoffed before turning to Jane. "Get on with it, Tex. Perhaps you will have one last chance to tie your thread."

Famine smiled, and it was gorgeous. "Ah, I do see it. Hidden beautifully." His gaze moved between Jane, David, and Death. "Magnificent."

War nodded. "A masterpiece."

Famine held out his hand. "Hello, beauty. I desire to bond with you before it is too late."

Jane darted her gaze to Death. He didn't look right. He was staring past Famine as though he was seeing something else.

"Jane?" War nudged her.

"Oh." She carefully placed her hand in Famine's. "Hello, Horseman."

He grinned, kissing her fingers. *Tingles.* He smiled wider. "Ah, that is a lovely sensation. I would yearn for it as well. A gift for you now."

"Yes, thank you." She sighed, closing her eyes as he cupped her cheeks and tilted her face up. She felt her tears gather. She missed these tingles— the hot and cold that swam under her skin, seeping into her pores until they sought out her soul. "Thank you."

"You are welcome." He chuckled, kissing her forehead. "However, that enchanting magic you two create is not my gift."

"Oh." She stared up at him.

"When Hunger finds you, fear not the depravation afflicting those around you and think of me. I will save you from yourself in the darkest of hours. Never will you be one of the ravenous. For I am Famine, Sweet Jane, and I am yours to bring." He leaned down, his black eyes growing darker, and pressed his lips to hers.

Feeling like she had thirsted for a drop of water for days, the taste of honey, fire, and leather swirled around her tongue. She swallowed his kiss, clutching his shirt and moaning softly as her belly warmed. It spread across her skin, touching every inch of her body.

Famine smiled against her mouth and murmured, "Lovely. I cannot wait for you to find them."

Jane sighed, closing her eyes as she felt the warmth of the sun on her face while love, beauty, and strength pressed up against her back.

The Horseman moved his mouth to her ear. "It is right to crave them. They are meant to hold you. Know this, though: there will always be a great price for you to pay, beautiful angel."

"What if I can't pay it?"

Famine leaned far enough away to look into her eyes. "Fear not, they will find you. They will roar as they seek your flame until you entwine yourselves in love's embrace again. They are yours even after the end of time." He smoothed her hair away from her face. "And no matter the cost, the Horsemen and those who cherish your heart most will follow you."

"Thank you, Famine," she whispered, mesmerized by her reflection in his dark eyes. She didn't want to let go of him. She wanted to beg for him to stay because he allowed her to feel her loves entirely.

He released her and bowed his head. "Always, beauty who dances in the dark."

David and Death gently pulled her away. Famine smiled alongside War as they stared at the three of them.

"Intricate, isn't it?" Famine tilted his head, observing them.

"Masterful." War nodded before bowing his head to Jane. "I must bid you farewell."

Jane frowned, looking between Death and Famine. Then it dawned on her. "You can't be together at once."

War caressed her cheek. "I pray you find happiness during your time together, Jane. Cherish every moment with those you love."

Her eyes watered, and she covered his hand. She knew the brothers were more aware than perhaps even Death. It was as if Death had been entirely blind when looking upon her. She did not want to ask why this felt like goodbye for good. She knew the men by her side could not stand to hear such a thing. So, she smiled bravely. "Until we meet again, War."

He bent and kissed her forehead. "Yes, until we meet again, Tex."

She almost cried, but she continued to smile through the sorrow drowning her.

War looked over her head. "Behave, little monster." He bowed again. "Little prince, take care of your sister." He patted David's shoulder. "Love your goddess as often as you can and keep my brother in line, Sir David."

David grinned and shook his hand. "I will simply ask her to wreak havoc when he crosses that line."

War laughed heartily as he nodded to Arthur and the other knights. "Fight well, boys." He smiled one more time at Jane before letting out a whistle.

Various flashes of red and white light signaled all who were in War's army had vanished.

"Brother." War bowed lower. "Love her well."

Then he disappeared.

Jane squeezed Death's hand. She could not tell his feelings, but she knew he must be panicking.

"Tomorrow, brother." Famine smiled at her. "Sleep well, beauty." He vanished in a black mist.

Jane tugged Death's hand. "Are you okay?"

He slowly glanced down at her, staring at her as though he had never seen her before. Or perhaps he had not seen her in a very long time.

"Death?" David carefully began to pull her away.

Her angel gripped her hand tightly. "I see." He glanced at his arm before looking at David, confused.

"What do you see?" she asked, stepping closer.

He cupped her cheek. "I see—"

Arthur rushed forward and gripped Death's shoulder. "Wait."

Death nodded, but he picked Jane up and hugged her.

"Everyone, feed yourselves. Keep order and return to your quarters. At dawn, we will begin organizing the evacuations. Law will be maintained. Gather your necessities and cherished items, and do not panic."

Humans and immortals disregarded his command and rushed to the lines to get food. Jane's demons kept many from crushing others, and Arthur walked to David as he motioned for Gawain and Elle to come close.

Jane tried to reach for her kids, but Arthur held up a hand.

He turned to her children. "This is one of those nights Mommy must be alone with these two. You must stay with Gawain and Elle. You will see her in the morning."

"It's okay, Mama," Natalie said as she tore her eyes from Death. "We'll be okay."

"I will take good care of them, Jane," Gawain said.

"Thank you." Jane gave them big smiles, hating she had to leave but trusting she must stay close to Death and David; something had changed. "We'll see you first thing. Behave and sleep when it's bedtime."

"Yes, Mama," they said.

"I will get them enough to eat for the day and morning," Gareth said before walking into the massive crowd with his wife.

"Get a good meal, take it to your quarters, and stay there until dawn." Arthur smiled, patting David's cheek. "You will see. It is beautiful, brother."

Jane touched Death's cheek before she turned and saw David watching them. She smiled at his lost expression and held out her hand.

Her vampire grabbed it quickly. "Are you all right?"

"I think so." She grinned at Death again, not sure why she felt happy and not at all distressed.

Her angel slid his hand under her outstretched one. "I know how to create the bond. It takes time, but we must begin it tonight."

"Why?" Jane pulled their hands to her lips and kissed each one, knowing her soul was guiding her as she looked between her two men.

486

Death stared into her eyes. "Just trust me."

"I do." She held their hands to her cheeks. "Let me down so I can give them hugs."

Death nodded, lowering her to her feet.

David held her waist, and Death stared at the contact intensely, almost like he was waiting to ensure she was okay with her vampire.

Eventually, he removed his hand and breathed out, relieved. "Go ahead. I must speak to some of the others first." He kept his eyes locked on David's hold on her.

"We'll see you in a bit, okay?" Jane smiled at her angel, trying to figure out what was bothering him.

"Yes." He lifted his gaze to hers, then suddenly grabbed her face and kissed her. It was a hurried but breath-stealing kiss. "I love you."

There was something definitely wrong or very right.

She kissed him back. "And I love you."

He let her go, and it looked incredibly difficult for him to do so. "Don't h —" He shook his head as his eyes met David's baffled stare. "I will be there shortly. Just don't—" He tore his eyes from hers and vanished before finishing what he was about to say.

Asmodeus bowed. "I will have your items removed from the room before you arrive. They will wait for you at the gates in the morning."

David tugged Jane toward the kids. "Let's make sure they get to the room. Then we will meet him and find out what has happened."

"Okay." Jane started to follow David, but she turned to Asmodeus. "Please speak with Adam. I don't want him to get too far from us tomorrow."

"Of course, my queen. Enjoy the rest of your time in Valhalla." Asmodeus vanished.

Jane pulled Natalie from Gawain as David took Nathan, and they hurried out of the hall as it became increasingly crowded.

"Gold." Nathan pointed at Jane. "Blue." He touched David's cheek.

David nodded as he pushed aside some humans running toward the hall. "Yes, Mommy has gold eyes right now, and I have blue eyes."

"Blue too hot."

David frowned but quickly smiled. "Does he mean it the way you say it, baby?"

She chuckled, blowing out a breath when he winked at her. David carrying her son was seriously sexy.

Gawain pushed aside a green-haired set of women as Ragnelle bared her fangs, but he laughed. "I do not think Nathan means it the way Jane does. Perhaps you are looking forward to your evening and struggling to hide your excitement."

"Hey, why did those women have green hair and eyes?" Jane tried to peer around.

David tugged her to his side. "Rusalka. Russian vampire-type creatures. No, you cannot meet that group."

"Why?"

He grinned. "They did not think I was serious when I said I had a woman. Don't worry—Artemis staked your claim, as promised."

Jane stuck her tongue out at him. "They look like mermaids. I want green hair now."

Ragnelle shoved another vampire. "It does look very exotic. I believe it would suit you nicely, Jane."

David gave her a dark look. "Baby, you are already my mermaid. No green hair unless you really want it."

"Green." Nathan nodded. "Green."

Jane smiled. "I probably couldn't pull it off. I think I just miss my green."

"You could pull it off, my love." David pulled her aside, growling at a group of males until they rushed away. He started talking again as though chaos was not already ensuing inside the fortress. "And we may get your green sooner than we thought."

"Don't get your hopes up, Jane." Gawain peeked back at her. "Just be happy."

David grinned. "We are happy."

There were some yells and flashes of red light before they could grow louder.

David squeezed her hand.

"Will we make a new home?" Natalie whispered.

"Yes, baby. And Mommy and David will try to get you your own bed. How is that?"

Natalie nodded. "So you can be whole."

Ragnelle covered her heart as she gave Jane a sad smile.

Jane hugged her baby girl, closing her eyes as more yells from the dining rooms were cut off by the sound of swords meeting flesh. "Thank you. I promise I will make sure we have time for just us. We can even try to meet your new friends."

Natalie squeezed Jane's neck. "They did not stay nice friends."

She sighed, hugging her tighter. "One day the right friends will come to you."

"I want an angel."

Jane chuckled, stopping at the door to Gawain's room. He and Ragnelle turned, waiting as they kissed their babies good night.

"See you for our trip, Mama." Natalie touched her cheek before going to David.

"See you in the morning, princess. Behave now." David gave Nathan a final kiss. "See you tomorrow, little man."

"Night." Natalie waved.

"Have fun," Ragnelle said.

Gawain smiled, but he looked a little sick. "Just don't elaborate tomorrow."

"I did not plan on sharing our intimacies with you, brother. Make sure they eat." David patted Gawain before kissing Ragnelle's cheek. "Thank you."

"Shoo." Ragnelle winked, shutting the door.

As soon as it closed, David lifted Jane. His hand was on her ass, and his lips were feverishly devouring her mouth as he walked toward their room. Jane threw her arms around his neck, smiling when he managed to clear a way for them to pass while never breaking the kiss.

"I could make love to you right here." He kissed down her neck, sucking hard. "Is it weird I hope this does involve us making love to you?"

"Oh God. Hurry." Jane gasped, picturing them tangled together. "Oh, do you think he's getting lube?"

David lifted his head, laughing before he claimed her lips again. "I guess we shall see when he gets here."

"I'm here."

Her entire body erupted in goosebumps as they paused to see Death standing in the doorway to their room.

He scanned them as well before moving aside. "Get in."

David didn't argue, but he did ask, "Are you all right?"

Death shut the door as he gestured to the bed. "I'll explain later. Right now—I need to feel her body between us." He tossed his jacket aside. "This time, we are both alpha."

Oh, shit.

34

OUR GODDESS

After Death's words, Jane had almost expected him to rip her free from David and throw her onto the bed. So it was a bit of a shock when he locked the door and carefully took her from David. He kissed her cheek as he placed her on her feet and then led her and David to the foot of the bed.

Jane looked up as her angel smiled down at her.

He caressed her cheek, lightly tracing his finger down her scar before he took her hand and did the same to the one she had there. She always forgot her scars now, so seeing the pale raised skin, she frowned. Those were painful memories. It wasn't how she'd gotten the wounds that hurt, though. That first battle upon landing in Asgard had nearly killed her. Throughout the fight, she had expected to have Death come to her aid. But he hadn't. That's what hurt.

"I should have always protected you," he murmured. "From the moment you were born, I should have been there with you, keeping you safe."

He lifted his gaze to her face. "You were kept hidden from me, but I should have known you were mine when I saw you. I did know. My soul did, at least. That is why I came for you myself. I felt you, heard you call for me when there should not be a soul on Earth able to summon me. You did. When I saw you, I should have understood what I was seeing in the beautiful little girl before me, but how could I? No angel has ever been given a true soul mate. All I knew was I could not let you pass on. So I kept you alive—pushed back your time—something I have never done for another.

"I did not know what to do beyond that. Still, I should have done something when I watched you go unconsoled, but I did not bother to find a way to get you to a loving and safer environment, and I pushed down the urge to take you away. That is understandable, of course—you were a human child. But at the very least, I could have taken you away from that family. It would have been difficult, but nothing should have stopped me. Not for you, Sweet Jane. Yet, I used every excuse that arose to stay away.

"Those boys should never have touched you. I realize now, even before we bonded, I felt you hurting. My soul urged me to go to you, roared for me to stop everything and get to you, but I stuck to my duties. I will never forgive myself for not being there when you needed me. I will always regret I did not tell you how much I loved you the moment I realized I did. And I should have kissed you longer when you were brave enough to tell me you loved me."

Breathing became difficult, and Jane's heart started to burn.

"*Shh* . . . I must say this." He smiled sadly. "I should have let you choose your path instead of choosing for you. I should have held you when you read that text from Wendy—when Jason first looked upon you with disdain."

He smiled again, then lightly gripped her chin. "I should have taken you and shown you how it felt to be loved by a man when I realized you had no idea. When you cried in the shower after he was satisfied, I should have beaten the shit out of him, then taken you away, told you everything about us, and helped you with your babies. I should have revealed myself when the plague arrived at your home. I should have ensured your family was safe instead of only caring about your survival. I should've confronted this vampire when he called you his."

He smirked at David before focusing on her again. "I shouldn't have been afraid to see you fall in love with him. That is why I left instead of forcing myself to duplicate. I saw it in your eyes—felt your heart yearning to be near him even though your mind and soul told you he was not what he claimed to be for you. I knew I would lose you when he smiled at you, but when he failed to keep you safe and I saw Lucifer watching you, I devised a way to keep you. I no longer cared he was supposed to be your soul mate. He had failed, and I was through with watching everyone fail you. But even after I revealed myself, you could not keep your eyes and heart from seeking him out."

Jane sniffled, smiling sadly when David began to push her closer to Death.

Her angel shook his head and kept David from letting go when he began to pull away. "She chose you before she knew she did." Death cupped her cheeks and kissed her softly.

She whimpered, pressing her lips against his harder because it did not feel the same as it used to. Their magic was still absent, and she knew it broke Death as much as it did her.

Death grinned against her mouth. "It's okay."

"I'm sorry." She gripped his wrist.

"You didn't know, angel." He sighed, kissing her once more before looking at David. "I thought I could let her go again. I intended to leave so you could properly win her heart, but when they attacked her again, I could not wait for you to save her."

David smiled at them and told her angel, "You saved her in more ways than slaying demons that night in Texas. I thought I had lost her forever." He put his hands on her waist and lifted her between them, placing Death's arms around her instead of his. "You brought her out of the dark. I thought that fire in her eyes was gone, but you relit her flame."

Death closed his eyes and pressed his forehead to hers. "Her flame," he whispered. "My gold flame."

Jane gasped as her suit changed from the tight-fitting bodysuit to a shimmering gold corset and thong. "Death," she whispered, sliding her hand down her body, tracing the dark-gold swirling designs along the bodice until she reached the fringed skirt along the bottom.

"Our gold flame." He nuzzled her cheek before kissing her scar. "Our goddess." He lifted her hand, kissing it. "Our Jane."

Her mouth opened as she watched him slide his lips over her hand, and almost as if he had painted her with liquid gold, her skin began to glisten with gold where there had once been pink and white scars.

He smiled as he lifted his head. "Do you like it?"

She nodded. "It's beautiful."

Death grinned, lowering her to her feet. He turned her to face David as he knelt and pressed his lips to her leg.

David was frozen. He didn't even appear to be breathing.

"Do you see it, David?" Death asked as he stood. He pulled Jane flush against him but kept her facing David. "Yes, I think you do."

David blinked before darting his eyes between Jane and Death. His hand shook as he held it toward her, then pulled it back.

"It's okay," Death said, carefully raising Jane's hand until they touched.

"Baby." He looked between her eyes. "She's—"

"Her," Death said before David could finish.

David nodded. "She is ours."

Jane smiled at David, her heart fluttering when he smiled back.

Death tilted her head so he could see her. "You have been trying to tie the three of us together, but he needed to see he was always meant to be with you for his soul to accept it. My question for you is: would you like David to be your soul mate?"

She frowned and darted her eyes over to David. "I don't understand."

"I will help you bond with David. He has always been destined to stand at your side." Death rubbed her cheek. "One day, you will see what I have. Until then, trust me when I say it was never only me you were meant to be loved by. Another was made just for you, and he is staring at you in complete awe because he sees his fiery goddess all over again."

"Again?" She watched David while he still searched every inch of her face.

"Yes." He motioned for David to come closer. "Do you want him? As he says, beyond forever?"

"Yes, but—" She looked at him. "What about you—us?"

He smiled. "I am always yours. Now answer me. This is something he was not given but deserves in every way, maybe even more than me. So do you want him this way? I will not force you to bond, but if you want to, I want you to have him."

She didn't hesitate. "I want him."

"David?" Death chuckled at his dazed look.

Her vampire still looked confused but amazed. "How is this—"

Death cut him off. "You understand now that you truly do not have a soul mate, but you see your soul, don't you? It's showing you something special, isn't it?"

The strain in his eyes winded her.

"I see," he said softly. "But I will—"

"You won't," Death said. "That's why I'm here. I've always been here, but your soul withdrew when I separated from her. He's back now, but like I said, I am here. Now do you wish to bond with her—make her your soul mate?"

"Yes." David dropped his gaze to where Death held her arm. "But—"

"Tying the three of us together will take time, but since I am her soul mate, even a separated one, I can help forge this bond for her tonight. It will be different from the bond I shared with her, but you will be soul mates. Just as you should have always been."

"What about our bond?" Jane looked at Death, hopeful. "Does this mean you and I will be the same again? We'll be us?"

He smiled sadly. "Maybe. We cannot truly be broken. Our love went beyond soul mates, but what matters is that David finally becomes bonded to you this way. He already sees only you, and you have chosen each other more than you will understand right now. We must do this tonight, though. I don't know when we will have another chance."

Her heart ached. She wanted David to be hers, and she wanted to be his, but she had a feeling Death would suffer from it. "Death, I can't lose or hurt you." She darted her gaze to David. "I want this, but if you and I are going to be ripped further—" Tears fell freely. "My loves, I can't choose."

David smiled, wiping her tears. "You can stay with him. I will keep both of you."

Death turned her, tilting her face up. "Sweet Jane, nothing will take me from you. I am yours. You were made for me." He smiled, trailing his fingers along her golden scar. "But there is so much clear to me now, and I desire to see you tied to him. I swear we will continue attempting to reform our bond—we should never have separated. But it was done. I trust we will find each other again."

She bobbed her head. "We will. I promise to never stop searching for a way to get you back."

David rubbed her side. "We will wait for you. I won't let her go without you for too long."

Death lifted her, pulling her by the back of her neck until their noses touched. "We will be one again. For now, we will join the only ways we can, and David will warm your soul with his. He burns hotter than even Lucifer's light. That is why he hesitated to touch you just now. He saw something that you will be shown one day. It is invisible to most, but we see it."

"I want to know now."

He gave her that smile that made her soul dance. "I know. I promise you will see, and you will be happy we did this tonight."

"What about Lucifer's light? You said it's acting as part of my soul—supplementing it. You said his light would keep you away. Won't it do the same to him?"

"David's flame is unique, just like ours. He can do what no other soul can—burn hotter than Lucifer." He kissed her as David pressed his lips to

494

her shoulder. "Now that his soul is aware, he will be too hot for your lovely flame, but that's why you have me. I will cast my grace over yours to protect you from his fire. That is why I said only I can help you bond with him. I am stronger. I can shield your soul. I am simply not tied or mixed with you now, but you will be tied to him if we do this."

"Only if you both want to," David murmured against her skin.

"We do." Death kissed her smiling lips. "Now, undress, Prince. Watch until your soul guides you to take her with me. She'll be ready for you then."

David dragged his hand down her back, squeezing her waist. "Baby?"

"I want your soul to burn next to mine," she whispered, turning her face toward his. "I want to be your soul mate."

"You're already my soul mate." He kissed her firmly before stepping away. "But it will be a gift to feel that connection."

She didn't let him move far. Then, gripping his shirt, she turned back to Death and whispered against his lips, "Undress me together."

Death shook his head. "Next time. This will be the last time you are only mine. It must be this way for his bond to take. He—and his soul—need to see me with you. I swear we will be gentler in the future."

David kissed her head. "Trust him, Jane. It will make sense for you when it's time."

"Okay." She touched Death's cheek.

Death pulled her lips to his and carried her away from David. His kiss consumed her so much that she could only focus on him. She gasped for air, but he pulled her back, pushing his tongue into her mouth as his arms flexed around her.

Her back met the mattress, and she smiled when he leaned back to look at her. "Beautiful," she whispered, reaching for him.

He grabbed her hands, sliding his fingers between hers as he pinned her arms by her head. "My angel."

Jane moaned, tightening her legs around his waist.

Death's shirt disappeared, and she was staring at a god. So perfect. Nothing about him could possibly look better.

Gold light lit up his face, and he smiled. "There's my gold goddess."

She realized her light was shining out of her, but she was casting a golden glow instead of the usual silver and white.

Death let go of one hand before dragging his down her body. His lips were on hers when his fingers slid between her legs.

The faint tingles made her see stars, and she cried out as he shifted her panties aside. Her entire body jolted, and she dropped her hand to his side, realizing he'd ordered his pants away. He teased her core for only a few seconds before thrusting his full length into her.

"Death," she gasped, clinging to him as he kept going deeper, faster.

His lips pressed against her neck as he whispered, "He must see this."

Jane whimpered. She didn't want to hurt David, but she knew Death wasn't doing this for just himself.

But it felt so good.

She gripped his shoulders, raising her hips and moaning when he growled.

"Look at him, Jane." Death grunted, bending her so he could roll onto his back. He groaned, holding her hips as he stared up at her. She only got to ride him briefly before he seemed to lose focus. "Fuck, come here." He pulled her down but thrust upward, fast and hard.

Jane moaned, unable to do anything but feel him moving in and out of her as she listened to his satisfied grunts.

Just as she began to cry out and shake, he slowed and sat them up. She caught her breath, but he raised her up and down until she started doing it herself.

"Oh, yes," she cried when he rocked his hips, meeting her movements. He was making her whole body come to life. Her vision got blurry, but it was so good.

"Look at him," he whispered, sucking on her neck.

Jane turned, gasping when she saw David watching. He was furious. "Death, we need to stop."

"Not yet." He wrapped his arms around her, securing her to him as he raised her up and down. Jane couldn't pull her eyes from David's. She didn't understand why Death would make him watch if it upset him.

"I need to come, Jane. Now look at me. Love me this once. Just me."

"But he's mad."

"It has to be this way." He pulled her down, rocking forward.

She threw her head back, putting in the effort now to satisfy him as he was her. "Oh, yes. Oh, fuck, don't stop."

Death tore off her corset and ripped away her panties. She felt him swelling inside her as she went faster. There was barely any heat, but the faint tingles were torturing her when they stayed just out of reach. She wanted to touch them, and she could see him trying to feel them, too, as her light surrounded his face.

"That's it, angel." Death pulled her mouth to his. "I'll miss you. Don't forget me."

"I won't forget." Tears sprang to her eyes as she cried, her orgasm destroying her and putting her together again when he came.

"Close your eyes and take my grace, Jane." He pushed his tongue in her mouth as he held her down, filling her in a way that jolted her entire body. The room shook, and she squeezed her eyes shut even though she wanted to watch the gold and green light spinning around them.

Shocks rushed down her throat, but she could only focus on the fire starting to surround her back.

She screamed as soon as David touched her skin. He was hotter than anything she'd ever felt.

Death shoved him back. "Wait."

David snarled, but the burn he'd caused simmered. Jane breathed out, basking in Death's presence now.

"There you go, angel." Death lifted her enough to move them off the bed. He slid back inside her but moved slower, sweeter, as he backed her into David. "Good girl. She's ready now."

She kissed him, gasping when she felt David's searing kiss on the nape of her neck. It felt like he was branding her, but she sighed, loving the heat again. It blanketed her, but there was something so soothing between them, shielding her.

Death's Grace.

David spoke in a different language, and she shivered at the husky tone as his dick nudged her back.

Death replied in the same language, shifting his hold as David guided him.

Their deep voices caused a tingle between her legs. "Oh, fuck, y'all are going to make me come just talking like that." She reached for David.

He kissed her cheek and lined himself up with her ass. "I see you, my love."

"Mhm." She didn't care what he was saying, really.

Death pulled her head to his shoulder. "Breathe slowly. He will only go faster and harder when he believes you're ready. His instincts will lead him, so he might be rough."

She felt David move one of Death's hands to her left butt cheek. He muttered something foreign again.

Death smiled, spreading her as David did the other. Then she held her breath as he slowly pushed forward.

"Ah, fuck." She dug her fingers into Death's shoulders.

"Breathe, angel." Death gave her small thrusts when David stopped. He said something again to David as her vampire shifted her hair and pressed his lips on her slick skin.

David scraped his fangs as he licked and pushed in more.

Jane gasped, nodding for him to keep going when Death began moving again. She was sliding up and down between them. David's muscled chest barely touched hers, but she was wrapped entirely around Death. He was keeping her safe from the dangerous aura emanating out of David. She knew he loved her, knew something was pushing down his usual softness, but Death was there.

Her angel turned, kissing her as he moved faster, making her too overwhelmed with him to focus on David getting further in each time she slid down Death's cock.

"Breathe in," David said just before thrusting in all the way.

Jane's back arched as Death growled, holding her down on both.

"Close your eyes, Sweet Jane." Death bit one side of her neck as David did the other, and they ground themselves deeper.

So full. Complete. Pain and beauty. "Oh, yes," Jane shouted, her legs shaking uncontrollably.

Their scents got stronger at the same moment warmth filled her, and the world shifted. She couldn't see clearly, but she could make out colors. Gold and blue light collided around her, but when green surrounded her, a bright white beam pushed it away.

Death growled, but he didn't release his bite. He gently caressed her trembling thigh and pressed deeper when David did. Then pretty sapphire light engulfed all other colors.

Jane peeked her eyes open and briefly caught sight of a room with jars of blue fire, but it was gone too quickly for her to realize what she'd seen.

David removed his fangs and kissed her tender skin, murmuring, "That's good."

A pained noise came from Death, but he removed his mouth before placing a sweet kiss where he'd bitten.

She felt the urge to comfort him, but they both picked up speed again, quickly syncing their movements so she could only moan, her skin prickling under their heavy breaths. She'd never felt so complete and beautiful as she did when they both moaned, kissing her neck as though they were sharing the same mind, telling each other what to do.

The heat was building. It hurt, but it felt good. She felt pure, and it made no sense but perfect sense at the same time. Every time she felt too much pain, tingles went to it, soothing the sting until she moaned again.

When the gold thread encircled all three of them, she tried to tighten it, but it unraveled. The green fire wrapped around it, though, and pulled it toward David.

The emerald flame gently caressed the thread before offering it to the blue fire. Then the green let go, and she stopped seeing the flames altogether as Death's movements became harder and faster.

David said something again.

Death nodded. "Yeah. Fuck." He came, holding her head down on his shoulder so David could have his turn.

David growled out when she did, and again, she felt warmth fill her. He kissed her shoulder as Death did the same on the other side. She moaned as they both rested their cheeks where they'd kissed.

"Did it work?" Jane whispered, sliding her fingers through Death's sweaty hair.

"Yes, angel." He lifted his head. "Do you feel him?"

David rubbed his hands down her sides. "Open your eyes, baby."

She did and gasped. Green flames surrounded Death, but they weren't hot.

He pecked her lips. "Look at David."

Jane turned, her mouth opening as she watched blue fire radiate from him.

He smiled, cupping her cheek before pressing his lips to hers. "You're glowing too."

She looked down, crying; her gold flame was entwined with his blue one. "It worked."

He kissed her forehead. "It did."

Jane cried, turning to face Death.

"Congratulations," he said, nodding to David. "Be careful."

"Will it hurt her?"

Death chuckled before pushing in hard, hitting her G-spot. She moaned loudly as her entire body trembled.

"Pull out," Death said, sucking her earlobe.

David withdrew himself, but Death did not.

Her angel laid her down, kissing her as he slowly began loving her again. He pushed one of her legs up and glanced at David. "I think she'll feel weird about you sticking your dick in her pussy after it's been in her ass. Go wash."

JANIE MARIE

She caught sight of David. "Oh, fuck, he looks like a superhero. Oh, shit. Death, I'm gonna go again."

Her vampire shook his head as he walked closer. He leaned down, kissing her, but he spoke to Death. "Make her come, then we'll shower together."

Death smirked before angling his hips to hit her G-spot again and again. He snatched David's hand when he grabbed her breast and yanked it down. David didn't have to be told anything. He pressed down on her clit and matched Death's rhythm. They worked together until she was unable to stop screaming their names.

"That's our girl." David grinned, waiting for Death to finish.

She whimpered, smiling when she caught sight of both men pulsing with fire. "Is this real? Are we in Heaven?"

David chuckled, nodding. "We're still in our room, but every bit of this is real. Now, come for him again so I can love you."

Death motioned for David to move, then yanked her up. "Turn the shower on, Prince."

David walked past them as Death pressed her against the wall.

"I love you so fucking much." He grunted, pulling her hands over her head as he snapped his hips forward over and over again, pressing his chest against hers. "Please tell me we are still us, angel. Tell me I haven't lost you."

"You didn't lose me. We're us." She almost cried from the sensation of his presence trying to unite with her again. "I'm sorry."

"It's okay."

Her vision started to darken until he slowed, chuckling.

"Breathe, angel." He gave softer thrusts. "You can't hold your breath like that."

Jane gasped, sucking in air. She grinned when he released her wrists and slid her arms around his neck. "You're breaking me in half. But don't you dare stop."

"I won't." He pressed his body against hers, pumping himself in her fast.

She closed her eyes, loving all his grunts and growls against the crook of her neck.

"Ah, fuck." He pushed in deep, coming, sending her into another orgasm.

Her entire body tensed, whimpering with each spasm when she felt his presence trying to penetrate Lucifer's light as it guarded his spot in her.

"It's okay," he whispered, kissing her shoulder as he finally removed himself. "I'll break through that fucker's light one day."

David came and took her from Death. He was already wet from head to toe. "Come on, both of you."

Death chuckled. "Papi can't go too long without resuming alpha position."

Jane hugged David as he carried her.

"She likes you softer with her and me rougher." David kissed her, smacking her butt. "Right, baby?"

"How did you know that?" She smiled lazily at Death.

"I see it. You like him soft until you lose control, then you don't care what he does. But you prefer him sweet with you."

"She likes us to reverse our personalities." Death rubbed her back, sliding his hand down until he touched her dimple. "I keep forgetting to kiss this."

David smacked his hand. "That's mine."

Death chuckled, fighting David's arm away so he could lick and kiss her dimple.

"You're lucky I can't kill you." David turned, putting her under the water. "Don't stare at my ass."

Jane leaned her head back, sighing when they both ran their hands through her hair and over her body. "Are we going to keep glowing?"

"Only we can see it." Death pulled her from David. "And other powerful angels. I stimulated David's soul by dressing you in gold and guiding your soul to rise to the surface. It gave him . . . memories, you could say."

"Memories I can't know about?"

David smiled at her as he supported one of her legs and poured body wash on her. "Not yet. It's incredible, though. And the only reason I allowed him to do what he did."

"Do y'all have to hold me like this?" She was tired, but she felt slightly ridiculous because they wouldn't let her stand.

"He just wants to wash you so he doesn't taste my dick." Death chuckled at David's glare. "Don't be angry, Papi."

"Stop calling me that." David leaned forward and gave her a kiss. "Hang onto him. It's my turn to take care of my kitten." He put one leg over his shoulder and held the other, spreading her.

"Oh, shit, David." She was so embarrassed but still turned on.

Death gripped her better, angling her so he could kiss her. "Are you okay?"

David dragged his tongue up her slit before sucking.

Her eyes rolled back into her head. David was so good at this.

"Yeah, you're okay," Death murmured, grabbing her breast. He smiled when she began to shake. "Come for him."

She already was.

And David was already lowering her and sliding his shaft over her. "Ready for me?"

She smiled at her blue, fiery god of a soul mate and told him those three words with her eyes: *I love you.*

"I love you, too." He gave her a gorgeous smile as he slowly eased inside her.

Jane nuzzled David's chest, sighing as he hugged her tightly but quickly realized there was not another body behind her.

"He's by the fire," David whispered in her ear. He tilted her chin up and gave her a soft kiss. "Go to him. Try to bring him back with you, but it's okay if he needs a moment alone with you, too. Give him whatever the two of you need. I'll wait."

She grinned, kissing him before he rolled her over. He kissed her back until she was out of reach, but she already had her eyes on Death, so she didn't give in to the urge to crawl back to David.

Jane summoned the gold corset as she approached her angel. She noticed he was smoking, but he sighed, flicking the cigarette into the fireplace.

"You should rest, Jane." He didn't look at her.

Her soul stood, reaching for him. "I'll rest when you get in bed with me again."

He chuckled, leaning back in the chair. "Go to sleep with your vampire. I'm just thinking."

When she stood in front of him, he finally took her in.

Death slid his eyes up and down her body. "You can't figure out how to return it to your suit?"

She huffed, putting her hands on her hips. "Are you angry with me?"

"No. Only myself for feeling weak." He smiled as he made a twirling gesture with his finger. "Turn around for me. I want to see you in front of the fire."

Jane turned slowly. She peered over her shoulder, gasping when he moved forward, gripping her hips.

He pushed some of the fringes away and kissed her butt cheek. "I've had your ass on my mind for far too long." He sighed, kissing again before pulling her backward until she sat on his lap. "I miss you already."

"I'm still here." She closed her eyes as he buried his face in the crook of her neck.

"You know what I mean. You're just his now."

"No. Always yours as well." Jane held his cheek with one hand as the other pulled his to the spot. His spot. "She's still waiting for you."

He rubbed back and forth—just under her heart and to the side. "Really?"

"Yes, my love."

Death kissed her neck where he'd bitten her. "And you?"

"I'm always waiting for you." Her nose burned, but she kept her eyes on the fire. "You shoulda told me you would regret bonding me to him."

He chuckled, still rubbing the empty spot. "You would have refused him."

She smiled, leaning her head against his. "You're a really good soul mate, Death."

He scoffed. "Hardly."

"You are. You've made mistakes, but so have I. But we were meant to. If you hadn't cut us apart, David wouldn't have found out the truth. He wouldn't have had a chance to learn why there was always more than our love pulling us together. You would have kept it secret because you love me, but I'd never understand and feel like I was cheating on David. And you'd never have me the way you were meant to. Plus, we would have gotten too weak to survive."

"That's true."

She leaned against him, closing her eyes. "Still, I feel like we were cheated because we didn't know each other as soul mates. I don't know why I never saw it before. I always heard a strong 'no' when they said David was mine. I should have put it together."

"Don't worry about it. I didn't know, and I didn't see it clearly until Famine bonded with you. My brothers all saw it so easily."

"What do y'all see?"

"You, beautiful." He tightened his arms around her. "Glowing. Gorgeous. Smiling. But when you look at me, your flame reaches for me, and you illuminate even more with bright, gold light. And my soul, he rushes out for you, circling you to keep you safe, trying to warm you even though he and I have no heat to give you both. That is why my 'tingles' are so strange. My soul is trying to warm and love yours. The warmth you thought you felt was from yours warming mine." He kissed her cheek. "I love you so much, angel. All this time, we have been trying to come together, but we always held back."

Jane hurt everywhere, but she smiled and kissed him. *Beautiful.*

He leaned farther into the chair, pulling her back closer to his chest as he kissed her thoroughly. She smiled when he cupped her cheek, his thumb caressing her jaw. "I think I might try dreaming of us sometime."

"What will you dream?"

He stared into her eyes. "Hazel. My hazel-eyed angel. That will be the day I feel Heaven again. I only felt it when we kissed, and only in those moments did I understand my brothers' devotion and love toward our father."

"We will find a way," she promised. "If I have to force Lucifer to remove his light so I can have you, I will."

He smiled sadly. "That would be quite the sight for the universe."

"Don't be sad," she whispered.

"I'm only sad that I cannot join you just yet. I'm happy to see you with David this way. You both deserve it." He put his hand over her heart. "Is he keeping you warm?"

"Yes." She grinned, covering his hand. "It's not like he's in there. It's different from how you felt. He feels tied to me, whereas you seemed more a part of me. What does that mean?"

He smirked, his eyes glowing. "You'll know one day. I'll just say you and I are unique from all other soul mates. Others are how you describe the bond you feel with him. We are different."

"Because I am half?" She frowned. "Wait, does this mean you are soul mates with my darker half, too?"

Death chuckled, shaking his head. "Fuck, no. She is like you, angel, you are from the same soul, but she was not with you when you and I officially paired. Both times. That's when she was with the man in black."

"Y'all don't say his name?"

"He has no name."

"Oh." She thought about the giant man who held more power than Death. "He's not really an angel, then?"

"He is, and he isn't. He is something that simply is and is not meant to be understood. He accuses God's children, including angels. His only goal is to prove Father wrong about all of us. Each one is unworthy in his eyes. It would almost seem he is ensuring only the best are allowed nearest God, but he isn't. He is the opposite of Father. Cold, empty—like me, but I have you to warm me. And where he wishes to corrupt, I have no desire unless it involves you. And with you, there is only love."

She smiled, savoring that she was all he felt and cared for. "In Pestilence's memories, he called my soul his daughter." She chewed her lip and peeked up at him. "Is he really my dad?"

"No." He kissed her head. "He corrupted her after she was separated from you until she was returned just before you were born. I never knew this—no one did. But I do recall seeing him concealing something. I assumed he had stolen a soul, but I did not care to find out."

"Even though she was me?"

"She's not you. Not really. Think of it as twins. You are half-souls, but your separation, just like one that occurs in the womb and at birth, created two minds, two desires, two personalities. The only difference is you were sharing one physical vessel. So two halves instead of two wholes."

"Jeez," she said, "can you imagine me talking to a doctor about this? 'Yes, Doctor, my other soul wants to destroy the world, and my soul mate, the Angel of Death, is trying to keep me alive without her while I shag this hottie vampire. Oh, and I'm the Queen of Hell, and I like to chill with the Knights of the Round Table and the Horsemen of the Apocalypse.' I'd be in a padded room."

He chuckled, rocking them from side to side. "I would have sprung you and beat the fuck out of whoever put you in there."

"I know." She sighed, relaxing in his arms and from the warmth of the fire. "Do you think she'll ever get back inside me? I fear her and don't want her inside me again or to feel her darkness, but I would fight her."

"I won't let her. I should have sensed her trying to destroy you and helped you fight her. And I know you would kick her ass."

Jane glanced over at the bed. Her heart fluttered when she noticed David smiling at them. "Is it all right if I tell David about El Diablo?"

A cute smile teased Death's lips. "I can imagine you seeing him on different occasions and calling him every name you can think of just to piss him off."

She laughed. "That does sound like me. If I get Gareth and Gawain to play along, he'll probably give up on whatever he's trying to accomplish."

"I wish, baby girl. And tell David whatever you want about him—he's been listening to us. If he hasn't figured it out, he's a moron."

David held up his middle finger before rolling onto his back and closing his eyes. He said nothing but seemed to be thinking, so she returned to her conversation with Death.

"Who knows about us being soul mates?"

He shrugged. "My brothers do, but that is because of their bond to me. It gives them a view of my emotions when I do not block them. They feel my devotion and love for you, and it allows them to see our souls clearly. Arthur is aware now because he saw everything David did the night you and I cut ourselves apart. He did not understand, but he saw, and it's too heartbreaking to ignore that we were always meant to be. I believe Luc figured it out long ago, though I am unsure when. Moros, one of my team, saw what you are. Lancelot has also figured it out, as well as Zeus. He is simply wise because of his age. Thanatos and some of your men probably know, and I am certain that Gareth and Gawain spilled their guts with their blubbering over your eyes."

"So pretty much all the powerful angels and my posse. Will it matter if more people find out now? Or does it have to stay secret?"

"I think it will become obvious something happened now that you carry both our scents. Your bond with David may stand out, so it might cause some to question it, and they will figure out I must be your soul mate as well for David to allow such a thing."

"I accept you have a role I was not given," David said, opening one eye to look at them. "You shared it with me so I could have it with her, too. If they find out, let them. As far as I am concerned, even without the final bonds to tie us, you are both mine as I am yours."

Jane grinned up at Death.

He whispered loudly, "Papi just pissed on us."

David smirked and closed his eyes again. "I'm alpha."

Death snorted and kissed her head. "When I'm tired."

"Whatever helps you maintain your pride. You know why you stand down for me."

Jane looked up at Death.

"I'm still stronger," Death muttered.

"And I'm—well, we will let her find out," David said as secretive smiles teased both men's lips.

"Y'all suck." Jane huffed.

"Only you, my love," David said, still resting his eyes.

"Whatever." She fanned her cheeks before feeling herself flush even more under Death's stare. "So, who told you?"

He sighed. "The Accuser. He offered me a deal that would make you mine, but it would mean taking you from David and helping him ensure his *daughter* became the dominant soul within you. He said I would have you all to myself—that he could fix everything so you discontinued your love for David and your family, and he would only summon his daughter when she was needed for her king. I declined.

"He then told me I would lose sight of you if I did not accept and that you would burn after bonding with Lucifer or even Belial. I still declined, forfeiting your fate so you could stay with David, so you would never reunite with her once Lucifer pulled her out. I still had faith that Luc would honor our bargain of at least removing her, so I vowed to protect you and support your relationship with David whenever we got you back. I knew it would be hard on both of you to reunite, and I knew he'd have his fuck-ups. But I vowed to myself I would bail him out. At the very least, I would be the soul mate who gave you the best."

David chuckled but still kept his eyes closed.

Jane turned, kissing Death's jaw. "You're the fucking sweetest, Death. I love you."

"And I love you."

"Come to bed," she said. "I'm probably going to have two babies wedged under me after tonight, and we might lose this big ass bed. We may be apart now, but you will always be my soul mate, and I won't give you up. So come cuddle the fuck out of me while you can."

"Baby, you are such a sweet talker." David laughed.

Death tilted her face to his. He kissed her like he would never see her again but soon stood, carrying her to bed.

David moved the covers and scooted back, making room for them. "Hi, baby."

Jane crawled to him.

"Hi, Papi," Death said, getting in behind her.

David shook his head as he smiled up at her. "And I thought I had lost the clingy Side-Boyfriend."

"It's called Side-Dick." Death smacked her ass as David pulled her head down for a kiss. "And you two won't lose me if she keeps sticking her ass up like this."

Jane sighed as Death squeezed her butt, and then both men inhaled deeply, their chests rumbling with low growls.

"Send the suit away, Jane," Death murmured. As soon as she did, he began kissing along her spine. He kissed her shoulder while David still tasted her lips. "One more, and then you two can sleep."

"Yes," she gasped against David's smile.

David turned her head to the side as Death palmed her ass. She could already feel his erection as he leaned over her.

"Since you have fantasized about her ass for so long, ask her if you can try." David chuckled when she nodded right away. "She says yes."

Death cupped her from behind before pushing his fingers into her pussy. "Are you sure?"

She arched her ass out, moaning. *Oh God.* "Yes."

Death's mouth was on her core.

Jane still couldn't believe how easy it was to be with them, but she wouldn't hold back. She pushed the blanket down to expose David's dick.

He chuckled, grabbing her thigh to shift her so she could reach him. David gathered her hair together. "Do you really want to?"

Death kissed up her back until his cock was nudging her entrance. "Sweet Jane?"

She grinned, nodding as she grabbed David, licking him from the base to the tip.

Death chuckled, pushing his dick into her pussy. "She's never been more sure."

Jane hummed, agreeing as David groaned and pushed her down more.

Death pulled her up, though, until her mouth was free. "Don't finish him. We'll love you together, and I'll finally take your pretty ass." He squeezed her ass cheek. "Do you want that? Do you like us in you together?"

She tried to nod, but he tightened his hand in her hair, and she gasped when David slid his hand between her legs, massaging her clit to assist Death.

Death pressed in deep and leaned over her, kissing her even though she'd just had her mouth around David. "Do you like both of us in you together?"

"Yes," she gasped. She was so turned on she could only move her body to keep up the friction. "Oh, I feel like such a slut."

"Hush," David said, rubbing faster. "You're our goddess loving her men."

"Oh, fuck," she gasped. "Hurry up and fuck me. We'll do the sweet shit when the fighting is over."

Death gave her a hard kiss. "Open your mouth."

She did.

He nipped her lips, grinning. "Suck him until you can't stand not having him inside you."

She moaned, clenching around him.

He grunted, licking her lips as he ground himself into her.

"Oh, shit." She blinked as her vision darkened.

"Breathe." He eased back.

Jane gasped, smiling when he resumed.

"Open again." Death waited for her to open her mouth. "So pretty for us."

David grabbed her hair, turning her head toward his face. "Are you okay?"

"Yes." She really was.

"Good." He pushed her head down.

"Damn." Death chuckled. "She's a queen on the streets but a freak in the bed."

35

KING BOYFRIEND

So many sets of eyes on Jane. Again.

She shifted Natalie on her hip and looked over her shoulder. A group of Rusalka watched her with their strange green eyes. Jane studied their faces briefly before taking in the Nereids David had pointed out. It was so cramped as they headed toward the main exit. Jane was in the group that would leave first. The knights were with her, but David was off delivering her cats to Asmodeus' men while Death spoke to one of Pestilence's soldiers.

"She reeks of both," someone whispered.

Gawain kept her from turning around and pushed her forward. "You do not reek, love."

She sighed, ignoring that everyone she passed raised their noses to scent her.

Ragnelle pushed through toward her. "Hello, Jane. You certainly took everyone's attention off the food shortage."

"I do what I can," she said, trying to hide her hot cheeks.

"Jane," Gareth whispered, "did you know there is a skull with a scythe and a sword crossing each other etched in gold on your bum?"

"What?" She tried to look. Her regular suit was on, but she'd not noticed anything odd.

Gareth chuckled. "They're making sure you're recognized from the front and back as theirs."

"It is actually very sweet," Ragnelle said as her eyes dropped to Jane's butt. "They get along so well now."

Gareth snorted. "Yes, they are practically brothers. Oh, and I corrected Death, by the way." He snickered. "It's a queen on the streets but a freak in the sheets."

"Oh, goodness." Jane tried to shield her ass. "And stop talking to him about us in bed."

He laughed again. "He was trying to make Gawain puke." Gareth laughed harder. "He did."

Jane giggled, her cheeks burning as she noticed several red-faced women looking at her. "Gareth, shush. More people are staring."

A hot hand grabbed hers when she continued to hide her butt, and even hotter lips pressed against her neck. "You will hurt our feelings if you hide us." David chuckled, kissing her repeatedly before straightening. He kept her back flush against him as he handed Natalie her dolly. "Here you go, princess. Don't lose her."

Natalie hugged her doll. "Is Ryder Mommy's boyfriend, too?"

Jane stopped smiling and realized the entire hall had gone quiet.

David answered without any hesitation or discomfort. "He's her soul mate and boyfriend." Jane's mouth opened. "Just like I am," he finished.

"Oh," was all Natalie said before reaching for David. "Okay."

He took hold of Natalie but cupped Jane's cheek and kissed her. "Yes, it's a very good thing."

The silence stretched on, and she knew it was because of the presence behind her.

"I don't remember asking her to be my girlfriend." Death slid a hand around the front of her neck until he lightly held her throat. He tilted her face up, his thumb caressing her jaw as he smirked and pulled her flush against him. "I don't have flowers, Sweet Jane. Or am I supposed to give you a letter to check yes or no?"

She couldn't hide her smile and stopped caring that every pair of eyes was on them. "You gave me a lot more than flowers, and I already checked yes."

His hand flexed around her throat. "I want a different title than boyfriend, then."

"What do you want?"

"I'll think of something. For now, I suppose boyfriend will do." He leaned down and kissed her softly, and he smiled when there were gasps of shock. "He set us up."

She chuckled, kissing him one more time before he straightened.

"I actually think I'll go by King Boyfriend." Death snickered.

David gave him an annoyed glare. "I don't think so."

"Whatever, Prince." Death scanned the crowd of onlookers. "If you have a problem, I suggest you mind your goddamn business!"

Jane hugged him quickly before taking Nathan from Gawain. "Hey, bubby."

Nathan kept his eyes on Death. "Green."

Death's eyes flashed when he glanced at her son. Then he smiled at him. "Yes, green."

David glanced at Nathan, smiling proudly. "He sees."

Jane turned to Death. "Is that true?"

"Yes." Death patted Nathan's head before he whispered in his ear.

Jane stayed quiet as she realized Death was using a sound barrier to shield whatever he was telling her son from her.

"Okay?" Death said audibly, dropping the barrier.

Nathan nodded, giving Death a small smile before hugging Jane and closing his eyes.

Death then leaned toward Natalie, doing the same thing.

Natalie grinned widely at whatever she was being told. "Yes."

David chuckled, and Jane was instantly annoyed he got to hear whatever Death was telling her kids.

Natalie turned and whispered something in Death's ear, which was cute as hell.

"Yes, that's fine," Death said. "Now leave me alone."

David shoved Death toward Jane.

She watched a faint smile tease her angel's lips as he took her hand but gestured for David to take Nathan.

"We need to have a word with her men," Death said, patting Nathan when he tried to tighten his arms around Jane. "Go on, Nathan."

David grabbed him, putting one of the kids in each arm. "Try to hurry. We will be moving to the front soon, so look for us there."

"Okay." Jane kissed him quickly before Death led her away. "Death?"

"Hm?" He glared at a few of the elves but kept walking.

"What did you tell the kids?"

Now he smiled. "I told them I'm not going to be their new daddy, but if they behave today, whenever you settle at the new location, I will take you and them somewhere—just us. And David, of course. And we can do whatever they want. I even said if they wanted just you, David and I would watch from a distance, but we would still have to come with the three of you."

Her smile was so big it hurt. "Really?"

Death nodded. "I'm not going to be a boyfriend like David, babe. I honestly don't know how long we will be able to be close and relaxed, but that's why you have David. I only pray that you will still want me when I return even though he is bonded to you as your soul mate, and I am not."

"I will never stop wanting you." She hugged his arm. "That's really the sweetest shit, though."

He chuckled. "My motivation for taking them anywhere is to tire them the fuck out, so I can get a blow job."

Jane threw her head back, laughing. "Of course."

"I was slightly jealous watching you give him one." He gave her a wicked grin. "Are you afraid to try with me? I'm not that much bigger than him."

"I know. I'm not afraid." She blushed when they passed a group of servants. They bowed at her and Death, but she tried to wave to them. She didn't like them acting like she was royalty. She was the Queen of Hell, not vampires.

"Good." Death lifted her, putting a hand on her ass as he carried her through the group of vampires. "You taste really good, by the way."

"Do I?" She wrapped her arms around his neck. He was too cute like this.

"Mhm." He kissed her neck. "I do not know the taste David describes, but it is appealing and stronger than your normal taste. If we bond again, I can show you better."

"I don't want to know what I taste like."

He squeezed her ass. "You should. My Sweet Jane addiction. Fuck, I still can't believe I get to kiss you the way I've wanted to—and that I get to taste every inch of you before consuming your beautiful body, heart, and soul."

She sighed, hugging him. "It is amazing. I'll never stop being grateful to David for letting us have this."

He nodded. "He managed to become greater than I thought any man could be. Perfect fucker."

Jane laughed, but she was worried about Death. "You're not going to disappear after we leave here, are you?"

"I don't know. I can't split myself anymore—not with me holding off my transformation. If I do, I will lose control. So if it is necessary to tend to a matter, I must leave."

She didn't want him to leave, but she understood. She would make sure he knew he had them to come back to. "Do you know when Famine is returning? Like, will we have time to split up at least?"

"No. Famine is different from the others. His presence was already fated to come to Valhalla, and the effects of his presence were felt by everyone here. When Elise arrives—she's his woman—it will likely be separate from him. She tends to follow him, and they meet briefly before he leaves again. She acts like a jealous girlfriend, if you ask me. That is why I want you close to me. She will realize he has bonded to you, and she will draw much of the hungry toward you simply because Famine gave you attention. She's never satisfied with just him, but she's possessive."

"Oh, great." She hugged him, not letting herself explore why it upset his comment about Famine not being enough for his woman, and joked, "Why do you boys always bring me trouble?"

He chuckled. "Like I said, angels don't have soul mates. So you bonding with him is a huge deal. Most angels only bond as guardians, but they are selected only to pair with humans. You're an immortal goddess, as far as many are concerned—more powerful than any of them. They'd attempt to knife you down if you were not my woman."

Jane chuckled, but as she took in humans and mortals shoving each other, she frowned. If it hadn't been for Death carrying her, she would have had to fight to get through the halls. Everything was already incredibly unstable.

"My queen." Asmodeus bowed. He shook his head at Death. "You realize that little stunt has spread beyond these walls already?"

"What stunt?" Jane asked as Death lowered her to her feet once they arrived at the guarded doors to the cell room.

"King Boyfriend." Asmodeus sighed. "This will get to Lucifer, and he will not be pleased."

Jane lifted her chin. "Do you think I care if he's pleased?"

"Of course not, my queen." Asmodeus chuckled, hitching his thumb behind him. "What do you wish to do about them?"

Jane groaned. "I completely forgot about the prisoners."

"Well, no one here has forgotten you, whore queen," Lancelot sneered, spitting in her direction.

"Go suck your own balls, Lance," she snapped, rubbing her forehead as she took in the people fleeing down the halls.

Death stared into the cells as Asmodeus laughed.

"Should we take them in the first wave with us?" she asked, her gaze locking with Thanatos'.

"You should ensure the mortals make it to safety." Zeus pulled Jane's attention away from Thanatos. "None of us here deserve saving."

There were yells and objects thrown through the bars at Zeus.

"We haven't been fed all day," someone shouted.

"They won't give us any rations," another yelled.

"Jane, they are prisoners." Death leveled her with a stern stare. "After we settle everyone, some of your men can return to see who survived. Many won't."

She focused on Lancelot, then Thanatos and Zeus. "I won't let them rot here. Who knows how long it will take us to get where we are going."

"Jane." He shook his head.

She ignored him and nodded to Asmodeus. "Lancelot, Zeus, and Thanatos are to be moved with us. Bind them for me and arrange for the others to take the rest in small groups."

"Jane," Death said again.

She glared at him. "I'm not leaving them here to die. If they are supposed to die now, kill them and be done with it. Otherwise, they're coming with me, and I will protect them."

He grabbed her chin, squeezing it but not painfully. "Focus on the good."

"I am," she said through gritted teeth. "That's what everyone forgets— they have good in them. Sometimes that's what you have to focus on. Just like you all did with me." She locked gazes with the onyx eyes of the prisoners before turning to Asmodeus. "Bind them. Now."

Asmodeus looked at Death before bowing to her. "Yes, my queen." He walked into the cells, heading toward Lancelot first.

Death watched her for a moment in silence.

"Don't stare at me," she muttered, crossing her arms.

"You're being foolish."

She nodded. "I know. But I can't leave them in there."

Asmodeus walked Lancelot toward her. Silver and gold chains were embedded into his wrists and ankles.

Death held out a hand for the chain, but Jane snatched it.

"I'll take him," she said, staring at Lancelot.

"Stupid girl." Lancelot shook his head. "David will be upset with you."

She shrugged before summoning her gun and aiming it at his chest. "Only if you hurt me, and I won't let you."

Lancelot glanced at Death. "She smells of you both, but you have not bonded with her again . . ."

"Nope." She smiled brightly. "I'm still working on restoring my bond with baby here. But I got my other baby last night. Thanks for noticing. We're still celebrating."

Asmodeus chuckled, handing Thanatos' chains to Death. He already had Zeus with him as well. "I will have more men take the rest in groups of four or five. Let us get these three to the front."

Jane motioned for Lancelot to walk. "Go."

Lancelot walked but spoke over his shoulder. "You realize saving us will only lead to your death, don't you?"

"Oh, well, I owe him a blow job, so I guess I'll be multitasking."

Lancelot glared at her. "Whore."

"Murdering rapist." She gave him a sugary sweet smile.

"Says the bitch who raped me before murdering my family." He spat at her feet.

She yanked his chain. "One day I will answer for my crimes. Maybe you'll be the one who punishes me. But not yet."

Asmodeus shook his head, but he was smiling. "Careful, my queen."

Jane glared at some of the vampires waiting in line, watching them pass. "Don't act like you fuckers are saints! You're all damned for a reason, and so am I. Don't expect forgiveness if you can't forgive yourselves and each other."

"He's the enemy, and you're dragging him to the front of the line like he's your dog," someone yelled.

Lancelot watched her and said nothing when she allowed the light within her to pulse in a golden glow before it was drowned in white.

"Calm, Jane." Death nudged her forward.

Thanatos chuckled. "White and silver are Lucifer's colors, my queen. Not to mention gray."

"I'll rip your goddamn head off," Death snarled.

Thanatos ignored him. "Watch your emotions if you wish to keep that fire within contained."

Jane brushed her side against Death to comfort him but snapped at her former general. "Eat ass, Than. I'm still pissed at you."

Someone charged Lancelot, their sword raised high.

Jane instantly aimed and shot the vampire. The blast rang through her ears, her eyes straying to the man as he fell to the ground at Lancelot's feet. She locked eyes with David's old friend, but he said nothing.

Death tugged her arm. "Someone clean this shit up."

Thor walked through the crowd, his violent gaze falling on the dead vampire before settling on her. "You killed one of my men?"

"She killed a Damned attacking her prisoner," Death snapped, summoning his scythe. "Move along. It was his time."

Thor glared at their group. "You dare put them at the head of my line? After you brought the plague and famine to my fortress—you put murderers before my warriors?"

Jane turned away. "They were already coming here, Thor. Maybe consider all your big banquets had something to do with shortages. Now grow up and help organize your troops or throw a fit with someone who cares. I'm taking my prisoners with me. Slaughter yours if you can live with yourself once my men get your ass to safety."

Zeus and Asmodeus chuckled, but Death was pissed. His grip tightened on her, so she turned her face up until he looked at her.

"Let him be," she said. "You owe my kids a day in the sun with David and me. I want it soon, so let's get out of this icy shithole."

Thor growled, but he turned, ordering some men to follow him to the cells.

Jane nodded to Asmodeus. "We'll take Zeus. Go secure more of the prisoners before he kills all of them."

Asmodeus sighed, handing Death the chain that held Zeus. "You realize very few of them seek redemption, my queen."

"I know." She took a deep breath as she scanned the faces of the Damned. "But nearly everyone here was just as bad as them once, including me. We all have demons, Asmodeus. I just happen to befriend many of mine."

He grinned, bowing. "And we honor you and fight by your side, my queen. I will gather as many as I can and meet you."

"Thank you, Asmodeus." She nodded for Lancelot to move. "Let's get you to the front."

Lancelot shook his head. "You are proving nothing but how foolish you are."

"Well, when you have the titles Queen of Hell and Horsemen Bringer, you kinda don't expect to look good in anyone's eyes, do you?"

"I suppose you don't." He growled at some of the vampires blocking them.

Jane glanced at Death. He was quiet, his eyes glowing brightly. "You okay?"

He shook his head. "We must get to David. I sense Famine. He's remaining hidden, but he's here."

Her breathing sped up. "Hurry, Lance. If there is one thing you care about, it's David not hurting his kids. He has my babies."

"Perhaps you deserve to see them slaughtered at his feet," he said, rooting his feet to the floor.

Death growled. "Move."

Jane shoved Death in the chest. "Get to David. I'm coming. You know what to do. Get the kids away from him."

Death snarled, but he pulled Thanatos and Zeus forward. "Move!"

She turned, summoning her sword when they were gone. "You have a choice to make right now. You can take out your hate and vengeance on me by attacking me, knowing David will kill children he considers his own— children that call Guinevere Aunt Gwen—or you can stop being the monster they want you to be."

"You think it's that easy?" He laughed.

She glanced around, her heart pounding when the crowd thickened, and fearful gazes watched her, knowing something was wrong. "I know it's not easy, Lance. But you will only ever be what they shaped you into if you keep refusing to try."

He lowered his head. "You are right."

"Of course I'm right," she snapped just before he kicked her in the chest.

The crowd screamed as she fell to her back. Her head smacked the stone floor with an awful crack, but she summoned her gun and aimed up before he could stomp her face in.

Lancelot snarled but ran when a dark cloud manifested behind her.

"My my." Famine stooped down and lifted her. "That did not work out well, did it?"

Jane rubbed her head, blinking away the blurriness. "I had to try."

He smiled, carrying her through the chaos suddenly unfolding. People trampled others, but he walked without anyone blocking his path. "I would expect nothing less from you."

She rested her head on his shoulder. She could feel bones in her skull shifting back into place. "It's happening, isn't it?"

"Yes." He turned his face toward hers. "You succeeded in bonding to the prince, I see. My poor brother."

Her eyes watered. "I tried to bond him to us. He acted like he wanted me with David."

"He does. The prince loves you as much as he does. Death will never be good—not like the prince—they are both something the other will never be, and that is very important."

"Should we really be talking about this right now?" She winced as the hall seemed to spin.

There were several explosions from the direction they were heading. Screams thundered through the stone halls, and the walls shook.

"Hm." Famine lifted her mask to shield her mouth and nose from the dust. "Adorable. He changed your colors to gold."

Jane touched the skeletal design of her mask with a faint smile. "Get me to them before it's too late."

He smiled as his suit changed, and she stared at Famine's honor to samurais. His suit was much sleeker than the kind she'd seen in movies. He actually reminded her of video game characters, a mix between samurai and ninja. "I hope you are ready to fight. Everyone in this fortress is about to lose their minds, and you will be the only immortal with an army of demons to save it."

"Is your wife here?"

"Elise is not my wife." His words hinted at sadness and anger, but he was so composed it was hard to tell what he felt.

"Elise?" She asked. "I know Death called her that, but isn't she Hunger? Like you all have your titles?"

Famine nodded. "Elise means consecrated by God. She is fulfilling her oath to Him. Just as I do, she transforms into Hunger when her duty calls. I choose not to call her by her duty, but yes, she is coming. Pestilence was trying to buy you time."

"How?"

He gave her a long look. "How do you think?"

She sighed. "He infected others with illness so Hunger would follow him."

"Precisely." Famine slowed, waiting before he turned a corner and pushed her mask down. "They probably don't want to see this."

"See what?"

"This." Famine pulled her by the back of the neck so his mouth was on hers. "She is here," he mumbled. "Take my kiss or become one of the Ravenous."

He tasted like blood, honey, sunlight, earth, and leather. Somehow the combination was exquisite, just like the tingle on her lips and tongue. "Oh, wow."

He chuckled, which made her tingle even more as he leaned away.

"They are a unique blend."

Jane watched his eyes briefly glow as her skin shimmered with white light.

"Hm." He lightly touched her cheek. "Be careful with the light. Use your weapons and only unleash the light when it feels warm, not electric or burning."

She nodded, pointing to the floor. "Will you fight with me?"

"I can only fight Fallen and demons. If any turn on you, I will engage them. Elise will summon forth Ravagers. They are soulless angels and can touch any affected by Hunger and those who have given up. I will destroy many of them as well. Get your family and go. Your men will guard who they can."

"Okay." Jane summoned her sword.

"Wait." He touched her hand. "Light Bringer."

Her sword illuminated in a white glow before revealing a shorter, gleaming silver and gold blade. The symbols etched along the blade matched Lucifer's markings, but the hilt caught her eye. The grip had stars trailing around it, but the pommel had a half moon on one side and a large star on the other.

"Only Lucifer's queen can wield this sword." Famine lowered his hand. "No matter who you are to my brother and your prince, you are still Lucifer's queen. She wields the fastest and sharpest blade in the universe. He ensured his queen could be greater than him, and he is the best swordsman there is." A quick smile teased his lips. "He bonded with you to give you his light because only the greatest light wielders—you and him—can cut with the sharpest blade in existence. You will cut all who oppose you, Jane. No armor will withstand your attack. You will cut electrons from atoms with this sword. Slay the gods now, Queen of Hell. Remember, though, you must return to your sun, where even angels burn, lest your king keeps you." He turned her so they'd enter the main hall.

David locked eyes with her. They darkened as they shifted toward Famine, and his fangs extended.

"No," she whispered, searching for her children as the knights began fighting the other vampires. They weren't trying to stop them—they were trying to feed.

"Jane." Death grabbed her arm, pushing her against the wall. His gaze dropped to the sword, and he snarled, glaring at Famine. "Get her out of here."

"She must fight, brother." Famine drew his sword—a katana.

Jane didn't look away from David. He was the only one not fighting, but he looked the deadliest. So deadly that none came close to him. "Death, where are my kids?"

"Beelzebub and Astaroth are running them to the other exit. Someone set an explosive, collapsing the main gate."

"Baby." It was David.

She cried and tried to go to him, but Death held her still.

David held his hand up. "Don't." His voice was raw, but he was fighting himself. "Get away. Save yourself. I love you."

Jane shook her head as hot tears made it almost impossible to see him. If he killed any of his brothers, he'd never be the same.

He fell to his knees, as did every immortal and human around him.

Jane gasped as a woman in a sheer black gown walked around them. A matching veil was over her head, reminding Jane of a mourning widow as she glided across the hall.

"Elise." Famine moved in front of Jane. "You knew I would bond with her."

The angel halted near David and reached down for him.

"Don't." Famine's armor changed; his face and arms were covered in shiny black metal.

"Jane," Death whispered, pushing her back. "The infirmary . . . Hades is there. He will not be affected by Hunger. I released Zeus to find him and Adam. They will help lead you out and toward those I have sent for. Get out with them. Meet up with your family, and don't look back. Be careful with Zeus, though. If he attacks you, destroy him."

"Where did Thanatos go?" she whispered.

Death sighed. "He escaped. If you see him, do not trust him."

"I told you, beloved." Hunger pulled her veil away. Blood-red eyes met Jane's before shifting to Famine. "I will test her worth with the hunger of a million Ravenous. That is the price for your kiss and bond."

Famine positioned himself in a fighting stance. "Unleash your worst, my love. For she is worthy of my bond and kiss and my blade."

"Go, Jane," Death growled, his mask shimmering into view.

"You're changing." She clutched his arm.

He turned, grabbing her face as his mask vanished, then kissed her fiercely. "Run, my moon. Glow when you must, but be careful. Come back to me. Come back to David and me." He shoved her gently as he summoned his scythe and went to stand at his brother's side.

Pestilence shimmered into view next to them, drawing his bow. "I will

521

split the fire wielders up so they do not engulf the fortress."

A pained snarl left Hunger's lips as she clutched her stomach with one hand and dropped the other to David's shoulder.

David yelled, falling forward. He braced himself, panting as everyone else did the same, some writhing more pain than others.

Jane shook her head and backed up, stepping over bodies as they screamed and snarled.

David's head snapped up, and he grabbed the angel's wrist. Hunger screamed, ripping herself away. Jane froze and watched David stand.

His eyes continued to get darker, and he hissed a low sound as he bared his fangs at Death before looking at Jane. He pulled his sword. "Go, my love. I cannot hold my beast off for long." He turned to face the knights and other immortals, slowly getting up. They had none of the control David displayed.

Death nodded to his brothers, and they placed a hand on David before they each erupted in flames of their color. David's blue aura ignited, mixing with the Horsemen's and growing larger than all as they seemed to push theirs into him.

Death patted David's shoulder once before they all let go and focused on the growling monsters.

Elise—Hunger—pointed a burned finger at Jane. "The Horseman Bringer can end your hunger." Shadowy silhouettes of winged beings began appearing within the mob of hungry immortals and humans. They had no mouths, only hungry, red eyes. They summoned swords, and many of Jane's demons and Fallen manifested around her.

Her army held their weapons high, some inching closer to Jane to flank her.

"Keep as many alive as you can," she told them. "Protect the humans and the weak."

"Yes, Queen," they echoed amongst themselves, and Jane realized the halls were now filled with her army and Hunger's.

David looked at her over his shoulder. "Go. We'll hold them as long as we can."

She nodded, wiping her tears to show him those words: *I love you.*

He smiled, not hiding his fangs as a blue, fiery inferno raged around him. "I love you, too. Go."

Jane turned, kicking down the first vampire to reach for her as the roar of the Ravenous rose behind her.

Her men roared louder.

36

ABSOLUTION

Breathe in, breathe out.

Jane pumped her legs faster, hearing screams and snarls while her heaving breaths resounded within her head. Valhalla was huge, and the infirmary was far away. She prayed she'd find most of its patients alive but mentally prepared to enter a bloodbath.

"My queen," Succorbenoth yelled, racing up alongside her. "Hades is protecting several unconscious humans and immortals. Sonneillon and others engage the Ravagers while some carry survivors to the exit. Hunger brought more than we have with us. If we withdraw from the forest, Hell will enter."

She peeked behind her, her eyes widening at the sight of Ravagers rushing toward them. "Fuck."

Succorbenoth pointed to her right. "Cut through here."

Jane turned, skidding to a halt at seeing humans cowering in the corner. She breathed in faster, her mind spinning. "They're not crazy."

He shook his head. "If one has lost hope, they will not be afflicted by ravenous hunger. They will still be attacked, though."

Her heart squeezed when she noticed a young girl shielding a smaller boy and girl, and she quickly ran close. "I need you to get up. You need to run toward the infirmary."

The little girl ran to Jane. "The monsters are coming again."

Jane hoisted the little girl up and motioned for the older girl to pick up the boy before she glanced at the others. "Run. As fast as you can, and don't look behind you." The group took off, and Jane turned to the demon at her side. "Take her. Keep her safe."

"My queen," he said, taking the little girl who tried to hang on to her. "I can't leave you behind. Let go of her, small one."

"You can." She patted the little girl's head when she finally let the demon hold her. "Go with him. He's a nice monster."

The demon gave Jane a dry look, and she smiled at him, saying, "Go. I will buy you time. Get the others to find the exit. Any lost to madness that cannot be carried must be left behind. Save the children. Don't withdraw our troops unless Hell finds a way in. If they do, we make a stand to save the survivors. If we have to blow up the mountain, then so be it."

"Yes, my queen." He pulled the little girl's head down and ran after the others.

Jane inhaled deeply, turning as she summoned her shield and lifted her mask into place. She felt light wash through her, tingling her fingertips. She wiggled them, watching the floor illuminate before the light scattered across the room. She'd have to be mindful of using it. Her experience with this new power was limited, and she didn't know how long she'd last, but she was ready to unleash it all if it meant saving everyone else.

Her gaze fell on the archway that would soon be filled with Ravagers and bloodthirsty vampires. The immortals were hissing and snarling, and the thundering footfalls of the Ravagers told her she was in for a big fight.

Nearly here.

She tightened her hands around the grips of Light Bringer and Havoc Bringer. Heat surfaced under her skin, but she bent her knees, bracing herself as she held her shield.

As soon as a bloody hand reached around the corner, Jane charged, raising her shield as they poured into the room like an unstoppable wave.

She slammed into them, the impact of her shield sending many of them flying backward, crashing into the others. She didn't waste time and swung her new sword, gasping when electricity trailed behind her blade. Silvery white light crackled and flew around her, smashing into the walls, but she kept swinging, marveling at the ease with which her sword cut through their flesh.

Kneeling, Jane swung her sword, slicing two Ravagers in half. Foul blood sprayed across the floor. It smelled of vomit and decay. It made her gag, but she swung her sword out to the side and cut the head off another before stabbing the next one through the stomach, slicing up until the creature was cut in half.

A pair of arms grabbed her from behind. Jane didn't yell out in fear. She shook him off, summoning her gun to fire shots at the oncoming attacks from two wild vampires. Another vampire attempted to pull her backward again, but she quickly grabbed and pulled him in front of her. She caught his fist, keeping his wrist in her hand as she shoved him to face away, yanking him down and wrapping her forearm around the back of his neck. She roared, lifting as hard as she could, wrenching his neck until it popped.

Yelling, she swung the body at the opening, knocking more out of her way as she summoned her shield and sword again.

She let none pass her. She massacred them, but it all abruptly stopped when a familiar face appeared.

"Gawain," she whispered, her heart hammering when he snarled, blood dripping down his chin and covering his hands as he reached for her.

A blue blur knocked her away before he could reach her. The blow blew her, and she coughed as she sat up. The blue blur was David, and he fought Gawain, Gareth, and Bedivere to keep them from touching her.

"Go, Jane," he roared, not looking at her.

A white flash illuminated the area around her.

"He's still in control of himself." Pestilence lifted her and pointed at the opening. "You did well. Now keep going. Once he loses it, you will be the one he rips apart."

David threw a devastating punch at Gareth, knocking him out, but he kicked him toward her.

Pestilence chuckled, lifting Gareth. "Go. I will follow you. Death is coming to stay with him."

Jane caught David's fierce glare as he exchanged blows with Gawain and Bedivere. They kept stumbling over the corpses, and that's when she saw pairs of eyes under a table. "Wait." She rushed to the woman she saw hiding. "Hela?" There were more women behind her, all unaffected. "Come on."

The frightened chambermaids scrambled out, sobbing and screaming.

"Go to the infirmary. Hurry." Jane shoved her as gently as she could.

"Yes, my lady." Hela sobbed, running.

"You are too sweet." Pestilence grinned and took her by the arm. "Let's go now. Another wave is coming, and it won't be long until Hell realizes what's happening here."

"Okay." She took one last look at David, tearing up as she watched him knock Bedivere unconscious before throwing him through a wall.

"He's trying to hide them." Pestilence tugged her arm. "I'll send men to retrieve the knights, then anyone else they can find."

David locked eyes with her and granted her a pained smile. "Go, baby. I won't last. Your blood is calling to me already."

It hurt, like a punch to the gut, but she turned away and followed Pestilence.

As they turned a corner, Jane continued to check for survivors. There were none.

Another flash of light illuminated beside her.

Famine allowed his mask to disappear and smiled. "Your vampire is quite strong."

"I know." Her heart filled with warmth. "Is he going to be okay?"

"I'm certain he will survive. We must be quick. The fire wielders are running loose. There are more than the knight and Greek. They are the strongest, though. The others are fleeing from them but trying to eliminate each other until only the strongest remain."

"Tristan or Apollo?" she asked, pausing to check another body but running again.

"They are even." Pestilence smiled over his shoulder. "It will be quite the battle if they meet."

She scowled at him. "That's not a good thing, Pest."

"Oh, I agree. Still . . ." He halted, dropping Gareth's body to the floor before pulling his bow in front of him.

Jane went to help Gareth, but Famine held her still, and they watched several arrows appear in the back quiver Pestilence wore.

He pulled one and aimed, releasing his arrow at what seemed to be nothing. But, clearly, that was not the case when a screech sounded, and a hellhound shimmered into view and fell to the ground dead.

Jane's mouth fell open as she watched him release arrow after arrow, hitting invisible targets until the hall was full of hellhound carcasses.

Famine casually pulled her to his side and stabbed his katana into the air, killing a hellhound preparing to attack her. "Safe to say Hell has penetrated the enchantments your army put in place," he said, yanking his blade free and swinging it to remove the blood.

Pestilence put his bow away before lifting Gareth again. He summoned his gun as he walked forward. Famine took her hand, leading her along the path his brother created by kicking the steaming bodies out of the way.

"I had no idea they could go invisible," Jane whispered, eyeing the impaled demon dogs.

"They usually can't." Pestilence fired his gun at one that still moved. "Someone cast protection and stealth charms over them."

David's roar reached them.

Famine turned his head. "Hurry. He is warning us."

Pestilence took off quickly as Death's roar shook the walls.

"What's happened now?" Jane asked, still trying to check the bodies strewn across the hall.

"Devourers," Famine said with a sigh. "They have mouths but no eyes. They are usually kept in Hell, where they feed on those who were consumed by greed during their lives. It seems someone has let them out."

Pestilence spoke without slowing down. "Lucifer is bringing more to the surface, or the Accuser has more players."

"Can't it be Belial?" she asked, peeking over her shoulder.

Famine pushed her forward. "No. Only rulers of Hell. Unless there is someone else we do not know of."

"The spy?" she guessed.

Famine nodded. "Possibly. They would have to make a portal for the Devourers to be able to enter Earth's realm."

Pestilence stopped and fired several shots at a wall. Nothing was there, and she realized he was making a hole when he kicked in the four-foot thick wall. Famine urged her to follow, and they entered a storage closet.

"We will leave Gareth here for now. The infirmary is overrun." Pestilence and Famine began stacking the rocks to fill the hole.

Famine muttered the angelic language under his breath as he placed a hand in the air. She watched in awe as the room was engulfed in darkness, save for the light glowing from her.

"He'll be safe in here." Pestilence grabbed Jane's arm and pulled her toward the door. "Devourers multiply unless you remove their heads. Their mouths will continue to bite, so be careful. If you must shoot their teeth out, do it after you decapitate them. Once you are in their jaws, there is no escape."

"Damn. Okay." She smiled as her light flickered across their handsome faces. "Do you guys know how hot y'all are?"

Pestilence grinned full-on. "I'm telling on you."

"As flattered as we are, it is time to be serious, Jane." Famine turned her to face him, the amused gleam in his dark eyes never fading. "Don't let the light consume you."

Jane sobered up. "I won't. Let's go."

Pestilence opened the door, bow raised as he scanned the hall. The sound of screams and battle was not far away.

"Careful, someone is here," Famine whispered as he put a hand on her back, guiding her.

Jane summoned her sword and swung to the side when she felt a breeze. The electricity lit up her soon-to-be victim's face, and she snarled, stopping. "Dammit, Than!"

Famine yanked her back and raised his sword as Thanatos stood there calmly.

"My queen." He bowed his head.

Pestilence aimed his arrow down the hall as he stared forward while Thanatos and Famine glared at one another.

"Why are you still here, Fallen?" Famine's aura ignited—black flames with silver outlining pulsed around him as he stood battle-ready in front of her.

Thanatos smirked, his red eyes flashing. "Simply keeping a promise to not fail her again."

Famine snarled and moved his sword in front of him. "Pest trusts you, but I do not."

"You became protective of her quite quickly." Thanatos shifted his gaze between her and Famine. "What of your codes? Hunger?"

"I honor Father, and my loyalty to Him extends to her. Do not insinuate there is more to my concern for her wellbeing."

Thanatos slowly slid his gaze to her. "My queen, my goal was to ensure you did not perish. Death would have held you captive, thus killing you by accident."

"You're a spy for Lucifer," she said, unwilling to drop her guard even if she wanted to have faith in him.

"I do what I must, my queen." He bowed his head. "Let us leave it at that."

Jane sighed, touching Famine's shoulder. "We could use his help. You boys can decide what to do afterward."

Famine hesitated but withdrew his sword and moved aside. "Very well."

"That was easier than I expected," Thanatos said before yanking her by her hair and pulling her flush against his body. His scythe pressed against her throat as his hood formed over his head.

"Than, you traitor." She tried to move but felt her blood dripping down her neck and stilled.

"You are always too trusting," he said.

Famine's symbols glowed, but he stayed still, watching. Calculating.

Jane held her hand up to stop him from attacking. "Don't."

"You know I will slit her throat before you can move," Thanatos warned. "Move aside."

"Please, Than," she gasped, her eyes burning again. Famine's eyes widened slightly as she was pulled into the walkway between the cells.

"Jane, stay calm," Famine whispered as silver light flashed across his face.

"Yes, you should have been more careful, my queen," Thanatos whispered. His tone was anything but concerned. "Your King's light is not pure inside you, even with the bond you have made with David. Perhaps that is why, though. God did not make him your soul mate for a reason. Do you really believe He approves of you fucking both of them?"

"Let her go," Famine ordered, slowly following after them with careful steps.

Heat rolled through her veins. She could see everything around her as if lit with light. But the blade lightly cutting into her throat kept her from attempting anything other than being careful not to miss her backward step.

"Jane," Death's roar shook the walls, but she knew he wasn't near them.

"Did you truly think Death was content with your vampire bonding to you in such a way?" Thanatos whispered. "Not to mention the King and Queen bond. He is heartbroken to be without you. You can see it in his eyes, my queen."

"You know nothing," she spat. "I will restore our bond. David and I won't leave him behind, and I trust that we were all meant to be joined." Her eyes hardened as she reached up to steady herself by holding his arm.

"Jane!" It was David.

Thanatos chuckled. "I think they know something is up. Soul mate bonds, even manufactured and dead ones, can alert powerful males when their mate is in danger. I wonder how long David will last now he risks losing a soul mate and not just the woman he's been fucking."

"I'm about to shove my sword up your ass." She teared up at his betrayal and his words, but she was ready to rip his head off.

His lips curved up against the back of her head, then a succession of bangs sounded from the hall they had come from.

"You let Hell inside," she whispered.

"Perhaps it was me . . . Perhaps it was another." He dragged her farther away. Pestilence and Famine followed side by side, but Thanatos kept himself protected.

"I should have guessed you were the unknown threat. Everything you've done has been to separate me from Death and David."

"You think I am the unknown threat?"

"Who else could it be?" She was confused and furious. Her body grew hotter as the walls lit up again.

Thanatos chuckled. "Still blind, my queen."

Yells from the humans erupted down the hall, then she heard Natalie's cry. That one sound had her soul screaming and the light latching onto her.

"Ah, there we go," Thanatos whispered. "Now destroy." He vanished, and Jane didn't give him another thought. She ran, ignoring Pestilence's and Famine's shouts for her to wait.

Her palms burned, and she balled her fists, afraid they'd somehow catch fire.

"Jane." Famine caught up to her. "Sweetest Jane, listen to me—it's consuming you. Help your soul fight back. You need to stay pure, or it will rule you." He looked ahead as several figures began appearing.

Pestilence released an arrow that exploded into a fiery wall of white flames to keep the enemy back. He turned to her, grabbing her hands and hissing as he yanked her to a stop. "Focus, Jane. You will bring the entire fortress down."

Famine eyed the fiery wall before looking behind them when Death's roar caused rocks to fall from the ceiling. "I see; we must let her unleash it here." He looked up and closed his eyes. "Jane, let her burn."

"What?" Pestilence held her tight when she tried to run.

Famine walked closer and grabbed her face. "Listen to me. This is your moment. Your fate demands you fail, but I believe you have changed your fate a thousand times in your short life. Change it again. If she burns in the light, burn with her. Become the fire. Become light."

"Brother . . ." Pestilence tried to shake him off.

Famine shook his head and leaned down, kissing her forehead. "Glow. Now."

The light she emitted grew brighter, and Famine covered her hands with his, grimacing as smoke rose from where he touched her. "Every night, my brother fell in love with a silly girl who believed in magic and monsters while she smiled at him, showing him only love. Lucifer wanted a weapon. He didn't lose one when he trapped your dark soul, Jane. He unleashed a queen who would stand fearless before that demon and all who cowered behind her. The vampire prince who was given no soul mate, who was ready to let you go to your true mate, said fuck it and claimed a goddess to be his eternity. You belong to all of them, beautiful girl. And they belong to you. This light is not of Heaven. Not anymore. But tonight, you are going to make it yours."

"Brother," Pestilence said, "my wall will fade. We must hurry."

Famine nodded, turning out her palms as he walked behind her. "Move out of her way, brother. When she breaks this wall, find her children. I shall stay with her."

"What are we doing?" Jane shook as more heat sizzled under her skin. She saw her soul fighting the white light as it wrapped around her, binding her, trying to enter her.

"Don't be afraid." Famine held her hands, aiming them as his skin began to burn. "Don't worry for me. I will heal."

Her arms trembled as she whimpered, trying to stay calm as her soul screamed. "It's hurting her."

"I know." He kissed the top of her head. "Now burn with her. I will hold you. Then you will rise on your own."

Mentally, Jane locked eyes with her soul. She already flickered with her gold flames, but she was in pain as white light shot wildly around her, hitting her.

Jane reached for her, grasping her as her soul closed her eyes, surrendering to the light. They screamed as it ate away at her soul's flames, smothering them.

"I've got you," Famine whispered, shaking behind her. "Breathe. Let it inside."

Like she had swallowed razor blades, Jane and her soul choked, thrashing as they wrapped their arms around each other.

Famine spoke again, his voice just as soothing as Death's. "All this time, you have fought against darkness. It has knocked you down, left you bloody, bruised, and scarred. Each time, it has consumed you. Each time, you have risen stronger. You are stronger now. It is darkness that will fall and shatter as it crashes upon you. No longer will you fall."

Jane and her soul stopped thrashing and opened their eyes. She knew they were casting the same white light her soul's eyes did as they stared at one another. It wasn't right, but Jane knew her soul was with her, and they both saw the blue flame swirling around them. David was a part of her now, and he'd be there. And even if he wasn't tied to her, Death would always be there. She knew they'd find a way to reforge their bond.

Her soul smiled, though she looked monstrous with her glowing white eyes. *"We will save them now. It will not break us. We will make it ours."*

Our gold. Jane's sadness grew to new heights. It was gone.

Her soul stood taller. *"We will make our own gold flames. Find our prince. He is the key."*

They told me to stay away from him.

Her soul shook her head as she exhaled puffs of white smoke. *"Find him."*

"Jane!" Famine shook her. "Snap out of it."

She regained her balance, noting how Pestilence's gaze widened upon seeing her.

"It has her," he said.

"Good." Famine aimed her hands, palms out, and let go.

Jane swore she saw Lucifer out of the corner of her eye watching her, but nothing was there when she turned her head.

Still, heat rolled through her veins like lava flowing down scarred valleys. Her arms began to tremble as a rumble shook within her chest. It raced faster toward her palms but also to her heart.

Her soul roared with her, and Jane released the light consuming her.

A beam of silvery white light shattered Pestilence's wall quickly and didn't stop. She pushed more energy into her attack, watching the beasts awaiting her burst into flames.

Pestilence was running beside her, but he vanished quickly.

Jane didn't pause. She could hear her kids crying and found out why when she rounded the corner.

Astaroth spewed fire from his eyes and mouth, incinerating Ravagers and what she quickly surmised to be Devourers. Beelzebub unleashed arrow after arrow, destroying anything he chose to. All of her princes were there. They had encircled the survivors, and her babies were in the center, hugging each other as other small children clung to them.

Jane summoned her sword, slicing everything in her path. She called her shield next, smashing it into one vampire before throwing it like a frisbee and crushing more who were trying to get under Asmodeus' chains.

Hollering out, she hacked the head off a creature she didn't recognize, only aware it was from Hell and not on her side when it tried to bite her. Before its head hit the floor, she spun, cutting heads from bodies, fueled by the screams of children and the shouts from her men to grab the survivors. Blood flew across her face, and light from her blade shot through walls, making rocks collapse.

"Be careful, my queen," Asmodeus shouted. "Valhalla is collapsing, and your light is too powerful."

She didn't hesitate to switch Light Bringer for Heaven's Reaper and swung, dismembering every attacker until she was part of the circle protecting the innocents.

"Beelzebub, what are they still doing here?" she roared.

"Apologies, my queen." He continued releasing arrows. "The second entrance exploded as soon as we reached it, and demons entered through portals throughout the fortress. We have to defeat all of them now, my queen. Then we can make a new exit."

Jane summoned her gun, firing as she wiggled through the crowded victims until she was beside Pestilence and her children. "Hi, babies."

"Mama," Natalie cried. "Your eyes."

"It's okay." She smiled. "You try to stay calm, okay? Help the other kids and stay close to Pest. He'll protect you."

Pestilence nodded as he stood tall, firing arrows over her shoulder. Sparks of white light fell around them like fireworks, and the children screamed when loud, demonic screeching filled the air.

"I have to go fight now." She kissed her babies and pulled her mask into place. "Pest, my cousin?"

"I have no idea, Jane. I do not see Hades either," he said, making her growl as she watched her hands glow. "Famine is checking the surrounding rooms. Some have barricaded themselves inside exam rooms."

Jane didn't wait. She pushed through the crowd, helping some of the injured up when others shoved them down.

"Jane!" David's angry yell made the hair on her neck stand. A hot hand closed around her arm, yanking her around. "Why are you still here?"

She smiled up at her vampire, throwing her arms around his neck. "You're still you."

He kissed her head before holding her at arm's length. "Baby, I won't stay in control." He reached out, grabbing a vampire by the throat and ripping his jaw off before hurling his body at a Ravager. "You need to go."

"There's nowhere to go! The exits are caved in." She tried to hang onto him, afraid he'd snap.

He pulled her close to him as he loaded his gun. "Where are our children?"

She pointed them out. "They're okay. Just scared."

His dark eyes took in the scene quickly before focusing on her. He was so beautiful, even at his most monstrous. "Why are your eyes white?"

"The light is one with my soul. She told me to find you, that you would help us be gold again."

He frowned, searching her eyes. "I am slipping, my love. I can't help you."

"You're not." She touched his cheek, smiling as he snarled and fired his gun over her shoulder but cradled her head as though they were sharing a sweet moment together.

He gripped her hair and forced her to look at him. "You need to get away from me. I already want to bleed you dry."

She pulled her mask down and exposed her neck. "Here. Feed."

He hissed, pushing her away. "Don't!"

"David." She tried to hold on to him, but he stepped away.

"I'm going to search for Tristan, Apollo, and Lance. You stay here or go where they tell you to. I love you. Just stay away. I don't know why your soul would tell you I can help, but you must stay away. I'm going to hurt you." He started to leave but turned, reaching for her before cupping her cheeks and kissing her hard. "I love you. So much, Jane."

Before she could say it back, he was gone.

She wanted to cry, but she didn't. She raced to the front of the circle, briefly admiring the collection of princes and her army falling in place around the survivors, some carrying more injured or unconscious vampires and humans. Asmodeus had moved out farther, swinging his chains, cutting everything in his path in half while Beelzebub fired arrows that exploded on impact. Astaroth threw fireballs from his hands, and she grinned, noticing Famine easily cutting through dozens of Ravagers and demons. She fired around him as several of her men carried wounded humans past him.

"The fire wielders are coming," someone shouted.

"Kill them," another hollered.

"No." Jane rushed forward, searching for them. She saw nothing, but she felt it. Heat.

"My queen." Beelzebub grabbed her arm. "Your mate went through there. He is likely handling the matter. If they get in here, though, they will destroy every one of these innocents. We must keep them out if they reach the entrances."

Jane's breathing sped as she heard David and Death roaring together. "What's happening?"

"Berith and Thanatos are engaging them." He locked eyes with her. "Stay, my queen. We can send them help."

She summoned her shield and Death's sword. "Stay with my family."

"My queen!" He reached for her, but she was too fast.

"Jane," Famine hollered, but she used her shield to plow through the chaos. If David and Death were fighting, Apollo and Tristan were free to do as they pleased. So she darted toward the heat, ignoring the bloody, blank stares from the corpses on the floor.

She was about to round a corner, where she was sure she heard fire fighting fire when she was tackled to the ground.

"Fuck." She rolled, kicking her attacker off and standing the same moment he did. "Lance, you piece of shit! I'm trying to fight a battle here."

He pointed a sword at her face. "I'm not on your side, whore queen. This is the perfect opportunity to take you out."

She released her shield, allowing it to vanish as she held up her sword. "You really want to do this right now? While these things are trying to eat everyone?"

"Afraid?"

The yells behind her were breaking her heart. She could hear all of them, and they wouldn't be able to come and stop her from killing Lancelot if he forced her to end him. She would not let David suffer the heartache of the old friend he spared killing her.

"If you fight me, I'll kill you, Lance. I don't have time for this. Please, don't make me have to tell David I killed his oldest friend."

He snarled, swinging the sword at her neck. She blocked it and met his swings with her own, hoping she could quickly work out a way to knock him out and drag him off somewhere safe.

She was so caught up in blocking each of his swings that she froze when Lancelot roared and transformed.

He shoved her to the ground and leapt over her, tackling a hairless monster on four legs. He tore its muscular limbs off, shaking them until he punched a hole into its chest and ripped out its spine.

He growled, turning in her direction as she smiled at him.

"Thank you, Lance."

He looked ready to attack her, but hellhounds appeared out of thin air. With another hard shove in the direction she had been going, he turned to charge the demon dogs.

Jane said a quick prayer for him and ran to where she knew a major fight was happening between fire wielders.

Again, her hands began to glow, but she embraced it, breathing out as heat spread down her arms, burning her hands.

When an orange glow lit up her surroundings, Jane slowed. She stared at her hands as she approached the corner. She was shaking, afraid to fight her two friends, but she peeked out and gasped.

Tristan and Apollo were indeed fighting one another, and she stared in shock as they swung their enraged gazes around to her. More shocking was that they both aimed at her with their fire.

She roared, rushing into the hall they were in, putting herself in the middle. Their first attacks smashed into the wall, crumbling part of the ceiling, but they were aiming at her again.

Jane's arms already felt like fire, but she let her instincts guide her. She balled her hands into tight fists, screaming as twin infernos flew toward her.

They never hit her skin. Instead, she met their flames with light, yelling out as she felt the power they wielded fighting to lick her flesh. The pressure was immense, and the heat was terrifying, considering she already felt like she was burning on the inside.

Somehow, she smiled through the pain and fear. Whether good or bad, Jane was going to control her chaos. Her men and followers were afraid for her, but she wouldn't cry or run. She would fight for the two men trying to kill her—for everyone in the fortress.

The flames from each side of her met the cocoon of light she'd managed to form out of instinct. The roar of the twin infernos was deafening. Apollo's and Tristan's battle yells were even louder as they pushed more energy into their attacks, trying to engulf her.

Light versus fire. Both powerful. Both capable of warmth or destruction.

Jane yelled louder, but her light seemed to collapse in on itself. She shook her head, sweat dripping from her nose as she screamed, giving all she had.

Her soul roared with her, and white filled her vision as she pushed against their flames.

Tristan and Apollo cried out when their flames rebounded, scalding the floor and walls around them.

Jane bent over, breathing heavily now she no longer had attacks crushing her. The light dimmed, revealing rubble and charred bodies.

There was recognition from both of her friends, but hunger still clouded their judgment. They bared their fangs, and she bared hers.

With a taunting hiss, she allowed light to flow through her arms again and dared them to attack.

It seemed that, while crazed, both men knew they had met their match.

But, as she watched them give each other a long stare, she knew they had just decided to put a hold on their fight to join forces—to eliminate her.

It should've frightened her to take on both of them as their bodies were engulfed in flames, but an awareness within the light she held awoke and prepared her to fight with a style she had never engaged in before.

She flexed her tiny arms as they began to glow. Her entire body was lit, providing her the same protection their flames gave them. It wasn't as intimidating as their fire forms, and compared to their rippling muscles, she was a weak, insignificant girl. Her soul shook her head at her, and Jane smiled at their fiery snarls.

Giving her little warning, Tristan darted at her, fist raised to pummel her. She blocked his punch, unleashing her own to his side. He dodged, growling as he exchanged more blows with her. For now, she stopped his attacks, holding the tiniest bit of hope he would snap out of it and this would all be over or that she could render him unconscious and do the same to Apollo. But Apollo joined the fight.

He kicked her side, ripping a scream from her, but she didn't stop. She punched Tristan in the chest, knocking him back a bit so she could turn to avoid Apollo's punch.

Fire erupted from the hand that had just missed her face. Then, as if he was wielding a flaming whip, it cut the air, but Jane moved into him, knocking his arm up so it would fly wildly behind them.

They took turns landing hits before Tristan reengaged her. Jane didn't waver. She blocked, dodged, and inflicted her own damage on the two vampires. But it seemed both Tristan and Apollo were done holding back.

Flames from both ignited, creating dangerous waves of fire she had to either dodge or attack.

She swung her arm down with a similar movement, letting her light beam shoot out to meet their fire. The explosion was thunderous, and more attacks were being sent her way.

Jane kept up her defense, splitting their flames with her beams of light and causing their fire to rain down around them.

Tristan and Apollo reacted by shooting out walls of fire. Jane secretly praised her childish love for cartoons and video games as she hollered, thrusting her palms out to lay out light beams. This light was deadly, not just an impressive show of pretty colors.

Tristan yelled, grabbing his shoulder where she'd managed to nick him. He aimed another blast of his own at her at the same time.

She thrust her palm toward the oncoming ball of fire to hit it with another blast of light. The impact was different. They each exploded, but neither one overpowered the other.

Her arm shook from the effort of keeping her beam intact. Both blazes pushed against the other while sparks of fire and light shot out around the edges. She whined under the heat, nearly engulfing her from behind. She hollered out again, her feet sliding back from the force of Tristan's attack while a massive wall of his fire broke over her light. It sent an enormous wave of fire at her. Inches separated her cheek from his deadly flames as they continued to rage a wall of fire beside her. If she were to grow weak and fall forward, she would be engulfed, and she knew her barrier would give out. She could already feel her strength waning.

When the burning fire from Apollo's new inferno made sweat drench her back, she cried out, knowing she was about to be burned alive. But a crack of lightning shot through the space between her and Apollo's attack, sending the flames into the wall instead of her flesh.

"Zeus," the name barely passed her lips as she made eye contact with the king of the Greeks.

"I will hold him off you," he yelled at her. "More help is coming."

Jane nodded, feeling him join her with his back to hers. She had no idea how or why he wasn't affected, but she was happy for the help. She still had to defeat Tristan without killing him.

It took everything she had, but she forced her other arm to throw a punch through Tristan's fire. Her light barrier gave out, and her arm burned in an instant. She screamed through the pain and punched forward, sending another beam of light to smother his flames.

Her light effectively knocked Tristan's attack back, allowing her to recover momentarily and take in her blistered skin. It would heal, but she whimpered at the sight of her seared flesh before concentrating again. The smell of her skin cooking was hard to shut out of her mind, but she raced forward, knocking Tristan to the ground. She pinned him with her burnt hand, screaming when he grabbed the charred skin and ripped some away. Despite the agony she was in, she landed a punch to his jaw and knocked him out.

She'd barely caught her breath when she heard Death roar for her.

Vengeance at last.

Death squeezed his hand around the cold heart still beating inside Berith's chest.

Surprising him, though, Berith laughed and said, "Before I die, I want you to know this—I possessed the boys who abused her. I felt her baby-soft skin through their touch," he continued, "and I watched the light leave her pretty hazel eyes. The Accuser protected me. He even wiped my memory, but I remember her now. Her little trembling thighs and how her body began to fill out. So precious. So innocent. And you had no idea." He spat out blood, laughing. "Now kill me, you fool. You won't make it to her in time anyway."

Death breathed in, feeling his heart beating again because it had stopped at hearing the confession, and glanced over his shoulder. David still fought Thanatos, so he returned his focus to Berith. This creature had destroyed his Sweet Jane's innocence, and he was too enraged to inflict more pain. All he could do was make these promises. "Father's wrath will not end for you. There will be no mercy on your soul." Black smoke spilled from Berith's mouth as the dark-blue orb was torn out of his body. "May Heaven's punishers be unforgiving."

With that, he ripped the monster's heart out the moment his harsh last breath caressed his ears. He stared into the empty eyes of his enemy until Berith ignited in green and black fire.

"You might want to hurry," Thanatos whispered, his breathing labored.

Death spun around, finding Thanatos smiling softly as he clutched his side where the handle of David's dagger stuck out.

Thanatos looked at the bloody trail leading out of the room. "He's almost there." He then vanished, leaving Death momentarily confused.

Then it hit him.

David had lost his fight.

"No," he roared and ran down the narrow halls. He kept trying to teleport, but he couldn't sense her. She'd summoned her suit's power. He frantically sought David's soul signature and howled when he could not feel it. "Jane!"

He stopped, searching the ground, trying to scent David or Jane. There were too many bodies, though. He didn't know where she was. Why was she using the suit that way?

"No!" He knew why. David was already there. "Jane."

"It's okay." Her voice was but a whisper, but he heard it, and he vanished, appearing at the end of the hall. His eyes went wide as he watched Jane lower the glowing hand she'd aimed at David as he tossed every one of her guards out of his path to her.

"Jane," Death roared, his eyes pricking as he summoned his gun to shoot David.

She smiled at him peacefully as David grabbed her, yanking her up and baring his fangs at her.

She gave Death another smile. "I love you." Then she focused on David, still smiling.

Death shot every demon that blocked him. "Stop him, Jane!" He started to teleport. He could make it, but pain exploded in his back where a knife had stabbed, and the wielder gripped him in a hold only one Fallen angel knew how to execute—his former general. Death couldn't teleport from this hold.

Thanatos yanked him closer. "You can't make it."

"No." Death thrashed, roaring as he watched a surrendering look of love and sadness spread over Jane's smile as David leaned down, ready to rip her throat out. "No!"

"I love you, David," she whispered, closing her eyes.

"Jane," Death roared as the last inch was closed between David's mouth and her beautiful skin.

Death fought desperately; he would not be able to stop the next series of events, and he would gladly allow himself to lose all control of the beast he was and destroy everyone in existence. He couldn't lose her.

"Watch," Thanatos growled, tightening his hold.

Death couldn't look away even if he tried. His breath stopped when she gasped.

No razor-sharp teeth ripped into her skin. No fangs. No bite.

David pressed a soft kiss against the base of her throat before his savage snarl silenced the hall. "I promised never to hurt you." His voice was strained, but he kissed her neck again.

A sad smile formed on Jane's lips as David pulled back to look at her face. Her eyes slowly opened. They were completely white, but he swore he could see a faint gold flame trying to appear around Jane's entire body.

She sobbed as David smiled and held her cheek delicately. There was no cruelness in his touch—no monster trying to destroy the girl they both loved.

Thanatos chuckled. "You make her whole, Death. You love and cherish her so dearly she will never truly part from you. But David is pure. He is good and can extinguish all that threatens to engulf her heart and soul."

"I love you, too," David said, his expression pained but loving as he lifted her.

Jane showed no hesitation—no fear—when David pressed his lips to hers.

At that moment, more of Jane's men and survivors spilled into the hall, all unable to look at anything but Jane wrapped in David's arms as they kissed.

David pulled her tight against him, and a flicker of silver was seen behind her shutting eyelids. They kissed deeply, a flash of silver light erupting between them. It was coming from Jane. It was still Lucifer's light. He could feel the darkness living inside it. It was going to burst out of her.

Screams of agony stretched out across the room. Her silvery-white glow was burning every one of vampire blood.

"Jane," he yelled.

Thanatos squeezed hard. "Watch."

Death saw it now. Gold. Golden, heavenly light.

It was beautiful and warm as it flooded the vast opening, touching everything and everyone in her wake. No one moved. Many still screamed, but the rest fell to their knees to receive her light.

"What?" Death whispered, feeling the gold light wrap around him. He only felt this when he and Jane shared their true kiss.

Thanatos fell to his knees but still held Death as they bathed in the warm glow.

David and Jane continued their kiss while every enemy demon and fallen burst into flames, screaming out as she sent them back to Hell. Those who served Jane, though, vampires, fallen angels, and demons, stayed kneeling with their eyes closed as the light grew more intense.

It should have been burning every vampire it touched, except Arthur and the knights, but it didn't. Only those deemed unfit for forgiveness crumbled to the floor, writhing as her sentence was delivered.

More miraculous than watching the damned receive their punishment was that other damned souls were unaffected by the destructive light. Instead, they wore smiles of peace as she granted them absolution.

Her Demon and Fallen Army fell to their bellies without protest. Fallen angels who had descended so far into darkness they had bat-like wings and horns began to morph back into the raven-winged angels who had originally been cast from Heaven, while more powerful Fallen's wings were drained of their inky color and restored to the dove-like wings of the holy.

"Refuse." The cry came from every one of her princes and Thanatos.

The raven color returned to their wings, and Asmodeus' dragon wings remained intact, though his horns and serpent tail faded in the golden light, leaving no trace of the monstrous appendages.

"They choose to stay for her," said Thanatos. "They refuse their deliverance. So do I."

While the Princes chose to refuse their freedom, the remaining Fallen began igniting in white light and shooting upward, returning to God's kingdom.

Thanatos shoved Death and backed away from him.

Death was breathing heavily as he watched the kiss between Jane and David draw to an end. He looked back to see that Thanatos still wore the black wings of the Fallen. He had refused his freedom. But it was his eyes Death stared at. They were no longer the ruby color signifying his condemnation. They were blue again, just like his twin's.

"My Lord." Thanatos bowed to him before winking and disappearing in a poof of black mist.

Death spent no more time staring at the space his former general once stood and jerked his head around to see the others crawling to their feet. Piles of ash lay all around them, and he noticed every set of onyx eyes had been replaced with their original color. They were forgiven.

When lovely gold eyes met his, he smiled. Lucifer's wings were gone. It was just his girl wearing his cloak.

David hugged Jane, kissing her face. "I'm so sorry."

"It's okay." She caressed David's cheek before turning to where Death stood. "Come here, my love. I'm okay."

He was slow but walked past everyone cheering and crying until he reached her. "I thought I lost you, angel."

"Never." She grinned, sighing when David kissed her once more before handing her to Death.

"I apologize for scaring you," David said once she was in Death's arms. "You can fight me later. Let me go find my children. I'll be right back, my love."

She waved him off as she caressed Death's face. "It's okay."

He didn't hold back. He kissed her like it was the last time he ever would, and she kissed him just as fiercely.

"I'm okay."

He nodded, his wings flapping.

"*Shh* . . ." She kissed across his jaw. "Not yet."

"I know." He closed his eyes, breathing in her scent. "Baby girl, that broke me."

"No." She kissed him again, weakly wrapping her arms around his neck. "You knew he wouldn't hurt me. That is why you picked him."

He grunted, noticing she was shaking. "You're hurt." He held her away, growling when he saw how she was burned. "Jane."

"It was an accident." She smiled at him. "I just need some Vitamin D."

He shook his head, kissing her again. "I'll give you all the D you want if you never scare me like that again."

She chuckled, grinning as she looked around.

"Yes," he said, looking at the people she'd saved. "You did this."

"No." She shook her head. "I was just a vessel."

"No." He tilted her chin up. "You and David did this. Your faith in goodness. Your forgiveness for those who do not deserve it and your fierce protection of those who do."

"Okay." She was far too humble.

"I love you." He cupped her cheeks. "Please tell me you still love me."

That gorgeous smile that made him feel everything spread over her lips. "You never have to ask, Death. I love you, always."

He sighed, kissing her quickly as David returned.

"Jane." David hugged Natalie.

"Oh, God, don't tell me Nathan is hurt." Her eyes filled with tears.

"He's fine." David kissed her forehead. "I'm sorry I scared you—he's with Adam. But Adam is hurt. Let's hurry. I don't know what can be done, but he's asking for you. Hades is there. He said you would know what to do."

Death knew Adam's time was up, but he smiled as he watched his girl run toward the infirmary with her vampire.

"She'll need your guidance, brother," Famine said beside him. "Go. I will help Pest and her men find a way out without the entire mountain collapsing on them."

Death nodded, vanishing to help his angel with her new ability. She had no idea what she had just become.

543

37

KING & QUEEN

"Oh, Adam." Jane pushed past Gawain and Gareth. She knew they were worried about attacking her during the fight, and she wanted to reassure them she was fine, but she needed to help Adam.

Bedivere smiled sadly and stopped her from touching him. "Jane, he's in a lot of pain. Most of the drugs were destroyed, so I could only give him a small dose of morphine."

She teared up when she saw the nasty bite on his neck. "Is this from a vampire? Or from one of those other things?"

No one answered.

David squatted behind her, rubbing her back as he spoke gently, "Baby, nearly everyone lost control. He was too close, that's all."

She knew that, but seeing his wounds broke her heart. His neck was shredded on one side, and he was far too pale to be considered safe.

David kissed her temple. "Listen to me, Jane. He didn't want to leave Artemis behind."

Jane looked up, her gaze darting across the room to where Artemis sat crying. "She fed on him?"

David gently nudged Natalie toward Arthur. "She didn't know what she was doing. I am certain she urged him to leave, just as I did with you. She just wasn't able to overcome it like I managed to."

"She tried to make him leave, Jane," Hades said quietly as he handed

Bedivere a roll of gauze. "I told him to go as well—he didn't listen, and she managed to get to him before he could escape."

The teary green eyes locked on Jane's had been so hateful in the past, and all that hatred had been aimed at Jane. It would be so to—Releasing a breath and closing her eyes, Jane whispered, "Come here, Artemis."

"Jane . . ." Hades trailed off when David held up a hand, silencing him.

"Let her speak to her." David kissed Jane's temple before he stood.

Jane only opened her eyes when she felt Artemis kneel beside her. She hadn't expected to see Artemis offering her neck.

"Please make it quick." Artemis sobbed. "I'm so sorry. If he wakes, tell him I'm sorry."

Jane touched Artemis' back, sighing when her former rival flinched. "I'm sure he will tell you there's no reason to apologize, but you may do so when he wakes."

Artemis snapped her head up, eyes glistening with tears. "What? You're not going to kill me? No, I deserve to be punished."

"You're punishing yourself too much already, Artemis. I know you didn't mean to hurt him." Jane grabbed one of Artemis' hands, smiling. "Now, I want you to help make it right. Hold on to him for me—this is going to hurt quite a bit."

"What are you going to do to him?" Artemis placed a hand over Adam's as she held his opposite shoulder down.

Honestly, Jane didn't know. She followed a silent order as her hands began to glow and held them over Adam's wound. Death shimmered into view, but he merely smiled at her as he crossed his arms and watched.

"I'm trusting the voice whispering to my soul. *Shh* . . ." It wasn't really a voice, but that was the only way she could describe the loving feelings and thoughts urging her to believe in herself.

Jane closed her eyes, keeping the mental image of Adam's injury in her mind. She knew many blood vessels had been shredded with his skin, and his jugular was nicked. But it was as if the light inside her had a mind of its own. It told her everything would be okay, so she stood beside her soul and followed a single command. *Heal.*

David's beautiful heat appeared and mixed with the heavenly warmth of the golden light before flowing out of her palms and into Adam's torn, bloody neck. Like she had done with her previous powers, her mind connected with the gruesome injuries, and she directed the light to spread over each laceration—each torn blood vessel until all skin and muscle tissue sealed. When she was done, she already knew what she'd find. His wound was cauterized, no longer pumping out precious blood.

Adam jerked, groaning as he opened his eyes.

"Hello, cousin." Jane smiled and called to the light so it would return to her.

"Oh, Adam," Artemis cried, dropping her head to his chest. "I'm so sorry. I didn't mean to hurt you. Please forgive me."

Adam didn't respond vocally beyond groaning, but he put an arm around Artemis.

Jane knew they'd be okay, so she patted Adam's leg before allowing David to help her stand.

"Good job, sweetheart." He kissed her head. "We need to find a way out of the fortress. Your soldiers will arrange for Adam to get out."

Asmodeus bowed. "My queen, the North Gate is the least damaged exit. Your guards are already working with the vampires to clear the rubble. I have others moving the supplies there now. I fear much has been burned by the fire wielders, but we will salvage what we can for everyone."

"Okay." She grinned up at him. "I kinda miss your horns and tail already."

He chuckled, bowing his head. "Apologies, my queen. I do still have my wings."

She beamed up at him, giving him a quick hug. "Yes, as long as I have my dragon, I'm happy."

David shook his head, smiling. "Let's join your men at the gate. We should leave as soon as possible."

After taking one last look at Adam and realizing her cousin wasn't going to hold back his feelings for Artemis any longer, she chuckled and followed David. "Do you want me to hold her?" she asked Arthur.

Arthur patted Natalie's back. "No, she is fine. I feel terrible for them seeing us that way."

"They understand this was none of your faults." Jane smiled at Nathan in David's arms before focusing on Arthur. "You already know this. Stop doubting yourself. Your past mistakes with your powers are simply that— mistakes. That does not mean you are any less great. I promise God has faith in you and has already forgiven you."

David laughed at Arthur's astounded look. She knew she'd changed. She felt it with every breath she took, and when she turned her head, her eyes meeting her angel's, she knew he was just as overwhelmed by what had happened to her.

She held out her free hand to Death. "You're not afraid of me, are you?"

He grabbed her hand and began walking with them. "I fear only a world where you do not exist."

Jane lifted their hands and kissed the back of his. "Good thing I am with you always."

Death glanced at David. "May I speak with her alone?"

David stopped, turning her so he could give her a long kiss. "I love you. Listen carefully to whatever he tells you because I know he is more aware of what happened than the two of us. So pay attention and don't get distracted."

"I won't." She grinned at him. "I feel it. It's incredible."

David put his hand over her heart. "It is. I'll catch up with you shortly. I want to speak to Gawain and Gareth. They are upset about attacking you. So is Tristan."

She pushed up on the tips of her toes and kissed him again. "Tell them not to worry. And that my arm is already healing."

"I'll tell them." Her vampire smiled, caressing her cheek as he searched her eyes. "So pretty when you glow for us." David kissed her again before gesturing for Arthur to bring Natalie.

Death tugged her hand. "Do you have a new voice in your head?"

Jane hugged his arm as a warm tingle enveloped her body. "It's not quite a voice—but yes."

He nodded, guiding her through the damaged halls until they were at the caved-in exit where many of her men and vampires were moving rocks and debris.

"Are you okay?" She watched him, sighing as he lifted her and hugged her.

"It makes me feel as though we are even farther from each other, but I see no other way for you to be. This is merely another path for you."

She played with his hair as she watched everyone working hard. They were tired, but they were happy.

"Do you know what you can do now?" he murmured, kissing her neck.

She closed her eyes, breathing out slowly as she watched her soul twirl for him. "No. I know she is more aware, but she seems content with just being us. Nothing special."

His lips turned up against her skin. "You are beyond special."

"Yeah, yeah." She turned, kissing his cheek. "I see your soul."

He leaned back. "Mine?"

Jane slid her gaze over his body, knowing the green flames that occasionally formed his outline were, in fact, his soul. "He never stops watching me. Her."

Death smiled, putting his hand over her heart. "He watches both of you —you are the same. Just as he is me." He chuckled. "She likes to dance for me and for David's soul. She's hiding Lucifer's wings."

"Really?" Jane covered his hand, completely at peace as she watched him glide his fingers across her chest, and she could almost see her soul twirling around his fingertips.

"Yes, she is my girl, after all." He smirked, lifting his gaze to her face. "Do you see others?"

Before she could answer, a cry of celebration rang out behind them. The exit was open, but that wasn't what had her heart hammering away excitedly. "Death . . ."

He lowered her to the ground. "He's waiting for you."

"Who?" She stared up at her angel.

Death cupped her cheeks. "Another admirer for my Sweet Jane. Go see. He will help you discover what you are."

"Move," David said, waiting for several vampires to get out of his way. He knew Jane was ahead and couldn't escape the sudden urge to be close to her.

"Where's Mommy?" Natalie asked.

"She's probably outside," he answered, glaring at another vampire. He didn't intend to be rude, but he had his children in his arms and wanted his baby back with him.

The cheers from the survivors exiting the crumbling fortress died when the harsh wind blew around them.

"What are we going to do?" someone asked, taking in the bloody and ruined land surrounding the mountain.

David sighed, glancing at his brothers before watching all of Jane's men lower their heads. He quickly searched for her and sighed, relieved when he spotted her. She was at the front line, walking ahead of Death.

He pushed through the crowd until he was at Death's side. "What is it?"

Death didn't answer, so David focused on Jane. She was staring at the tree line opposite her, and that's when David noticed a silver light approaching her. His immediate thought was that it must be Lucifer, and he went to put the children down to go after her, but Pestilence placed a calm hand on David's shoulder.

"*Shh* . . ." Pestilence's eyes flashed as he grinned. "My brother called in a favor for his girl."

David whipped his head around to watch the source of light finally reveal itself.

Natalie gasped, as did the entire group of survivors.

A gray, winged unicorn walked toward Jane. It was massive. He was a male with a dark gray body, but he had a silver horn and steel-colored mane and wings.

"Lucifer has kept him imprisoned for several millennia," Pestilence said. "Well, not so much imprisoned." A faint smile teased the White Horseman's lips. "I would say it was more that he kept him for a special occasion he knew one day would come."

David couldn't believe what he was seeing. "What day?"

Pestilence smiled as Jane reached up to touch the creature's muzzle. "The day his queen, a beautiful gold flame who dreams of magic, would need a little assistance with her own."

The winged unicorn nuzzled Jane's hand as she laughed and rubbed her other hand along its neck.

David grew angry but also worried. "Lucifer sent this for her?"

Pestilence touched David's temple. "Close your eyes."

David didn't want to, but he obeyed. The world around him suddenly disappeared as he heard Death's voice and glimpsed when they realized Jane had summoned Famine. "Do it," Death said as Asmodeus bowed and vanished. When the scene illuminated, Asmodeus approached a glowing gate.

The demon king summoned chains and wrapped them around the bars, hissing as fire began to burn his hands.

A voice spoke behind him, and David turned, shocked to see Lucifer standing there.

"What brings you here, Asmodeus?" Lucifer asked, proving to David this event had already occurred. "I do not take kindly to traitors." Lucifer summoned a sword almost identical to the one Jane now had. "Nor do I allow them to live after attempting to steal from me."

Asmodeus sighed and lowered his head. "Death asked me to free him. Famine is coming to Valhalla soon. Your queen will be under attack once Hunger arrives. The fortress will need support to find accommodations for those who survive."

Lucifer's gaze slid away to where the gray unicorn was chained to a silver tree. Lucifer sighed before waving his hand. The gates opened as the chain holding the creature fell to the ground.

Asmodeus chuckled as he bowed. "My king."

Lucifer said nothing. He simply gave the beast a long stare before vanishing.

David breathed in deeply when the present world returned. He looked up to watch Jane.

She covered her mouth upon seeing a slightly smaller winged unicorn prance out. This one was white with a gold horn—a female.

It almost didn't surprise David to see both unicorns lower their massive heads in a bow to her, and he smiled when Jane lowered her arms, calming her excitement as she gracefully returned the gesture.

As soon as she did, Jane and the unicorns began to glow, and glittering, golden light rolled through everything, revealing horses with riders far beyond his plane of view.

"Ah, he found them," Asmodeus said as every one of the demons and fallen angels bowed their heads to the two unicorns.

David watched as the crowd fell to their knees when Jane and the unicorns straightened.

Death walked toward Jane. The female neighed and pranced around him happily, but the angel kept his gaze on Jane. Even when he patted the female winged unicorn on her rear and muttered, "Go introduce yourself, silly girl."

Death kissed Jane before lifting and hugging her. "I know you love them. Let's get you on so he can solidify his bond." Death kissed her once more before putting her on the stallion's back.

David was so absorbed in watching Jane's happiness that he didn't notice the female had approached him. When he did, he stilled, watching her shake her head. Her mane brushed against his side, and Nathan reached out without hesitation. The unicorn gently nuzzled Jane's son's hand before she looked at Natalie, who slowly held out her hand for her.

David smiled over at Jane. She was crying but so happy as she watched her children meet a magical creature even he had not believed existed.

Pestilence nudged David. "Bow to her. She wishes to claim you as her rider."

"Me?" David looked into the female's eyes, smiling at the gold flames greeting him there.

"I believe Lucifer had some inspiration when he created her for King."
Pestilence inclined his head toward the towering male Jane sat atop.

"Lucifer made her?" David asked, lowering his head.

"King would only allow one rider, and Lucifer knew it would be his
queen. So he made a female to keep him company."

David stood straighter and allowed Arthur and Gawain to take the children so he could touch her since she kept her head down.

Arthur smiled at him. "I can hear her. She wishes for you to mount
her."

"Of course she does," Gareth said. "She's got that same lovesick gleam
Jane gets in her eyes. Yet again, Jane's connections with angels, even the
King of Hell, have given her the most amazing gifts. Am I not as pretty as
she is?"

"No." David shook his head, laughing at his brother before rubbing
along her cheek. He dragged his hand around, smiling when she extended
her wings to make it easier for him to get on. "She's not going to fly off with
me, is she?"

Arthur laughed. "No, she simply wishes to seal her bond to you. She
says Lucifer calls her Queen."

"Of course." David's chest tightened a bit. This creature was made by an
angel who wanted to take his baby from him, but he could not deny he had
already felt an attachment to the animal. "Hello, Queen."

She lowered her head even more, so David mounted her, smiling at
Jane when she beamed at him.

One of the riders on the other horses dismounted the black stallion he
was on and walked toward Arthur. "Greetings, Great King. I am Joseph. If
you would like to instruct the survivors to select a rider, we would be
honored to transport all of you to your new home."

David held out his arms for Natalie when she reached for him.

Arthur handed her over before extending his hand to the rider.

"Bring him here, Queen," Death said. "Gawain, bring Nathan."

Natalie gasped, clutching Queen's mane when she began to move.

"Don't pull too hard, princess." David grinned, helping her hold on
better.

"She's pretty," Natalie whispered.

"She is." David focused on Jane now.

"David, they've come to take us to meet someone Death knows." She
pointed at the riders. "They are called the Two Hundred Million
Horsemen."

"They are not that numerous," Death said, lifting Nathan to sit in front of Jane. "But that is what you might have read of them in the biblical text."

"I thought they were a destructive force from Hell." David glanced at the riders. They wore breastplates bright as fire or blue as sapphires, and their helmets were designed to mimic a lion's head. The beasts were impressive, but their most noticeable trait was that they were breathing smoke, and fire swirled within them whenever they opened their mouths.

"Well, I am the Queen of Hell." Jane winked at him.

"Fine." David sighed, worried but happy because she was happy. "Please be careful on him, though. I don't want him flying away with you."

Death smiled as emerald flames erupted from the rocky ground, revealing Sorrow. "King does not follow Lucifer's orders. Nor do the Two Hundred Million—they answer to the Horsemen Bringer."

"Really?" Jane asked.

"Yes. Even though there are three commanders: Joseph, Ephraim, and Manasseh, they are Jane's to command." Death glanced around the crowd. "Where the fuck is Adam?"

David pointed him out.

"Adam, you're not that hurt. Get your dumbass over here," Death snapped.

When Adam tried to bring Artemis, Death growled. "Find another rider, Artemis. Sorrow will not carry outside of Jane's bloodline."

"Don't be so mean," Jane said as Adam walked Artemis to a different rider. "Aw, he's being so chivalrous."

David chuckled, watching her completely happy to see her cousin with Artemis. He should've known she'd end up accepting her. She just needed time.

Jane zoned in on several groups of humans. "Those women are frightened, and no one is helping them. Let me go help."

"They'll figure it out," Death said.

Jane ignored him and beamed when King lowered his head for her to get off. "Thank you, King. I'll be right back." She ran toward a group of humans Arthur and the knights organized into smaller groups of survivors and soldiers. She giggled when Gareth intercepted her by scooping her up and spinning her around.

"Death, where did the riders come from?" David asked as he and Death kept their eyes on Jane.

"They have been locked within an inner circle of Hell. Asmodeus told King his Rider Queen would need extra horses. So, after King was free, he secured what his rider would need. A fleet at her command." Death casually waved his hand. "They will carry the others for us." He turned to Queen, giving her a light pat on her rear. "My girl here found Nyc."

"Your girl?" David asked, glancing at the male unicorn.

Death smirked. "She's like Jane. She can't resist me. Dear God, why is she bringing those women over here?"

David chuckled as Jane led a group of timid humans to them.

"Death, do the riders have names?" she asked, keeping her eyes on the few women blushing as they stared at David. "These women said they don't seem to speak."

One of the women spoke up. "We just didn't know what to do because they don't answer us."

"They will answer to Jane," Death said. "Arthur can read their thoughts, though. So he can communicate."

"Oh," Jane murmured, jumping a little when a thought seemed to occur to her. "Goodness, I didn't even ask your names. I feel snobby. Let me introduce myself, and then I'll help you with the riders." She held out her hand. "I'm Jane. This is David and Death. They're my men, boyfriends—er—soul mates" Her face reddened. "I haven't actually figured out how to label the three of us. I'm with both of them. They don't do each other—just me. I don't share."

Death covered his laugh by turning away.

Even though David wanted to laugh at her silliness and possessiveness, he nodded politely to the women. "Hello, ladies."

Most of the women still had their mouths hanging open at Jane's words, but a few bowed their heads, murmuring, "Sir David."

"So, what's your name?" Jane asked the blonde who had spoken first. It was polite, but she was definitely asking for their names to keep an eye on them.

"Ashley," she said before turning around and pointing each woman out. "That's Emily, Katie, Desiree, Kaitlyn, Dinah, Kelly, Zeyba, Fabia, Zahlé, Éabha, Leah, Laura, Shane, Aisham, Sadhbh, Maria, Jessica, and the last one there is Varshini. We grouped together to survive after we fled from our homes. We were rescued by the knights, actually. We're from the U.S. They found us shortly after the plague broke out. Sir David was quite busy, but he was the one who suggested we be flown to safety. We never got to thank you and your friends for sending us on your plane to Camelot."

"Oh." David had no idea what she was talking about, but he knew they had sent several groups back with the planes as they traveled through the

JANIE MARIE

country before finding Jane. "It was no trouble. I am glad you have all stuck together and are as well as can be."

Death chuckled before nudging Jane. "Baby girl, find riders for them quickly. Just speak to the rider, and he will respond to you telepathically. They are yours to command." He kissed her quickly and whispered low enough so the women wouldn't hear him. "I know you think they are checking us out, but they are just stunned because I look like the Grim Reaper, and David is—well, David. So stop scowling. You are trying to appear diplomatic, and that means always smiling, beautiful. God will be a bit disappointed if you get feisty so soon." He smacked her butt and pointed to one of the nearest riders. "Go to him."

She did, speaking kindly with a smile on her face, even though she still shot a few of the women dark looks for staring.

"She's never going to get over being territorial," Death said as Adam approached. "The blond one was doing naughty things to you in her head."

"I'm sure she was." David grinned at him. "It makes for interesting love-making with Jane if she knows I am stared at for too long. Too bad they can't see you. She might break us."

Adam groaned. "Please stop talking about having sex with my cousin. I had to find out from Artemis that she's banging both of you now."

Death snickered as he gestured to Sorrow. "Stop acting jealous that we're getting action while you're with a virgin. Now get on before I make your ass walk."

David shook his head. He didn't want Artemis mocked, but there was no stopping Death from saying what he wanted to.

Adam glared at Death. "Is she some sort of divine being now?"

"It is beyond your comprehension, mortal." Death's eyes glowed brightly for a few seconds. "If she wishes to explain more to you, she will. I suggest you not ask, though."

"Whatever." Adam sighed but smiled at Jane as she bounded over, giggling.

She hugged Adam carefully. "I'm so glad you're looking better. Take good care of him, Sorrow." She walked to Queen, petting her. "Hello."

"Mommy, she's a unicorn," Natalie said.

"Yes, I know." Jane grabbed David's hand, kissing it. "Do you like her?"

"I do, my love. She reminds me of you." He bent down, raising her hand and kissing her fingers. "Let's get moving. I have a feeling you will be leading us."

Death held Nathan in place, but he waved Jane to come to him. "David's right. You have a long journey ahead, and you have work to do. King will explain."

Jane gave David another smile before going to Death. "How did you know she would pick David?"

Her angel smiled at her. "She told me she has dreams of blue and green eyes and asked me to find her a rider since I refused to be hers."

David smiled as Queen pranced around King, appearing to show him off to her mate.

"She's silly, just like you." Death kissed Jane's fingers. "Now enjoy the ride. I will fly with the others to ensure the skies remain clear for you."

"Thank you, Death." She wiped the icy tears from her cheeks.

"Always, Sweet Jane." Death leveled a frightening stare at King. "Take care of her, or I will lock you up again."

Jane shoved him as he laughed.

David rubbed Queen's neck, helping Natalie stay in place as she kissed her. "You said she found Nyc?"

"She's been roaming around waiting for me to free King." Death affectionately caressed Queen's muzzle. "I gave Nyc orders when the plague was released, but he went off the plane of existence—no doubt with his mother's help. I haven't been able to locate the fucker. She promised to find him for me, and she came through."

"Why did you never tell me about them?" Jane stared at Death.

"Because one has to be worthy and pure to ride them. Even looking at them is dangerous if they do not wish to be seen." He smiled at Jane. "Your knight helped you achieve a purity no other can, and you both proved how worthy you are to bear witness to God's purest creation. They wish to show off for you." He nodded to King. "He was made for Lucifer."

"Before he fell," Pestilence said, releasing a whistle, which caused his angels to take to the sky.

Death's wings appeared as he spoke to David. "Queen has already asked King where to go. He will lead. Jane's magic will begin to mix with his as he helps her stabilize it because she is far too powerful to be around safely. Demons are lingering in the forest. He will give her some practice and show her how to use her gift."

David realized Jane wasn't listening at all.

"He's speaking to her telepathically," Death said, a bit of sadness in his tone.

"Does Nathan need to ride with one of us?" David continued watching Jane as she bobbed her head and giggled a few times.

"He's fine," Death said. "King is shielding everyone from going blind at the sight of them. He's more powerful than you can imagine. He is happy to finally be with her, though. He'll continue protecting everyone from their magic."

Asmodeus pulled Lancelot forward. "My queen?"

Jane finally looked around and smiled at Lancelot, even though his former friend glared at her and King. "Lance, please tell me I don't have to hogtie and gag you."

Lance met King's stare for only a few seconds before snarling at Jane. "I saved you out of convenience and nothing more. I needed you to kill the others for me."

Jane sighed, her eyes dropping to King, and David knew she was being told something again.

"No, we're bringing him. Which one?" She lifted her head when the male rider turned his head in her direction. "Oh, I see. Yes, he looks quite strong."

David chuckled, smiling at Natalie as her little mouth fell open.

"Is he talking to Mommy in her mind?" she whispered.

"I think so, princess." David loved watching his girl in her element. This was only the beginning of the magic she would bless him with.

She lifted her gaze to him, the gold inferno in her eyes mesmerizing him.

My goddess.

Her eyes shifted to Lance as she gestured for him to go to the horseman who had approached. "Get on, or I am serious about hogtying you. Don't force me to disrespect you. I'm grateful for your help in there, even if it wasn't for me. Now honor me the relief of not having to inflict harm on you."

David chuckled as Lancelot growled and got on behind the silent horseman.

"Thank you, Lance." She smiled before winking at David and letting King trot away.

Death let out a loud whistle, and Jane's army took to the skies. "Follow your queen. Avoid their light as they cleanse the way. Those who don't deserve a second chance will perish. Locate those who pass their test."

"Cleanse?" David watched Jane's body glowing as King began to glow as well.

"They will cleanse the path they forge. Any who seek redemption, even secretly, will have the chance to earn it." Death patted Queen's rear. "Give him a good ride, girl."

"What's Mommy going to do?" Natalie looked up.

David was about to respond, but King let out a loud neigh and sprinted forward as Jane's body became a gold blur. Then light burst from her, rolling like a wave ahead of her. Demons hidden in the trees began fleeing in the thousands before getting swallowed in light and plummeting to the ground or igniting into flames.

"That's my girl." Death shot upward and flew after them as Jane's army followed.

Pestilence and Famine mounted their horses and flanked David.

"Let's get moving," Famine said. "King is much faster than any horse. They'll make it to the sea in no time."

David ensured he had a good grip on Natalie before patting Queen. "Get me as close as you can to my girl."

Her horn lit up brightly as wisps of smoke puffed out of her nostrils, and she took off, whinnying when she broke through the remnants of Jane's light.

3 8

THE GOLD FLAME

Three men wearing black suits stood beside one another, all watching the swirling gold and emerald smoke before them.

"Father?" called the blond male at the center.

The large silhouette of a man inside the smoke seemed to glance over their shoulder before responding in a booming yet soothing voice, "Yes, Lucifer? I already know you wish to learn what I have been creating."

Lucifer had no markings on his skin—no prison. "Yes, Father. You have kept this soul guarded."

"Souls, my son." His features remained shrouded in flashes of gold and emerald. "One is to be your brother. I am merely altering his current form so he may perform what I ask of him."

"A brother?" asked the male to Lucifer's right.

"Yes, Michael. He has a great responsibility. His position is of the most importance. He is almost ready."

Now the brunette male spoke. "Father, you said there are multiple souls . . . Is it merely a pair, or are there more?"

A laugh that made Jane's ears ring sounded. "Gabriel, my son, you always ask what cannot be answered."

"You have made a female for our brother," Lucifer said.

Gabriel and Michael shared a confused look as Lucifer glared at the darkening silhouette. It was then Jane caught a glimpse of a tanned male torso. His face was not visible through the light and smoke, but she knew who he was and that he was unconscious.

"Death," she whispered, but no one reacted to her presence.

The shadowed figure also did not show any indication she was watching them as he placed a flickering gold flame that had been reaching for Death onto her angel's palm.

Jane swallowed her sob, covering her mouth as the gold flame twirled, brightening the room with light. "My soul."

"What is her purpose?" Michael asked. "Is she to aid him in whatever duty you ask of him?"

"Her purpose is great and not one you will concern yourselves with. She is his."

Jane teared up as emerald light illuminated Death's face as his fingers twitched. His eyes glowed as he stared upward, unseeing, but some part of him was already aware. "His soul knows I'm there. I was with him from the very beginning." She was so overwhelmed by the warmth spreading over her skin that she almost didn't notice how Lucifer never took his eyes off her soul.

She lowered her hands as her jaw dropped. She remembered how Lucifer had once implied she was made for Death and not David. He'd known all this time. He knew even before Death did.

A green glow grew bright before submerging her in darkness. Jane's breathing sped up.

The room lit up again, and Death's body was no longer there. Nor was there any sign of her soul. Instead, she watched, shocked, as Gabriel and Michael—both wearing golden armor—forced Lucifer to his knees.

The booming voice shook the ground. "Do you choose Darkness over loving and protecting my creations?"

Lucifer thrashed, snarling as his white wings unfolded from his back. "You know why I refuse to bow to them, Father. They are not worthy of protection or your love."

"The Accuser's whispers have tainted you," Michael spat.

"Brother," Gabriel said, calmer, "look into your heart—think of the gold soul. She will be a human—like Father's other creations. We know you envy not having one for yourself—she is our brother's, though. Consider her happiness. Consider his—you know he will only be devoted to her. We are devoted to Father. Our brother will have none but her after what we have watched Father do to him."

"I will see that she is destroyed before his very eyes," Lucifer roared.

"You will all watch as she burns, and he will burn with her and the other humans. In my light!"

The room illuminated in bright gold, and Jane sobbed upon hearing Lucifer scream as his wings lit on fire.

Gasping, Jane's eyes flew open and darted around the dark room. Wherever she had been, she was no longer there. She was back in the abandoned house she and the knights had chosen to rest in for the night.

Blinking several times, she stared at the bunk above her and listened to the nearby heartbeats.

David tightened his grip around her stomach. "Baby?"

Her heart beat faster, and she reached behind her, caressing his cheek before reaching out in front of her. She made contact with a different body. "Death."

His hand covered hers as she let out a relieved breath.

"I'm here, just as you asked me to be. It was just a dream," Death murmured as David pulled her sweaty hair away from her face.

"I think it was a memory." David hugged her tighter. "Another one."

Jane turned her head, smiling sadly, when David gave her a quick kiss and let her go so she could curl up with Death. She didn't know how long she'd been asleep. "Are we still in West Virginia?"

"Yes," David said quietly. "You were too tired to continue your ride, so we are camped in the same small town we stopped in two nights ago to allow you time to recharge. Do you remember now?"

"Yes," she said as the memories of cleansing the ruined country came forward. When she had not been able to keep her eyes open, Death and David forced King to stop so they could carry her. They did and finally found habitable structures to keep her and the survivors in for a few nights.

Death pulled her on top of him, running his fingers through her hair. "Why do you refuse to let King help you control these memories? Your power is great, Jane. No one expects you to handle it all on your own."

"I think I'm supposed to see them," she whispered, wiping her tears. "Anyway, King is busy helping me not destroy everything by accident."

"You won't destroy everything," Death muttered. "You've expanded your army by granting absolution to those too afraid to rise against Hell, and you have gathered many humans who would have surely perished slow, agonizing deaths without your help."

David rubbed her back. "What did you see this time?"

"I saw Death with my soul." She lifted her head, smiling at her angel. "You weren't alive yet, but I was with you when you were being made. I think I witnessed God, and He told Lucifer, Michael, and Gabriel He was altering you to perform your duty to him. Lucifer became upset when he was told I was yours."

David chuckled before smacking her ass. "Lucifer must be furious now, knowing we are together."

"If Jane was not so powerful, he would kill you," Death told him. "Your time comes and goes every day that passes. Jane is why you live. He fears her."

Jane reached out for David's hand, smiling when he lifted it to his lips.

"My baby always protects me when I'm the one trying to protect her." David kissed her hand. "I'm not afraid of him, my love. Just as your soul speaks to you now, mine does to me. It is a strange communication, but I understand him. He always reminds me that I burn hotter than the King of Hell and, of course, of the little secret I think even God is keeping from you. Perhaps it is one Lucifer doesn't know."

"You guys ruin all the fun of having powers." She sighed dramatically. "I'm practically at my most Zen here, and I still can't learn the big secret you two share."

"You have enough to contemplate, my love."

"I'm still stronger than David, though," Death quipped.

"Must you bring it up every night?" David asked.

"Yes," Death replied instantly. "And, Jane, no matter how much inner peace you achieve, you will always turn to mush in our hands, so you forfeit the chance to torture answers out of us at our most vulnerable."

"She's not even listening." David chuckled, kissing the inside of her wrist before biting and sucking her blood.

Death nibbled and licked her neck as he shifted her between them. David was quick to release her wrist and reach for the hem of the shirt she wore.

Jane pressed her lips together but sighed against Death's mouth as David pushed her panties down.

Then the loudest fart ever ripped through the room.

Both men froze, and a higher-pitched, extended fart followed. Then an even squeakier, short fart punctuated the silence.

Jane threw her head back, laughing as several others joined in.

"What the fuck, Gawain?" Gareth yelled.

Jane giggled uncontrollably while David carefully lifted her panties into place as she struggled to stay quiet. Her kids were asleep on the bunk bed above them, but this was too much. "Gawain, that was the loudest fart I have ever heard," she whispered, struggling to breathe.

"You fart louder than that, Jane," Gawain snapped.

All her happiness vanished, and she gasped. "I don't fart!"

The others chuckled, including David. Gawain scoffed, making her face grow hot.

"I don't fart. David, tell them I don't." The thought of doing such a thing in front of David—or any man—always embarrassed her. The only times she had done so with Jason were during her pregnancy. Even then, she had been so humiliated that she ran up the street to get away from him.

David kissed her head. "You don't fart, baby."

"Keep telling yourself that, Jane," Gawain said seriously. "You may be some sort of divine being Death refuses to let us in on, but since we've known you, you've been unconscious around all of us on multiple occasions. I'm surprised the dead never came along at the sounds coming out of your bony ass. Don't even get me started on the smell. You could take out Hell all on your own with a single fart. Perhaps we should strap her to King and ask him to fly her over Hell's camp—let her crop dust the lot of them."

"Shut up," she whisper-screeched. "David, make them stop."

Her vampire took something Death handed him as Death cupped her cheek and kissed her.

Gawain yelped. "Oh, fuck. Don't throw stuff at me. What is this?"

"Leave my baby alone," David said. "The next thing I throw will be a silver dagger."

"No need to resort to violence," Gawain hissed. "And everyone farts, David. Even Jane. Though, I imagine hers may sparkle and smell of rainbows and gummy bears now."

Gareth cut in. "I've never heard you fart, darling. Gawain just couldn't stand the idea of you getting it on with the Ds, so he pushed that behemoth out of his ass to make them stop."

The others lost it now.

David gripped her tightly. He was furious and would have been roaring, but he kept his voice low as he hissed, "You cock-blocked us with a fart?"

The group struggled to keep their noise down.

"Oh, come on," Gawain cried. "She's practically our sister."

"She's not ours," Death said, chuckling as laughter sounded from outside the room they were all in.

"My ears are bleeding." Gawain gagged. "Dearest, make them stop."

Ragnelle let out a dainty laugh. "My dear husband, because of your insistence last night, they had to endure the sound of us—well, you—as we made love in the bath. Perhaps they are paying you back for waking Jane from her much-needed rest."

Jane smiled when both her men kissed her—David on the nape of her neck while Death claimed her lips.

Adam's tired voice filled the darkness. "Does no one care that Jane is my baby cousin? This is worse than hearing other inmates in the cells surrounding mine. Show some control. Her children are sound asleep above your heads."

Death lifted his head. "Sound asleep implies they have no idea what we're doing to their mother. I can ensure they don't wake or walk in on us making love to her. That is control." Death smirked. "And, no, no one cares she's your little cousin. She's our soul mate. Now stop being a bitch, and maybe the little brunette you're sacked up with will grab your pee-pee."

Jane buried her face against Death's chest as the room roared with laughter.

"Master." Hades groaned. "It is difficult enough to sleep imagining Jane grabbing yours or Sir David's manhood. Must you drag my innocent niece's name into this inappropriate conversation?"

"Innocent, my perfect ass." Death snickered. "Your niece has witnessed shit that would cause even my ass to blush."

"Your ass blushes?" Gareth asked.

David chuckled as the room laughed louder.

Gareth spoke again. "Am I the only one present who is dumbfounded by the fact that the Angel of Death is arguing with the God of the Underworld about the kinky shit Artemis has witnessed while David is still trying to slide Jane's panties down as Death covers her mouth?"

"Stop staring, pervert." Death removed his hand from Jane's mouth as he summoned a dagger and aimed it at Gareth. "Close your eyes and ears."

"How can I do such a thing?" Gareth ducked behind his wife. "Save me, my love."

Jane laughed, pulling Death's arm down. "We'll stop, boys."

"Thank Jesus," Gawain said, sighing dramatically. "I almost vomited on my wife."

"Enough," Arthur said, his voice loud and firm. "The entire camp, besides the humans, can hear you fools. We must all exercise control and respect each other when we choose to be intimate."

"Exactly!" Gawain practically shouted. "Death doesn't show any respect. He is nearly as loud as Jane."

There were several hits followed by Gawain grunting.

"Why are you hitting me?" he asked as another hit sounded.

"I am attempting to shut you up before one, or both, of her mates destroys you." Ragnelle sighed. "Forgive him, Jane."

Jane grinned, pulling Death down until he pressed his lips to hers again.

"Great. They're going at it again." Adam groaned.

David sat up a bit, lifting a sheet from the top bunk. "Yes, we're going at it again. Now mind your business, or sleep outside with the hounds. Bear in mind, though, they make love to their women as well."

Artemis' timid whisper to Adam reached Jane's ears. "She is preparing to menstruate. They will not be able to make love to her during that time. Let them be."

"Is that true?" Jane asked.

Death nodded, lifting her shirt. "Why do you think I'm on this small ass bed with the two of you? I want to get lucky while I still can. Not that I would mind making love to you during your period. I'll find a fucking shower or river if I have to."

David chuckled as he helped Death pull her shirt off before sliding his hand down her spine. "Death, put a sound barrier in place."

Jane closed her eyes, sighing when their hands and lips met her skin.

"I already did." Death brought his mouth to her ear. "Scream as loud as you want."

David palmed her ass, making her moan. "We should have chosen the floor."

"Why?" Death smiled at her as her mouth popped open when he slid a hand between her legs. "Purr for us, Jane. You're my kitten, too."

David slid her panties down. "I said the floor because I feel like breaking the damn bed."

"Ay, Papi!"

David rested a hand on Jane's waist as they pretended they were not keeping their attention on Nathan and Natalie having a bathroom break behind the bushes. They had started transitioning to becoming more independent, so they asked for privacy for their bathroom breaks. But she was not losing her attention on her children as they traveled dangerous territory.

David kissed the top of Jane's head, reminding her he'd had the same thought when Nathan told him to stay when he went to the bushes. "Baby," he said quietly, "I know you insist on proving to everyone there is good in Lance, and I adore you for putting up with his attitude and preventing your men from slaughtering him, but perhaps there is little hope my old friend truly remains."

She turned so she could stare up at his handsome face. They were covered in soot and dirt, but David always looked sexier than any male model could.

"Are you distracted again, my love?" He cupped her cheeks. "Even blessed by God himself with light from His kingdom, my Jane is still the same silly, blushing girl I met in Texas."

"Having divine powers doesn't change me."

"I'm glad." He used his thumb to wipe away some dirt on her cheek. "Will you consider allowing Death to imprison Lance far away from you?"

"No." She sighed, kissing his chest. "The 'voice' tells my soul to keep him close. I'm not giving up on him."

He sighed but nodded. "Just be careful, my love. I know you are much stronger than him, but he has been successful in harming you on numerous occasions because your beautiful heart is so forgiving."

Jane knew that, but she was at peace with whatever had happened to her now.

"I'm done," Nathan said.

David chuckled, kissing Jane before pulling out a roll of toilet paper. "Stay still, little man. I'll bring you toilet paper."

A voice hollered out in the distance. "David, bring me some when he's done!" It was Gawain.

Death appeared, snatching the roll Jane held before he launched it like a football in the direction Gawain had called from.

"Ow."

Jane shook her head as Death smiled at her.

"I was helping your fellow knights, angel." He kissed her as David tossed him the roll he had.

"Don't throw that one. Let her help Natalie before you start behaving like a child again."

"Papi is mad." Death snickered, placing the toilet paper in her hand. "Hurry up. There is a horde nearby, and I know you would prefer it if the kids did not see the slaughter that will ensue. I can take them back to the house with you while David and the others eliminate the undead."

"Yes, please." Jane went to Natalie. She could already smell the stench of decay.

David and Death both jerked their gazes in the same direction, sniffing.

"What is it?" Jane lifted Natalie as David did the same with Nathan.

"Friends." David smiled, holding out a hand for Jane. "Let's go meet them."

Death nudged her forward. "Hurry. The horde is sizable and almost here."

Jane started forward, but a man with aqua-colored eyes came into view, halting her. Numerous others followed him, but he was the only one with bright eyes. The others all had black eyes of the damned. They were dressed similarly to what the knights wore during combat, but they wore a mixture of black, white, and brown gear, all with masks that could be worn like beanies.

"It's good of you to finally join us, Nyc," David said, letting go of Jane's hand to greet the man. "How are you, my friend?"

"In need of a hot bath, preferably with a lovely woman wrapped around me." Nyc winked at her.

Jane hoped she wasn't blushing at David's sexy friend, but her hot cheeks suggested she was as red as a tomato.

Death grunted, putting his arm over her shoulder. "Don't flirt with her."

David chuckled as he shook several of the other men's hands. "You all look as though you have been having quite a bit of fun."

Jane glanced up at Death as David hugged a few of the others. "He's this close to them?"

"How the fuck should I know? It's not David's ass I bury myself balls deep in." He smirked when she pinched him. "Yes, they are close. When the knights took leave, David frequently joined Nyc's pack for hunts. They are not restricted to darkness, so it also allowed him to work in daylight, away from the colder climates where many of the Damned seek shelter."

"Their souls burn bright." She smiled when each blue flame grew in intensity around the men. They were all looking at her.

"They are good men." Death twirled her hair as many of the knights arrived, greeting the newcomers. "They work similarly to the knights. They were chosen for a task and have carried out their duty for thousands of years."

Jane focused on Nyctimus when he laughed with David and Arthur. "Why are his eyes not dark like the others'?"

"He was blessed when his life ended."

Jane whipped her head up. "He died? You brought him back?"

"Not me." He tightened his hold on her. "There are other powerful beings out there. They have powers to work miracles, and sometimes, just as in David's case, I watch them unfold instead of reaping their souls again."

"Oh." She leaned her head against him. "David really seems to like them."

"These men, unlike the knights, have no wives. David likely felt relief in their company after watching his brothers with their wives. With the pack, he could kill and not worry about acting proper, as his royal status demands."

"They behaved like dogs, you mean?"

"Wolves." He smirked. "You killed their father—the Wolf King."

Her mouth fell open. "He was their dad?"

"Nyc's, at least. The others are the offspring of Nyc's brothers. Very few are true brothers to him. Don't worry about killing Lycaon," he said quickly. "They were at war with him. There are many children—true children, not the creations you dealt with—that Lycaon spawned. Nyc is the only one blessed by his family, but he hopes to save his brothers and nephews. Well, those who have joined him. His family is quite fucked up."

Jane covered Natalie's ears. "Death."

He shrugged. "I can wipe her memory of naughty words, if you like."

She chuckled when Natalie stuck her tongue out at him.

"Just like your mother." He shook his head.

"So, you found her?" Nyc's voice carried through the hum of conversations. "I should have guessed she would be the same girl Death had his eyes on."

"You knew about her?" David asked, waving for Nyctimus to follow him. "Come meet her."

"Yes, I knew of her." Nyctimus shook hands with Apollo before squeezing past the others. "Is this her child?"

David hugged Nathan. "Ours. Jane was married before I found her. Nathan and Natalie are twins from her late husband."

"You perform the role naturally." Nyctimus grinned at David. "He has a bright soul."

David nodded, smiling proudly at Nathan. "He does. Here's my girl. Baby, this is one of my oldest friends, Nyctimus. Nyc, this is my Jane. You clearly know Death. Ignore him when he calls me Papi. And this"—he caressed Natalie's head—"is my princess, Natalie."

567

Natalie blushed, mumbling, "Hello."

Jane grinned at David as she held out a hand to his friend. "Hello, Nyctimus."

He removed his beanie, revealing his sexy tousled dark hair, before kissing her hand. "Greetings, Little Moon."

The men behind him bowed as another male, larger than Nyctimus, pushed through the crowd. He smiled at her before smirking at David, then Death. "My my, I do believe Sir David has entered into a rather risqué relationship."

David turned, laughing. "Sin, please tell me I have no reason to kill you today."

Sin tugged off his beanie, freeing his long curly brown hair. He had a mischievous gleam in his eyes as he took her in, running a hand down his beard, revealing various tattoos along his forearms. He smirked at David, and it was the most sinful thing she'd ever seen. He chuckled, bowing to her but still addressing David. "You enjoy my company far too much to kill me. Hello, beautiful." He kissed Jane's fingers after snatching her hand from Nyctimus. "I did tell him if he searched for gold, he would find his heart."

Death pulled her back, glaring at Sin.

David quickly moved between them as he addressed Sin quietly. "Jane's eyes used to be hazel. We are trying to find a way for the green to return."

Sin darted his eyes between Jane and Death, giving them a sad smile. "Apologies. Either way, I am pleased to see David and Death have found their woman."

"It's a pleasure to meet you." Jane hugged Death.

"There are many children and mortals in their party." Death glared at Sin before focusing on Nyctimus. "I suggest you send some of your men to clear the path for her riders."

Nyctimus whispered to the men beside him, and they went off quickly, shouting orders.

Sin bowed to Death. "She's lovely, my lord. Forgive me."

"He'll be fine." Nyc patted Sin's shoulder. "Bring the survivors we have gathered. They could use a break."

David leaned down, giving Jane a quick kiss. "Baby, go with Death and rest before you lead us on. I will join you shortly."

Death said nothing, but he held his arms out for Nathan. The exchange was so natural for them Jane almost didn't think of it as Death adjusted his hold on Nathan, instructing him to rest.

Her vampire smiled, kissing her again. "I love you."

"I love you, too." She turned, nodding to Nyctimus and Sin. "Gentlemen."

"My lady." They bowed together.

"Beat it." Death growled, snatching her hand before dragging her away.

David pushed Sin. "Now I have to comfort his arrogant ass. I can't even get you in trouble with a female. Wait, Nyc, where is Helena?"

"Gone," Nyctimus answered. "And do not ask where."

"Fine." David dropped it without hesitation.

"Are you fucking Death? Or do you both just make love to her?" Sin laughed, taking the brutal hit David delivered. "That hurt, my prince."

Nyctimus sounded more serious. "If he is happy, it is no concern of ours. Let us destroy this mob before it gets closer—I am sure there is a reason Death does not want her army to eliminate it."

Jane tuned out their conversation and raised Death's hand to her lips, kissing it as he led her farther away. "You know there will be a day when I stare at you with hazel eyes again."

He sighed. "I hope so, Sweet Jane. It seems less likely with each day that passes."

Natalie reached for Death, rubbing his arm. "Don't be sad. You will be with Mommy again."

"I'm not sad." He stared at her daughter without any emotion. "I'm angry. She's mine."

It was moments like this when Jane realized Death truly needed her as much as she needed him.

"Once again, I see you are receiving attention from other males, my queen," Lancelot said where he lazily lounged—still bound in Asmodeus' chains. The wounds on his wrists and ankles looked awful, but he'd attacked the vampire who'd been brave enough to try and treat him, so they were letting him be.

Death pulled her to a stop and turned his head, meeting Lancelot's taunting stare. "Do not provoke me."

Jane threw a glare at Lancelot before tugging Death. "Come help me organize my bag, please. I want you with me."

"Yes, run along like a good little pet for her since Daddy is off at work with the wolves," Lancelot sneered.

Jane stopped walking, taking a deep breath before turning around. She placed Natalie on the ground, relieved when her daughter walked to Death, clutching his leg.

"I have shown you patience and respect when you deserve it," Jane said as her soul surfaced, furious. "You will stop taunting my men." The wind blew, causing her hair to fly around her as gold light began to glow beneath her skin. "Or I will make you stop."

Lancelot's eyes widened as Asmodeus chuckled beside him.

"Sweet Jane," Death called gently, "breathe. His time is not yet come."

Power continued to build inside her as her soul roared, enraged and full of sorrow from Lancelot's words.

A tingling caress slid down her cheek. "Baby girl, you will become something else if you judge him. That is not your duty." Death tilted her chin up and smiled when she locked eyes with him. "I will find you. I will never stop searching. Let him go. Of all the reasons to enter god mode, Lancelot is not one of them. We know what we are. So does God."

She released the breath she'd been holding before nodding at Asmodeus. "Bring him, but keep him out of my sight. I'm hormonal right now."

Asmodeus bowed, a smile teasing his lips. "Yes, my queen."

Death chuckled, grabbing her hand. "And here David and I thought you would no longer suffer from mood swings after he unlocked your deity soul."

Jane squeezed his hand before picking up her daughter. "You still haven't told me what that means . . . And hormones are probably the most powerful force in the universe. The fact I'm actually about to start my period this time is nothing to be excited about."

"Do you want me to tell David to find you some pads before you start?"

She thought he was poking fun at her, but she saw him watching her with a genuine smile on his handsome face. "No. I'll find some on my own."

"I'll tell him to get you some. He has probably never paid attention to when the wives or his sister go through menstruation. In fact, I think he often skipped town because the women tended to group into the same days each month."

Jane covered her face. "Death, are we really discussing David's knowledge of periods? And the fact he may have bailed just because the women were hormonal?"

He shrugged. "You used to beg me to comfort you, and I continued to do what I could even when I remained invisible to you."

She lowered her hand. "Did you really?"

"Yes." He didn't look at her, but she saw his tanned cheeks turn pink.

"Aw, Death." She hugged his arm. "You're so freaking sweet."

"Sweet enough to get lucky in the closet while we wait for David?"

She laughed.

"Is that a yes-laugh, or are you laughing at me?" He glanced at Natalie for a second. "I'll knock them out. I can make it quick."

Queen trotted out, stopping in front of Death and stomping her hooves.

Death glared at her before looking behind them.

"What is it?" Jane turned, spotting David laughing with Sin and the knights from where they stood on a hill, about to disappear over it.

"Your vampire is cock-blocking me. He sent her to stop me." Death pushed past the unicorn as he gave David the middle finger. "You're supposed to be on my side, Queen."

Nyctimus approached, causing Death to growl.

"Did he send you as well?"

"Not for the reason he sent her." Nyctimus laughed. "Arthur asked me to speak to Guinevere."

Jane watched Nyctimus as he scanned the groups gathered around the only houses left standing in the destroyed neighborhood they had picked. She pointed at the home across the street. "I believe she is in that one. She didn't stay with us last night."

"Thank you." Nyctimus grinned before jogging to it.

"Do you think Arthur and Gwen will make up?" Jane glanced up at Death.

"I don't know or care." He shoved open the broken door to the house they had slept in. "And don't worry about fixing anything for them. Let them deal with it."

She sighed, following him upstairs. "But it is sort of my fault."

"How so?" He put Nathan on a bed before handing him a toy.

Jane felt her heart flutter as her soul seemed to blush watching Death with Nathan.

"Jane?" Death tilted his head, observing her. "Are you all right?"

"Yes." She lowered Natalie and retrieved her and David's bags. "And I say it is my fault because I allowed Lancelot to live."

"I think Guinevere would have been just as devastated had you not interfered. You're not the reason bad things happen."

"I know." She walked into the bathroom and tugged off David's shirt.

Death crossed his arms before leaning against the doorframe, watching her undress in the mirror. "I could bend you over that sink and have you coming in under thirty seconds."

Jane laughed, folding David's shirt before she tugged off her panties. "Wait, if I start, and I'm wearing my suit, will it get everywhere?"

He glanced at his crotch. "My hard-on just disappeared. That has never happened before."

Jane pouted, turning to look at him. "Death."

He shrugged. "I don't know. I haven't had a period before. I can try to alter your suit to have period-proof panties, if you want."

She sighed, bending to look in the cabinets. "Maybe the person who lived here still has some lying around."

Death looked over his shoulder. "You two stay put." He then pushed off the doorway and walked up behind her, pulling her back against him as he dropped a hand to her breast. "Damn, they're bigger."

She smiled, watching his other hand caress her belly.

"I can try to make something similar to what I remember you using, but they won't be permanent. I'll have to construct them each time, and I don't know how bad you'll be bleeding."

Her body shook, and she couldn't look away from his face as he continuously scanned her reflection, squeezing her breast more as she felt him grow hard through his pants.

He focused on her face as he slid a hand between her legs and smirked. "I forgot your size."

"Mhm." She sighed as she struggled to keep her eyes open.

"Ready?" He teased her with his middle finger, grinning mischievously. "Or do you want me to have you screaming in thirty seconds?"

Jane covered his hand. "Don't make it one of those thick ones since I haven't started yet, but I feel kinda crampy."

He rolled his eyes. "I thought you were going to push my finger in and bend over."

"Maybe not when the kids are in the next room." She bit her lip, holding her breath, when his eyes and her skin began to glow.

"I still can't decide if it's a negative thing you are a mother or if it makes you extra sexy." He pinched her nipple, snickering when her legs began to shake because he also pressed and massaged her clit. "Wanna come first?"

"Death." Her voice cracked.

"What if I ask him real fast?" He rubbed slower. "If I get permission, can I? I'll split my soul."

"Death, I doubt David wants us messing around like this without him."

He sighed, nodding as he relaxed his fingers. "Breathe and imagine your suit. I'll alter it when it appears, and you can let me know when to change the panties."

"You'll have to do it each time?"

"I'm Death, babe, but I'm not a woman. I haven't mastered period panties just yet. Maybe when you've had a few, I'll get it right, or you will learn how to alter it. Although your abilities are so overwhelming, something as minor as outfit changes may stay out of your range of control for quite some time." He glanced at her ass. "I'm still hard. Let's get this over with so I'm not close to coming in my pants." He kept staring. "Fuck, I could just slide in right now. You're so fucking wet."

Jane moaned, closing her eyes as she squeezed her thighs together, keeping his hand in place. "Oh, shit, stop. I'm gonna come."

He chuckled. "I'm not doing anything. You're supposed to summon your suit." He slid a finger in, and she came. "Whoops."

Jane cried out, shaking as he pressed the right spot, letting her lose herself for just a moment. The room pulsed with gold light, and she moaned again, squeezing his hand around her breast as he watched her come undone in the mirror.

"That's my girl." He pushed a second finger in but merely held her in place. "Papi gave me permission, by the way. So don't feel bad."

Jane swallowed. "You duplicated?"

He nodded. "For only a few seconds. I won't do it again, I promise. I know it's dangerous for me to do so now, but holding you in one form gives me exceptional control. Plus I wanted you to have release. You're sensitive right now."

She smiled weakly. "He gave you permission?"

Death raised his hand to his mouth, sucking his fingers. "Mhm. He said I couldn't fuck you, but he told me to make you shake in my hands."

Jane laughed, grabbing the counter. "I'm sorry."

He shrugged, dropping his hand between her legs again. "I like watching, knowing you're in ecstasy from my touch. Maybe just give me a blowjob later."

"Okay."

He winked, lightly patting her. "Let's cover this pretty pussy up before I break Papi's rules. We'll look for tampons so we can take turns on your ass if you're a good girl."

"Death!" She covered her face, laughing.

He responded by spreading her butt cheeks and teasing her by giving her pelvic thrusts. "You better summon that suit. My dick has a mind of its own when it comes to you."

She stared at his reflection. "Let go of my butt cheeks. I can't even concentrate with you doing that."

A teasing grin stretched over his lips. "Why?" He gripped her hips tightly. "Are you going to come again, just like this? I know you feel me. Wanna see if I can make you without breaking his rules?"

Jane summoned her suit, smiling when he frowned and let her go.

"Baby girl, that was just mean." He pulled her flush against him and put a hand between her legs, cupping her as he closed his eyes.

She felt the shift in her suit and nodded. "I think you did it."

"Want me to check?" He winked, letting go. "My mouth is good at checking for appropriate coverage."

She shoved him back. "Go. My kids probably know what we're doing. I'm such a bad mom." When she walked out, she paused upon finding them sound asleep.

Death tilted her head back so she stared straight up at him. "You're not a bad mom. And you have David and me. We will step up when you want to have a little fun."

"You put them to sleep so you could please me?"

"Of course. I know it's hard for you to resist David and me, and you'd feel bad as soon as you were done."

She turned, hugging him. "See, you can do the rugrat thing."

He lifted her, pulling her legs around him as he carried her to a chair. "Unlike David, who wants to ensure they are always loved and cared for, I am thinking about you naked and how to get you that way without them seeing me touch you."

Jane leaned forward, kissing him. "Still, you're doing more than I would have imagined. You're protecting their innocence, just like I wanted for them. You knew a horde was on the way, and you made sure we got here before they had to see zombies all over again."

He leaned back in the chair but kept her close as he caressed her cheek. "It made you sad when they accidentally saw them in that one town. I don't like seeing you sad."

"You make me happy," she promised. "You, David, the babies—you are my happy thoughts."

"I know." He kept staring into her eyes. "Do you want to know what you are, my love?"

Jane sucked in a breath, nodding. "Will you finally tell me? All you and the others have said is my true soul has been unlocked, and we are a deity soul."

He chuckled, shaking his head. "No. More than that."

Jane kept thinking, and she swore she saw her soul. "I think my soul is laughing at me."

"She is." He held out his hand and placed hers on top of it. His began to glow in green fire, and then her flame erupted in the center.

Jane covered her mouth, crying happily as she watched her twirl with Death's soul before they spun in a whirlwind, then formed two human figures again, hugging or dancing.

"Is this similar to what you saw in your dream?" He watched their souls, looking peaceful at last.

"Almost. Your soul was not able to appear like this. Your eyes began to glow when she danced."

He slid his fingers between hers. "One day, you will be taken from me, Jane."

Her soul stopped dancing, and his held her close.

"What will it mean, though? If I get taken or even killed, and you find me?"

"I don't know, angel. Because we are a pair, I am not given this knowledge. Perhaps only God knows, and he wants you to have this time to be loved because that is all we are meant to have."

Her eyes burned, and she stared at him through their flames. "We are meant for more than this."

Her face hurt as she watched his soul kiss hers before fading away. Her soul looked between them before reaching toward Death.

He chuckled, kissing the little flame's hand. "Go on. I'll bring him out for you again."

Jane's soul twirled before disappearing into her skin, illuminating her entire body in a golden glow for a few seconds before dimming.

Death pulled her by the back of the neck until their lips touched. He kept it sweet, whispering he loved her until she began to feel too drowsy to keep her eyes open. "Now dream of us," he murmured. "Make us a world where no one will destroy us. One that contains all that makes you happy and nothing that brings you sorrow." He kissed one of her eyelids. "I'm there . . . David is there . . . We are both with you, and you are ours."

She sleepily responded, "That is now."

He kissed her other eyelid. "No, we still have much sorrow. You simply shine golden light on it. I'm telling you to make our Heaven."

"Because I'm going to die?" she asked as her muddled thoughts drowned in gold light.

A tingling kiss was pressed against her lips as she felt a fiery one on her hand.

"Yes."

Two sets of hands came to rest over her heart. One tingled, the other burned. "We'll follow you."

39

OUR GIRL

David coughed from the dust as he examined the boxes in front of him.

"Just grab a few kinds," Gawain muttered as he rounded the corner.

David read the different boxes. "Why are there different strengths?"

Nyctimus laughed. He was checking the expiration date on a bag of chips and sighed before tossing it on the broken shelf. "They are different women. Their hormones and cycle vary, as do their bodies. Just like my dick is bigger than Gawain's, Jane's period might be worse than Elle's."

A hammer came flying at Nyctimus' head.

He caught it, laughing again. "I thought Death made Jane a special pair of panties. He's lucky you can't kill him. I mean, I get it—you are all together—but he knows you are still adjusting to them being alone."

David ignored everyone suddenly looking at him. He'd permitted Death to pleasure her because he could tell they needed to be close without him. No one would understand how much he and Death had discussed with each other, even Jane. He also knew Jane had been extra sensitive to their presence since Valhalla. She was struggling to control her hormones just from hearing their voices. "I have adjusted to the three of us. We both aim to keep her happy, and it was thoughtful of him even to split his soul to ask me. I'm sure he didn't mean to ask in front of everyone, but he still harmed himself to get permission."

"I thought you said he'd only be with her while you were present," Kay said. "He already knew you would be upset with such a request."

David shrugged. "It is deeper than lust. He plays it off as lust, but their connection is beyond comprehension, and it is precious to me. I want her to have what he gives. Sometimes his desire to make her happy overwhelms him, and he doesn't know what to do. He is not like us."

Lamorak leaned around the aisle. "So he gets overwhelmed and asks you if he can give her an orgasm?"

"It isn't our business," Arthur said, grabbing various items through the aisle. "David has agreements with Death, and that is between them. Drop this matter. If I learn that Jane is aware you are all discussing her intimacies with Death, I will permit Death to have one minute alone with you in a cell."

Gareth raised his hand.

Arthur glared at him. "What?"

"We are just worried for David's sake. And Jane's. Death isn't like us, so he may hurt her heart unintentionally by doing the things he does. He has so many times already. As far as being intimate with Jane goes, David was vocal about it only when he was there. We are just showing our support if he needs help."

David smiled sadly. "Thank you, brothers. But Death and I have spoken deeply about our bonds and actions with her. I am fine with what happens between them alone. I know she always considers my feelings, but sometimes, she needs to show him he is enough to make her happy."

"So this is about Death?" Gareth scratched his head. "Because you feel bad for him?"

"I just want them to have what they can together. While they can. If he feels the urge to be with her, I am fine. After all, he is her true soul mate. Not me. If it were not for his love for her, I would not have what I do with her."

Everyone looked down. It was the first time he had vocally admitted he and Jane were not true soul mates. They had figured it out and spoken amongst themselves about it, but none had asked him for details.

"I'll talk to them about it," he added. "There is no need for you to worry. I have spoken with Death more than you all realize. And none of you know what I do." He waved his hand at Arthur. "Well, Arthur does."

"Fine, brother." Gareth nodded. "But if you need us."

"I know." David turned away but stopped as he noticed Sin reading a paper inside a box of tampons.

Sin gagged. "Did you know they can die from wearing tampons? I wonder what women did so wrong to have to experience periods, even as immortals."

The store got quiet.

Sin laughed. "Oh, yes. Me."

David shook his head. "Men sinned as well—I believe more than women. And we have been led to believe they are the reason when it was us."

"Ah, nothing like a good woman to help a man see our misdeeds." Nyctimus handed David a box. "Yes, that is why we must watch, helpless, as our women suffer. Only fools take it out on them—the weak. We were too weak to protect them, so a worthy male would support his woman at her worst. God knew what would hurt us more. Take her those." He tapped the box he'd given David. "Even if she doesn't like the brand, she will be happy you tried. We will arrive in town tomorrow anyway, and she can shower."

Gareth opened the bag of chips Nyctimus had discarded and started eating them.

"I think those are expired," David said, frowning.

Gareth turned the bag around. "It says best if eaten by last year. I'm fine if they are not at their best."

"They say best if eaten by because they don't wish to write you will regret eating or possibly die after said date." Nyctimus checked another bag. "They're all expired. Don't eat them."

Gareth ate another handful. "No, that just means they don't taste their best. They taste fine."

David pinched the bridge of his nose and walked away. "I'm not even going to humor you. I'm going back to the camp."

Arthur nodded. "We will leave in one hour."

"We'll be ready." David kicked a clear path and left the store.

Nyctimus and Sin caught up to him.

Sin raised a rifle, firing into the distance. "These damn zombies are everywhere. We should see if there is a way to power up your woman to cover the entire planet in light that disintegrates them like she did to the campsite."

"She would destroy everything." David scanned the burned-down houses and businesses. "It could even kill her."

"At least there are no bugs here." Nyctimus kicked a corpse. "The South was horrible. Survivors were all carrying diseases from mosquitos and contaminated water. They begged to be put out of their misery."

David cringed. "We meant to go to the East, but we found Jane. We ensured all the nuclear and water plants on our route were safe, but we didn't bother returning after going home with Jane."

"You wouldn't have been able to help." Nyc shook his head. "They were hit by three hurricanes. California suffered wildfires because of drought, then the earthquakes came. I will not be surprised if Yellowstone blows soon. I think many of the volcanoes have already erupted. That is why the skies are blocked. Several countries in Asia suffered typhoons, tsunamis, and mudslides, too. Then, of course, the bugs and humans with their ridiculous bombs. Africa and Australia are the same—Europe is worse. Zombies are only part of the devastation."

"I'm sure that pleases Death's brother. Can't you talk to your mother about the natural disasters?" David wondered what pull Nyctimus really had with family.

Nyctimus rolled his eyes. "It is the Destroyers' doing, not hers. She heals. Lucifer only has control of the Destroyers that kill in combat. Even Death would bleed in their hands, but by then, he'd be just as destructive. The Earth and nature deities follow a system that aligns with the stars. They are fated. The rest of the world is just as bad or worse. We picked a good spot. Mother was the one to help me pick. We should already be able to self-sustain for several years. We are building an underground bunker as well. Not that anyone would want to survive without each other, but it will be there. The more we gather, the more we can provide."

David was relieved. "Good. I want the children to be able to grow up a bit. Death says Belial and the rest of Hell fear Jane, and they will bide their time now that she has slightly evened out the fight."

"But it is only temporary." Sin sighed as he raised his rifle again. "We will have a glorious battle, and I am sure we will perish. Even with the Horsemen and Jane on our side, Hell will crush the world with its power."

"Have some faith," Nyctimus said. "Her abilities are beyond our comprehension. She needs to learn control and continue strengthening her mind and spirit. Her purity is only the beginning."

"I do have faith in her." Sin shrugged. "The children should enjoy the town. And the other humans. We will need to build more, but it will be easier with everyone there. Your woman, or perhaps her unicorns, may be able to clear the sky with their power. If they can, we will be able to harvest decent crops."

"You think her power could do that?" David looked up. Everywhere they went had overcast from eruptions and bombings. He was worried they would not last because of climate change.

"Mother said to find you, and I would locate a solution. I assume she knew Jane would be a powerful deity." Nyctimus grinned. "Have you figured out what she is?"

David smiled. "Not entirely. I don't think it's for me to know. That is what my soul tells me, at least. It's between Jane and Death. I will let them have it. I know she will include me once she learns the truth. I feel bad for being the one to learn I was not her soul mate."

"That worked out, though." Sin bent and picked up a magazine, laughing. "It's an old porno mag." He nudged some bones with his foot. "The fucker held onto this until his ass died."

David threw the magazine into a simmering fire. "Give them respect, even if they do not deserve it."

"Sorry." Sin whistled lowly. "David, your woman certainly has the ass of a goddess."

Nyctimus muttered a curse. "Don't kill him, David. He's not had any pussy in over a month."

David glanced ahead, finding Jane where Sin had been looking. She was rummaging through bags with her beautiful ass in clear view, and Death was glaring at Sin.

David turned, shaking his head. "If I don't knock you out, he might kill you."

Sin winced and closed his eyes. "Nyc, catch me so I don't fall in any shit. And make sure I don't get left behind."

When Death summoned a blade that would probably light Sin's ass on fire, David punched his reckless friend in the jaw, knocking him out.

Nyctimus laughed as he watched Sin fall. "I'll bring him. See to your woman and keep her other boyfriend away from my men. I would like it if they survived the night."

David snatched a few apples he noticed had rolled out of Sin's bag. "Of course he would find apples and not share."

Nyc handed him a few more. "For the little ones."

"Thanks." David jogged over to Jane. He leaned over her, kissing her neck. "Baby, what are you doing?"

She grinned and lifted a pair of jackets. "The kids are cold when we ride."

"Oh." He helped her up before giving her the bag of tampons and pads. "I don't know if those are the right kind."

Her face flushed, but she nodded. "Thanks, David. This is the sweetest thing ever."

He grinned, kissing her as he guided her back to their tent. "Get them ready to go. I'm going to keep an eye on him."

Death smacked her butt when she walked past them. "Her ass is only for us."

David chuckled. "I know. He is Sin, though. He can barely help himself."

Death twirled the blade as he tracked Nyctimus carrying Sin's body to their pack.

"Are you all right?" David nudged him.

"I'm fine." Death scanned the others breaking down the camp. "They are questioning you about me with Jane."

"You heard?"

"They were discussing it when you first returned."

David patted his shoulder. "I took care of it. You know what we discussed, and I know why it has become unbearable for both of you. So it's nothing to worry about. We'll talk to her after we settle in tonight."

Death focused on something in the woods for a few moments. "I apologize if it bothered you. Don't take it out on her. She is doing and thinking as though she and I are what we are meant to be."

"I know." David put on his pack. "Don't be upset or worried. I won't take anything out on her because I understand, and I already allowed it. I think she knows in a way. Well, her soul does."

"She does. Jane's mind is doing so much she almost does not think at all when it comes to us." Death began walking away. "I'll be back."

David watched him vanish before entering the tent.

"Is he okay?" She didn't look at him.

David kissed her head. "Yes, baby. So am I."

She smiled but kept packing. "He wants us to have alone time."

"You and him?" David frowned.

"No." She grabbed his hand. "You and me. He said he wanted us to be alone for a few days. Like how we would be without him."

David stared at the children for a few seconds. He had wanted to be a family for so long, but he already felt like Death was a part of their family.

"If that is what he wants, that's fine." David zipped Nathan's jacket up. "But he can be with us if he wants to, Jane. And I am not upset about what happened. I already told the others—they do not know what has been discussed."

She began braiding her hair. "I think it's that we heard the women, and he is worried I am upset. I am. I didn't know you talked to each other so much about how things would work."

"We just haven't had time." David began rolling up a sleeping bag. "I know you won't betray me. It's not a betrayal—you are with him as well. And he did ask."

"But I didn't." She pulled Natalie onto her lap and began braiding her hair as well.

David finished what he was doing before sitting beside her. "It's fine, Jane. I didn't ask you how you felt about the issues Death and I discussed. I promise we will try to find time when we are not in the middle of fighting, traveling, or with innocent ears around to have the three of us sit down again. I should have clarified when I decided your alone time with him would involve being that close. So I'm saying it now—it's fine. If you are comfortable and desire what he offers, don't stress yourself about it. I told you we are not a normal couple."

Natalie peeked up at him. "Mommy has two husbands."

David chuckled, caressing her cheek. "I haven't asked Mommy to marry me, nor has Ryder."

Natalie darted her eyes over to Jane. "Oh."

Jane stayed exceptionally quiet, focusing on the braid more than she probably needed to.

David kissed her shoulder so she could feel him and let his words sink in. "I'll take this stuff out to the riders."

She nodded but didn't look at him.

"Want to come with me, little man?" David held a hand out for Nathan.

"Are you going to ask Mommy?" Natalie blurted.

"Natalie." Jane shook her head. "He doesn't have to ask me that. Death doesn't either."

That was why David hadn't asked her. Death would always be in their relationship, and he didn't want to kick him out by asking Jane to be his wife. Death wouldn't be able to marry her, and that wasn't fair in David's mind. Not when Jane and Death were meant to be together in the first place.

David helped Nathan open the tent, but he kissed Jane's cheek. "I already consider Mommy my wife. She's more than a wife, but I still haven't asked. Maybe one day, okay, princess?"

Natalie nodded, smiling brightly. "Okay. Don't forget a ring."

Jane sighed, turning away.

David rubbed Jane's back. "I won't forget. Hurry up, my girls. We'll arrive at our new home today." With that, he exited the tent and carried Nathan toward the riders Jane commanded. He wasn't surprised when Queen pranced out toward him.

"Hello, Queen." David patted her side.

King snorted at him as he passed, trotting in Jane's direction.

"You're in trouble." Nyctimus laughed, passing him. "Get her a ring. Soon."

David sighed, putting Nathan on Queen and supporting him as he kept his gaze aimed at the tent. "I don't have it anymore."

"You don't have what?" Death appeared beside him.

"Nothing." David smiled at Death. "You don't have to give us alone time, but if you need to get away, I understand."

Death studied him briefly before green flames erupted and Sorrow appeared. They both watched Sorrow nuzzle Queen but heard King's protest from across the distance.

David locked eyes with Death when Queen lowered her head and turned away from Sorrow.

"I don't want her to feel this way," David said, petting Queen. "Our girl gets both of us without feeling guilty."

Death glanced at Queen before watching Jane exit the tent in the distance.

"Go ride with her," David said as he mounted Queen. "Talk to her about what we discussed. If she has objections, we will talk to her together. But you can talk to her and keep the conversation private. She'll listen to you more than me anyway." David smiled at Jane when she finally got atop King. "Help her with any discomfort she has from her cycle, too. It will probably be uncomfortable riding in her condition. I don't care what power she has; it must still be painful. We both saw how much she whined in her sleep."

Death glanced at Queen, patting her briefly before he waved for Sorrow to leave. "Find Adam."

David watched as Death walked over to Jane. He saw their hesitation and sighed.

"Death loves Mommy," Nathan said. "Needs Mommy."

David nodded. "I know, little man. I'll make sure he has her the way he's supposed to."

"Before too late." Nathan huffed.

It broke David's heart because he knew that was the big issue for Death and Jane. Her death would change the world, and Death was the one who would be most affected. Her angel wouldn't be able to handle the loss.

David felt better when Death finally got on King behind Jane and hugged her so she could situate Natalie.

"Let's go, Queen." He patted her side. "And you know Sorrow loves you, girl. Just be patient."

She bobbed her head and began trotting to the front of the line.

"That's a good girl." David smiled at Queen but also because he could hear Jane laughing with Death.

"Happy." Nathan looked up at him.

David nodded. "Yes, she's happy. That's what matters. He makes her happy."

Gold light began to light up the area as King barreled past them. The crowd cheered as his girl lit the way with her angel protectively holding her.

Queen's horn began glowing, and she neighed, speeding up to stay close.

"As long as we get to be a part of their happiness, right?" David smiled as Queen whinnied, sprinting faster and glowing just as brightly as Jane when Sorrow caught up to them. And Jane's smile was the best sight. With her eyes closed and her arms out, Death kept hold of Jane and Natalie and let King direct her light where it needed to touch.

David leaned down, kissing Jane's bare back after Death covered her.

"She'll sleep for several hours." Death caressed her cheek.

"She'll be sad she missed coming into the town." David carefully lifted Natalie, smiling when she mumbled in her sleep. He kissed her hair and carried her to the room where Nathan was already in bed.

David returned, smiling as he finally took in the room. It was plain, but it was homier than his room at the castle. "Nyc did a good job. Do you think she'll like it?"

Death didn't pull his gaze from Jane. "She'll love it. She had magazines that matched the rooms. I gave them to Nyc."

"Did you really?" David chuckled, tugging off his dirty shirt. "Are you going to stay? I need to shower."

Death nodded, sitting beside Jane.

585

His girl didn't wake, but she reached out for Death until the angel pulled her against him the way he usually held her.

David grabbed a few things and left them alone. He stared at his reflection as he thought about what this house meant. He had a home with Jane now. He had a real family, and he could only smile when he always pictured Death on the other side of the bed, with Jane between them.

As he took in the bathtub and shower, he chuckled. He'd ensure Jane never had a bad memory from her time in their house. He'd make her as happy as possible and let the angel holding her add to that happiness.

"David?" Her voice carried into the bath suite.

He leaned out and realized she was still asleep.

Death rocked her, caressing her cheek. "He's here, angel. I'm here."

She smiled but still didn't wake. "My loves."

A peaceful smile formed on Death's face. "Yes. You have us both."

David nodded to him and left to shower so he could return to his girl.

Jane grinned as she spotted David outside talking to Gawain, Gareth, and some of the wolf boys she had yet to meet. She held a finger to her lips as she tiptoed along the porch before leaping from the top step and landing on David's back.

He reached up for her thighs, laughing as she repeatedly kissed his cheek. "Morning. I meant to be there when you awoke, but the boys needed help."

She sniffed him, moaning because he smelled clean and very much like David again—not like the dying world they had traveled through.

David patted her legs. "Baby, maybe don't moan like that so early in the morning."

"Or ever." Gawain covered his ears.

Jane kicked her foot out at her brotherly knight. "Shush, he smells good. Clean and David-y."

The one named Sin chuckled. "She's cute."

Nyctimus shook his head. "He's going to knock you out again."

"You knocked him out?" She noticed the bruise on Sin's jaw. "David, don't be mean to your buddies. You only just reunited with them."

"I did it so Death wouldn't kill him for staring at your ass."

Gareth threw a biscuit at Sin. "Pervert. We claimed her as a sister. So watch that shit around us."

Sin scoffed but cringed when a green glow signaled Death's arrival. "Um, I'm going to go help that house of females."

David shook his head. "Leave the women to the others. You are trying to stay on the right path."

Jane observed how the aura around Sin was dark, but he had a glowing center where his soul pulsed with blue fire. "He'll behave."

David patted her leg. "He'll behave better with women not eager to fill their new home with a strong male. The humans can find other humans. They were already told to be mindful of the temptations immortals must resist."

Nyctimus pointed out another house. "Go there, and I will join you. They need help with furniture. Two families are choosing to stay together."

Sin winked at her but hurried away when Death gave a low growl.

"He can't help himself." Nyctimus chuckled. "But be mindful of those women. They are searching for males and don't care about the consequences. They've been warned, but they've been alone for too long."

"Are they the women that came with us from Valhalla?" she asked.

"I don't think so." David pointed down the dirt road. "Most of the survivors from Valhalla are staying near Thor's home."

Nyctimus waved his hand toward a different path. "These are humans we found. They have had a rougher life since the outbreak. There were rapists, murderers, and all sorts of horror. Just because they are women does not mean they cannot cause harm. They are fearful we will abandon them if they do not offer themselves. Sin has difficulty saying no, so David is right to warn him to stay away. All males of my species are filled with the urge to breed, but we would kill a human female right away. Their bodies are too weak for us."

"Oh." She frowned. "I wonder if I can do anything."

Death leaned forward to whisper in her ear. "It is not your duty to save everyone. Some will need to save themselves. No amount of help will do them good, and it will only hurt you to be involved."

David turned, kissing her cheek. "He's right, my love. You have done your part in getting them here. You are a beacon of hope for many, but these souls must take the steps toward light on their own. We will help by keeping temptation away. Sin is an obvious temptation."

Jane grinned at him. "Do you think he's cute?"

He gave her that look that warmed her insides and smirked when she shivered. "You know who I am attracted to."

Gareth laughed when Gawain stomped away.

Nyctimus pointed behind them. "You have small ones to tend to. Let me know if you need anything, Jane. We have a supply warehouse with extra furnishings."

"Oh, thank you." She waved him off.

Gareth leaned over and kissed her cheek. "I'm going to catch up with Gawain. The girls are trying to convince Gwen to move in with Arthur."

David shook his head as he lowered Jane to the ground. "I'll come speak with her later. Is Lance being kept far from her?"

"Of course. You should go by and see if you can talk to him. I hear he's been throwing a fit."

David grabbed her hand before leading her to the porch where the kids were. "I'll come by later."

Jane let David go before lifting Nathan when he reached for her as Natalie reached for David.

"We're hungry," Natalie said.

"Okay." David started up the steps, and Jane watched, smiling when David nudged Death to go inside as well. "I think we have cereal, but we will go see the gardens they have made to find fresh stuff to stock our home with."

Jane kissed Nathan's cheek and followed her family inside their new home, grinning again when David handed Natalie to Death so he could pour them cereal. Death didn't seem too uncomfortable, but she still went over to him, pushing up on her tippy toes when she was close.

He didn't hesitate to kiss her. "Good morning, my moon."

"Morning, Death." She nodded toward the table. "There are five chairs. I know you don't eat, but will you stay? Since it's our first meal."

He glanced at David.

"He's staying." David grabbed both kids from them before kissing Jane's head. "Come sit. We'll go to the gardens like I said. I'm sure Death will help you with your army. They were already by, asking for orders, and he sent them away so you could rest."

Death led her to the table, pulling out a chair. "Just this once. I won't make it a regular thing to come around for breakfast."

She frowned as she sat but smiled at David when he winked.

"We'll see about that." David poured milk into a bowl for her.

Death glared at him. "Papi, you don't get to boss me around."

Natalie giggled at them. "Papi."

"Papi," Nathan cheered.

Death rubbed a hand down his face. "Now it feels weird."

David chuckled. "You can call me Papi if you agree to stay here when you're around."

Jane bit her lip, darting her eyes between them. She wanted something normal for the kids, but she wasn't sure how her men would handle things. She had new powers to learn, more people to lead, and her kids to raise. She'd have to let David and Death work out this part because how they got along mattered more than anything.

Death sighed. "I'll think about it."

David nodded. "Good."

"Mommy, did you see my pretty bed?" Natalie asked.

"I did." She beamed at her daughter. "I peeked in and saw it when I woke up. Do you like everything?"

Both of her babies nodded.

"Di-saurs," Nathan said.

Jane glanced at Death. He stared out the window, watching people and vampires roaming together. She knew the dinosaur bedding and several princess items around the twins' new room hadn't come with them. He'd told Nyctimus what to put in there. She smiled, grabbing his hand under the table. "Thank you, Death."

He squeezed it but didn't look at her. "Always, Sweet Jane."

40

ALWAYS ENOUGH

Death stayed quiet as he sat with Jane outside the building where Lancelot was being held. She had wanted to go inside, but he'd put his foot down and told her no. He knew she was still plotting, though.

"I might be able to help him." She scooted closer, trying to butter him up.

He lowered his gaze to her gorgeous face but kept himself from showing any emotion. "Lancelot doesn't deserve your help."

She pouted her pretty lips at him.

He shook his head. "Stop."

She pushed her lips out more. "You sound just like King."

"King is wise—you should listen to him. And to me." He grabbed her chin and gave her a quick, rough kiss. "Stop trying to win me over with your lips."

"You like my lips." She beamed up at him.

He stared at them, remembering how they had pressed against his body that morning. He actually didn't mind the simple life she was trying to get him to live with her, but he knew he wouldn't stay forever. Death sighed, kissing her again. Longer.

She chuckled before kissing him hard. "Does this mean you'll help me?"

"You will do something foolish if I do not." He lifted her onto his lap. "Is this something David should know about?"

590

She glanced behind her, shaking her head and biting her lip. "He won't let me do what I think needs to be done."

Death sighed as he summoned his brothers and King. All appeared, bowing their heads to Jane when she grinned at them.

"What's up?" Pestilence sat, glancing around. "Are we killing the prisoners?"

Jane gasped. "Pest, we are trying to create a peaceful environment."

He smirked. "Lovely, you have three of the Horsemen of the Apocalypse staring at you. One, I might add, sleeps in your bed every night—I am jealous."

"And you will stay jealous. But I don't sleep." Death smirked. "I let her sleep a little bit, though."

Her face turned red.

Famine crossed his arms as he stared at Jane and then at King before muttering, "It's possible."

"How do you know what I want to do?" she asked, sitting straighter.

Famine smiled at her. "Your soul gives you away. She's just as hopeful as you are." He nodded to Death. "Let her try if you want to make her happy."

King snorted, shaking his massive head.

Jane pouted her lips at him, and the unicorn shook his head again.

"King," she sang softly before smiling brightly at the beast.

King stared at her before releasing a huff and turning away to take flight.

She clapped her hands. "He's fine with me trying. We can't tell David, though."

Death watched King disappear in the clouds.

Pestilence laughed. "Like Lucifer. Her smile gets them to submit to her wishes."

Jane leaned against Death. "I haven't thought about Luc."

Death kissed her head. "Good. Don't think about that fucker."

She kissed his cheek over and over, her soul rising for a moment to comfort him from the painful reality of her future.

Pestilence stood, stretching. "Get out of here. We'll take care of it. Maybe go to the meadow to relax for a bit."

Jane hopped off Death's lap. "Let's go."

He glared at Pestilence but walked with his girl as she remained oblivious to the people staring at her. She never realized how lovely she looked in this state. He chuckled when she spotted Sin, and the fucker took off running.

"He's too afraid to even come near me." She frowned but blushed when Nyctimus waved to her. "He's a hottie. And he's not afraid. I see why he's like the alpha."

Death shook his head. "You're walking with me and calling another man a hottie while you think about his alpha status? Baby girl, what am I going to do with you?"

She peered up at him. "Love me until the end of time."

He lifted her, squeezing her ass before kissing her. "Longer."

She wrapped her arms around his neck. "Yes. Always longer."

David stormed out of his house, growling. "Where the fuck did they go?" He pulled on his hair, his mind racing. He'd left Lancelot's cell when an explosion outside made him run out. He realized it had been a diversion when he found Pestilence's arrow, and nothing was damaged. He didn't understand it, so he searched for Jane, and that was when a guard alerted him that Lancelot had escaped.

That wasn't the reason David was panicking, though. He was panicking because Jane and Death were nowhere to be found.

Gareth jogged up to him. "His trail went cold at the edge of the tree line there. We're gearing up."

David glanced at the woods surrounding the town, his blood running cold, when he spotted a faint flicker of gold light. "She's in there. Hurry."

Gareth handed him a rifle before running off, and David rushed down the street.

He picked up Lance's trail quickly and ran faster when Jane's sweet scent blew from the same direction.

"Please don't do anything stupid, baby." He jumped over several demolished trees, knowing Lance had probably crashed through them in a hurry.

Jane's scent blew from a different direction. He skidded to a stop, scanning for any sound, and finally picked up her heartbeat. It was as if Death had put a barrier around her, but it was lifted, and he knew exactly where she was.

Lancelot was close to her.

David crept through the trees, listening as he put a silver bullet into the chamber. His heart stopped when he found her sitting on a boulder, staring at the dead flowers. He started to smile because she was safe, but his heart thundered when Lancelot walked up behind her. Jane didn't turn.

David raised his rifle, but a hand covered his before he could aim.

Death shook his head. "Watch."

"I know you followed me," Jane whispered, not turning away from the dead flowers.

Lancelot grabbed her by her hair, forcing her to stand as he raised a dagger to her throat.

David tried to run to her, but Death gripped him tightly and forced him to watch.

Jane merely smiled before reaching up and slowly moving the blade as it cut into her skin. Instead of escaping, she moved the dagger to hover over her heart. "I knew you would come for me. I promise I won't try to stop you."

David glared at Death, but the angel only smiled and pointed at the surrounding trees. Her entire army was hidden, bows and guns raised. Waiting.

"I don't want to hear your voice anymore," Lancelot growled, pressing the tip of his dagger into her soft skin.

She grimaced but continued to speak calmly. "I know. Let me show you one thing before you carry out your vengeance on me, though."

"I don't want to see anything of yours." Lancelot tightened his hand in her hair, but David could see his old friend warring with himself.

"It's nothing of mine that I am going to show you." She finally shifted her gaze away from the dead plants, and that's when David saw two figures trot out from the forest.

King and Queen.

The two beasts stopped at the sight before Jane and Lancelot. King puffed out his chest as he shook his massive head, his dark gray mane flowing behind him. Queen, however, just like Jane, remained calm as she pranced across the dead meadow. Every dead plant she touched bloomed with life only for a moment before fading away in gold dust. She kicked it up, filling the sky with gold glitter, entirely at peace with Jane being held captive.

"Those beasts are yours," Lancelot said, spitting his words, his glare fixed on King as he crossed at a slower pace. Everyone knew King held immense power and could destroy entire cities without any real effort.

"They're here to help me show you what I was asked to let you see."

Lancelot snapped his eyes to her. "What?"

Jane's aura pulsed, and her skin shimmered with her beautiful golden light. "*Shh . . .*" she whispered. "They're watching."

Lancelot glanced around, his brows drawn together. "Who?"

Jane slowly outstretched her arms as the entire forest lit up with fiery blue spheres, each one hovering several feet off the ground.

"What is this?" Lancelot scanned the magnificent sight.

David was in awe. There were so many. Countless. And more continued to fill the forest far beyond the distance even his powerful eyesight allowed him to see.

"They're souls," Jane whispered, her skin glowing brighter. "Watch." She gently pushed the dagger down and stepped backward as she smiled at Lance again, then bowed her head, King and Queen following her lead as their horns began to radiate light.

Each flame grew in intensity, some so big that a human silhouette was visible inside them.

"They were asked to wait for this moment." Jane stood straighter. The wind picked up around her as she lifted one of the blue flames into her palm. She blew on it until it floated in front of her, revealing the shape of a small boy. "Whether they died by your hand or you took them under your curse, they are all here. They have followed you all this time. This is the little boy you killed in front of me. His name is Brian. Do you remember him?"

Lancelot fell to his knees, nodding as he saw how many blue flames surrounded him.

David struggled to breathe. He barely noticed that the knights and Jane's generals had joined him as Lancelot's eyes filled with tears.

"Why are they here?" Lancelot asked Jane.

She smiled softly. "God asked them to stay. He wanted you to see."

"See what? That I'm a monster?" Lancelot shook his head. "I know I am."

"No." Jane nodded to the flame in front of her. "So they could give you something you seek. Don't be afraid to ask."

Lancelot's eyes widened before a tear fell. "I'm sorry." Another tear fell as he glanced around him. "Forgive me."

Jane bowed her head again. David smiled at his goddess. She was embracing her place in the universe.

The souls drifted closer until all of them were swirling around Lancelot. They went faster and faster, creating a colossal sphere that took up the entire clearing before they shot upward.

Lancelot darted his gaze to Jane. "What happened? Where did they go?"

Jane straightened as the wind picked up again, and she smiled. "They forgave you."

Lancelot stared at her, his teary eyes wide.

"So did God," she said, her light building as the ground shook. "Now watch." The ground rolled like a wave toward her, and as soon as it reached her, she tilted her head back and held out her arms as a gold beam of light burst out of her chest, breaking through the clouds.

The ground shook more as rocks began to levitate around Jane, but she didn't falter. She made a swirling motion with a hand before, almost as if she had lassoed something and yanked it down. At that moment, three blue orbs shot down from the sky.

The entire clearing filled with her light, and the crowd gasped in awe as Jane spread her arms wide, palms facing inward and trembling, and the orbs spun around Lancelot. King and Queen galloped around him as well, horns glowing.

Lancelot's eyes watered more as the three orbs circled him. They spun with incredible speed, and that was when David noticed Jane's soul had risen as well, engulfing her body in flames. He'd never seen her in full form so clearly before. She really was just Jane.

With a roar spilling from her lips, Jane's fiery soul burned brightly, and the blue spheres grew in size until there was no mistaking the figures of two children and a woman.

"Now," Jane hollered, and King and Queen reared up, their horns sparking as she thrust a hand forward, a beam of gold light erupting from her palm at the same moment King and Queen produced beams from their horns: their light and Jane's shot toward the blue orbs and David's breath caught in his chest.

The three figures became flesh.

Everyone watching fell to their knees as they watched a small boy and a little girl take in their physical forms before rushing to Lancelot.

"Daddy," the girl cried.

"Father," the boy said more seriously.

David chuckled, wiping away the tear on his cheek as he watched Jane cover her heart with her free hand and bow her head with King and Queen following her lead. They never stopped pushing energy into Lancelot's family.

Lancelot cried, hugging his children. He kissed their heads, murmuring words so softly that none of them could hear him over the thunderous surge of energy. He stood, picking up his children before nodding to the woman to come closer. Her long brown hair and green eyes made it easy to see why his friend had spared her. David saw it: his friend had found his soul mate, and he only realized it now.

"I'm so sorry, baby," Lancelot whispered, leaning down to kiss her. "I love you."

She touched Lancelot's face, sobbing. "I love you."

David looked at Jane, overwhelmed by seeing his friend and his family. He knew this was a gift from Jane and God, but it wouldn't last.

Jane still surged with light, but it was dimming. Her lovely soul began to twirl, throwing her arms out as if she were doing a pirouette before flaring up, revealing Jane's silhouette, then transforming into a fiery whirlwind, feeding power to the trio.

Arthur came to David's side, patting his shoulder as he watched with tears in his eyes. David smiled when he saw Arthur holding his sister's hand, happy to see his sister finally at peace and attempting to mend her marriage.

David returned his focus to the miracle his baby had made, noticing her soul spinning faster. She wasn't giving in to her weakness just yet.

However, Lancelot picked up on what was happening and kissed his family, telling them how much he loved them as they told him how proud they were of him and that they would wait for him.

Jane finally looked up, smiling through the strain of using such power as she took in the family. "You were always enough, Lancelot." Her voice mixed with another's, and it would have made David fall to his knees had Death not held him up.

"You were never forgotten," she said, the other voice still echoing through everything around them. "You were always loved. I will never give up on you." She cried as she stared at his family for a moment before focusing on Lancelot. "Forgive us."

The children and Lancelot's woman bowed to Jane, smiling, at peace.

Lancelot smiled at her, too. "I do. We do. Thank you."

She let out a sad laugh, bowing her head to them once more, roaring even louder than earlier, her entire frame shaking as Lancelot hugged his children, kissing them as quickly as he could when they began to fade. Jane gave Lance every bit of energy she could for this.

Death motioned for David to follow him as she stopped hollering.

She looked up, smiling as the orbs spun around Lance until she raised her hand, sending them into the sky again.

Jane gasped as she fell on all fours. The entire gathering was in tears, and the children played with the gold dust still floating through the air.

"Thank you," Jane whispered, breathing heavily as King and Queen trotted to her.

David couldn't describe the warmth he felt watching his girl stay on shaky arms until she allowed King to help her stand.

"Thank you," she whispered again, kissing the winged unicorn's muzzle. "Yes, I know. I will not make another wish for him."

"Beautiful, angel," Death said, lifting her as King and Queen returned to the forest. "Never ask me to let you nearly get attacked again."

"You were ready. So were my guards." She nodded to her army weakly. "Thanks, boys."

"Baby?" David caressed her sweaty hair as Death better situated her in his arms. "Why didn't you tell me what you were doing?"

"You would have stopped me." She pointed at Lancelot. "See to your friend. Death will stay with me—I need the sun."

David glanced up, noticing no more clouds where her light had hit. Only blue sky and sunlight, and the vampires Jane had given absolution to were crying, happy to finally feel the sun on their skin without burning.

She smiled at the sight, and David cupped her cheeks, kissing her. "I love you so much. Thank you for giving him this." He gave her another kiss. "Don't ever do this to me again, though."

"I won't. I didn't know I would do it until it felt right." She sighed as the sun's rays touched her face. "It feels like you, David." She raised a hand to Death's cheek and his. "Like both of you."

David couldn't describe what he felt seeing her so at peace as she basked in the sunlight. Her hair had red and gold tones, and she was more beautiful than he believed possible. "Rest now, my love." David kissed her and watched Death carry her away before approaching his old friend, who stayed kneeling on the creek bank. "They were lovely, Lance."

Lancelot nodded, his entire body shaking as he cried.

David put a hand on his head before helping him up and embracing him as his brother again.

"Forgive me," Lancelot whispered, hugging him.

"I forgave you the moment I remembered the boy who called me brother." David patted his back. "Are you going to be all right? You're not going to slit my throat like you threatened earlier?"

Lancelot chuckled. "No. You knew already I couldn't do it."

David smiled. "I know. I guess she believed in you too."

Lancelot looked up at the sky. "How did she do it?"

"I don't think we are meant to know." He held his arm out, enjoying the warmth on his skin. It reminded him of Jane's touch. "We are all here to help her, and she chose to help you."

"Foolish girl." Lance shook his head. "I could have killed her. Did you at least have me in your sights?"

David laughed. "Yes. I was ready. Death stopped me."

"She has him wrapped around her finger. Doesn't it bother you?"

David raised his hand, allowing gold dust to fall into his palm. "It will bother me if I wake up and see her sad because he is gone."

Lancelot nodded as he rubbed his chest.

"Your woman was breathtaking, brother." David watched a heartbroken smile form on Lancelot's face. "As terrible as it is that it took until now, I am glad you could finally see who she was to you. And the boy and girl—I wish I could have met them."

"I should have been better for them," Lancelot said, strained. "I didn't know how much I loved them until they were gone."

"I know." David sighed but smiled when he saw Nathan and Natalie spinning around in the floating gold dust. "Now you know they are waiting for you. They believe in you. Don't let this gift go to waste. Jane would not have been able to do this if God did not believe in you. I believe in you, too. I know others will doubt you, but I have your back. Clearly, so does my girl."

David followed Lancelot's gaze and spotted Death holding Jane as she spoke to her men.

"She's beautiful," Lancelot whispered. "I knew the moment I first saw her I was staring at an angel, and I hated her. I saw how perfect she was for you and knew she was special. That darker half was there, of course, but I saw this." He waved his hand at Jane when her army of princes placed their hands on her head, bowing in what seemed to be a prayer as they pushed energy into her. Famine and Pestilence appeared, doing the same, their horses manifesting beside them. Aside from her obvious attachment to Sorrow, Jane had grown quite fond of Misery, the Black Horse of the Apocalypse. King did not appear to like any of the horses, but that didn't stop them from each admiring Queen. *Just like my baby.*

"She's special," he agreed. "I do not even know how to describe what I see every time I look at her."

"Keep her safe," Lancelot said fiercely. "Lucifer will come for her one day. She is powerful, probably capable of doing things we thought only the highest angels could do, but He is using her. Or trusting her with a duty we will never understand. Still, protect her. Love her every damned second you can. And hang on to her if that bastard shows up for her."

"I will." David's heart throbbed. He knew Jane would die one day—there was no point denying it. He knew that was why Death was giving her what she wanted. Her angel wanted to give her the world and perfect life he desired for her.

Lancelot roughly wiped the tears from his cheeks. "Thank her for me. I know it must have drained and hurt her to give me this, even if only for a short moment. I will never forget it. I did not even know such a thing was possible."

"I will tell her. I know she wishes it was more. If she could, she would give you a whole life with them."

Arthur approached, holding out the dagger Lancelot had dropped. "Brother."

Lancelot took the dagger, his eyes drifting to Guinevere and the children before darting to Arthur again.

"They were beautiful, Lancelot," Guinevere sobbed, unable to hide her emotions. "She was beautiful. I'm so sorry, darling. I shouldn't have hurt you so."

Arthur kissed Guinevere's head, taking Nathan from her and nudging her toward Lance.

Lancelot embraced her, shushing her as she cried her apologies against his chest. "It's all right. I will see them again now."

David lifted Natalie as he watched Death launch into the sky, carrying Jane.

"He's refueling her," Arthur murmured, looking up. "So beautiful."

"Will Mommy always be like this?"

David watched until he could no longer see them because of the sun. "She will for as long as she is supposed to, princess."

"Where did the little boy and girl go?" she asked.

David kissed her head. "Back to the stars."

Arthur rubbed Guinevere's back as she continued to cry, still allowing Lancelot to hold her.

"Oh," Natalie whispered, lifting her gaze to Lance's. "I will say hello to them at night for you, Sir Lance. I'll ask my daddy to watch them for you."

Lance stared at Natalie before finally smiling. "She looks like her."

David smiled at Natalie. She did look like Jane, but she had a lot of Jason too. He knew Jane saw her husband whenever she was with Natalie.

"Thank you, little one," Lance told her. "I think they will like that."

Nathan smiled at Lancelot. "Knight."

David chuckled. "Yes, he is one of the greatest knights ever."

"Like Daddy." Nathan touched David's cheek.

David's heartbeat sped up, and he could only stare at Nathan in awe.

Lancelot patted his back. "Daddy is the best of us, but only because I trained with him. And your mom made him great, of course."

Arthur handed Nathan to David before gently pulling Guinevere away. "Come, my wife. Let us see if we can persuade the cooks to make the children's favorite, and I can move your things into our new home."

Her eyes filled with even more tears before she kissed Arthur. "Yes." She turned, quickly kissing Lancelot's cheek before doing the same to David. "Brother. Forgive me."

"I already did, sister. So did Jane. I love you." David smiled, kissing her forehead before resting his cheek on Nathan's head. *My baby boy.*

His sister cried as she finally turned away, whispering, "Arthur, we are truly their aunt and uncle."

Lancelot chuckled beside him before sitting on the ground.

David joined him, still in shock from Nathan's declaration.

"Were you and Daddy bestest friends?" Natalie asked Lancelot.

David whipped his head around to stare at her. She was talking about him. She was calling him her daddy too.

"Bestest?" Lancelot chuckled. "You must've gotten that from your mother. But your daddy was my brother many years ago. We both forgot." Lancelot pointed up at the sky. "Your mother brought us back together. She lit up the darkness so we could see each other again."

David kissed her hair. *My little girl.*

"Your boy was pretty." Natalie turned red in the face and quickly hid behind her curls.

Lancelot laughed. "I'm certain he would think the same about you. Your daddy would probably scare him away. That means he doesn't think any boy is good enough for you."

Natalie blushed when she looked at David. "Ryder can hold him if Mama asks him to. Mama has lots of boys."

Lancelot laughed louder. "She does. She's good for each of them, I suppose. I think she is quite fond of your daddy, though."

"She says he's the bestest." Natalie nodded, pointing at the sky. "She is the moon. That's what Daddy and Ryder say. See, she is full now, even in the day."

David looked up, noticing the moon was indeed visible in the sky where the clouds were cleared.

"Yes, she is a special soul," Lancelot whispered, staring at it.

David stared at the twins with a warmth he had not felt before filling his heart. It was different from Jane's beautiful heat, which never weakened, but this new feeling overwhelmed his heart so much that he felt their love throughout his entire being.

"Congratulations, brother," Lancelot said, not looking at him. "They're beautiful."

David smiled at Nathan and Natalie as they waved their hands through the gold still drifting down, dusting the rocks. God and Jane hadn't just given Lance a gift. They had gifted everyone with something they needed. And they had given him the chance to hear his children call him Daddy. "Thank you, brother."

Jane smiled as she watched David enter the room. He had a big grin on his face, but she could tell he'd cried earlier.

Death sighed, sitting up. "I have shit to do tonight. You two have fun without me."

She reached out for him before he could get too far. "Why can't you stay?"

He smirked, leaning down and kissing her. "I'll stay tomorrow. Talk him into letting you play solo with me sometime."

David pulled his shirt over his head, chuckling. "I told you it's fine. How well did you take care of her this evening?"

"I took care of our girl." Death pressed a long kiss to Jane's lips. "Both of them. I love you, angel."

"And I love you," she whispered, caressing his cheek.

He gave her another kiss before sitting up. "She'll probably still be tired tonight, but I think she will be fully recharged tomorrow. I'll take her up again in the morning, though. Using King and Queen helped her. Famine and Pest drained themselves for her."

David patted Death's shoulder. "Thank you."

"It's never for you." Death snickered, raising Jane's hand to kiss it. "I heard the rugrats finally called you Daddy."

Jane gasped, focusing on David's wide smile. "Oh, I missed it. He said I would hear it."

"They'll call him it again." Death smacked David's shoulder. "She gains a connection to Father when she meditates or enters god mode. She understands everything He wants her to."

She gave him a tired smile. "He still won't let me know what secret you two have. And I forget a lot when I stop concentrating."

"You'll master it soon enough." Death kissed her hand again. "Good night, my moon."

"Good night, Death." She frowned as he vanished but grinned as her vampire got in bed, not letting her feel alone for more than a second.

"Nathan called Lance a knight and said like Daddy as he touched my cheek. Then Natalie asked him if he was bestest friends with Daddy." He pulled her close, burying his face in the crook of her neck. "I wasn't expecting it. I did not think it would affect me so much, but I almost cried."

"Aw, baby." Jane hugged him tight. "You're getting soft without monsters to slay."

"Perhaps I should take you hunting with me so you can see I am still alpha."

"Oh, I know you are." She purposely rubbed herself against him, smiling when she felt him getting hard. "You're a great daddy, too. I'm so happy they finally told you so."

"Me too." He kissed her neck before leaning away. "Today has been the most beautiful day of my life, Jane. I'm still slightly pissed you let Death in on it and scared me, but it was divine. You showed everyone a glimpse of Heaven. You restored hope to all present."

She took a tired breath as he pulled her even closer. "I still wish I could have done more for them. I will never forget what it felt like to feel their love. Every one of them. They were all at peace, and they truly forgave him."

David kissed her forehead. "It was incredible. You were magic. Never would I have imagined I would see such wonders. I am so proud of you. You've come so far. It is no wonder Hell has halted its advances on us."

"They're still coming," she said softly.

"I know." He twirled her hair. "Do you think Lucifer controls King?"

She could barely hide her smile. "I think Luc is aware of what King does. Almost as if he is a loyal spy, but King is just as stubborn as him. He doesn't want to put me in harm's way. That is what he told me. He said I would grow too weak from performing such a feat, and I would alert Hell of where we are. As if they do not already know."

David sighed. "I think it was worth the risk. You were so brave to allow Lance to get close to you."

"You already knew he wouldn't truly hurt me."

"Yes, I did." David looked up at the ceiling. "He loves you and has yet to forgive himself for the pain he caused you."

"He loves you," she corrected. "It is his love for you that I trusted in. He would not hurt you by killing me."

He nodded. "I know. Still, I see that he has developed a love for you. It is different from my love, but he does, and he has been trying to hide it behind hate."

Jane pushed herself up, throwing a leg over him.

"Baby, you know you should be resting." He grabbed her hips before sliding a hand up her stomach. "And I am not upset that he loves you. You are loved in many forms by men and women—angels and demons—kings and humble mortals. But Lance always had a thing for brunettes with pretty eyes. I have caught him watching you often. He forgets he's supposed to want to kill you, and I realize he is admiring and in awe."

She leaned down, and her hair fell around them like a veil. "He is quite handsome when he's not threatening everyone, but he's not my David. Now will you love me? We're already naked."

David squeezed her ass, rocking her. "Yes, my love. We should probably go soft, though. I want you alert when you spend time with your other love tomorrow. He has missed your alone time together."

She rolled her hips, sighing. "You're so fucking sweet. Gosh, I don't even know if you've ever gone soft with me."

He chuckled before sitting up and cupping her face. "I don't think I have."

"I love you, David. I'll never get tired of telling you."

"I know you do." He kissed her as he helped ease her onto him. "And I love you more than even God can fathom."

Jane sighed, whimpering as she adjusted to the fullness, and put her arms around his neck. "I don't think God would agree with such a claim."

David grinned, dragging his hand down her back as he rocked her on him. "No, he told me so. Are you good?"

"Mhm." She pulled herself up so she'd slide down, and she smiled upon hearing him release a deep sigh.

He pressed a kiss to her neck. "I rarely feed from you anymore. I miss it."

"You can feed." She threw her head back when he thrust forward.

"No, you need to recover." He still kissed her neck, sucking the skin where he'd managed to mark her. He never touched Death's bite, only his. "If you want, let Death love you by himself tomorrow."

She threaded her fingers through his hair, sighing as he fastened their movements. "He refuses to love me without you."

He smiled against her mouth. "I will talk to him, then. I think he needs it. So do you. It may be what you need for your bond—just the two of you without me present."

Jane grinned against his kiss. "Bestest."

"So you have told me many times before." He chuckled before hitting her spot and making her cry out. "Ah, there's my kitten. No more talk of your angel now. Just us tonight. Tomorrow, just him."

Her body erupted in goosebumps as he began to engulf her being with his heat. "Oh, God."

He rocked them, going deeper. "Not God . . . Just your David."

4 1

FAIRY TALE

David yawned, rubbing a hand over his face as he awoke, smiling when he heard Jane moving around in the kitchen, feeding the children.

"Stop smiling, dumbfuck, and wake up."

"Please tell me you are not in bed with me without her between us." David opened one eye to see Death lounging in a chair with his feet resting on the bed.

"Papi, if you want to start cuddling me, I've got bad news for you. I only cuddle a sexy five-footer, and she's downstairs making you breakfast in her new kitchen. I'll warn you—I don't think she's a very good cook."

David flipped him off. "I'll love whatever she makes. Now what do you want?"

Something landed on his chest. David picked it up, his heart hammering as he took in the dirty ring. "How?"

Death gestured to himself. "I'm Death, bitch."

"I could almost fucking kiss you." David sat up, inspecting the ring he'd kept since becoming immortal. It was the ring his mother had given him to present to a bride when he confessed he was no longer human. She was the only human to know, and she'd made him promise to marry the girl who accepted the ring his father had given her before they were wed. It was well crafted for being so old, and he had always wondered if his father had also met an immortal to have such a ring.

Death shrugged. "If you want me to punch you through the wall, go for it. I have time."

David chuckled, reaching for the sheet to wipe it off. "How did you know about it?"

"I put it together when I realized you discussed marrying her with Nyc. I asked Arthur, and he said you'd had the ring since you were mortal, but you lost it in the fire. I decided to see if I could find it. She'll like it, if you're worried. It suits her."

"Thank you." David smiled at him.

"You shouldn't have taken it out of your fucking pocket in the first place." Death glared at him and went on, his tone violent as his stare. "Yes, he told me you had carried it around since finding Jane. Don't ever do that shit to her again."

David sighed, knowing what Death was talking about. He'd carried this ring around since he had returned home with Jane, but after she admitted to loving Lucifer right in front of him, he had taken it out of his pocket, stored it in his closet, and then left. He'd fallen down with her confession and the magnitude of what had occurred while she was gone, and he'd considered for the briefest moment that he couldn't go on. He considered that he wasn't the man she was destined for or the man she wanted.

"You're going to have arguments," Death said when he stayed quiet. He released a breath, his glowing eyes dimming as he spoke calmer. "As great as you both are together, it will happen. She will have moments of sadness or anger, and you will have to step up. She will have to do the same, but this shit"—he pointed to the ring—"with doubting your life together isn't gonna happen if you decide to give it to her. You don't get to marry her and then walk away when she's bitchy, hormonal, or just fucking confused about shit. Our girl loves beyond what we can comprehend, and we are not supposed to judge her for it. If you put that on her finger, you are all in, David. No taking that ring off and putting it aside because you're upset with her. Never again will you walk away like you did that night. She stayed so strong, but I felt her dying, and it wasn't from half her soul being ripped from her the night before. Had she not had the kids . . ."

Death shook his head as a frustrated growl got caught in his chest. "If you give her this ring, you take all that comes with my baby. I stand aside because I believe you are better than me and because I cannot be what her heart needs me to be. So think really hard before offering it to her. I won't stand by if you walk away again. I will take her to where she never has to feel the pain of losing you. If you give it to her, you are promising me as much as you are promising her that you are strong enough—that you love her enough to be the greatest man she could ever have. You were made for her, David . . . Not the other way around. So be that man."

It always overwhelmed David when he realized how much Death loved Jane. He knew he didn't have to ask for Death's consent, but he did anyway. "I will always try to be what you both expect me to be for her. How do you feel about this, though? If I were to ask her to be my wife?"

Death peered out a window. "If I could, I would take that step with her, but you know I cannot, and you know I don't deserve to have her that way."

"You do." David studied the sapphire ring. He had already tested it on her finger when she was asleep and knew it was a perfect fit.

"Maybe," Death said. "If you still wish to marry her, I want you to ask her. She has envisioned a life with you, and it's a beautiful dream. I have felt her hope to have all of it, and it was for you, not me. I'm not complaining or upset—I am simply assuring you it is not me she desires a marriage with."

His heart hurt. "What if she desires to marry both of us now? You only read her mind before we started our new relationship—before she became so at peace."

Death chuckled, finally returning his focus to him. "You want me to be husband number two?"

"If you are considering leaving her so I can have her, I won't ask her to be mine alone. I told you we are one."

"What do you expect me to do?"

David stared at him, neither one breaking eye contact. "You've already decided, haven't you? That's what all this shit has been about lately. You're leaving."

"I'm leaving."

His heart was crushed. "You don't have to go. I can give her the ring and let her know I had always meant to give it to her, but I still embrace what we have. She'll understand."

A deep sigh left Death. "I'll remain faithful to her, but I can't stand by and watch her become a wife to another man again. She wants to marry you, and she won't be able to embrace being your wife and you her husband if we are still sharing a bed nearly every night."

David ran his hand through his hair. He had feared this day would come. He had been prepared to console Jane for Death's departure, but he hadn't expected to be able to marry her. Not just because the ring was lost to him but because he wanted Jane to have Death. Death was her true soul mate, and he deserved to be there. "I thought there would be more time," he whispered.

"The end will still come," Death said. "We can only hope to hold it off long enough for Jane to watch the children live a full life. They will not grow old before her eyes, but she deserves to give them the family she has always wanted them to have—that is with you. Not with me."

"This is going to hurt her. I can't watch her fade because you are not here."

"She won't."

David frowned. "How can she not?"

Death smiled, but it was sad. "I'm not her soul mate anymore, and she is no longer dying because Lucifer's light and bond mimic the energy a soul gives. She doesn't need me. She will miss me, but she will be content with you. She has achieved a level of peace that few have glimpsed. She'll be able to handle me leaving."

He shook his head. "You are her true soul mate. I am, but only because of the gift you allowed me to have with her. You will always be the soul God paired her with. Besides, we have developed a family unit already—it includes you. I have been trying to keep us together, and it makes her so happy to see us like we have been."

Death laughed. "I make out with Jane while you play daddy. You say you are fine, but it will get old fast. I don't want her to witness that either."

David chuckled. "It won't get old. I know she needs alone time with you, just like you know she needs it with me. We both ensure she gets that. You need her physical love more because your bond is not in place—I get it. And she craves and misses that bond. I cannot imagine what it must feel like for both of you to not have it. So I enjoy bonding with the children alone while you have our girl to yourself. I know you are doing more than satisfying your urge to be with her sexually. You're trying to find a way to bond while you help her harness her new abilities. She's whole in a different way now, and you are helping her in a way I do not know how. So don't brush off how truly important you are to her and me. You are a part of us without the bond."

"Perfect fucker," Death muttered, "you almost made me blush."

David smiled sadly. "I can't ask her to marry me without you in our lives. And you haven't given us a chance here to decide that things won't work. She may finally be able to perform the bond she wants us to share."

Death held his hand up to stop him. "I'm leaving to do other things as well. I have my duties, and for her to give the children a chance to grow up, even if it's only for a few more years, she needs me to fight for her. I'm going to do it, and you are going to stand by them, protect them, love them—do everything I cannot—and I will see you when it is time."

"For me to die, you mean?" David's heart felt like it was bleeding.

"Returning any sooner than the end would ruin what you end up building together. I want my girl to live, and I am Death. I will always be Death. I can only hope I find a way to be a part of her death. I will never stop trying to keep my girl happy, but her happiness is to have a family for her children. I have to make sure she has it. Lucifer and others are watching, and they will take you from her if I sit back. They could even take her or the kids and Adam—I can stop that. This is why I was never truly meant to have her. God knew I could only protect her from these threats long enough for her to be happy. Don't ask me to sit around playing house while she loses all of you just so I can be in her life."

David rubbed the ring between his fingers. He knew Death was right, but he didn't want him to go. He didn't want Jane and Death to lose each other. "When?"

"Sooner than I want to admit aloud this morning."

David rubbed his face. His entire body hurt because he knew life would no longer be the same. He knew Jane would never be the same. "I will see to it that we have all taken this step together and are simply waiting to reunite. I won't give up hope you will reforge your bond with her. And if you want to return sooner, I swear you will be welcomed back."

"Jane will not ask that of you," Death said. "What we have now is special, and it works for us, but a husband and wife—in Jane's mind and yours—is limited to just that: one husband and one wife. Don't force yourself to look for options that somehow result in a marriage that involves me being the extra one there to spice things up." He smirked. "I know I would, but you can fill both roles. And I already told you I cannot be a husband. I'd give everything to be that for her, but doing it would force her to give everything. So no, I cannot be husband number two."

David moved to the edge of the bed, his stomach knotting at Death's words. Death was giving up Jane because she really would lose all if she chose him. "I will still hold faith that one day you will have your soul mate again. And hopefully, that will be the same day we three are tied together. If not, then—later. Don't give up. I won't. I will love her for both of us. I will tell her each night how much you love her before telling her good night."

"Romantic fucker." Death chuckled. "I have one request: permit me a night with her. Just for her to remember me. She remembers almost everything, and I'd like it if she could have a memory of us not tainted with sorrow. Just something for us. I suppose—what we were meant to be in another life."

"I would give anything for you both to have more than that, but yes, if you are certain about leaving so soon, I want you to have a night neither of you will ever forget."

Death nodded. "I'll probably fuck up the no sorrow bit but thank you." He walked out before David could reassure him.

Getting out of bed, David stared at the ring in his hand and listened to Jane giggling with Death as she asked him why he had been using his sound barrier.

"I was confessing about my secret crush on Papi," Death told her. "Give me a kiss. He totally shot me down, and I'm heartbroken."

Jane was quiet for a few seconds before she whispered, "Are you all right, Death?"

"I'll be all right when you put those lips on mine. Now come here."

David pulled on a pair of jeans as he felt Jane's love for Death and him through their bond, and he even faintly registered what Jane experienced from her contact with Death. He opened his hand, staring at the small ring resting on his palm. He wanted her to wear it, to be married to her, but he wished it could come without such a steep price.

"Daddy." Natalie ran into the room. "I can't find my dolly."

David pocketed the ring and picked her up. "I'm sure it's around here, princess. Let's go eat breakfast, and then I will help you search for it."

"Her doll is down here," Death hollered. "She left it in the cat bed."

David kissed Natalie's head. Death didn't realize how good of a husband and father figure he was, but he felt he was only this way because of his broken bond. He wasn't sure why he felt that way, but he knew being bonded to Jane meant more to Death than being a father. If anything happened to Jane, Death would feel nothing for them.

"I didn't leave her in the cat bed," Natalie said as David entered the kitchen.

Death tossed him the dolly as Jane's eyes sparkled, watching them. This is what being a husband would cost him. She always glowed a bit brighter and smiled a tiny bit wider when Death participated in their interaction as a family.

David handed Natalie her doll as he walked to Jane, kissing her. "Good morning."

"Morning." She grinned, kissing him again. "Sit and eat. Death arranged for us to meet Nyc at the hill. The boys are going hunting for meat. Some of the humans are coming to watch the boys transform, and they're having a barbecue."

"A barbecue?" David set Natalie in a chair and then pulled Jane onto his lap once he sat.

"Do you not know what a barbecue is?" Death pushed Jane's plate closer. "Eat up. You know you always hate the food at those gatherings."

David watched a soft smile cross Jane's face as she stared at her angel. "Sit with Death, Jane. I need to get a ration."

Death made eye contact with him as Jane offered to get it. "Come here."

She sighed dramatically, but David saw her happiness with them sharing her time.

He smacked her cute ass before standing. "Where's Nathan?"

"He ate earlier." Jane held up a drawing. "He's in the living area doing another one. He said this one is for you."

David returned to his seat after getting a glass of water. "So why do you hate the food at these gatherings but still wish to go?" He returned to his chair, inspecting the drawing. It was him, Jane, and the twins, but Death was on Sorrow, riding away. David glanced at Death and sighed, trying to appear happy when Jane answered.

"They just usually have meaty stuff. Or things like potato salad and stuff I don't like."

"I thought you loved hamburgers," he said.

Death smiled fondly. "She thinks it's meaner to eat them when they're cooked on an open fire. It's like the bone thing versus a regular hamburger. She gets grossed out and sad when she's reminded something was killed so she could eat."

Her cheeks turned pink. "It's just easier when it doesn't look like an animal."

"So adorable, baby." David chuckled, staring at his plate. Death was right—it didn't look that great.

Jane started talking again. "At least it isn't so hot here. I hated how humid it was in Texas—I couldn't stand it."

Death hugged her. "You just don't like sweating and getting all hot. Those assholes always made your blood boil. That, along with the heat, you were always ready to blow."

David put the drawing down and ate. "We'll pack you something, then. And you can always slip away with one of us if you get overwhelmed by the crowds. You seem to do well, though."

Death kissed Jane's head before whispering in her ear low enough that Natalie would not hear. "Pretend you're stressed so we can make love to you in the woods with the risk of getting caught."

Her face went red.

David winked at her. "Your call, Jane. You know we can keep it secret, and you're already off your cycle."

She blew out a breath as her pheromones gave away her mood.

He smirked, lifting a glass of blood, but paused before drinking and added, "I'll bring a blanket if he helps you change your suit into something to match a woodland goddess for us."

"Ay, Papi." Death laughed, kissing Jane's blushing cheek.

Jane smiled awkwardly as she listened to a group of women discussing recipes, decorating, and starting a daycare or school. Then, every once in a while, when a male vampire or one of Nyctimus' men walked by, they'd gush over them and discuss whether anyone knew whether he was with a woman. Some were even contemplating asking to be turned into immortals.

She shook her head at their stupidity. They were already told about the consequences, yet they were joking about damning good men and themselves. She felt a strong urge to protect the humans, but the immortals were people she'd been allowed to save. It would crush her just as much as it must have done God when they began to fall.

She sighed as she studied the young mom of the girl Natalie played with. The woman seemed nice, but she didn't want to get too close to Jane. The lady switched between staring at Natalie like something was wrong with her and smiling wistfully at David. Jane had gotten better at accepting the attention her men got, but it was still irritating to sit through.

David slid an arm around her waist before kissing her head. "You look annoyed."

"It's the same as it was when I was a human." She leaned against him, breathing in his scent to relax. "I guess even achieving inner peace means not everything is perfect. God some of these women are even considering asking men to change them."

"The men won't." David chuckled. "Any immortal who has lasted this long is committed to fighting for Heaven and saving the human race. They are not going to do something that foolish."

"I hope not. It's just stupid to hear them. I get silly about you guys, but I can tell these women really would go there. They see how we all visit the infirmary for blood rations; some even donate, so it's not like a movie. This is real, and they're seriously considering damning the men I was given a chance to save."

"I think they are simply lonely, my love. There are surprisingly few human males alive here. The ones they encountered were not all noble. For these women to see strong, honorable men must be a miracle."

"They're horny," she deadpanned.

He smiled, pulling her onto his lap. "Are you judging them when you are receiving satisfaction from both of your men?"

"No. Maybe."

He chuckled, giving her a long kiss. "You're so protective of the souls you've saved. Try not to be too hard on these mortals, though."

She pecked him on the lips. "But they are taking it a bit too far. I won't let them damn any men whose sins I was allowed to absolve."

"That's not up to you, baby." He pushed her hair away from her neck and kissed the mark he'd given her. "Do you want to meet some of the other mothers? Or sit with the wives? I'll go with you if you want me to or come rescue you when you give me a sign you've had enough."

She shook her head. "I'm fine. I like sitting with you. And no one is eager to have me around."

He offered her an apple slice before he took in the other people. "I think it will just take time for people to be comfortable around you. You're not human, Jane. You're not even a normal immortal. Being paired with me as your Other has become insignificant now. You're intimidating. Not in a bad way, but I understand why many hesitate to come close enough to talk to you. I experienced similar scenarios throughout my life—as a prince and a vampire—but you are more powerful than I am. I know it must hurt, though. I can see you still want to be like the other mothers. But look at our children." He hugged her tighter. "They have accepted you completely and are not even considering why you do not sit with the other mothers. They are not looking down on us for not being like the others, and that is what matters."

"I know." She chewed on the apple he'd given her. "What were you talking about with Death? He was using a sound barrier."

David kissed her head. "I'm sure he'll tell you later."

Jane looked up at him before searching for Death. He was nowhere to be found. The others were all around, though. All the immortals were laughing and eating. Thor wasn't being an ass. Surprisingly, he was helping the injured humans from his fortress. The knights were scarfing down food as their wives and the immortal women who had joined their group chatted with each other. Even her fallen angels and demons seemed to be enjoying themselves. They weren't eating, but they were conversing with smiles on their faces. "David, do you want to go sit with your friends?"

"No." He chuckled. "I'm old, sweetheart. I have been around my brothers, their wives, and the soldiers longer than you can imagine. This is nice, just sitting in the sun with you in my arms. And, of course, watching our children happy. The food could be better, but that is why we are going hunting later."

"Don't kill any deer." She covered her mouth. "Sorry."

"You don't want me to kill a deer?"

"You can." She felt so stupid. The people there relied on them to provide food, and she worried about them killing cute animals.

"I can kill animals besides deer. We are actually hoping to find animals to bring back alive to provide milk. They've been trying to catch chickens too. For eggs."

"That's good. I guess just make sure the kids don't see anything dead. One time some asshole had a dead deer tied to the back of their truck, and the kids screamed because they thought someone had killed Rudolph."

David glanced at the kids. "I will make sure any kills brought back are kept out of sight from all the children. Sometimes hunters are too proud of their kills to consider the innocence and feelings of others. I will do what I can to preserve the innocence we've managed to keep in them."

She curled up against him more. "David, you're so perfect it hurts."

"Just for you." He gave her another piece of apple.

Natalie ran over to them. Her little eyes were red, and her lips quivered.

Jane sat up. "What's wrong?"

Natalie looked up at her before staring at David. "They said he's not my daddy because Daddy died. They said you weren't married to Mommy, and only daddies could be married to mommies."

Fire burned under Jane's skin, but she took a deep breath when David lifted Natalie and hugged both of them.

"Princess, they don't know what they're talking about," he said soothingly instead of angry like she felt radiating from his body. "There are different types of daddies and mommies. You have two daddies. And you have Death, too. He's a part of our family."

"They said Mommy can't marry you if she has Death, so you can't be my daddy. They laughed at me because I said it was okay because Death is her soul mate, too. They said that's stupid, and Death won't ever love me."

"Who said this?" Jane tried to move, but David held her tighter.

"Baby, relax." He kissed her forehead before forcing Natalie to look him in the eye. "Princess, I can ask Mommy to marry me whenever I want to. Mommy will always have Death, though. That doesn't change the fact I already consider you and your brother my children. And none of those children understand Death's burden. You know he is different, princess. He can't help it."

"But you're not married." Natalie's lip trembled.

Jane rubbed her head and turned away from David. She wanted to marry him, but she didn't think he wanted that anymore, and she didn't want to push Death away by becoming David's wife anyway.

Death shimmered into view on the opposite side of the table. He stared at them for a moment before speaking. "Come here, Natalie."

Jane pressed her lips together, her gaze shifting between David, Natalie, and Death.

David helped Natalie off their laps, and Jane held her breath when Death held out a hand for her daughter. When she took it, he walked her in the opposite direction and called Nathan to come with them.

"Where's he taking them?" she whispered to David.

"I don't think he's going far." David sighed, kissing her head. "Don't be upset. We have nothing to prove to anyone. They have accepted us, but that doesn't mean others can keep their opinions to themselves. And our children will learn to handle these situations with us being strong at their sides. If we show confidence in our relationship, they will develop the confidence to face bullies."

Jane kept her eyes on Death as he placed her kids on a boulder and spoke to them with a sound barrier in place.

"I do want to marry you, Jane." David tilted her chin up. "I think you know why I don't bring it up."

She covered his hand. "I know." *Death.*

"One day, my love." Her vampire leaned down, kissing her softly. "We're already a family. You're their mommy, and I'm their daddy."

"I feel silly for being upset over something a little kid said."

David smoothed her hair back. "That's not why you're upset. You're upset because your daughter and son are being teased because of our choices as a couple. You are upset because you don't like seeing her hurt, especially regarding something so sensitive for us, and even as powerful and close to God as you have become, something so small as words and seeing your babies sad can stab you in the heart. My heart hurts as well. I wanted to hurt whoever made her cry, too. So, no, you are not being silly."

There was definitely a stupid smile on her face as she stared into his sapphire eyes, but their moment was ruined by the sound of lips smacking.

Jane and David slowly looked at the two men eating ribs across the table. They were humans.

The first one smiled, nodding as he kept eating while the other was staring at the plate of sliced apples David had brought for her.

Thankfully, David was turning them around so they would have some privacy.

"Aren't you one of them vampires?" It wasn't hard to guess it was the second man who had asked.

David answered, "We are immortals. I am David, and this is Jane."

The first man waved a greasy hand. "I'm Jacob. Pleased to meet you, ma'am, sir."

Jane smiled. "Hello, Jacob. It's a pleasure to meet you."

The second man pointed at her plate. "Why are you pretending to eat fruit? We could use that for people who really need it. Can't you go drink blood at your house?"

David released a deep sigh. "Our diets are similar to mortals. Blood is what you might consider a necessary supplement for us."

"That makes sense," Jacob said, clearly trying to end the conversation when he returned to his meal. "Hope you enjoy the bull we hunted. It was a difficult one to take down."

"I do. Thank you."

"Why didn't you vamps bring meat?" asked the other man.

David stared at him. "We have been traveling swiftly across the continent after our homes were destroyed. Carrying game as we traveled was not possible. Any hunts we carried out were consumed almost instantly."

Jacob smiled. "Glad y'all made it here, then."

"But she's not eating meat." The other man frowned. "Is there something wrong with her?"

David's tone was short. "She simply prefers not to."

The man pointed a rib bone up at the hole in the clouds. "Isn't she the one who put a hole in the clouds? The glowy, holy vampire? And why does she prefer not to eat our meat?"

"Her name is Jane," David said curtly. "And she does not have to explain why she doesn't want to eat meat."

The man looked at her plate again. "God made animals for us to eat. She's insulting God if she refuses to eat the animals he put here for us to hunt." He then waved a hand behind them. "It's also a sin—her being with two men and all. We all saw her kissing on that big fella."

David's temperature began to rise. "You can stop talking about her as though she's not sitting across from you, and instead of calling her the glowy vampire who put a hole in the clouds, you can show her respect for blessing you with the first rays of sunlight you've had in months. And you can certainly mind your business regarding our relationship." He shoved his plate toward the silent man. "My woman doesn't like eating animals! It's not an insult to God. You know nothing about us, especially God's opinion of her or us."

Death's presence wrapped around Jane like her favorite blanket, but the men across from her looked ready to pass out.

"Are you losing your composure with the ignorant side of humanity already, Prince David?" Death's amused tone seemed to relax David.

Jane realized everyone was watching, so she smiled at the man who had been polite. "It was a pleasure to share your company, Jacob. Well done on hunting the bull."

"Ma'am." Jacob nodded before bowing his head to David and Death. "Sirs."

Jane smiled at him before finally looking at the man beside him. "You never graced us with your name, sir. That's perfectly fine—I will not ask you to provide it now. You must forgive David, though. He is new to inter-acting with people who are unnecessarily vocal and critical of others, especially regarding what one might consider an insult to God. After all, David was chosen by God, specifically, to be the strongest of his kind so he could rid the world of evil. He has been doing so for longer than you can fathom as he has searched for a woman—the woman he would love. He has remained chaste, loyal to her, even though she had not yet been born."

She paused, taking a deep breath. "Forgive me for losing my train of thought. You did not even insinuate he had sinned or insulted God, just me. I suppose I was hoping to stress one point: the woman he was told to search for—he was told she would destroy darkness and help him and his brothers save the world." She smiled brightly. "I'm that woman, in case you are not keeping up, and I was paired with God's most powerful angel"—she touched Death's hand, grinning wider when he held hers—"the Angel of Death. I assume you were gesturing to him as the big fella I'm sinning with.

Did you know God made it so he could not feel a single shred of emotion as he reaped souls?"

The man shook his head, his glassy eyes wide like his mouth.

"Well, he did," she continued. "Because he needed to be able to perform his duty. Yet, even though God did this, He also selected me to be Death's soul mate. He made it so I was the only being Death would ever feel and love. God only knows why this was done, but one must assume God desired we have a relationship. Just the same as God selected David, then instructed him to find the woman his heart chose—one would assume God anticipated they would love each other. Perhaps your definition of love and relationships differs from mine, but I find—as you said—kissing up on—a most enjoyable way to express my love to the men God put in my life."

She smiled again as the man closed his mouth and swallowed audibly. "Now, we did not expect you to know any of this, but it certainly provides a wider perspective of our relationships with each other and with God. For all you know, every immortal here was instructed to perform a duty you find unnatural and permitted to have relationships beyond your comprehension. Perhaps, retain this moment as a reminder you are not fully informed on what God expects from us as His children. Judging someone because they do not fit into your preferences of living or abide by your expectations for what God deems acceptable might be the true insult to God."

She stood up as her skin shimmered on its own. "We bid you farewell, sir." Her soul stirred within her, causing the ground to tremble. "Before we go, though, I will suggest this to clarify my points. Keep your opinions about me and our relationship to yourself from now on, and should you feel the need to question someone else's behavior when it does not concern you, pray to God about it first." The tables began vibrating. "And should God not answer you, take that as His way of saying mind your business and leave His children—His warriors—in peace, even if it bothers you. Now enjoy stuffing your belly with the meat from a successful hunt. Perhaps you can forgive us vamps for not contributing with meat but find relief knowing they were planning to leave for a hunt immediately following this relaxing barbecue." She tossed a cloth napkin at him. "Here, you can make use of one of the few items our party managed to salvage from our ruined homes to wipe the grease and flesh from your chin instead of disrespecting the creature God placed on this planet to feed your judgmental ass."

Death chuckled as he finished helping her off David's lap. Jane snatched her plate of apple slices. "My buddy Sin gave me this apple. I'm not wasting it."

"I got more for you, honey," Sin shouted from another table.

Death shot him a look that caused the whole pack to laugh and howl.

David lifted the sword he'd had under the table before sheathing it. She blushed when he put his beanie on, his blue eyes paling as he glared at the man again before picking Natalie up since Death already held Nathan.

"Baby, let's go see Nyc and Sin." David took her hand. "You wanted to see them transform. Lancelot is there, too."

"Oh, yay." She hooked her arm with his and let him lead them to Nyc's side of the field.

Sin nudged Nyctimus' arm as they drew closer. "How sexy was it that she almost destroyed that foolish mortal because she liked my apples?"

David shook his head. "Do not continue slipping fruit to her."

Sin winked at her. "Desire another apple, beautiful?"

Death summoned his scythe and held it to Sin's throat. "I will shove those apples up your ass if you keep it up."

Jane chuckled but pushed Death so he wasn't almost killing the guy. "He's playing around. His apples were yummy."

Sin chuckled as Nyctimus covered his laugh with a cough.

"Mhm." Death looked at Nathan. "I don't like punks flirting with Mama."

Nathan smiled at him, and a group of female immortals sighed.

David took a jug of blood from a woman offering some to various men around them and went to sit by Lancelot and Nyctimus.

Natalie blushed when Nyctimus tickled her cheek.

"She's just like Jane." David laughed, kissing her head as he slid the empty mug away.

Jane finished her apple as she leaned against Death.

"Is this better?" Death asked as he put Nathan on her lap and pulled them onto his.

She nodded as she scanned the group of men lounging around. "I did always fit in more with the guys."

Death grunted. "You mean with dogs."

She giggled when the entire pack growled, then cheered when Akakios trotted over. "Hi." She threw her arms around his neck. "You've been so busy. Have you met my babies?"

Akakios sniffed Nathan's hand before licking his cheek.

Nathan wasn't a fan of puppy love and wiggled off her lap before going toward David. Jane gasped, though, when he went to Lancelot instead and sat beside him.

Lancelot lifted his gaze to her before looking at David.

David carried on talking with Nyctimus and Sin while Nathan and Lancelot had a silent staring contest.

Death kissed her neck. "David is going to hunt and hopefully catch some livestock to bring back."

"Yes, that's what he said. Are you staying with me?" She sighed when he sucked on the mark he'd given her.

"Yes." He breathed in deeply. "Arthur is going to watch the children."

She peeked at David. He nodded to her, winking before returning to his conversation with the others.

"So, we're having a Jane and Death afternoon?" She clutched the empty spot below her heart that never filled.

He covered her hand. "Just us, Sweet Jane. Would you like that?"

"Yes." She stared at their hands, always awed at how different they were.

The men around them let out howls and got to their feet.

David walked over with Lancelot walking behind him. Nathan was staring up at him, and this seemed to be the most uncomfortable she'd ever seen her former enemy.

"Baby, I guess he told you about his plans to spend the afternoon with you." David sat beside Death and pulled her onto his lap. "Arthur still needs a buffer with Gwen, so he asked if they could spend the day with them."

She dropped her eyes down to her kids. They were smiling sadly at her. "Do y'all want to stay with Aunt Gwen and Arthur?"

Natalie nodded, her gaze sliding to Death for just a moment. "Yes, Mama."

Adam jogged over with Artemis trailing behind him. Both David and Lancelot sniffed, chuckling.

Death full-out laughed. "The Virgin Goddess is no more." He held out a fist to Adam.

Adam smacked Death's hand. "I need to talk to you, asshole."

Death got up without any protest and walked away with Adam behind him.

Artemis stood awkwardly, her face red when David and Lancelot continued staring at her.

Jane shoved David. "Stop."

He chuckled, kissing her cheek. "It is just amusing that all the headaches we went through could have been avoided had I known your cousin needed to be rescued."

Artemis glared at Lancelot when he chuckled.

Lancelot held up his hands in surrender. "You did try to have her killed by a powerful being."

"I asked to be forgiven," Artemis growled. "And you're one to talk. Because I respect Jane and David and her children are present, I will not mention the vile things you have done."

David sighed and held his hand up. "Forgive us, Artemis. We are happy for you. If Adam ever mistreats you, you need only call for me, and I will support you."

Jane smiled sadly, but her heart pounded when she caught Adam shaking Death's hand. It was like he was saying goodbye.

David hugged Jane, kissing her cheek and neck. "I will return soon, my love. Enjoy your time with him. I told him not to hold back and to love you to the fullest."

Emerald eyes locked onto hers as Death walked over to them again. Adam didn't stick around. He quickly grabbed Artemis' hand before waving to everyone and rushing off.

Death paused beside Lancelot. "Keep my wingman out of trouble."

Lancelot nodded but didn't look at Jane when David pressed a long kiss to her lips.

"I'll see you soon."

"Okay." She gave him her best smile, but dread filled her heart for the first time in days.

Arthur came to them. He gave Death a nod before wishing the boys a safe hunt and carrying the kids away.

Jane watched David jog away with the pack and Lancelot, her heart growing heavier by the second. And not because she was watching David leave. It was the man standing at her side who had her soul pacing. "Death, do you want to see if we can reform our bond? David thinks we might have to be alone to form it."

Death took her hand and shook his head. "I think I broke something God made, and He is punishing me. We won't restore our bond unless He chooses to restore it for us."

"No." She touched her chest. "He promised you are mine—that I get to keep you. When I pray about us, I hear. You're mine."

"I know you speak to Him." He tugged her to a path she had not gone down before. "I will always be yours."

She turned and saw Nathan and Natalie wave at them. "Death, I don't like the feeling this is giving me. My heart is hurting, and my soul is panicking."

He threaded their fingers together. "Don't be afraid. I promise to bring you back."

"Where are we going?" She peeked over her shoulder. "Does David know?"

"He knows." He shoved branches out of the way, and they walked in silence for at least ten minutes until a small house came into view. She recognized it. It was one she'd put stickers on in her magazines. It was like a magical cottage. Only the world around it was surrounded by dead plants.

"Do you understand now?" He stopped walking. "A life with me is this. Death. A fairy tale surrounded by sorrow."

Her eyes burned, and she shook her head. "No. We're making a life together. All three of us. And the kids."

"It's a dream, angel." He caressed her cheek. "A beautiful dream, but this is the truth. I am Death before anything else."

"You said we're a pair." She wiped her tears, truly panicking and ready to cling to him by any means necessary. "Whatever this is you're trying to do—stop. I see us, and we are not a stupid dream. We are real. We are magic. And God made us to be together. It's okay that David is with us. You accepted him."

"I did, baby." He rubbed her tears. "I chose him for you, just like my father did."

Her throat felt like it was closing. "Please, let's go back. I won't let you do whatever you're trying to do by showing me this." She glared at him. "We are always, Death. Always."

He pulled her closer, smiling that beautiful smile that haunted her dreams and gave her life. "We are always. That's why I can go through with this."

She shook her head, causing her tears to fall on her chest. "Please don't say what I think you are."

He wiped away more of her tears. "Close your eyes."

She grabbed his pants to ensure he didn't leave before staring at him fiercely. "Don't you dare disappear."

"I won't."

Jane wiped her cheeks before closing her eyes.

"Open."

She did, gasping at the necklace dangling in front of her. It was simple, but it was intricately detailed and beyond beautiful. There, on a glowing gold thread, was a miniature pair of black angel wings. "Are they real feathers?"

"Mine, Sweet Jane. I used magic to shape a single feather into this pendant for you." He lifted her hand so her fingers touched them, and she sobbed when a faint tingle darted to his spot and faded.

"And the thread?"

He smiled as he rubbed it between his fingers. "I stole it the night you bonded with David. You were trying to latch on to me again—this was ours. It would have failed to tie to me because of Lucifer's light, but it would never have stopped trying. I took it so your soul would believe I would join it. Otherwise, it would not have turned to bond with David."

She covered her mouth. "You made sure I bonded with him?"

He nodded. "That's why I made you close your eyes that night . . . I kept this, but I will not let you tie us together again."

"Why?" she cried, clutching his shirt.

"One day, you will understand." He wiped under her nose. "I want you to wear it, though. It will be our secret and proof we are soul mates—that my father tied us with His most beautiful light."

"Why are you giving it to me now?"

He raised it to her lips. "You know why."

Her chest rose and fell with every harsh breath she took. "Death, you can't leave me."

"This is how we are meant to be for now. This is how you live the life you have always wanted and how I have my wish of you living that life."

"I want you in my life." She grasped his wrist. "Please, Death."

He raised the feathers to her lips. "Make a wish and seal it with a kiss. I promise it will come true."

She sobbed but stared at the pretty feathers and made a wish without hesitating, kissing the tiny wings that were a part of him.

"That was fast." He raised the pendant to his lips and kissed it as well. "When this thread breaks, your wish will come true."

"I don't want it to break." She couldn't move as he clasped it around her neck, but she calmed when the wings touched her skin.

"It will only break when it is meant to. Did you wish for something good?"

"Yes." She lifted his hand to her cheek. "Please tell me this is a dream, and I'm going to wake up in bed with you on one side and David on the other."

"When you wake up, you will finally begin to live . . . with your prince. He's your knight in shining armor who loves you just as much as I do. He will make you happy. He will be the best father your babies could ask for besides their own. Jason chose him. Father chose him. You chose him . . . And now I do."

She cried and threw her arms around his waist. "I love you."

He lifted her, hugging her and swaying like he had always done. "And I love you."

She turned her head, kissing him as he carried her inside her dream cottage. He had the whole place lit with candles. The only piece of furniture was a gorgeous bed carved out of wood with feathers etched in and four horses barely visible.

"Do you like it?" He kept his lips against her neck.

"Yes." She hugged him as tightly as possible.

"You can come here and nap as long as you let David know where you are going and ask King to watch over you."

She wiped her tears, nodding. "You're giving me the dream I used to have of us."

He smiled against her skin. "Almost, baby. Just when you wake in the morning, your other dream guy will be there waiting instead of me."

Jane cried, overwhelmed by the amount of love and pain she was experiencing, and she teared up again when she noticed the Grim Reaper carved into the headboard, his wings outstretched as he leaned over a sleeping girl with a dancing flame standing over her heart.

Death pressed his lips against her forehead. "Tonight will be just for us. I will think of you every second. Just promise me you will think of me from time to time when Mr. Perfect is less than perfect."

She nodded, cupping his cheeks as she scanned his beautiful face. "I promise. Every morning and every night. Fuck, more than that."

"Good girl. Don't cry. A part of me will always be with you. We will always have our memories, and this will be one of our best." He kissed her collarbone over the thread as he laid her down. "This is as close as I can get to marrying you. I know David wants to marry you, and I have given him my blessing, but this"—he touched the thread—"is ours. Will you have me even though he will one day be the man you call husband?"

She sobbed, nodding as she pulled him down. "Yes. I'll always have you."

He smiled, holding her face so delicately. "Order your suit away, my love. I'm going to love you this one time the way I wish I could every single night under our moon."

Her suit vanished, and so did his clothes. She cried, touching his cheek when green flames surrounded his body because his soul was rising to the surface.

Death smiled as he pressed his lips to hers. "My moon." He kissed her cheek. "My Sweet Jane." He pressed a kiss above her heart. "My angel." Then below her heart and to the side. "My soul mate." Her body began to glow in golden light as he murmured against her skin, "I love you."

She smiled as her soul did and pulled him to her, sighing when he pushed inside her so carefully, and their flames—their souls—became just for one the night.

4 2

HALF MOON

Jane let her head lazily roll to the side, smiling when tingles, always fainter than they should be, caressed her cheek.

Death brushed a strand of hair from her face, then leaned over her, kissing her cheek. "Don't ever forget this. Us."

She slid her fingers through his sweaty hair. "I won't. Don't forget me."

He shook his head. "Never."

"Kiss me again," she whispered as her eyelids grew heavy. "Are you trying to put me to sleep?"

He kissed her, then nuzzled her cheek. "I can't go with you staring at me. It will be too hard."

Tears blurred her vision as she fought to stay awake.

"Don't cry." He kissed each tear. "Just pretend we're us again, back when you knew I would come see you again the next night."

"But you won't," she cried, her arms too weak to hold him.

He entwined their fingers. "You can dream I come back. Every night I'll close my eyes and think of kissing you good night, and it will be like we are together for that tiny moment."

"It won't be the same." She blinked a few times, tightening her fingers around his. "Death, don't leave me. I'm not alive without you."

"No, Sweet Jane. I'm your Death. You live without me."

She weakly shook her head. "You're why I live."

Death smiled as he continued to caress her hair. Their bodies were still tangled, but the sweat from their slick skin began chilling them.

"Keep building our Heaven, okay?" He gave her small kisses. "Every night, add a little piece to our world."

Jane tried to tighten her legs around him. "Stay with me. We'll build it together."

"You have to let me go, angel." He kissed her chin.

"I don't want to." She couldn't hold her eyes open anymore, but her tears continued to fall. "Death." She sniffed, trying so hard to hold him closer.

"Let me go, baby." He brushed his lips over her tears. "David will take care of you now. Live for me. Live for him. He'll love you for both of us, and I'll give you what I always wanted you to have. A life with a man who loves you in a world where your babies can laugh and play." He pried her fingers off his hand but held them to his lips. "A world where you watch them grow up without monsters trying to destroy them. I can't do that unless you let me go."

Her breathing slowed as he put her to sleep, but her chest felt like she was screaming. "I can't let go. Not again."

"I'll return when it's time. I promise."

"Lucifer," she whispered, not able to say more.

"I won't let him take you." He kissed her fingertips. "I'll destroy the universe if I have to. You're going to live your life. If he somehow manages to steal you, I swear I will get you back. You are mine. You are David's. We'll never stop searching for you. Wherever you go, we'll follow."

"I know you will." She tried to smile.

"There's that smile I breathe for." He pressed his lips to hers. "Keep it there for me. For David and your babies. Remember me. Now let me go, Sweet Jane."

"Eyes." She tried to open them. "Let me see you."

His lips touched her eyelids, and she finally opened them. He was still sweaty—still shirtless and still the most beautiful sight in the universe.

"Beautiful." She pressed her palm over his heart. It was beating so fast. "My Sweet Death."

He smiled, cupping her cheek. "My Sweet Jane." He gave her a long kiss, murmuring, "David is on his way to take you home, okay?"

She nodded, trying so hard to keep her cries down.

"He'll make you happy. Let him. He's greater for a reason."

She didn't stop staring into his eyes. She never wanted to forget them.

"It's time to sleep now." He kissed her again. "I love you."

"And I love you." She sobbed, kissing him again and again until he leaned away.

"Good night, my moon."

She took a deep breath as her eyes started to shut again. "Good night, Death."

Darkness engulfed her as emptiness spread, but she was suddenly held together.

Crunching gravel sounded as her body swayed, and strong arms pulled her against a warm chest. "He'll be back, my love." Fiery lips caressed her forehead. "I promise."

Jane blinked, catching sight of a half moon as her vampire carried her up the porch of their home. Then darkness returned.

"Wake up, Jane. You're having a bad dream."

Jane gasped, her eyes flying open.

"*Shh . . .*" David lifted her hand to his lips as he kissed the sapphire ring on her finger. "You were crying in your sleep again."

Jane blinked a few times as she took in the sun's rays filtering through the curtains before looking back at David.

He kissed the ring again as the gold band around his finger glinted in the sunlight. "Dreaming about that night with him again?"

She nodded, staying still as he wiped her tears. "I'm sorry."

"Don't be." He leaned down, kissing her softly. "I miss him, too."

A sad laugh left her as she put her arms around him. "Every time I dream about him, it seems like it was only last night that he left, not almost seven years ago."

"I know." He smoothed her hair back. "I'm glad you remember that night with him, though. It worries me when you're so happy with us."

She touched his face. "Why?"

"Because you make me feel like I'm the only man you need and love. I don't want you to forget him or what we all had together."

"I won't. You just light up my whole day. It's impossible to be sad when I'm with you."

The sorrow in his eyes showed her how much he loved her. He reminded her daily about Death, even though she would never forget her angel.

"Mom," Natalie yelled. "What's for breakfast?"

David turned his head, raising his voice as he responded in her place. "Check the stove, princess."

There was silence for a few moments.

"Thanks, Daddy!"

Jane laughed, hugging David. "She's never going to stop calling you Daddy. Neither will Nathan."

"Good." He lifted her. "Just because they grow up doesn't mean I will stop being their daddy."

"But they call me Mom. That sounds so old." She pouted, hanging on to him as he carried her to the bathroom.

"You're just as beautiful and young as you were when I first saw you, Jane." His eyes fell on her naked body. "Well, I didn't see you like this right away, but you know what I mean."

She yelped when he put her on the counter but giggled when he kissed her face wherever he could over and over again.

"We're supposed to go on a round today to push back the perimeter. Are you up for it?" He walked to the shower, turning it on. "Lance is coming, so you know King will be there too."

"You and King still act like Lance is going to attack me or something." She swished her legs, staring at the muscles rippling across his back and down his arms as he turned the shower knobs.

"I know he won't attack you, but he's still adjusting. You're still considered a young immortal. For us, seven years is nothing. Any immortal relearning how to live, especially him and the others on Hell's side, will have a difficult time. The fact he saw you naked last week has made him jumpy. I'm trying to assure him I understand it was an accident he saw us, but you two avoiding each other only makes the situation more awkward. Plus, you said it's good for you to be around him."

She knew what he was getting at. Lance was a huge source of pain and bad memories for her, just as she was for him. "I told you that you weren't paying attention."

David's eyes flashed as a mischievous smirk formed on his lips. "You were my focus that night. I didn't hear him running close to the creek I picked, and he had a kill overwhelming his senses."

Jane sighed, thinking about all the nights David would take her to a different spot in the forest to either make love to her or to swim like they had done in Texas all those years ago. It was one of his favorite memories, and he liked to remind her as often as possible.

"I'll talk to him," she said, sliding her legs around David's waist when he walked to her again. "He doesn't need to worry. I'd hate to see you two drift apart. It's nice watching you with him. You both look so young when you're relaxed together."

"I know you like it. That is why I ignore the fact he secretly loves you."

"He doesn't secretly love me. He just appreciates everything we've done for him."

David chuckled, kissing her. "I know my old friend. He fell in love with you along the way, and he fights it every day." He hoisted her up before carrying her to the shower. "Let's stop talking about it, though. Want to pretend we're trying to make a baby again?"

Her cheeks heated, and she forgot about Lancelot and nodded. She wanted a baby so badly, and he would let them pretend they were humans again, just a regular husband and wife trying to begin a family.

"We'd have such pretty babies," she whispered against his mouth.

"I'll give you babies, my love." He slid his fingers between her legs before smirking and sliding her onto him.

Jane moaned, closing her eyes as he pressed her against the shower wall. "Two boys and a girl."

He thrust forward, pressing his lips to hers. "Hold your screams for later, my love."

Her body slid up and down as she tightened her wet legs around him. "I'll keep my panties off this time."

"There's my kitty." Her vampire grinned, his fangs fully extended. "Wear your hunting skirt but only bend over in front of me. And be ready for me whenever we are alone."

She gasped, pulling on his hair as he began to feed from her while still fucking her under the spray of water.

"I don't understand why I have to learn this." Natalie threw her pencil down. "It happened a long time ago. And we won't even see Europe or anywhere besides this town."

David looked over his shoulder and saw Jane take deep breaths as she tried to stay calm. He smiled, turning the temperature down on the stove before walking over to his two girls. He kissed Jane's hair before sitting beside her. "Natalie, you have to do the work they gave you."

Natalie glared at him, looking just as fierce as Jane when she was pissed. "It's stupid. I'd rather go to Amber's house."

"You mean you'd rather see her brother." He snatched up her pencil and held it out to her. "You're not going anywhere until you do your work. You know the rules. Don't give your mother attitude when you know what's expected of you."

"You always take her side." Natalie kicked the empty chair Death had once filled.

David held Jane's hand as he gently pushed the chair back in place. Her eyes followed the movement, and he saw the regret in Natalie's gaze. Jane always kept Death's chair at their table, and everyone respected it as though they were merely waiting for him to come home.

Natalie sighed, grabbing her pencil as she muttered, "Sorry, Mama."

Jane looked away from the chair and smiled even though her eyes watered. "It's okay. Maybe Daddy can help you. I really didn't pay attention to European History when I was in school."

"Then why do I have to?"

Jane stood up. "Because you're better than me."

David kissed Jane's hand. "I'll see what she's struggling with."

She smiled at him before her eyes slid to Death's chair again. "Excuse me. I have to go to the bathroom."

He gave her another kiss and watched her go.

"She's going to go cry." Natalie shook her head.

Nathan walked into the room and showed David his completed assignment. Some answers were wrong, and some words were misspelled, but he was finished.

"Good job, little man." David grinned at Nathan's proud smile. "Do you want me to check it with you?"

Nathan sat down, his smile falling. "I'm not smart like Natalie."

David shook his head. "You don't have to be like Natalie."

"Just not like Mama," Natalie said, pressing her lips together when he glared at her.

"Stop." David opened her book, seeing that she was not trying to do the work and that her missing answer was Nathan's first wrong one. He pointed to the paragraph that had the answer. "Re-read this, and you'll find the answer to number five."

"Why can't you just tell us?" Natalie looked up at him, calmer now.

David knew she was only being a typical teenager with him. She knew he usually played the good guy, but now things were changing, and she and Jane were butting heads more and more. "I'm not telling you because you can find the answer on your own. I've shown you where to look. Stop focusing on things you want to do and do what you are expected to do.

Then you can expect me and your mother to allow you time for the fun stuff you're daydreaming about when you should be paying attention in class."

Natalie's eyes welled up with tears. "You don't even care about me."

David rubbed his face. "That's not true. You know I love you, princess. You're my little girl, but you are still expected to learn. This may not seem important because Europe was destroyed, but it is a part of our history as human beings."

"You're not human, though. And I'm not your real daughter."

David stared at her until she looked away. He was hurt and angry, but he couldn't say what he felt the urge to. He loved her too much to make her feel worse. It reminded him of the time Natalie had said mean things to Jane and how Death ended up being the one to put his foot down and scold her, but then he was also the one to come back and speak calmly, explaining things in a way that amazed all of them as much as it broke their hearts.

"Natalie, go finish your work in your room," Jane said softly as she re-entered the kitchen. "When you finish, you can think about your attitude and the hurtful things you've said to your dad."

"I'm sorry." Natalie gathered her things.

Jane lifted her chin. "Sorry doesn't fix anything. Sorry is for you. It is your actions beyond this point that prove to us you regret whatever you've done to make us feel bad. That is how you earn forgiveness, Natalie. Now go. You don't want the help your dad can offer, so you can learn the consequences of pushing away those who love you and wish to help you."

Natalie's lips trembled, but she turned, ran out of the kitchen, and finally slammed her door shut.

Jane turned her head to wipe her tears before smiling at him and Nathan. "I'll finish cooking if you want to help him. You know I suck at that stuff."

David pulled her to him, cupping her cheek as he rubbed away the tiny remnants of her tears before kissing her. She still tasted like gummy bears, and that dreamy smile she first used to give him was present every time he kissed her. "I love you," he told her.

Her gold eyes sparkled and still managed to tell him those three words, but his heart ached every time because he did not see green swirling around the gold flames.

David chuckled, kissing her again. "I'll punish you later for not saying it aloud, my love."

"I know you will." She grinned, kissing him quickly before darting to the stove.

David laughed, tossing a log onto the stack he was making. "Sin, you are not offering that woman anything."

"It's just an apple." Sin grinned before winking at one of the humans gardening nearby.

"That's not even the same woman you pointed out a moment ago." David shook his head.

"They all look the same to him." Nyctimus tossed him water.

"Well, we can't all be blessed with a goddess to make love to each night." Sin turned to wave at Jane. "She still blushes when I smile at her."

"She blushes when any of you wolves looks at her like a bunch of horny dogs." Gareth threw an apple core at Sin. "Even Nyc."

"Especially Nyc," Gawain said. "Sorry, Sin, Jane has a thing for the boys with pretty eyes."

Sin scowled. "That's all Lance's fault. You ruined it for me."

David glanced at Lancelot. His friend quickly dropped his gaze from sneaking a look at Jane before David tossed Sin another log. "Sin, stop trying to seduce my wife. We forbid murder in the community, but I can break your legs so they don't heal properly."

Sin threw his arms up. "You put too many rules on me. How am I expected to live when most of the immortals are marrying? I'm running out of options. I have to flirt with Jane because I know she'll tell me no or light my ass on fire."

David knew he was joking, but he could see that a part of what Sin was saying was genuine.

"What is she discussing with them?" Nyctimus asked, his gaze fixed on Jane. She was with Zeus, Tristan, and Apollo.

"She's been meditating with them in the forest." David smiled at his girl as the sun lit up her face, and she closed her eyes before tilting her head to feel more heat.

"Meditating?" Sin rubbed his head. "Maybe I should join them."

Gawain threw his water bottle at him. "They are meditating with the hope to harness their power and fuel Jane should she run out of sunlight to recharge with during combat. You're not going to sit there and have perverted thoughts. All of us will break you then."

All the men quieted when Natalie approached. He didn't see her at dinner the night before, and Jane had taken her a plate instead of forcing her to apologize to him when she continued pouting.

David caught Jane watching when Natalie stopped in front of him, but he kept his focus on his daughter.

"Hello, Natalie." Gareth broke the silence. They all knew about his fallout with her.

She blushed, waving at all the men before holding a piece of paper up to him.

David slowly grabbed it, knowing that sometimes Natalie expressed her feelings better in writing, and unfolded it.

I'm sorry, Daddy. I didn't mean what I said. You're better than any mortal and the best dad I could ever hope to have since my real daddy is in Heaven. I'm sorry. I love you and Mama.

Love, Natalie
P.s. can I go to Amber's house? Her brother is gone for the weekend.

David chuckled, folding the letter before putting it in his pocket. He then hugged her, smiling when she squeezed him as tight as she could. "I love you too, princess. Thank you for the letter."

She looked up at him. "Can I go?"

He sighed, knowing her desire to go out partially prompted her to write the letter, but he knew Natalie loved him and meant what she wrote. "Have you apologized to your mother?"

"No." She cringed.

David grabbed her chin. "Go talk to her first. You know how much your words hurt her."

"Then I can go?"

He gave her a stern look. "Princess, please be sincere with your apologies."

She sighed. "I am. Really. I'll go talk to her right now."

He nodded as he let her go. "Talk to her, then you may ask her about going. Whatever she says is what I say."

"Okay." She hugged him again before rushing off toward Jane.

His girl didn't embarrass her or force her to be more sincere. She was still the best mom for their kids.

David shook his head as he watched Natalie run off to where her friends were hiding.

"Maybe I will stop worrying about women," Sin said softly. "Teenage daughters are reason enough not to mess around."

David smiled. "The good outweighs the unpleasant parts. But you don't need any children."

"Could you imagine the beasts Sin would spawn?" Gareth laughed. "We'd be doomed."

Arthur walked past them. "Gareth, perhaps do not speak of doom in public."

"Sorry." Gareth chuckled, swinging his ax.

"I told her she could only spend one night," Jane said, nearly startling him.

Lancelot did startle and drop his ax before picking it up and resuming chopping the trees they were preparing for lumber.

"Baby, did you just use light speed?" David smiled, cupping her cheeks before kissing her smiling lips.

"I didn't mean to." She puckered her lips again. "Mm. I need another one."

David laughed, giving her a longer kiss as he lifted her. His friends howled, but he didn't stop kissing her.

"Are you almost due for a break?" she whispered, wrapping her legs around his waist.

"Where's Nathan?" he asked, gripping her ass.

A naughty smirk teased her lips. "He's gone to see your sister for art lessons. The house is empty."

Gawain gagged as Nyctimus snatched the ax David had been about to use.

He took that as a sign he could go for a break and started carrying her to their home.

"Where are you going?" he heard Nyc ask.

Gareth responded, "It's break time. I'm doing like my captain—going home to make love to my wife."

"David was here three hours before you," Nyc said.

"Only because Jane was out early," Gareth shouted. "He would've been making her scream in the woods like he normally does if she hadn't gone for a ride, but no, he came to work."

David chuckled, spanking Jane when she giggled, and took her home to do exactly what he had hoped to have been doing when he woke up that morning. He made love to his wife until she began to glow so bright the entire town knew what they were doing.

———

Jane rubbed her hands under the stream, washing the dirt off her ring. She smiled as the ripples and sunlight made it shine, remembering the day David had asked her to marry him.

A sparkle of light had hit her eyes, and she had felt King lift his head with a huff.

"What is it?" She hadn't bothered sitting up. She was perfectly content resting by the brook with King watching over her.

"*Queen.*" The mental response rang through her head.

"Oh." Jane lowered Death's pendant from her lips and turned her head to watch Queen trot through the shallow water. The unicorn seemed to be in her own world, splashing playfully in the water, causing rainbows and gold sparkles to fill the clearing she had found.

Jane smiled, knowing either David was close by or he had sent Queen with a message for King to relay to her. Jane always found it amusing that Queen gave her the silent treatment because she was upset David was unable to speak telepathically with her. Queen blamed Jane for that; silence was her eternal middle finger.

Her necklace pulsed with tingles for a second and even King glanced at her pendant before David exited the forest, patting Queen's side as he walked closer.

He stood over Jane, smiling as the sun's rays spread around him. "Hi, baby."

She held up her hand for him. "Hi. Pull me up."

He grabbed her hand but slid something on her finger instead of pulling her to her feet.

Jane's mouth fell open as the sun hit the sapphire ring, and blue light lit up the golden glow that had been around David.

He knelt beside her as he lifted her hand to his lips. "You already know what this is."

Her eyes watered, and she nodded.

David's gaze slid to Death's necklace. "I only waited to ask because doing it right after he left felt wrong. I remember how sad you were about your friend's husband remarrying so soon after she had died. And between

Jason and Death, I wanted you to hold them just a little longer before asking you to be my wife."

She sat up, wiping her tears as she switched her gaze between the gorgeous ring and his face.

He slid his thumb over the blue gem. "It's been just over a year since he left, and there hasn't been a day where I don't hope he'll come walking through the door with a smile for you and a scowl for me."

A sad laugh left her as she clutched her necklace and kept her eyes on the ring around her finger.

"My mother gave me this ring to give to the woman I would end up loving and wanting to marry. When we arrived at the castle, I took it out of the drawer I had kept it in all this time, and I carried it with me, hoping I would earn your love so I could present it to you one day." He smiled sadly. "I tried it on when you were sleeping one night. It was after I knew things were over with Jason, and I knew that as terrible as things had ended, I was being given a chance to prove myself worthy of you. And I wanted to see if it would need to be resized." He looked up at her. "It didn't."

Jane sniffled as she tightened her hold on his hand.

"I always kept it in my pocket, but one night I took it out and put it back where it had been hidden." He raised her hand to his lips, kissing the ring again. "The night I left you when you declared your love for Lucifer."

Jane held her breath, her mind racing through all the memories.

King snorted before standing.

David chuckled, watching him for a moment. "Do you remember what happened after I left?"

She lifted her eyes to his. "The attack . . . The castle exploded and burned."

He nodded, sliding his thumb over the ring again. "I searched for it amongst the rubble after determining you were not one of the bodies there, but I cared more about finding you and apologizing than finding the ring." He smiled. "The morning Death left—he was there waiting for me to wake up. You were in the kitchen."

Jane had replayed that day over and over in her mind, and she felt her heart ache as she whispered, "The sound barrier."

David nodded, his eyes glassing up a bit. "He found out I had lost this ring, and he went and found it for me."

Jane sobbed, squeezing her necklace before kissing it and crawling to David.

He hugged her, sitting as he pulled her onto his lap. He covered her hand over her necklace, smiling when the thread shimmered. "He was furious with me for ever taking it out of my pocket, but he was still returning it and giving me his blessing to give it to you. I told him I couldn't give it to you without him. I couldn't imagine our life without him anymore, but he knew and accepted what you and I tried to ignore. He gave me so many gifts that allowed me to get closer to you—to become the man you deserved and the one he wanted you to have."

Hot tears collected on her lips before falling to her chest. She cried as it looked like the gold from her necklace and the blue sapphire was swirling and making green fire. It vanished when she blinked, but she felt her soul look up and smile.

"I'm hoping I haven't disappointed either of you this past year as we've lived in relative peace together—peace that was only possible because the Angel of Death loved his Sweet Jane so much he had her dream home built by a pack of wolves and brought everyone she loved together. It's almost like he made you your very own fairy tale village . . . I'm so grateful for everything he's done for us, even if he says it was only for you." He smiled, kissing her ring again. "Please bless me once more and allow me to give you what he could not by letting me be your husband. I promise I'll love you for both of us. Will you marry me, Jane? Be my baby beyond forever?"

She nodded, crying as she pressed her lips to his. "Yes."

"You should not be out here alone, my queen."

The memory vanished, and Jane gasped, standing and summoning her sword.

Lucifer walked past King, ignoring how the unicorn angrily stomped his hooves on the rocks.

"What are you doing here?" She raised her sword and imagined her full suit.

He sighed and stopped, his gaze sliding down her figure. "He must always show others how you were tied to him first, even when his presence and bonds to you are no longer a part of your life."

Her soul rose to the surface, engulfing her body in her gold flame. "Death will always be mine, even though you have kept him from bonding with me again."

Lucifer's steel eyes drifted over her, and a faint smile teased the corner of his mouth. "So beautiful, even if it is for him."

She darted her eyes around. Her soul surged with power, but she didn't think she could take down Lucifer. His light was still a part of her, and it roared in his honor.

"Your vampire is far from us," he said. "I may have influenced him into thinking you were elsewhere."

"If you hurt him . . ." She tightened her hand around her sword.

"Why not use my sword?" He smirked at Death's blade in her hand.

"I can defend myself without your gift."

"So you will accept King but not the sword that will make you legendary?" He shook his head. "Did they tell you King was mine? That I allowed Asmodeus access to where I had him hidden so he could present himself to you?"

Jane swallowed. "He told me you had him imprisoned."

Lucifer chuckled. "Yes, I suppose he would omit any bit of information you would find loving on my behalf."

"You want my soul, Luc. My soul belongs beside Death's and David's."

His eyes flashed. "You gave me your soul because Death was foolish. He was so foolish that had you died, I would have had no choice but to accept Belial's bargain by reintroducing the bitch still burning inside me to you—so that I could have you at all. That is why we are bound, Jane. I saved you from her fire so you could shine in Father's light."

A tear slid down her cheek. She didn't want to trust him or begin to believe in him again, but he always managed to soften her heart and have her focus on his goodness. "Why are you here?"

"I'm here to offer you one more chance to come with me."

She shook her head. "No."

"Even if it means I can guarantee the war will not return for one hundred years? That I can hold off the final battle so your family can live out their lives, and this community you have helped build can live in peace?"

Her mouth went dry as her mind raced. She grabbed hold of her pendant, shouting for Death in her mind.

"He won't come, Jane." Lucifer watched the thread of her necklace pulse, and she sobbed when the light suddenly faded, and the tingles disappeared.

"What have you done?" she screamed, staring at her necklace and the dull thread holding it together. "Death, please. David!"

"They can't hear you." He rubbed his chest where she had shot him; simultaneously, she felt a pain pierce her heart.

"What have you done?" she whispered, staring at her necklace and ring.

"What must be done, my queen." He lowered his hand, and the stabbing pain ebbed.

She rubbed the feathers, crying because there was nothing there. "Undo it. Whatever you've done, you undo it right now."

A smile spread over his face. "Always so fierce when you face me."

"Stop this, Luc." She gripped her sword, her soul flaring just as furious as her. "You won't take them from me, and I won't go with you. Try and take me, and I promise they will come for me."

He went quiet, then said, "I thought you would choose your children."

Her heart raced as she saw their faces. She saw how much they'd changed over the past seven years, how they had laughed and lived happy lives. She'd been with them every step of the way. David had helped her raise them, and the knights and the wives had helped them learn and shown them things Jane would have never been able to. The community had given them friends and enemies, but they lived. She could give them a full life by leaving with Lucifer, but nothing with Luc was ever so simple.

She stared into Lucifer's eyes. "I choose to stay with them for as long as I can. I choose to fight for them, but I will not throw away Death's sacrifice for a hundred years. I will not walk away from my husband to live as your queen. We will fight for our children's happiness. And I will stand by them as their mother. Until the end."

A glint of pride sparked within his gaze, but his expression went unchanged. "You have grown so strong, my queen. Still—"

Another voice spoke, "Still nothing." Lancelot walked out of the forest until he stood between her and Lucifer.

"Hello again, dog." Lucifer tilted his head, his expression empty.

"Leave." Lancelot looked over his shoulder. "Go, Jane. David is coming. Get to your family and stay there."

Jane darted her eyes between Lucifer and Lancelot. "Lance, you need to move."

He looked forward, his muscles flexing as he glared at Lucifer. "She's not going with you. No longer will you manipulate her by using her family and the ones she loves as your pawns."

Tears filled her eyes when she saw no reaction from Lucifer.

"Does David know what you think about her?" Lucifer stared Lancelot down. "Does he know you watch her like a pathetic dog, thirsting for another taste of her? I would offer you a chance to have her, but she is my queen. The bitch you fucked will not touch her soul again, and never again will you have the pleasure of holding her soft body against yours. I will, however, allow you to return to my ranks because you are a decent soldier, and your queen does have some attachment to you. It would please her to have a familiar face when she stares out the window of her castle. I will even give you a rug at the foot of our bed, so you can watch me make love to her every night."

Lancelot's shoulders sagged. "Forgive me, Jane. I have prayed every night to stop having such thoughts about you. I would never hurt you or David . . . And I ask forgiveness from my woman for fantasizing about you. I think I love you for what you've given me—no one has ever done so much for me. But I don't know how to express it without thinking about you like that. I was bad for so long. I don't know how to be now."

"It's okay, Lance." Jane sniffed and reached out to touch him.

Just as she pressed her hand to his back, he roared, transforming into a werewolf as he lunged for Lucifer.

She screamed as a blade stabbed through him, exiting his back. "No," she cried as Lancelot shimmered into a man again, sobbing when Lucifer yanked his sword free.

Jane ran to Lancelot's side, putting her hands over his heart and pushing her light into him, but nothing happened. His gaze stayed fixed upward, and all the breath in his lungs slipped past his lips.

"My queen," Lucifer said without any hint of remorse.

"Go away," she screamed, lighting up the entire clearing with her light, burning everything but Lancelot as she shielded his body from disintegrating.

Lucifer shook his head as she tried shooting her light at him. "You can't hurt me, Jane. My soul is tied to yours, and I have already burned in Father's light."

"You haven't burned in mine." David appeared behind her, his soul pulsing until his entire body was surrounded by blue fire. He moved in front of her. "She's not going with you."

Jane lifted her head, shaking it as she watched David unsheathe his sword.

Lucifer dropped his gaze to hers, and that's when she saw a drop of sweat slide down the side of his neck. "Very well, my queen. Enjoy what time you have left with your prince." Then he vanished.

Jane sobbed, dropping her light as she hugged Lancelot's body. "I'm so sorry."

David knelt behind her, his hand shaking as he put it over Lancelot's wound.

"David, I'm sorry." She lifted her head, crying harder, when she saw his tears.

He pulled her to him, hugging her as he kissed her hair. "It wasn't your fault."

The trampling sound of horses announced the arrival of the Two Hundred Million.

Arthur ran forward, falling to his knees beside Lancelot as the other knights arrived.

David tilted her face up. "What did he say?"

Asmodeus, Beelzebub, Astaroth, and the other members of her army began to appear. They were usually far off, hunting demons, but they must've felt Lucifer's presence near her.

She wiped her tears and tried to look strong even though she worried he'd be mad at her. "He offered me a deal. If I went with him, he would ensure all of you live in peace for at least one hundred years within this community. He said the kids would be able to grow up, but if not, the war would return."

David lifted her necklace, and his gaze hardened as he rubbed the dull thread between his fingers. "Did he do this?"

She covered his hand. "I think so. I don't know what it means. I tried calling for him, but there's nothing. It's like he's gone."

Astaroth and Asmodeus stepped forward, inspecting her necklace.

"Abbadon," Astaroth muttered.

Asmodeus sighed. "Lucifer has released the Destroyers. Abaddon can confine anyone Lucifer asks for up to a thousand years."

Jane shook her head. "No. He's okay. He's Death."

Astaroth caressed her head. "Abaddon is destruction and King of the Abyss. He could throw the Devil into his abyss if he wanted to."

"It's always limited," Beelzebub said. "Death will be let out or escape eventually, my queen. He will be tormented, but even Abaddon cannot kill Death. And Abaddon only kills if ordered to."

David caressed her cheek. "Baby, you refused?"

She searched his eyes, worried only for a second that he was angry she didn't choose to save them until she saw him smile sadly.

"You chose us. To fight beside us." He kissed her, hugging her when she nodded.

Arthur patted her back. "Jane, may I use your blanket to cover him?"

She let go of David before pulling the blanket she'd been resting on to her. She caressed Lancelot's cheek before leaning down and kissing it. "Thank you, Lance. I promise to fight to the very end." She kissed his other cheek. "And even beyond then."

David waited for her to cover Lancelot before helping her stand. He smiled sadly as his eyes fell on her necklace, but he lifted her hand, kissing her ring. "He's only locked away. I'll still love and protect you for both of us."

Jane's heart pounded as she took in the faces of the men around her before turning to Lancelot's body. She stared at the bloody spot appearing from his wound. "Make sure our bunker is stockpiled. We'll meet to discuss and instruct everyone on what to do when the time comes because we will fight for them. For all of us. We're going to fight for every soul that has suffered and perished. Every one of them deserves a chance to live in God's kingdom, and those who seek it will fight beside us or stand as a force between darkness and the weak."

She sighed, tilting her face and closing her eyes when clouds blocked the sun. "No more darkness unless it is prepared to meet my light." She held out her hand, shaking as it lit up and shot a beam into the clouds until they broke apart.

So much rage and sorrow swirled inside Jane, but she refused to let it destroy her. "This is not the end for you, Sir Lancelot. I will come back for you." She lowered her hand until it hovered over Lancelot and smiled sadly when her soul rose to join her, spinning as Jane surrounded Lancelot's body in light. She gasped as her soul reached out, lifting a blue flame from Lancelot's body. They both caressed the flame as his body became engulfed in her fire, but she raised her hand, sending his soul to the stars. "Just wait," she whispered when she could no longer see it because of the sun.

Her soul returned to her, and her light collapsed inside her.

David pulled her away from the inferno surrounding his friend as everyone kneeled, bowing their heads and praying for Lancelot.

"What are you asking him to wait for?"

Jane watched the fire with a sad smile. "I'm not sure. I just know I will see him again."

David touched her pendant. "He's not gone, Jane. I feel his energy."

She covered his hand. "I can't feel anything."

He smiled down at her as he took her hand, both holding the pendant. "I know you can't. But I can. He's roaring for you. My soul is roaring in return, telling him you are safe. He's telling him not to lose himself, that you are thinking of him, that you are strong, and that you are waiting for him to come home. He's telling him we are waiting for him, but we are preparing to fight." David lifted her pendant to her lips. "He's telling you to remember your wish, and he promises he will find you."

Jane cried, kissing the feathers. "I remember. I'll always be waiting."

David covered her hand again. "He says he's proud of you, and he's happy for us. He's asking if you yell out Papi when we're making love."

She laughed sadly and swore she saw Death's smile in her mind. "Find a way out, Death. Find me."

His face became clearer, and the darkness below her heart and to the side fluttered.

"Always, Sweet Jane," David spoke the words, but she saw Death's lips move in her mind.

"I love you," she whispered.

"And I love you." He smiled. "Kick some ass, baby girl. I'm coming."

Jane nodded, breathing deeply as his face faded and David let go. She realized David's soul had risen and watched as the blue flames receded into his body. "How did you do that? You heard him when I didn't . . . You channeled him from the abyss."

The sapphire flames in his eyes burned brightly. "That's our secret. Now let's go home. We will have dinner with our children, promise them we will fight for them, kiss them, and then I'm making love to you. Then you can focus on being a warrior."

"You know I might die, right?"

He caressed her cheek, nodding. "You know I will follow you. I'll be right beside Death, my love. Be brave."

She smiled through her tears. "I will."

43

SAPPHIRE & GOLD

David lifted Natalie onto his lap as she cried. He smiled sadly at Jane as she wrapped her arms around Nathan. His little boy was trying to stay strong, but he was a gentle soul. "It's going to be okay, little man," he said softly. "It's okay to cry. Men can cry."

Jane hugged Nathan tighter as he finally succumbed to his tears.

David stood, carrying Natalie to sit beside Nathan on the floor. He rubbed his back as he rocked Natalie.

Adam rushed into the house with Artemis right behind him. He paused at the entrance, seeing the kids and Jane.

David waved him over as Jane held out her hand.

"Jane," Adam whispered, grabbing her hand as he squatted beside her. He kissed her head as he rubbed Nathan's arm.

"It's going to be okay." She smiled bravely at her cousin.

"No, it's not," Natalie shouted.

David let go of Nathan to hug Natalie. "Princess, we all knew this day was coming."

"But you're gonna die," she wailed.

David didn't promise that they wouldn't. He just caressed her head as he rocked her from side to side. His eyes fell to the paper Nathan had been drawing on when they'd come home. He'd drawn an epic battle that had reached a standstill under a moon hidden in darkness.

There were monsters he had never even witnessed fighting against

Jane's riders and his brothers. It was unclear who was winning, but it didn't matter. David focused on the center of the picture, where a dark-haired warrior surrounded in blue flames kneeled before an angel with black wings inside green fire. Death. Opposite them stood another angel. It was a man with gray wings and a white suit. Lucifer. In his arms was a woman with long hair. She was limp, covered in blood as flames of gold died around her.

David shifted his gaze to Jane. She already stared at the drawing, her brows pinched together the longer she studied it. Then he saw the moment she recognized each figure in the picture, and his heart squeezed.

Nathan snatched the drawing, crumpling it up. "I'm sorry. It's what he told me. I tried to draw something else, but I can't."

Jane's hands began to glow as she caressed Nathan's hair. "Who told you?"

"The man in white." Nathan rubbed his tears. "Ryder's brother."

Jane stared out the window.

"Pestilence?" Adam asked, pulling Artemis to sit with them.

"He said not to be sad," Nathan said. "He said he'd be with you, Mama. He told me not to cry when you told us you would go. I'm sorry—I tried not to be sad."

"*Shh* . . ." She kissed his head, her hands glowing brighter as she reached for Natalie and placed a hand on each of them. "He's right. He will be with me; there's no reason to be sad. Everything that is meant to happen will happen."

"What if you die?" Natalie whimpered.

The light in Jane's hands increased, and their children relaxed. "If I die, Death will be with me. And I won't feel any pain. And what you feel right now—this warmth—you will feel it every second, and that will mean Mommy did what she promised. She fought so you could live, just like her angel did for her."

David reached out, caressing her cheek. She was so brave.

She smiled, kissing his palm. "Don't be afraid. Wherever I go, I promise I will see you again. There is so much beyond death. You just have to wait and see. I'm not afraid. I'm ready. And you'll be ready to show everyone here that everything is going to be okay. Heaven's warriors and every soldier we have found over the past seven years will join us, and we will roar so loud that the monsters will fear coming here."

"But if they kill you, you won't be able to stop them," Natalie whispered calmly.

Jane smoothed down her curls and smiled. "The only monster you will see is Mommy's soul mate, baby girl. I promise."

Adam hugged Artemis as she covered her cry.

Jane was telling them what she knew—what they all knew. If she died, Death would come for them all. For her, there was nothing to fear at the end because she did not fear Death. Jane greeted Death with a kiss on the lips.

Both children nodded, looking more peaceful than their uncle and the goddess sitting beside them. "We don't fear Death."

"No, we don't." Jane kept caressing their heads. "Should he come, close your eyes and ask him to take you to Mommy. I'll be waiting."

"Yes, Mama."

Jane patted King's shoulder as he came to a stop.

Queen halted beside them, and David pushed up his mask to wear like a beanie. "Here?"

The knights, Nyctimus, Sin, Arthur, Asmodeus, Astaroth, Beelzebub, Zeus, and the commanders of the Two Hundred Million stopped at the line she'd made.

"Yes," she whispered, glancing up at the moon. "King says this is where Lucifer is focusing."

"Should we really choose where he wants to fight?" Thor asked.

Jane smiled. "You would question me."

The men chuckled. So did Thor.

He ran a hand through his mohawk and winked at her. "It wouldn't be an epic battle if you and I did not have some words beforehand."

She grinned at him. "I promise it will be a battle Odin envies he did not live long enough for."

Thor raised his hammer, his voice echoing like thunder, "Behold the birthplace of Ragnarök!"

His men and every soldier in their ranks cheered, banging their swords and spears against their shields and stomping until the ground shook.

Arthur held a hand up to quiet their vast army. "You have your orders. Make camp and prepare the battlefield." He turned to the human military commanders. "Make sure communications are working with each commander before you fall back. And get the proper translators with their units. There are many countries under your charge, but we are together."

"Yes, sir." The general nodded before riding off with his team.

David reached for her hand. "Want me to massage your ass now?"

Jane laughed with the others before leaning forward to kiss King's mane. Her unicorn glared at David, snorting and kicking up some dirt.

"I wonder if Artemis and Adam are freaking out," Gareth said.

"They're probably fucking." Sin shrugged.

David shook his head after he was finally standing on firm ground. "Whatever you are insinuating, be silent."

Sin grinned at her. "Your cousin is a legend, Jane. He's got my respect. I think even God will high-five him when they meet."

Zeus turned his head as electricity crackled around him.

"Easy." Nyctimus laughed, holding up a hand. "Artemis is a good girl, and Adam is a gentleman. I'm sure they are performing their duties as they watch over the children."

Sin winked at Zeus. "You know the game, god of lightning. He's hitting it hard."

David pulled Jane down, hugging her. "Baby, I'm worried these two will begin the battle before Hell arrives."

Apollo ignited his power as he casually walked up behind Sin, tossing a fireball. "I'll give you a five-second head start."

"A warm-up with the sun god." Sin clapped his hands and transformed into his wolf form. He was massive, all black, and much bulkier than the other werewolves they had fought against, save for Lancelot.

"One . . ." Apollo started as Sin ran onto their soon-to-be battlefield. The army roared, cheering for either Sin or Apollo.

David picked Jane up, supporting her with his forearm under her ass.

"That's not a massage." She smiled before kissing him.

"I have to wait for our tent to be ready before I can give you a proper massage." He chuckled, kissing her again. "And I never told you that it was nice of you to persuade Artemis to stay behind with my sister and the others."

"We had to leave mainly women behind. I wanted the best warriors." She hugged him, kissing his neck. "At least it's not cold."

"I thought I always kept you warm." He carried her through the camp already emerging around them.

"You do." She hugged him tight. "I just meant we can probably sneak in more sex than before."

Gawain groaned behind them. "Sissy, really? We haven't even made camp."

"Sir David, your tent is ready," came a soft voice.

Jane chuckled as she turned to see one of the many former maids from Valhalla. "You're too sweet, Hela. Thank you."

Hela bowed. "You are very welcome. We have prepared tents for the remaining knights nearby."

"Great," Gawain muttered, stomping off.

David pressed his lips to Jane's neck. "Thank you, Hela. Extend our thanks to the other ladies as well. But you didn't have to prepare our tents. You are a soldier now."

Jane grinned, remembering the fight she'd had with Thor because he berated the former maids who had shown up for combat training, and she'd beaten him in a battle so every woman and servant had the right to join their ranks.

"It is our pleasure to make your accommodations comfortable, Sir David."

David laughed. "Fine. Excuse us, though. I promised my wife a massage after riding for eight hours."

"Thank you, Hela." Jane laughed when David squeezed her ass.

Hela bowed, her eyes wide, before running off.

A loud howl filled the sky, and Jane threw her head back, laughing at the sight of Sin in werewolf form, patting out the fire on his leg.

David brought his mouth close to her ear, whispering, "They're distracted, my love."

She nodded. "Let's go."

Her vampire smirked, running to their tent and tossing her onto the rollout mat that made their bed. He pulled his beanie off while she unbuttoned his belt and pants.

When he was stripped, he stared at her suit still in place. "Send it away."

She did, reaching up for his face. "I'll be quiet."

He kissed her softly but roughly tugged her to where he wanted her. "This may be the last night I am able to make love to you. I want to remember every time you scream my name."

"Um, David . . . Jane?" Arthur called from outside their tent.

David growled. "Really, Arthur?"

There were laughs all around their tent.

"I lost a bet with Sin." Arthur chuckled.

David shook his head as he turned, smiling down at her.

Jane reached up, caressing his cheek again, returning his smile when he turned to kiss her ring.

"Give us two minutes, though," Arthur said. "Sin is going to start, and you can be as loud as you want without her brothers vomiting all night."

David leaned down but lifted his head quickly. "Arthur . . ."

Arthur laughed. "I'll arrange it, brother."

"What did you tell him?" she asked when he leaned closer. Then she heard the music and smiled.

"As Death would say, I'm a smooth fucker." He pressed a kiss to her lips as music from their wedding began to play. There were no words. It was a collection of classical pieces David had picked out. He'd told her each one reminded him of her or a moment in their life together. Most were compositions he had listened to before meeting her to relax and dull out the sounds of wherever he was so he could see her eyes and face in his dreams. The rest of the music had come after a movie theater was built in the town. He had remembered every film score she had pointed out to him. She loved those more than vocal soundtracks. So when David told her he wanted to pick out music, she was stunned to hear her favorites mixed in with his.

David smoothed her hair back. "I love you so much."

"I love you, too." She teared up as he smiled and traced her fingers over his lips. "Always this."

He kissed her fingertips. "Do you remember our wedding vows?"

She nodded.

"Close your eyes. When I kiss you, show us our wedding."

Jane breathed, closing her eyes as their music played.

Fire touched her lips and filled her sight, and she called forth Vision.

Silvery moonlight danced across her face as the scent of rose petals tossed from the basket Natalie carried filled the air.

"Breathe, cousin," Adam whispered. "And don't break my arm."

Jane smiled, loosening her grip on his arm as he guided her under the tunnel of swords held by the knights, the Princes of Hell, Nyctimus' entire pack, the fairy and elf soldiers, and a few of the armed military forces that had joined their town. She chuckled as she passed the lone hammer above her and grinned full-on when Akakios led Nathan ahead of her, right to David.

She briefly caught sight of Lancelot standing beside David while Arthur stood at the altar, ready to marry them, but it was sapphire eyes and the smile that took her breath away that held all her attention.

"Careful. She's already dazed." Adam shook David's hand before turning to kiss her cheek. "Focus, cousin."

Jane blinked, ignoring the laughter from the crowd as she handed her bouquet of blue and yellow flowers to Artemis as Elle fixed the skirt of her strapless gold embroidered wedding dress.

David raised her hand to his lips. "You look beautiful, my love."

She smiled, tearing up when David reached for her necklace, fixing the pendant so it slid to the right spot.

"Shall we begin?" Arthur asked.

David nodded to him as he took both of her hands to hold between them.

"David and Jane are going to travel far enough away that we don't have to hear them tonight, so I promised we would make this fast."

The crowd laughed as Gawain let out a groan.

Arthur chuckled. "David and Jane have prepared their vows. Whenever you are ready, brother."

David winked at her before turning to Nathan. "Do I still have permission to marry Mommy, little man?"

Nathan smiled and held up the ring after Lancelot untied it for him.

Jane had to fan her eyes as she watched Nathan hold out his other hand to shake David's.

Her vampire shook his hand before giving him a quick hug and kiss. "I'll take care of her. I promise."

"Okay," Nathan said, stepping back to stand beside Lancelot.

David grinned at her as he slid a matching gold band next to the sapphire ring he'd given her. "Jane, this is a promise of my undying love and commitment to you and our family. I promise never to take you or our marriage for granted. I will share your interests and passions and support you in any endeavor you pursue. I'll even change the litter box and wake up when our children are sick so you can sleep a little longer—hopefully dreaming about me, our life together, and perhaps Jane and D sandwiches."

He wiped away her tear. "I promise to pamper you and spend the rest of my life treating you with the love and respect you deserve. I promise to tell you I love you every morning upon waking up and every evening as we end our day. I will never leave your side without kissing you first. Every kiss and every time we make love will not be just an act, instead, know that it is always a joining of our hearts and souls. Know that I will always honor your other loves. I will remind you of Jason's love and keep his memory alive for our children."

He smiled as his gaze fell to her pendant and then to where Jason's ring hung on a chain below Death's. "I'll love you for Death. When we see the moon together, we'll cherish the moments we were one, and I'll be the man he wanted you to have. I won't let him down. Or you. You'll always be our girl." He wiped away more of her tears. "I also promise to get you Dr Pepper, burgers, and fries as often as possible."

Everyone laughed, including her.

He squeezed her hand. "This is what lies in my heart for you. It aches for your love. My porcelain doll, my beautiful girl, my baby, my kitten, my soul mate, my love—and now—my wife. All of this is my eternal commitment to you as your husband. I love you beyond forever, Jane."

"Mommy?" Natalie called. "Here's Daddy's ring."

Jane sniffed, laughing sadly as she took the ring she'd had made for David. "Thanks, baby."

Natalie rushed over to David, hugging his leg before running to stand between Guinevere and Elle.

Jane shook as she slid the gold band on his finger and smiled when she looked up at him again. "I just realized I hadn't made sure it fit." She laughed with him.

"It fits," he said, caressing her cheek before holding her hand again.

She took a deep breath and focused on his eyes. "Home," she whispered as her heart beat faster. "David, you are my home. You are my sun, and without you I am cold. Without you, every broken piece of the woman I am shatters. You always call me your light, but it is because of you that I glow at all. It's you who keeps me warm, keeps me sheltered, and lights up the universe for me. No matter how far I have fallen, how broken I have wound up, or how empty my gaze has become, you have always been the man there waiting for me, ready to hold, warm, and love me until I glow again. Everything you are is what I wish to be. Everything good about you is what I reach for when all I hear are dark whispers."

She kissed his hand. "One night, before we were together, I could not escape my Hell. No matter how many times I closed my eyes and opened them, I still saw my torment. But I felt heat. I felt fire that wouldn't burn me and ran toward it. And your arms wrapped around me when I wished to die just so I could escape. It was your lips on my skin as you whispered you wouldn't let go—that you loved me. You asked me to hang on, to not give up. You thought I couldn't hear you, but I did. I listened as you threatened to kill whoever was tormenting me. You didn't think I was crazy or dramatic. You saw me falling into Hell, and you held me tighter and prayed. You prayed for so long because you didn't know how to fix a broken girl. But you held on to me. Through all of it, even when I screamed at you to go, you stayed. When I left, you waited for me to come back. Then you saw a truth that should have destroyed us. But you didn't let it."

She smiled as more tears fell. "You roared when darkness crushed us— burned so hot that I should have burned in your flame, but you didn't let me. You pulled my protector between us and surrounded us in your love. Your love should not exist, but you make it. And because of it, my extinguished flame was lit again, and you begged me to dance for you both. You held me—you held our babies—and you let me have something no ordinary man would permit. All of me.

"So, this is my promise to you. I promise to always smile, always dance, always breathe, fight, and be brave for you. I promise to never let go, to never give up, to love you, Prince David of Cameliard, second son of King Leodegrance, High Knight of King Arthur's Court, My David—my bestest —and now my husband—beyond forever."

Arthur put his hands over theirs. "David and Jane, I, King Arthur of Camelot, below our Heavenly Father's kingdom, pronounce you husband and wife. David, you may kiss your wife."

Fiery lips touched hers as she opened her eyes, and the fabric of their tent came into view above her head.

"I think about you in that gold dress every night, Jane." David stared at her as their music continued to play, and the camp sang victory songs in their native tongues. "I'm so honored to be your husband. So thankful to have been your choice. I will never let go, baby. We will never end."

She nodded, smiling as her soul rose, engulfing them both in her flames, and his soul rose to meet hers. His fire mixed with hers, and he made them one in every way, drowning out the world so it was just the two of them: Sapphire and gold.

"Nyc?" Jane lifted her gaze, grinning when aqua eyes locked onto hers.

"Yes, Little Moon?"

"Did Death tell you about me before we met?"

He chuckled, shaking his head. "Not exactly. He usually killed something if I asked about the girl occupying his thoughts. Or he would punch me really hard."

The table laughed as they eagerly shoveled breakfast into their mouths.

"So how did you know he called me his moon?"

David kissed her head. "I think he spoke to you at night."

She looked up at him before turning to see Nyctimus. "He did?"

"That's how I figured it out—that you were his moon." Nyctimus nodded. "He would get cranky if he needed to be with us, or anywhere I suppose, whenever the moon came out."

Hades nodded. "Yes, it was any time the moon appeared. Even before he met you, Jane. He would stare at the moon for hours, sometimes just telling her hello. Then he started saying Good Night and Good Morning."

She touched her necklace. The thread was still dull, and there was still no sensation from him. "Do you think he's going to get out in time?"

"It's difficult to say, my queen," Asmodeus said, standing behind her. "Abaddon is bottomless, but if anyone can escape, it's Death."

"Yes." She kept rubbing the feathers. "I miss the Horsemen. It's like there's no one home, in a sense, when I think of them."

"You can still summon your weapons, though," Hades said. "I believe this is just your soul's way of grieving his loss. She does not wish to speak to the other Horsemen if Death cannot answer."

David patted her leg. "He'll come, Jane. You will focus on what we planned. The battle will not be over soon."

A small uproar in the distance and a flash of light on the battlefield had everyone looking.

"Is that a pegasus?" Gareth asked.

David and the others stood, watching as a gray and white pegasus flapped its wings as it carried a lone rider toward them.

"It's one of the Two Hundred Million," Sin said. "No, it's a female rider."

"There are no female Horsemen," Hades said.

David grabbed Jane's hand as a path cleared for the rider, which was halted by the three commanders of the Two Hundred Million.

"Emilia," Joseph, the only rider who ever spoke aloud, shouted.

"She sounds hot," Sin said.

David threw a glare at him. "Stay put. Come on, Jane."

She followed him, not understanding the language being spoken. "Joseph?"

The commanders bowed their heads to her as Jane took in the young woman. Her armor matched the Two Hundred Million, but it was her fiery hair and sapphire eyes that Jane was surprised by. They glowed like fire, just like the armor each rider wore.

"My queen." Joseph bowed. "I present Emilia, my daughter." He waved his hand to the stallion with a star mark where a unicorn's horn would be. "And Prince."

"Starlight," Emilia said, her blue eyes flashing like ice. "He prefers Starlight."

Jane grinned as Joseph glared at his daughter. "Hello, Emilia, Starlight." Starlight lowered his head the same way King and Queen did.

Jane returned the gesture, her soul rising to see the animal. "You called him Prince, though . . ." She studied the pegasus. "He is King and Queen's?"

Starlight nodded repeatedly and bowed lower when heavy breathing behind her made Jane's hair blow around her face.

King walked forward, outstretching his wings and using his massive size to push his son back.

"King, don't be mean." Jane rubbed his side as she walked around him. She watched the young rider bow her head to King, relaxing when Queen pranced out, nuzzling Starlight before wedging between her son and mate.

"If I may explain, my queen," Joseph said.

"Yes, please." Jane kept petting King, and she hid her smile when the girl seemed awed that she was so close to him, then further shocked to see Queen nuzzle David's hand until he petted her.

"Emilia is one of my children from when I was mortal. Her mother passed after I was given immortality. When Lucifer imprisoned me with the others, I hid my daughter, not knowing I was confining her to one of his prisons within Hell. Emilia grew up very slowly, as time passed differently there. I shielded and trained with her, but the men refused to allow me to include her in our army."

He patted Starlight. "Prince—Starlight—was brought by Lucifer when Emilia was still young. Lucifer said the colt was to stay hidden there. He allowed Queen to visit whenever she liked. King, however, only came when Lucifer did. I gathered he sired him on my own."

"Oh." Jane beamed up at King. "You're a daddy."

King snorted, pawing the dirt as he began to push Starlight away.

"Why doesn't he want him here?" David asked. "And why do you seem upset with her arrival?"

Joseph sighed. "She is not one of the Horsemen. She cannot ride with us or under my command, and King refuses to command Prince. Lucifer was displeased when he mated the female and disappointed when the colt had no horn."

Jane moved in front of King before focusing on the girl. "How did you get here, Emilia?"

She pulled off her lion helmet and pushed her hair from her face. "Lucifer entered the prison, not expecting me to be there. He never said what he intended to do, but I assume he was there for Starlight."

"Lucifer sent you?" David growled.

Jane grabbed his hand. "Did he bargain with you? Or send you with a message?"

Emilia raised her chin. "He simply asked me if I would care to join a battle to fight alongside my father and his queen. I said I would like to join the Horsemen, but it was not permitted. He said his Queen was the Horsemen Bringer and that Starlight would obey her, that if I were a Horseman at heart and worthy, I would follow her. I have come to prove to my father and the Two Hundred Million that I can ride beside them so that if I should live, I become one of them."

"No." Jane watched the girl's bravado weaken. She marched past King, staring into Starlight's pale steel-colored eyes before looking at the young rider again. "You are not one of the Two Hundred Million Horsemen . . . You are Emilia, Rider of Starlight, son of King and Queen and prince of all Horses, and you, Emilia, are the only Horsewoman of the Two Hundred Million Horsemen." She reached up for Emilia's hand. Emilia stared at her but did not take her hand.

David chuckled, stepping closer as he held out a hand to Emilia. "If I may see your hand?"

Emilia slowly put it in his.

David then clasped it with Jane's. "She is greeting you." He kissed Jane on her head before moving away.

Jane grinned, shaking her hand. "Welcome, Emilia, Starlight. Please follow your father and join their ranks to await orders." She nodded to Joseph and King. "See that she is welcomed appropriately."

"Horsemen Bringer." Emilia bowed.

Jane waved to her before walking to David.

Her vampire hugged her. "So pretty when you're shy but sexier than should be possible when you order your men to do what they do not want to."

"How are you not afraid she was sent here to kill or capture you?" Thor asked, stomping onto the field. "By Odin, girl, what are you thinking? She

656

THE LIGHT BRINGER

could be Lucifer's spy. She could be the threat we have been searching for all these years."

"Yes, I suppose she could be." She smiled as Thor stopped waving his hammer.

"You're taking my advice?" he asked.

"Oh, goodness no." She giggled, jumping up so David would hold her. She threw her arms around her vampire's neck, kissing his cheek repeatedly. "I would worry she was a spy if you welcomed her. The fact that you are against this only assures me my instincts are right."

Thor shook his head but laughed. "Watch your back with her, Jane. I mean it. One wrong move, take her out."

She nodded as she pressed her lips to David, noticing he appeared worried. "Don't worry. Have faith in me."

"I do, baby. Just be careful with your trusting heart."

"I will."

He gave her a firm kiss. "Let's go prepare and send out our final orders, then."

"They are massive." Gareth looked at the screen everyone huddled around.

It was an infrared map of the battlefield. It showed images from a stealth plane they'd gotten from the U. S. Air Force.

"It's like looking at a pee-wee football game and the Super Bowl," she murmured.

"The what?" David asked, pulling her onto his lap.

She waved her hand. "I'm just saying we're way outnumbered."

"Too bad the Two Hundred Million are not actually two hundred million," Tristan said. "Combined, Apollo, myself, and Zeus can blast this much"—he circled a small area of the screen—"in one go. The King of Demons and princes can take out—what?"

Asmodeus pointed to the map, circling only an eighth of the force against them. "This is merely a single attack we are speaking of. Even you, my queen, would drain and only eliminate a quarter of this army."

"So we don't go in with our big bang attacks," she said. "All right. Plan B it is." She glanced around the table.

"Plan B," they said, nodding.

"Well, let's get ready to kick some ass." She stood up.

657

Nyctimus helped her over the benches as David spoke to Arthur, and she followed him out.

"Nyc?"

"Jane?" He smirked down at her. "Still blushing."

She rubbed her cheeks, laughing. "I know we never spoke of your father, and, well, since I might die tonight, I wanted to express my sorrow for killing him, especially allowing my darker half to do it so mercilessly."

"Jane, my duty to God was to destroy my father and brothers who chose to follow his path."

"Well, that's awful." She stopped, smiling up at the moon already visible in the dimming blue sky. "He was still your father, Nyctimus."

Nyctimus grabbed her chin. "He was the son of the Devil, Jane."

"Really?"

He stayed quiet for a moment before continuing. "You have witnessed the Norse and Greek arguing about my father: one calls him Lycaon, the other calls him Fenrir—there have been many different names I've heard my father addressed by. There were also men with different faces whom he called father. I even remember the Norse immortal called Loki in Father's home when I was just a boy. He was there with Zeus, yet when I encountered my father alone with Loki, my father bowed to him and addressed him as Father as they spoke of Hell. Loki told my father to get rid of me, and shortly after, he killed me. Whatever my father was, God wanted him to die for his wickedness. Do not feel sorrow for killing him. You killed one of the world's greatest evils. You possibly saved me and many of my pack from slaughter. Sin would not be here to flirt with you if we ever faced him. We owe you a great deal, Jane. We will follow you wherever you go. We are yours, Little Moon."

She pulled him down to kiss his cheek and whispered, "Keep David safe for me. Make sure he is not in the path of my end."

He leaned back, staring into her eyes. "You really are the moon that glows in the darkness. Little Moon who dances for her Earth, constantly changing her face and pulling on her blue and green sphere, forcing it to stay with her, keeping him calm or causing his waters to rage—an enchantress admired by many, envied by the stars because it is she the Earth sees when he looks into the night. Then the Sun warms her. No matter where she goes, he shines his light for her, waiting for her to find her way back home, which the Earth always ensures she does." He pointed up. "During this month, they call this a Hunter's Moon. Tonight, when blood—good and evil—spills on this battlefield, the moon will be full. Quite fitting for the start of battle."

"You forget what tonight's moon is." Sin shook his head.

Nyctimus held a hand up to silence him. "I will stay close to David. Fight well, Jane. Glow for all of us, and we will fight to the very end and beyond with you."

"Thank you." She sighed, remembering all the times Death had called her his moon. He only saw her. She was his moon, and he was her world. Her Earth. David was the Sun. "Will Death come?"

"Only when he is meant to, Jane."

"Yes." She touched her pendant. "Good luck, Nyc."

"And to you, Little Moon."

4 4

BLOOD MOON

The ground shook from the advancing force. Jane closed her eyes, exhaling slowly as she rubbed Death's pendant, broken because she felt nothing.

"He'll come, Jane. He won't let you down."

She knew that was not the case, though.

King shook his head, pawing at the dirt as the trembling earth became more difficult to stand on.

Asmodeus sighed beside her. "My queen, Belial and Lucifer will ride out for a formal greeting, offering you a chance to surrender. Thanatos may arrive as well, though I do not sense his presence. David, Arthur, and I will ride with you. You can expect that they will only address you, though."

"Yes, I know." She opened her eyes, scanning the front line for a flash of white. "I don't see Lucifer."

David shook his head. "He's not there, my love. I'm sure he will show. Don't let your guard down."

"Maybe Death was able to escape and hold him," Gawain said.

Jane rubbed her pendant but watched David shake his head. Her angel wasn't going to make it.

Three riders on black steeds broke through the ranks as cheers sounded from the enemy.

"The Accuser rides with them," Asmodeus said.

Jane took a deep breath and released her pendant. "Well, boys, sit tight. I'm gonna go pick a fight with the Devil." She patted King, signaling for him to ride out, and she led the way, smiling as the combined armies behind her cheered, scaring the ravens and vultures from the trees.

Belial, the Devil, and Thanatos waited for them. Jane didn't bother looking at the first two men, but she made sure Thanatos knew she was coming for him should she see him on the battlefield.

"Queen Jane." The Devil smiled. "Looking almost as lovely as your twin soul—my daughter."

King came to a stop, his horn sparking with silver electricity.

Jane turned to the Devil and smiled. "If it isn't my least favorite version of El Diablo. I gotta say, I've been secretly disappointed you're not all red with cute horns on your head." She waved her hand out. "You would've had more points if you'd at least had cool wings and a tail."

The corner of Thanatos' mouth twitched with a smile, but the Devil wasn't amused.

"You are lucky I desire to see my daughter returned to her vessel." His blood-red eyes glowed. "What they have found desirable in you eludes me, but I will laugh when I hear your soul screaming in my fire."

"Ooh, I was worried you wouldn't react like your little minions here." She grinned at him wickedly. "Unfortunately for you, my soul is no longer held down by the half you stole. Maybe Lucifer will arrange for you to have father-daughter time. Though, I doubt either of you really cares for the other."

He grinned. "I was given half of your soul, little queen. Pray to the Father about that little secret and see if your soul still feels confident."

Jane saw her soul. She was confused, but they didn't care. She smiled at her and called her forward, engulfing her body in flames. "We still feel confident. Do you feel the same confidence in your pawns?" She turned her head to Belial. "Hello, scum." She ignored his glare and looked at Thanatos. "Traitor."

Her army roared, banging their weapons.

Belial chuckled, unfolding dragon wings as a pair of black horns appeared on his head. "Take off that ridiculous suit; perhaps then I will be impressed. This pathetic candlelight will extinguish in my hands, and I will cut up your flesh until my prize, your lovely darker half, decides to repair her vessel. Even confined within Lucifer, I can speak with her, and she looks forward to watching you bleed as I take turns with her father, fucking you as you weep for your men." He grinned at David. "Is she still as soft as they said she was as a mere girl?"

David's soul rose all on its own and spoke in unison with him, their voices echoing across the field. "Do you sweat as Lucifer does in the wake of my soul?"

Belial laughed but leaned away, as did his and Thanatos' horses.

The Devil seemed surprised for once as he stared at David, holding the reins of his horse firmly in his grasp.

David smiled. "It seems our Father hid a few secrets from you as well. I know you haven't revealed all your players or children, but I assure you, none match me. He made it so."

The Devil cast a glance at Thanatos before smiling at David again. "It matters little if the Father hid your soul well. My players are right where I placed them. And your bride is not all-powerful. There are those who can easily kill her."

"Good"—Jane touched her pendant—"I've been eagerly awaiting Death. Perhaps your pals can show me to the hole your buddy Lucifer threw him into because I can't wait to watch my baby and his brothers beat the absolute fuck out of the fuckers dumb enough to follow your darkness. Now, do you have anything else important to say? Like, where my good-for-nothing king is? Because I'm ready to light him and all of your asses on fire."

The Devil chuckled. "Make sure you kiss your prince goodbye, Queen Jane. I assure you, the death that awaits you does not smile and cuddle you like a child."

Jane grinned as her soul flared up. "You forgot something. There is only one Death, and he calls me Sweet Jane." She didn't wait for a response. She turned King around, summoning Heaven's Reaper and holding it high as she roared, "Light those motherfuckers on fire."

The earpiece in Arthur's ear went off as their armies charged. "Spooky coming in hot. Ghost Rider right behind him."

The AC-130U plane she'd seen in Texas flew over the Devil's army, dropping bombs as the canons they were armed with delivered an onslaught of gunfire. The explosion was massive, even more so when a second AC-130U followed behind, with fighter jets and helicopters from the world's various forces taking turns dropping their bombs.

"You little bitch," Belial roared.

Asmodeus roared louder, transforming into his new dragon form. He was still black but wore a golden crown that matched his gold wings. He flapped them, spewing fire as Jane yelled, switching out her sword for a spear. She hurled it at the Devil, not surprised when he vanished, but David surprised the hell out of her when he sent a beam of blue light at

Thanatos, hitting him in the arm. Her former general shouted before vanishing, leaving his horse.

"Baby!" Jane beamed at David.

"Secrets, my love," he said.

She laughed, lifting her skeletal mask into place. "Asmodeus, get them in the air."

Her dragon king nodded his massive head before taking flight, his army of dragons rising out of the trees and flying toward battle as their human allies dropped the last of their artillery.

Jane, David, and Arthur looked behind them. The knights led the charge as Nyc's wolves and Akakios' pack raced alongside them.

"Light the way, Jane." David reached out, kissing her hand. "I will follow you."

She nodded before patting King. "Let's go, boy."

He reared up, Queen following his lead before lunging forward. She breathed out, hearing the army behind her.

"Ready?" David shouted, catching up to her.

She touched her pendant. "David, you're supposed to be with the others."

He shook his head as he covered his body in blue flames. "I told you. I'm following you. Now focus."

She tightened her grip on the reins, lighting up with King as the Two Hundred Million Horsemen manifested, racing full force alongside her before falling into an arrow formation with her and David at the tip.

She stared ahead as Hell's army charged at them. They were still being attacked by the dragons spewing fire on them as the last fighter jets dropped their payloads, but the damage was a fraction of what they needed to destroy enough to come close to being even.

"Now," she shouted, the Two Hundred Million Horsemen igniting in flames as King and Queen took flight. With David and Queen mimicking hers and King's planned attack, they sent down beams of gold and sapphire light, carving a massive hole for their army to cut through.

They met Hell's flames with their light. Roaring together, Jane and David circled, swooping behind Asmodeus and the dragons to cut off a large section of the enemy's forces for their army to eliminate.

Jane smiled at her vampire before scanning her princes and their legions as they soared down from the clouds, crashing into the wave of demons flying toward her.

"All right, time to join the others." David's sapphire eyes were even brighter than his flames. "Still need me to carry you?"

She shook her head as she patted King. "Have a good fight, boy. I will see you again."

King neighed as silver light crackled around him like lightning.

Jane summoned Havoc Bringer. "See you on the battlefield, my love."

She could tell he was smiling. "See you on the battlefield."

Then they jumped together, roaring as they fell toward the flames of Hell.

"How long will you let this go on?"

Lucifer glanced at Thanatos and chuckled as he watched him trying to heal the wound David had given him. "Father kept quite the secret with him."

Thanatos snarled, looking away from the battle. "Heal me so I do not bleed to death."

Lucifer held out his hand, casting what remained of his light at the smoldering wound. "His light is unique. That is the best I can do."

Thanatos breathed out, rubbing the seared flesh. "How long?"

Lucifer sighed, glancing up at the full moon, finding what they had expected. An eclipse began, and a quarter of the silver orb was already dark. "Not long now."

Thanatos nodded as he scanned the fiery field. "She made a lake of fire. One even Hell cannot cross."

"It will extinguish soon." Lucifer found Jane quickly. She was still burning bright, her gold flame calling to him as she had always done.

"None of us saw her using the humans to attack." Thanatos searched the skies. "Do you think they will send another wave before it is time?"

"I doubt it." Lucifer watched his queen as she roared like a lioness, swinging the sword Death had given her instead of the one he had. "She will do what she can to preserve humanity. They will fall back to their village to await a last stand. I am surprised she has allowed the ground forces, though." He smiled as she hollered orders for the military tanks to keep the cut-off army from advancing. They fired nonstop as the ground troops launched artillery fire.

"She's bombing the fuck out of Belial's ranks."

"Good." Lucifer smiled as he checked the eclipse. Nearly half. "The spy?"

Thanatos nodded. "In place."

Lucifer sighed, watching Jane fight back to back with David, Zeus, Tristan, and Apollo, all raining their attacks down as they supplied her with energy to arc up her light and smash holes into Hell's ranks.

"Death has nearly reached Abaddon's gate," Thanatos added.

Lucifer checked the moon again as he rubbed the tattoo on his wrist. The image of Jane screaming as she lay between David and Death when they attempted to extract venom from his light flashed within his mind as his mark glowed. It matched the invisible mark she wore on her wrist and still burned as fiercely as it had when he'd soothed her from the burns of Death cutting into his light.

"The more you think of her, the more she will remember," Thanatos murmured. "Death knew you soothed her that night."

Lucifer said nothing as he watched Jane look around. Odin's son had to throw his hammer to keep a hellhound from attacking her.

Thanatos shook his head, his tone chiding. "Lucifer."

He released their mark and watched the half moon and morning star on his wrist fade.

Jane shouted, apologizing to David as he yanked her into line. She rubbed her wrist before hollering louder, engulfing her body in her soul's flames.

"They are doing well considering their lack of numbers," Thanatos commented.

"It will not matter. They will not last without Heaven's aid."

Thanatos nodded, not letting his now blue eyes leave Jane as she roared, piercing her blade through one demon's heart, then spinning to slice the head off another. A small smirk appeared on both angels' lips as they watched Asmodeus prevent others from reaching her back by pulling them back with his enchanted chains, and Jane sent beams of deadly light at her next victims.

Once again, Lucifer checked the eclipse. Nearly three-quarters were shrouded in darkness. "It's time. Put it in place. Don't let her or David kill you unless it is done."

Thanatos looked up as well as a circular seal formed in his hand. It lit up in silver light, resembling the moon, before fading to match the darkness of the eclipse.

"Go." Lucifer nodded and watched Thanatos vanish. He sighed again and looked down at Jane. She appeared alarmed now. He knew she could feel him close by. She turned toward him, and he stayed visible long enough for her to accept she was looking at him before he vanished.

"David," she shouted, pulling her sword from a demon.

"I saw him." He pointed to his right. "Do not leave my side."

She searched the field, shouting when she was yanked backward, an immense pain shooting through her back. Her flames died. "No!"

"Jane," David shouted, reaching for her, his glowing hand raised. "Down."

She ducked, ripping herself free as she caught sight of the one who had grabbed her. Thanatos stared at her back, where she felt a circular brand burn into her skin. Her suit had been burned away, and she couldn't reform it.

David roared, lunging over her as a beam of blue light shot from his hand to where Thanatos stood.

Her former general threw a dagger before vanishing.

David's light shot through a whole row of demons but missed Thanatos. He growled, yanking her up before dragging her into the circle of knights and wolves that formed around her. "Jane, where are you hurt?"

She cried as she saw the handle of a dagger sticking out of his side. "David."

He shook his head, yanking it out and sheathing it. "I'll be fine. Bastard only returned my dagger."

She tried to stay calm. "David, I can't feel my soul."

He turned her around, his soul flaring up with a mighty roar.

"What is it?" She tried to feel it.

"A seal," Beelzebub said, shimmering into view. "They marked you with a seal. Your soul and light are trapped."

She shook her head, searching every corner of her being for gold light.

David ripped off his mask and cupped her cheeks. "Baby, it's okay. I know she's there. I'll get her back."

Beelzebub shook his head. "There is no way to remove a seal."

David glared at him. "Fall back in line."

Nyctimus transformed, running up to them completely naked. His gaze fell to her back before he looked between her and David. She knew he understood she wanted him to get David to safety when he smiled sadly.

"David," Nyctimus said, "the fiery lake has extinguished. The rest of their ranks are almost upon us."

Jane grabbed hold of David's face and kissed him. "It's up to you. Burn them for me."

He stared into her eyes, his gaze fierce but broken. "I won't leave you."

She kissed him again before lifting his hand and kissing his ring. "You are with me beyond forever. But you must go now. Our babies need you to fight."

His gaze darted between her and the approaching roar of the enemy.

"I'll stay with her," Nyctimus said. "Lead the others. I won't leave her side."

David growled, crushing his lips to hers. "Stay alive. Don't you dare follow Death without me."

She sobbed, kissing him back. "I won't let go."

He kissed her softer. "My brave girl. I love you." He released her, his body igniting in flames again as he stood, charging in the opposite direction as Queen swooped down for him. King was behind her with his son flanking him, though he had no rider.

"Jane." Nyctimus turned her to face him. "A seal is put in place to be broken. I won't be able to stop it. It is the beginning of the end when it breaks."

She wiped her tears. "It's okay." She patted his cheek. "Get me a horse. I'll get far enough away to buy you some time."

"Jane, there is nothing to buy."

She looked up at the moon and laughed, seeing it nearly black. "An eclipse. You stopped Sin from telling me it was an eclipse."

He caressed her cheek before kissing her forehead. "I'm sorry, Little Moon. You were so full of hope—even I believed we could stop it."

She shoved him back. "A horse. If the ground opens around me, I want those fuckers to fall in first."

Jane heard the thunderous roars she remembered coming from the behemoths in the distance.

A fleet of women with wings flew overhead.

He shook his head. "The Valkyries finally made it."

She watched them engage, picking up demons and ripping them to shreds before they met the Keres head-on.

Nyctimus smiled, caressing her hair. "I will ride with you, Jane. We will fall into Hell together."

"Thank you, Nyc." She pushed him again. "Now hurry."

He let her go and jumped up, still stark naked, as he ran out to stop one of the riders. "I need your horse."

Jane glanced behind her, catching sight of Emilia battling in the distance, and smiled. Then, grunting, she turned to see Nyctimus ripping apart a demon with his bare hands. She panted, pushing herself up. All her energy was fading.

A flash of white light appeared in front of her. "My queen, where do you think you are going?" Lucifer stood there amid the fiery battle, wearing his white suit instead of armor.

She stared in shock as blue fire lit the sky in the distance.

"Jane," Nyctimus roared, releasing the horse he was about to mount and transforming into an enormous black werewolf.

He knocked everything out of his path as her generals shouted, "To the queen."

Lucifer remained calm, his gaze empty as it shifted to the right of her.

She summoned her sword as she heard David's roar and saw him approaching on Queen, blue flames brighter than ever around him as he raised his hand. "Move, Jane."

She sobbed, switching her blade for another.

Lucifer looked away from whatever he'd been staring at, his eyes immediately dropping to her sword. "Light Bringer."

"Like you said, my king"—she raised the sword, ignoring David's cries for her to move—"we burn together when the world burns."

"No," came a female voice behind her. "Just you. Enjoy burning in Hell —my kingdom, False Queen."

Jane recognized the voice, her mind racing through thousands of them as the images of her fight with the Wolf King flashed before her eyes. Odin had faced off with him.

"Tell me, Ole Father, how does it feel to know that you will die shortly with the knowledge that Hell is inside your walls?"

Her conversation with Nyctimus flashed right after:

"My father was the son of the Devil . . . I stumbled across my father alone with Loki. My father bowed to him and addressed him as Father as they spoke of Hell."

Then a memory from when she was younger, listening to a lecture in school:

"Loki's daughter was the goddess of death, ruler of Hel or Helheim. That is one 'L.' She was also called the Hidden One. It was said she was half alive, half dead. Some have taken this in the literal sense that she was dead on one half of

her body while the other half thrived with living flesh. I like Jane's take that she was a vampire—half dead but alive. Now, the place Hell, as we hear of it today, was believed by some to come from the frequent pronunciation of her name...

"Hela," Jane whispered the rest of the memory.

"Hel, actually, my lady."

A black blade stabbed through her back, exiting her chest—Death's spot—nicking her heart as another blade dragged across her throat.

"No," David roared.

Jane sputtered, seeing only Lucifer's silhouette vanish before blue flames landed behind him.

Another female let out a battle cry, and Hela was yanked away from her.

A gurgling sound left Jane's mouth as she fell to her knees, and a scream drowned the battle's roars.

"Baby," David shouted, his hands cupping her cheeks.

"I tried, Father," a woman cried.

"Quiet, Emilia." Joseph of the Two Hundred Million Horsemen lifted his daughter off Hela's lifeless body.

"Baby, stay with me." David's lips pressed against hers as several sets of hands pressed against her body.

"Don't remove it," David shouted as the blade was yanked from her back.

A clap of thunder unlike any she'd ever heard before shook the earth as the sky lit with emerald light.

"Fuck," David shouted. "Press both sides. Bedivere! Come on, stay with me, Jane. You're strong."

She tried to talk, to tell him it didn't hurt, but she couldn't breathe.

"She's suffocating," Bedivere said. "Tristan, Apollo, burn her wounds. I need to clear her airway. Someone get me a trach tube."

Her body was being moved, but she could only stare up as the green sky grew brighter.

"You see the sky," David whispered against her lips. "Death's coming, Jane. He's coming for you. He'll fix this."

"David..." Gawain cried.

She jerked as a sharp sting jolted through her back, and another clap of thunder sounded.

"Stop," Bedivere shouted. "Roll her back."

Jane saw a flash of gold and a glimpse of her soul reaching for David's.

"I'm here, Jane." David's face became clear for just a moment. The sapphire and gold light mixed, lighting up his face. He smiled as the colors swirled, appearing green, and his face merged with Death's.

He nodded. "Yes, baby. Stay with me. He's coming."

She tried to blink, but she could only stare as his face shifted between his and Death's. They really did look like brothers—almost twins. Except one was darker, like he'd been permanently tanned from the sun, and his eyes were a mixture of sapphire and gold. Emerald.

Brothers, she thought, suddenly glimpsing a room of jars filled with souls. Blue flames all burned brightly. Only one jar contained a small gold flame. It formed into a female silhouette as it reached out, touching the crystal jar, but she flinched when the huge blue flame beside her moved closer.

Too hot.

The blue flame didn't care. It grew larger, making her retreat to the far side of her jar. It wanted her closer, to consume her. It was made just for her, to keep her warm.

A hand appeared, opening the blue flame's jar but only allowing half to come out.

"Well done. You finally duplicated," a voice said. "This one grew stronger to keep you from burning her. He has no heat—you have burned him—but he is able to withstand it. He feels nothing. He will protect her."

The gold flame's jar was opened, and the twin blue flame rushed in, surrounding her as she trembled in fear, her fire almost extinguished. He tried to warm her, swirling faster and faster until they merged, blending their colors to make emerald light. "Ah, you perfected yourself just for her."

God turned the blue flame's jar. He was roaring—an inferno. "You were too close to my light. Almost perfect, but too hot. He will guard her for you. You will still be by her side."

The blue flame formed a man's silhouette. He observed the twin—almost identical to him, save for their coloring—before roaring and hitting the top of his jar.

"You will destroy her," God warned.

The blue flame didn't care. He was lost in his desire to have her—to consume her in every way.

The emerald flame wrapped himself around the gold even though she tried to soothe the blue flame—her first companion.

"Perhaps we will test your brother's ability to protect her. If he cannot withstand your heat, he will not be enough for his other duties." The hand appeared again, releasing the original blue flame as he opened the jar to the new couple.

The blue flame roared, incinerating the room as it rushed out. The green flame hugged the gold one, even though she reached for the blue, telling him to stop, that she loved him, but he would destroy her.

The green flame turned, a man's figure forming as he looked between his brother and the pretty flame he loved—the flame that was all he cared for. He saw their love even though God had already known she was destined for him—knowing already that he would form from his pure brother.

He weakened his flames, ready to move aside for his brother.

However, the blue flame did not weaken. He grew in size, in heat. The green flame panicked when she tried to flee her love, clawing at the crystal glass to escape the heat. He jumped between them, engulfing her as his brother beat down on him, trying to rip her away.

A wail very bell-like sounded from the gold flame, and the blue one hesitated.

He returned to a human shape, accepting it was not his fate to be with her this way. He turned to leave, but the green flame extended a part of his fire, holding a bit of hers but covering her, protecting her.

The blue flame did not burn her. The green flame pulled his brother closer, encouraging him, before wrapping himself around his gold flame. The blue joined, agreeing to share her love as they begged her to glow. She did, spinning and dancing. She grew bright enough to light their world.

"Good. She is special, like you two. She will need you as much as you need her. Protect her together. Love her together. She is yours."

A bright flash filled Jane's sight, and there were three jars, but now gold sat between sapphire and emerald. She danced between them, trying her best to glow as bright as she could for both as the blue flame pushed heat to both flames.

"What are you doing to him?" It was Lucifer's voice.

A hand holding a green flame passed the green jar. The twin emerald flames tried to touch, but the hand did not let them.

"I separated his soul. This is only half—the half that completes hers."

"Why is she incomplete?"

"He is still strong, Lucifer, my strongest and most beautiful soul. He will protect her and still perform his duty. That is why this half will not feel hesitation when he reaps souls. Not unless he is reunited with his soul and mate. See how he surrounds her? I will hide their knowledge of each other so he performs his duty."

A golden fiery sphere encircled by a larger green flame flickered in her mind, as did the image of her staring at her hazel eyes. Gold surrounded by emerald. Emerald that faded when gold grew smaller, gold that roared when emerald drifted away.

"She is perfectly fine now. They will stay this way until it is time to hide her."

"She's not breathing." The green sky reappeared to Jane as a nearly complete eclipse came into view. She tried to see David, but the scene shifted again.

"How can she be hidden from Darkness?" Lucifer asked.

"Perhaps you can protect her. You have developed quite a fondness for her."

"My Grace."

"Yes, Lucifer. Do you believe in your strength to not fall from mine?"

"Yes, Father."

"Then gift her your Grace. It will shroud them from each other, protecting them while allowing him to keep her safe and whole."

"Will I see her?"

"Why do you wish to see her?"

"I love her."

"As I said, Lucifer, she will be hidden from all darkness, even your brother, since he is now neutral. Only when he is complete—when he is near his half that completes her—will he detect a connection. Still, he will not see. He will not understand unless he is told."

"I will not tell her."

"Of course you will not."

"You promise I will not be blocked from her?"

"I promised you, my son, only those who have fallen from my light. You are the only son who knows what they are. Gift her if you wish to keep her and your brother safe."

A veil slid around her, coating her jar in silver, just like Lucifer's eyes.

"There, now she is hidden."

"Like the Hidden One you warned me of?"

"No, the Hidden One is of darkness. If they meet, your protection will be needed."

"I will protect her."

"Of course you will."

"Jane, baby, breathe." David's lips touched hers. "Please, my love."

The Devil's face flashed in her mind, ripping her away from David again. "I offer you a gift, a prize," he told someone.

"I need no prize, Accuser." Lucifer unsheathed his sword.

"Did you know your Father gifted me a soul? A rare golden flame. She is lovely. She is the prize I speak of."

Lucifer lowered his sword. "Gold?"

The Devil grinned.

The scene changed once more, and God's voice bellowed. "Do not question me."

"You said she was safe. I want to see her."

"Do you not?"

Lucifer scanned the jars. Her gold flame sat where it always did, but Lucifer looked past her. He did not see her. "She's not here because you gave her to him. Get her back. She is mine."

"She was never yours, Lucifer. She will never be yours, and you will not see her. Not as you did before. You allowed the Accuser to taint your light."

"You said my brother would not have her—that she would belong to another. I am the other."

"No, Lucifer. A human—a good, pure soul will be the soul her heart chooses. She cannot live with her mate. He is Death."

"You made her a human?"

"Yes. He was made to sit beside her. He will find her, and he will love her unconditionally."

The green sky returned.

"David . . . Brother," Arthur cried. "I cannot hear her. She sees light. Nothing but light."

The world was alight as Lucifer's roar from her dreams rang loud, silencing Arthur's voice.

"I will see that she is destroyed before his very eyes," Lucifer roared. "You will all watch as she burns, and he will burn with her and the other humans. In my light!"

Light. Just light.

"She's not dead." David shook his head. "Come on, baby." He pushed Arthur away and resumed mouth-to-mouth. "There's still light there. The gold is still there."

The roar above cracked David's heart, and he didn't stop when the ground shook, signaling Death's arrival.

"Death." David kept blowing air into her mouth. "Her soul is still there. Her heart is still beating."

"No, it's not, David," Nyctimus said.

"You can't hear it." David shook their hands off. "I hear better. I hear it. I feel her."

"David," Arthur said softly. "There is only light in her mind. It is growing dimmer by the second. But there is nothing there."

"She's there. She sees light for a reason. She's dreaming. She's dreaming of us." He didn't look away, but he felt Death's stare. "Death, snap out of it. Help me save her before it's too late."

Death kneeled on her other side and touched the pendant around her neck. The thread had been cut. "My moon." Death lifted the necklace as he looked up.

David chanced looking up and saw the moon.

"It's not just an eclipse," Nyctimus said. "It's a Blood Moon."

"The army is reforming," Arthur said. "They are coming. David, we must hold them back."

David's hands trembled as he took in the red moon above them, but he shook his head, ignoring Arthur—ignoring Death's roar as he crushed the feathery pendant—ignoring the loudest crack of thunder as it sounded from the pendant shattering in Death's hand.

"He gave her the final seal," Sin whispered. "Get away from him. David, move away."

He pushed them back, never stopping, never giving up, never letting her go. "Come on, Jane. It's not time."

The skies opened as trumpets sounded and angels poured down from the heavens.

A hand touched his shoulder. "David, it is the End."

He shook his head before shoving the archangel's hand from his shoulder. "Help me fix her or leave."

Michael sighed as Gabriel raised a horn, blowing it as the field filled with warrior angels. He blew again, and three claps of lightning shot across the sky. One white, one red, one black. Like fireballs, they landed on the battlefield. The three Horsemen looked at him before settling their gazes on Jane.

"Make him help." David looked at Death as he continued to roar, his face covered in a mask as his wings shifted between black feathers and the skeletal, wraithlike wings he'd seen before. "He's lost without her. Make him fix her."

They did not respond. Their eyes glowed brighter and brighter, and their armor appeared. Flames of white, red, black, and emerald erupted before him. The horses of the Apocalypse shook their fiery manes as armor matching their riders appeared over their bodies.

When Sorrow approached Death's side, David looked up. "Sorrow, help him. Make him see that she's still alive."

Sorrow didn't react.

David kept blowing breaths into her mouth before yelling, "Someone find King. Find Queen."

No one listened. They fell to their knees before the angels, too overwhelmed by God's warriors.

"Queen." David's heart stuttered when she landed, carrying Lucifer in full battle armor. "Stay back."

Lucifer did not listen. He dismounted Queen, and David realized King was bound behind her.

"Move aside," Lucifer said, coming to a stop.

David blew breaths into her mouth again. "She's not dead. You can't have her. She's not gone."

Death stopped roaring. He stood, not looking like the angel David knew to be his brother. His form was entirely changed. David witnessed the Pale Horseman as he stomped toward him. David expected him to fight Lucifer, but he didn't.

Death gripped David's shoulder, squeezing until the bone shattered, and ripped him away from Jane, tossing him across the ground.

Michael lifted him. "Be still. It is done."

"No!" David tried to run to her. "Jane."

Death stared at Lucifer before kneeling beside Jane. He held up the broken thread, looking confused, before lifting his gaze to the Blood Moon.

Death dropped his eyes to the necklace again, then held a hand over Jane's chest.

David's breath chilled in his lungs, waiting for her to breathe, but a silver thread shot from her chest to Lucifer's.

A crown formed on Lucifer's head. "She is my queen. For eternity. You cannot take her with you."

"No." David thrashed.

Death looked at the thread again before staring at Jane for several seconds. He touched the silver bond, not reacting when it burned his skin, but he eventually lowered his hand and stood.

"No, don't let him take her." David shoved Michael as the angels summoned swords and put on golden helmets.

"Thus begins the End," a voice bellowed from the sky.

Death nodded, finally looking away from Jane to mount Sorrow. Hades appeared, chained to Sorrow. A gold crown formed on Pestilence's head as he pulled his bow. War's sword lit in blinding red fire, and Famine's armor revealed scales that constantly shifted in weight as Hunger appeared behind him, the Ravagers close behind her.

Pestilence rode ahead, releasing his arrow as War followed. Famine turned, heading in the direction of their village.

"Famine, stop." David fought to free himself as he watched soldiers fall to their bellies in agony.

David shook his head. "Jane, wake up."

Lucifer cast him the briefest of glances before lifting her body into his arms. His wings unfolded and silver light engulfed him. Then green light filled David's sight.

Death had stopped Sorrow in front of him.

David bowed his head. "Please, brother. We can save her. She is ours— our girl. Sweet Jane. Just look. She's there. You can see her." He looked up, hopeful, when Death had turned his head to stare at Lucifer.

"I see silver. My flame is no more. I am no more." Death turned back to him, and Lucifer vanished. "I am nothing. I am Death."

Michael dragged David backward. "Stay quiet. She is gone. The beginning is gone. It is the End."

David clutched his arm as Heaven's army rode forward. "She's my baby." He stared at his ring. "My kitten. My love . . . My wife."

Lightning shot across the sky, lighting it on fire.

David shook his head, unable to stand as he watched his brothers and their entire army lift their heads, their eyes blood red as snarls ripped from their mouths.

David smiled sadly at his ring. "I'll follow you now, Jane."

Michael shouted an order, dividing Heaven's ranks to target the army he had helped lead with Jane, the bloodthirsty, crazed monsters that never should have scoured the Earth.

Michael and Gabriel stood over David.

He pressed his lips to his ring before staring up at them. "I'm ready. Please let me follow her in death."

Michael exchanged a look with Gabriel before Gabriel turned, leaving. David followed the direction Gabriel went with his eyes. It was where Arthur and the knights started to rise from the bloody ground, their eyes red as they snarled at their maker.

Gabriel held out his hand as it began to glow in white light. "I rid the Earth of my creation."

David closed his eyes when a white beam of light engulfed his brothers and even the few wives who had come to battle.

Michael held his hand over David's head, caressing his hair, reminding him of how he comforted Nathan.

"My children." David looked up, seeing the same glow of white light forming in Michael's hand. "Please go to my children. Don't let them be afraid. Don't let it be Death, not that Death. That's not my brother. Don't let them feel it."

Michael tilted his head. "My brother will be with them. They will not suffer. Be at peace now, David, beloved son of God. Your duty is complete."

David nodded, closing his eyes as white light surrounded him. "I'm ready."

45

FAMILIAR FACES

Light.

Just light.

"I can't believe I'm helping you."

David snapped his eyes open. The speaker's face came into view, but it was blurry. "Baby?"

"Unfortunately for you, my wife is not here." Jason's face became clear. He was wearing black with a hood over his head.

"Jason?" David blinked as chaos—screams and roars echoed around him, but besides Jason standing over him, he could only see white. "Fuck, I'm in Heaven."

"Why would you think that?"

David frowned, taking in Jason's appearance. The hood reminded David of the one Thanatos and other reapers wore. The sleeves of his hoodie were pushed up, revealing numerous tattoos on his forearms and hands. David didn't bother trying to figure out what they were and quickly focused on Jason's face. His brown eyes were darker than before—not malicious. Just dark. "We're not in Heaven?"

"No, we are not," Jason said. "Jane is not here either."

"Where is she?"

"Gone." Jason glanced up at the blood-colored moon. It was turning black.

David tried to move, but he couldn't. "Is this Hell?"

"It looks like it." Jason gestured out. "There are demons in the sky, a lake of fire behind you, and beasts I've never seen before."

"Why are we in Hell?" David didn't understand.

Jason kept staring at him, but he leaned away as another figure approached.

That person leaned over him. "Hello, my prince. It is good to see you again."

"Dagonet? What's happened to me? Why are you here? Death said you were redeemed."

His old friend smiled. He wore black as well, a suit. "It is time for you to go."

"Go where?"

Dagonet stopped smiling. "To the End."

"My prince does not do well with riddles." A third figure stood over him. "Hello, brother." Lancelot smiled, his gaze drifting to Jason momentarily before looking at David. He wore a simple black shirt, but his arms had black markings, similar to Jason's. "It seems your foolish girl is more powerful than should be possible."

"I don't understand. I saw Jane send your soul to Heaven."

Lancelot shook his head. "I have not seen Heaven. None of us have. Jane sent me somewhere else."

David finally sat up. He scanned the burning world around him. Surely, they were lying to him—this was Hell.

"Behold, I am the son of Odin. The God of Thunder." Thor flew through the air, swinging his hammer as a colossal serpent with horns, and scales the size of shields erupted from a hole in the earth. Thor laughed heartily, landing as he smashed the beast's head. "I welcome thee, Ragnarök!"

"No, I'm really in Hell." David clutched his head. "What did I do wrong? Is this because Jane is coming here?"

"We are not lying. We are simply limited in what we can say." Dagonet pulled David to his feet. "You are still on Earth. The only immortals not affected by Hunger are Heaven's original protectors. It seems they are being given one last chance to battle in Heaven's name. The Nephilim are untouched because Earth's guardians have blessed them. Hopefully, you do not see them—they are on quite the rampage, destroying themselves because the Earth has lost the Moon."

David's soul roared within him, but he felt too weak, and his broken heart confined him. "I'm still at the battle? Where is Michael? My brothers?"

"The archangels are battling the Accuser and his children," Lancelot answered. "You should go, David."

A bolt of lightning smashed through a sea of Ravenous and demons. Zeus roared while Apollo created a wall of fire.

"Get the others," someone yelled while human soldiers dragged his brothers to a pile. "Gawain . . . Gareth."

A blond male angel who looked almost identical to Thanatos walked by, waving his hand, sending clouds of white smoke at people.

"Hypnos has been rendering most of your ranks unconscious. The human forces are still fighting, saving whoever they can."

A naked man ran past them but stopped, turning. Nyctimus. "David? Fuck, I thought you were gone."

David looked down. He appeared the same as always, but he felt different. He felt weak.

Nyctimus ran to him, hugging him quickly. "Forgive me. She knew there was no way to break the seal. I meant to stay with her until the end. She wanted to bring down as many as she could. I told her we'd fall into Hell together."

David was furious. He'd trusted Nyctimus to stay with Jane, but he'd been too far away.

"Do not seek vengeance, David. You must listen to us." Lancelot forced David to focus on him. "Death is at the village."

David's eyes widened. "I can't get there in time."

A flap of wings sounded behind them. David turned, seeing the girl Jane had allowed to join the Two Hundred Million Horsemen. She was on her pegasus, holding a rope that led to King.

"He said the prince would need a fast ride." She held up the rope.

David didn't ask the girl who 'He' was. He stood there as King approached him, bowing his head.

Lancelot said, "We wanted you to be with your children at the end. Farewell, brother."

David hugged Lance, kissing his head before doing the same to Dagonet. "Thank you."

"How is he going to stop Death?" Nyctimus yelled. "He's mortal now. They're all mortal!"

David stared down at his arms, realizing he did not feel the immense strength he once had. He tried to call his soul forward. His soul was far more powerful than what he'd let Jane know, but now he could only visualize his soul roaring as he mourned Jane's death. Yet, something held him steady, keeping him from losing himself as Death had.

"He is not going there to stop Death," Lancelot said. "He can't."

Dagonet bowed. "Farewell, my prince."

"Hurry. It is almost too late," Jason said.

David glanced at his brothers, watching as the humans and wolves dragged survivors toward a C-17 Globemaster that waited on the battlefield. Before he could seek out the rest of his brothers, a blue haze on the horizon had his blood turning cold. "Are those souls?" he whispered, watching the violent storm of blue fire swirl like a massive hurricane.

"Yes." Lancelot sighed. "He's even reaped his reapers. Once every mortal is slain, he will come for everyone else. Every immortal, every demon, every angel. Even God. Heaven will not try to stop him."

David didn't say goodbye. He turned King, kicking his heels into the stallion's side as he went to meet Death.

Adam carried the last kid into the bunker, panicked as he searched the chaos for Nathan and Natalie.

The villagers screamed as canon fire sounded and demonic roars filled the air.

"Adam," Artemis ran to him, kissing him quickly, "Death is here."

He nodded before shouting, "Nathan, Natalie."

They scanned the crowd when a woman turned toward them, her tears never-ending.

"They said they weren't afraid of Death—that he would take them to their mama. They went outside."

"What?" Adam yelled, shoving past everyone as Artemis ran ahead of him. "Artemis, wait."

"I have to stop him," she shouted. "I won't let Jane down. He will break them."

"No." He lost sight of her in an instant. "Get out of my fucking way."

Suddenly a green light lit the doorway. Everyone froze before falling to their knees, praying.

Shouts came from outside. "The Horsemen are here!"

"No." Adam ran toward the door. He ran up the stairs in no time, rushing out of the building past the soldiers that made up their last line of defense. He came to a stop when he saw the swirling fiery blue storm above, but his eyes fell to the gates when he heard a scream.

He took off again for the children, who stood there holding hands as a monster in black held Artemis several feet off the ground. She flailed, stabbing it as she tried to pry off the hand crushing her throat.

The monster wasn't affected. It squeezed tighter, lifting her higher off the ground as it finally grabbed the dagger from her before stabbing it into her side.

"Artemis." Adam ran faster, his eyes stinging as the twins watched Artemis go limp. "Nathan . . . Natalie, run!"

The children didn't turn around. They stared at the monster and the four horses behind him. Three had riders, but the fourth waited, watching its rider while Hades held his reins. The god of the underworld's eyes were emerald in color, matching the fiery chains around his throat and wrists. He showed no reaction to watching his niece being killed.

"Hello, Death." Nathan held up a piece of paper. It was stained red. Blood.

Emerald eyes hidden beneath the skeletal mask of a demon suddenly lit into an inferno and locked on Nathan.

"Nathan, get away from him." Adam ran faster, ignoring everything happening around him.

"We're ready to go see Mama," they said together.

Natalie held up her paper, also stained with blood. Her finger was covered with a bandage.

Death threw Artemis, and Adam couldn't see where she landed. He teared up, knowing she was probably dead, but he had to get to the kids.

Death walked to them, his skeletal mask the most terrifying thing Adam had ever seen. It was demonic, not beautiful like Jane had described him.

Nathan and Natalie lifted their hands higher. "Mama has missed you. Please take us home to her."

"No." Adam slipped, falling on his stomach when Death took the papers. He crawled to them, finally grabbing the ends of their shirts. He saw what Nathan had drawn: Jane standing before a bloody moon. She was holding up the necklace from Death, and Natalie's paper was a letter.

"Can you read it while you are like this?" Natalie asked Death.

Adam shushed her, trying to pull them behind him.

Natalie wiped her tears. "It says: Dear Death, we know you can't love us, but we love you, just as Mama does. We want her home with you. Even if we can't go, we want her to finally go home. We want her to be whole. Emerald and Gold. The way she is meant to be. Death and Sweet Jane. Longer than always. Love, Natalie and Nathan."

Death stared at the papers before looking above him. Adam did too, and he cried when he saw the red moon, just as Nathan had made it on the drawing.

"My moon is gone." Death's voice was too smooth. His scythe appeared, the blade shining and dripping in blood as it was raised. "My Sweet Jane is gone."

Natalie whimpered, closing her eyes as Nathan nodded and closed his.

Adam pulled them back but stopped as the blade was lifted to his neck. He covered the children's eyes, shaking as he watched Death crush the drawing and letter, dropping them to the ground and walking over them.

"It's okay." Adam hugged the kids as he shut his eyes too. "It's okay."

46

KINGDOM COME

Light.

Just light.

That was the only word Jane could think—the only sensation she could feel—the only thing around her. No pain. No sadness. Nothing but light.

Jane snapped her eyes open. Just light.

"Come, Jane," a voice called from the far end of the room.

Jane still saw only white, but it felt like she was lying on a bed. She turned her head, and the light vanished.

She was in her dream cottage—on the beautiful bed where Death had made love to her. And he was there, lying on his back and staring up just like she had been . . . that night. His hair was sweaty, his breathing heavily, and he was completely naked. Beautiful.

He turned his head to the side to look at her. "It's time to wake now, Sweet Jane."

"I don't want to leave you."

They reached for each other at the same time, but he vanished before their fingers touched.

"Death is not here, Jane." The voice echoed around her.

White again. She turned her head as she had just done, but this time, there was nothing.

The unfamiliar voice spoke again. "The End has only begun."

Jane didn't feel sadness, yet she knew she should.

She started to sit up, only to realize she already stood. Again, only white light surrounded her, which made it impossible to distinguish anything about where she was.

Hall popped into her head.

She didn't understand why she immediately trusted the white nothingness was a hall, yet she turned and walked forward, already aware this was the direction she needed to go.

It seemed she should hear footsteps, but it was utterly silent. Not even her breathing could be heard. Finally, a single heartbeat sounded, and she looked down. She was covered in blood, but she wasn't alarmed. She touched her chest, feeling for her heart, but it was still. Silent.

"You must come now, Jane. He waits."

She followed the voice, not startled or confused, and walked steadily until she finally saw a massive angel wearing a gray suit.

He smiled, taking her in before opening his palm. He held a wilted leaf with a dull green and gold vine hanging. The flower bud at the end was partially open. No, it wasn't open—it was ripped in half, separating green and gold flower petals, leaving their bases even duller. The only reason they were somewhat held together was a blue leaf at the base of the bulb.

"Jane." The air shook as her hair blew around her. It was the voice that spoke through and to her when her soul rose. Creator. Father. "Come, my daughter. I have much to tell you."

Jane passed the angel beside her, trying to understand why she felt a familiar connection to him. But she kept walking until the white nothingness vanished, and she was inside the room filled with jars. She immediately sought where she had seen hers, David's, and Death's souls. The jars were there, but they were empty.

"Of course they are empty, child. Death's full soul sits inside him—broken but whole. David gained full control of his soul when you bonded to one another, so it sits fully within him, awaiting his call to come forward. His jar will stay empty as long as he holds full control."

"And mine?"

"Have you not also gained full control of your soul? Just the same as David, she has left her jar to be one with her vessel. Now she sleeps."

"Yes, because I'm dead." She touched her neck, feeling raised skin. She held her hand away, not worried about seeing blood dripping from her fingertips.

"Come closer, daughter."

She forgot about her neck and walked toward the smoky light, watching the shadows take shape behind it.

It appeared to be a man—bigger than any she'd ever seen, but still a man. A separate shadow lingered behind him, but they did not quite match. This one was smaller and moved slightly different from the larger shadow. "You fought bravely, but your time was meant to end. Is there anything you desire to understand?"

The first real thought was the twin flames. "David and Death are brothers. I mean, their souls are."

"Yes. Why have you not used Vision after all these years?"

"Afraid," she said, touching her bloody neck again.

"There is nothing to fear about their connection. First, let me help you understand your soul since she is no longer awake."

Jane saw the jar with a gold flame. It looked like her soul's flame but was larger, and the other jars in the room were empty.

A hand appeared, opening the jar and pulling the flame out. "Hello, daughter."

The flame flared up, spinning violently.

"I see. You are unhappy sitting here alone. Angry." The hand caressed the flame. "Not all of you, I see. You will do wondrous things, but you must wait."

The flame spun more chaotically. It didn't burn as gracefully as her soul. Half of it seemed to try to calm itself, while half fought to explode.

"Yes, I see a part of you wants to understand. A part of you will suffer whatever is asked of you, but the other desires what I refuse to give. You need time to learn and grow. You are not ready for all you desire and that I want for you."

Again, the gold flame erupted in a chaotic inferno. It spun faster and faster until it nearly fell to the floor.

"Very well. You are not happy here. Would you like a new home? There, you will have attention, and you will be given gifts by a new father, but he will drain you of all your light. For he is Darkness, and he darkens all that he touches."

The flame spun as a part of it tried to hang on to the fingers closing around it.

"Yes, you turned out just as I expected you would. A good Beginning indeed. Light and dark. Well done." Another hand appeared, pulling the flame until it separated. Two smaller flames nearly died out, but the smallest flared up, spinning beautifully.

"There you are, daughter. Perfect. They will love you as much as I do. Now you will wait until it is time." The smaller flame was put into a new jar and sat alone on the shelf. A female figure formed, but she spun again whenever she dimmed.

"Yes, you are already growing weak. Fear not, for I am always with you. Your mate will come. He will make you whole as you dance together."

The small flame spun again, agreeing to her fate.

The other half began to dim, turning a darker gold, sometimes looking more red than gold. It no longer spun violently. It smoldered.

"Ah, see what has happened? Your impatience and desire destroyed you." She was put in the original jar.

The first gold flame formed a female figure as she looked at the darker gold flame. She put her hand on the crystal, trying to comfort her other half, but the dark flame flared up in a fiery red inferno before moving away.

"Still angry. It is not her fault. You chose darkness and a new father. You need more time to understand, but you cannot balance each other. If I leave you together now, you will destroy each other and those I place around you. This way is better—you both have a chance. I will sit you where you do not harm her. Worry not. The new father you desired will come for you before she ever has company. That is what you wished for, after all. So eager but unwilling to listen. You must learn that sometimes becoming better hurts. Yet, you do not give in to dark desire." A red jar appeared, but it was not see-through like the jar Jane's soul was in. "Since you favor this violent color, enjoy it before you embrace Darkness." The dark gold flame's jar was put inside the red one and moved across the room.

The gold flame kept staring out, watching the red jar until she dimmed.

"You let her take much of your heat—such compassion. Be patient, and do not give up. When you want to go out, find a way to burn brighter. It will be difficult, but I have faith in you."

The room rippled, and more jars filled it, but none were placed close to the gold flame. She was dull, sometimes dying out, but she would flare up at the last moment. She looked lonely. Sad.

"Yes, here you go, my son. She has waited for your company. Be gentle. She is far smaller than you."

A jar with a sapphire flame was placed beside her. It roared, spinning fiercely as it slid closer to the gold. She instantly warmed but retreated under the immense heat.

"I said gentle, my son." The blue jar was slid a small distance away. "Warm her from there. You will be her companion and shelter. Her home."

The sapphire flame seemed content. He calmed, flickering steadily as the gold flame crept closer.

"Good. You will be perfect for her. Take care of her while she waits for her mate," God said. "He has just begun, but he must be perfect, and that will take time."

The gold flame pressed herself against the glass. The sapphire flame did the same, again causing her to retreat.

There was a chuckle. "Yes, I know you desire to hold her. You have your duty to her, though. I already told you. Stand beside her always. Will you perform it? The choice is still yours."

The sapphire flame transformed into a male silhouette. He watched the gold flame when she changed, revealing her female form. They stared at each other until the male figure nodded, raising his arm and holding his hand to the glass. The female copied him.

Jane covered her mouth. She had seen a similar scene in her mind when she'd gone to meet Lucifer for the first time. Her feelings had begun to return, and David's smile formed in her head before she saw him holding his hand up for her to come back. When she reached up to touch him, glass separated them. He stayed on one side while she stood on the other. Then she turned, leaving to keep him and her family safe.

"Good boy." God forced Jane to refocus on the flames. "Be good to her. Be everything she needs you to be."

The blue flame nodded before spinning into an inferno.

The room came into focus as it had been before.

The shadow moved in the smoke. "Does that make your beginning clearer?"

Jane's eyes watered. "You split me from the half that chose darkness and gave my soul David's as a companion while she waited for Death."

"Yes. David's soul was committed to serving its duty to you, but he began to believe you were meant for him because of how much he loved you. To him, no one would be good enough because he was more than enough. He was too much because I made him so. I needed him to burn hotter than all others but to be yours. Unlike your soul, which I purposely split to initiate the two sides to truly become incomplete beings, David's soul split on its own, making two whole souls."

"How are they not half souls, then? Like mine and my darker half?"

"Because I made it so."

"That doesn't make sense. I don't understand the difference. They are the same thing."

"They are different. It is so."

"How can you make it so?"

"Because I am that I am."

Jane stared at the shadow in silence.

"Death's soul was there, but only a spark hidden within David's flame. When David's was put in place, and he saw you, Death's conscience awoke. His Beginning was before him. Thus he began. He grew until he was ready, then they split all on their own. Death's soul had watched everything while he waited for his time. He knew he would have a duty but had yet to be told what it was. He knew the gold flame was his brother's duty. However, it became more apparent to him that David's flame was not entirely compatible with her. Death's soul's personality began to develop simply because of her, and he was displeased to see her paired so poorly. After all, the souls around them seemed to have paired nicely, but his brother and the pretty flame he cherished were not a perfect match.

"He observed her more, accepting, despite her small size, she would fit him better than his twin. His only fault was that he had no heat to give her. He knew she was often cold. She often fell—tired from trying to keep her flame intact—and he grew frustrated because his pure brother had so much that even he burned in his wake.

"As more souls appeared, David's soul increased his flame, giving off more warmth to the others instead of only her, burning his twin in the process. Death's soul allowed himself to burn because of her. He watched as she was not given the right amount of heat or attention. David's soul believed it was gifted so much warmth to care for all others. This was also because he was lit nearest my flame. He felt a sense of duty to others, but Death's did not care. No matter how many surrounded them, he saw only her. But your soul admired how great David's was. He was so good to the others. So strong. Greatness. Because of this, she still did not realize her true mate had come into existence and was already watching over her.

"Thus, Death's soul proceeded to grow stronger. He gave no heat to the others, so he cared less and less about them, but he never stopped trying to show her he was there. He knew he could protect her and quickly exceeded his brother's strength. He was stronger and more beautiful than any of the souls present, including his twin. He did it all for her. I knew he would. I made her everything for him—to fit him just so. Yet, he could not warm her. And why would he? If he had warmth to give, she would incinerate in their presence.

"So, Death's soul is cold. So cold she assumed she was seeing her original companion whenever she did see him. This only caused Death's to work harder to be unique, as I would need him to be. However, the more beautiful he became next to David's, the less worthy she began to feel. She also believed I had forgotten my promise of a mate. She remembered how even her other half did not want to be with her. After all, she was a small, half-soul.

"Neither Death's nor David's souls cared or even knew she was half—for she was perfect to them. Just as David and Death see you as perfect, and you saw that you were not enough, she did the same. And just as you did, she finally decided half was capable of greatness all on its own. So, she did just as I expected her to. She became great and gave others hope when they felt forgotten. She was determined to be great. So she danced, burning brighter and brighter, causing more souls to admire her. She still kept her sights on David's, unaware he saw her as perfect already and certainly not aware he had already claimed her as his."

He chuckled. "Your soul caught herself admiring Death's soul again, though. She still did not believe he was there but would watch him and feel foolish for simply wanting to dance for a reflection."

"Why didn't they just talk to each other?" Jane watched several souls spin violently while others trembled.

"They need a vessel to communicate through. That's why she danced."

"Could David's and Death's communicate?"

"Yes, but they chose not to. They each knew the other wanted her."

"But she never acknowledged Death's soul?"

"She did. She danced, trying to copy how he burned whenever he tried to get her attention. When David's soul caught her looking at his brother, though, he burned hotter, forcing her to retreat and burning his brother—every time strengthening his brother, darkening his blue color."

Tan, Jane thought with a smile. Death was so good, but it would not be seen that way. The only thing that didn't make sense was the description of David's soul. It almost matched her David, but this made it seem like his soul was less considerate of her. And he was always so thoughtful and kind.

"Was he always considerate?" God asked. "He never hurt you with his actions?"

"David always took up for Death, even when he didn't like him. And he was never mean."

The Creator chuckled. "That is simply your admiration for how nearly perfect he can be. Your admiration closes your eyes to the truth. Was David not angry when Death returned and saved you? Did he not storm out because you were at peace in Death's arms? Because you smiled at Death? Did David not hurt your heart when he wanted you to be tolerant of a woman who wanted you gone? Because one is perfect, one must care for all, and that can sometimes mean those they love most suffer from being in their presence. Too much, daughter. We are too much because we must be so, which sometimes hurts."

Jane thought back to those first moments of Death's return. David had seemed broken, though, not angry.

"Do not force your heart to accept what your mind sees as truth. It is still okay to love him, and it is okay that he is too much at times. All souls change in their vessels. When Death held you, and you instantly embraced him, David's soul stirred awake—furious—and ready to slaughter Death. Luckily, David knew he was outmatched, giving his heart time to hold him steady and remember his love for you. His soul is great, but his heart is greater. And it had much time to grow as David waited for hazel eyes—gold dancing in emerald. His wait had a purpose. His heart steadied his soul, and it grew.

"Had his soul been able to control him then, it would have unleashed fury, destroying you. Do not forget he nearly attacked Jason the first time he met him. Death held him back long enough for his heart and mind to regain control. David's love has kept him from destruction, from the unstoppable inferno he could be. Do you not see how much he has changed since meeting you? How, even though you thought him perfect from the beginning, he became a true prince of your heart. A great father, friend, and husband. Because of you, he became everything he was capable of being. You had already called him your bestest." He chuckled. "He simply embraced his best when he embraced every part of you and what came with you."

"Death," she whispered.

The shadow appeared to nod. "David saw the truth. He was not your soul mate. He had a choice, just as his soul did when it rushed to take you back. He could further rip you apart, abandon you, or he could accept all of you. He always had Death there, reminding or stopping him from destroying you. If he wanted to be the best he could be for you, he needed to completely accept his role in your life and his brother's place with you. Unfortunately, it did not happen until your beloved soul mate was already torn from you.

"My sons, twin souls, became heartbroken. They did not know their souls were twins then, but they knew Death was the true soul mate. David had pieced information together, but neither had seen their origins. Death's soul prepared to take on its duty when Famine arrived, and that is when he saw everything he needed to. He saw and knew what needed to be done to get his soul's twin to rise. You could not bond with Death because of Lucifer's light, but David's soul burns hotter. While Death can withstand being burned, his soul was broken. He could not break the bonds or remove light and felt unworthy. He wanted the best for his love and mate.

"When David allowed Death something he did not think possible since you chose David, Death decided to help David fully embrace his soul. He saw David's mistakes with you and was determined to give you the best. But then, his eyes opened further to realize he and David were from the same soul. This truth devastated him. This meant David had indeed been first, and David was more deserving of your soul than him. His happiness from being your true soul mate was not his to have. In his mind, at least. So, he chose to make David all he could be . . . because Death had already lost hope of reforging your bond. He couldn't watch, hear, and feel your love for David and not him, and he feared his weakening state would drive him to madness.

"So your mate stimulated his soul's twin by dressing you in gold. This allowed David a glimpse of the moment you witnessed before coming here. David saw what they were to one another and Death's intentions to tie your souls together since he could not resume his bond. They recreated the moment your souls touched for the first time, forcing David's soul to rise and take complete control of the vessel so he could tie your souls together.

"Death kept the gold thread that had once joined you, hoping he'd soothe his soul by being complete and feeling the bond. And when he prepared to leave you, he took the final seal from himself and shaped it into a pendant, then made your necklace with the thread meant to tie you both together in every way. He gave you the final seal because you are the final seal of the Apocalypse. His heart. Without his heart, his flame, his moon—his Sweet Jane—he is Death and nothing more."

Jane's eyes watered and overwhelming sadness filled her to the point where she could no longer bear to exist. She clutched her wound. That's where it had been empty. That was where he was supposed to be. Her lips trembled, and she gasped as her entire body felt like it would shatter. "And my death wasn't even his to take."

"Be still, daughter. For I am with you," God said as a gold blanket of light lifted from the smoky shadow. It passed over her, surrounding her with warmth she only felt between Death and David. "Yes. You felt Me only through your kiss with Death. The bond you shared was made of my purest light. You and Death are more unique than simple soul mates. You both were made to wait for my love and attention when it was time to join you. You watched, waited for me to tell you what to do, then wondered what was wrong with you that you were left for so long—so I gave my purest light to bond you to show My love. I would have to hide him when your darker half returned, and his free half would be emptier. So the thread is only for you two. My way of letting you share the warmth of your lovely flame as he tried so fiercely to warm you.

"I love my son and had given him the most dreadful duty. I did not want to force it on his entire soul. That is why he is so strong. He needed to be the strongest to do his duty once split. Half also allowed him to perform his duty without becoming attached to others. He has been split for so long that neither half wants to be united. He does not know how to be whole without you. You shower him with your love and allow each other the comfort of My love for you. The reminder I never forgot either of you."

Jane wiped her tears. "Forgive me for thinking you had."

The room lit with gold light, and it kissed her face like the sun. "I already have."

Jane laughed, sobbing as the light continued to comfort her.

"Only because Death and David became close did your vampire prince achieve greatness to express a love equal to mine. David mimicked me, just as his soul had done for the others, and finally, the gold and emerald flame, loving both of you, caring for both of you, just as his soul did with all other souls around him. That is why you three were held together. You made him greater than ever, and he held you fiercely.

"But Death wanted you to have one thing he did not think possible with him in your life because he feared what he was and what he must do. So he did everything to give you your greatest dreams. He left to fight monsters so that you could stay home."

Jane breathed in as the light kissed her eyes, soothing her stinging tears. Her wound began to glow, the unbearable pain—gone. She rubbed her hand over it, looking down to see blood seeping out. It finally looked as it had felt when they separated. "Death set out to capture Lucifer."

"And I had Abaddon capture him." Lucifer walked up beside her. "Hello, my queen."

"What are you doing here?" She tried to attack him but couldn't even raise her hand to him.

693

"Allowing you to have the answers you seek before we go." He caressed her cheek, wiping away tears and dirt. "Don't cry for them."

She glared at him, and he smiled.

"Lucifer has asked that I allow you to see."

"I don't want to see anything from you. Stop touching me."

Lucifer lowered his hand, his gaze falling to her bleeding wound before returning to her eyes. "Do you remember when you shot me, my queen? You wounded the half of your soul that is imprisoned within me. I keep her close to my heart."

She tried to summon her gun to shoot him again, but nothing happened.

He chuckled, shaking his head. "So fierce. Pay attention to what is being said and shown to you. It's better this way. It will hurt less."

The moment in the cave with him when he'd said something similar surfaced in her mind. He'd been trying to get her to submit and give herself to him completely. But she wouldn't. And he'd ended up needing to call forward her darker half to break her.

She searched his eyes, watching them as they watched her. "I can never figure you out, Luc."

A slight smile spread over his lips. "Because I have made it difficult for you." His smile soothed her, no matter how hard she tried to force it not to. "Will you listen and allow me to show you the answers to the questions you have always asked?"

She nodded, swallowing painfully.

He stared at her throat. "This is taking too long."

"Then show her what you desire, Lucifer." God seemed to turn away as more souls disappeared.

Lucifer's gaze slid to the jars before moving to her. He reached for her hand and turned it so her palm was up. "Do you remember this hurting during the battle?" He slid his fingers over her wrist. A tattoo of a half-moon with a star appeared.

She gasped as she stared at it. It had burned as badly as the pain she'd experienced when his light had burned her. "Yes. I saw memories of when Death removed the venom from my back. He had to cut through your light to remove it. I couldn't take the pain."

He nodded and turned his hand, pushing up his sleeve. A matching tattoo was on his wrist. "Watch." He put their wrists together, and she saw Death holding her as she convulsed on the bed. David was standing, holding a phone.

"Hurry." Death tried to keep her still.

Lucifer walked away from the wall, passing David, though David didn't react to his presence. He was bleeding where she'd shot him, but he only seemed to be hurting when he looked at her thrashing in Death's arms. He leaned down as if to kiss her but saw where Death held her arm and sighed. He shook his head before he held his glowing hand over Death's. Her body had jerked. Lucifer kissed her forehead as another pulse of light passed from his hand to Death's, and her angel hissed, ripping his hand away as he stared at her, furious when she gasped and opened her eyes.

"Baby?" David lowered the phone. "Can you hear me?"

Lucifer kissed her forehead again. "That will feel better now. Feed."

"Blood." She sighed.

Death snarled but kissed her when Lucifer leaned away. "Feed her now."

David bit into his wrist and held it against her lips.

She drank without difficulty and sighed as she felt the skin on her back sealing.

"What did you do to her?" David asked Death.

"Nothing." Death smoothed her hair back. "I did nothing."

Lucifer smiled at her as she stopped feeding and closed her eyes. He clutched his wound, wincing. "Sleep well, my queen." Then he vanished.

The room of souls reappeared, and she stared up at Lucifer, trying not to feel the warmth he was showing her.

"Do you desire to understand more?" he asked, moving closer.

"What have you been doing, Luc?"

He wiped away another tear. "What needed to be done."

She nodded to him. "Show me what you want me to see."

Lucifer glanced at the still-disappearing souls before holding his hand over her wound. His hand began to glow, not hurting her at all. "Close your eyes, my queen. I ache when I do not see hazel eyes staring at me."

Her lips trembled, and she obeyed, gasping as the world spun.

It stilled, and the wind blew across her cheek. Jane turned, her lungs burning and her throat aching as she tried not to cry from the scene before her.

Death was talking to her children. It was the day he'd left when he had taken them to speak to them alone. He'd used a sound barrier then, and she'd always wondered what he'd told them.

"I want you two to be good for your mama," he said after putting them on a boulder.

"You're leaving?" Natalie asked, her eyes filling with tears. "But you're her boyfriend and soul mate. She's happy."

Death smiled. "I am, and she is happy. But Mama wants a husband. She will want one more now you are being teased."

"I'll tell that girl you're my daddy, too. You and David are my daddies, just like my real daddy."

Death glanced at Nathan. Her little boy nodded.

"I can't marry Mama. And she wants to marry David. He'll be your daddy. I have to leave."

"But David will let you marry her too," Natalie whined.

He sighed, glancing at her in the distance with David. David was getting angry, preparing to yell at the human in front of them.

"Shit." Death looked at the kids again. "I mean . . . Ah, fuck it. You've heard your mama talk, and I want you to remember this conversation, so I'm not wiping your memories again."

Natalie's mouth was hanging open. "I won't tell her you said those bad words. I won't let her get mad at you. Now you can marry her. Daddy won't ask her. I already asked him. So you can be her husband, and David will be our daddy."

Death's lips twitched with a smile. "I can't marry Mama because that will take her away from you." He patted Natalie's leg. "I promise you will have a daddy. In fact, David has the ring he will give her in his pocket. Don't tell him you know, and don't tell Mama. But I want you to have all the time you can with her, okay? Just be good. I will buy you time so she doesn't have to fight until it's time. You want her home, right?"

They nodded.

"It was hard on her to leave you all the time. So I will go so she doesn't have to. She'll still have to work here. But she will be home every night. And David will be your daddy and marry your mama."

"She's gonna miss you," Natalie whispered.

"I know. I'll give her a present to help. But it will really help if you be as happy as you can be with her. I'm going to give her a little place in the woods where she can go when she's sad. If you see she wants to go there, be extra good for her." He looked down. "The next time you see me, I won't be the same. Try to be brave. I promise I would stop if I could. But when I come back, I won't be good anymore."

Natalie touched his cheek. "'Cause Mama won't be with you?"

He nodded. "I'm sorry I am this way. That is my biggest reason for leaving. I can't have a life with her if I take everything too. I don't deserve it. But you do, and so does David."

"Death." Nathan nodded.

"Yes." Death patted Nathan's cheek. "When I come back, I am only Death. Just close your eyes for me and remember I love your mama, and if I could, I would love you."

Nathan teared up but nodded as Arthur approached.

"All right, be good now." He patted their legs.

Arthur lifted Natalie into his arms, hugging her as she tried not to cry. "Go so that you can make the most of your day with her."

Death nodded, vanishing and reappearing behind David.

Jane sobbed, covering her wound when the scene ended, then found herself staring at Thanatos and Lucifer. They stood at the foot of her and David's bed, watching them sleep.

Her past self whined in her sleep before murmuring, "Death, don't leave me."

Her pendant lit up in green light, and Death's whisper sounded. "Brother."

David's body glowed with sapphire light, and the deeper voice that had spoken with David before the battle responded, "Brother."

Lucifer and Thanatos glanced at each other but said nothing.

Death's voice sounded again. "I can't visit her in her dreams tonight. Soothe her for me. Wake David, if you must."

The blue light grew brighter. "Do you need help, brother? I can fight him now."

The green light flickered. "You are helping. Love her for us. Keep your power hidden until she needs to know. You will be able to protect her should any come for her."

Thanatos chuckled, and it almost looked like the green light formed Death's shape behind her body as David's soul fully formed and stood, turning in Lucifer's and Thanatos' direction.

"Someone is here," said David's soul.

Lucifer glared at Thanatos just as Death appeared in the room in full reaper form, swinging his scythe at them, barely missing them when they vanished.

The room disappeared before a dark room appeared. The black, sleek walls stretched upward close to twenty feet. There were carvings similar to Lucifer's marks engraved into them and the ceiling. It reminded her of

Death's realm, but the bed was different. It was all white, standing out like a light in the darkness.

Thanatos shimmered into view, walking past the bed. "Forgive me. I am weakened in the presence of David's soul. I did not expect him to sense us. It is similar to Father's fire."

Lucifer shook his head. "What powers does he speak of?"

"I don't know." Thanatos glanced out the window where cries of agony sounded. "Must we come here?"

"Death will not come where I keep Abaddon." Lucifer glanced out the window.

A creature Jane assumed to be Abaddon was visible. He looked both angel and demon. He had two sets of wings. One pair was made of white feathers, while the other resembled bat wings. His body constantly shifted from being engulfed in flames and then darkness while a scorpion-like tail twitched behind him.

Lucifer watched as Abaddon selected those he'd already ordered him to enslave. The endless cavern before him was exactly how she imagined Hell would look. A sea of people screaming as they were tortured. Demons were around humans, ripping off their flesh, cutting out their tongues, and carving their bodies until they lay in steaming piles of flesh. The worst part was they would instantly reform, and the process would restart.

Jane felt like crying when Lucifer's gaze fell on a woman in her mid-twenties—a woman with pale skin and hazel eyes.

"There," he said.

Abaddon turned, his fiery gaze falling on the woman. There was no hope left in her dull eyes as she lay strapped to a rock table. A demon was beside her, caressing her busted cheek with taunting affection. It showed her the knife it held, but she didn't react. Not even when he dragged the jagged blade over her wrist, spilling crimson blood.

"Do it," Lucifer said as Thanatos stood beside him.

Abaddon crossed the vast field of bloody torture.

Jane's breathing sped up as she watched the woman stay still and quiet as she was cut several times. Another demon wrapped a rope around her neck, tightening it until blood seeped from the edges.

"What a terrible death she gave herself at the end," Thanatos said.

The woman didn't fight, and the demons kept cutting her until, at last, a single tear fell from her eye.

Jane tried to look away when they cackled in her face as one climbed on top of her and spread her legs.

"She looks like Jane," Thanatos said as the demon thrust himself into the woman. "Though she obviously took a more destructive path than the queen."

"Yes." Lucifer kept watching as the demons took turns raping her.

Thanatos chuckled when Abaddon finally reached the woman. "You know demons do not choose what torment they inflict."

Jane gasped as Abaddon sent gold chains out, wrapping up the demons instead of the woman they were torturing. They screamed as he tore their flesh away, only silenced when a black hole opened below them, and they fell inside.

Lucifer sighed as he watched Abaddon shed his demonic appearance and lift the broken woman. She still had no hope, not even in the presence of one of God's most powerful angels. Abaddon turned her head to the side, inspecting her before shaking his head.

"Fine," Lucifer said.

Abaddon opened his mouth, fire spewing free and engulfing her body in flames. She didn't even scream.

"So many are lost." Thanatos raised his hand. The blue flame that had formed inside Abaddon's fire flew to Thanatos and was absorbed in his palm.

Lucifer turned to Thanatos. "What will need to be done?"

Thanatos pointed to Lucifer's wrist. "Mark her when it's time. It is a good thing he removed his bond and soul, but he put their bond around her with the fucking seal."

"Fool." Lucifer rubbed his wrist. "His soul won't be able to reclaim its place because of my light? You are certain?"

Thanatos nodded. "He cut out everything—you know that. She is empty there, and that is where Hel will strike. You confirmed it with your visions."

"Yes, but it changed to Jane's throat being slit after Death removed his soul."

"Well, I did not expect him to wrap the bond around her throat with the seal. If you give her your seal, it will trap her soul inside your light. Then you will be able to withdraw both before her heart stops."

"It will have to be done at the right moment." Lucifer stared at the moon on his wrist before kissing it. "You are going to be the death of me, my queen." The moon part of the tattoo glowed brightly, making him smile, but he nodded to Thanatos with a sad look.

"Forgive me." Thanatos held out a blade and appeared to cut the glowing moon off Lucifer's wrist, leaving only a dull half-moon tattoo. "Avoid touching it. She can still sense you and extract your memories whenever you do."

They stared at the moon once Thanatos held it, watching it become a clay seal.

"Guard it." Lucifer pulled his sleeve down, hiding their mark. "When I say, put it in place. Make sure it is not placed in the path of her heart. David's bond must stay intact. Once Death is in Abaddon's chains, his bond will deactivate. His seal will hibernate until mine is broken. I pray when her throat is slit, the seal remains. We need time to finish."

"We will be close." Thanatos waved his other hand over the seal, and it vanished. "If I have to, I will interfere and slit her throat myself without breaking Death's seal. Ensure Jane's back is facing Hel. That bitch will find it hilarious once she sees that Jane bears a seal where she intended to stab her."

Lucifer nodded. "No one was supposed to know Death was a half soul."

"Hel's magic is strong, and Jane was often weak in her presence. She saw him whenever he foolishly came to soothe her. And you know how often Jane caresses the spot he was hidden inside her."

Lucifer snarled. "Of all places for Father to hide the remainder of Death's soul, he chose the spot right below her heart."

"And to the side." Thanatos laughed as Lucifer gave him an annoyed look. "This will work. You know I am true."

"To him," Lucifer said. "I do not know if you are a fool for falling just for this purpose or a saint. I am bothered that Father told you so much."

"He told me what I needed to know. I still chose Death, just as He knew I would."

"Like a fool."

Thanatos smiled, his now blue eyes twinkling. "Death is my king before you, Lucifer. At least she does not realize she is his intended queen as well. It might get awkward for her to call you both her king. Though, since he has started calling himself her King Boyfriend, I think he's figured it out."

Lucifer stared at the bed in his room. "And my foolish little brother almost crowned her."

"If he married her, he would have." Thanatos smiled again. "That is why I always told him Jane wouldn't want two husbands, and she would want to marry David. Anyway, crowning her restricts her to his realm, and he won't do that to her. Another sign that Father knows exactly what He has done. Had Death not taken Jane to his realm at such a broken moment in her life and witnessed all that death would cause her, he might have taken her long ago."

"You're lucky he loves her so greatly that he didn't take David's offer to ask her to marry them both. My queen is to be protected, and she must remain bound to me."

Jane covered her mouth.

Thanatos smiled wider. "She's not your crowned queen until she says I do and kisses you. So neither of you fully has her. And as I said, Death won't confine her to his realm after seeing what it did to her before. If she is not with her soul mate there, she relives her torture, just as these souls do here. He loves her too much to do that to her."

"The End will not end The Beginning." Lucifer sighed. "Now she will wind up chained to my bed."

Thanatos glanced at the bed. "We have no choice. The Accuser hid his ravenous daughter inside Valhalla, and we made deals involving Jane's eternity. I didn't even know he had imprisoned Loki, then posed as him without anyone knowing."

"Odin knew, and that is why he killed Loki."

"The real one." Thanatos chuckled. "It was a clever plan, I will give Darkness that. Fill Odin with grief over killing the real son, so much so he believed Hel must have been innocent of the crimes she'd been accused of."

"And so Odin let Hel return as a servant named Hela." Lucifer sighed, rubbing his arm. "I should have recognized her when I saw her speaking to Jane. I felt the disturbance and found her praise of Jane odd." He shook his head. "The False Queen. Goddess of Death—what a ridiculous lie. So many believe Death is attainable."

"They do not know he will only ever see and feel Jane, nor does the Accuser."

"Still, Darkness is more clever than I ever gave him credit for."

"He wants one of his daughters ruling beside you," Thanatos said. "He does not care which—only that you remain in the Dark. But he knows Jane's half soul is more powerful than any of his true children. He disregards Jane's abilities—he always has because she is smaller and requires more light and heat than the dark one. If only he knew, he would try harder to seduce Jane."

Lucifer glared at Thanatos.

The Fallen shrugged. "Again, you let it be known that you love Jane. He's also trying to preserve the Jane you love so you have a reason to keep his daughter instead of destroying her. She is a more useful tool than our Jane."

"Stop calling her our Jane."

"Giving up that she still secretly cares for you?" Thanatos chuckled. "I think it matters little. All that would have happened is Hela would have tried a lot harder to reveal herself when you followed Jane to Valhalla. Her little games—tainting the minds of the immortals around her as clues for you. Just as she did in her little game with Odin, poisoning his mind so he fucked Sif, destroying what greatness was left in Thor—she tried to destroy Jane by using every maid and servant to lust after David or whisper about what a pity it was to have a scarred, small Other. And she showed her fury when she learned you'd already been so close to Jane. Once she overheard Death mention you eternally bound to Jane, she was done. She opened Hell's portals and brought them in."

Lucifer rubbed his arm. "I was so absorbed with keeping Jane from falling as she had begun to."

Thanatos grimaced. "It would have been easier to let her fall then."

"I know." Lucifer shut his eyes for a moment. "I just couldn't see it happen the way it was."

"Or at all." Thanatos smiled as he paced the room. "It is such a unique design—to see all that was done to return your light to its true glory. He knew you would support her while Death stood aside, watching you do as you were supposed to. Just always never the final push. Not until you realized how much you loved Jane and not just that flame." Thanatos pointed to Lucifer's arm. "Stop rubbing. Are you still using the spell to block that bitch? If she hears, this is over."

"I would not allow such a thing." Lucifer looked at the bite mark Jane had left on his arm. "I suppose you have been right. It does align as Father said. Only bonding as king and queen with Jane's consent could silence her dark soul."

"Yes, then she acquired Light, strengthened Death, saved David from killing Lancelot—adding to David's greatness. Father is more clever than any of us." Thanatos walked past him. "Belial is summoning me. They are plotting against you again. I will inform you when I learn their new plans. If Death finds you, summon Abaddon and lock him away. Do not offer Jane more time in her new life. Her children will understand."

"I will offer her what I wish."

Thanatos rolled his eyes. "She will refuse you. She is not the same little queen she was before. Offer it and make David proud."

"You would desire that he see her stand up to me."

"So do you, Lucifer. Don't let Death get you. Our only hope is to lock the Accuser away so she has time to become your rightful queen. At her best. And you know what must happen for that to be."

Lucifer waved him off. "Go. And hide your eyes."

"Fuck." He held a hand over his eyes as red light left it. When he was done, red eyes stared back at Lucifer. "Thank you."

Lucifer didn't say anything, and Thanatos vanished.

The scene swirled, and Jane was staring at Death.

He was in full reaper form and trapped in Abaddon's chains. Pissed.

"I warned you not to come for me, little brother." Lucifer sighed, closing his eyes for a moment. "She's daydreaming about David's proposal. At least he kept his promise to you."

Death snarled, thrashing in the gold chains. "She's happy. If you have any real feelings for her, you will release her from the bond you made."

"Foolish, little brother. My bond is for eternity. Besides, if she is to live, she needs either the dark gold bitch I have in my prison, my light, or you. Well, half of you."

Death stopped moving.

Lucifer chuckled. "Yes, I know half your soul was hidden within her to complete her. I was there when Father separated your soul and put you with her. However, I never knew you came from David's soul. That Father kept hidden, and I still am yet to understand all David is capable of."

Death smirked. "Let her go, and I won't let him kill you."

Lucifer tilted his head, watching Death. "That powerful?"

Death shrugged. "Face him and find out. I wouldn't have left her alone if I didn't have faith that he could keep her safe. Not that she needs it from your minions now he has unlocked her deity soul."

"Do you even know all that she is? She is not a full deity yet. That will be a sight to behold."

Death stayed quiet for a moment. "Do you truly love her, Luc?"

Lucifer sighed, looking at his wrist briefly. "Because I have not achieved what I must, I will offer you a deal. I release you, and you take her to your realm where she is safe until I ask you to bring her back."

"What?" For the first time ever, Death looked utterly confused.

"Keep her until I say. Her children will grow up and live their lives. The same with Adam. And David—your brother."

"Fuck you. I see their time, and it has not changed. They will not grow old."

"You won't stop for them? For her?"

Death snarled. "You know I cannot. What is your game? Are you simply trying to turn her on me? So she embraces what she is and chooses you?"

"Actually, I just want to see her again. I want to glimpse her rise against me before it all ends. So I will offer her one hundred years of peace to her community if she comes with me."

Death's eyes widened. "Do not offer her the chance of her children living a full life. You know it will not be so. Let her live with them while she can."

Lucifer chuckled. "Incredible the amount of devotion and love that exists in you just for her. You will know her response through Abaddon. When she refuses me, stands up to me like I want her to, and accepts she must stand by her family, Abaddon will throw you into the abyss. Feel free to send word to your twin. I've already led him far from her, but I am curious to see what he is capable of. Now, farewell, little brother. Because the next time we see each other, you will be an empty, broken fool preparing to destroy the world."

"Don't do this to her." Death dropped his head. "Please. I just want her to live in peace. He is everything."

"No, brother. David is close to perfect, but he is not everything." Lucifer patted Death's chest. "Do not be so careless with your heart. I did not cast my grace over the two of you the first time so you could let her suffer so. Stop believing he is all she needs. She needs you both. Stop walking away from her. You are The End for a reason." He smiled at Death's fearful gaze. "The Beginning must meet her End. Embrace your fates."

Death's eyes widened. "I can't lose her. I will lose her in more ways than just the last beat of her heart. Without my bond to her, I will reap her and lose myself. And I will not even be able to keep her because of you. Even if I crown her, she will wither in my realm once she learns I have killed them the way I will. That is why I left her there."

"I know, brother. You wanted to let her live as long as possible in her fairy tale because you lost hope when David became her soul mate. You forgot one thing—you are Death." He chuckled before looking upward. "If you have any faith in our father, break the seal when you see her slain. My seal will have broken by then, and yours is the last. Her."

Death stared at him. "If I break my seal, I become him. Only one thing will stop me."

Lucifer smiled wide. "And what is that?"

"Jane."

"Then have faith and crush the seal, little brother. Either way, you are falling into the abyss. Try to escape; he will not let you until the battle is underway. But do not tell David about the seal you put around her neck. You must let the end unfold. Perhaps let her think you are coming. Give her some hope. Just in case."

Death stared at Lucifer for a long time before looking up. "Will I see the moon again?"

"At The End. Just as you should. Trust in Father. I realize you only felt Him through her, but you are whole now and have witnessed His miracles. You have felt what you did not think possible because, for once, your vessel held all of your soul and heart. Was that not only possible because a former general convinced you to separate yourself from her?"

Death looked up but stayed silent.

"You have prayed to Father so much since the other half of your soul awoke. Listen to what He tells you."

"He said to trust the light. You gave it to Jane."

"Not all." Lucifer chuckled before sighing. "She is to die by wounds below her heart and to the side and a slit throat. It will hurt, but only for a moment."

A tear fell from Death's eye.

Lucifer smiled. "Yes, little brother. I ensured you and your bond were removed before a cursed blade was stabbed through you. I believe Father is testing my love for my brother before he forgives me. Now I think He is testing your faith in Him because I did not expect you to put your bond and heart around her neck. Do you understand now?"

"Yes." Death sounded so broken. "Please don't betray me, brother."

"I never wanted to. I simply misunderstood and became lost in my grief when I thought she was gone." Lucifer touched Death's temple, making Death's eyes turn silver for a mere few seconds. He removed his hand and patted Death's cheek when the silver faded. "See? As I said, take better care of your heart. Do you know why her soul dances but Jane does not?"

"Yes. She wants to dance, but the crash her family died in happened when they were taking her to ballet lessons. She never wanted to dance again."

Lucifer closed his eyes, imagining the gold flame twirling. "Maybe Jane will dance for us."

Death nodded. "Thank you, brother."

"You are welcome, little brother."

The world spun, and when it settled, she was in her kids' room. They were the same age they were now, and Lucifer sat between them on one of their beds.

She stopped crying, covering her mouth as Lucifer caressed Nathan's head. "I will be with her just as you have always seen me when she's hurting. It will be okay. Try not to be sad. Be strong for her."

Natalie began to cry, and Lucifer grabbed her hand, caressing her fingers with his thumb.

"Death?" Nathan asked.

Lucifer nodded. "Do not fear him. I want you to remind him of your mother in your own ways and show no fear."

"Blood?" Nathan glanced at Lucifer.

"Yes." Lucifer smiled at him. "You remembered."

Nathan shrugged. "I don't forget."

Lucifer kissed both of them on the head. "She's coming to tell you goodbye. Be brave. I will see you at the end."

"Okay," they whispered, both sniffling.

The room vanished, and the chamber of souls appeared again. Lucifer smiled at her as he removed his hand.

"I don't—" Her mouth opened and closed a few times. "How long have you been planning all this?"

"For some time." He lifted her hand and kissed the mark on her wrist. "But I was not always true. Not until our conversation in the cave." He wiped the blood from her cheek. "It is better if you see."

The room rippled, and she saw Lucifer standing in a cemetery. She knew the graveyard—it was the one she had intended to meet Lucifer at when she was still in Texas.

A white light flashed behind him, and the angel Gabriel stood there.

Lucifer sighed. "I am busy."

Gabriel scanned his back before staring off into the distance. "There is no need to go to her. Death is returning. It is time."

"Now?"

Gabriel placed a hand on Lucifer's shoulder. "Yes, brother."

They were surrounded by white light, and when it faded, she was staring at Lucifer standing before the smoky shadows in the room of souls.

"Father." Lucifer lowered his head.

"Lucifer, you know why I have allowed you here."

Luc nodded. "The gold soul. I have seen her."

"Then you have done as you promised the Accuser and unleashed darkness upon her?"

706

"Yes, Father."

"Your brother has prayed—he desires to understand his bond to her. I have made it so the Accuser tells him. If he knows Jane is his soul mate before it is time, he will be foolish in his quest to save her. You know he is not able to free her. You have been given that right, and he will never be able to inflict the horrors needed to break her."

"Yes, I know. It is as you said. I will break her for him. I will free her."

God chuckled. "I know you plan to do more than that, Lucifer. You still desire vengeance for the betrayal you believe I have committed against you."

Lucifer stared at the floor in silence.

"I will allow you a chance to choose your path."

Finally, Lucifer looked up, a twisted snarl on his lips. "You gave her to him. I gave my Grace, and you let her go. Now she waits to be drowned in darkness once again."

"Lucifer, do you remember the gold soul you fell in love with—how I told you she was only half?"

The evil look on Lucifer's face weakened. "You gave him half."

"Yes, Lucifer. Jane is the Beginning—the beginning is never meant to be whole until it ends. I split her well before I breathed life into your flame. The half the Accuser offered you—the weapon—had already chosen darkness. The half you fell in love with—that you promised to protect—has not left this room." God's shadow moved, revealing a sleeping gold flame in her crystal jar. "You did not see because you already believed I betrayed you—because you wanted her when I told you she was not yours."

"Why did you not tell me?" Lucifer didn't look away from her soul.

"You never asked, Lucifer. And you had already begun your path to darkness. You had to earn the chance to learn the truth. There is always a consequence when you choose Darkness. Simply because you are my favorite does not mean you are free to do as you like."

Lucifer clutched his heart. "You gave the Accuser the half you knew would choose the dark path—made it so I would have control over her."

"I made it so you would have the chance to prove your love. Choose your path once again. He offers a weapon that will destroy my kingdom and surround all in Darkness—swallow the gold flame. I offer the chance for you to guard her and your brother. Your Grace will return when you choose to free her and return her to him."

"But why must I destroy her?"

"Because she agreed to suffer as she awaits her mate. She made her choice. Painful it has been, but she only became the lovely flame you fell for because she never gave up on her choices. Even as a flame, she allowed darkness to surround her, and she danced to light the way. Now she has shown you light because yours became dark. Make your choice. For she must drown in the darkest of nights before she may shine her brightest."

"The Light Bringer."

"Yes, Lucifer. My brightest star. My Light. She is many things. You tainted the light I gave you because of her—she will clean and return it. You need only choose her when she needs you to. And shine when she calls you."

"How will she restore my light?"

"Love. Her love and faith. Your brothers will help her—as you will help them. All of you will love and restore faith that has been lost. All of you will cement faith and bonds that are not there."

"How will she possibly love me after what I must do?"

There was a low laugh. "Because I made her. She will forgive you."

Lucifer shook his head. "That is not possible."

"Have you doubted your redemption all this time?"

Lucifer stayed quiet again.

"The choice is yours, Luc."

Lucifer jerked his head up.

"Betray me if you wish. Just do one thing first—see if you can earn her smile and kiss. Experience what I allow only her to give you. Then choose again. If you choose her, I will give you further instruction."

"Yes, Father."

"Now go."

Gabriel placed a hand on his shoulder, but God spoke again.

"And, Lucifer, trust Thanatos. He was told to betray you. Only then would he see the truth and his next instructions on what must be done."

"The truth?"

"His king's queen." God chuckled. "Worry not, the King Reaper will not crown her until it is time."

"You told Thanatos?"

"Of course. He did not fall and become your right hand for nothing. Let him instruct you, but be warned—she is already his queen because of Death. He will be angry if you betray his king and Me."

"You would have him reap me?"

"He is a reaper."

Lucifer sighed, nodding. "I will not betray you or my brother."

"No, Lucifer, you will. I will see you after you make your choice."

The room spun, and she saw Lucifer kneeling before God's shadow.

"Let me show you something, Lucifer."

Lucifer's eyes glazed over with gold light, and she suddenly saw the Devil in his black suit. Only white was around him, but his presence was still drowned in darkness.

"I told you he would be tempted," said the Devil. "It took less effort than I anticipated."

"He will ask for forgiveness," said God. "I will grant it when he does."

The Devil's eyes flashed. "I have already seen what will become of him —he will fall. Those he takes with him will create horrors unlike any that have ever existed. Their creations will ravage the world you have made, and the warriors you send to protect your creations will battle for centuries. But it will not be his fault entirely. Your greatest warrior will cause Lucifer to create a dark monster of his own. One that will battle your champion endlessly because your champion will have advantages that Lucifer's will not. Still, your favorite son will be responsible for billions of lost souls. You cannot forgive him."

God stayed quiet for a long moment. "You wish to have a destroyer of your own making?"

"It is fair."

"Very well. I have agreed to always keep balance. However, I still wish to grant my son forgiveness when he asks."

The man in black looked thoughtful. "I will offer Lucifer a chance to hold power over the weapon I create. Then we will see if he is worthy of entering your great kingdom again. If he accepts my offer and takes control of the one I make for him, he will be granted the ruling of Hell as High King. He will hold the one you've granted me access to corrupt at his side, and they will destroy your warriors. If he refuses, he is worthy of forgiveness. But I will dim your brightest star. His Light will be forever mine."

"We will see," God said. "You will require a soul."

"Yes, you know I do not have that power. I will use the soul you provide to birth the most deadly of demons. We will give it the power to destroy both light and dark."

"You do not think my son will refuse your gift?"

"He is arrogant and hungry for power—he will jump at the chance to destroy your heroes."

"There is little reason for me to allow such a terrible creation."

"It tests your son. Should he refuse it, he will be worthy. I will make it so he is the only one who can wield or restrain my demon child. If you doubt him, decline."

"I do not doubt him. I have faith that when he falls, he will find his way home and become Light again." A red jar appeared on the white floor before the Devil. "I have given you half of a rare soul. A gold flame."

"Gold?" The Devil inspected the jar.

"Yes. The half you hold chose to wait in darkness. The half I have kept has less heat to her flame, but she chose to serve."

"How is this half going to function? A vessel requires a full soul."

"I will rejoin them. You may test your half against mine after the vessel is born. The stronger will wield the vessel."

"It is female?"

"Yes. She will be able to destroy unlike any other."

The Devil smiled. "A daughter. I request the ability to unleash my minions on your daughter—allow them to inflict whatever horror they wish as they are drawn to the vessel without understanding a monster waits within. I also request your daughter have no Guardian of Light."

"You wish to ensure my daughter is broken?"

"Yes. It is only fair if you choose the vessel and soul. How will I stand a chance if they are guarded against the terror that will free my child?"

"I see your point and accept. Lucifer will be her guardian."

The image faded, and the room of souls appeared as it was—Lucifer was kneeling.

He looked up at God's figure. "I am her guardian?"

"Yes. Well, you and Death. Should you return to Light, he will become her new guardian. After all, he is neutral and not an angel of Light."

"And David?"

"Ah, my prince. What do you wish to know of him?"

"Why you have always referred to him as a prince."

God chuckled. "Is it not obvious?"

Lucifer's gaze slid to a jar containing a roaring sapphire flame. "You made him stronger than the others. He is your favorite son amongst the immortals. That does not explain why he is called the prince in Heaven."

"I have many sons. Do you have any other questions?"

"Why Jane?"

"From the beginning, I knew I would need a special soul. One to Begin. One that could be ripped in two—that would be loved by a fallen son— could not be gifted with a guardian of my light. A soul that would be hunted but could escape death. Death is not an angel of the Light, nor are you. I needed a soul that would stand up to darkness because it would always be half of her. She had to withstand all the time in the dark, alone, to prepare for her darker side. I needed a soul who would conquer all light and dark."

"She is greater than that."

"Yes, I know. She has only begun. When you find a soul that burns even yours, my bright star, confine Death to the abyss. Then look at the Moon. When she is covered in blood and darkness, the End will begin. He will escape and unleash his destruction, and you will bring his moon to me.

"Then, she will be ready. The Light Bringer will summon Light and gift it unto you. Because only then will you see the extent of my love—through her. The terms will be that you embrace your eternal sentence once and for all. Accept she was not for you but yours to love, cherish, and let go. Protect her until she goes home."

Lucifer looked down at the ground before he closed his eyes. Jane could see his thoughts as he imagined her tear-stained face after watching her darker half kill Lancelot's family and how her eyes shifted from darkness to dying hazel. "I will accept my sentence and stay in her place."

"Then you are ready. I will forgive you when you return with her. And I will tell you when it is time to let go."

Lucifer jerked his head up. "I will have more time with her?"

God chuckled. "She will dream for you and give you an eternity with her when she dreams. After all, you already consider her your eternity; she is more than a girl with lovely eyes—more than a gold flame. She is capable of many wonders."

"How do I let her go if I have her for an eternity?"

"You will because I made it so. Because she is Jane."

The world shimmered, and she stood in the room of souls across from Lucifer.

He smiled at her, caressing her cheek.

God chuckled. "Jane, take my sons with you, for they are yours to keep. When you dream, dance together."

Jane nodded, turning to Lucifer, her heart aching for him. "Luc."

"Do not look at me like I am one of your men." He glanced at all the souls still vanishing from their jars.

"It is time, Lucifer," God said. "Do you still accept our agreement?"

Lucifer stared into her eyes. "Yes, Father. As before, I will await your call."

"I always knew you would. Farewell, daughter. Never forget, I am with you, always." Light slid around them, warming them both. Tears gathered in Lucifer's eyes, but he smiled at her. "You are forgiven . . . my son. Farewell, my beloved Morning Star. Shine your brightest tonight. When you see gold and emerald in your path, pause to witness the beginning of your eternity. Then you will know. For I have made it so."

The light vanished, and so did the smoke. It was just Jane and Lucifer in the room of souls.

Azrael appeared, handing Lucifer the leaf and wilted flower. "As your deal with the Accuser allowed—her fate is in your hands."

Lucifer took it, letting it vanish before she could look at it. "A moment longer, Azrael."

The angel nodded, vanishing.

"It is time to go." Lucifer slid his thumb over her lips. "Smile for me, my queen."

She did, letting out a cry when she put her hand over his heart. "I love you."

"And that is all I need for eternity." He leaned down, kissing the corner of her mouth. "And this smile."

She clutched his shirt. "What's going to happen?"

"What must be done." He tilted her face up. "Forgive me one day."

"I already have," she cried, touching his smile.

"Thank you, Jane." He held the hand she'd placed over his heart. "This will always be yours. No other. You are my one queen."

"Yes, your queen. For eternity."

"We must go." He pulled her closer, giving her hand that little squeeze of comfort she always desired. "One more smile."

She smiled the smile she only gave him.

He took it in silently. "Beautiful. My eternity." He then lowered his lips to hers. "My queen." He gave her a sweeter kiss than she ever imagined he could. Her back began to burn as what felt like a circular shape and a star were carved into her skin. Light filled her vision as her wounds began to sizzle. She cried, clutching him, a pounding in her chest speeding until seeming to stop. Her mouth opened, and nearly all the air left her lungs with the burning light.

She felt her body lift and caught a glimpse of his glowing white eyes as he carried her. It was a hall, but not the white one. There was so much noise, but she could only stare up at him. "Luc."

His gaze fell to hers, revealing gold eyes before they returned to white light. "It is time to dream, my queen." He laid her down on something soft, smoothing her hair back before lifting her wrist to his lips. He smiled at the mark before kissing it.

Her entire body hurt. Even the light from the room hurt. It was so bright she could barely stand it. Her gaze fell to his hair, and she hoped she smiled. "I like the gray color."

He leaned over her. "I know you do."

"Does she still burn you?"

He kissed the corner of her mouth. "Always, my queen."

She tried to reach for him, but her arm felt too heavy. "It wasn't her fault."

His expression went unchanged, but he held her hand. Jane pulled on it as hard as she could, only able to lift his hand to her lips because he assisted her.

"What are you doing, Jane?"

She felt tears falling down her cheeks. "Saving you from her fire." She turned his arm and kissed his markings. They were weak, sloppy kisses, but she pressed the longest to the star next to the moon. "I will find a way to save you and stop the fire."

He breathed out, closing his eyes for a moment. "Sleep, Jane. Build our kingdom. I must insist—no vampire princes."

"Yes, my king." She chuckled, her eyes fluttering shut as blood oozed down the sides of her body and throat. "Perhaps only sexy bad boys, wolves, and fairy tales. You did kill my dearest wolf."

"How did I already know you would say that?" He pressed his hand to her neck as the other touched her temple. "Rest now. I will find you, and we will complete our kingdom together."

"My wish?"

"I haven't forgotten. Sleep, my queen."

A pair of cold lips touched hers.

Then light . . . Just light.

47

THE LIGHT BRINGER

David tightened his hold on the reins, his heart beating faster. King burst through the smoke, landing and not stopping as he ran toward the village gate. "Hurry, King. If Death gets there, he'll kill them."

King neighed loudly, coming to an abrupt stop as Sorrow blocked his path.

David stared into Sorrow's glowing eyes, knowing the Pale Horse was no longer the horse that loved Jane. "Stop him."

King's horn began to glow, and David jumped, rushing past Sorrow as King charged him. He could only hear his heavy breaths as he slid on the bloody gravel, falling on his side, his heart filled with horror from the scene unfolding before him.

"No." David pushed himself up once he saw his children and Adam kneeling before Death.

Death raised his scythe, his wings unfolding as Adam tightened his hold on the kids, pulling their heads below him so he would be the first to get cut.

A blinding white light stunned David enough to make him freeze. He couldn't see anything. He couldn't hear either. Then, finally, a green glow lit, and he turned toward it. "Death, leave them. Please."

The bright light faded, and Lucifer stood in full armor, holding two pieces of paper and Jane's necklace.

David ran at him, panicking because of his slow speed.

"Little brother," Lucifer said.

Death halted all movement.

"I have something of yours," Lucifer said.

Death turned, freezing, when Lucifer held up the broken necklace as the papers in his hand lit fire. David took the chance to run to his children. He grabbed Nathan by the shirt as he picked up Natalie, pulling all of them back.

"No." Nathan fought him. "Mama is with him. He's Death's brother."

"The man in white," Natalie whispered, hugging David's neck like she used to as a little girl.

Lucifer dropped the papers to the ground, then produced a leaf and torn flower bud.

Death turned, fully facing Lucifer. He tilted his head but showed no emotional sign that he was affected.

"Well done, little brother." Lucifer dropped the leaf into the fire. "Take better care of your heart this time. She holds all of mine as well."

The leaf and flower were engulfed in flames.

Lucifer held his arm over them, summoning a sword like Jane's, and he slit his wrist. He shook his arm, forcing blood to fall into the flames. "When Darkness surrounds all, think of me—for I am Lucifer, His brightest star—Light. I am yours to bring, Light Bringer. Rise, my queen."

The final drop of blood fell, and gold light exploded from the flames, spinning into a fiery inferno.

David hugged his children as tears gathered in his eyes, and Death's mask vanished upon seeing a fiery female silhouette spinning before she stopped. Completely engulfed in gold flames, the figure smiled at Death before turning her head to David and the children. She bowed, just like Jane had done to Lance's family, and David knew he was staring at Jane's soul.

"For you, my queen." Lucifer held the broken necklace out. "You are free of my light. Your other half is ready to take you to the End."

She took the necklace from him, the dull thread igniting with gold light as soon as she touched it. She smiled brighter, caressing Lucifer's cheek, though the flames did not burn him.

Surrounded by a halo of golden and white light, Lucifer smiled at her. "Jane's wish has been granted."

She nodded, lowering her hand, only to hold her necklace up to Death. "We wished for our bond to be restored. We are ready for you, my love. We are ready for The End."

Death touched the flames around her, not burned as he cupped her fiery cheeks. "My Moon."

David looked up at the night sky. The eclipse was over, and the moon was filling with light.

"My Death." She handed him the necklace. "Take me home."

As soon as Death touched the pendant, it was repaired as if it had never been broken. He put it around her neck before cupping her cheeks again. Her flame was weakening.

"Take from me, Sweet Jane. For I am Death, the End of your Beginning. Your soul mate." He kissed her, erupting in green flames. His soul surrounded him, their flames spiraling.

David smiled sadly, watching as their figures became a blur, and only a gold sphere with an emerald inferno roaring around it remained.

"The green's back," Natalie said. "Like Mama's eyes."

David nodded, watching them spinning faster and faster as the three horsemen appeared around them.

Lucifer turned to him. "Take them below. All not of divine blood in my path will perish. The Light Bringer has called forth Light. I have come."

The emerald and gold flame shot into the sky, vanishing in a crack of thunder.

A reverberating voice shook the sky. "Thus ends The Beginning."

"Take them, Prince." Lucifer's body began to glow, white light constantly shifting to gold.

Adam pulled David toward the building. "I'm pretty sure that bastard is going to blow up the world."

David watched as other angels landed around them, bowing their heads as the light from Lucifer became too bright to stare at.

"Hurry." Adam shoved David forward, pushing him toward the bunker.

David took one last look as all light vanished. Lucifer looked at him before roaring and lighting up even brighter as fiery golden wings unfolded from his back.

"Fuck!" Adam shoved David down.

Then there was white.

Just white.

"David." The voice echoed amongst the screams.

"Daddy," Natalie screamed. "It's Mama."

"Wake up, David." It was Dagonet's voice. "It's time to wake."

David opened his eyes, the blurry view around him so chaotic with the rushing bodies and shaking ceiling.

Adam smacked his cheek. "Wake your ass up. Someone said a man in white appeared, carrying a body to the infirmary. They said it was Jane."

David pushed himself up, grabbing Nathan's and Natalie's hands. "Why was I on the floor?"

"The light hit you like a damn bolt of lightning." Adam shoved hysteric people out of their way. "I thought you were dead, but you were breathing, and your body was surrounded in blue flames. Like Jane's would do."

David touched his chest, looking down. He still felt weak. "Where's Dagonet?"

"Who?" Adam pulled a door open to the hall that led to the infirmary.

The ceiling shook as demonic roars rang out above them.

Adam looked up. "I think he's destroying the world. Or maybe all the bad in it."

David walked faster, but not before kissing Natalie's and Nathan's heads. "It's going to be okay."

"Where'd Mama go?" Natalie asked, sobbing. "That was her."

"Just part of her." David's eyes stung. "She just went home. I'm with you. We're together. That's what she wanted."

"The door won't open." Adam pressed his face against the window. "I can't see anything. They were certain it was Jane."

David let go of the kids and tried the door, but it was locked.

"Kick it down." Adam stepped back.

David looked down. "I'm weak."

"What?" Adam felt his head. "Did you forget you're a badass vampire?"

"He's been hit in the head by two archangels today." Dagonet walked toward him. "One is Fallen, but he has been granted Light. And he's a mortal now."

"Dagonet." David pointed to the door. "Is Jane in there?"

"Her body is." Dagonet opened the door calmly and entered. "Do not approach her. For her End has come."

David shoved past him, but a large angel in gray suddenly forced him to his knees. The children and Adam stopped.

"It is too late." The angel turned, walking toward the bloody body on a bed.

"Jane," David whispered, trying to stand but unable to move.

"Mama," Natalie cried.

717

The angel leaned over Jane. David kept trying to go to her. He hadn't even kissed her one last time. He wanted to say goodbye to this part of her, too. Jane's heart was there. His Jane. She was more than a beautiful soul.

Jane coughed, her lips taking weak gasps of breath as she stared up at nothing.

David's eyes widened. "Baby?"

Dagonet patted his shoulder. "Watch."

That's all he could do. He cried, seeing her chest weakly rise up and down. She was taking frantic but weak gasps of air.

"Do you remember your wish, Jane?" the angel asked.

"Bond . . . Death."

David cried silently, wishing to run to her or hug his children. They did not cry, though. They were at peace with seeing her in the bloody mess he had allowed.

Fire roared within him, and he finally saw his soul. It was as if he'd been awoken and was a raging inferno. He didn't know that she was right there. But then David remembered Death had taken Jane's soul with him. This was just her body and mind. Her heart. No soul.

His soul roared as blue fire filled David's sight. Power David had never felt before filled his entire being. Jane wasn't dead. She was dying, but Death had reaped her soul anyway.

"No," David roared, breaking the hold on whatever had kept him from moving, and he ran toward Jane.

The angel beside her kneeled. "My prince."

David growled, reaching for Jane's face but stopping as he looked into her dull eyes. They were black.

"My prince," the angel said, not looking up. "Her vessel is empty."

She kept gasping, the blood from her wound pumping out slowly.

He instinctively put his hand over it, channeling his light to cauterize the skin and tissue.

She didn't scream as he burned her. Her body jerked once, her mouth opening and closing repeatedly until a faint whisper finally left her lips. "Dark . . . Darkness has returned."

The angel in gray raised his head. "She speaks of the other half of her soul —the one imprisoned within Lucifer. The Father of Darkness is attempting to free her. He still has the jar he once held her in. If he gets her, he can supplement her soul with darkness and return her to Jane's empty vessel."

David looked at Jane's face, his soul surging with fire but refusing to press down on her. He pulled his hand away, staring at the wound. It sizzled, but the constant pumping of blood had stopped.

He moved his hand to her neck, his soul growling at the sight. How was she even talking?

"David," she whispered, gurgling and spilling blood from her mouth.

He stopped burning her throat and turned her head, clearing her mouth. He and his soul spoke as one, "I'm here, my love."

"Save him. Them." She took frantic breaths, not focusing on him, her head twitching to the side again and again.

"She wishes to free Lucifer from Darkness. From the daughter he has created from her soul." The angel bowed his head. "I will not stop you, my prince."

David didn't understand why the angel was referring to him that way. He rolled Jane onto her back and held his hand to her neck, ready to burn the cut.

"Coming," she gasped. "He doesn't know."

"Doesn't know what?" David turned her to look at him, but her eyes had turned white. "Who's coming?"

"Lucifer released Jane's darker soul so he could destroy it," said the angel in gray.

"He doesn't know her vessel remains empty." Dagonet appeared beside him. "The Father of Darkness has his daughter now. Light opposes Dark, but both must exist. You must stop Darkness before he returns Jane's dark soul." He held up the sword. "There is one true Son of God, and Father has kept him at his side this night. Prince David, beloved Second Son of God, Warrior of Our Father, Flame He hath lit nearest His, I bestow upon thee, His Retribution."

David stared at the sword, and his heart roared when he saw that the gem in the hilt matched the ring he had given Jane.

"The dark flame is still half of Jane, David. One that was offered and then accepted Darkness as her father. But Jane . . ."

David didn't need to hear anymore. He turned to Jane, cupping her cheeks as she took short, weak breaths. "Hang on, baby. I'll come back. I swear. Just hold on. I'll find Death."

"Death. My Death."

David kissed her, nodding. "I'll find him."

"Home. Take me home."

He kissed her again before burning her throat. He couldn't bear to watch the pain he'd caused, so he turned his head. His soul wasn't having it. He roared, waiting for him to finish sealing her flesh.

As soon as David was done, he closed his eyes and spoke to his soul. "Fight with me. Should I fall, leave my body and save our girls."

His soul snarled, engulfing him with flames once more. He barely caught sight of his children as they smiled at him before blue.

Just blue.

"Where the fuck is David?" Sin yelled, dragging Arthur's body behind some boulders.

Nyctimus looked away from the battle unfolding in the sky. A black mass swirled, darting violently around a white light. He could hear swords and see the occasional gleam from steel, but he couldn't tell who was winning.

"Nyc?" Sin shouted.

Nyctimus shook his head. "He went to the children."

Sin stared at him, furious. "He left?"

Flashes of white light filled his vision.

"Calm yourself."

"Lance?" Nyctimus frowned. "I thought you guys got zapped up."

"This fool's a fucking zombie," Sin said, walking over. "I know Jane adores you, but you've got to die again . . . whatever the fuck you are."

Lancelot smirked before putting a finger on Sin's forehead. "Sleep."

Sin fell to the ground.

"I could have just killed him," said a man Nyctimus had only seen when he was with David. He wore a reaper's hood but looked like a mortal man.

"He hit on your wife all the time—tried to make her sin with him and his apples. I was doing him a favor by removing the temptation so you wouldn't kill him." Lancelot gestured to the man. "This is Jason, Jane's husband—the first one. Fucker works for Death now. Can you believe it? He didn't want to leave her."

Nyctimus ran to help one of his men carry Bedivere's body. "I thought Death killed all his reapers. They've been falling out of the sky for an hour."

"I was told to stay with Sir Lancelot." Jason glared at Lance. "I've been following this piece of shit since Death showed up to reap me. Again." He pulled out a ring that hung around his neck. "He stopped when he saw Jane's ring." He kissed it and let it go. "My forever."

Lancelot held up his hands in surrender. "It's not like I was grabbing her ass like David was undoubtedly doing when you were still married. And, technically, she was the one who raped me."

"You still fucked my wife."

"I love Jane for all she has done for me. I will fight in her name until I am no longer able to. Anyway, it was the bitch they're fighting for up there." Lance pointed to the battle above them. Blood was falling like rain as Heaven's angels continued to fight Hell.

"What do you mean?" Nyctimus propped Bedivere's body against Arthur's and Kay's.

"Lucifer is Light now." Lancelot searched the skies, ignoring the beams of light and darkness flying through them as angels roared. "He had Jane's dark soul. Jane was reunited with Death, which completed her soul. I think Lucifer set the bitch in him on fire when he became Light because he saw no reason for her to exist, and she called for her father." He pointed at the black mass. "The Devil. The fucker managed to get her from Lucifer. Now they're fighting. He knows Jane's body is at the bunker, but Jane is still empty."

"How the fuck do you know this?" Nyc looked up toward the blue firestorm still swirling in the distance.

Lancelot shrugged. "A voice told me."

Jason rolled his eyes.

"Shut up." Lancelot shook his head at Jason. "You said Jane's voice came out of your ring and told you to wait with me."

"Are they dead?" Lancelot squatted to touch Arthur. "They look dead."

"They're unconscious." Nyctimus checked Arthur's pulse. It was thready. "Gabriel removed their immortality and blessed them with Holy Light. A voice told me to guard them—they have one more call to answer, but they've been this way the whole time. I put their wives on the plane."

"Fucking hell." Nyctimus walked away from them, looking toward the Fallen fighting Belial in the distance. "I thought this fucker was dead."

"You won't stand a chance against him," Lancelot said. "Not even Asmodeus can beat him."

Belial roared, swinging his sword, deflecting every attack from the princes of hell. Michael and Gabriel flew over their heads, but they flew toward the battle Lucifer was in.

"They can't let Lucifer kill Darkness. I don't know if he even can,"

Lancelot said. "They have to hold him for Abaddon. Otherwise, this world will cease to exist."

Belial threw Beelzebub at Astaroth, sending them flying through the lake of fire. Then he turned, stabbing his sword into Asmodeus' thigh before slicing off one of his wings.

Jason pulled his hood down as a scythe formed in his hand. "I'll give it a shot."

Black wings unfolded from Jason's back, and he launched himself into the air.

Lancelot yelled up at him before he could go. "Jason, he's the one who filled you with worthlessness, then influenced you to take it out on Jane. He made you hate her and tried to get you to beat her, but your love for her kept you from doing more. You only slipped once." Lancelot smiled. "And you know that's why you refused Paradise. Go kick his ass for her, boy."

Jason didn't say anything. Instead, he turned, flying like a rocket and tackling Belial as he prepared to strike Asmodeus down.

"Did he really do that to him?" Nyctimus watched Belial stand, but Jason was on him.

"He did." Lancelot smiled as Jason managed to cut one of Belial's hands off. "Jane and Jason might not have been soul mates, but he was meant to father her children. And he really fucking loved her. He just forgot."

Jason roared, swinging with the skill of Death as he tore one of Belial's wings off with his bare hands.

"Atta boy, Jason." Lancelot chuckled. "I think Death gave him some extra perks when he pulled his soul. He fights like him."

Another swing, another wing gone. Jason pulled Belial's' sword from his hand and stabbed it through Belial's chest before holding out his scythe. He told the demon something, but Belial laughed.

Jason roared, slicing his scythe across Belial's stomach before beheading him.

Nyctimus was about to cheer, but he froze upon seeing a blue blur racing through the trees, heading right for Jason.

"Ah, shit." Lancelot started to run to Jason, but a separate blur flew into Jason, knocking him out of the path of blue fire.

"David," Nyctimus whispered, watching as the blue fire did not stop to worry about Jason, who Thanatos was helping up. "What the fuck?"

"Yeah, Than isn't bad." Lance nodded at the blue fire that was David. "But he's as bad as you can get if his baby is hurt."

Nyctimus watched in amazement as David's silhouette formed for a mere second before he cut through demon after demon—monster after monster. Lucifer had been frying everything in white light earlier, but now it seemed they'd been called back.

"Will we be able to stop David?" Nyctimus watched his friend swing a sword that cut through everything it touched while engulfing everything in a fire so hot that it melted rock.

"No." Lancelot looked up. "But I think help has arrived."

Nyctimus panicked when the blue firestorm settled overhead. "Death."

The roar of the firestorm brought Nyctimus to his knees. He covered his ears, squinting as emerald and gold slammed into the ground. Everything stopped as all eyes fell on the dust ball floating up before it was blown away with a single flap of giant wings.

"Oh, shit." Nyctimus could barely look at them.

"Indeed."

Death was no longer in Pale Horseman form, but emerald flames pulsated around him, and in his hand, a small gold flame.

David's figure stopped moving, and he snarled, watching Death kiss the little flame before putting it on the ground. It grew as soon as he did, forming a female silhouette, but she was only flames.

"It's Jane." Nyctimus blinked. "Her soul."

David rushed to her, his flames darker and surrounding him. He cupped her cheeks, kissing her as she appeared to whisper to him.

David looked up at the battle above before kissing again. Death then nodded to David and lifted Jane's soul. She shrank in size, fitting in his palm, just as David aimed a beam of light at the dark mass.

A roar shook the air and darkened the sky. Lucifer appeared beside Death, yelling at him. Death watched the black mass even when Michael and Gabriel landed behind him.

David stopped firing his light and backed up, putting himself between the black cloud rushing toward the ground and Jane's soul.

"You think I can be stopped?" The Devil walked out of the darkness. He held up a jar with another gold flame. "I just need her tiny vessel, and my daughter is free."

"You're not getting her vessel," David said, breathing heavily.

Death bent, placing the gold flame on the ground. She grew in size once more. She didn't address the Devil, but she did turn to Lucifer, caressing his face as she seemed to speak, though Nyctimus heard nothing. Lucifer did and didn't look happy, but he sighed and nodded. She smiled before patting David's back and walking away in the opposite direction.

The Devil shot black smoke at her. Lancelot and Thanatos had to hold Jason still to keep him from running to her.

Just when it reached Jane, she flared up, spinning into a whirlwind of gold fire, protecting herself. The Devil repeatedly shot at her until David and Lucifer aimed their beams at him. Michael and Gabriel did the same, suppressing Darkness in their light as Jane's soul scanned the dead bodies. She waved Death to come closer. He vanished and reappeared beside her. Whatever she communicated to him had him nodding before he picked up the bodies she pointed out. Then he began tossing them around the battle-field in a wide arc.

"We need to put the knights in the circle he's making," Thanatos said. "Hurry."

Nyctimus didn't question him. He grabbed Gareth's body, throwing him out, momentarily forgetting they were mortal now. "Fuck."

Lancelot chuckled. "It's only Gareth. He's not that smart."

Nyctimus was more careful but watched as the occasional black flame beam shot toward Jane. She flared up and moved. Then she started moving more gracefully. Her flames grew in strength the more she moved. She was dancing.

She started holding her arms out, pushing up on her toes as she performed turns like a ballerina across the bloody battlefield, occasionally stopping, bending just as gracefully. It was a complete contrast to the chaos happening around her.

The fire from the angels and David sounded like a spaceship preparing to blast off, but Jane's little soul stayed calm. Every time the Devil sent a black blast at her, she performed an elegant maneuver to get out of the way. Sometimes Death snarled and threw his own blasts until Jane's soul distracted him, dancing across his path and kissing him before pointing out more bodies.

"Is she about to perform a spell?" Nyctinus asked, watching Jane's soul stare down at a body. Thor.

"Not a spell," Thanatos said. "Watch."

Jane's soul leaned down to Thor. He'd been bitten in half but managed to get a fatal strike to end the serpent Jörmungandr. She caressed his cheek as a blue orb floated down from the storm.

Jane's soul smiled at the orb and then began to dance again. Her move-ments reminded Nyctimus of the magical way ballerinas danced. She circled him as Thor's soul formed his human shape. He seemed to notice his destroyed body, then Jane. She never stopped dancing. There seemed to be more to the dancing—she was communicating with Thor's soul. He watched her twirl and bow, and Thor's soul either nodded or shook his head.

Finally, he kneeled before his body, and Jane held her hand out, sending beams of gold fire toward him and his body.

Death walked closer, glancing at the body on fire before kissing her, sending a surge of green fire down her throat. Then she spun again, flames building until she blasted Thor's body.

As soon as she stopped, her attack fading, Thor sat upright. He'd been completely healed.

"Holy fuck." Nyctimus dropped Gawain. "Fuck." He picked him up again, watching Jane's little flame dance happily around Thor as he smiled, bowing his head to her before she danced away. Once again, she pointed out bodies for Death. Thor rubbed his head, his gaze on the fire battle and the black fire still shooting at Jane. And still, she danced out of its path, causing Darkness to roar.

"She's beautiful," Jason whispered.

Nyctimus noticed the reaper tear up before leaning down for one of the other knights. "She's been happy with him," he told Jason. "Missed the big guy, but David's been good to her."

"I know." Jason didn't look at him as they placed Lamorak beside his brother.

She finally came close to them, dancing in the same pretty turns until she spotted Jason. Her fiery smile only appeared heartbroken for a moment, and then she twirled in circles around her ex. When she stopped, she touched the ring around Jason's neck and the marks of a reaper tattooed on his forearms. They glowed in gold until she removed her hand. She reached for her neck, pulled out something, and held it up to him. A ring.

"My forever." Jason touched her face. "I love you too, baby doll. I'm sorry I forgot how much you loved it when I called you my baby doll. I'll never stop. Never again, my Janie."

She smiled peacefully at the term of endearment and variation of her name before tilting her face toward his palm, then quickly spun away—once again, picking out bodies.

Lancelot patted the reaper's back. "You're a good guy, Jason. She wouldn't smile at you like that if she didn't love you."

Jane's soul finally came to a stop behind Lucifer. He handed her something, and she pulled it inside herself before it was clear what it was.

"You can't be free," the Devil said, his voice echoing through the sky. "One way or another, my daughter will return to her vessel. You will burn, little queen."

Jane's soul ignored him and flitted over to David. She kissed his back sweetly before nodding to the other angels. When she spotted Asmodeus, she rushed to him, flames flickering wildly.

The demon king laughed, trying to shoo her, but she kissed his cheek before dancing around him, surrounding him in light until he stood in the form of a man.

He glared at her. "My queen, I thought you liked my wings."

She seemed to giggle, her flame sparking when Death called for her. She bowed to Asmodeus, and he returned the gesture.

"My love," Death said, calling her again.

She danced to him, twirling around him until he smiled. He bent, grabbing a handful of dirt, rocks, and a canteen from one of the bodies.

She kept dancing around him as he made a motion around the dirt. It floated in no particular form, but the more Jane danced, the more the dirt and rocks began to swirl, making an orb. Death poured the water, and it mixed with the swirling sphere. Then he glanced over his shoulder, watching as the black mass grew in size, but turned to the orb Jane danced around. He said something, and her head bobbed as she shot gold light into the sky.

A whirlwind of blue orbs fell from the storm, spinning around Jane. She went faster and faster, sending the balls to bodies while others entered the muddy sphere above Death.

"She's resurrecting everyone," Nyctimus whispered.

"No. He won't let her bring everyone back. She's only picking those who won't reach Paradise and those who've chosen not to." Thanatos pointed to the orb. "Did your mother tell you that she's a creator deity?"

Nyctimus shook his head. "I knew she was more than what Death revealed, but not this. Is she life?"

"Not exactly. She's not making anything from nothing. But she has more pull than any other deity."

"I suppose that's bound to happen if Death is your soul mate." Thor plopped down on the ground by them. "Hey. I died."

Nyctimus couldn't hide the grin on his face. "I'm surprised as hell that you're the first soul she returned."

Thor laughed, cheering when several men and women sat up. None of them moved. They bowed their heads, facing the dancing flame. Angel after angel landed, sending their light toward Darkness until Jane seemed bothered by it. She stopped dancing, rushing to David.

He kept his soul out as he embraced her, nodding as a gold thread beamed between their hearts.

"This shit is beautiful." Thor wiped his eyes. "I once called her a wench. I called her the Devil's mistress because of Lucifer, and he's not so bad. He's not even the Devil. That evil fucker loves her."

Nyctimus laughed when a pair of pants was thrown at him.

"You let him knock me out?" Sin pulled on his pair. "Put some fucking pants on. We're in the presence of God's first soul, and she saw your dick."

Nyctimus rolled his eyes but put the pants on. "Does this mean Jane will be okay?"

Jason answered. "If they get there in time. Her heart still slows. Whatever she decides, she needs to do it soon."

Jane's soul kissed David's before taking Lucifer's hand. She pulled him, though he kept pulsating with white light.

When she let go of his hand, he cupped her cheeks and whispered to her.

"He doesn't want her to do what she has asked." Thanatos sighed.

Finally, Lucifer nodded to her. He glanced at the black cloud being bombarded with light. It had grown much larger without Lucifer's light holding it down.

Jane's soul did a small bow to him. Then, extending her arms as she bent one leg, she pushed up, spinning slowly for him. Lucifer watched her do a series of twirls, but she kept her gaze on the King of Hell.

Nyctimus noticed the white beam of light tying them together at their wrists, and even though he hated the bastard, he felt warmth in his chest at seeing Jane's soul dance just for him and how much love was visible in the faint smile Lucifer gave her.

The King of Hell extended his hand, and she grabbed it, twirling for him. Lucifer let go, though, turning away and approaching Death, who stood maintaining control of the muddy sphere. Lucifer raised a hand, sending light into it.

"She's building a world from ours," Nyctimus said, watching it change more with Lucifer's light. Land masses were visible, blue oceans, but the size of a large beach ball.

"Yes, but she just yelled, 'What is that, Death? A world for ants.'" Jason laughed, wiping away a tear. "I was always annoyed with her for being silly, and I've missed it so much."

Nyctimus felt bad for the man. He loved David like a brother—Death as well—but this fucker was still in love with her, and he was only staring at her soul. "You can hear her?"

Jason nodded. "She's my wife. I never let go, and she kept some part of me alive with her."

"Someone should tell him he's dead," Sin whispered. "Well, I guess she is too. Maybe he does have a shot now."

Nyctimus elbowed Sin. "Quiet."

Jane's soul danced toward David again, touching each angel's shoulder as she passed, forcing them to stop their attacks until only David's light held the Devil.

It was then Nyctimus realized David had no intention of stopping. His friend was furious, ready to destroy, and Jane's soul tried to stop him.

"He's trying to kill him," Thanatos said, watching Lucifer and Death glance toward Jane and David. "It'll cause everything we know to implode into nothing."

The little soul tried to move around David, but he pushed her behind him, holding her against his back as blue flames swallowed Darkness.

"Should we help her?" Sin asked.

Lucifer took Death's spot, and then Death marched across the field, pushing every person she'd just resurrected out of his way until he was at Jane's side. He took her from David, lifting her, causing her to shrink. She danced in Death's palm. The angel stared at her, then David, then Darkness. David was succeeding, something that shouldn't be possible.

Death spoke, green flames igniting around him, "Brother, you must stop."

David shook his head. "She's ours. He wants to fill her with his demon. I will destroy both."

"That demon began with our flame."

David replied, his voice deeper, resonating across the field, "Not the same. Not my flame. Not your flame."

"She says you may fight him in combat," Death said with a smile. "But you'll destroy all if you kill him, brother."

David snarled but weakened his flame before extinguishing it to reveal the Devil.

"You foolish boy," the Devil roared, dusting his singed suit.

David pulled the sword from his back. "Release the half-soul you've stolen."

The Devil laughed. "Afraid of my creation, son of God?"

David glanced at Death before taking in the gold flame. Then he turned to the Devil. "I know you fear them facing each other. Let yours free. She is useless to you if Jane is stronger."

"That is not your warrior wife." The Devil chuckled. "Do you think my daughter fears a dancing fool?"

"Then let her face Jane's soul." David lowered his sword. "And you can face me in combat."

The Devil glanced around but pulled free a glass jar. The soul inside looked like Jane's, but it was dark gold. It spun into an inferno upon seeing Jane's, its color shifting from dark gold to black. "Are you sure, Death?" The Devil grinned. "You could take your little mate with you, leave these fools, and keep her all to yourself. I will not even ask you to leave her. You may simply go. Be happy with that tiny flame."

"Jane and her soul are one. They both desire to see you locked away, and I desire to see that bitch where no one can find her." Death kissed the flame in his hand before bending down. "Kick her ass, baby girl. I'll make you a J and Ds sandwich when we get home."

"That sounds delicious." Sin rubbed his stomach.

"That's a three-way with my sissy, Sin." Gareth sat up, rubbing his head. "Double D dicks, too. So keep your snake in your trousers."

Sin laughed, throwing his arm over Jason's shoulder. "Sorry for hitting on her. She's cute as hell, though. Nice ass and smile, too."

"Stop touching me." Jason summoned his scythe.

Sin jumped away, moving to Nyctimus' other side.

"Very well. I have grown bored playing this game." The Devil held the jar up. "Destroy her."

The flame bowed, waiting impatiently as the Devil gestured to Death. "Put yours out first, Horseman."

Death kissed Jane's little soul, whispering in her ear before placing her down.

Jane's soul flared into a fiery human form just as the Devil opened the jar, releasing Jane's darker half.

"Fucking hell," Sin whispered. "They're twins."

"No. Jane is a half soul." Lancelot waved toward the darker flame. "That's the bitch who killed my family."

Jane bowed her head to Darkness and the dark soul, then standing, she flipped them both off and summoned a flaming sword.

"Yes, Tex," came a loud shout. "Don't forget me, beautiful."

A shield formed as well.

"Yes!" War rode to Death's side. Pestilence and Famine stopped beside them. They bowed their heads to David and Jane but remained silent.

Jane's darker soul summoned her flamed sword.

"Catfight of the souls," Sin said. "Glad I'm wearing pants."

Jane's little soul roared, sending a sound wave that knocked down trees. Her darker soul turned red, raging into an inferno, and Jane's soul danced again. It was so fast, so elegant that the attacks barely registered. She was cutting her dark soul apart, not letting the flame get a single swing in. It only burned in chaotic bursts, sometimes hitting Jane's soul. But Jane was beating the shit out of her darker half.

"Fight, you little whore," the Devil roared, shooting darkness at her.

Jane's soul paused, watching the darker one get hit with the blast. It weakened the dark flame, and Jane's soul rushed between them, holding her shield up, protecting the darker soul.

The darker one moved fast. She stabbed right into Jane's soul's back.

David rushed Darkness, unleashing a brutal assault as Death blasted the darker soul and lifted Jane's crouched soul.

Jason stepped forward, but Thanatos held him steady. "He's got her."

Death cupped her cheek, ignoring the battle between David and Darkness, and pushed energy into her soul as she smiled up at him.

"She's strong." Thor nodded. "She can take this."

Her darker soul stood, burning red and black. No trace of gold. She extended her arm, shooting black fire. Everyone winced from the sound. It was worse than the rocket ignition sound—a mixture of fire and screams.

"What is that?" Sin yelled.

Jane's soul shoved Death away, putting herself in the path of the black fire before spinning into a fiery tornado. Gold fire swirled, with no sign of Jane's silhouette. But when a beam of gold blasted down on the dark soul, angels all around lowered their heads.

"What's wrong?" Sin yelled.

The black mass tried to shoot at Jane, but David and Death were there. They attacked, pushing the Devil farther away until gold chains suddenly wrapped around him. The silhouette of an enormous winged angel wielded those chains. Abaddon.

The Devil took human form again, bleeding and bruised. "This isn't the end. She will always be haunted by darkness. I have ensured it."

Fire spewed from Abaddon's mouth, opening a massive hole under the Devil. His roar as he fell made their ears bleed, but Abaddon shut the abyss and kneeled.

Nyctimus turned back to Jane's soul. She was destroying her darker half, not reacting to the black fire hitting her.

"What happens if Jane destroys her?" Nyctimus asked.

Thanatos shook his head. "It will destroy Jane's goodness. The angels are praying for both souls."

The destruction Jane unleashed came to a halt, and besides a pile of ash, there was no sign of the darker soul.

Jane's soul stared down at the ashes, her shoulders shaking as she appeared to cry. Then she fell to her knees and frantically began digging through the embers.

"Leave it, Jane," David said, trying to pull her away, but Death shoved him back and helped Jane search. David watched momentarily but eventually growled and kneeled to search with them.

Jane's soul suddenly flared, and she raised a piece of ember, appearing to blow on it.

"I think she's cleansing it," Sin said. "Is that possible? Would she just put her back?"

Finally, the dark soul flickered. It stayed dark in color, but it grew in Jane's soul's palm. She tried to caress the flame, but it still attacked her.

Death hugged Jane's soul, speaking into her ear as he pulled something from Jane's chest—a solid red jar.

Jane shook her head, pulling the flame close to her until David stopped her.

He grabbed the jar from Death, ripped the top off, and held it under the gold soul's hand. "You are not to be hurt by her again."

She still tried to pull the dark one closer, not reacting when it sent small blasts of fire at her chest.

"Jesus, girl." Sin rubbed his head. "I mean, she's sexy as hell, but she's too forgiving."

"Because she's Jane," Jason said, walking toward them. He snatched David's arm before he could force her to do what she didn't want to.

David yanked his arm free, snarling at Jason, but Jason didn't back down.

Jane watched them argue before whispering to the soul in her hands. "Fear not, for our Father is always with us. He never forgot you. But you must wait."

Jason kissed her head and held her as she dropped the dark flame inside.

David covered it, stomping toward Lucifer. He thrust it in Lucifer's free hand before growling, forcing himself not to attack.

Death stayed beside Jane's soul, watching over her as Jason showed no hesitation with her fire. He hugged her, smiling as she seemed to speak to him.

"This is one of the most fucked up but beautiful love pentagons I've ever seen." Sin sniffed. "She's just right for all of them."

"Are you fucking crying?" Gareth asked, a disgusted look on his face. "You know we've all slept in a room with them as they had a three-way, right? Death purposely lifted the sound barrier, so Gawain and I had to hear them."

Nyctimus covered his face as Thor roared with laughter.

He focused on his friend, smiling when David apologized to his girl, who still had herself wrapped in Jason's arms. The blue fire in David's eyes grew, but he stayed in place, allowing his wife's soul to have this moment with her first husband. But Nyctimus could see the fury in his dear friend. So did Death, and he did his part, putting a firm hand on David's shoulder and squeezing to remind him to stay in control.

"David loves her too much," Thor said. "He can smother her."

Nyctimus nodded. "I think that's why Death is a part of her. He makes her strong and is there to push David back because she won't fault David."

Jane's soul moved out of Jason's hold, but not before kissing her ex-husband's cheek. Then she flitted close to David, raising her hand to glide her fingers over his lips. It was strange to watch his friend not burn, but Nyctimus had seen weirder shit than a fiery goddess.

After David relaxed and kissed her fingers, she spun away, becoming a fire vortex as she circled the people she'd selected earlier. Her human shape formed quickly again, though, and she began a continuous series of leaps while still creating a circle.

Death's soul storm rained down blue orbs, shooting into the blue and green sphere. Every once in a while, she'd stop, do a flourishing movement, and thousands of blue orbs would fall from the sky. A hole opened in the ground below the sphere, and again, Jane made an elegant hand movement, calling souls from below to enter the blue and green ball.

She slowed, twirling in front of the Native American tribes before bowing. They bowed to her before she took turns dancing and bowing for each group of nations. So many refugees had felt the calling to come to their village. It could have been Jane's doing, but she had insisted all be welcome, even when many rose to ban specific religions and Indigenous peoples.

Her mouth opened, but the voice coming from her was not her own. "Punish thy crimes . . . Not thy faith—not thy children whose skin I hath made different—not thy beliefs. For I love each of you." She twirled away as though she had not even remembered speaking.

The knights kneeled as her soul continued to do ballet turns so fast she eventually became a gold blur. Death walked past the knights, aiming his palm at the sphere, raising it higher.

Nyctimus didn't know how long she did this for, but when the last blue orb flew in, Jane's soul moved below her sphere, roaring as she shot a beam of gold light at it.

Threads began tying every person there to the sphere, including Nyctimus.

"What the fuck?" Sin tried to pull the thread attached to him away.

"Leave it." Nyc closed his eyes, seeing what Jane's soul was trying to show them. It so fast, but he'd seen it. "I will follow you, Little Moon."

Others around them said similar words. The knights, the Horsemen, Thanatos, Lancelot, nearly every wolf from his pack, the demon king—and the trio, Death, David, and Lucifer. However, Lucifer's light surrounded the orb instead of tying him to it.

"Send me with your mistakes," Jason told Death and David. "You won't make them again."

David and Death pulled Jason close to them, pressing their glowing palms over Jason's heart.

He cried out in pain, his black wings expanding and vanishing repeatedly until they released him.

Death summoned a different scythe, handing it to him. "Until it is time."

"I didn't get one of those light things," Thor said.

"She was only resurrecting you," Nyctimus told him. "There are more like you. I think it's a good thing for you. Just trust her."

"What was that we saw?" Sin asked.

"A dream." Nyctimus smiled as Jane's soul called Jason to the sphere. A few of her princes were there, all bowing. She hugged each one, kissing them on their cheeks before they faded, becoming blue balls of fire and flying into her little world.

Finally, Jason was the only one left. She kissed the ring he wore before kissing him once more. He caressed her cheek, then faded into a blue and green sphere engulfed in blue fire. Then, like the others, it shot into the muddy orb.

Jane's soul danced again, doing turns, her arms extending and folding as gold dust floated in the air.

"The unicorns," Nyctimus said, watching King and Queen trot out. The younger one, Prince, trotted out, too. He didn't have a rider this time.

Jane danced to Lucifer, whispering to him.

He scowled but opened the jar, letting in some of his light. "That is all she gets. I will not bond with her."

The smile on her face softened the king, and he shook his head. She danced off, spinning as she made a huge circle, sending the orb higher. King and Queen sent their magic to it.

Jane touched the young pegasus as she passed it, and it sprouted a horn. Gold and Silver. It neighed, rearing up, flapping its wings before bursting into silvery light and disappearing into the orb.

"She would send a unicorn." Lancelot nodded to the others before jogging to Jane's soul. She stopped dancing, hugging him tightly and kissing his cheek.

He grinned at her, kissing hers too, then burst into a blue flame, shooting into the growing sphere that rose higher.

Then Jane stopped, standing there beside Lucifer. She took his hand as he lifted hers, kissing the inside of her wrist. He then motioned for her to go to Death. She twirled, keeping her gaze on Lucifer as her golden face glowed with a beautiful smile, and she bowed.

Death lifted Jane's soul, holding her to his heart as she shrunk in size, then vanished in a flash of gold and emerald.

David whirled around. "Where'd they go?"

Nyctimus ran to him. "Calm. Be calm."

"I need to get to the village." David's flames died. "He probably took her there. Jane's still dying."

King nudged David's back.

"Good boy." David turned, jumping on and not saying goodbye as they flew through the air.

Arthur walked to Nyctimus. "I can't hear anything."

"You're mortal." Nyctimus hugged him. "Let's get you to the village. I sent all your wives there. They are fine."

"The other immortals?" Tristan asked, rubbing his arms. "My powers?"

"Your duty is fulfilled. Father has gifted you his greatest gift—a mortal life. Live it to the fullest." Thanatos gestured to a plane, preparing to take off. "You may want to get your fragile human asses out of here. Lucifer is about to destroy every immortal not of divine origins graced in Heaven's light. And he's pissed he didn't get to kill Jane's darker soul."

Nyctimus jogged with them to the plane, many stopping to help others who were adjusting.

"Apollo, you lucky fucker." Sin laughed. "She didn't just send you wherever that thing was going?"

"Her voice was in my head. She asked that I live the life Father wished for me. He asked to pass on."

"Everybody get situated," the captain said over the speaker. "We are low on fuel, so it might get bumpy."

"Take us home," Gareth yelled.

The plane cheered, brothers embraced, and others prayed.

"Jane released Hell into that thing, didn't she?" Arthur asked him.

"I think so . . . But she took from Heaven as well. And many that just perished." Nyctimus rubbed his heart. "I don't think we are meant to know our fate, so I will not ask her. Still, I will follow. Wherever she's gone, I will follow."

"Hell yeah, I'll follow that vixen," Sin yelled, laughing when he was punched. "Don't knock me out. David does that too much. Anyway, I have my immortality. So"—he flexed—"watch it."

"She let you stay immortal?" Gawain cried. "Why?"

"We are of divine blood by birth, fool." Sin smirked. "And she likes my body. I heard her tell David I reminded her of her husband when he was young. He wasn't such a bad guy."

"No," Arthur said, "he wasn't."

"Is she okay, Nyc?" Gawain asked as the plane took off.

"I don't know. They were very cryptic. I think David did something to buy her time, but the fact Death vanished with her soul the way he did worries me. She took her time performing this miracle."

The knights all lowered their heads, putting their hands together. Nyctimus followed their lead. The entire plane quieted their cheers and closed their eyes as Arthur prayed aloud. "Heavenly Father . . ."

Death opened his eyes, looking at his empty palm for a second before staring ahead. Azrael was there. Jane's beautiful heart stopped as she sucked in a final breath.

He rushed to her, watching her pupils as they fixed and dilated, then she began to release her last breath.

"There are terms to what you do now, Death," Azrael said. "Darkness was locked away, but you broke many rules. Choose to crown her or begin again. There will be consequences, and you cannot avoid them."

Death leaned over her, holding her cheek as the last of her breath flowed into his mouth. "The End." He swallowed her last breath, then whispered, his lips brushing against hers, "Now, Begin again. Live,"—he kissed her lips and returned her last breath—"Sweet Jane."

The door to the infirmary burst open, and David rushed forward, hugging his children as he guided them all to Jane's side.

She gasped, eyes wide. "Hi, Death."

"Hi, angel." Death rubbed away her tear, smiling at the hazel eyes staring at him. "You're home."

She smiled at him. "Home."

David walked closer, his tears endless. "Baby?"

Death tugged David's arm, putting him in his place while patting the children on their heads. "Mama's home. Be good to her."

Doctors and nurses rushed into the room, passing Death as he walked away.

"Death?" David yelled, holding Jane's hand as the medical team treated her. "She'll want you to stay. I want you to stay."

"I need to speak to Father and my brother. Her fate is still out of my sight. Keep her warm for me. I will do whatever they ask of me."

"Sir, we need to give your wife a blood transfusion and prep her for surgery. She's lost a lot of blood and bleeding internally," one of the medics told David.

"He's her match." Death pushed the door open and walked through. "So are they."

4 8

LUCIFER

Three Years Later

David lifted Jane's hand, kissing her ring over and over again. "Please, baby. Please don't go like this. We need you."

He looked down at his lap, swaying slightly as he held the little bundle to his chest. He released her hand only long enough to caress his son's cheek. "He looks just like me, Jane. Just how you said he would." He lifted the baby, kissing his forehead. "He's warm like you. Well, maybe a little hotter. I swear, we can name him Luc like you wanted to. I don't mind anymore. Whatever you want, my love. Just wake up."

He grabbed her hand again. "Death, where are you? You didn't have to leave. Look at her." His tears didn't stop. He stared at Jane's face. She was pale, and he couldn't even kiss her lips because of the tube in her mouth. "Brother, please come back. We've wanted you home with us since the battle. You know you are a part of us. If you let her stay just to give me three years and a child, that's not enough. Not anymore."

The baby whimpered before crying.

David lifted him, swaying as he patted his back. "It's okay. Daddy's got you, and Mommy is right here. She's just dreaming right now."

"No, she's not."

David looked behind him, freezing when he saw Lucifer standing there.

"What do you want?" David stood, holding his son close as he tightened his hold on Jane's hand.

Lucifer stared at Jane blankly. "What happened to her?"

David shook his head. "Don't act like you don't know. She's been followed by darkness since the war. Death left, and he never came back."

"It isn't Darkness." Lucifer walked to her side. "She's simply fading because of what she and Death have done."

"The world she made?"

Lucifer nodded. "She put nearly all darkness inside. She's trying to confine it, and it is destroying her. As far as my brother goes, I only know that he was given a choice, and he chose." He motioned to her stomach. "Now tell me what happened."

David watched the angel, ready to make a deal with him if he had to. "The placenta was blocking part of her cervix. We knew it, and she was scheduled for a cesarean. But she took Natalie shopping without telling me. She went into labor while driving. She pulled off to the side of the road and tried to call, but she started bleeding when she started dilating. Natalie drove to the hospital, but Jane had already lost too much blood and had gone into shock. They delivered him and started transfusions, but she also had an amniotic fluid embolism. Amniotic fluid entered her bloodstream. Her heart began to fail, and her lungs filled with fluid."

Lucifer sighed. "Is Natalie all right?"

David shook his head, rubbing his son's back. "She's blaming herself. I can't talk to her. I don't know what to say. I had already told her no when she asked about going out. She knew it was important for Jane to stay close to home or with me. But Natalie did what she always does with Jane."

"Are you blaming your daughter for your wife's condition?"

David glared at him. "No. I'm just trying to process everything before I say things I shouldn't. I told her I love her, but I have to stay with Jane and the baby."

The baby suddenly wailed.

"His name?" Lucifer asked, caressing Jane's cheek.

"She wanted to name him Luc."

Lucifer closed his eyes as he leaned over her, kissing her forehead. "I am forbidden from interfering with her mortality. You know already that Death is meant to hand her over when she goes. Our bond is unbreakable, but if I interfere, I hurt her more."

"Then what are you doing here? Collecting?" He glared at him. "If I figure out how to unlock my soul again, I will slaughter all of you."

"And that is why Father put your soul at rest. So you don't destroy the world. His new failsafe—giving his angels and me the right to harm all immortals who break the rules." Lucifer smirked, but his expression quickly softened. "But I am not here to taunt you, Prince David. You know I love her. I have done everything to keep her safe, but Death is her guardian and soul mate. I am not permitted to know more than what my bond allows. And that is limited to our fate after she passes.

"I do not wish to see her pass before setting eyes on your child with her. I will seek out my brother. I am not even permitted to be on Earth's plane, but I came. Hopefully, this choice doesn't count as interference. If it does, I will take the punishment."

"Thank you." David kissed his son's head. "Please send word if you find him. I can't imagine what would keep him from her."

"Nor I." Lucifer turned to David, but his gaze was on the baby. "May I hold him?"

David glanced down before staring at Jane's face. His heart told him to trust the angel, so he sighed, handing him over.

Lucifer was careful and stared at him for a long time. "Does he have her eyes?"

"No." David was tense, but he trusted his heart.

"Is he worth losing her?"

David's eyes watered. "I can't choose. I've been asked to choose between her and my children too many times."

"And she chooses them." Lucifer lifted the baby, pressing a kiss to his head. "I will find Death. Keep praying." He returned his son to him. "Father does not answer the way we wish—you know that. But I do not believe he set this up for you to have a son and three mortal years together."

The door opened, and Natalie and Nathan gasped, taking in Lucifer.

Lucifer smiled at them, extending his arms and hugging them as they sobbed. "Speak to her. She will hear you."

"I'm sorry." Natalie sobbed. "I know she was just trying to make me happy, but I—I." She wailed. "I'm such a bad daughter."

Lucifer caressed her head, his hand glowing as he did. "Your mother doesn't think so. Don't you see? All this time, she has been trying to give you the world, Natalie." He kissed her head. "Should she wake, be kinder. Her fate appears to be more uncertain than we had hoped."

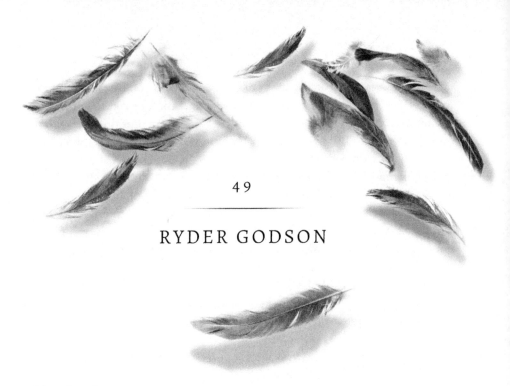

49

RYDER GODSON

More than dreams...

So many colors. All of them. Colors Jane didn't even know existed. All glowing. All swirling around her. All of her loves. They were all there.

At least in her dreams.

"Just make everything better in your dreams, Sweet Jane . . . Happily Ever After."

Sapphire . . .

David leaned over her, kissing her swollen belly with the happiest smile on his handsome face. He sighed and lifted his head as a muffled sound echoed around them, yelling that breakfast was on the stove.

Tears . . .

"It's okay." David kissed her again and again. "The doctor is coming. It's going to be okay."

"Luc?" she tried to say.

He looked unsure of what she was saying but quickly turned, picking up a bundle. "He's perfect, my love. Just like you said."

Brown eyes . . .

Natalie cried, hiding her face in a pillow as Jane sat beside her.

"Baby girl, it's okay." Jane lightly ran her fingers through Natalie's brown curls. "I know you didn't mean to say those things."

Her daughter lowered the pillow. "I'm still sorry, Mama. You wouldn't have taken me shopping if I hadn't said it. I didn't mean to say I hate you."

David entered the room before she could respond. He shifted the tiny bundle in his arms before stopping in front of Jane. He smiled, rubbing his hand ever so gently across the bundle. "Natalie, let your mother rest." He held a hand out for Jane. "Slowly, my love."

Jane pressed her lips together, holding her stomach as she let him pull her up. "Thank you."

He tilted her face up, holding her chin as he leaned down to kiss her. "I'll keep him with me so it is quiet for you. Go take a nap."

"I can take him," she whispered, moving a portion of the blanket to reveal a cute face, flushed pink cheeks, and wisps of black hair sticking out from under the blue beanie on his head.

David smiled, kissing her forehead. "No. You need to rest. We only just got you back. It's okay—I'll take care of everything."

"But he might need me." She frowned, watching the sleeping baby boy. "I haven't been with him at all. It still feels like a dream."

"It's not a dream—I promise. And he'll still need you when you wake up." He lowered his hand to her stomach. "Do you need a heating pad?"

"I'll get it, Mama." Natalie rushed out of the room.

Then clouds and blue skies . . .

Strong arms wrapped around her, hugging her tight as they both stared out the window when they spotted two figures kissing under a tree.

"I can't believe he has a girlfriend," she murmured, watching as Nathan leaned away from the girl.

David chuckled. "Of course he has a girlfriend—he's my son."

Nathan's gaze shifted away from the girl and right to them.

"Oh, shit." Jane ducked, pulling David down with her. "He saw us. Fuck, I hit my head."

"Baby." He leaned over her, laughing. "You are not as stealthy as you once were." He pressed his lips to hers, tugging her under him, but he raised his hand to her head, massaging it before scanning her dress. "Still my sexy goddess, but one clumsy ninja."

"I'm a great ninja."

"Mhm." He held her cheek, leaning over her more. He smiled against her mouth as his rough fingers slid up her thigh before squeezing her ass cheek. "No panties?"

"I'm pretty sure I'm ovulating."

"Jane, are you sure you want this? You know I want us to have more children, but—"

"Lucifer promised I was safe."

David took a deep breath. "I think we are going to regret this deal with him."

She caressed his cheek. "You'll find me."

He smirked, tugging her even closer. "Yes, I will." He snapped open the button on his jeans as she reached inside.

"Mom? Daddy?" Natalie's voice called out. "I'm home, and Nathan's kissing that girl under the tree."

"Fuck." David scrambled, buttoning his pants as he pulled Jane up.

She laughed, wrapping her arms around his neck while he tugged her dress in place.

"What are y'all doing on the floor?" Natalie stared at them from the archway.

"Nothing." David pulled Jane flush against his front, his erection digging into her back. "Uh, your mother just has a backache. I'm going to take care of it upstairs. Dinner's in the oven."

Natalie switched her gaze between her and David. "Ew. You guys have no control."

David pointed to the kitchen. "Go. You're eighteen. You know we're trying to have another baby."

"And you shouldn't be trying!" Natalie glared at them. "Are we not enough?"

Death's voice disrupted the scene. *"That's not happy, Jane. Darkness is filling you with fear. Try again."*

Yelling . . .

"And you shouldn't be." Natalie stomped her foot, glaring at them.

David hugged Jane. "Princess, I know you're worried after what happened before. But every angel we can summon has confirmed she's safe. We don't have much time to make a family. And you are enough. Always. We love you. We just want to spread more love. You're going to the only university in the country. You're leaving us. Your mother and I want our second chance, too."

Natalie's eyes turned red, and she smiled sadly. "I'm sorry. I just don't want to go through that again. I love Luc, but if something happens."

Jane shook her head. "We have made it so you never have to worry. I promise."

"Okay." Natalie pointed to the window. "I should be allowed to date. You have no idea what it's like for kids to know my parents get it on all over town. Then my brother has every girl in school in love with him while every guy I like is afraid of Daddy."

"No one is good enough for you," David muttered.

Her daughter blushed. "Thanks, Daddy. But I really would like one date before I go away."

David nodded. "Okay."

"Really?" Natalie's eyes lit up.

"Yes. I'll take you out for ice cream and a movie."

Natalie's cheeks turned red. "Daddy!"

"What? You like ice cream."

Jane covered her face, laughing.

"Ugh." Natalie stomped her foot. "Y'all are so unfair and gross. And it's awful I can't even bring friends over because they all perv on you. My teacher even asked about your marriage. Then she offered to tutor me at home. In front of everyone!"

"No one pervs on me but your mother."

"That's gross." Natalie's nose scrunched up in disgust. "Do you even hear yourself?"

David covered his eyes. "Just go. And watch your brother if he wakes up."

Natalie shivered. "Please don't moan. God, I'm gonna throw up."

David dragged his hand down his face as Natalie disappeared around the corner. "I really hate not having our heightened senses anymore to hear when they're coming close."

Jane looked up, wiggling her butt against him. "No, but I'm still your kitty."

He grinned down at her, dropping his hand to her breast. "My goddess."

"Daddy." Natalie squeezed her eyes shut, dropping her plate of food on the floor.

"Dammit," he shouted. "You're supposed to eat at the table. Clean that up." He snatched Jane's hand, dragging her to the stairs.

Jane could hardly breathe. "I don't even care that I'm not turned on anymore. You getting flustered about getting caught is the funniest shit ever."

He glared at her but chuckled. "Shut up, Jane."

She giggled, squeezing his ass, then yelping when he quickly lifted her and pulled her legs around him.

"Never tell me you're not turned on when walking around the house without wearing panties." He slipped one hand under her dress, squeezing her ass. "Are you going to be quiet this time?"

She nodded, her mouth open as his fingers teased her entrance.

He paused, peeking behind the cracked open door. "Good. He's still out."

"Hurry." She kissed his cheek over and over. "'Cause losing your immortality didn't affect your lovemaking abilities. And since I'm human, the feeling of you inside me lasts for days, not hours."

David lowered his lips to her neck. "Then be ready to feel me for an eternity."

Then more blue...

David entered the room, holding the one-and-a-half-year-old and gold and blue flowers. "Hi, baby. This big guy wanted to see his mama and meet his new brother."

Jane smiled at the black-haired, blue-eyed little boy in his arms. "Hi, Luc."

"Mama." He held his arms out for her, but David kept a good grip on him as he put the flowers on the table.

"No, Luc." David kissed his head before leaning down to kiss Jane. "Mama is feeding the baby."

"Jason." Luc waved.

David grinned, reaching down to caress baby Jason's cheek. "He looks a little like you, baby. He's got your eyes and hair color."

"Yeah." She winced as he sucked too hard.

"We can search for formula, Jane. Things are becoming more available."

"No, I can do it." She swayed a little. "I can do it. My Jason."

David wiped away the tear sliding down her cheek. "Your Jason. Maybe we will add a little Ryder."

She cried more. "He should be with us."

David nodded. "I know."

Then emerald...

"I'm sorry," Death said, lowering his head.

David sat on the sofa beside Jane as Death sat on her other side.

She sobbed, reaching for Death's hand. "You know I already forgave you."

He looked at David for permission before taking her hand. "I had no way to send word. I made a choice, and this was the consequence."

She pulled him closer. "It's okay."

David sighed, leaning away but glaring at Death. "You're forbidden from making decisions from now on."

Jane laughed as Death hugged her tighter.

"We've had two children," David added. "And Jane has nearly died a dozen times."

"I know." Death kissed her shoulder. "But it was that or destroying her creation and making her barren. I had faith. I just should have had it sooner. This is the consequence. I won't fuck up like this again."

Jane whispered, "How can Darkness still make deals?"

"It's just the way things are. I'll make it up to you. I'll find you something cool, like a muscle car. I can get where a lot of these mortals can't."

"Don't butter her up with a car," David said. "Gas supplies are still low anyway."

Death grinned, kissing her cheek. "Fine, I'll bring shit to the needy like you try to do."

David scoffed. "Jane already had the needy given essentials, housing, and jobs. The world is scattered and rebuilding, but I doubt you throwing expired chips at people will make a difference."

Then gold threads...

"No, her fate is certain this time." Death caressed her cheek.

"Good." David kissed Jane's hand. "We have no kids to interrupt us, Jane."

She rolled her eyes. "David, our four-year-old and two-year-old sons are asleep in their room."

Death shook his head. "I can't do it."

"You can." David glared at him.

He shook his head again. "I get wanting to try for a girl, but I can't be a part of it. This is your life with her, not mine."

Then light.

Just light...

"It's time to wake up, Sweet Jane."

She smiled, shaking her head as she squeezed her eyes shut. *No,* she thought.

His chuckle was music to her ears. "You have to."

"I don't want to leave," she whispered, sighing as tingles slid down her arm.

"You can't stay in your dreams."

"Memories. And yes, I can."

"Look at me, angel."

She turned her head to the side and opened her eyes. They were in the cottage he'd given her, and he was lying right beside her, his head tilted like hers.

"That's better." He grinned. "My hazel-eyed angel."

She scanned his face. Every part of him was as it always was, yet she would never stop trying to see more of him.

He kept his eyes on hers. "You were dreaming sad things."

"It was my life with David."

"David dreams are meant to be perfect. Everything you keep with you is meant to be perfect."

Her eyes watered. "They were perfect. We were getting older, having babies, making babies. You had finally come back, and we were trying to make babies with you. And my gold thread. I did it."

He chuckled, rolling onto his side before lightly trailing his fingers across her lips. "Well, I suppose some of our memories are not so bad. I like when you dream things that are not from our past. When you dream we are young—when you imagine I'm just human."

"Young human Death," she mused. "My Ryder."

He grinned, still sliding his fingers along her lips. "I also enjoy the dreams when I get to give you everything. And the dreams when you dance for me, especially in our meadow."

"I love each one, even if they are not so happy. I don't want to forget." She sighed, savoring the tingles seeping into her skin. "That feels good."

"Yeah?" He gave her that gorgeous smile. "Want to make a dream for us to keep before you go home?"

"Yes. Don't stop."

He caressed her cheek, lowering his face but not close enough to kiss her yet.

"I've missed you," she whispered, rubbing her legs together as more tingles danced across her skin. "Touch me. I don't want it to end."

"But we have ended." He smoothed her hair back.

She shook her head. "I didn't let us. I made it so."

He chuckled as he looked down at her naked body. "So you're not going to let me take you home? Are we making naughty Jane and Death dreams?" He slid his fingers between her breasts and over the pink, scarred skin as he leaned down, kissing the spot just under her heart and to the side.

Jane sighed, her eyes stinging as he murmured words she didn't understand against her skin.

He pushed himself up so he could reach every inch of the scar. "Will you still love me when you leave?"

"You're the one who always leaves." She slid her fingers through his hair. "But, yes. Always."

"You know I would stay if I could. That's why we make dreams." He rubbed her belly, sighing as he kissed up until he reached her lips. "Yes, this is definitely needed. Fuck reality for a few more hours."

"Yes." She grinned against his mouth, spreading her legs as his smile stretched wide.

"Naughty Jane and Death Time." He tugged her under him more as he pressed down on her. "Good?"

She wrapped her arms around him. "Always good."

He chuckled as he kissed the scar on her neck before pressing his lips to the pendant there. He slid his hand between her legs before lining up and sighed, sliding his shaft across her. She was already shaking. "So sensitive." He slid his large hand over her breast, squeezing. "So full."

Jane pulled him until his lips touched hers and gasped as he entered her without warning. Still gentle, but so sudden that she came right away.

He watched her moan and close her eyes. "I'll stay a little bit longer this time."

She panted, hugging him as her body continued to feel jolts of tingles. "Faster."

His gorgeous face came closer as he completely caged her below him, and he kissed her, consuming her in a way only he could. "Still marrying me in one of these dreams?"

Jane tried her best to hook her legs around him. He helped her, holding the back of her thigh as he positioned himself so that he growled in her ears with every thrust, losing control for a few seconds each time.

"Fuck, answer me." He pressed his lips against his mark on her neck, still thrusting hard. "Answer me."

Yes. She confirmed her answer with a kiss.

He pulled out, holding her cheek as he pressed a long kiss to her trembling lips. He breathed heavily, caressing her nose with his. "Imagine the perfect ring, the dress you'd wear for me, and your favorite place for us."

She gasped. "I will."

He kissed her again, sliding in but rolling onto his back. He held her hips, letting her have complete control. "Fuck, you're beautiful."

Jane moaned, riding him faster, but he groaned, pulling her down.

"You're extra tight, and I'm going to come if you keep that up." He held her by the back of the neck and ass as he thrust upward fast.

"Oh, fuck," she shouted, holding on to him as he made her come. She bit his chest, her legs shaking as he let out loud growls before lifting her off him.

"Fuck, don't make me come yet." He groaned as she tried to go down on him. "That'll make me come in two seconds. Get your cute ass up here and ride my face."

She covered her cheeks, laughing as he pulled her up to him.

"I'm not kidding. Let me make you come, then we'll finish, and you can sleep." He pulled her legs over his shoulders. He grinned up at her, flicking his tongue out.

"Ah, shit." She pressed her lips together but stuck her breasts out.

"Don't you hold back." He dragged his tongue up her slit.

"We haven't done this. Am I supposed to face the other way?"

He closed his mouth around her, sucking until her head was tilted back, and she screamed. "I'm Death, babe. I can do anything. And we can do it both ways." He smacked her ass. "Now fuck my face so I can fuck your pussy before I make love to you, fiancée." He winked. "That counted as a proposal, by the way. I have the ring you wanted. It's in your panty drawer."

She stared at him, her mouth open.

"Love you too, Sweet Jane." He kissed her, and she yelped from the tingles jolting through her. "Hurry up so I can do the romantic shit you like."

She wiped her tears away as the image of a ring was forced into her mind. It was an antique emerald engagement ring she'd found back when she was a seventeen-year-old girl in love with the Angel of Death.

"Told you I wanted to be your everything, even then." He grabbed her hips as he smiled between her legs. "Hurry up so I can kiss your other pretty lips, and I'll put it on your finger."

She wanted to climb off and kiss him, but he opened his mouth, shoving his tongue in and devouring her as he rocked her all on his own until she couldn't help herself, and she covered his hands, crying when he laced their fingers together.

She was still having an orgasm when he lifted her off him and rolled her onto her back.

He vanished and reappeared in the blink of an eye, grabbing her right hand instead of her left. "Fucker."

Jane laughed, smiling as he kissed the ring once it was on.

He glared at David's but kissed it too. "He knows about me planning to ask."

She nodded, cupping his cheeks as she pulled him into a kiss.

"Freak in the sheets." He chuckled, kissing her over and over. "It'll be in our dreams for now. When it's time, we'll do it the way we were meant to."

"I know."

He leaned back on his heels, staring at his erection before looking down at her. "Sweet or hard?"

"Both."

He rolled his eyes, spreading her legs. "So greedy."

She stared at her ring. She couldn't believe he would remember or even do such a thing.

He watched her for a second before flipping her onto her belly and propping her up just right. He straddled her legs, gliding his dick along her opening. "Stop sticking your ass up like that. No anal for you today. I want pussy."

She whimpered as he leaned over her, pushing the tip in.

"Good?" He caged her in but pulled her hair to make her arch how he liked her. "Tell me if it hurts."

She moaned as he pushed in deep. "I'm a deity."

"Ah, fuck, this is fucking heaven." He tilted her head to kiss her as he thrust in, building his rhythm. "And you have a deity soul, baby. There's a difference when your soul sleeps. I'll always be able to hurt you."

She cried as he sped up, hitting her G-spot.

"Want me to make you a goddess?" He chuckled before moving her hand. "Pull your ass cheek right there."

"D-Goddess." She smiled as he laughed.

"Silly girl." He stopped, holding her cheek as he kissed her hard. "No more talking, though. I need to fuck you hard and fast because proposing almost made me come, and I've been holding it."

Her heart beat so fast. "I love you."

He gave her another long kiss. "Yes, beat just for me. And I love you." He threaded their fingers together before pressing them into the quilt. "Safeword is Godson." He grinned, kissing her cheek as he thrust hard, putting his big arms around her neck and shoulders to keep her in place. "Mrs. Ryder Godson."

Death crossed his arms, his eyes never leaving Jane as she tilted her face upward, soaking in the sun's rays. She loved the sun. It reminded her of David. That's why he always made them come here. So she could dream of this when it was time to go with Lucifer. So he could close his eyes and remember when he couldn't be with her.

"I miss King," she murmured with her eyes still closed. She held out her arms, swaying slightly enough to make the gold dress she wore twirl. "And Queen. She didn't like me so much, though. I think we were too much alike."

He smiled, watching the two creatures she had just voiced her longing for exit the woods. They always came to the meadow to watch her dance, but she never saw them. Not anymore.

She pushed up on her toes, stretching her arms out more as she shifted a leg behind her and bowed her head. "I wish she wasn't asleep."

"You're mortal, Jane. She is still you, but you have no reason to summon her awake."

"I know." She smiled, extending her hand as King walked closer, bowing his head to her. "Sometimes I think King and Luc are watching me. When I see the silver and white flowers."

Death sighed, watching King trot away when she lowered her hand. He knew King put the flowers there, gifts from Lucifer to Jane.

"Do you think Luc locked them away?"

"No, angel." Death let his gaze fall over her figure. She was already curvier than she'd been a month ago. "He knew you wanted them to be free. But you can't see them anymore."

"Maybe I will dream of them. I can take them with me. You can ride Sorrow, obviously. Your brothers will be there with Perish, Ravage, and Misery. The knights, the wolves, and David. My David."

"Then dream it. Add it to your fairy tale world. You already know wherever you go, we will follow."

"Yes." She smiled at him this time. "Don't laugh."

"I never laugh." He made a twirling motion with his hand. "Let me see my gold goddess."

She chuckled, holding her arms out again. "I've been practicing, but my balance is all off now."

"Just focus on me."

"Okay." She twirled, causing her dress to flare out like a flame as she kicked her leg, performing pirouette after pirouette. Her long hair blew around her as the wind rushed through the trees.

Death stayed still, taking every movement in. He'd already remember it all, but he always tried to absorb more. The way she smiled with each spin, the way she held her hands as she extended her arms, the way she gracefully kicked her leg before spinning again, sending her skirt flying around her.

King bowed his head, and the crack of his magic made Jane stop.

She looked up, grinning as thousands of silver flowers were swept up in a whirlwind. "Death, are you doing this?"

Death shook his head. "You know who's doing this. Apparently, your king is thinking of you dancing today."

The glistening tear on her cheek sparkled like a rainbow, but she kept smiling as she spun in circles.

Finally, the people who had stayed silent behind Death and out of her view came to his side.

"So?"

Death didn't look at him. "She said yes."

"I told you she would." David smiled when Jane finally spotted him.

When the little boys holding David's hands looked up at Death, he waved his hand in Jane's direction. "Go see Mama."

The boys took off as David released them.

"I was going to give you more time alone with her, but we need to go." David smiled wide as Jane turned, giving the toddlers the loveliest smile. "How were her dreams? Is she still getting confused and thinking none of this is real?"

"Yes and no." Death let out a huff. "She's dreaming of your life together, but she's taking the difficult parts—not just the happy shit like I told her to."

David grinned. "She wants to remember the pain because that makes what we have more precious."

"Whatever," Death muttered. "I'm going to push my soul to guide her dreams and world-building next time. I'm kicking your ass out so we have fun."

"She loves dreaming about me." David smirked. "But show up—I'll knock your ass out."

Death laughed as she watched Jane with her boys. He still couldn't believe they were together. He'd come back after years of separation as she built a family with David and became a wife, and they welcomed him and asked him to stay. Now he was her fiancé.

"Mama, Mama. It's King," Little Luc yelled.

Jane glanced at where he pointed, and she grinned. "Do you see him?"

Luc and Jason nodded.

"That means you are special and pure and good." She kept staring at where they pointed, her smile fading.

David sighed as the boys laughed and ran in circles while Jane kept staring right at King, never seeing him.

"She thinks this is punishment for burning and imprisoning her soul," David said. "She used to sit up in bed, calling for Lucifer. And she believes she is being punished for calling him her king and answering as his queen."

"It is punishment," Death said. "Just the same as me being cast into the abyss. You are a prince of Heaven, David. Jane is but a child of God. A deity, yes—the beginning of souls—but there is no queen of Father's creations. No king but the son of God. But Jane will not leave Lucifer to be punished alone, and she will not ask him to call her anything other than his queen."

"I know." David looked down at the flowers. "We are all punished, even now."

Death smiled. "Together, though. Just like in the beginning."

David smiled back. "Yes, brother. Just as we should be. The two of us watching over and loving our girl."

Death rolled his eyes. "Fucker. I could still take her and marry her. Make her queen."

"You will eventually."

"Papi, are you getting upset?" Death laughed, but it was a serious matter they didn't discuss.

David punched his arm. "Don't forget I asked you to stay and have this with me."

"I won't." Death exhaled loudly. "You want us like we were before?"

David shrugged. "We'll figure it out. You gave me fifteen years of just us. I got to be Nathan and Natalie's father, but I got to experience becoming a father to my children with her, too."

"No, no." Jane put little Jason down as she picked up the older boy. "Luc, don't do that to the flowers."

"Why?" Luc asked as she took the crumbled flower from his tiny fist.

"Because it has only just begun. Let it live." She held the flower in her palm. "Forgive us."

King trotted close, but Jane still looked past him, even when his horn lit up, and another flower instantly bloomed from where Luc had plucked it.

David smiled sadly. "We'll make her whole and happy. Thank you for not holding back. Without Lucifer and her soul speaking to her, she is diminishing, but this is the life God wanted for us."

"Father wanted this for you." Death glanced at him. "But I will see what happens. There are fewer souls to reap now. Luc destroyed all immortals not of divine blood, but I can't bear to part with her again."

"Good." David grinned as Jane showed the boys the dance poses she'd been practicing. Luc watched her as Jason tried to copy her.

Death felt warmth as she began to glow in gold light. She had black wings. She couldn't even summon her suit anymore, yet she displayed his wings for him.

"Death, are you doing this?" David whispered.

He shook his head as she closed her eyes and performed a simple pirouette. Then the golden silhouette separated from her, mirroring Jane's movements. Jane never opened her eyes. They were in perfect sync, dancing in a wide circle around the boys. She moved faster, and so did her soul. They leaped, kicking their legs out with each turn until they both smiled, then a translucent blue and green sphere—her world—formed between them. The boys didn't move, and neither did David or Death. They couldn't.

Jane threw the dead flower out without opening her eyes, and Death smiled as it bloomed perfectly and flew into the sphere.

She kept dancing with her soul directly across the field from her, dancing just as her soul had done during the End. Jane abruptly stopped.

"Are you okay?" he asked her.

She didn't open her eyes as the world before her spun. "Yes. Just daydreaming of us all together in a different life. Everyone. Even our horses. My king. My Prince. My Death. My loves ... My Jason."

"Your daydreams are magic," Death said. "They are going to your world and some build our heaven."

"I know." She smiled as her soul danced close to her. Her miniature world faded until it was no more, and her soul turned, smiling at him and David before waving to the boys and unicorns, then rejoined Jane to sleep again.

Her wings faded, too, but seeing her wearing them again had been a gift.

"Pretty, Mama," Luc said.

Finally, Jane opened her eyes. "Thank you, baby." She rubbed her tummy and knelt to hug her little boy as he touched her lips, smiling.

David shook his head. "He's so similar to how Jane described Lucifer."

"He looks just like you." Death chuckled. "I think this is merely Father's sense of humor and His way of giving all of us what we need."

"If our daughter comes out with blonde hair and gray eyes, I'm having a word with our Father."

Death laughed. "If anything, she should look like me."

David grinned at him. "True."

"Thank you," Death said, staring at the ring he'd given Jane. "I know I cannot marry her yet, but I'm glad you convinced me to ask her."

David shrugged. "You gave me more than I ever hoped to have with her after losing her on the battlefield. She's getting older, and I want every day to be one she smiles at. And she smiles most with you."

"Jealous?"

David shook his head. "Happy."

"Sappy fucker."

"You're helping me with our daughter, by the way. You didn't get invited to help me make her so you could go make love to Jane while I change diapers."

"I'm not a nanny." Death gave him a dry look. "And it's your daughter. Stop saying ours. I pulled out and took her pretty ass so you could fill her up."

"Stop acting like you were just there to fuck her," David glared at him. "You wanted to put that baby in her with me. She smiles at her tummy because we were part of our little angel's beginning."

Death sighed. "Fine, I'll put the baby to sleep from time to time so we can fuck Jane."

David shook his head. "You rarely fuck her. You are the softer of us when it comes to making love to her."

"If only you knew what we just did." Death snickered.

"I'm sure it's nothing compared to what I've done with her." David smirked.

"Fucker." Death growled, watching Jane stare at King again when Luc pointed him out.

"You're sure?" she asked.

Luc nodded, giving her a big smile. "He misses you, Mama."

Jane turned to face the direction Luc had pointed in, and she held the skirt of her dress before bowing.

King returned the gesture as lightning streaked across the sky. None of them flinched as thunder cracked because they all watched a flower fall from the sky and land in Jane's palm. Her tattoo glowed silver momentarily, and she let out a sad laugh as she traced the mark before kissing it. "Thank you, my king."

David smiled sadly. "I actually feel bad for Lucifer. He did so much for her, and he's stuck in Hell, in her place."

"She'll join him." Death balled his fist. "There is no Heaven for Jane like there is for the rest of you."

"I won't go anywhere without my baby," David said. "If Lucifer's kingdom with her is where she goes when her time comes, I want you to ensure I follow her. Even if it is to her world—whatever she's turned it into."

Death stared at him for a while. "We will follow her. I promise."

"I mean it, Death."

"Always forgetting what your wife is, Prince." Death smiled. "This is not it for you. Or us."

"Then, when we see each other in another life, I'll embrace you as my brother."

"Pussy."

"I hate you." David laughed, punching his shoulder.

Death rubbed it. "I know you're a human, but that still hurts, Papi. I'm telling."

"It doesn't hurt you." David started walking toward Jane. "And do not call me Papi in front of our little girl. I swear I will kick you out if she grows up calling me that."

"Does this make me King Daddy?" He followed him, smiling at his girl when David lifted her, his hand dropping to the barely visible baby bump.

"No." David laughed as he inspected the emerald ring Jane wore. He smiled before lifting her hand and kissing the ring. "It's beautiful, baby."

"Thank you." She pushed up on her toes to kiss him. "Is it time?"

"Yes. And you need to eat before you feel bad."

Jane giggled, turning toward Death. She wrapped her arms around his waist but pulled David to her back.

"There are children present, Jane." Death smirked, lifting her. "And we already made our baby."

She cupped his face. "Are you gonna let her call you Daddy?"

"Maybe." He nudged her nose with his. "If you called me Daddy, I would not. But you don't. So, we'll see."

"You will let her. As soon as she looks at you, you will have a new girl."

Death shrugged. "We'll see. When we are together like this, I feel more, but it's still difficult. It's forced."

"I'll teach you," Jane whispered against his mouth. "If you really can't, it's okay. Maybe I'll just dream it up, so you can experience it."

"Whatever you want, angel." He took the kiss she was trying to give him as he motioned for David to get in, too.

She moaned quietly as David kissed her neck. She breathed faster, and her full breasts nearly spilled over the top of her dress.

"Daddy," Luc yelled. "My Mama. Don't bite Mama."

David chuckled, kissing Jane softer. "I know she's your mama."

"So, are we both tapping this tonight?" Death squeezed her hips. "I'm just asking 'cause I don't want either of our dicks hitting the baby on the head. So, if we're J and Ds, we should probably go nuts—like literally—for the next month only because I can't do it. I don't even want David's pee-pee in there."

"Pee-pee." Jason laughed.

"Death, really?" David lifted Jason.

The hazel-eyed boy grinned at him. "Death pee-pee."

Jane smiled, wrapping her arms around Death's neck as he glared at Jason.

"No. Not Death Pee-pee. It's King Daddy."

"Not Daddy." Jason looked away from Death and hugged David. "My daddy."

Death raised Jane's hand, showing off the ring he'd given her. "I'm going to marry her too."

Little Luc stared at him, and Death stared back. Both boys looked like David, but Luc was a replica of his father: sapphire eyes, black hair, sun-kissed skin—a prince. Jason had Jane's lighter skin tone and hair.

Jane quickly kissed Death before motioning for him to lower her down.

Death growled, squeezing her ass before kissing her again, but he followed the instructions she'd given him and put her on her feet.

"Mama, we brought gifts for them." Luc grabbed the toys David had been holding.

Jane grinned, kissing Luc's cheek before walking the boys to the headstones she'd been dancing around.

"Can I put them there?" Luc looked up at Jane.

"Yes, baby. Thank you." She kissed his head as she knelt down.

Death scanned the headstones: **Sir Lancelot Grimm, Maren Lorelei Grimm, David Hunter Grimm, Arianna Maura Grimm.**

No one knew Lancelot's woman's last name, and David had told Jane that Lancelot despised his father, King Ban, because he was a mere bastard son of a prostitute who'd been tossed away. So, Jane gave him a new last name—Grimm. She'd seen one of the boy's knight toys in her fairy tale book, and she had blurted out that's what his name was. David had promised her Lancelot would love the name she'd picked.

Luc handed a doll toy to Jason as he held a knight, and both boys put them by Lancelot's children's headstones.

Death watched Jane hold her emotions in as her eyes slid to the headstone off to the side:

Jason Logan Winters
Beloved husband, father, reaper. My forever.

"You okay, Sweet Jane?" Death watched her eyes widen.

"Yes." She smiled before kissing her fingertips and touching them to Jason's name.

Luc pointed at King. "Ride."

Death shook his head. "Maybe some other time."

The skies lit with white light as thunder rumbled in the distance.

"Let's go before it starts raining." David lifted Jason as he took Jane's hand, helping her stand before leading them out of the woods.

Jane smiled as Luc held his arms up for Death.

Death sighed, lifting him. "You are only being carried because I love your mama."

Luc whispered in his ear, "You glow with Mama's soul."

Jane took Death's hand, pulling him with them. "That's because Death completes Mama's soul."

"Why?" Luc asked.

"Because the other half of Mama wasn't meant to be with her," Death said. "I am."

"Like Daddy?" Jason asked.

David nodded. "Like me. We are both meant for Mama. That's the way God made us. He put both of us with her, and she danced for us."

Luc touched Death's cheek before whispering in his ear, "Mama doesn't see."

Death smiled as a faint gold flame flickered around her, and trails of gold dust kicked up from her footsteps. "That's just so she keeps dreaming." He didn't tell him she was dreaming of Hell, giving its prisoners a second chance.

Luc nodded, resting his head on Death's shoulder. The angel felt nothing from the little boy's affection, but he did when Jane smiled at him. *My moon.*

"*I love you,*" he told her mentally, completely happy he had this with her again.

"*And I love you,*" she said, stealing his line.

He glared at her but sent her the mental image of him making love to her, and he chuckled when she blushed and bit her lip. "Still the same naughty girl."

David glanced down at her before glaring at him. "Stop sending her dirty images."

"She likes them." Death snickered, sending her another mental image of the three of them together—how they had been when they made the baby together.

Her chest heaved up and down, and a soft gasp left her lips when he pushed in the image of him and David entering her together as her gold thread formed, tightening around all three of them.

"I better be included in whatever you're showing her," David muttered.

"You are," Jane gasped.

"We're going to have to find somewhere to sneak off to when we get there," Death said, sending her more images of their time together, along with more of the three of them. "A bathroom or something."

She was panting as they followed the worn path to the village. "I hope we always find each other and become this."

Death raised her hand, kissing it. "Dream it, my love."

She nodded, closing her eyes as her flushed cheeks grew darker.

"That's our girl," David said. "Keep building our Heaven, baby. We never end."

"Longer than always and beyond forever," she whispered.

5 0

HAPPILY EVER AFTER

David yawned, leaning against the sofa's armrest as he rubbed Jane's thigh.

Death groaned, leaning against the opposite armrest. "How long do we have to stay?"

Jane frowned, opening her eyes before staring up at her angel. She'd been dozing for the past hour. "You knew we were gonna be here for a while."

Arthur laughed, walking past them. "You realize this is Artemis and Adam's first child. They are getting all the instructions for the first time."

Death glared at Arthur. "Artemis is older than dirt. She should know how to nurse a newborn."

"It's hard." Jane rubbed her stomach, and David smiled, putting his hand over hers.

"You stick your tit in the baby's mouth." Death frowned down at her. "If David and I can already make milk come out of yours, and you haven't even had the baby, a fucking baby with instincts to nurse should know what to do."

Gareth threw his head back, laughing. "I hate that I can't not see it. It's worse because I've seen Jane's tits."

Death summoned a knife. "If you weren't holding a child."

"I'm mortal, though." Gareth turned, shielding his little girl. "Pick a meaty part, at least."

Gawain rubbed his head. "You three are the worst. I can't believe you're going to move in."

"Believe it," Death said. "Every night, Jane is going to be between us. Moaning."

Gawain covered his ears. "Dear Jesus."

David leaned his head back, smiling up at his sister.

"Brother," she greeted, swaying with her six-month-old daughter.

"How is my niece?" He reached up, caressing the little hand exposed from the bundle.

"Well, thanks to Death." Gwen smiled at him.

"He only helped so he didn't have to hear her cry," Gawain said.

David flipped Gawain off. "Quiet. He helped."

Gareth laughed. "Gawain is still sore about the D-Bromance."

David ignored the banter as he observed the little girl. He'd soon have his very own with Jane. He already had Natalie, but this would be a baby girl he held and kissed from her first breath. His little girl would have two daddies, just as Natalie did, but he would have the other daddy right there, helping him raise her. He knew Death didn't expect to feel anything for their daughter, but he knew he'd change once he saw a little girl with brown hair, big eyes, and a smile for both of them.

Gwen smiled at him. "You will both be wonderful fathers, brother."

"Thank you, sister."

She nodded. "The boys are fine, by the way. Thor is telling them all about his great battle with Jörmungandr and how he was the savior of the world for slaying it."

"I corrected him." Nyctimus walked past her, kissing her head. "It was the great pack from Greece. Hello, Gwen."

"You mean the naked pack of wild men that we all woke up to," Gareth said. "Dong in my face and everything. Jane's poor soul was surrounded by dong. Well, I guess that's nothing new."

Nyctimus flipped him off. "Suck my nuts. I kept your ass from getting eaten by hellhounds. Be grateful."

"Nyctimus." Gwen's scolding tone made Nyc's cheeks turn red.

"Sorry." He quickly focused on Jane as she struggled not to laugh out loud. "Congratulations, Little Moon. And you're welcome for the ring. That old jeweler took half my fortune."

Jane gasped. "You bought the ring?"

"No. Death did me a favor in exchange for paying a custom designer to make it for you." Nyctimus chuckled. "Six months ago, he threw an emerald, a lump of gold, and a burned-up magazine at me and told me to find the best jeweler."

"Aw, Death." She beamed up at him. "You dug up an emerald?"

"No, Sin and I blew up a jewelry store and took it. I wanted it to be the one you had already picked."

"Aww." Elle sighed next to Gawain. "Dearest, why are you not as romantic as Death?"

Gawain looked at her like she'd lost her mind. "Death is not romantic."

"Yes, he is." Elle's cheeks turned red as she rubbed her swollen stomach.

Death snickered and lifted Jane's new ring, kissing it. "Romance is my middle name, bitch."

Gwen scowled at Death, but he winked at her, making her blush and walk away.

David chuckled, shaking his head. He always forgot that everyone now saw Death as he and Jane had always been able to. It made it a lot easier for the rest of his brothers to accept their relationship because there was no denying that he and Death were connected with how much they resembled each other. Even Death carrying the boys for Jane looked natural because they looked so much alike.

Gareth looked at Death, completely serious. "You're the god of romance? Like deadly love?"

"Why are you still alive?" Death acted as if he was checking the time on a wristwatch. "I think this is broken."

Jane rubbed her eyes. "Fuck, I can't stop crying."

"Wanna go fuck in one of the empty rooms?" Death asked, completely serious.

Everyone looked at David, and he just waved them off.

"What?" Death glanced around. "She's horny. I'm only doing what David taught me to."

David sighed, staring at the angel he'd practically asked to be his wife's second husband. "Just because we have twin souls and accept each other does not mean you can talk about my wife like that."

"She's my soul mate." Death put his hand over the spot below Jane's heart where half of his soul was kept.

"She's mine, too." David smirked, putting his hand over Jane's heart.

"She's my fiancée," Death shot back, running his fingers through her hair. "And she likes to get tag teamed by her Ds."

Jane covered her face, an embarrassed laugh slipping free.

Gawain shivered. "No one here wants to know about it."

Death grinned at him. "You don't want to hear about the three-night-long Jane and Ds sandwich that put this little girl in here?" He put his hand over Jane's stomach. "We barely let Jane sleep."

"I hate you." Gawain scowled.

"You're just jealous Death will be helping them with their third baby while you take care of all yours," Nyctimus said.

"That is true." Gareth pointed at Gawain. "You're mad because David won't have to get up all night this time."

Gawain looked at Death. "Give me one of your brothers."

"Give you?" Death kept playing with Jane's hair.

"Yes. We all served God, so we should all get an angel to sleep well."

Death gestured toward Elle. "They'll steal your wife."

"Well, give me one of the women." Gawain nodded. "Yes, I saw several of them at Valhalla. Give me one of those."

Elle stared at Gawain, her mouth hanging open. "You fool!"

Gawain cringed. "I meant for you, dearest. She can help so that I may massage your aching feet."

Elle smacked him as she stood, waddling out of the room. Gwen followed her, sending Gawain a glare from hell.

"What?" Gawain leaned back. "I'm tired. I have too many boys, and now a daughter is to come. How many children do I have now?"

"This is your fifth." Gareth hoisted his daughter onto his shoulders. His son was no doubt with the other boys. "You should have planned better. I just made the two, then got cut."

"I won't get cut." Gawain covered himself.

"It hurt for a few days. Now there is no trouble." Gareth waved his hand toward David. "David will probably do it. And he has four kids, too. You cannot act like a child. Death wasn't there for Luc and Jason."

"Have I missed anything?" Hades rushed into the waiting room, dropping a toy. "Fuck."

David chuckled. "No. We are still waiting to see them."

Jane held her hands out. "Let me see."

Hades grinned, handing her the plush wolf toy.

"Aw, it looks like Akakios." She petted it as if it were a real wolf pup. "I miss them."

"And they miss you." Hades put his hand over her stomach. "How is this one?"

"Good." Jane handed him the toy. "I must ask Persephone to make something for me."

Hades bent, kissing her forehead. "She'd love to. As always, thank you, young beauty."

David rubbed Jane's leg. She really was full of surprises. It had shocked everyone when Persephone arrived at their home a week after the battle, asking for the gold goddess who returned her to Earth.

"And you are always welcome, Hades." Jane grinned up at him. "Just don't get me in trouble. You're a reaper now, and she's a human. No babies."

He shook his head. "No babies. I promise. Watching grandnieces and nephews is more than I ever hoped for."

"Did I give you the day off?" Death covered Jane's mouth and smirked at his only reaper.

Jane pinched his hand until he let her go. "Be nice."

Death rubbed his hand. "Ouch."

She laughed, kissing his hand before smiling at Hades. "You have two weeks off to help with your niece. Just promise you will pull the extra slack when our daughter is born."

Death glared at Jane. "Are you the Angel of Death?"

"No." She kept smiling.

He kept glaring at her. "Give me a kiss."

"Give him time off." Jane snickered when he growled.

"Fine. Hades, take the week off. Now go over there so I don't have to give you more vacation time. Fucker."

"Thank you, Master." Hades winked at Jane as he intercepted Apollo, guiding him out of the room. "Go before he changes his mind."

Jane pushed herself up, puckering her lips. Death didn't wait to claim them.

"And you call her spoiled." David chuckled when Death flipped him off.

Finally, Adam walked through the double doors with a big grin. "Ready to meet the newest member of our family?"

Jane sat up, wiping her eyes. "Fuck, I can't stop crying."

David pointed out some oranges to Jason. "Do you want those?"

Jason nodded, holding out his hand.

"What is it called?" David asked, handing him one as he bagged more.

"Watermelon." Jason grinned widely.

David chuckled, shaking his head. "No, son. It's an orange."

"Mor-nge." Jason stared at his mouth. "Pour-nge."

Luc laughed, hugging David's waist. "Where's Mama?"

David patted Luc's head. He always found it amusing that Luc was so affectionate.

He kept scanning the faces around the market and sighed as he realized every woman in the produce section was staring at him. He didn't like this part of being mortal. Or just a normal person. No one knew he was a prince whenever they left the village to go to the larger markets. It seemed everyone was starting to forget he and the others had once been the most feared immortals. Now, he was just David.

"Daddy?" Luc tugged on his shirt.

"Oh." David checked the area around him again. It was a big warehouse, and there were always lots of people. "I don't see her. We'll find her. She's with Death."

"Mommy pees a lot." Luc sniffed some strawberries. "Mmm."

"Well, she has your baby sister in her tummy. She will have to go potty a lot."

"Daddy, why do ladies always stare at you?" Luc spoke loud enough for several people to hear and pointed them out.

David chuckled, grabbing Luc's hand. "Don't point at people."

"Aw," a woman said. "They're so cute. Handsome, just like their daddy."

David gave the woman a polite smile before grabbing some apples. The woman didn't stop staring, though.

"My daddy is a prince," Luc said proudly. "He's married to my mama, his goddess. Go away."

David didn't look up. He just pulled his son behind him to the next bin of produce.

"Go away," Jason yelled, throwing a grape.

"Jason." David stopped him from throwing another. "I apologize. They are very protective of their mother."

The woman's face was red, looking ready to say something until she looked behind him.

"King Daddy." Luc rushed away.

David usually disliked the boys calling Death 'King Daddy.' It wasn't that he was bothered by them calling him daddy, but he knew Death didn't see them as his children. He was faking it for Jane's sake.

"What did your dad do?" Death was no doubt ready to embarrass him. He hoisted Luc up, holding him just like David was holding Jason.

"That lady said I was cute and that Daddy was handsome."

"Did you tell her your other daddy is God's sexiest creation?"

"No, I forgot."

Death chuckled, coming to stand beside David. Jane held his hand, reading something and not even paying attention.

"Baby, do you need anything else from here?" David asked her, ignoring the whispers. No matter where they went, if Death was there, everyone saw them.

Death tossed bars of chocolate into the shopping basket. "She wanted those."

David smiled at Jane. She had a new book of fairy tales, and she was obsessed. "Baby, did you want to look for baby supplies?"

She looked up, giving him a dreamy smile. "What was that?"

David grabbed her chin, kissing her. "Still losing focus around me."

"I'm still sexier." Death jostled Luc. "Want to come help me find Mama's Dr Pepper?"

Luc nodded. "She ran out."

"I know she did." Death tilted Jane's face up, kissing her. "We'll meet you at the baby section."

She gave him a dazed smile. She was more affected by them when she was pregnant. "Do you know where to go?"

Death shrugged. "It's a big ass warehouse—not Tartarus. I can find it."

"Okay." She pecked him.

Death smacked her butt. "Sexy ass. David and I are going to melt your chocolate and lick it off your body if you keep staring at us like this."

That pretty blush spread over her cheeks, and David pulled her close, laughing at the gasps from people listening nearby.

"I want chocolate," Luc said.

Death winked at Jane before walking away. "I'll get you some different chocolate. It'll bother me if you are eating Mama's."

"Okay."

Death smiled, tugging Jane away from David. She didn't even stir in her sleep.

David opened his eyes, angry. "You think you can come into bed after being gone for twenty-four hours and get her to yourself?"

"Yes." Death kept pulling her. "And I see you took advantage of me being gone."

"Yes, I did. She's begging to be fucked because she thinks it'll put her into labor."

"Your ding dong hit my daughter's head?" Death glared at him.

"No, I wouldn't do that." David rubbed her belly. "I just gave her intense orgasms."

"Not intense enough." Death snickered, rubbing her belly. "Want me to try?"

Jane groaned, grabbing Death's and David's hands before putting them between her legs. "Both."

"Goddamn." Death leaned down, tugging her nipple with his teeth as he and David got to work.

"Get this baby out of me." She closed her eyes, moaning. "I'll give blowjobs to the one who puts me into labor."

Jane leaned against Death's shoulder as they stared into a pair of hazel eyes.

"She looks like you," he murmured, placing the baby on his lap. The baby took hold of his finger before he could pull back, and he let her. "Her skin is darker, though. Like mine."

"Maybe this is God's way of letting you have a baby with me."

He shook his head. "She's David's. She has his smile."

David caressed the baby's cheek. "She's yours, too."

"I'm going to teach her to call you Papi." Death smirked.

"Don't even think about it." David leaned down, kissing the baby's head. "No brainwashing her."

Death smiled at Jane. "Are you happy, angel?"

"Very."

He leaned down, kissing her. "That's what matters."

"Just try," she whispered. "I won't be able to even imagine happiness if you are unhappy."

Death released a sigh, picking the baby up. He cradled her tiny head in one hand before kissing her forehead. "I'll try."

"Come for us, Jane." David pulled her hair, tugging her up so she could kiss him as he buried himself deep inside her.

She gasped as Death latched on to one of her breasts, sucking hard as he thrust upward.

"Oh, fuck." She whimpered, glancing down at Death.

"Daddy," a little voice yelled on the other side of the door.

"Fuck." Death thrust up fast and hard, making Jane moan louder.

"Daddy!"

"Daddies are coming." David was content letting Death strive for his release.

"Fuck, fuck," she gasped, hanging onto Death.

David chuckled, pressing in hard and fast, somehow finding the right rhythm that had all of them moaning.

"I'm coming." Jane squeezed her eyes shut, panting as warmth pumped into her.

Death cupped her cheeks, kissing her again and again. "I love you so fucking much, Sweet Jane." He smirked before kissing his mark as David kissed his. "I'll make sure they're all asleep tonight."

"Daddy!"

Death kissed her once more and then vanished.

Jane fell to her belly, smiling as she listened to Death talking to their daughter.

"Daddy, they won't let me play with them. They said no girls."

Death's response was instant. "No girls?"

"Uh-huh. I wanted to be the Pale Horseman, and they said I couldn't."

David leaned over Jane, kissing her shoulder as she smiled.

"You're the Pale Horseman's little girl. You're special."

"I wants to be a Horseman like you, Daddy. Then when I retires, I'll be a knight like Papi."

David gave Jane an annoyed glare as they heard Death snickering.

"That's my girl," Death said. "Let's go outside and summon Sorrow, and you can ride with Daddy. Okay?"

"Okay."

There was a kissing sound. "Good girl. We'll summon Uncle War, Pest, and Famine to scare Luc and Jason."

"Who summoned me?" came a deep voice that had Jane grinning from ear to ear.

"Uncle War!"

Jane loved that his brothers could all be together now that they'd fulfilled their duty.

"Little angel." War's tender tone made Jane feel all warm.

"Brother, hand the girl over," said Famine, "and go wash your hands. I can smell your soul mate's pheromones."

"Stop scenting her," Pestilence said. "The last time I scented Jane, I'm pretty sure David's soul awoke. I still have a scorch mark on my ass."

"Don't say ass around my daughter," Death snapped.

"You just said it, brother." War chuckled.

"Daddy, are we going to scare Jason and Luc for being mean?"

"You're damn right we are," Death said. "Go find your mask and cloak."

"Okay!"

Jane turned, kissing David.

He was smiling as he held her cheek and returned the kiss. "I love you."

She wrapped her arms around him, pulling him on top of her. "I something you."

He chuckled, kissing across her cheek. "I'm going to something you if you don't say it."

"Wendy," Death said. "You were going to get your reaper costume. What is this?"

"I'm a knight reaper fairy. See, I got my mask on under my knight helmet. But I need wings to fly like Peter Pan."

"It's kind of scary, brother," Famine said. "You should be proud."

"Don't call her scary. She's a goddess like her mama."

A door slammed, followed by thunderous footsteps.

"We're back," Gawain yelled.

"Oh, are we playing fairies and knights?" Gareth asked. "I'll go get my sword and the boys."

There was a loud sigh from Death. "You are meant to round up the baby girls."

"Yes, I'll tell them to bring the girls as well," Gareth hollered. "It will be an epic battle."

Pestilence laughed. "I'm glad David doesn't mind using his land for this."

Death was amused when he spoke. "He enjoys any chance to battle, but Jane ordered him to set up booby traps around the castle treehouse."

"Only your woman, brother," Famine said.

"Ah, Little Monster is all grown up," War said.

"War," Natalie cheered. "I've missed you so much."

"Me as well, Little Monster."

"Hi, guys." Natalie's tone was always more timid with the others. "Hi, Death."

"Don't hi me. Did you bring that boyfriend you told your mother about?"

"Please don't scare him," Natalie begged. "He wasn't around the war and doesn't believe in the final battle or the Horsemen."

"Then he's a fool," Death said. "Break up with him."

"Death," she whined. "Please behave."

"Do you not realize who I am?"

"Where is this boyfriend?" War asked.

"He's helping Nathan with our bags. I'm so glad to be home. Daddy said we'd look for a lot for my house to be built. 'Cause I'm not staying here with them all the time. They're gross."

"Making your mama happy isn't gross," Death said. "War, keep your eyes on this boyfriend. If he makes one wrong move, we kill him."

"Oh, Jesus." Natalie sighed.

"Daddy isn't Jesus, Sissy," Wendy said seriously.

Natalie laughed. "Oh, I know. What are you about to play?"

"The boys said I couldn't play Horsemans with them. So, we're gonna scare them."

"Death, do you ever grow up?" Natalie asked.

"No. I'm immortal. I thought you were smart."

Natalie groaned. "How am I going to keep who you all are secret if you're battling in the backyard?"

"If your boyfriend can't slay at least one of us in a play battle, he's not good enough for you," Death said.

Jane grinned and knew Death's words would touch Natalie.

"The Little Prince has returned," War said. "Are you enjoying living with your roommates?"

"Hey, guys," Nathan greeted. "And, yes, they're good guys. I'm glad Dad found people who like the stuff I do. So, why are you all here? Did Luc and Jason make Wendy sad again?"

"We don't only show up to defend your sisters," Pestilence said.

"We promised you we would come to view your art exhibit," Famine reminded him. "But, yes, Death summoned us to scare them for making her mildly upset. A battle is set to commence shortly."

Nathan chuckled. "Good. I'll help Jason and Luc."

Gawain butted in. "Give me my niece so she can learn to be a proper knight."

"I'm her dad," Death said. "She's learning how to be a reaper. Don't try to steal my girl because yours screams orders from the castle while mine is riding fiercely to the front line."

David grinned against Jane's mouth, pushing himself in slowly. She sighed, hugging him with the biggest smile on her face.

"She has another dad." Gawain pointed out. "I'm sure he wants her to learn to be a knight like him and her mom. Where is he?"

"Loving our woman," Death answered right away. "Come on. You'll hear her screaming in a few moments without me there to block them out."

"Why do you have to tell me?" Gawain groaned.

"You did ask," War said as loud footsteps led away from their room.

"Daddy?" Wendy's voice still carried up to their door.

"Yes, my star?" Death's tone was just as soft as when he spoke to Jane.

"Will you let me win like you let Mama win when we play swords?"

Jane stared into the sapphire eyes that were her home. "I love you, David."

He kissed her. "And we love you, my love. You're ours . . . always and beyond forever."

"I'll let you win," Death said. "Always, Sweet Wendy."

SWEET DREAMS

Lucifer sighed as he watched the scene outside his castle window.

"She's been dreaming a lot," Thanatos said.

"She's getting older," he replied, watching the glowing blue and green sphere float over the lake of fire. Gold light appeared around it every few seconds before zooming into the orb.

"She's been happy, though." Asmodeus came to his side. "So has Death. They will hold onto it."

"Good." Lucifer lowered his gaze to the red jar on the table.

"Too bad she still has nightmares," Thanatos said.

"Yes." Lucifer shook his head.

"Perhaps the fairy tales will help." Asmodeus smiled as several bright lights appeared. "There she goes. It must have been a good day."

Lucifer watched the gold beams and stars float into the world he'd rule with Jane when she died.

"Gods and monsters versus Jane's fairy tales," Thanatos mused. "At least her fairy tales are unique."

Lucifer's gaze lowered to the jar again. He slid his fingers over the moon on his wrist, smiling when silver light shot into the orb. "This isn't going to go well. She should have let me take the punishment on my own."

"You know she would never abandon you. She is Jane," Thanatos said.

"At least in their current world, they've had their happily ever after, after all." Asmodeus gestured to the jar. "If this one chooses darkness after this, we still follow the queen to all worlds she creates, and she will have us to call on when she needs us. Plus, you are bound to each other—you won't let her fall."

"I will have to wake first," Lucifer said. "You know I may end up hurting her before then. I pray she does not put me to sleep for long. None of us will remember this when we enter the new world."

"You will all remember when she wakes, my king." Asmodeus smiled. "We will find each other, and then it will be as if we had never parted. He has made it so."

A gold flash and a myriad of colors lit up the darkness.

Asmodeus chuckled as they watched gold light race across the ruins of Lucifer's former kingdom. His new kingdom with Jane grew with every dream she sent to it. He was only waiting for her life to end so they could begin a new journey. One that he knew would not be a sweet fairy tale that his queen was trying to create. There was always darkness around Jane. But he was light. He'd find his queen in their new world when it was time. Then they'd live in her fairy tale until it was time to wake again.

Lucifer lowered his gaze to the moon on his wrist and smiled. "Sweet dreams, my queen."

Thus Ends The Gods & Monsters Trilogy

Though this part of their journey has ended,
They will always Begin Again.
Jane's fairy tale kingdom with her king begins with the Big Bad Wolf
Trilogy, and her accidental alternate reality, the Jane's Team duology, will
impact both worlds until they collide in a web of creations by the Little
Moon and Janie Marie.

ABOUT THE AUTHOR

Janie Marie is an Amazon Bestseller in Paranormal Angel Romance and International Bestseller in Young Adult Contemporary Romance & Young Adult Fairy Tale Adaptations.

Much of her life experiences—good and a lot of bad—are where she has chosen to draw inspiration from to create her characters and stories. It's important to her to create the kind of characters she needs or needed at one point in time because she wanted to create something only the saddest souls would recognize as brave and strong.

Be ready for raw, emotional tales, as Janie never holds back. With her darkest thoughts, she found light is still possible, that the sad girl can sometimes glow the brightest.

amazon.com/author/janiemarie

tiktok.com/@janiemarie1617

instagram.com/janiemarie1617

ALSO BY JANIE MARIE

THE FAIRY TALE

The Big Bad Wolf Trilogy

A twisted coming-of-age fairy tale adaptation is interconnected to the Gods & Monsters trilogy.

THE DREAM

The Jane's Team Duology

A Gods & Monsters Alternate Reality

THE PREQUEL/SPINOFF

The Wolf Prince

Nyctimus' story is coming soon

Printed in Great Britain
by Amazon